THE HISTORY OF
MISS BETSY
THOUGHTLESS

ELIZA HAYWOOD
Introduced by Dale Spender

London and New York

This edition first published in 1986
by Pandora Press (Routledge & Kegan Paul plc)

11 New Fetter Lane, London EC4P 4EE

Published in the USA by
Pandora Press (Routledge & Kegan Paul Inc.)
in association with Methuen Inc.
29 West 35th Street, New York, NY 1000

Set in Ehrhardt 10 on 11½ pt
by Columns, Reading
and printed in Great Britain
by
The Guernsey Press Co Ltd
Guernsey, Channel Islands

Introduction © Dale Spender 1986

Library of Congress Cataloging in Publication Data
Haywood, Eliza, 1693?–1756
The History of Miss Betsy Thoughtless
I. Title
PR3506.H94H5.   1986   823'.5   85-29860
British Library CIP data also available

ISBN 0-86358-090-4

CONTENTS

Introduction by Dale Spender vii

Volume the First

Volume the Second

Contents

Volume the Third

Volume the Fourth

INTRODUCTION

To get married, to the right person – and to stay married – these can be among the most difficult achievements in a woman's life. It is not just a question of being able to tell who the right man might be (though this in itself is an issue for endless debate), or even what to do if he turns out to be the wrong man; there is also the possibility that a woman may not want to marry at all, and this makes it very difficult indeed.

This was the experience of Betsy Thoughtless who had little inclination to be married – but who at the same time was not averse to being admired. According to the author, Eliza Haywood, the problem for Betsy Thoughtless was that 'though she could not love she was pleased with being loved' and this meant that the young heroine had much to learn.

Today, if women are not inclined to marry there are other options open to them, although given how mandatory marriage is still made, there are not perhaps as many alternatives as there sometimes seem. But there were even less in Eliza Haywood's day when women were deprived of education and denied any legitimate influence in the public and professional realm. A woman's occupation was to be a wife, which is one reason that Eliza Haywood takes as the theme of her novel the necessity for Betsy Thoughtless to come to terms with the necessity of marriage. No other possibilities are entertained in this book.

For Eliza Haywood such a conclusion may have been the product of a bitter experience. She left her own husband to lead a life of independence and to earn her living by her pen. And while very little is known about how she fared – financially or emotionally – sufficient is known about the period for it to be appreciated that she must have had her troubles. Perhaps she wanted to 'protect' her heroine from some of the problems she herself had faced.

Not that there's much of the 'protective' nature in Eliza Haywood's writing. On the contrary, in keeping with the permissive values of her time, she exposes some of the more seamy sides of life in a rather bawdy manner. So her work stands in sharp contrast to much of the fiction which followed. Because the Victorians would have ostensibly been scandalised by much that she described, it is doubtful whether this remarkable writer would have been permitted publication a century later. Perhaps this partially explains her fall from literary grace for although the most prolific writer of her day (and the most popular) she slipped from notice after her death.

Even her racy language would have given offence in the nineteenth century. While it gives her work a modern flavour, there is still something rather startling about finding such blatant words as 'pregnant', 'prostitute', and 'abortion' scattered through these pages. And although it is possible to trace some of the literary links between Eliza Haywood and Jane Austen, it is also possible to see that there were paths that Eliza Haywood would fearlessly tread, and where Jane Austen would never follow.

But if there are differences there are similarities as well, and Jane Austen was indebted to the literary traditions which Eliza Haywood helped to found. For in the writing of Eliza Haywood we see the novel being shaped in a way that Jane Austen would later use. . . to perfection. And if Jane Austen's novels are people with young women who must learn about life and values, Betsy Thoughtless is among the first of the female characters in fiction to appear in this guise.

This is one of the most significant contributions Eliza Haywood makes to the development of the novel. Prior to her entry to the literary stage, most narratives had centred on a male character, and the predominant story line was one which concerned itself with the way a man's honour was tested. Traditionally the man was an aristocrat and it was a women who tried to dissuade him from his duty.

But with Eliza Haywood – and particularly with *The History of Betsy Thoughtless* – we are introduced to a new dimension. We have a heroine, not a hero; she is an ordinary, not an aristocratic woman; and in Betsy Thoughtless we have a woman and not a man's honour being tested.

The emerging middle class provides the heroine; and it is no accident that the upper class provides most of the villains. Eliza Haywood was a political writer who dramatised the conflict of interest between the classes and between the sexes. And no one had done this before.

So Eliza Haywood provides a real reversal. It is an ordinary young woman who interests the author (and whom she assumes will interest the reader): a middle-class young woman who must find her way through the tricks and the traps that are set by men. In incident after incident, Betsy Thoughtless must use her wits – and her physical strength – to avoid harassment, seduction, and even a forced marriage. And much of this – the author assures us – is because Betsy does not think, because she doesn't think about what she's doing.

If the events are to some extent repetitious they are certainly not boring or tiresome. Each drama is different from the one before (clearly there is a lot for Betsy to think about) and the humorous and satirical touch of the author is never far away. Even when Betsy is married and the reader could be forgiven for assuming that there might be a reduction in pace, there are still surprises in store. There is one scene where Lord ...... tries to seduce the married Betsy – who protests, and who defies convention in the process:

> She struggled with all her might, but her efforts that way being in vain, she shrieked and called aloud for help. This a little shocked him; he let her go:
>
> 'What do you mean, Madam?' said he, 'Would you expose yourself and me to the ridicule of my servants?'

However, this is one situation where no amount of 'thought' on Betsy's part would have been of much help for Lord ...... used a variety of tricks to get her on her own. The point that Eliza Haywood makes though is that men are not to be trusted and that women must always be on their guard.

Which makes finding the right man a real problem. There seems to be only one decent man to every ten rogues in this novel. And even the most desirable of men – Mr Trueworth – doesn't always appear in a good light. He goes off and marries someone else because Betsy is undeniably thoughtless – but a little more thoughtfulness on his part would not have gone astray.

Much of this fiction is facetious, but much is serious as well. Eliza

Haywood is concerned to make value judgments, about people and about life. And in *The History of Betsy Thoughtless* it becomes clear that the days of telling a simple narrative story in prose have passed. The author is interested in ethical questions – particularly as they relate to women's lives; she is fascinated with human nature, particularly as it affects women's choices in the world. And Eliza Haywood alerts her readers to her interests and her meanings in the naming of her characters. Not only do we have Betsy Thoughtless, and Mr Trueworth, we have Mr Staple (another contender for Betsy's hand), and such personages as Mr Goodman, Sir Ralph Trusty, and Miss Forward!

It is in the company of Miss Forward that Betsy's tale begins. And there can be no doubt about where being 'forward' gets a young woman; fortunately, Betsy avoids Miss Forward's dire fate.

One reason that she survives – to make more mistakes another day – is that she does learn from experience; she does shrewdly assess her situation and make the necessary changes when they are required. And it is this which helps to make her so endearing; it is this, along with her liveliness and spirit, which makes her so likeable. For while Betsy may be silly and vain – and thoughtless – on occasion, she is never nasty. And here she is contrasted with Flora Mellasin who is malicious, but whose behaviour can be explained (if not excused) by her lot in life.

It is a mark of Eliza Haywood's considerable achievement that she was able to create such convincing and contrasting characters and this constituted an imaginative leap from some of the earlier novels – her own included. Another considerable achievement is that she created such coherent and cohesive plots. For *Betsy Thoughtless* is no rambling tale but an integrated series of events and relationships. While there are times when the 'seams' do show, and the odd new character suddenly appears, such 'lapses' in no way detract from the great gains that her work represents.

But probably her greatest achievement is the introduction of serious matters into the novel; ethical questions are opened up for debate and fundamental issues of human nature are explored in a way that was illuminating then and which is still relevant now.

Should a woman have to marry? How should she choose? And should she have to stay married if the husband proves to be far from what he seemed? Can he be changed? Can she change? Does it matter anyway?

Interestingly, Betsy Thoughtless leaves her first husband and not for any grave offence that he commits. Even more interestingly the world does not end. There is not the slightest suggestion that Betsy has committed a sin, or that she will be punished for her actions. Which makes this novel more immediate in its concerns than many that have been published in the intervening years.

Likewise, Eliza Haywood's criticisms of the married state have a distinct ring of modernity:

> Mr Munden's notions of marriage had always been extremely unfavourable to the ladies – he considered a wife no more than an upper-servant, bound to study and obey, in all things, the will of him to whom she had given her hand; and how obsequious and submissive soever he appeared when a lover, had fixed his resolution to render himself absolute master when he became a husband.

Eliza Haywood didn't approve of such sentiments in husbands; and Betsy Thoughtless certainly didn't approve. And when the husband took the money that the wife had saved from the housekeeping by her own good management. . . we are meant to understand that this is sufficient grounds for separation.

Betsy leaves; and Betsy learns from her mistakes. And like so many of the heroines who follow her in the pages of women's fiction, she does live to be happy ever after. But it is *after* numerous escapades, after flirting with some of the more adventurous aspects of life that later heroines would never know about. The freedom of movement that Betsy enjoyed – the sights she witnessed and the affairs she experienced – would not have been available to a well brought up middle-class young lady fifty years later. It was because Betsy did not have to have a chaperone – because she lived on her own for a while – that she received some of the attentions that she did. By the time Fanny Burney, Maria Edgeworth and Jane Austen were writing, no decent heroine could have been taken home by an unknown young man, concerned to obtain a mistress, and made the sort of offer that Betsy had no difficulty in resisting:

> I have been bit once and have made a vow never to settle upon any woman while I live again; but you shall fare never the worse for that, I will make you a handsome present before we part; and if you can be constant will allow you six guineas a week.

Throughout her writing, and throughout *The History of Betsy Thoughtless*, Eliza Haywood holds up to scrutiny the values of her day and she does not hesitate to focus on the sexual double standard and its inherent injustice. And because Betsy Thoughtless seeks to be an independent woman – and because Eliza Haywood clearly endorses this stand – the novel is still relevant and illuminating today.

That Eliza Haywood should have been erased from the literary records – that Betsy Thoughtless should have been excluded from the gallery of heroines – is not only surprising, it is also sad. For this woman writer (and the characters she creates) occupies a central place in women's literary history. Both Eliza Haywood and Betsy Thoughtless deserve to be better known, more highly respected, and much more widely enjoyed.

Dale Spender

VOLUME THE FIRST

CHAPTER I

———————————•———————————

Gives the reader room to guess at what is to ensue,
though ten to one but he finds himself deceived

IT was always my opinion, that fewer women were undone by love
than vanity; and that those mistakes the sex are sometimes guilty of,
proceed, for the most part, rather from inadvertency, than a vicious
inclination. The ladies, however, I am sorry to observe, are apt to
make too little allowances to each other on this score, and seem
better pleased with an occasion to condemn than to excuse; and it is
not above one, in a greater number than I will presume to mention,
who, while she passes the severest censure on the conduct of
her friend, will be at the trouble of taking a retrospect on her
own. There are some who behold, with indignation and contempt,
those errors in others, which, unhappily, they are every day falling
into themselves; and as the want of due consideration occasions the
guilt, so the want of due consideration also occasions the scandal;
and there would be much less room either for the one or the
other, were some part of that time which is wasted at the toilette,
in consulting what dress is most becoming to the face, employed
in examining the heart, and what actions are most becoming of
the character.

Betsy Thoughtless was the only daughter of a gentleman of good
family and fortune in L—e, where he constantly resided, scarce ever
going to London, and contented himself with such diversions as the
country afforded. On the death of his wife, he sent his little favourite,
then about ten years old, to a boarding-school, the governess of
which had the reputation of a woman of great good sense, fine
breeding, and every way qualified for the well-forming of the minds

of those young persons who were entrusted to her care.

The old gentleman was so well pleased with having placed his daughter where she was so likely to improve in all the accomplishments befitting her sex, that he never suffered her to come home, even at breaking-up times, when most of the other young ladies did so: but as the school was not above seven or eight miles from his seat, he seldom failed calling to see her once or twice a week.

Miss Betsy, who had a great deal of good-nature, and somewhat extremely engaging in her manner of behaviour, soon gained the affection not only of the governess, but of all the young ladies; but as girls, as well as women, have their favourites, to whom they may communicate their little secrets, there was one who above all the others was distinguished by her. Miss Forward, for so she was called, was also very fond of Miss Betsy. This intimacy beginning but in trivial things, and such as suited their age, continued as they advanced nearer to maturity. Miss Forward, however, had two years the advantage of her friend, yet did not disdain to make her the confidante of a kind of amorous intrigue she had entered into with a young lad, called Master Sparkish, the son of a neighbouring gentleman: he had fallen in love with her at church, and had taken all opportunities to convince her of his passion; she, proud of being looked upon as a woman, encouraged it. Frequent letters passed between them, for she never failed to answer those she received from him, both which were shewn to Miss Betsy; and this gave her an early light into the art and mystery of courtship, and consequently a relish for admiration. The young lover calling his mistress angel and goddess, made her long to be in her teens, that she might have the same things said to her.

This correspondence being by some accident discovered, the governess found it behoved her to keep a strict eye upon Miss Forward: all the servants were examined concerning the conveying any letters, either to or from her: but none of them knew any thing of the matter; it was a secret to all but Miss Betsy, who kept it inviolably. It is fit, however, the reader should not remain in ignorance.

Master Sparkish had read the story of Pyramus and Thisbe; he told his mistress of it, and in imitation of those lovers of antiquity, stuck his letters into a little crevice he found in the garden-wall, whence she pulled them out every day, and returned her answers by the same friendly breach, which he very gallantly told her in one of his epistles, had been made by the God of Love himself, in order to favour his suit: so that all the governess's circumspection could not hinder this amour from going on without interruption; and could they have contented themselves with barely writing to each other, they might probably have done so till they both had been weary: but though I will not pretend to say that either of them had any thing in their inclinations that was not perfectly consistent with innocence, yet it is certain they both languished for a nearer conversation, which the fertile brain of Miss Forward at last brought about.

She pretended, one Sunday in the afternoon, to have so violent a pain in her head, that she could not go to church; Miss Betsy begged leave to stay and keep her company, and told the governess she would read a sermon or some other good book to her: the good old gentlewoman, little suspecting the plot concerted between them, readily consented.

Nobody being left in the house but themselves, and one maid-servant, young Sparkish, who had previous notice at what hour to come, was let in at the garden-door, the key being always in it. Miss Betsy left the lovers in an arbour, and went into the kitchen, telling the maid she had read Miss Forward to sleep, and hoped she would be better when she waked. She amused the wench with one little chat or other, till she thought divine service was near over, then returned into the garden to give her friends warning it was time to separate.

They had after this many private interviews, through the contrivance and assistance of Miss Betsy; who, quite charmed with being made the confidante of a person older than herself, set all her wits to work to render herself worthy of the trust reposed in her. Sometimes she made pretences of going to the milliner, the mantua-maker, or to buy something in town, and begged leave that Miss Forward should accompany her; saying, she wanted her choice in what she was to purchase. Sparkish was always made acquainted when they were to go out, and never failed to give them a meeting.

Miss Forward had a great deal of the coquette in her nature; she knew how to play at fast-and-loose with her lover; and, young as she was, took a pride in mingling pain with the pleasure she bestowed. Miss Betsy was a witness of all the airs the other gave herself on this occasion, and the artifices she made use of, in order to secure the continuance of his addresses: so that, thus early initiated into the mystery of courtship, it is not to be wondered at, that when she came to the practice, she was so little at a loss.

This intercourse, however, lasted but a small time; their meetings were too frequent, and too little circumspection used in them not to be liable to discovery. The governess was informed that, in spite of all her care, the young folks had been too cunning for her: on which she went to the father of Sparkish, acquainted him with what she knew of the affair, and intreated he would lay his commands on his son to refrain all conversation with any of the ladies under her tuition. The old gentleman flew into a violent passion on hearing his son had already begun to think of love; he called for him, and after having rated his youthful folly in the severest manner, charged him to relate the whole truth of what had passed between him and the young lady mentioned by the governess. The poor lad was terrified beyond measure at his father's anger, and confessed every particular of his meetings with Miss Forward and her companion; and thus Miss Betsy's share of the contrivance was brought to light, and drew on her a reprimand equally severe with that Miss Forward had received. The careful governness would not entirely depend on the assurance the father of Sparkish had given her, and resolved to trust neither of the ladies out of her sight, while that young gentleman remained so near them, which she knew would be but a short time, he having finished his school-learning, and was soon to go to the university. To prevent also any future strategems being laid between Miss Betsy and Miss Forward, she took care to keep them from ever being alone together, which was a very great mortification to them: but a sudden turn soon after happened in the affairs of Miss Betsy, which put all I have been relating entirely out of her head.

CHAPTER II

---●---

*Shews Miss Betsy in a new scene of life, and the
frequent opportunities she had of putting in practice
those lessons she was beginning to receive from her
young instructress at the boarding-school*

THOUGH it is certainly necessary to inculcate into young girls all
imaginable precaution in regard to their behiaviour towards those of
another sex, yet I know not if it is not an error to dwell too much
upon that topick. Miss Betsy might, possibly, have sooner forgot the
little artifices she had seen practised by Miss Forward, if her
governess, by too strenuously endeavouring to convince her how
unbecoming they were, had not reminded her of them: besides,
the good old gentlewoman was far stricken in years; time had
set his iron fingers on her cheeks, had left his cruel marks on
every feature of her face, and she had little remains of having
ever been capable of exciting those inclinations she so much
condemned; so that what she said seemed to Miss Betsy as spoke out
of envy, or to shew her authority, rather than the real dictates
of truth.

I have often remarked, that reproofs from the old and ugly have
much less efficacy than when given by persons less advanced in years,
and who may be supposed not altogether past sensibility themselves
of the gaieties they advise others to avoid.

Though all the old gentlewoman said, could not persuade Miss
Betsy there was any harm in Miss Forward's behaviour towards
young Sparkish, yet she had the complaisance to listen to her with all
the attention the other could expect or desire from her.

She was, indeed, as yet too young to consider of the justice of the
other's reasoning; and her future conduct shewed, also, she was not
of a humour to give herself much pains in examining, or weighing in

the balance of judgment, the merit of the arguments she heard urged, whether for or against any point whatsoever. She had a great deal of wit, but was too volative for reflection; and as a ship without sufficient ballast is tossed about at the pleasure of every wind that blows, so was she hurried through the ocean of life, just as each predominant passion directed.

But I will not anticipate that gratification which ought to be the reward of a long curiosity. The reader, if he has patience to go through the following pages, will see into the secret springs which set this fair machine in motion, and produced many actions which were ascribed, by the ill-judging and malicious world, to causes very different from the real ones.

All this, I say, will be revealed in time; but it would be as absurd in a writer to rush all at once into the catastrophe of the adventures he would relate, as it would be impracticable in a traveller to reach the end of a long journey, without sometimes stopping at the inns in his way to it. To proceed, therefore, gradually with my history.

The father of Miss Betsy was a very worthy, honest, and good-natured man, but somewhat too indolent; and, by depending too much on the fidelity of those he entrusted with the management of his affairs, had been for several years involved in a law-suit; and, to his misfortune, the aversion he had to business rendered him also incapable of extricating himself from it; and the decision was spun out to a much greater length than it need to have been, could he have been prevailed upon to have attended in person the several courts of justice the cause had been carried through by his more industrious adversary. The exorbitant bills, however, which his lawyers were continually drawing upon him, joining with the pressing remonstrances of his friends, at last rouzed him from that inactivity of mind which had already cost him so dear, and determined him not only to take a journey to London, but likewise not to return home, till he had seen a final end put to this perplexing affair.

Before his departure, he went to the boarding-school, to take his leave of his beloved Betsy, and renew the charge he had frequently given the governess concerning her education; adding, in a mournful accent, that it would be a long time before he saw her again.

These words, as it proved, had somewhat of prophetick in them. On his arrival in London, he found his cause in so perplexed and entangled a situation, as gave him little hopes of ever bringing it to a favourable issue. The vexation and fatigue he underwent on this account, joined with the closeness of the town air, which had never agreed with his constitution even in his younger years, soon threw him into that sort of consumption which goes by the name of a galloping one, and, they say, is the most difficult of any to be removed. He died in about three months, without being able to do any great matters concerning the affair which had drawn him from his peaceful home, and according to all probability hastened his fate. Being perfectly sensible, and convinced of his approaching dissolution, he made his will, bequeathing the bulk of his estate to him whose right it was, (his eldest son) then upon his travels through the greatest part of Europe; all his personals, which were very considerable in the Bank, and other public funds, he ordered should be equally divided between Francis his second son, (at that time a student at Oxford) and Miss Betsy; constituting, at the same time, as trustees to the said testament, Sir Ralph Trusty, his near neighbour in the country, and Mr. Goodman, a wealthy merchant in the city of London; both of them gentlemen of unquestionable integrity, and with whom he had preserved a long and uninterrupted friendship.

On the arrival of this melancholy news, Miss Betsy felt as much grief as it was possible for a heart so young and gay as her's to be capable of; but a little time, for the most part, serves to obliterate the memory of misfortunes of this nature, even in persons of a riper age; and had Miss Betsy been more afflicted than she was, something happened soon after which would have very much contributed to her consolation.

Mr. Goodman having lived without marrying till he had reached an age which one should have imagined would have prevented him from thinking of it at all, at last took it into his head to become a husband. The person he made choice of was called Lady Mellasin, relict of a baronet, who having little or no estate, had accepted of a small employment about the court, in which post he died, leaving her ladyship one daughter, named Flora, in a very destitute condition. Goodman, however, had wealth enough for both, and consulted no other interest than that of his heart.

As for the lady, the motive on which she had consented to be his wife may easily be guessed; and when once made so, gained such an absolute ascendancy over him, that whatever she declared as her will, with him had the force of a law. She had an aversion to the city; he immediately took a house of her chusing at St. James's, inconvenient as it was for his business. Whatever servants she disapproved, though of ever so long standing, and of the most approved fidelity, were discharged, and others, more agreeable to her, put in their places. In fine, nothing she desired was denied; he considered her as an oracle of wit and wisdom, and thought it would be an unpardonable arrogance to attempt to set his reason against her's.

This lady was no sooner informed of the trust imposed in him, than she told him, she thought it would be highly proper for Miss Betsy to be sent for from the school, and boarded with them, not only as her daughter would be a fine companion for that young orphan, they being much of the same age, and she herself was more capable of improving her mind than any governess of a school could be supposed to be; but that, also, having her under her own eye, he would be more able to discharge his duty towards her as a guardian, than if she were at the distance of near an hundred miles.

There was something in this proposal which had, indeed, the face of a great deal of good-nature and consideration for Miss Betsy, at least it seemed highly so to Mr. Goodman; but as Sir Ralph Trusty was joined with him in the guardianship of that young beauty, and was at that time in London, he thought it proper to consult him on the occasion; which having done, and finding no objection on the part of the other, Lady Mellasin, to shew her great complaisance to the daughter of her husband's deceased friend, sent her own woman to bring her from the boarding-school, and attend her up to London.

Miss Betsy had never seen this great metropolis; but had heard so much of the gay manner in which the genteel part of the world passed their time in it, that she was quite transported at being told she was to be removed thither. Mrs. Prinks (for so Lady Mellasin's woman was called) did not fail to heighten her ideas of the pleasures of the place to which she was going, nor to magnify the goodness of her lady, in taking her under her care, with the most extravagant encomiums: it is not, therefore, to be wondered at, that neither the tears of the good governess, who truly loved her, nor those of her dear Miss Forward, nor of any of those she left behind, could give her any more than a momentary regret to a heart so possessed with the expectations of going to receive every thing with which youth is liable to be enchanted. She promised, however, to keep up a correspondence by letters; which she did, till things, that seemed to her of much more importance, put her L——e acquaintance entirely out of her head.

She was met at the inn where the stage put up, by Mr. Goodman, in his own coach, accompanied by Miss Flora: the good old gentleman embraced her with the utmost tenderness, and assured her that nothing in his power, or in that of his family, would be wanting to compensate, as much as possible, the loss she had sustained by the death of her parents. The young lady also said many obliging things to her; and they seemed highly taken with each other at this first interview, which gave the honest heart of Goodman an infinite satisfaction.

The reception given her by Lady Mellasin, when brought home, and presented to her by her husband, was conformable to what Mrs. Prinks had made her expect; that lady omitting nothing to make her certain of being always treated by her with the same affection as her own daughter.

Sir Ralph Trusty, on being informed his young charge was come to town, came the next day to Mr. Goodman's to visit her: his lady accompanied him. There had been a great intimacy and friendship between her and the mother of Miss Betsy, and she could not hold in her arms the child of a person so dear to her without letting fall some tears, which were looked upon by the company as the tribute due to the memory of the dead. The conjecture, in part, might be true, but the flow proceeded from the mixture of another motive, not suspected – that of compassion for the living. This lady was a woman of great prudence, piety, and virtue: she had heard many things relating to the conduct of Lady Mellasin, which made her think her a very unfit person to have the care of youth, especially those of her own sex. She had been extremely troubled when Sir Ralph told her that Miss Betsy was sent for from the country to live under such tuition, and would have fain opposed it, could she have done so without danger of creating a misunderstanding between him and Mr. Goodman, well knowing the bigotted respect the latter had for his wife, and how unwilling he would be to do any thing that had the least tendency to thwart her inclinations. She communicated her sentiments, however, on this occasion, to no person in the world, not even to her own husband; but resolved, within herself, to take all the opportunities that fell in her way, of giving Miss Betsy such instructions as she thought necessary for her behaviour in general, and especially towards the family in which it was her lot to be placed.

Miss Betsy was now just entering into her fourteenth year, a nice and delicate time in persons of her sex; since it is then they are most apt to take the bent of impression, which, according as it is well or ill directed, makes or mars the future prospect of their lives. She was tall, well-shaped, and perfectly amiable, without being what is called a compleat beauty; and as she wanted nothing to render her liable to the greatest temptations, so she stood in need of the surest arms for her defence against them.

But while this worthy lady was full of cares for the well doing of a young creature who appeared so deserving of regard, Miss Betsy thought she had the highest reason to be satisfied with her situation; and how, indeed, could it be otherwise? Lady Mellasin kept a great deal of company; she received visits every morning, from ten to one o'clock, from the most gay and polite of both sexes; all the news of the town was talked on at her levee, and it seldom happened that some party of pleasure was not formed for the ensuing evening, in all which Miss Betsy and Miss Flora had their share.

Never did the mistress of a private family indulge herself, and those about her, with such a continual round of publick diversions! The court, the play, the ball, and opera, with giving and receiving visits, engrossed all the time that could be spared from the toilette. It cannot, therefore, seem strange that Miss Betsy, to whom all these things were entirely new, should have her head turned with the promiscuous enjoyment, and the very power of reflection lost amidst the giddy whirl; nor that it should be so long before she could recover it enough to see the little true felicity of such a course of life.

Among the many topicks with which this brilliant society entertained each other, it may easily be supposed that love and gallantry were not excluded. Lady Mellasin, though turned of forty, had her fine things said to her; but both heaven and earth were ransacked for comparisons in favour of the beauty of Miss Flora and Miss Betsy: but as there was nothing particular in these kind of addresses, intended only to shew the wit of those who made them, these young ladies answered them only with raillery, in which art Miss Betsy soon learned to excel. She had the glory, however, of being the first who excited a real passion in the heart of any of those who visited Lady Mellasin; though, being accustomed to hear declarations which had the appearance of love, yet were really no more than words of course, and made indiscriminately to every fine woman, she would not presently persuade herself that this was more serious.

The first victim of her charms was the only son of a very rich alderman; and having a fortune left him by a relation, independent of his father, who was the greatest miser in the world, he was furnished with the means of mingling with the *beau monde*, and of making one at every diversion that was proposed.

He had fancied Miss Flora a mighty fine creature, before he saw Miss Betsy; but the imaginary flame he had for her was soon converted into a sincere one for the other. He truly loved her, and was almost distracted at the little credit she gave to his professions. His perseverance, his tremblings whenever he approached her, his transports on seeing her, his anxieties at taking leave, so different from what she had observed in any other of those who had pretended to lift themselves under the banner of her charms, at length convincing her of the conquest she had made, awakened in her breast that vanity so natural to a youthful mind. She exulted, she plumed herself, she used him ill and well by turns, taking an equal pleasure in raising or depressing his hopes; and, in spite of her good-nature, felt no satisfaction superior to that of the consciousness of a power of giving pain to the man who loved her: but with how great a mortification this short-lived triumph was succeeded, the reader shall presently be made sensible.

CHAPTER III

—————•—————

*Affords matter of condolance, or raillery, according to
the humour the reader happens to be in for either*

WE often see, that the less encouragement is given to the lover's suit,
with the more warmth and eagerness he prosecutes it; and many
people are apt to ascribe this hopeless perseverance to an odd
perverseness in the very nature of love; but, for my part, I rather take
it to proceed from an ambition of surmounting difficulties: it is
not, however, my province to enter into any discussion of so nice
a point; I deal only in matters of fact, and shall not meddle with
definition.

It was not till after Miss Betsy had reason to believe she had
engaged the heart of her lover too far for him to recal it, that she
began to take a pride in tormenting. While she looked on his
addresses as of a piece with those who called themselves her
admirers, she had treated him in that manner which she thought
would most conduce to make him really so; but no sooner did she
perceive, by the tokens before mentioned, that his passion was of the
most serious nature, than she behaved to him in a fashion quite the
reverse, especially before company; for as she had not the least
affection, or even a liking towards him, his submissive deportment
under the most cold, sometimes contemptuous, carriage, could afford
her no other satisfaction, than, as she fancied, it shewed the power of
her beauty, and piqued those ladies of her acquaintance, who could
not boast of such an implicit resignation and patient suffering from
their lovers; in particular, Miss Flora, who she could not forbear
imagining looked very grave on the occasion. What foundation there
was for a conjecture of this nature was nevertheless undiscoverable

till a long time after.

As this courtship was no secret to any of the family, Mr. Goodman thought himself obliged, both as the guardian of Miss Betsy, and the friend of Alderman Saving, (for so the father of this young enamorato was called) to enquire upon what footing it stood. He thought, that if the old man knew and approved of his son's inclinations, he would have mentioned the affair to him, as they frequently saw each other; and it seemed to him neither for the interest nor reputation of his fair charge, to receive the clandestine addresses of any man whatsoever. She had a handsome fortune of her own, and he thought that, and her personal accomplishments, sufficiently entitled her to as good a match as Mr. Saving; but then he knew the sordid nature of the alderman, and that all the merits of Miss Betsy would add nothing in the balance, if her money was found too light to poise against the sums his son would be possessed of. This being the case, he doubted not but that he was kept in ignorance of the young man's intentions; and, fearing the matter might be carried too far, resolved either to put a stop to it at once, or permit it to go on, on such terms as should free him from all censure from the one or the other party.

On talking seriously to the lover, he soon found the suggestions he had entertained had not deceived him. Young Saving frankly confessed, that his father had other views for him; but added, that if he could prevail on the young lady to marry him, he did not despair but that when the thing was once done, and past recal, the alderman would by degrees receive them into favour. 'You know, Sir,' said he, 'that he has no child but me, nor any kindred for whom he has the least regard; and it cannot be supposed he would utterly discard me for following my inclinations in this point, especially as they are in favour of the most amiable and deserving of her sex.'

He said much more on this head, but it had no weight with the merchant; he answered, that if the alderman was of his way of thinking, all the flattering hopes his passion suggested to him on that score, might be realized; but that, according to the disposition he knew him to be of, he saw but little room to think he would forgive a step of this kind. 'Therefore,' continued he, 'I cannot allow this love-affair to be prosecuted any farther, and must desire you will desist visiting at my house, till you have either conquered this inclination, or Miss Betsy is otherwise disposed of.'

This was a cruel sentence for the truly affectionate Saving; but he found it in vain to solicit a repeal of it, and all he could obtain from him, was a promise to say nothing of what had passed to the alderman.

Mr. Goodman would have thought he had but half compleated his duty, had he neglected to sound the inclination of Miss Betsy on this account; and in order to come more easily at the truth, he began with talking to her in a manner which might make her look on him rather as a favourer of Mr. Saving's pretensions than the contrary, and was extremely glad to find, by her replies, how indifferent that young lover was to her. He then acquainted her with the resolution he had taken, and the discourse he had just had with him; and, to keep her from ever after encouraging the addresses of any man, without being authorized by the consent of friends on both sides, represented in the most pathetick terms he was able, the danger to which a private correspondence renders a young woman liable. She seemed convinced of the truth of what he said, and promised to follow, in the strictest manner, his advice.

Whether she thought herself, in reality, so much obliged to the conduct of her guardian in this, I will not take upon me to say; for though she was not charmed with the person of Mr. Saving, it is certain she took an infinite pleasure in the assiduities of his passion: it is, therefore, highly probable, that she might imagine he meddled in this affair more than he had any occasion to have done. She had, however, but little time for reflection on her guardian's behaviour, an accident happening, which shewed her own to her in a light very different from what she had ever seen it.

Lady Mellasin had a ball at her house; there was a great deal of company, among whom was a gentleman named Gayland: he was a man of family – had a large estate – sung, danced, spoke French, dressed well – frequent successes among the women had rendered him extremely vain, and as he had too great an admiration for his own person to be possessed of any great share of it for that of any other, he enjoyed the pleasures of love, without being sensible of the pains. This darling of the fair it was, that Miss Betsy picked out to treat with the most peculiar marks of esteem, whenever she had a mind to give umbrage to poor Saving: much had that faithful lover suffered on the account of this fop; but the fair inflictor of his torments was punished for her insensibility and ingratitude, by a way her inexperience of the world, and the temper of mankind in general, had made her far from apprehending.

While the company were employed, some in dancing, and others in particular conversation, the beau found an opportunity to slip into Miss Betsy's hand a little billet, saying to her at the same time, 'You have got my heart, and this little bit of paper will convey to you the sentiments it is inspired with in your favour.' She, imagining it was either a sonnet or epistle, in praise of her beauty, received it with a smile, and put it in her pocket. After every body had taken leave, and she was retired to her chamber, she examined it, and found, to her great astonishment, the contents as follows –

'Dear Miss,
I must either be the most ungrateful, or most consumedly dull fellow upon earth, not to have returned the advances you have been so kind to make me, had the least opportunity offered for my doing so; but Lady Mellasin, her daughter, the fool Saving, or some impertinent creature or other, has always been in the way, so that there was not a possibility of giving you even the least earnest of love: but, my dear, I have found out a way to pay you the whole sum with interest; which is this – you must invent some excuse for going out alone, and let me know by a billet, directed for me at White's, the exact hour, and I will wait for you at the corner of the street in a hackney-coach, the window drawn up, and whirl you to a pretty snug place I know of, where we may pass a delicious hour or two without a soul to interrupt our pleasures. Let me find a line from you tomorrow, if you can any way contrive it, being impatient to convince you how much I am, my dear creature, yours, &c. &c.

. J. GAYLAND.'

Impossible it is to express the mingled emotions of shame, surprize, and indignation, which filled the breast of Miss Betsy, on reading this bold invitation; she threw the letter on the ground, she stamped upon it, she spurned it, and would have treated the author in the same manner, had he been present; but the first transports of so just a resentment being over, a consciousness of having, by a too free behaviour towards him, emboldened him to take this liberty, involved her in the utmost confusion, and she was little less enraged with herself, than she had reason to be with him. She could have tore out her very eyes for having affected to look kindly upon a wretch who durst presume so far on her supposed affection; and though she spared those pretty twinklers that violence, she half drowned their lustre in a deluge of tears. Never was a night passed in more cruel anxieties than what she sustained; both from the affront she had received, and the reflection that it was chiefly the folly of her own conduct which had brought it on her; and what greatly added to her vexation, was the uncertainty how it would best become her to act on an occasion which appeared so extraordinary to her. She had no friend whom she thought it proper to consult; she was ashamed to relate the story to any of the discreet and serious part of her acquaintance; she feared their reproofs for having counterfeited a tenderness for a man, which she was now sensible she ought, if it had been real, rather to have concealed with the utmost care both from him and all the world; and as for Lady Mellasin and Miss Flora, though their conduct inspired her not with any manner of awe, yet she thought she saw something in those ladies which did not promise much sincerity, and shewed as if they would rather turn her complaints into ridicule, than afford her that cordial and friendly advice she stood in need of.

These were the reasons which determined her to keep the whole thing a secret from every one. At first she was tempted to write to Gayland, and testify her disdain of his presumption in terms which should convince him how grossly his vanity had imposed upon him; but she afterwards considered that a letter from her was doing him too much honour, and though ever so reproachful, might draw another from him, either to excuse and beg pardon for the temerity of the former, or possibly to affront her a second time, by defending it, and repeating his request. She despised and hated him too much to engage in a correspondence with him of any kind, and therefore resolved, as it was certainly most prudent, not to let him have any thing under her hand, but when next she saw him to shew her resentment by such ways as occasion should permit.

He came not to Mr. Goodman's, however, for three days, possibly waiting that time for a letter from Miss Betsy; but on the fourth he appeared at Lady Mellasin's tea-table. There were, besides the family, several others present, so that he had not an opportunity of speaking in private to Miss Betsy; but the looks she gave him, so different from all he had ever seen her assume towards him, might have shewn any man, not blinded with his vanity, how much she was offended: but he imagining her ill-humour proceeded only from the want of means to send to him, came again the next day, and happening to find her alone in the parlour, 'What, my dear,' said he, taking her in a free manner by the hand, 'have you been so closely watched by your guardian and guardianesses here, that no kind moment offered for you to answer the devoirs of your humble servant?' – 'The surest guardians of my fame and peace,' replied she, snatching her hand away, 'is the little share of understanding, I am mistress of, which I hope will always be sufficient to defend my honour in more dangerous attacks, than the rude impertinences of an idle coxcomb.'

These words, and the air with which they were spoke, one would think should have struck with confusion the person to whom they were directed: but Gayland was not so easily put out of countenance; and, looking her full in the face – 'Ah, child!' cried he, 'sure you are not in your right senses today! "Understanding – impertinences – idle coxcomb!" Very pleasant, i'faith! but, upon my soul, if you think these airs become you, you are the most mistaken woman in the world!' – 'It may be so,' cried she, ready to burst with inward spite at his insolence; 'but I should be yet more mistaken if I were capable of thinking a wretch like you worthy of any thing but contempt.' With these words she flung out of the room, and he pursued her with a horse-laugh, till she was out of hearing, and then went into the dining room, where he found Lady Mellasin, and several who had come to visit her.

Miss Betsy, who had gone directly to her own chamber, sent to excuse coming down to tea, pretending a violent head-ache, nor would be prevailed upon to join the company till she heard Gayland had taken his leave, which he did much sooner than usual, being probably a good deal disconcerted at the shock his vanity had received.

CHAPTER IV

———————•———————

Verifies the old proverb, that one affliction treads upon the heels of another

As Miss Betsy was prevented from discovering to any one the impudent attempt Gayland had made on her virtue, by the shame of having emboldened him to it by too unreserved a behaviour; so also the shame of the disappointment and rebuff he had received from her, kept him from saying any thing of what had passed between them: and this resolution on both sides rendered it very difficult for either of them to behave to the other, so as not to give some suspicion. Betsy could not always avoid seeing him when he came to Lady Mellasin's, for he would not all at once desist his visits for two reasons; first, because it might give occasion for an enquiry into the cause; and, secondly, because Miss Betsy would plume herself on the occasion, as having, by her scorn, triumphed over his audacity, and drove him from the field of battle. He therefore resolved to continue his visits for some time; and to pique her, as he imagined, directed all the fine things his common-place-book was well stored with, to Miss Flora, leaving the other wholly neglected.

But here he was little less deceived than he had been before in the sentiments of that young lady; the hatred his late behaviour had given her, and the utter detestation it had excited in her towards him, had for a time extinguished that vanity so almost inseparable from youth, especially when accompanied with beauty; and she rather rejoiced, than the contrary, to see him affect to be so much taken up with Miss Flora, that he could scarce say the least complaisant thing to her, as it freed her from the necessity of returning it in some measure. Her good sense had now scope to operate; she saw, as in a mirror, her own late follies in those of Miss Flora, who swelled with all the pride of flattered vanity on this new imaginary conquest over the heart of the accomplished Gayland, as he was generally esteemed, and perceived the errors of such a way of thinking and acting in so clear a light, as, had it continued, would doubtless have spared her those anxieties her relapse from it afterwards occasioned.

In these serious reflections let us leave her for a time, to see in what situation Mr. Saving was, after being denied access to his mistress. As it was impossible for a heart to be more truly sincere and affectionate, he was far from being able to make any efforts for the banishing Miss Betsy's image thence; on the contrary, he thought of nothing but how to continue a correspondence with her, and endeavour, by all the means in his power, to engage her to a private interview. As his flame was pure and respectful, he was some days debating within himself how to proceed, so as not to let her think he had desisted from his pretensions, or to continue them in a manner at which she should not be offended. Love, when real, seldom fails of inspiring the breast that harbours it with an equal share of timidity; he trembled whenever he thought of soliciting such a meeting; yet, without it, how could he hope to retain any place in her memory, much less make any progress in gaining her affection! At length, however, he assumed enough courage to write to her, and by a bribe to one of the servants, got his letter delivered to her, fearing if he had it sent by the post, or any publick way to the house, it would be intercepted by the caution he found Mr. Goodman had resolved to observe in this point.

Miss Betsy knowing his hand by the superscription, was a little surprized, as perhaps having never thought of him since they parted, but opened it without the least emotion either of pain or pleasure: she knew him too well to be under any apprehensions of being treated by him as she had been by Gayland, and was too little sensible of his merit to feel the least impatience for examining the dictates of his affection; yet, indifferent as she was, she could not forbear being touched on reading these lines –

'Most adored of your sex,
I doubt not but you are acquainted with Mr. Goodman's behaviour to me; but, oh! I fear you are too insensible of the agonies in which my soul labours through his cruel caution. Dreadful is the loss of sight,

yet what is sight to me, when it presents not you! Though I saw you regardless of my ardent passion, yet still I saw you – and while I did so, could not be wholly wretched! What have I not endured since deprived of that only joy for which I wish to live! Had it not been improper for me to have been seen near Mr. Goodman's house, after having been forbid entrance to it, I should have dwelt for ever in your street, in hope of sometimes getting a glimpse of you from one or other of the windows: this I thought would be taken notice of, and might offend you; but darkness freed me from these apprehensions, and gave me the consolation of breathing in the same air with you. Soon as I thought all watchful eyes were closed, I flew to the place, which, wherever my body is, contains my heart and all it's faculties. I pleased myself with looking on the roof that covers you, and invoked every star to present me to you in your sleep, in a form more agreeable than I can hope I ever appeared in to your waking fancy. Thus I have passed each night; and when the morning dawned, unwillingly retired to take that rest which nature more especially demands, when heavy melancholy oppresses the heart. I slept – but how? Distracting images swam in my tormented brain, and waked me with horrors inconceivable. Equally lost to business, as to all social commerce, I fly mankind; and, like some discontented ghost, seek out the most solitary walks, and lonely shades, to pour forth my complaints. O Miss Betsy! I cannot live, if longer denied the sight of you! In pity to my sufferings, permit me yet once more to speak to you, even though it be to take a last farewel. I have made a little kind of interest with the woman at the habit-shop in Covent Garden, where I know you sometimes go; I dread to intreat you would call there to-morrow; yet, if you are so divinely good, be assured I shall entertain no presuming hopes on the condescension you shall be pleased to make me, but acknowledge it as the mere effect of that compassion which is inherent to a generous mind. Alas! I must be much more worthy than I can yet pretend to be, before I dare flatter myself with owing any thing to a more soft emotion, than that I have mentioned. Accuse me not, therefore, of too much boldness in this petition, but grant to my despair what you would deny to the love of your most faithful, and everlasting slave,

H. SAVING.

P.S. The favour of one line, to let me know whether I may expect the blessing I implore, will add to the bounty of it. The same hand that brings you this, will also deliver your commands to yours as above.'

Miss Betsy read this letter several times, and, the oftener she did so, the more she saw into the soul of him that sent it. How wide the difference between this and that she received from Gayland! 'Tis true, they both desired a meeting, each made the same request; but the manner in which the former was asked, and the end proposed by the grant of it, she easily perceived were as distant as heaven and hell. She called to mind the great respect he had always treated her with; she was convinced both of his honour and sincerity, and thought something was due from her on that account. In fine, after deliberating a little within herself, she resolved to write to him in these terms –

Sir,
Though it is my fixed determination to encourage the addresses of no man whatever, without the approbation of my guardians, yet I think myself too much obliged to the affection you have expressed for me, to refuse you a favour of so trifling a nature as that you have taken the pains to ask. I will be at the place you mention to-morrow, some time in the forenoon; but desire you will expect nothing from it but a last farewel, which you have promised to be contented with. Till then, adieu.'

After finishing this little billet, she called the maid, whom Saving had made his confidante, into the chamber, and asked her, when she expected he would come for an answer. To which the other replied, that he had appointed her to meet him at the corner of the street very early in the morning, before any of the windows were open. 'Well, then,' said Miss Betsy, smiling, and putting the letter into her hands, 'give him this. I do it for your sake, Nanny; for, I suppose, you will have a double fee on the delivery.' – 'The gentleman is too much in love,' answered she, 'not to be grateful.'

Miss Betsy passed the remainder of that day, and the ensuing night, with that tranqillity which is inseparable from a mind unincumbered with passion; but the next morning, remembering her promise, while Lady Mellasin and Miss Flora were engaged with the beaux and belles at their levee, she slipped out, and taking a chair at the end of the street, went to the milliner's according to appointment. She doubted not but the impatience of her lover would have brought him there long before her, and was very much amazed to find herself the first comer. She knew not, however, but some extraordinary accident, unforeseen by him, might have happened to detain him longer than he expected; and from the whole course of his past behaviour, could find no shadow of reason to suspect him of a wilful remissness. She sat down in the shop, and amused herself with talking to the woman on the new modes of dress, and such like ordinary matters; but made not the least mention of the motive which had brought her there that morning: and the other, not knowing whether it would be proper to take any notice, was also silent on that occasion; but Miss Betsy observed she often turned her head towards the window, and ran to the door, looking up and down the street, as if she expected somebody who was not yet come.

Miss Betsy could not forbear being shocked at a disappointment, which was the last thing in the world she could have apprehended. She had, notwithstanding, the patience to wait from a little past eleven till near two o'clock, expecting, during every moment of that time, that he would either come or send some excuse for not doing so; but finding he did neither, and that it was near the hour in which Mr. Goodman usually dined, she took her leave of the woman, and went home full of agitations.

The maid, who was in the secret, happening to open the door, and Miss Betsy looking around and perceiving there was nobody in hearing, said to hear, 'Nanny, are you sure you delivered my letter safe into Mr. Saving's hand?' – 'Sure, Miss!' cried the wench, 'yes, as sure as I am alive; and he gave me a good Queen Anne's guinea for my trouble. I have not had time since to put it up,' continued she, taking it out of her bosom; 'here it is.' – 'Well, then, what did he say on receiving it?' said Miss Betsy. 'I never saw a man so transported,' replied she; 'he put it to his mouth, and kissed it with such an eagerness, I thought he would have devoured it.' Miss Betsy asked no farther questions, but went up to her chamber to pull off her hood, not being able to know how she ought to judge of this adventure.

She was soon called down to dinner; but her mind was too much perplexed to suffer her to eat much.

She was extremely uneasy the whole day for an explanation of what at present seemed so mysterious, and this gave her little less pain than perhaps she would have felt had she been possessed with an equal share of love; but in the evening her natural vivacity got the better, and not doubting but the next morning she should receive a letter with a full eclaircisement of this affair, she enjoyed the same sweet repose as if nothing had happened to ruffle her temper.

The morning came, but brought no billet from that once obsequious lover: the next, and three or four succeeding ones, were barren of the fruit she so much expected. What judgment could she form of an event so odd? She could not bring herself to think Saving had taken pains to procure a rendezvous with her, on purpose to disappoint and affront her; and was not able to conceive any probable means by which he could be prevented from writing to her. Death only, she thought, could be an excuse for him, and had that happened she should have heard of it. Sometimes she fancied that the maid had been treacherous; but when she considered she could get nothing by being so, and that it was, on the contrary, rather her interest to be sincere, she rejected that supposition. The various conjectures, which by turns came into her head, rendered her, however, excessively disturbed, and in a situation which deserved some share of pity, had not her pride kept her from revealing the discontent, or the motives of it, to any one person in the world.

CHAPTER V

———•———

Contains nothing very extraordinary, yet such things as are highly proper to be known

I THINK it is generally allowed that there are few emotions of the mind more uneasy than suspense. Not the extreme youth of Miss Betsy, not all her natural cheerfulness, nor her perfect indifference for the son of Alderman Saving, could enable her to throw off the vexation in which his late behiavour had involved her: had the motive been the most mortifying of any that could be imagined to her vanity, pride and resentment would then have come to her assistance; she would have despised the author of the insult, and in time have forgot the insult itself; but the uncertainty in what manner she ought to think of the man, and this last action of his, made both dwell much longer on her mind than otherwise they would have done. As the poet truly says –

'When puzzling doubts the anxious bosom seize,
To know the worst, is some degree of ease.'

This is a maxim which will hold good, even when the strongest and most violent passions operate; but Miss Betsy was possessed of no more than a bare curiosity, which as she had as yet no other sensation that demanded gratification, was sufficiently painful to her.

It was about ten or twelve days that she continued to labour under this dilemma; but, at the expiration of that time, was partly relieved from it by the following means.

Mr. Goodman, happening to meet Alderman Saving, with whom he had great business, upon Change, desired he would accompany him to an adjacent tavern; to which the other complied, but with an air much more grave and reserved than he was accustomed to put on with a person whom he had known for a great number of years, and was concerned with in some affairs of traffick, they went together to the Ship Tavern.

After having ended what they had to say to each other upon business – 'Mr. Goodman,' said the alderman, 'we have long been friends; I always thought you an honest, fair-dealing man, and am therefore very much surprized you should go about to put upon me in the manner you have lately done.' – 'Put upon you, Sir!' cried the merchant; 'I know not what you mean; and am very certain I never did any thing that might call in question my integrity, either to you or to any one else.' – 'It was great integrity, indeed!' resumed the alderman, with a sneer, 'to endeavour to draw my only son into a clandestine marriage with the girl you have at your house.' Mr. Goodman was astonished, as well he might, at this accusation; and perceiving, by some other words that the alderman let fall, that he was well acquainted with the love young Saving had professed for Miss Betsy, frankly related to him all that he knew of the courtship, and the method he had taken to put a stop to it. 'That was not enough, Sir,' cried the alderman, hastily; 'you should have told me of it. Do you think young folks, like them, would have regarded your forbidding? No, no! I'll warrant you they would have found some way or other to come together before now; and the boy might have been ruined, if I had not been informed by other hands how things were carried on, and put it out of the power of any of you to impose upon me. The girl may spread her nets to catch some other woodcock, if she can. Thanks to Heaven, and my own prudence, my son is far enough out of her reach!'

Mr. Goodman, though one of the best-natured men in the world, could not keep himself from being a little ruffled at the alderman's discourse; and told him, that though he had been far from encouraging Mr. Saving's inclinations, and should always think it the duty of a son to consult his father in every thing he did, especially in so material a point as that of marriage, yet he saw no reason for treating Miss Betsy with contempt, as she was of a good family, had a very pretty fortune of her own, and suitable accomplishments.

'You take a great deal of pains to set her off,' said the alderman; 'and since you married a court-lady not worth a groat, have got all the romantick idle notions of the other end of the town as finely as if you had been bred there. A good family! – Very pleasant, i'faith. Will a good family go to market? Will it buy a joint of mutton at the butcher's, or a pretty gown at the mercer's? – Then, a pretty fortune! you say – Enough, it may be, to squander away at cards or masquerades for a month or two. She has suitable accomplishments too! – Yes, indeed, they are suitable ones, I believe! – I suppose she can sing, dance, and jabber a little French; but I'll be hanged if she knows how to make a pye, or a pudding, or to teach her maid to do it!'

The reflection on Lady Mellasin, in the beginning of this speech, so much incensed Mr. Goodman, that he could scarce attend to the latter part of it: he forbore interrupting him, however; but, as soon as he had done speaking, replied in terms which shewed his resentment. In fine, such hot words passed between them, as, had they been younger men, might have produced worse consequence; but the spirit of both being equally evaporated in mutual reproaches, they grew more calm, and at last talked themselves into as good harmony as ever. Mr. Goodman said he was sorry that he had been prevailed upon, by the young man's intreaties, to keep his courtship to Miss Betsy a secret; and the alderman begged pardon, in his turn, for having said any thing disrespectful of Lady Mellasin.

On this they shook hands; another half-pint of sherry was called for; and, before they parted, the alderman acquainted Mr. Goodman, that to prevent entirely all future correspondence between his son and Miss Betsy, he had sent him to Holland some days ago, without letting him know any thing of his intentions till every thing was ready for his embarkation. 'I sent,' said he, 'the night before he was to go, his portmanteau, and what other luggage I thought he would have occasion for, to the inn where the Harwich stage puts up; and, making him be called up very early in the morning, told him he must go a little way out of town with me upon extraordinary business. He seemed very unwilling; said he had appointed that morning to meet a gentleman, and begged I would delay the journey to the next day, or even till the afternoon. What caused this backwardness I cannot imagine, for I think it was impossible he could know my designs on this score; but, whatever was in his head, I took care to disappoint it. I listened to none of his excuses, nor trusted him out of my sight; but forced him to go with me to the coach, in which I had secured a couple of places. He was horribly shocked when he found where he was going, and would fain have persuaded me to repeal his banishment, as he called it. I laughed in my sleeve; but took no notice of the real motive I had for sending him away, and told him there was an absolute necessity for his departure; that I had a business of the greatest importance at Rotterdam, in which I could trust nobody but himself to negociate; and that he would find, in his trunk, letters, and other papers, which would instruct him how to act.

'In fine,' continued the alderman, 'I went with him aboard, staid with him till they were ready to weigh anchor, then returned, and stood on the beach till the ship sailed quite out of sight; so that if my gentleman had a thought of writing to his mistress, he had not the least opportunity for it.' He added, that he did not altogether deceive his son, having, indeed, some affairs to transact at Rotterdam, though they were not of the mighty consequence he had pretended; but which he had, by a private letter to his agent there, ordered should be made appear as intricate and perplexing as possible, that the young gentleman's return might be delayed as long as there was any plausible excuse for detaining him, without his seeing through the reason of it.

Mr. Goodman praised the alderman's discretion in the whole conduct of this business; and, to atone for having been prevailed upn to keep young Saving's secret from him, offered to make interest with a friend he had at the post-office, to stop any letter that should be directed to Miss Betsy Thoughtless, by the way of Holland: 'By which means,' said he, 'all communication between the young people will soon be put an end to; he will grow weary of writing letters when he receives no answers; and she of thinking of him as a lover, when she finds he ceases to tell her he is so.'

The alderman was ready to hug his old friend for this proposal, which, it is certain, he made in the sincerity of his heart; for they no sooner parted, then he went to the office, and fulfilled his promise.

When he came home, in order to hinder Miss Betsy from expecting to hear any thing more of Mr. Saving, he told her he had been treated by the alderman pretty roughly, on account of the encouragement that had been given in his house to the amorous addresses which had been made to her by his son: 'And,' added he, 'the old man is so incensed against him, for having a thought of that kind in your favour, that he has sent him beyond sea – I know not to what part: but, it seems, he is never to come back, till he has given full assurance the liking he has for you is utterly worn off.'

'He might have spared himself the pains,' said Miss Betsy,

blushing with disdain, 'his son could have informed him how little I was inclinable to listen to any thing he said, on the score of love; and I myself, if he had asked me the question, would have given him the strongest assurances that words could form, that if ever I changed my condition, (which Heaven knows I am far from thinking on as yet) I should never be prevailed upon to do it by any merits his son was possessed of.'

Mr. Goodman congratulated her on the indifference she expressed; and told her, he hoped she would always continue in the same humour, till an offer which promised more satisfaction in marriage should happen to be made.

Nothing more was said on this head; but Miss Betsy, upon ruminating on what Mr. Goodman had related, easily imagined, that the day in which he had been sent away, was the same on which he had appointed to meet her, and therefore excused his not coming as a thing unavoidable; yet, as she knew not the precaution his father had taken, was not so ready to forgive him for not sending a line to prevent her waiting so long for him at the habit-shop. She could not, however, when she reflected on the whole tenor of his deportment to her, think it possible he should all at once become guilty of wilfully omitting what even common good manners and decency required. She soon grew weary, however, of troubling herself about the matter; and a very few days served to make her lose even the memory of it.

CHAPTER VI

May be of some service to the ladies, especially the younger sort, if well attended to

MISS Betsy had now no person that professed a serious passion for her; but, as she had yet never seen the man capable of inspiring her with the least emotions of tenderness, she was quite easy as to that point, and wished nothing beyond what she enjoyed, the pleasure of being told she was very handsome, and gallanted about by a great number of those who go by the name of very pretty fellows. Pleased with the praise, she regarded not the condition or merits of the praised, and and suffered herself to be treated, presented, and squired about to all publick places, either by the rake, the man of honour, the wit, or the fool, the married as well as the unmarried, without distinction, and just as either fell in her way.

Such a conduct as this could not fail of laying her open to the censure of malicious tongues: the agreeableness of her person, her wit, and the many accomplishments she was mistress of, made her envied and hated, even by those who professed the greatest friendship for her. Several there were who, though they could scarce support the vexation it gave them to see her so much preferred to themselves, yet chose to be as much with her as possible, in the cruel hope of finding some fresh manner wherewith to blast her reputation.

Certain it is, that though she was as far removed as innocence itself from all intent or wish of committing a real ill, yet she paid too little regard to the appearances of it, and said and did many things which the actually criminal would be more cautious to avoid. Hurried by an excess of vanity, and that love of pleasure so natural to youth, she indulged herself in liberties, of which she foresaw not the consequences.

Lady Trusty, who sincerely loved her, both for her own sake, and that of her deceased mother, came more often to Mr. Goodman's than otherwise she would have done, on purpose to observe the behaviour of Miss Betsy: she had heard some accounts, which gave her great dissatisfaction; but, as she was a woman of penetration, she easily perceived, that plain reproof was not the way to prevail on her to reclaim the errors of her conduct; that she must be insensibly weaned from what at present she took so much delight in, and brought into a different manner of living, by ways which should rather seem to flatter than check her vanity. She therefore earnestly wished to get her down with her into L—e, where she was soon going herself; but knew not how to ask her without making the same invitation to Miss Flora, whose company she no way desired, and whose example, she was sensible, had very much contributed to give Miss Betsy that air of levity, which rendered her good sense almost useless to her.

This worthy lady happening to find her alone one day, (a thing not very usual) she asked, by way of sounding her inclination, if she would not be glad to see L—e again; to which she replied, that there were many people for whom she had a very great respect; but the journey was too long to be taken merely on the score of making a short visit; for she owned she did not like the country well enough to continue in it for any length of time.

Lady Trusty would fain have persuaded her into a better opinion of the place she was born in, and which most of her family had passed the greatest part of their lives in; but Miss Betsy was not to be argued into any tolerable ideas of it, and plainly told her ladyship, that what she called a happy tranquil manner of spending one's days, seemed to her little better than being buried alive.

From declaring her aversion to a country life, she ran into such extravagant encomiums on those various amusements which London every day presented, that Lady Trusty perceived it would not be without great difficulty she would be brought to a more just way of thinking; she concealed, however, as much as possible, the concern it gave her to hear her express herself in this manner; contenting herself with saying, calmly, that London was indeed a very agreeable place to live in, especially for young people, and the pleasures it afforded were very elegant; 'But then,' said she, 'the too frequent repetition of them may so much engross the mind as to take it off from other objects, which ought to have their share in it. Besides,' continued she, 'there are but too frequent proofs that an innate principle of virtue is not always a sufficient guard against the many snares laid for it, under the shew of innocent pleasures, by wicked and designing persons of both sexes; nor can it be esteemed prudence to run one's self into dangers merely to shew our strength in overcoming them: nor, perhaps, would even the victory turn always to our glory; the world is censorious, and seldom ready to put the best construction on things; so that reputation may suffer, though virtue triumphs.'

Miss Betsy listened to all this with a good deal of attention; the impudent attempt Gayland had made on her came fresh into her mind, and made this lady's remonstrances sink the deeper into it. The power of reflection being a little awakened in her, some freedoms also, not altogether consistent with strict modesty, which others had offered to her, convinced her of the error of maintaining too little reserve; she thanked her kind adviser, and promised to observe the precepts she had given.

Lady Trusty, finding this good effect of what she had said, ventured to proceed so far as to give some hints that the conduct of Miss Flora had been far from blameless; 'And therefore,' pursued she, 'I should be glad, methinks, to see you separated from that young lady, though it were but for a small time;' and then gave her to understand how great a pleasure it would be to her to get her down with her to L—e, if it could be any way contrived that she should go without Miss Flora.

'As I have been so long from home,' said she, 'I know I shall have all the gentry round the country to welcome me at my return; and if you should find the company less polite than those you leave behind, it will at least diversify the scene, and render the entertainments of London new to you a second time, when you come back.'

Miss Betsy found in herself a strong inclination to comply with this proposal; and told Lady Trusty, she should think herself happy in passing the whole summer with her; and as to Miss Flora, the same offer might be made to her without any danger of her accepting it. 'I am not of your opinion,' said the other: 'the girl has no fortune, but what Mr. Goodman shall be pleased to give her, which cannot be very considerable, as he has a nephew in the East Indies whom he is extremely fond of, and will make his heir. Lady Mellasin would, therefore, catch at the opportunity of sending her daughter to a place where there are so many gentlemen of estates, among whom she might have a better chance for getting a husband than she can have in London, where her character would scarce entitle her to such a hope. I will, however,' pursued she, 'run the risque, and chuse rather to have a guest whose company I do not so well approve of, than be deprived of one I so much value.'

Miss Betsy testified the sense she had of her ladyship's goodness in the most grateful and obliging terms; and Lady Mellasin and Miss Flora coming home soon after, Lady Trusty said she was come on purpose to ask permission for Miss Flora and Miss Betsy to pass two or three months with her down in L—e.

Lady Mellasin, as the other had imagined, seemed extremely pleased with the invitation; and told her, she did her daughter a great deal of honour, and she would take care things should be prepared for both the young ladies to attend her on her setting out. Lady Trusty then told her she had fixed the day for it, which was about a fortnight after this conversation; and some other matters relating to the journey being regulated, took her leave, highly pleased with the thoughts of getting Miss Betsy to a place, where she should have an opportunity of using her utmost endeavours to improve the good she found in her disposition, and of weaning her, by degrees, from any ill habits she might have contracted in that Babel of mixed company she was accustomed to at Lady Mellasin's.

CHAPTER VII

Is a medley of various particulars, which pave the way for matters of more consequence

MISS Flora had now nothing in her head but the many hearts she expected to captivate when she should arrive in L—e; and Lady Mellasin, who soothed her in all her vanities, resolved to spare nothing which she imagined would contribute to that purpose. Miss Betsy, who had the same ambition, though for different ends, made it also pretty much her study to set off, to the best advantage, the charms she had received from nature. The important article of dress now engrossed the whole conversation of these ladies. The day after that in which Lady Trusty had made the invitation to the two young ones, Lady Mellasin went with them to the mercer's to buy some silks; she pitched on a very genteel new-fashioned pattern for her daughter, but chose one for Miss Betsy which, though rich, seemed to her not well fancied; she testified her disapprobation, but Lady Mellasin said so much in the praise of it, and the mercer, either to please her, or because he was desirous of getting it sold, assured Miss Betsy that it was admired by every body; that it was the newest thing he had in his shop, and had already sold several pieces to ladies of the first quality. All this did not argue Miss Betsy into a liking of it; yet between them she was over-persuaded to have it. When these purchases were made, they went home, only stopping at the mantua-maker's in their way, to order her to come that afternoon: Lady Mellasin did no more than set them down, and then went in the coach to make a visit.

The young ladies fell to reviewing their silks; but Miss Betsy was no way satisfied with her's: the more she looked upon it, the worse it appeared to her. 'I shall never wear it with any pleasure,' said she; 'I wish the man had it in his shop again, for I think it quite ugly.' Miss Flora told her, that she wondered at her; that the thing was perfectly handsome, and that my lady's judgment was never before called in question. 'That may be,' replied Miss Betsy; 'but certainly every one ought to please their own fancy in the choice of their cloaths: for my part, I shall never endure to see myself in it.' – 'Not when their fancy happens to differ from that of those who know better than themselves what is fit for them,' cried Miss Flora; 'and, besides, have the power over them.' She spoke this with so much pertness, that Miss Betsy, had had a violent spirit, was highly provoked. 'Power over them!' cried she, 'I do not know what you mean, Miss Flora; Mr. Goodman is one of my guardians, indeed; but I don't know why that should entitle his lady to direct me in what I shall wear.'

Mr. Goodman, who happened to be looking over some papers in a little closet he had within his parlour, hearing part of this dispute, and finding it was like to grow pretty warm, came out, in hopes of moderating it. On hearing Miss Betsy's complaint, he desired to see the silk; which being shewn him, 'I do not pretend,' said he, 'to much understanding in these things; but, methinks, it is very handsome.' – 'It would do well enough for winter, Sir,' replied Miss Betsy; 'but it is too hot and heavy for summer; besides, it is so thick and clumsy, it would make me look as big again as I am: I'll not wear it, I am resolved, in the country, whatever I do when I come to town, in the dark weather.'

'Well,' said Mr. Goodman, 'I will speak to my lady to get it changed for something else.' – 'Indeed, Sir,' cried Miss Flora, 'I am sure my mamma will do no such thing, and take it very ill to hear it proposed.' – 'You need not put yourself in any heat,' replied Miss Betsy; 'I don't desire she should be troubled any farther about it – but, Sir,' continued she, turning to Mr. Goodman, 'I think I am now at an age capable of chusing for myself, in the article of dress; and as it has been settled between you and Sir Ralph Trusty, that, out of the income of my fortune, thirty pounds a year should be allowed for my board, twenty pounds for my pocket expences, and fifty for my cloaths, I think I ought to have the two latter entirely at my own disposal, and to lay it out as I think fit, and not be obliged, like a charity-child, to wear whatever livery my benefactor shall be pleased to order.' She spoke this with so much spleen, that Mr. Goodman was a little nettled at it, and told her, that what his wife had done was out of kindness and good-will; which since she did not take as it was meant, she should have her money to do with as she would.

'That is all I desire,' answered she, 'therefore be pleased to let me have twenty guineas now, or, if there does not remain so much in your hands, I will ask Sir Ralph to advance it, and you may return it to him when you settle accounts.' – 'No, no,' cried the merchant hastily, 'I see no reason to trouble my good friend, Sir Ralph, on such a frivolous matter. You shall have the sum you mention, Miss Betsy, whether so much remains out of the hundred pounds a yet set apart for your subsistence, or not, as I can but deduct it out of the next payment: but I would have you manage with discretion, for you may depend, that the surplus of what was at first agreed upon, shall not be broke into, but laid up to increase your fortune; which, by the time you come of age, I hope will be pretty handsomely improved.'

Miss Betsy then assured him, that she doubted not of his zeal for her interest, and hoped she had not offended him in any thing she had said. 'No, no,' replied he, 'I always make allowances for the little impatiences of persons of your sex and age, especially where dress is concerned.' In speaking these words, he opened his bureau, and took out twenty guineas, which he immediately gave her, making her first sign a memorandum of it. Miss Flora was all on fire to have offered something in opposition to this, but durst not do it; and the mantua-maker that instant coming in, she went up stairs with her into her chamber, leaving Miss Betsy and Mr. Goodman together; the former of whom, being eager to go about what she intended, ordered a hackney-coach to be called, and taking the silk with her, went directly to the shop where it was bought.

The mercer at first seemed unwilling to take it again; but on her telling him she would always make use of him for every thing she wanted in his way, and would then buy two suits of him, he at last consented. As she was extremely curious in everything relating to her shape, she made choice of a pink-coloured French lustring, to the end, that the plaits lying flat, she would shew the beauty of her waist to more advantage; and to atone for the slightness of the silk, purchased as much of it as would flounce the sleeves and the petti-coat from top to bottom; she made the mercer also cut off a sufficient quantity of a rich green Venetian sattin, to make her a riding-habit; and as she came home bought a silver trimming for it of Point D'Espagne: all which, with the silk she disliked in exchange, did not amount to the money she had received from Mr. Goodman.

On her return, she asked the footman, who opened the door, if the mantua-maker was gone; but he not being able to inform her, she ran hastily up stairs, to Miss Flora's chamber, which, indeed, was also her own, for they lay together: she was about to bounce in, but found that the door was locked, and the key taken out on the inside. This very much surprized her, especially as she thought she had heard Miss Flora's voice, as she was at the top of the stair-case; wanting, therefore, to be satisfied who was with her, she went as softly as she could into Lady Mellasin's dressing-room, which was parted from the chamber but by a slight wainscot; she put her ear close to the pannel, in order to discover the voices of them who spoke, and found, by some light that came through a crack or flaw in the boards, her eyes, as well as ears, contributed to a discovery she little expected. In fine, she plainly perceived Miss Flora and a man rise off the bed: she could not at first discern who he was; but, on his returning to go out of the room, knew him to be no other than Gayland. They went out of the chamber together as gently as they could; and though Miss Betsy might, by taking three steps, have met them in the passage, and have had an opportunity of revenging herself on Miss Flora for the late airs she had given herself, by shewing how near she was to the scene of infamy she had been acting, yet the shock she felt herself, on being witness of it, kept her immoveable for some time; and she suffered them to depart without the mortificiation of thinking any one knew of their being together in the manner they were.

This young lady, who though, as I have already taken notice, was of too volatile and gay a disposition, hated any thing that had the least tincture of indecency, was so much disconcerted at the discovery she had made, that she had not power to stir from the place she was in, much less to resolve how to behave in this affair; that is, whether it would be best, or not, to let Miss Flora know she was in the secret of her shame, or to suffer her to think herself secure.

She was however, beginning to meditate on this point, when she heard Miss Flora come up stairs, calling at every step, 'Miss Betsy! Miss Betsy! where are you?' Gayland was gone; and his young mistress being told Miss Betsy was come home, guessed it was she who had given an interruption to their pleasures, by coming to the door; she, therefore, as she could not imagine her so perfectly convinced, contrived to disguise the whole, and worst of the truth, by revealing a part of it; and as soon as she had found her, 'Lord, Miss

Betsy!' cried she, with an unparalleled assurance, 'where have you been? how do you think I have been served by that cursed toad Gayland? He came up into our chamber, where the mantua-maker and I were, and as soon as she was gone, locked the door, and began to kiss and touze me so, that I protest I was frighted almost out of my wits. The devil meant no harm, though, I believe, for I got rid of him easy enough; but I wish you had rapped heartily at the door, and obliged him to open it, that we both might have rated him for his impudence! – 'Some people have a great deal of impudence, indeed,' replied Miss Betsy, astonished at her manner of bearing it off. 'Aye, so they have, my dear,' rejoined the other, with a careless air; 'but, pr'ythee, where have you been rambling by yourself?' – 'No farther than Bedford Street,' answered Miss Betsy; 'you may see on what errand,' continued she, pointing to the silks which she had laid down on a chair. Miss Flora presently ran to the bundle, examined what it contained, and either being in a better humour, or affecting to be so, than when they talked on this head in the parlour, testified no disapprobation of what she had done; but, on the contrary, talked to her in such soft obliging terms, that Miss Betsy, who had a great deal of good-nature, when not provoked by any thing that seemed an affront to herself, could not find in her heart to say any thing to give her confusion.

When Lady Mellasin came home, and was informed how Miss Betsy had behaved, in relation to the silk, she at first put on an air full of resentment: but finding the other wanted neither wit nor spirit to defend her own cause, and not caring to break with her, especially as her daughter was going with her to L—e, soon grew more moderate; and, at length, affected to think no more of it. Certain it is, however, that this affair, silly as it was, and, as one would think, insignificant in itself, lay broiling in the minds of both mother and daughter; and they waited only for an opportunity of venting their spite, in such a manner as should not make them appear to have the least tincture of so foul and mean a passion; but as neither of them were capable of a sincere friendship, and had no real regard for any one besides themselves, their displeasure was of little consequence.

Preparations for the journey of the young ladies seemed, for the present, to employ all their thoughts, and diligence enough was used to get every thing ready against the time prefixed, which wanted but three days of being expired, when an unforeseen accident put an entire stop to it.

Miss Betsy received a letter from her brother, Mr. Francis Thoughtless, accompanied with another to Mr. Goodman, acquainting them, that he had obtained leave from the head of the college to pass a month in London; that he should set out from Oxford in two days, and hoped to enjoy the satisfaction of being with them in twelve hours after this letter. What could she now do? it would have been a sin, not only against natural affection, but against the rules of common good manners, to have left the town, either on the news of his arrival, or immediately after it: nor could Lady Trusty expect, or desire she should entertain a thought of doing so; she was too wise and too good not to consider the interest of families very much depended on the strict union among the branches of it, and that the natural affection between brothers and sisters could not be too much cultivated. Far, therefore, from insisting on the promise Miss Betsy had made of going with her into the country, she congratulated her on the happy disappointment; and told her, that she should receive her with a double satisfaction, if, after Mr. Francis returned to Oxford, she would come and pass what then remained of the summer-season with her. This Miss Betsy assured her ladyship she would do; so that, according to all appearance, the benefits she might have received, by being under the eye of so excellent an instructress were but delayed, not lost.

CHAPTER VIII

———•———

*Relates how, by a concurrence of odd circumstances,
Miss Betsy was brought pretty near the crisis of her
fate, and the means by which she escaped*

MR. Francis Thoughtless arrived in town the very evening before the
day in which Sir Ralph Trusty and his lady were to set out for L—e.
They had not seen this young gentleman since the melancholy
occasion of his father's funeral, and would have been glad to
have spent some time with him, but could no way put off their
journey, as word was sent of the day in which they expected to
be at home; Sir Ralph knew very well that a great number of
his tenants and friends would meet them on the road, and a letter
would not reach them soon enough to prevent them from being
disappointed: they supped with him, however, at Mr. Goodman's,
who would not permit him to have any other home than his house
during his stay in town. Lady Trusty, on taking leave of Miss
Betsy, said to her, she hoped she would remember her promise
when her brother was returned to Oxford; on which, she replied,
that she could not be so much an enemy to her own happiness
as to fail.

Miss Betsy and this brother had always been extremely fond of
each other; and the length of time they had been asunder, and the
improvement which that time had made in both, heightened their
mutual satisfaction in meeting.

All that troubled Miss Betsy now was, that her brother happened
to come to London at a season of the year in which he could not
receive the least satisfaction: the king was gone to Hanover, all the
foreign ministers, and great part of the nobility attended him; and the
rest were retired to their country seats; so that an entire stop was put

to all publick diversions worth seeing. There were no plays, no operas, no masquerades, no balls, no publick shews, except at the Little Theatre in the Hay Market, then known by the name of F—g's scandal shop, because he frequently exhibited there certain drolls, or, more properly, invectives against the ministry; in doing which it appears extremely probably that he ahd two views; the one to get money, which he very much wanted, from such as delighted in low humour, and could not distinguish true satire from scurrility; and the other, in the hope of having some post given him by those whom he had abused, in order to silence his dramatick talent. But it is not my business to point out either the merit of that gentleman's performances, or the motives he had for writing them, as the town is perfectly acquainted both with his abilities and success; and has since seen him, with astonishment, wriggle himself into favour, by pretending to cajole those he had not the power to intimidate.

But though there were none of the diversions I have mentioned, nor Ranelagh at that time thought of, nor Vauxhall, Marybone, nor Cuper's Gardens, in the repute they since have been, the young gentleman found sufficient to entertain him: empty as the town was, Lady Mellasin was not without company, who made frequent parties of pleasure; and when nothing else was to be found for recreation, cards filled up the void.

Nothing, material enough to be inserted in this history, happened to Miss Betsy during the time her brother stayed; till one evening, as the family were sitting together, some discourse concerning Oxford coming on the tapis, Mr. Francis spoke so largely in the praise of the wholesomeness of the air, the many fine walks and gardens with which the place abounded, and the good company which were continually resorting to it, that Miss Betsy cried out, she longed to see it – Miss Flora said the same.

On this the young gentleman gave them an invitation to go down with him when he went; saying, they never could go at a better time, as both the assizes and races were to be in about a month. Miss Betsy said, such a jaunt would vastly delight her. Miss Flora echoed her approbation; and added, she wished my lady would consent. 'I have no objection to make to it,' replied Lady Mellasin, 'as you will have a conductor who, I know, will be very careful of you.' Mr. Goodman's consent was also asked, for the sake of form, though every one knew the opinion of his wife was, of itself, a sufficient sanction.

Though it is highly probable that Miss Betsy was much better

pleased with this journey than she would have been with that to
L—e, yet she thought herself obliged, both in gratitude and good
manners, to write to Lady Trusty, and make the best excuse she
could for her breach of promise; which she did in these terms.

'To Lady Trusty
'Most dear and honoured madam,
My brother Frank being extremely desirous of shewing Miss Flora
and myself the curiosities of Oxford, has obtained leave from Mr.
Goodman, and Lady Mellasin, for us to accompany him to that place.
I am afraid the season will be too far advanced to take a journey to
L—e at our return; therefore flatter myself your ladyship will pardon
the indispensible necessity I am under of deferring, till next spring,
the happiness I proposed in waiting on you. All here present my
worthy guardian, and your ladyship, with their best respects. I beg
mine may be equally acceptable, and that you will always continue to
favour with your good wishes, her, who is, with the most perfect
esteem, Madam, your ladyship's most obliged, and most obedient
servant,

E. THOUGHTLESS.'

The time for the young gentleman's departure being arrived, they
went together in the stage, accompanied by a footman of Mr.
Goodman's, whom Lady Mellasin would needs send with them, in
order to give the young ladies an air of dignity.

They found, on their arrival at that justly-celebrated seat of
learning, that Mr. Francis had given no greater eulogiums on it than
it merited: they were charmed with the fine library, the museum, the
magnificence of the halls belonging to the various colleges, the
physick-garden, and other curious walks; but that which, above all
the rest, gave the most satisfaction to Miss Betsy, as well as to her
companion, was that respectful gallantry with which they found
themselves treated by the gentlemen of the university. Mr. Francis
was extremely beloved amongst them, on account of his affability,
politeness, and good-humour, and they seemed glad of an opportunity of shewing the regard they had for the brother, by paying all
manner of civilities to the sister: he gave the ladies an elegant
entertainment at his own rooms, to which also some of those with
whom he was the most intimate were invited. All these thought
themselves bound to return the same compliment: the company of
every one present was desired at their respective apartments; and as

each of these gentlemen had, besides, other particular friends of their own, whom they wished to oblige, the number of guests was still increased at every feast.

By this means, Miss Betsy and Miss Flora soon acquired a very large acquaintance; and as, through the care of Mr. Francis, they were lodged in one of the best and most reputable houses in town, their families known, and themselves were young ladies who knew how to behave, as well as dress, and receive company in the most elegant and polite manner, every one was proud of a pretence for visiting them.

The respect paid to them would, doubtless, have every day increased during the whole time they should have thought proper to continue in Oxford, and on quitting it, have left behind them the highest idea of their merit, if, by one inconsiderate action, they had not at once forfeited the esteem they had gained, and rendered themselves the subjects of ridicule, even to those who before had regarded them with veneration.

They were walking out one day, about an hour or two before the time in which they usually dined, into the park, where they were met by a gentleman-commoner and a young student, both of whom they had been in company with at most of the entertainments before mentioned. The sparks begged leave to attend them, which was readily granted: they walked all together for some time; but the weather being very warm, the gentleman-commoner took an occasion to remind the ladies how much their beauties would be in danger of suffering from the immoderate rays of Phœbus; and proposed going to some gardens full of the most beautiful alcoves and arbours, so shaded over that the sun, even in his meridian force, could, at the most, but glimmer through the delightful gloom; he painted the pleasures of the place, to which he was desirous of leading them, with so romantick an energy, that they immediately, and without the least scruple or hesitation, consented to be conducted thither.

This was a condescension which he who asked it, scarce expected would be granted; and, on finding it so easily obtained, began to form some conjectures no way to the advantage of those ladies reputations. It is certain, indeed, that as he professed a friendship for the brother, he ought not, in strict honour, to have proposed any thing to the sister which would be unbecoming her to agree to; but he was young, gay to an excess, and in what he said or did took not always consideration for his guide.

They went on laughing, till they came to the place he mentioned, where the gentlemen, having shewed their faire companions into the gardens, in which were, indeed, several recesses, no less dark than had been described: on entering one of them, Miss Betsy cried, 'Bless me! this is fit for nothing but for people to do what they are ashamed of in the light.' – 'The fitter then, Madam,' replied the gentleman-commoner, 'to encourage a lover, who, perhaps, has suffered more through his own timidity than the cruelty of the object he adores.' He accompanied these words with a seizure of both her hands, and two or three kisses on her lips. The young student was no less free with Miss Flora: but neither of these ladies gave themselves the trouble to reflect what consequences might possibly attend a prelude of this nature, and repulsed the liberties they took in such a manner as made the offenders imagine they had not sinned beyond a pardon.

They would not, however, be prevailed upon to stay, or even to sit down in that darksome recess, but went into a house, where they were shewn into a very pleasant room which commanded the whole prospect of the garden, and was sufficiently shaded from the sun by jessamine and honey-suckles, which grew against the window: here wine, cakes, jellies, and such like things, being brought, the conversation was extremely lively, and full of gallantry, without the least mixture of indecency.

The gentlemen exerted all their wit and eloquence, to persuade the ladies not to go home in the heat of the day; but take up with such entertainment as the place they were in was able to present them with. Neither of them made any objection, except that, having said they should dine at home, the family woud wait in expectation of their coming: but this difficulty was easily got over; the footman, who had attended Miss Betsy and Miss Flora, in their morning's walk, was in the house, and might be sent to acquaint the people that they were not to expect them. As they were neither displeased with the company, nor place they were in, they needed not abundance of persuasions; and the servant was immediately dispatched. The gentlemen went out of the room, to give orders for having something prepared, but staid not two minutes; and on their return, omitted nothing that might keep up the good-humour and sprightliness of their fair companions.

Persons of so gay and volatile a disposition as these four, could not content themselves with sitting still, and barely talking; every limb must be in motion, every faculty employed. The gentleman-commoner took Miss Betsy's hand, and led her some steps of a minuet, then fell into a rigadoon, then into the louvre, and so ran through all the school-dances, without regularly beginning or ending any one of them, or of the tunes he sung; the young student was not less alert with Miss Flora; so that, between singing, dancing, and laughing, they all grew extremely warm. Miss Betsy ran to a window to take breath, and get a little air; her partner followed, and taking up her fan, which lay on a table, employed it with a great deal of dexterity, to assist the wind that came in at the casement for her refreshment. 'Heavens!' cried he, 'how divinely lovely do you now appear! the goddess of the spring, nor Venus's self, was ever painted half so beautiful! What eyes! what a mouth! and what a shape!' continued he, surveying her, as it were, from head to foot, 'How exquisitely turned! How taper! how slender! I don't believe you measure half a yard round the waist.' In speaking these words, he put his handkerchief about her waist; after which he tied it round his head, repeating these lines of Mr. Waller's –

> 'That which her slender waist confin'd
> Shall now my joyful temples bind;
> No monarch but would give his crown,
> His arms might do what this has done.'

'O fie upon it!' said Miss Betsy, laughing, and snatching it from his head, 'this poetry is stale; I should rather have expected from an Oxonian some fine thing of his own extempore, on this occasion, which, perhaps, I might have been vain enough to have got printed in the monthly magazine.'

'Ah, Madam!' replied he, looking on her with dying languishments, 'where the heart is deeply affected, the brain seldom produces any thing but incongruous ideas. Had Sacharissa been mistress of the charms you are, or had Waller loved like me, he had been less capable of writing in the manner he did.'

The student perceiving his friend was entering into a particular conversation with Miss Betsy, found means to draw Miss Flora out of the room, and left them together, though this young lady afterwards protested she called to Miss Betsy to follow; but if she did it was in such a low voice that the other did not hear her, and continued her pleasantry, raillying the gentleman-commoner on every thing he said, till he finding the opportunity he had of being revenged, soon turned his humble adoration into an air more free and natural to him. As she was opening her mouth to utter some sarcasm or other, he catched her in his arms, and began to kiss her with so much warmth and eagerness that surprized her; she struggled to get loose, and called Miss Flora, not knowing she was gone, to come to her assistance. The efforts she made at first to oblige him to desist, were not, however, quite so strenuous as they ought to have been on such an occasion; but finding he was about to proceed to greater liberties than any man before had ever taken with her, she collected all her strength, and broke from him; when looking round the room, and seeing nobody there, 'Bless me,' cried she, 'what is the meaning of all this! Where are our friends!' – 'They are gone,' said he, 'to pay the debt which love and youth, and beauty challenge; let us not be remiss, nor waste the precious moments in idle scruples. Come, my angel!' pursued he, endeavouring to get her once more into his arms, 'make me the happiest of mankind, and be as divinely good as you are fair.'

'I do not understand you, Sir,' replied she; 'but neither desire, nor will stay to hear, an explanation.' She spoke this with somewhat of an haughty air, and was making towards the door, but he was far from being intimidated; and, instead of suffering her to pass, he seized her a little roughly with one hand, and with the other made fast the door. 'Come, come, my dear creature,' cried he, 'no more resistance; you see you are in my power, and the very name of being so is sufficient to absolve you to yourself, for any act of kindness you may bestow upon me; be generous, then, and be assured it shall be an inviolable secret.'

She was about to say something, but he stopped her mouth with kisses, and forced her to sit down in a chair; where, holding her fast, her ruin had certainly been compleated, if a loud knocking at the door had not prevented him from prosecuting his design.

This was the brother of Miss Betsy, who having been at her lodgings, on his coming from thence met the footman, who had been sent to acquaint the family the ladies would not dine at home; he asked where his sister was, and, the fellow having told him, came direclty to the place. A waiter of the house shewed him to the room: on finding it locked he was strangely amazed; and both knocked and called to have it opened, with a great deal of vehemence.

This gentleman-commoner knowing his voice, was shocked to the last degree, but quitted that instant his intended prey, and let him enter. Mr. Francis, on coming in, knew not what to think; he saw the gentleman in great disorder, and his sister in much more. 'What is the meaning of this?' said he. 'Sister, how came you here?' – 'Ask me no questions at present,' replied she, scarce able to speak, so strangely had her late fright seized on her spirits; 'but see me safe from this cursed house, and that worst of men.' Her speaking in this manner made Mr. Francis apprehend the whole, and perhaps more than the truth. 'How, Sir,' said he, darting a furious look at the gentleman-commoner, 'what is it I hear? – Have you dared to –' 'Whatever I have dared to,' interrupted the other, 'I am capable of defending.' – 'It is well,' rejoined the brother of Miss Betsy, 'perhaps I may put you to the trial: but this is not a time or place.' He then took hold of his sister's hand, and led her down stairs: as they were going out, Miss Betsy stopping a little to adjust her dress, which was strangely disordered, she bethought herself of Miss Flora; who, though she was very angry with, she did not chuse to leave behind at the mercy of such rakes, as she had reason to think those were whom she had been in company with. Just as she was desiring of her brother to send a waiter in search of that young lady, they saw her coming out of the garden, led by the young student who, as soon as he beheld Mr. Francis, cried, 'Ha! Frank, how came you here? you look out of humour.' – 'How I came here, it matters not,' replied he sullenly; 'and as to my being out of humour, perhaps you may know better than I yet do what cause I have for being so.'

He waited for no answer to these words; but conducted his sister out of the house as hastily as he could: Miss Flora followed, after having taken leave of her companion in what manner she thought proper.

On their coming home, Miss Betsy related to her brother, as far as her modesty would permit, all the particulars of the adventure, and ended with saying, that sure it was Heaven alone that gave her strength to prevent the perpetration of the villain's intentions. Mr. Francis, all the time she was speaking, bit his lips, and shewed great tokens of an extraordinary disturbance in his mind; but offered not the least interruption. When he perceived she had done, 'Well, sister,' said he, 'I shall hear what he has to say, and will endeavour to oblige him to ask your pardon.' And soon after took his leave.

Miss Betsy did not very well comprehend his meaning in these words; and was, indeed, still in too much confusion to consider on any thing; but what the consequences were of this transaction, the reader will presently be informed of.

CHAPTER IX

Contains such things as might be reasonably expected, after the preceding adventure

WHEN in any thing irregular, and liable to censure, more persons than one are concerned, how natural is it for each to accuse the other; and it often happens, in this case, that the greatest part of the blame falls on the least culpable.

After Mr. Francis had left the ladies, in order to be more fully convinced in this matter, and to take such measures as he thought would best become him for the reparation of the affront offered to the honour of his family, Miss Flora began to reproach Miss Betsy for having related any thing of what had passed to her brother: 'By your own account,' said she, 'no harm was done to you: but some people love to make a bustle about nothing.' – 'And some people,' replied Miss Betsy, tartly, 'love nothing but the gratification of their own passions; and having no sense of virtue and modesty themselves, can have no regard to that of another.' – 'What do you mean, Miss?' cried the other, with a pert air. 'My meaning is pretty plain,' rejoined Miss Betsy: 'but since you affect so much ignorance, I must tell you, that the expectations of a second edition of the same work Mr. Gayland had helped you to compose, though from another quarter, tempted you to sneak out of the room, and leave your friend in danger of falling a sacrifice to what her soul most detests and scorns.' These words stung Miss Flora to the quick; her face was in an instant covered with a scarlet blush, and every feature betrayed the confusion of her mind: but recovering herself from it much sooner than most others of her age could have done; 'Good lack,' cried she, 'I fancy you are setting up for a prude: but, pray, how came Mr.

Gayland into your head? – What! because I told you he innocently
romped with me one day in the chamber, are you so censorious as to
infer any thing criminal passed between us?' – 'Whatever I infer,'
replied Miss Betsy, disdainfully, 'I have better vouchers for the truth
of, than your report; and would advise you, when you go home, to get
the chink in the pannel of the wainscot of my lady's dressing room
stopped up, or your next rendezvous with that gentleman may
possibly have witnesses of more ill-nature than myself.' – 'That can
scarcely be,' said Miss Flora, ready to burst with vexation: 'but don't
think I value your little malice; you are only angry because he slighted
the advances you made him, and took all opportunities to shew how
much his heart and judgment gave the preferences to me.' These
words so piqued the vanity of Miss Betsy, that, not able to bear she
should continue in the imagination of being better liked than herself,
though even by the man she hated, told her the solicitations he had
made to her, the letter she had received from him, and the rebuff she
had given him upon it; 'So that,' pursued she, 'it was not till after he
found there was no hope of gaining me, that he carried his devoirs to
you.'

Miss Flora was more nettled at this eclaircissement than she was at
the discovery she now perceived the other had made of her intrigue:
she pretended, however, not to believe a word of what she had said;
but willing to evade all farther discourse on that head, returned to the
adventure they had just gone through with the Oxonians. 'Never
expect,' said she, 'to pass it upon any one of common sense, that if
you had not a mind to have been alone with that terrible man, as you
now describe him, you would have staid in the room after I was gone,
and called to you to follow.'

It was in vain that Miss Betsy denied she either heard her speak, or
knew any thing of her departure, till some time after she was gone,
and the gentleman-commoner began to use her with such familiarities as convinced her he was sensible no witnesses were present.
This, though no more than truth, was of no consequence to her
justification, to one determined to believe the worst, or at least seem
to do so: Miss Flora treated with contempt all she said on this score,
derided her imprecations; and, to mortify her the more, said to her,
in a taunting manner, 'Come, come, Miss Betsy, it is a folly to think
to impose upon the world by such shallow artifices. What your
inclinations are, is evident enough: any one may see, that if it
had not been for your brother's unseasonable interruption, no-

body would ever have heard a word of these insults you so heavily complain of.'

Poor Miss Betsy could not refrain letting fall some tears at so unjust and cruel an inuendo: but the greatness of her spirit enabled her in a few moments to overcome the shock it had given her; she returned reproaches with reproaches; and, as she had infinitely more of truth and reason on her side, had also much the better in this combat of tongues: nevertheless the other would not give out; she upbraided and exaggerated with the most malicious comments on it every little indiscretion Miss Betsy had been guilty of, repeating every censure which she had heard the ill-natured part of the world pass on her conduct, and added many more, the invention of her own fertile brain.

Some ladies they had made acquaintance with in town coming to visit them, put an end to the debate; but neither being able presently to forget the bitter reflections cast on her by the other, both remained extremely sullen the whole night; and their mutual ill-humour might possibly have lasted much longer, but for an accident more material, which took off their attention, as it might have produced much worse consequences than any quarrel between themselves could be attended with. It happened in this manner.

The brother of Miss Betsy was of a fiery disposition; and though those who were entrusted with the care of his education were not wanting in their pains to correct this propensity, which they thought would be the more unbecoming in him, as he was intended for the pulpit, yet did not their endeavours for that purpose meet with all the success they wished. Nature may be moderated, but never can be wholly changed: the seeds of wrath still remained in his soul; nor could the rudiments that had been given him be sufficient to hinder them from springing into action, when urged by any provocation. The treatment his sister had received from the gentleman-commoner, seemed to him so justifiable a one, that he thought he ought not, without great submissions on the part of the transgressor, to be prevailed upon to put up with it.

The first step he took was to sound the young student, as to what he knew relating to the affair; who freely told him, as Miss Betsy had done, where they met the ladies, and the manner in which they went into the house; protesting, that neither himself, nor (according to the best of his belief) the gentleman-commoner, had at that time any designs in view but mere complaisance and gallantry.

'How then, came you to separate yourselves?' cried Mr. Francis, with some earnestness. 'That also was accidental,' replied the other; 'your sister's companion telling me she liked the garden better than the room we were in, I thought I could do no less than attend her thither. I confess I did not consult whether those we left behind had any inclination to follow us or not.'

The air with which he spoke of this part of the adventure, had something in it which did not give Mr. Francis the most favourable idea of Miss Flora's conduct; but that not much concerning him, and finding nothing wherewith he could justly reproach the student, he soon after quitted him, and went to the gentleman-commoner, having been told he might find him in his rooms.

Had any one been witness of the manner in which these two accosted each other, they would not have been at a loss to guess what would ensue; the brother of Miss Betsy came with a mind full of resentment, and determined to repair the affront which had been offered to him in the person of a sister, who was very dear to him, by calling the other to a severe account for what he had done. The gentleman-commoner was descended of a noble family, and had an estate to support the dignity of his birth, and was too much puffed up and insolent on the smiles of fortune: he was conscious the affront he had given demanded satisfaction, and neither doubted of the errand on which Mr. Francis was come, nor wondered at it; but could not bring himself to acknowledge he had done amiss, nor think of making any excuse for his behaviour. Guilt, in a proud heart, is generally accompanied with a sullen obstinacy; for, as the poet says –

'Forgiveness to the injur'd does belong;
But they ne'er pardon who have done the wrong.'

He therefore received the interrogatories Mr. Francis was beginning to make, with an air rather indignant than complying; which the other not being able to brook, such hot words arose between them as could not but occasion a challenge, which was given by Mr. Francis. The appointment to meet was the next morning at six o'clock; and the place, that very field in which the gentleman-commoner and his friend had so unluckily happened to meet the ladies in their morning's walk.

Neither of them wanted courage, nor communicated their rendezvous to any one person, in hopes of being disappointed without danger of their honour; but each being equally animated with the ambition of humbling the arrogance of the other, both were secret as to the business, and no less punctual as to the time.

The agreement between them was sword and pistol; which both having provided themselves with, they no sooner came within a proper distance, than they discharged at each other the first course of this fatal entertainment: that of the gentleman-commoner was so well aimed, that one of the bullets lodged in the shoulder, and the other grazing on the fleshy part of the arm of his antagonist, put him into a great deal of pain. But these wounds rather increased than diminished the fury he was possessed of: he instantly drew his sword, and ran at the other with so well-directed a force, that his weapon entered three inches deep into the right-side of the gentleman-commoner. Both of them received several other hurts, yet still both continued the fight with equal vehemence; nor would either of them, in all probability, have receded, till one or other of them had lain dead upon the place, if some countrymen, who by accident were passing that way, had not, with their clubs, beat down the swords of both, and carried the owners of them, by mere force, into the village they were going to; where they were no sooner entered, than several people who knew them, seeing them pass by in this manner, covered all over with their own blood, and guarded by a pack of rusticks, ran out to enquire what had happened; which being informed of, they took them out of the hands of these men, and provided proper apartments for them.

By this time they were both extremely faint through the anguish of their wounds, and the great effusion of blood that had issued from them. Surgeons were immediately sent for; who, on examining their hurts, pronounced none of them to be mortal, yet such as would require some time for cure.

Mr. Francis suffered extreme torture in having the bullet extracted from his shoulder; yet, notwithstanding that, and the weak condition he was in, he made a servant support him in his bed while he scrawled out these few lines to his sister; which, as soon as finished, were carried to her by the same person.

'To Miss Betsy Thoughtless.

My dear sister,
I have endangered my life, and am now confined to my bed by the wounds I have received, in endeavouring to revenge your quarrel: do not think I tell you this by way of reproach; for, I assure you, would

the circumstances of the affair have permitted it to have been concealed, you never should have known it.

I should be glad to see you; but think it not proper that you should come to me, till I hear what is said concerning this matter. I shall send to you every day: and that you will be perfectly easy, is the earnest request of, dear Betsy, your most-affectionate brother, and humble servant,

F. THOUGHTLESS.'

The young ladies were that morning at breakfast in the parlour, with the gentlewoman of the house, when the maid came running in, and told her mistress she had heard, in a shop where she had been, of a sad accident that had just happened: 'Two gentlemen,' cried she, 'of the university, have been fighting, and almost killed one another; and they say,' continued she, 'it was about a young lady that one of them attempted to ravish.'

Miss Betsy and Miss Flora, at this intelligence, looked at each other with a good deal of confusion, already beginning to suspect who the persons were, and how deeply themselves (one of them especially) were interested in this misfortune. The gentlewoman asked her servant if she knew the names of those who fought. 'No, Madam,' answered she, 'I could not learn that as yet: but the people in the street are all talking of it; and I doubt not but I shall hear the whole story the next time I go out.'

The good gentlewoman, little imagining how much her guests were concerned in what she spoke, could not now forbear lamenting the ungovernableness of youth; the heedless levities of the one sex, and the mad-brained passions of the other. The persons to whom she directed this discourse, would not, at another time, have given much ear to it, or perhaps have replied to it with raillery: but the occasion of it now put both of them in too serious a temper to offer any interruption; and she was still going on, inveighing against the follies and vices of the age, when Miss Betsy received the above letter from her brother, which confirmed all those alarming conjectures the maid's report raised in her mind.

The mistress of the house perceiving the young man who brought the letter came upon business to the ladies, had the good-manners to leave the room, that they might talk with the greater freedom. Miss Betsy asked a thousand questions; but he was able to inform her of no farther particulars than what the letter contained.

The moment he was gone, she ran up to her chamber, threw herself upon the bed, and in a flood of tears gave a loose to the most poignant vexation she had ever yet experienced. Miss Flora followed; and, seeing her in this condition, thought she could do no less, in decency, than contribute everything in her power for her consolation.

By the behaviour of this young lady in other respects, however, the reader will easily perceive it was more through policy than real good-nature, she treated her afflicted companion with the tenderness she did now: she knew that it was not by an open quarrel with Miss Betsy she could wreak any part of the spite she had conceived against her; and was therefore glad to lay hold of this opportunity to be reconciled.

'I was afraid, my dear,' said she, 'that it would come to this, and that put me in so great a passion with you yesterday, for telling Mr. Francis any thing of the matter: the men are such creatures, that there is no trusting them with any thing. But come,' continued she, kissing her cheek, 'don't grieve and torment yourself in this manner; you find there is no danger of death on either side; and as for the rest, it will all blow off in time.' Miss Betsy said little to this; the sudden passion of her soul must have it's vent; but, when that was over, she began to listen to the voice of comfort, and by degrees to resume her natural vivacity, not foreseeing that this unhappy adventure would lay her under mortifications which, to a person of her spirit, were very difficult to be borne.

CHAPTER X

———————•———————

Gives the catastrophe of the Oxford ramble, and in what manner the young ladies returned to London

IF the wounds Mr. Francis had received, had been all the misfortune attending Miss Betsy in this adventure, it is probable, that as she every day heard he was in a fair way of recovery, the first gust of passion would have been all she had sustained; but she soon found other consequences arising from it, which were no less afflicting, and more galling to her pride.

The quarrel between the two young gentlemen, and the occasion of it, was presently blazed over the whole town: it spread like wild fire; every one made their several comments upon it; and few there were who endeavoured to find any excuse for the share Miss Betsy and Miss Flora had in it.

The ladies of Oxford are commonly more than ordinarily circumspect in their behaviour; as indeed, it behoves them to be, in a place where there are such a number of young gentlemen, many of whom pursue pleasure more than study, and scruple nothing for the gratification of their desires. It is not, therefore, to be wondered at, that being from their infancy trained up in the most strict reserve, and accustomed to be upon their guard against even the most distant approaches of the other sex, they should be apt to pass the severest censures on a conduct, which they had been always taught to look upon as the sure destruction of reputation, and frequently fatal to innocence and virtue.

This being pretty generally the characteristick of those ladies who were of any distinction in Oxford, Miss Betsy and Miss Flora immediately found, that while they continued there, they must either be content to sit at home alone, or converse only with such as were as disagreeable to them, as they had now rendered themselves to those of a more unblemished fame.

They had received several visits, all of which they had not yet had time or leisure to return; but now going to pay the debt, which complaisance demanded from them, they were denied access at every place they went to; all the persons were either abroad or indisposed: but the manner in which these answers were given, easily convinced Miss Betsy and Miss Flora that they were no more than mere pretences to avoid seeing them. In the publick walks, and in passing through the streets, they saw themselves shunned even to a degree of rudeness: those of their acquaintance, who were obliged to meet them, looked another way, and went hastily on without vouchsafing a salute.

This was the treatment their late unhappy adventure drew on them from those of their own sex; nor did those of the other seem to behave to them with greater tenderness or respect, especially the younger students, who all, having got the story, thought they had a fine opportunity of exercising their poetick talents: satires and lampoons flew about like hail. Many of these anonymous compositions were directed to Miss Betsy, and thrown over the rails into the area of the house where she lodged; others were sung under the windows by persons in disguise, and copies of them handed about throughout the whole town, to the great propagation of scandal, and the sneering faculty.

Never, certainly, did pride and vanity meet with a more severe humiliation, than what these witticisms inflicted on those who, by their inconsiderate behaviour, had laid themselves open to them. Neither the assurance of Miss Flora, nor the great spirit of Miss Betsy, could enable them to stand the shock of those continual affronts which every day presented them with. They dreaded to expose themselves to fresh insults, if they stirred out of the doors; and at home they were persecuted with the unwearied remonstrances of their grave landlady: so that their condition was truly pitiable.

Both of them were equally impatient to get out of a place where they found their company was held in so little estimation: but Miss Betsy thought her brother would not take it well, should she go to London and leave him in the condition he then was. Miss Flora's importunities, however, joined to the new occasions she every day had for increasing her discontent on staying, got the better of her apprehensions; and she wrote to her brother in the following terms.

'To Mr. Francis Thoughtless.

Dear Brother,

Though I am not, to my great affliction, permitted to see you, or to offer that assistance which might be expected from a sister in your present situation; yet I cannot, without the extremest regret, resolve to quit Oxford before you are perfectly recovered of those hurts you have received on my account. However, as by your judging it improper for me to come to you, I cannot suppose you are wholly unacquainted with the severe usage lately given me, and must look on every affront offered to me as an indignity to you. I am apt to flatter myself you will not be offended, that I wish to remove from a place where innocence is no defence against scandal, and the shew of virtue more considered than the reality.

Nevertheless, I shall determine nothing till I hear your sentiments; which, if I find conformable to mine, shall set out for London with all possible expedition. I would very fain see you before I go; and, if you consent, will come to you so muffled up as not to be known by any who may happen to meet me. I shall expect your answer with the utmost impatience; being, my dear brother, by friendship, as well as blood, most affectionately yours,

E. THOUGHTLESS.'

When this letter was dispatched, Miss Flora made use of all the arguments she was mistress of, in order to persuade Miss Betsy to go for London, even in case her brother should not be altogether so willing for it as she wished he would. Miss Betsy, though no less eager than herself to be out of a place she now so much detested, would not be prevailed upon to promise any thing on this score; but persisted in her resolution of being wholly directed how to proceed, by the answer she should receive from Mr. Francis.

Miss Flora was so fretted at this perverseness, as she called it, that she told her, in a very great pet, that she might stay if she pleased, and be the laughing-stock of the town; but, for her own part, she had more spirit, and would be gone the next day. Miss Betsy coolly replied, that if she thought proper to do so, she was doubtless at liberty; but believed Mr. Goodman, and even Lady Mellasin herself, would look on such a behaviour as neither consistent with generosity nor common good-manners.

It is, indeed, scarce possible, that the other had the least intention to do as she had said, though she still continued to threaten it, in the most positive and peremptory terms; and this, if we consider the temper of both these young ladies, we may reasonably suppose, might have occasioned a second quarrel between them, if the servant, whom Mr. Francis always sent to his sister, had not that instant come in, and put an end to the dispute, by delivering a letter to Miss Betsy; which she hastily opening, found it contained these lines.

'To Miss Thoughtless.

My dear sister,

It is with an inexpressible satisfaction that I find your own inclinations have anticipated the request I was just about to make you. I do assure you, the moment I received your letter, I was going to write, in order to persuade you to do the very thing you seem to desire. Oxford is, indeed, a very censorious place: I have always observed it to be so; and have frequently told the ladies, between jest and earnest, that I thought it was a town of the most scandal, and least sin, of any in the world. I am pretty confident some of those who pretend to give themselves airs concerning you and Miss Flora, are as perfectly convinced of your innocence as I myself am: yet, after all that has happened, I would not have you think of staying; and the sooner you depart the better. You need be under no apprehensions on account of my wounds: those I received from the sword of my antagonist are in a manner healed; and that with the pistol-shot in my shoulder is in as fine a way as can be expected in so short a time. Those I had the fortune to give him, are in a yet better condition; so that I believe, if it was not for the over-caution of our surgeon, we might both quit our rooms to-morrow. I hear that our grave superiors have had some consultations on our duel, and that there is a talk of our being both expelled: but, for my part, I shall certainly save them the trouble, and quit the university of my own accord, as soon as my recovery is compleated. My genius is by no means adapted to the study of divinity: I think the care of my own soul more than sufficient for me, without taking upon me the charge of a whole parish; you may, therefore, expect to see me shortly at London, as it is highly necessary I should consult Mr. Goodman concerning my future settlement in the world. I should be extremely glad of a visit from you before you leave Oxford; more especially as I have something of moment to say to you, which I do not chuse to communicate by letter; but cannot think it at all proper, for particular reasons, that you should come to me, some or other of the gentlemen being perpetually dropping into my chamber; and it is impossible for you to disguise yourself so as not to be distinguished by young fellows, whose curiosity would be the more excited by your endeavours to conceal yourself. As this might revive the discourse of an affair which I could wish might be buried in an eternal oblivion, must desire you will defer the satisfaction you propose to give me till we meet at London; to which I wish you, and your fair companion, a safe and pleasant journey. I am, with the greatest tenderness, my dear sister, you affectionate brother.'

F. THOUGHTLESS.'

The receipt of this letter gave an infinity of contentment to Miss Betsy; she had made the offer of going to take her leave of him, chiefly with the view of keeping him from suspecting she wanted natural affection; and was no less pleased with his refusing the request she made him on that account, than she was with his so readily agreeing to her returning to London. Miss Flora was equally delighted: they sent their footman that instant to take places in the stage-coach; and early the next moring set out from a place, which, on their entering into it, they did not imagine they should quit either so soon, or with so little regret.

CHAPTER XI

Lays a foundation for many events to be produced by time, and waited for with patience

MISS Betsy and Miss Flora, on their coming home, were in some perplexity how to relate the story of their Oxford adventure to Lady Mellasin and Mr. Goodman; and it is very likely they would have thought it proper to have kept it a secret, if the unlucky duel between Mr. Francis and the gentleman-commoner, which they were sensible would be a known thing, had not rendered the concealment of the whole utterly impracticable.

As there was no remedy, Miss Flora took it upon her to lay open the matter to her mamma; which she did with so much artifice, that if that lady had been as austere, as she was really the reverse, she could not have found much to condemn, either in the conduct of her daughter or Miss Betsy: as to Mr. Goodman, he left the whole management of the young ladies, in these particulars, entirely to his wife, so said little to them on the score of the adventure; but was extremely concerned for the part Mr. Francis had in it, as he supposed it was chiefly owing to that unlucky incident, that he had taken a resolution to leave the college; and he very well knew, that a certain nobleman, who was a distant relation of his family, and godfather to Mr. Francis, had always promised to bestow a large benefice in his gift upon him, as soon as he should have compleated his studies.

This honest guardian thought he should be wanting in the duty of the trust reposed in him, to suffer his charge to throw away that fine prospect in his view, if by any means he could prevent him from taking so rash and inconsiderate a step; and as to his being expelled, he doubted not, but between him and Sir Ralph, interest might be made to the heads of the university, to get the affair of the duel passed over. The greatest difficulty he had to apprehend, in compassing this point, was from the young gentleman himself, who he had observed was of a temper somewhat obstinate, and tenacious of his own opinion; resolving, however, to try all means possible, he wrote immediately to him, representing to him, in the strongest and most pathetick terms he was master of, the vast advantages the clergy enjoyed, the respect they had from all degrees of people; and endeavoured to convince him that there was no avocation whatever, by which a younger brother might so easily advance his fortune, and do honour to his family.

He also sent a letter to Sir Ralph Trusty, acquainting him with the whole story, and earnestly requesting that he would write to Mr. Francis, and omit nothing that might engage him to desist from doing a thing so contrary to his interest, and the intention of his deceased father, as what he now had thoughts of doing was manifestly so. These efforts, by both the guardians, were often repeated, but without the least success; the young gentleman found arguments to oppose against theirs, which neither of them could deny to have weight, particularly that of his having no call to take upon him holy orders. During these debates, in which Miss Betsy gave herself no manner of concern, she received a letter from her brother, containing these lines.

'To Miss Betsy Thoughtless.

My dear sister,
Though I flatter myself all my letters afford you some sort of satisfaction, yet by what little judgment I have been able to form of the temper of your sex, have reason to believe, this I now send will meet a double portion of welcome from you. It brings a confirmation of you beauty's power; the intelligence of a new conquest; the offer of a heart, which, if you will trust a brother's recommendation, is well deserving your acceptance: but, that I may not seem to speak in riddles, you may remember that the first time I had the pleasure of entertaining you at my rooms, a gentleman called Trueworth was with us, and that the next day when you dined with that person, who afterwords treated you with such unbecoming liberties, he made one of the company; since then you could not see him, as he was obliged

to go to his seat, which is about thirty miles off, on an extraordinary occasion, and returned not till the day after you left this town. He seemed more than ordinarily affected on my telling him what had happened on your account; and, after pausing a little, "How unhappy was I," said he, "to be absent! had I been here there would have been no need for the brother of Miss Betsy to have exposed his life to the sword of an injurious antagonist, or his character to the censure of the university. I would have taken upon myself to have revenged the quarrel of that amiable lady, and either have severely chastised the insolence of the aggressor, or lost the best part of my blood in the attempt!" I was very much surprized at these words, as well as the emphasis with which they were delivered; but, recovering myself as soon as I could, "We are extremely obliged to you, Sir," said I; "but I know not if such a mistaken generosity might not have been fatal to the reputation of us both. What would the world have said of me to have been tamely passive, and suffer another to revenge the affront offered to my sister? What would they have thought of her, on finding her honour vindicated by one who had no concern in it?" – "No concern!" cried he, with the utmost eagerness; "yes, I have a concern, more deep, more strong, than that of father, brother, or all the ties of blood could give; and that you had before now have been convinced of it, had I not been so suddenly and so unfortunately called hence."

Perceiving I looked very much confounded, as well I might, "Ah, Frank!" cried he, "I love your charming sister; my friends have, for these six months past, been teazing me to think of marriage, and several proposals have been made to me on that score; but never till I saw the amiable Miss Betsy, did I behold the face for whom I would exchange my liberty: in fine, 'tis she, and only she, can make me blest; and I returned to Oxford full of the hopes of an opportunity to lay my heart, my person, and my fortune, at her feet."

It would require a volume, instead of a letter, to repeat half the tender and passionate expressions he uttered in your favour. What I have already said is enough to give you a specimen of the rest. I shall only add, that being impatient to begin the attack he is determined to make upon your heart, he is preparing to follow you to London with all possible expedition. I once had thoughts of accompanying him, but have since thought it proper to have Sir Ralph Trusty's advice in something I have a mind to do, and for that purpose shall take a journey into L—e, as soon as I receive remittances from Mr.

Goodman, to pay off some trifling debts I have contracted here, and defray my travelling expences; so that if things happen as I wish they may, my friend's passion will have made a considerable progress before I see you.

Indeed, my dear sister, if you have not already seen a man whose person you like better, you can never have an offer that promises more felicity: he left the college soon after I came into it, beloved and respected by all that knew him, for his discreet behaviour, humanity, and affability; he went afterwards on his travels, and brought home with him all the accomplishments of the several countries he had been in, without being the least tainted with the vices or fopperies of any of them; he has a much larger estate than your fortune could expect, unincumbered with debts, mortgages, or poor relations; his family is ancient, and, by the mother's side, honourable; but, above all, he has sense, honour, and good-nature – rare qualities, which, in my opinion, cannot fail of making him an excellent husband, whenever he comes to be such.

But I shall leave him to plead his own cause, and you to follow your own inclinations. I am, with the most unfeigned good wishes, my dear sister, your affectionate brother, and humble servant,

F. THOUGHTLESS.

P.S. Mr. Trueworth knows nothing of my writing to you in his behalf; so you are at liberty to receive him as you shall think proper.'

Miss Betsy required no less a cordial than this to revive her spirits, pretty much depressed since her ill usage at Oxford.

She had not time, however, to indulge the pleasure of reflecting on this new triumph, on her first receiving the news of it. Lady Mellasin had set that evening apart to make a grand visit to a person of her acquaintance, who was just married; the young ladies were to accompany her, and Miss Betsy was in the midst of the hurry of dressing when the post brought the letter, so she only looked it carelessly over, and locked it in her cabinet till she should have more leisure for the examination. They were all ready; the coach with the best hammer-cloth and harnesses was at the door, and only waited while Mrs. Prinks was drawing on her lady's gloves, which happened to be a little too tight.

In this unlucky instant one of the footmen came running into the parlour, and told Lady Mellasin that there was a very ill-looking woman at the door, who enquired for her ladyship, and that she must needs speak with her, and that she had a letter to deliver, which she would give into nobody's hand but her own. Lady Mellasin seemed a little angry at the insolence and folly of the creature, as she then termed it; but ordered she should be shewed into the back-parlour: they were not above five minutes together before the woman went away, and Lady Mellasin returned to the room where Miss Betsy and Miss Flora were waiting for her. A confusion not to be described sat on every feature in her face; she looked pale, she trembled; and having told the young ladies something had happened which prevented her going where she intended, flew up into her dressing-room, followed by Mrs. Prinks, who appeared very much alarmed at seeing her ladyship in this disorder.

Miss Betsy and Miss Flora were also surprized; and doubtless had their own conjectures upon this sudden turn. It is not likely, however, that either of them, especially Miss Betsy, could hit upon the right: but, whatever their thoughts were, they communicated them not to each other, and seemed only intent on considering in what manner they should dispose of themselves that evening, it not being proper they should make the visit above-mentioned without her ladyship. As they were discoursing on this head, Mrs. Prinks came down; and, having ordered the coach to be put up, and sent a footman to call a hack, ran up stairs again in a great hurry to her lady.

In less time than could almost be imagined, they both came down: Lady Mellasin had pulled off her rich apparel, and mobbed herself up in a cloak and hood, that little of her face, and nothing of her air, could be distinguished; the two young ladies stared, and were confounded at the metamorphosis. 'Is your ladyship going out in that dress?' cried Miss Flora; but Miss Betsy said nothing. 'Aye, child,' replied the lady, somewhat faltering in her speech, 'a poor relation, who they say is dying, has sent to beg to see me.' She said no more, the hackney-coach was come, her ladyship and Mrs. Prinks stepped hastily into it; the latter, in doing so, telling the coachman in so low a voice as nobody but himself could hear, to what place he was to drive.

After they were gone, Miss Flora proposed walking in the Park; but Miss Betsy did not happen to be in a humour to go either there or any where else at that time; on which the other told her she had got the spleen: 'But,' said she, 'I am resolved not to be infected with it, so you must not take it ill, if I leave you alone for a few hours; for I should think it a sin against common sense to sit moping at home without shewing myself to any one soul in the world, after having taken all this pains in dressing.' Miss Betsy assured her, as she might do with a great deal of sincerity, that she should not at all be displeased to be entirely free from any company whatsoever, for the whole evening; and to prove the truth of what she said, gave orders that instant to be denied to whoever should come to visit her. 'Well,' cried Miss Flora, laughing, 'I shall give your compliments, however, where I am going;' and then mentioned the names of some persons she had just then taken into her head to visit. 'As you please for that,' replied Miss Betsy, with the same gay air; 'but don't tell them it is because I am eaten up with the vapours, that I chuse to stay at home rather than carry my compliments in person; for if ever I find out,' continued she, 'that you are so mischievous, I shall contrive some way or other to be revenged on you.'

They talked to each other in this pleasant manner, till a chair Miss Flora had sent for was brought into the hall, in which she seated herself for her intended ramble, and Miss Betsy went into her chamber, where how she was amused will presently be shewn.

CHAPTER XII

———•———

Is little more than a continuance of the former

MISS Betsy had no sooner disengaged herself from the incumbrance of a formal dress, and put on one more light and easy, *al fresco*, as the Spaniards phrase it, than she began to give her brother's letter a more serious and attentive perusal, than she had the opportunity of doing before.

She was charmed and elated with the description Mr. Francis had told her, she had inspired in the breast of his friend: she called to her mind the idea of those persons who were present at the entertainments he mentioned, and easily recalled which was most likely to be the lover, though she remembered not the name; she very well now remembered there was one that seemed both times to regard her with glances, which had somewhat peculiar in them, and which then she had interpreted as the certain indications of feeling something in his heart of the nature her brother had described; but not seeing him afterwards, nor hearing any mention made of him, at least that she took notice of, the imagination went out of her head.

This account of him, however, brought to her memory every thing she had observed concerning him, and was very well convinced she had seen nothing, either in his person or deportment, that was not perfectly agreeable; yet, not withstanding all this, and the high encomiums given of him by a brother, who she knew would not deceive her, she was a little vexed to find herself pressed by one so dear and so nearly related to her, to think of him as a man she ever intended to marry: she thought she could be pleased to have such a lover, but could not bring herself to be content that he ever should be a husband. She had too much good sense not to know it suited not with the condition of wife to indulge herself in the gaieties she at present did; which though innocent, and, as she thought, becoming enough in the present state she now was, might not be altogether pleasing to one who, if he so thought proper, had the power of restraining them. In fine, she looked upon a serious behaviour as unsuitable to one of her years; and therefore resolved not to enter into a condition which demanded some share of it, at least for a long time; that is, when she should be grown weary of the admiration, flatteries, and addresses of the men, and no longer find any pleasure in seeing herself preferred before all the women of her acquaintance.

Though it is certain that few young handsome ladies are without some share of the vanity here described, yet it is to be hoped there are not many who are possessed of it in that immoderate degree Miss Betsy was. It is, however, for the sake of those who are so, that these pages are wrote, to the end they may use their utmost endeavours to correct that error, as they will find it so fatal to the happiness of one who had scarce any other blameable propensity in her whole composition.

This young lady was full of meditation on her new conquest, and the manner in which she should receive the victim, who was so shortly to prostrate himself at the shrine of her beauty, when she heard somebody run hastily up stairs, and go into Lady Mellasin's dressing-room, which being adjacent, as has been already taken notice of on a very remarkable occasion, she stepped out of the chamber to see who was there, and found Mrs. Prinks very busy at a cabinet, where her ladyship's jewels were always kept: 'So, Mrs. Prinks,' said she, 'is my lady come home?' – 'No, Miss,' replied the other; 'her ladyship is certainly the most compassionate best woman in the world: her cousin is very bad indeed, and she has sent me for a bottle of reviving drops, which I am going back to carry.' With these words she shuffled something into her pocket, and having locked the cabinet again, went out of the room saying – 'Your servant, Miss Betsy; I cannot stay, for life's at stake.'

This put Miss Betsy in the greatest consternation imaginable: she knew Lady Mellasin could have no drops in that cabinet, unless they were contained in a phial of no larger circumference than a thimble, the drawers of it being very shallow, and made only to hold rings, croceats, necklaces, and such other flat trinkets: she thought there was something very odd and extraordinary in the whole affair. A strange woman coming in so abrupt a manner, her refusing to give the letter to any one but Lady Mellasin herself, her ladyship's confusion at the receipt of it, her disguising herself, and going out with Prinks in that violent hurry, the latter being sent home, her taking something out of the casket, and her going back again; all these incidents, I say, when put together, denoted something of a mystery not easily penetrated into.

Miss Betsy, however, was not of a disposition to think too much, or too deeply, on those things which the most nearly concerned herself, much less on such as related entirely to other people; and Miss Flora coming home soon after, and relating what conversation had passed in the visits she had been making, and the dresses the several ladies had on, and such other trifling matters, diverted the other from those serious reflections, which might otherwise, perhaps, have lasted somewhat longer.

When Miss Flora was undressed, they went down together into the parlour, where they found Mr. Goodman extremely uneasy, that Lady Mellasin was not come home. He had been told in what manner she went out, and it now being grown dark, he was frighted lest any ill accident should befal her, as she had no man-servant, nor any one with her but her woman, whom, he said, he could not look on as a sufficient guard for a lady of quality, against those insults, which night, and the libertinism of the age, frequently produced.

This tender husband asked the young ladies a thousand questions, concerning the possibility of guessing to whom, and to what part of the town, she was gone, in order that he might go himself, or send a servant to conduct her safely home: but neither of them were able to inform him any thing farther than what has already been related; that she had been sent for to a sick relation, who, as it appeared to them, had been very pressing to engage her ladyship to that charitable office.

Mr. Goodman then began to endeavour to recollect the names, and places of abode, of all those he had ever heard her say were of her kindred, for she had never suffered any of them to come to the house, under pretence that some of them had not behaved well, and that others being fallen to decay, and poor, might expect favours from her, and that she would suffer nobody belonging to her to be burdensome to him.

He was, notwithstanding, about to send his men in search of his beloved lady, though he knew not where to direct them to go, when she and Mrs. Prinks came home: he received her with all the transports a man of his years could be capable of, but gently chid her for the little care she had taken of herself, and looking on her, as Mrs. Prinks was pulling off her hood, 'Bless me, my dear,' said he, 'what was your fancy for going out in such a dress?' – 'My cousin,' replied she, 'is in very wretched circumstances, lives in a little mean lodging, and, besides, owes money; if I had gone any thing like myself, the people of the house might have expected great things from me. I am very compassionate, indeed, to every one under misfortunes; but will never squander Mr. Goodman's money for their relief.'

'I know thou art all goodness,' said the old gentleman, kissing her with the utmost tenderness: 'but something,' continued he, 'methinks, might be spared.' – 'Leave it to me, Mr. Goodman,' answered she; 'I know best; they have not deserved it from me.' She then told a long story, how kind she had been to this cousin, and some others of her kindred, in her first husband's time, and gave some instances of the ill use they had made of her bounties. All she said had so much the appearance of truth, that even Miss Betsy, who was far from having a high opinion of her sincerity, believed it, and thought no farther of what had passed; she had, indeed, in a short time, sufficient businesses of her own to take up all her mind.

Mr. Goodman, the very next day, brought home a very agreeable young gentleman to dine with him; who, though he paid an extraordinary respect to Lady Mellasin, and treated her daughter with the utmost complaisance, yet in the compliments he paid to Miss Betsy, there was something which seemed to tell her she had inspired him with a passion more tender than bare respect, and more sincere than common complaisance.

She had very penetrating eyes this way, and never made a conquest without knowing she did so; she was not, therefore, wanting in all those little artifices she had but too much made her study, in order to fix the impression she had given this stranger as indelible as possible: this she had a very good opportunity for doing; he staid the whole afternoon, drank tea with the ladies, and left them not till a crowd of company coming in, he thought good manners obliged him to retire.

Miss Betsy was filled with the most impatient curiosity to know the name and character of this person, whom she had already set down in her mind as a new adorer: she asked Miss Flora, when they were going to bed, as if it were a matter of indifference to her, and merely for the sake of chat, who that gentleman was who had dined with them, and made so long a visit; but that young lady had never seen him before, and was as ignorant of every thing concerning him as herself.

Miss Betsy, however, lost no part of her repose that night, on this account, as she doubted not but she should very soon be informed by himself of all she wished to know: she was but just out of bed the next morning, when a maid-servant came into the chamber and delivered a letter to her, which she told her was brought by a porter, who waited for an answer.

Miss Betsy's heart fluttered at the mention of a letter, flattering herself it came from the person who at present engrossed her thoughts; but on taking it from the maid, found a woman's hand on the superscription,and one perfectly known to her, though at that instant she could not recollect to whom it belonged: she was a good deal surprized, when, on breaking the seal, she found it came from Miss Forward, with whom, as well as the best of the boarding-school ladies, she had ceased all correspondence for many months. The contents were these.

'To Miss Betsy Thoughtless.

Dear Miss Betsy,
Though, since I had the pleasure of seeing or hearing from you, so many accidents and odd turns of fortune have happened to me, as might very well engross my whole attention, yet I cannot be so far forgetful of our former friendship as to be in the same town with you, without letting you know, and desiring to see you. Were there a possibility of my waiting on you, I certainly should have made you the first visit; but, alas! at present there is not. Oh, Miss Betsy! I have strange things to tell you; things fit only to be trusted to a person whose generosity and good-nature I have experienced. If, therefore, you are so good to come, I must intreat you will bring no companion with you, and also that you will allow me that favour the first leisure hour, because I am in some hopes of returning to L—e in a short time. Please to enquire for the house of one Mrs. Nightshade, in Chick Lane, near Smithfield; where you will find her who, in spite of time, absence, and a thousand perplexing circumstances, is, with the most tender regard, my dear Miss Betsy, your very sincere, though unfortunate friend,

A. FORWARD.

P.S. Be so good to let me know, by a line, whether I may flatter myself with the hopes of seeing you, and at what time.'

Though Miss Betsy, through the hurry of her own affairs, had neglected writing to this young lady for a considerable time, yet she was extremely pleased at hearing from her: she could not imagine, however, what strange turns of fortune they were she mentioned in her letter, and which she supposed had brought her to London. Equally impatient to satisfy her curiosity in this point, as to see a person with whom she had contracted her first friendship, she took pen and paper, and immediately wrote this answer.

'To Miss Forward.

Dear Miss Forward,
The satisfaction of hearing you were so near me would be compleat, were it not allayed by the hints you give, that some accidents, not altogether pleasing, had occasioned it. I long to hear what has happened to you since last we saw each other, and will not fail to wait on you this afternoon. I know nothing of the part of the town you are in, but suppose a hackney coach will be able to find it's way. I will detain your messenger no longer than to tell you that I am, with the most perfect amity, dear Miss Forward, your very affectionate friend, and humble servant,

E. THOUGHTLESS.'

Miss Flora had not been present when the maid delivered the letter to Miss Betsy; but coming into the chamber just as she had finished, and was sealing up the answer to it, 'So,' said she, 'have I catched you? Pray what new lover have you been writing to this morning?' It was in vain that Miss Betsy told her she never had yet seen the man she thought worthy of a letter from her on the score of love: the other persisted in her asseverations; and Miss Betsy, to silence her raillery, was obliged to shew her some part of the letter she had received from Miss Forward.

It being near breakfast-time they went down together into the parlour, and as they were drinking their coffee, 'Well, pretty lady,' said Mr. Goodman to Miss Betsy, with a smile, 'how did you like the gentleman that dined here yesterday?' This question so much surprized her that she could not help blushing. 'Like him, Sir!' replied she, 'I did not take any notice of him. I remember a stranger was here, and staid a good while, and that is all; for I neither observed any thing he said or did, or thought on him since.' – 'The agreeable confusion,' cried Mr. Goodman, gaily, 'you are in at my mentioning him, makes me believe you remarked him more than you are willing to acknowledge, and I am very glad of it: you do him but justice, I assure you; for he is very much in love with you.'

'Lord, Sir!' said Miss Betsy, blushing still more, 'I cannot imagine what makes you talk so; I don't suppose the man thinks of me any more than I do of him.' – 'That may be,' rejoined he, laughing out-right. Lady Mellasin then took up the word, and told her husband he was very merry this morning. 'Aye,' said he, 'the hurry of spirits I have put poor Miss Betsy in has made me so; for I can assure you the thing is very serious: but,' continued he, 'you shall know the whole of it.'

He then proceeded to inform them, that the person he had been speaking of was the son of one who had formerly been a merchant; but who, having acquired a large fortune by his industry, had for several years past left off business, and lived mostly in the country; that the young gentleman had seen Miss Betsy at St. Paul's Rehearsal, when they were all there to hear the musick; that the next day after, he had come to him at a coffee-house, which it was known he frequented, and after asking many questions concerning Miss Betsy, and hearing she was not engaged, declared he was very much charmed with her, and entreated his permission, as being her guardian, to make his addresses to her. Mr. Goodman remembered the affront he had received from Alderman Saving on a like occasion, and was determined not to lay himself open to the same from Mr. Staple, (for so he was called) and plainly told the young lover that he would encourage nothing of that sort without the approbation of his father; that after this he had a meeting with the old gentleman, who being fully satisfied by him of Miss Betsy's family, fortune, and character, had no objections to make against his son's inclination. 'Having this sanction,' continued Mr. Goodman, 'and believing it may be a very proper match for both of you, I brought him home with me to dinner yesterday; and should be glad to know how far you think you can approve of the offer, before I give him my consent to make it.'

'I have already told you, Sir,' replied Miss Betsy, 'that I took but little notice of the gentleman; or if I had, should never have asked myself the question, whether I could like him or not; for, as to marriage, I do assure you, Sir, it is a thing that has never yet entered into my head.' – 'Nay, as to that,' returned he, 'it is time enough, indeed. A good husband, however, can never come unseasonably. I shall tell him he may visit you; and leave you to answer the addresses according to the dictates of your heart.'

Miss Betsy neither opposed nor gave consent to what her guardian said on this score; but her not refusing seemed to him a sufficient grant: so there passed nothing more, except some little pleasantries usual on such subjects.

CHAPTER XIII

───────●───────

Contains some part of the history of Miss Forward's adventures, from the time of her leaving the boarding-school, as related by herself to Miss Betsy

MISS Betsy had now her head, though not her heart, full of the two new conquests she had made: Mr. Trueworth was strongly recommended by her brother, Mr. Staple by her guardian; yet all the ideas she had of either of them, served only to excite in her the pleasing imagination, how, when they both came to address her, she should play the one against the other, and give herself a constant round of diversion, by their alternate contentment or disquiet. 'As the barometer,' said she to herself, 'is governed by the weather, so is the man in love governed by the woman he admires: he is a mere machine – acts nothing of himself – has no will or power of his own, but is lifted up or depressed, just as the charmer of his heart is in the humour. I wish,' continued she, 'I knew what day these poor creatures would come – though it is no matter – I have got, it seems, possession of their hearts, and their eyes will find graces in me, let me appear in what shape soever.'

These contemplations, however, enchanting as they were to her vanity, did not render her forgetful of the promise she had made Miss Forward; and as soon as dinner was over, she ordered a hackney-coach to be called, and went to the place Miss Forward's letter had directed.

It is scarce possible for any one to be more surprised than she was, on entering the house of Mrs. Nightshade. The father of Miss Forward was a gentleman of a large estate, and of great consideration in the county where he lived, and she expected to have seen his daughter in lodgings suitable to her birth and fortune; instead of which, she found herself conducted by an old ill-looked mean woman, who gave her to understand she was the mistress of the house, up two pair of stairs, so narrow that she was obliged to hold her hoop quite under her arm, in order to gain the steep and almost perpendicular ascent: she was then shewed into a dirty little chamber, where, on a wretched bed, Miss Forward lay, in a most melancholy and dejected posture. 'Here is a lady wants you,' said the hag, who ushered in Miss Betsy. These words, and the opening of the door, made Miss Forward start from the bed to receive her visiter in the best manner she could: she saluted, she embraced her, with all the demonstrations of joy and affection; but Miss Betsy was so confounded at the appearance of every thing about her, that she was almost incapable of returning her caresses.

Miss Forward easily perceived the confusion her friend was in; and having led her to a chair, and seated herself near her, 'My dear Miss Betsy,' said she, 'I do not wonder you are alarmed at finding me in a condition so different from what you might have expected: my letter, indeed, gave you a hint of some misfortunes that had befallen me; but I forbore letting you know of what nature they were, because the facts, without the circumstances, which would have been too long to communicate by writing, might have made me appear more criminal than I flatter myself you will think I really am, when you shall be told the whole of my unhappy story.'

Miss Betsy then assured her she should take a friendly part in every thing that had happened to her, and that nothing could oblige her more than the confidence she mentioned: on which the other taking her by the hand, and letting fall some tears, said, 'O Miss Betsy! Miss Betsy! I have suffered much; and if you find a great deal to blame me for, you will find yet much more to pity.' Then, after having paused a little, as if to recollect the passages she was about to relate, began in this manner.

'You must remember,' said she, 'that when you left us to go for London, I was strictly watched and confined, on account of my innocent correspondence with Mr. Sparkish; but that young gentleman being sent to the university soon after, I had the same liberty as ever, and as much as any young lady in the school. The tutoress who was with us in your time, being in an ill state of health, went away, and one Mademoiselle Grenouille, a French woman, was put in her place: the governess had a high opinion of her, not only on the score of the character she had of her, but also for the gravity of her behaviour. But as demure, however, as she affected to be before her, she could be as merry and facetious as ourselves when out of her sight, as you will soon perceive by what I have to tell you.

'Whenever any of us took an evening's walk, this was the person to whose care we were entrusted, the governess growing every day more infirm, and indeed unable to attend us.

'It was towards the close of a very hot day, that myself, and two more, went with Mademoiselle Grenouille, to take a little air in the lane, at the back side of the great road that leads up to Lord ****'s fine seat. We were about in the middle of the lane, when we heard the sound of French horns, double curtalls, and other instruments of wind-musick: Mademoiselle at this could not restrain the natural alertness of her country, but went dancing on till we came very near those that played.

'You must know, my dear Miss Betsy,' continued she, 'that my Lord ****s park-wall reaches to the bottom of this lane, and has a little gate into it: having, it seems, some company with him, he had ordered two tents to be erected in that part of the park; the one for himself and friends, the other for the musick, who sounded the instruments to the healths that were toasted; but this we being ignorant of, and delighted with the harmony, wandered on till we came close to the little gate I mentioned, and there stood still listening to it. Some one or other of the gentlemen saw us, and said to the others, "We have eve-'s-droppers!" On which they quitted their seats, and ran to the gate. On seeing them all approach, we would have drawn back, but they were too quick for us; the gate was instantly thrown open, and six or seven gentlemen, of whom my lord was one, rushed out upon us. Perceiving we endeavoured to escape them, they catched hold of us – "Nay, ladies," said one of them, "you must not think to avoid paying the piper, after having heard his musick."

'Mademoiselle, on this, addressed herself to my Lord ****, with as much formality as she could assume, and told him we were young ladies of distinction, who were placed at a boarding-school just by, and at present were under her care; so begged no rudeness might be offered. His lordship protested, on his honour, none should; but insisted on our coming into the park, and drinking one glass of whatever wine we pleased; upon which – "What say you, ladies?" cried Mademoiselle; "I believe we may depend on his lordship's protection." None of us opposed the motion, as being as glad to accept it as herself. In a word, we went in, and were conducted to the tent in the midst of which were placed bottles, glasses, jellies, sweetmeats, pickles, and I know not what other things, to regale and quicken the appetite. Servants, who attended, cooled the glasses out of a silver fountain, on a little pedestal at one end of the tent, and filled every one a glass with what each of us chose. One of the company perceiving our conductress was a French woman, talked to her in her own language, and led her a minuet around the table; and, in the mean time, the others took the opportunity of entertaining us: he that had hold of me, so plied me with kisses and embraces, that I scarce knew where I was. Oh! the differences between his caresses and the boyish insipid salutes of Master Sparkish! The others, I suppose, were served with the same agreeable robustness I was; but I had not the power of observing them, any more than, as I afterwards found, they had of me.

'In short, never were poor innocent girls so pressed, so kissed; every thing but the dernier undoing deed, and that there was no opportunity of compleating, every one of us, our tutoress not excepted, I am certain experienced.'

'Heavens!' cried Miss Betsy, interrupting her, 'how I envied your happiness a moment since, and how I tremble for you now!'

'O Miss Betsy,' replied Miss Forward, 'every thing would have been done in that forgetful hour; but, as I have already said, there was not an opportunity. My lover, notwithstanding, (for so I must call him) would not let me get out of his arms, till I had told him my name, and by what means he should convey a letter to me. I affected to make a scruple of granting this request, though, Heaven knows, I was but too well pleased at his grasping me still faster, in order to compel me to it. I then gave him my name; and told him, that if he would needs write, I knew no other way by which he might be sure of my receiving his letter, but by slipping it into my hand as I was coming out of church, which he might easily do, there being always a great concourse of people about the door: on this he gave me a salute, the warmth of which I never shall forget, and then suffered me to depart with my companions; who, if they were not quite so much engaged as myself, had yet enough to make them remember this night's ramble.

'The tutoress knew well enough how to excuse our staying out so much longer than usual; and neither the governess, nor any one in the family, except ourselves, knew any thing of what had passed. I cannot say but my head ran extremely on this adventure. I heartily wished my pretty fellow might keep his word in writing to me, and was forming a thousand projects how to keep up a correspondence with him. I don't tell you I was what they call in love; but certainly I was very near it, and longed much more for Sunday than ever I had done for a new gown. At last, the wished-for day arrived – my gentleman was punctual – he came close to me in the church-porch – I held my hand in a careless manner, with my handkerchief in it behind me, and presently found something put into it, which I hastily conveyed into my pocket; and, on coming home, found a little three-cornered billet, containing these lines.

"To the charming Miss Forward.

Most lovely of your sex,
I have not slept since I saw you – so deep an impression has your beauty made on my heart, that I find I cannot live without you; nor even die in peace if you vouchsafe not my last breath to issue at your feet. In pity, then, to the sufferings you occasion, grant me a second interview, though it be only to kill me with your frowns. I am too much a stranger in these parts to contrive the means; be, therefore, so divinely good to do it for me, else expect to see me carried by your door a bleeding deathless corpse – the victim of your cruelty, instead of your compassion to your most grateful adorer, and everlasting slave,

                                        R. WILDLY."

'In a postscript to this,' pursued Miss Forward, 'he told me that he would be in the church-porch in the afternoon, hoping to receive my answer by the same means I had directed him to convey to me the dictates of his heart.

'I read this letter over and over, as you may easily guess, by my remembering the contents of it so perfectly; but it is impossible for me to express the perplexity I was in how to reply to it. I do not mean how to excuse myself from granting the interview he so passionately requested; for that, perhaps, I wished for with as much impatience as he could do; but I was distracted at not being able to contrive any practicable method for our meeting.

'O Miss Betsy, how did I long for you, or such a friend as you, to assist me in this dilemma! But there was not one person in the whole house I dared trust with such a secret: I could not eat a bit of dinner, nor scarce speak a word to any body, so much were my thoughts taken up with what I should do. I was resolved to see him, and hear what he had to say, whatever should be the consequence: at last I hit upon a way, dangerous indeed in every respect, and shameful in a girl of my condition; yet, as there was no other, the frenzy I was possessed of, compelled me to have recourse to it.

'You must remember, my dear Miss Betsy,' continued she, with a deep sigh, 'the little door at the farther end of the garden, where, by your kind contrivance, young Sparkish was introduced: it was at this door I determined to meet Mr. Wildly. This, you may be sure, could not be done by day without a discovery, some one or other being continually running into the garden: I therefore fixed the rendezvous at night, at an hour when I was positive all the family would be in bed; and ordered it in this manner.

'Chance aided my ill genius in my undoing; I lay at that time alone; Miss Bab, who used to be my bedfellow, was gone home for a fortnight, on account of a great wedding in their family; and I thought I could easily slip down stairs, when every body was asleep, and go through the kitchen, from which, you know, there is a passage into the garden. I took no care for any thing, but to prevent the disappointment of my design; for I apprehended nothing of ill from a man who adored me, and of whose will and actions I foolishly imagined I had the sole command.

'The settling this matter in my mind engrossed all my thoughts, till the bell began to ring for divine service; and I had only time to write these lines in answer to his billet.

"To Mr. Wildly.

Sir,

I have always been told it was highly criminal in a young maid, like me, to listen to the addresses of any man, without receiving the permission of her parents for so doing; yet I hope I shall stand excused, both to them and you, if I confess I am willing to be the first to hear what so nearly concerns myself. I have but one way of speaking to you; and, if your love be as sincere and fervent as you pretend, you will not think it too much to wait between the hours of eleven and twelve this night, at a green door in the wall which encompasses our garden, at the farther end of the lane, leading to that part of Lord ****'s park, where we first saw each other. You will find me, if no cross accident intervenes, at the time and place I mentioned: but impute this condescension to no other motive than that compassion you implore. I flatter myself your intentions are honourable; and, in that belief, am, Sir, your humble servant,

A. FORWARD." '

Miss Betsy, during the repetition of this letter, and some time before, shook her head, and shewed great tokens of surprize and disapprobation: but offering no interruption, the other went on in her discourse in this manner.

'I protest to you, my dear Miss Betsy,' said she, 'that I had nothing in view by this letter but to secure him to me as a lover. I never had reason to repent of the private correspondence I carried on with Mr. Sparkish; nor knew it was in the nature of man to take advantage of a maid's simplicity: but I will not protract the narrative I promised, by any needless particulars. Every thing happened but too fortunately, alas! according to my wish: I found Mr. Wildly in the church-porch, gave him the fatal billet, unperceived by any one. Night came on – all the family were gone to their repose – and I, unseen, unheard, and unsuspected, quitted my chamber; and, taking the route I told you of, opened the garden-door, where, it seems, the person I expected had waited above half an hour.

'His first salutations were the most humble, and withal the most endearing, that could be. "My angel," said he, "how heavenly good you are! Permit me thus to thank you." With these words he threw himself on his knees, and taking one of my hands, kissed it with the extremest tenderness. But, oh! let no young woman depend on the first professions of her lover; nor in her own power of keeping him at a proper distance!'

Here a sudden gush of tears prevented her, for some minutes, from prosecuting her discourse; and Miss Betsy found herself obliged to treat her with more tenderness than, in her own mind, she thought the nature of her case deserved.

CHAPTER XIV

—————•—————

Concludes Miss Forward's narrative, and relates some farther particulars of Miss Betsy's behaviour, on hearing a detail she so little expected

HOW sweet are the consolations of a sincere friend! How greatly do they alleviate the severest of misfortunes! – Miss Forward soon dried up her tears, on a soft commiseration she saw they excited in Miss Betsy; and stifling, as well as she could, the rising sighs with which her bosom heaved at the remembrance of what she was going to relate, resumed her mournful story in these terms.

'You may very well suppose,' said she, 'that the garden-door was not a proper place to entertain my lover in: good manners forbade me to use him in so coarse a manner; besides, late as it was, some passenger might happen to come that way; I therefore led him into the arbour at the end of the terrace, where we sat down together on that broad bench under the arch, where you so often used to loll, and call it your throne of state. Never was there a finer night; the moon, and her attendant stars, shone with uncommon brightness; the air was all serene, the boisterous winds were all locked in their caverns, and only gentle zephyrs, with their fanning wings, wafted a thousand odours from the neighbouring plants, perfuming all around. It was an enchanting scene! Nature herself seemed to conspire my ruin, and contributed all in her power to lull my mind into a soft forgetfulness of what I owed myself – my fame – my fortune – and my family.

'I was beginning to tell him how sensible I was, that to admit him in this manner was against all the rules of decency and decorum, and that I hoped he would not abuse the good opinion I had of him, nor entertain the worse of me for my so readily complying with his request, and such-like stuff: to which he gave little ear, and only answered me with protestations of the most violent passion that ever was; swore that I had more charms than my whole sex besides could boast of; that I was an angel! – a goddess! – that I was nature's whole perfection in one piece! then, looking on me with the most tender languishments, he repeated these lines in a kind of extasy –

"In forming thee, Heav'n took unusual care;
Like it's own beauty it design'd thee fair,
And copied from the best-lov'd angel there."

'The answers I made to these romantick encomiums were silly enough, I believe, and such as encouraged him to think I was too well pleased to be much offended at any thing he did. He kissed, he clasped me to his bosom, still silencing my rebukes, by telling me how handsome I was, and how much he loved me; and that, as opportunities of speaking to me were so difficult to be obtained, I must not think him too presuming if he made the most of this.

'What could I do! – How resist his pressures! The maid having put me to bed that night, as usual, I had no time to dress myself again after I got up; so was in the most loose dishabille that can be imagined. His strength was far superior to mine; there was no creature to come to my assistance; the time, the place, all joined to aid his wishes; and, with the bitterest regret and shame, I now confess, my own fond heart too much consented.

'In a word, my dear Miss Betsy, from one liberty he proceeded to another; till, at last, there was nothing left for him to ask, or me to grant!'

These last words were accompanied with a second flood of tears, which streamed in such abundance down her cheeks, that Miss Betsy was extremely moved: her good nature made her pity the distress, though her virtue and understanding taught her to detest and despise the ill conduct which occasioned it; she wept and sighed in concert with her afflicted friend, and omitted nothing that she thought might contribute to assuage her sorrows.

Miss Forward was charmed with the generosity of Miss Betsy, and composed herself as much as possible to make those acknowledgements it merited from her; and then proceeded to gratify her curiosity with that part of her adventures which yet remained untold.

'Whenever I recollect,' resumed she, 'how strangely, how suddenly, how almost unsolicited, I yielded up my honour, some lines, which I remember to have read somewhere, come into my mind, and seem, methinks, perfectly adapted to my circumstances. They are these –

> "Pleas'd with destruction, proud to be undone,
> With open arms I to my ruin run,
> And sought the mischiefs I was bid to shun:
> Tempted that shame a virgin ought to dread,
> And had not the excuse of being betray'd."

'Alas! I see my folly now – my madness! But was blind to it too long. I upbraided not my undoer; I remonstrated not to him any of the ill consequences that might possibly attend this transaction; nor mentioned one word concerning how incumbent it was on him to repair the injury he had done me by marriage. Sure never was there so infatuated a wretch! Morning began to break in upon us; and the pang of being obliged to part, and the means of meeting again, now took up all my thoughts. Letting him in at midnight was very dangerous, as old Nurse Winter, who, you know, is very vapourish, often fancies she hears noises in the house, and rises to see if all the doors and windows are fast: besides, Mr. Wildly told me it was highly inconvenient for him, being obliged to make a friend of my Lord ****'s porter to fit it up for him.

'I was almost at my wit's end; til he recovered me, by saying he believed there might be a more easy way for our intercourse than this nocturnal rendezvous. "Oh, what is that!" cried I, earnestly. "The French woman," replied he, "who lives here, is good-natured, and of a very amorous complexion; at least, Sir John Shuffle, who toyed with her in my lord's park, tells me she is so. But," continued he, "I dare take his word: he knows your sex perfectly; and, I dare answer, if you will get her to go abroad with you, the consequence will be agreeable to us all."

"What," said I, "would you have me make her my confidante?" "Not altogether so," said he; "at least, not till you are upon even terms with her; I mean, till you have secret for secret."

"How can that be?" demanded I. "Leave that to me," said he; "do you only get her out to-morrow a walking: let me know, what time you think you can best do it, and Sir John and I will meet you as if by chance." I told him I would undertake to do it if the weather were fair, and that they might meet us going towards the town; but it must be past five, after she had given her French lesson to the ladies. This being agreed upon, we parted, though not without the extremest reluctance; at least, I am sure, on my side it was sincerely so. I then went back with the same precaution I had gone out; locked all the doors softly, and got into my chamber before any of the family were stirring.

'I was more than ordinarily civil to Mademoiselle all the next day; I said every thing I could think on to flatter her: and, having got an opportunity of speaking to her alone, "Dear Mademoiselle," said I, in a wheedling tone, "I have a great favour to beg of you." – "What is that, Miss?" replied she. "Any thing in my power you may command." I then told her I had got a whim in my head for a new tippet, and that I wanted her fancy in the choice of the colours. "With all my heart," said she; "and when we go out a walking this evening, we can call at the milliner's, and buy the ribbands." – "That will not do," cried I; "I would not have any of the ladies know any thing of the matter till I have made it, and got it on; so nobody must go with us." – "Well, well," answered she, "it shall be so; but I must tell the governess. I know she will not be against humouring you in such a little fancy, and will send the other tutoress, or Nurse Winter, to wait upon the other ladies." I told her she was very good, but enjoined her to beg the governess to keep it as a secret; for my tippet would be mighty pretty, and I wanted to surprize them with the sight of it.

'The governess, however, was so kind as to let us go somewhat before the time we expected, in order to prevent any one from offering to accompany us: but, early as it was, the two gentlemen were on the road. They accosted us with a great deal of complaisance: "What, my Diana of the forest!" said Sir John to Mademoiselle, "am I so fortunate to see you once again?" What reply she made I do not know, being speaking to Wildly at the same time; but he also, by my instigations, made his chief court to Mademoiselle, and both of them joined to intreat she would permit them to lead her to some house of entertainment: her refusals were very faint, and, perceiving by my look, that I was not very averse, "What shall we do, Miss?" said she to me; "there is no getting rid of these men. Shall we venture to go with them? It is but a frolick." – "I am under your direction, Mademoiselle; but I see no harm in it; as, to be sure," replied I, "they are gentlemen of honour."

'In fine, we went into the first house that had the prospect of affording us an agreeable reception. It is not to be doubted but we were treated with the best the place we were in could supply; Sir John declared the most flaming passion for Mademoiselle, and engrossed her so much to himself, that Wildly had the liberty of addressing me, without letting her see his choice gave me the preference.

'Sir John, after using Mademoiselle with some freedoms, which I could perceive she did not greatly resent, told her, there was an exceeding fine picture in the next room; and asked her to go and look upon it. "O yes!" replied she, "I am extravagantly fond of painting. – Are you not, Miss?" continued she to me with a careless air. "No," said I, "I had rather stay here, and look out of the window: but I would not hinder this gentleman," meaning Mr. Wildly; who replied, "I have seen it already, so will stay and keep you company."

'I believe, indeed, we might have spared ourselves the trouble of these last speeches, for our companions seemed as little to expect as to desire we should follow them; but ran laughing, jumping, and skipping, out of the room, utterly regardless of those they left behind.

'Thus, you see, my dear Miss Betsy,' continued she, 'Wildly had, a second time, the opportunity of triumphing over the weakness of your unhappy friend. Oh! had it been the last, perhaps I had not been the wretch I am: but, alas! my folly ceased not here; I loved, and every interview made him still dearer to me.

'On Mademoiselle's return, we began to talk of going home: "Bless me," cried I, "it is now too late to go into town. What excuse shall we make to the governess for not having bought the ribbands?" – "I have already contrived that," replied she; "I will tell her, that the woman had none but ugly old-fashioned things, and expects a fresh parcel from London in two or three days." – "Oh, that is rare," cried I; "that will be a charming pretence for our coming out again." – "And a charming opportunity for our meeting you again," said Sir John Shuffle. "If you have any inclination to lay hold of it," rejoined Mademoiselle. "And you have courage to venture," cried he. "You see we are no cowards," answered she briskly. "Well, then, name your day," said Wildly; "if Sir John accepts the challenge, I will be his second: but I am afraid it cannot be till after Thursday, because my lord talks of going back to ****, and we cannot be back in less than three days."

'Friday, therefore, was the day agreed upon; and we all four were punctual to the appointment. I shall not trouble you with the particulars of our conversation in this or any other of the meetings we had together; only tell you, that by the contrivance of one or other of us, we found means of coming together once or twice every week, during the whole time these gentlemen staid in the country, which was upwards of two months.

'On taking leave, I pressed Wildly to write to me under cover of Mademoiselle Grenouille, which he promised to do, and I was silly enough to expect. Many posts arriving, without bringing any letter, I was sadly disappointed, and could not forbear expressing my concern to Mademoiselle, who only laughed at me, and told me, I as yet knew nothing of the world, nor the temper of mankind; that a transient acquaintance, such as ours had been with these gentlemen, ought to be forgot as soon as over; that there was no great probability we should ever see one another again; and it would be only a folly to keep up a correspondence by letters; and added, that by this time, they were, doubtless, entered into other engagements. "And so might we too," said she, "if the place and fashion we live in did not prevent us."

'I found by this, and some other speeches of the like nature, that it was the sex, not the person, she regarded. I could not, however, be of her way of thinking. I really loved Mr. Wildly, and would have given the world, had I been mistress of it, to have seen him again; but, as she said, indeed, there was no probability of my doing so; and therefore I attempted, through her persuasions, to make a virtue of necessity, and forget both him and all that passed between us. I should in the end, perhaps, have accomplished this point; but, oh! I had a remembrancer within, which I did not presently know of. In fine, I had but too much reason to believe I was pregnant; a thing which, though a natural consequence of the folly I had been guilty of, never once entered my head.

'Mademoiselle Grenouille seemed now terribly alarmed, on my communicating to her my suspicions on this score: she cried 'twas very unlucky! – then paused, and asked what I would do, if it should really be as I feared. I replied, that I knew not what course to take, for if my father should know it I was utterly undone: I added, that he was a very austere man; and, besides, I had a mother-in-law, who would not fail to say every thing she could to incense him against me.

"I see no recourse you have, then," said she, "but by taking physick to cause an abortion. You must pretend you are a little disordered, and send for an apothecary; the sooner the better, for if it should become visible, all would infallibly be known, and we should both be ruined."

'I was not so weak as not to see, that if any discovery were made, her share in the intrigue must come out, and she would be directly turned out of doors; and that, whatever concern she pretended for me, it was chiefly on her own account: however, as I saw no other remedy, was resolved to take her advice.

'Thus, by having been guilty of one crime, I was ensnared to commit another of a yet fouler kind: one was the error of nature, this an offence against nature. The black design, however, succeeded not: I took potion after potion, yet still retained the token of my shame; which at length became too perspicuous for me to hope it would not be taken notice of by all who saw me.

'I was almost distracted, and Mademoiselle Grenouille little less so. I was one day alone in my chamber, pondering on my wretched state, and venting some part of the anguish of my mind in tears, when she came in; "What avails all this whimpering?" said she; "you do but hasten what you would wish to avoid. The governess already perceives you are strangely altered; she thinks you are either in a bad state of health, or some way disordered in your mind, and talks of writing to your father to send for you home." "Oh Heaven!" cried I. "Home, did you say? – No; I will never go home! The grave is not so hateful to me, nor death so terrible, as my father's presence." – "I pity you from my soul," said she: "but what can you do? There will be no staying for you here, after your condition is once known, and it cannot be concealed much longer." These words, the truth of which I was very well convinced of, drove me into the last despair: I raved, I tore my hair, I swore to poison, drown, or stab myself, rather than live to have my shame exposed to the severity of my father, and reproaches of my kindred.'

"Come, come," resumed she, "there is no need of such desperate remedies; you had better go to London, and have recourse to Wildly: who knows, as you are a gentleman's daughter, and will have a fortune, but you may persuade him to marry you? If not, you can oblige him to take care of you in your lying-in, and to keep the child: and when you are once got rid of your burden, some excuse or other may be found for your elopement."

"But how shall I get to London?" resumed I; "how find out my undoer in a place I know nothing of, nor ever have been at? Of whom shall I enquire? I am ignorant of what family he is, or even where he lives." – "As to that," replied she, "I will undertake to inform myself of every thing necessary for you to know; and, if you resolve to go, I will set about it directly." I then told her, I would do any thing rather than be exposed; on which she bid me assume as chearful a countenance as I could, and dpend on her bringing me some intelligence of Wildly before I slept.

'The method she took to make good her promise was, it seems, to send a person whom she could confide in to the seat of Lord ****, to enquire among the servants, where Mr. Wildly, who had lately been a guest there, might be found. She told me that the answer they gave the man was, that they knew not where he lodged, but that he might be heard of at any of the coffee-houses about St. James's. As I was altogether a stranger in London, this information gave me but little satisfaction; but Mademoiselle Grenouille, whose interest it was to hurry me away, assured me that she knew that part of the town perfectly well, having lived there several months on her first arrival in England – that there were several great coffee-houses there, frequented by all the gentlemen of fashion, and that nothing would be more easy than to find Mr. Wildly at one or other of them. My heart, however, shuddered at the thoughts of this enterprize; yet her persuasions, joined to the terrors I was in of being exposed, and the certainty that a discovery of my condition was inevitable, made me resolve to undertake it.

'Nothing now remained but the means how I should get away, so as to avoid the pursuit which might, doubtless, be made after me; which, after some consultation, was thus contrived and executed.

'A flying-coach set out from H— every Monday at two o'clock in the morning; Mademoiselle Grenouille engaged the same man who had enquired at Lord ****'s for Mr. Wildly, to secure a place for me in it. The Sunday before I was to go, I pretended indisposition to avoid going to church: I passed that time in packing up the best of my things in a large bundle; for I had no opportunity of taking a box or trunk with me. My greatest difficulty was how to get out of bed from Miss Bab, who still lay with me; I thought, however, that if she happened to awake while I was rising, I would tell her I was not very well, and was only going into the next room, to open the window for a little air: but I stood in no need of this precaution, she was in a sound sleep, and I left my bed, put on the cloaths I was to travel in, and stole out of the room, without her perceiving any thing of the matter. I went out by the same way by which I had fulfilled my first fatal appointment with Mr. Wildly. At a little distance from the garden-door, I found the friend of Mademoiselle Grenouille, who waited for me with a horse and pillion; he took my bundle before, and me behind him, and then we made the best of our way towards H—, where we arrived time enough for the coach. I alighted at the door of the inn, and he rode off directly to avoid being seen by any body, who might describe him, in case an enquiry should be made.

'I will not trouble you with the particulars of my journey, nor how I was amazed on entering this great metropolis; I shall only tell you, that it being dark when we came in, I lay that night at the inn, and the next morning, following the directions Mademoiselle Grenouille had given me, took a hackney-coach, and ordered the man to drive into any of the streets about St. James's, and stop at the first house where he should see a bill upon the door for ready-furnished lodgings. It happened to be in Rider Street; the woman at first seemed a little scrupulous of taking me, as I was a stranger, and had no recommendation; but on my telling her I would pay her a fortnight beforehand, we agreed on the rate of twelve shillings a week.

'The first thing I did was to send a porter to the coffee-houses; where he easily heard of him, but brought me the vexatious intelligence that he was gone to Tunbridge; and it was not known when he would return. This was a very great misfortune to me, and the more so as I had very little money: I thought it best, however, to follow him thither, which I did the same week.

'But oh! my dear Betsy, how unlucky every thing happened; he had left that place the very morning before I arrived, and gone for London. I had nothing now to do but return; but was so disordered with the fatigues I had undergone, that I was obliged to stay four days to compose myself. When I came back, I sent immediately to the coffee-house: but how shall I express the distraction I was in, when I was told he had lain but one night in town, and was gone to Bath.

'This second disappointment was terrible indeed; I had but half-a-crown remaining of the little stock I brought from the boarding-school, and had no way to procure a supply but by selling my watch, which I did to a goldsmith in the neighbourhood, for what he was pleased to give me, and then set out for Bath by the first coach.

'Here I had the good fortune to meet him; he was strangely surprized at the sight of me in that place, but much more so when I told him what had brought me there: he seemed extremely concerned at the accident. But when I mentioned marriage, he plainly told me I must not think of such a thing; that he was not in circumstances to support a family; that, having lost the small fortune left him by his friends at play, he was obliged to have recourse, for his present subsistence, to the very means by which he had been undone: in short, that he was a gamester. The name startled me: treated as I had always heard it, with the utmost contempt, I could not reconcile how such a one came to be the guest and companion of a lord; though I have since heard that men of that profession frequently receive those favours from the nobility, which are denied to persons of more unblemished characters.

'Wildly however, it is certain, had some notions of honour and good-nature; he assured me he would do all in his power to protect me; but added, that he had been very unfortunate of late, and that I must wait for a lucky chance, before he could afford me any supply.

'I staid at Bath all the time he was there: he visited me every day; but I lived on my own money till we came to town, when my time being very near, he brought me to the place you find me in, having, it seems, agreed with the woman of the house for a certain sum of money to support me during my lying-in, and keep the child as long as it should live. The miseries I have sustained during my abode with this old hag, would be too tedious to repeat. The only joy I have is, that the wretched infant died in three days after it's birth, so has escaped the woes which children thus exposed are doomed to bear. Wildly has taken his last leave of me, and I have wrote to an aunt, entreating her to endeavour to obtain my father's forgiveness. I pretended to her that I left L—e for no other reason than because I had an ardent desire to see London; and as I think nobody can reveal to him the true cause, have some hopes of not being utterly abandoned by him.'

Here this unfortunate creature finished her long narrative; and Miss Betsy saw her in too much affliction to express any thing that might increase it: she only thanked her for reposing a confidence in her; 'Which,' said she, 'may be of great service to me some time or other.'

Before they parted, Miss Forward said she had gone in debt to Mrs. Nightshade, for some few things she wanted, over and above what is generally allowed in such cases, and had been affronted by her for not being able to discharge it; therefore intreated Miss Betsy to lend her twenty shillings; on which the generous and sweet-tempered young lady immediately drew her purse, and after giving her the sum she demanded, put two guineas more into her hand. 'Be pleased to accept this,' said she; 'you may possibly want something after having paid your debt.' The other thanked her, and told her she doubted not but her aunt would send her something, and she would then repay it. 'I shall give myself no pain about that,' said Miss Betsy: and then took her leave, desiring she would let her know by a letter what success she had with her friends. Miss Forward told her she might depend not only on hearing from her, but seeing her again, as soon as she had any thing to acquaint her with.

CHAPTER XV

Brings many things on the carpet, highly pleasing to Miss Betsy, in their beginning, and no less perplexing to her in their consequences

THE accounts of those many and dreadful misfortunes which the ill conduct of Miss Forward had drawn upon her, made Miss Betsy extremely pensive. 'It is strange,' said she to herself, 'that a woman cannot indulge in the liberty of conversing freely with a man, without being persuaded by him to do every thing he would have her.' She thought, however, that some excuse might be made for Miss Forward, on the score of her being strictly debarred from all acquaintance with the other sex. 'People,' cried she, 'have naturally an inclination to do what they are most forbid. The poor girl had a curiosity to hear herself addressed; and having no opportunity of gratifying that passion, but by admitting her lover at so odd a time and place, was indeed too much in his power to have withstood her ruin, even if she had been mistress of more courage and resolution than she was.'

On meditating on the follies which women are sometimes prevailed upon to be guilty of, the discovery she had made of Miss Flora's intrigue with Gayland came fresh into her mind. 'What,' said she, 'could induce her to sacrifice her honour? Declarations of love were not new to her. She heard every day the flatteries with which our sex are treated by the men, and needed not to have purchased the assiduities of any one of them at so dear a rate. Good God! are innocence, and the pride on conscious virtue, things of so little estimation, as to be thrown away for the trifling pleasure of hearing a few tender protestations? perhaps all false, and uttered by one whose heart despises the early fondness he has triumphed over, and ridicules the very grant of what he has so earnestly solicited!'

It is certain this young lady had the highest notions of honour and virtue; and whenever she gave herself time to reflect, looked on every thing that had a tendency to make an encroachment on them with the most extreme detestation; yet had the good-nature enough to pity those faults in others, she thought it impossible for her to be once guilty of herself.

But, amidst sentiments as noble and as generous as ever heart was possessed of, vanity, that foible of her soul, crept in, and would have it's share. She had never been thoroughly attacked in a dishonourable way, but by Gayland, and the gentleman-commoner at Oxford; both which she rebuffed with a becoming disdain. In this she secretly exulted, and had that dependence on her power of repelling all the efforts, come they in what shape soever, that should be made against her virtue, that she thought it beneath her to behave so as not to be in danger of incurring them.

How great a pity it is, that a mind endued with so many excellent qualities, and which had such exalted ideas of what is truly valuable in womankind, should be tainted with a frailty of so fatal a nature, as to expose her to temptations, which if she were not utterly undone, it must be owing rather to the interposition of her guardian angel, than to the strength of human reason: but of that hereafter. At present there were none had any base designs upon her: we must shew what success those gentlemen met with, who addressed her with the most pure and honourable intensions. Of this number we shall speak first of Mr. Trueworth and Mr. Staple; the one, as has been already said, strenuously recommended by her brother, the other by Mr. Goodman.

Mr. Staple had the good fortune (if it may be called so) to be the first of these two who had the opportunity of declaring his passion; the journey of the other to London having been retarded two days longer than he intended.

This gentleman having Mr. Goodman's leave, made a second visit at his house. Lady Mellasin and Miss Flora knowing on what business he was come, made an excuse for leaving him and Miss Betsy together. He made his addresses to her in the forms which lovers usually observe on the first declaration; and she replied to what he said, in a manner not to encourage him too much, nor yet to take from him all hope.

While they were discoursing, a footman came in, and told her a gentleman from Oxford desired to speak with her, having some commands from her brother to deliver to her. Mr. Staple supposing they had business, took his leave, and Mr. Trueworth (for it was he indeed) was introduced.

'Madam,' said he, saluting her with the utmost respect, 'I have many obligations to Mr. Thoughtless; but none which demands so large a portion of my gratitude, as the honour he has conferred upon me in presenting you with this letter.' To which she replied, that her brother must certainly have a great confidence in his goodness, to give him this trouble. With these words she took the letter out of his hand; and having obliged him to seat himself, 'You will pardon, Sir,' said she, 'the rudeness which my impatience to receive the commands of so near and dear a relation makes me guilty of.' He made no other answer to these words than a low bow; and she withdrew to a window, and found the contents of her brother's letter were these.

'To Miss Betsy Thoughtless.

My dear sister,
I shall leave Oxford tomorrow, in order to cross the country for the seat of Sir Ralph Trusty, as I suppose Mr. Goodman will inform you, I having wrote to him by the post: but the most valuable of my friends being going to London, and expressing a desire of renewing that acquaintance he had begun to commence with you here, I have taken the liberty of troubling him with the delivery of this to you. He is a gentleman whose merits you are yet a stranger to; but I have so good an opinion of your penetration, as to be confident a very little time will convince you that he is deserving all the esteem in your power to regard him with; in the mean time doubt not but you will receive him as a person whose success, in every thing, is much desired by him, who is, with the tenderest good wishes, dear sister, your most affectionate brother,

F. THOUGHTLESS.'

As she did not doubt but by the stile and manner of this letter, that it had been seen by Mr. Trueworth, she could not keep herself from blushing, which he observing as he sat, flattered himself with taking as a good omen. He had too much awe upon him, however, to make any declarations of his passion at the first visit: neither, indeed, had he an opportunity of doing it; Lady Mellasin and Miss Flora, thinking they had left Mr. Staple and Miss Betsy a sufficient time together, came into the room. The former was surprized to find he was gone, and a strange gentleman in his place; but Miss Flora remembering him perfectly well, they saluted each other with the freedom of persons who were not entire strangers: they entered into a conversation; and other company coming in, Mr. Trueworth had an opportunity of displaying the fine talents he was master of. His travels – the observations he had made on the curiosities he had seen abroad, particularly at Rome, Florence, and Naples, were highly entertaining to the company. On taking leave, he told the ladies, he hoped they would allow him the favour of making one at their tea-table sometimes, while he remained in London; to which Lady Mellasin and her daughter, little suspecting the motive he had for this request, joined in assuring him he could not come too often, and that they should expect to see him every day: but Miss Betsy looking on herself as chiefly concerned in his admission, modestly added to what they had said, only that a person so much, and she doubted not but so justly, esteemed by her brother, might be certain of a sincere welcome from her.

Every body was full of the praises of this gentleman; and Miss Betsy, though she said the least of any one, thought her brother had not bestowed more on him than he really deserved. Mr. Goodman coming home soon after, there appeared some marks of displeasure in his countenance, which, as he was the best humoured man in the world, very much surprized those of his family: but the company not being all retired, none of them seemed to take any notice of it, and went on with the conversation they were upon before his entrance.

The visitors, however, were no sooner gone, than, without staying to be asked, he immediately let them into the occasion of his being so much ruffled; 'Miss Betsy,' said he, 'you have used me very ill; I did not think you would have made a fool of me in the manner you have done.' – 'Bless me, Sir,' cried she, 'in what have I offended?' – 'You have not only offended against me,' answered he, very hastily, 'but also against your own reason and common understanding: you are young, it is true, yet not so young as not to know it is both ungenerous and silly to impose upon your friends.' – 'I scorn the thought, Sir, of imposing upon any body,' said she; 'I therefore desire, Sir, you will tell me what you mean by so unjust an accusation.' – 'Unjust!' resumed he; 'I appeal to the whole world, if it were well done of you to suffer me to encourage my friend's courtship to you, when at the same time your brother had engaged you to receive the addresses of another.'

Miss Betsy, though far from thinking it a fault in her to hear the proposals of a hundred lovers, had as many offered themselves, was yet a little shocked at the reprimand given her by Mr. Goodman; and not being able presently to make any reply to what he had said, he took a letter he had just received from her brother out of his pocket, and threw it on the table, with these words – 'That will shew,' said he, 'whether I have not cause to resent your behaviour in this point.' Perceiving she was about to take it up, 'Hold!' cried he, 'my wife shall read it, and be the judge between us.'

Lady Mellasin, who had not spoke all this time, then took the letter, and read aloud the contents, which were these.

'To Mr. Goodman.

Sir,

This comes to let you know I have received the remittances you were so obliging to send me. I think to set out to-morrow for L—e; but shall not stay there for any length of time: my intentions for going into the army are the same as when I last wrote to you; and the more I consider on that affair, the more I am confirmed that a military life is most suitable of any to my genius and humour. If, therefore, you can hear of any thing proper for me, either in the Guards, or in a marching-regiment, I shall be infinitely thankful for the trouble you take in the enquiry: but, Sir, this is not all the favours I have to ask of you at present. A gentleman of family, fortune, and character, has seen my sister, likes her; and is going to London on no other business than to make his addresses to her. I have already wrote to her on this subject, and I believe she will pay some regard to what I have said in his behalf. I am very well assured she can never have a more advantageous offer, as to his circumstances, nor be united to a man of more true honour, morality, and sweetness of disposition; all of which I have had frequent occasions of being an eyewitness of: but she is young, gay, and, as yet, perhaps, not altogether so capable as I could wish of knowing what will make for her real happiness. I therefore intreat you, Sir, as the long experienced friend of our family, to forward this match, both by your advice, and whatever else is in your power, which certainly will be the greatest act of goodness you can confer on her, as well as the highest obligation to a brother, who wishes nothing more than to see her secured from all temptations, and well settled in the world. I am, with the greatest respect, Sir, your most humble, and most obedient servant,

F. THOUGHTLESS.

P.S. I had forgot to inform you Sir, that the name of the gentleman I take the liberty of recommending with so much warmth, is Trueworth; that he is descended from the ancient Britons by the father's side, and by the mother's from the honourable and well-known Oldcastles, in Kent.'

'O fie, Miss Betsy!' said Lady Mellasin, 'how could you serve Mr. Goodman so? What will Mr. Staple say, when he comes to know he was encouraged to court a woman that was already pre-engaged?' – 'Pre-engaged, Madam!' cried Miss Betsy, in a scornful tone; 'what, to a man I never saw but three times in my whole life, and whose mouth never uttered a syllable of love to me!' She was going on; but Mr. Goodman, who was still in a great heat, interrupted her, saying, 'No matter whether he has uttered any thing of the business, or not, it seems you are enough acquainted with his sentiments; and I doubt not but he knows you are, or he would not have taken a journey to London on your account. You ought therefore to have told me of his coming, and what your brother had wrote concerning him; and I should then have let Mr. Staple know it would be to no purpose to make any courtship to you, as I did to another just before I came home, who I find has taken a great fancy to you: but I have given him an answer. For my part, I do not understand this way of making gentlemen lose their time.'

It is probable these last words nettled Miss Betsy more than all the rest he had said; she imagined herself secure of the hearts of both Trueworth and Staple, but was vexed to the heart to have lost the addresses of a third admirer, through the scrupulousness of Mr. Goodman, who she looked upon to have nothing to do with her affairs in this particular: she was too cunning, however, to let him see what her thoughts were on this occasion, and only said, that he might do as he pleased – that she did not want a husband – that all men were alike to her – but added, that it seemed strange to her that a young woman who had her fortune to make, might not be allowed to hear all the different proposals that should be offered to her on that score; and with these words, flung out of the room, and went up into her chamber, nor would be prevailed upon to come down again that night, though Miss Flora, and Mr. Goodman himself, repenting he had said so much, called to her for that purpose.

CHAPTER XVI

———•———

Presents the reader with the name and character of Miss Betsy's third lover, and also with some other particulars

THOUGH Lady Mellasin had seemed to blame Miss Betsy for not having communicated to Mr. Goodman what her brother wrote to her in relation to Mr. Trueworth, yet in her heart she was far from being averse to her receiving a plurality of lovers, because whenever that young lady should fix her choice, there was a possibility some one or other of those she rejected might transmit his addresses to her daughter, who she was extremely desirous of getting married, and had never yet been once solicited on honourable terms: she therefore told her husband, that he ought not to hinder Miss Betsy from hearing what every gentleman had to offer, to the end she might accept that which had the prospect of most advantage to her.

Mr. Goodman in this, as in every thing else, suffered himself to be directed by her judgment; and the next morning, when Miss Betsy came down, talked to her with his usual pleasantry. 'Well,' said he, 'have you forgiven my ill-humour last night? I was a little vexed to think my friend Staple had so poor a chance for gaining you; and the more so, because Frank Thoughtless will take it ill of me that I have done any thing in opposition to the person he recommends: but you must act as you please; for my part I shall not meddle any farther in these affairs.'

'Sir,' replied Miss Betsy very gravely, 'I shall always be thankful to my friends for their advice; and whenever I think seriously of a husband, shall not fail to intreat yours in my choice: but,' continued she, 'one would imagine my brother, by writing so pressingly to you, wanted to hurry me into a marriage whether I would or no; and though I have as much regard for him as a sister can or ought to have, yet I shall never be prevailed upon by him to enter into a state to which at present I have rather an aversion than inclination.'

'That is,' said Mr. Goodman, 'you have rather an aversion than an inclination to the persons who address you on that score.' – 'No, Sir,' answered she, 'not at all; the persons and behaviour both of Mr. Trueworth and Mr. Staple appear to me to be unexceptionable: but sure one may allow a man to have merit, and be pleased with his conversation, without desiring to be tacked to him forever. I verily believe I shall never be in love; but if I am, it must be a long length of time, and a series of persevering assiduities must make me so.'

Mr. Goodman told her these were only romantick notions, which he doubted not but a little time would cure her of. What reply Miss Betsy would have made is uncertain, for the discourse was interrupted by a footman delivering a letter to her, in which she found these lines.

'To Miss Betsy Thoughtless.

Fair creature,
I am no courtier – no beau – and have hitherto had but little communication with your sex; but I am honest and sincere, and you may depend on the truth of what I say. I have, Heaven be praised, acquired a very large fortune, and for some time have had thoughts of marrying, to the end I might have a son to enjoy the fruits of my labours, after I am food either for the fishes or the worms – it is no great matter which of them. Now I have been wished to several fine women, but my fancy gives the preference to you; and if you can like me as well, we shall be very happy together. I spoke to your guardian yesterday, (for I love to be above-board) but he seemed to lour, or as we say at sea, to be a little hazy on the matter, so I thought I would not trouble him any further, but write directly to you. I hear there are two about you; but what of that? I have doubled the Cape of Good Hope many a time, and never failed of reaching my intended port; I therefore see no cause why I should apprehend a wreck by land. I am turned of eight and forty, it is true, which, may be, you may think too old: but I must tell you, dear pretty one, that I have a constitution that will wear out twenty of your washy pampered landmen of not half my age. Whatever your fortune is, I will settle accordingly; and, moreover, will secure something handsome to you at my decease, in

case you should chance to be the longest liver. I know you young
women do not care a man should have anything under your hand, so
expect no answer; but desire you will consider on my proposals, and
let me know your mind this evening at five o'clock, when I shall come
to Mr. Goodman's, let him take it how he will. I can weather out any
storm to come at you; and sincerely am, dear soul, your most faithful
and affectionate lover,

J. HYSOM.'

There were some passages in this letter that set Betsy Thoughtless
into such immoderate fits of laughter, as made her a long time in
going through it. Having finished the whole, she turned to Mr.
Goodman, and putting it into his hands – 'Be pleased, Sir, to read
that,' said she; 'you shall own, at least, that I do not make a secret of
all my lovers to you.' Mr. Goodman soon looked it over; and, after
returning it to her – 'How troublesome a thing it is,' said he, 'to be
the guardian to a beautiful young lady! Whether I grant, or whether I
refuse, the consent required of me, I equally gain ill-will from one
side or the other.'

Lady Mellasin, who had all this morning complained of a violent
headache, and said nothing during this conversation, now cried out,
'What new conquest is this Miss Betsy has made?' – 'O Madam!'
replied Miss Betsy, 'your ladyship shall judge of the value of it by the
doughty epistle I have just received.' With these words, she gave the
letter to Miss Flora, desiring her to read it aloud, which she did; but
was obliged, as Miss Betsy herself had done, to stop several times
and hold her sides, before she got to the conclusion; and Lady
Mellasin, as little as she was then inclined to mirth, could not forbear
smiling to hear the manner in which this declaration of love was
penned. 'You are all very merry,' said Mr. Goodman; 'but I can tell
you, Captain Hysom is a match that many a fine lady in this town
would jump at; he has been twenty-five years in the service of the
East India Company; has made very successful voyages, and is
immensely rich: he has lived at sea, indeed, the greatest part of his
life, and much politeness cannot be expected from him; but he is a
very honest good-natured man, and I believe means well. I wish he
had offered himself to Flora.' – 'Perhaps, Sir, I should not have
refused him,' replied she, briskly; 'I should like a husband
prodigiously that would be abroad for three whole years, and leave
me to bowl about in my coach and six, while he ploughed the ocean

in search of new treasures to throw into my lap at his return.'

'Well, well,' said Miss Betsy, laughing still more, 'who knows but when I have teazed him a little, he may fly for shelter to your more clement goodness!' – 'Aye, aye,' cried Mr. Goodman, 'you are a couple of mad-caps, indeed; and, I suppose, the captain will be finely managed: but, no matter; I shall not pity him, as I partly told him what he might expect.'

After this Mr. Goodman went out; and the young ladies went up to dress against dinner, diverting themselves all the time with the poor captain's letter. Miss Betsy told Miss Flora that, as he was for coming so directly to the point, she must use all her artifice in order to keep him in suspense; 'For,' said she, 'if I should let him know any part of my real sentiments concerning him, he would be gone at once, and we should lose all our sport: I will, therefore,' continued she, 'make him believe that I dare not openly encourage his pretensions, because my brother hath recommended one gentleman to me, and Mr. Goodman another; but shall assure him, at the same time, that I am inclined to neither of them; and shall contrive to get rid of them both as soon as possible. This,' said she, 'will keep him in hopes, without my downright promising any thing particular in his favour.'

Miss Flora told her she was a perfect Machiavel in love-affairs; and was about to say something more, when a confused sound of several voices, among which she distinguished that of Lady Mellasin very loud, made her run down stairs to see what was the occasion; but Miss Betsy staid in the chamber, being busily employed in something belonging to her dress; or, had she be less engaged, it is not probable she would have troubled herself about the matter, as she supposed it only a quarrel between Lady Mellasin and some of the servants, as in effect it was; and she, without asking, was immediately informed.

Nanny, the upper house-maid, and the same who had delivered Mr. Saving's letter to Miss Betsy, and carried her answer to him, coming up with a broom in her hand, in order to sweep her lady's dressing-room, ran into the chamber of Miss Betsy, and seeing that she was alone, 'Oh, Miss!' said she, 'there is the devil to do below.' – 'I heard a sad noise, indeed,' said she, carelessly. 'Why, you must know, Miss,' cried the maid, 'that my lady hath given John, the butler, warning; and so, his time being up, Mrs. Prinks hath orders to pay him off this morning, but would have stopped thirty shillings for a silver orange-strainer that is missing. John would not allow it; and

being in a passion, told Mrs. Prinks that he would not leave the house
without his full wages; that, for any thing he knew, the strainer might
be gone after the diamond necklace. This, I suppose, she repeated to
my lady, and that put her in so ill a humour this morning, that if my
master had not come down as he did, we should all have had
something at our heads. However,' continued the wench, 'she
ordered Mrs. Prinks to give him his whole money; but, would you
believe it, Miss! my master was no sooner gone out, than she came
down into the kitchen raving, and finding John there still, (the poor
fellow, God knows, only staid to take his leave of us) she tore about,
and swore we should all go; accused one of one thing, and another of
another.' – 'Well, but what did the fellow mean about the diamond
necklace?' cried Miss Betsy, interrupting her. 'I will tell you the
whole story,' said she; 'but you must promise never to speak a word
of it to any body; for though I do not value the place, nor will stay
much longer, yet they would not give one a character you know, Miss
Betsy.'

Miss Betsy then having assured her she would never mention it,
the other shut the door, and went on in a very low voice, in this
manner.

'Don't you remember, Miss,' said she, 'what a flurry my lady and
Mrs. Prinks were in one day? how her ladyship pulled off all her fine
cloaths, and they both went out in a hackney-coach; then Mrs. Prinks
came home, and went out again?' – 'Yes,' replied Miss Betsy, 'I took
notice they were both in a good deal of confusion.' – 'Aye, Miss, well
they might,' said Nanny; 'that very afternoon John was gone to see a
cousin that keeps a pawnbroker's shop in Thieving Lane; and as he
was sitting in a little room behind the counter, that, it seems, shuts in
with glass doors, who should he see through the window but Mrs.
Prinks come in; she brought my lady's diamond necklace, and
pledged it for a hundred and twenty, or a hundred and thirty guineas,
I am not sure which he told me, for I have the saddest memory: but it
is no matter for that, John was strangely confounded, as you may
think, but resolved to see into the bottom; and when Mrs. Prinks was
got into the coach, popped up behind it, and got down when it
stopped, which was at the sign of the Hand and Tipstaff in Knaves
Acre; so that this money was raised to get somebody that was arrested
out of the bailiff's hands, for John said it was what they call a
spunging-house that Mrs. Prinks went into. Lord! how deceitful
some poeple are! My poor master little thinks how his money goes:

but I'll warrant our house-keeping must suffer for this.'

This gossipping young hussey would have run on much longer, doubtless, with her comments on this affair; but hearing Miss Flora's foot upon the stairs, she left off, and opening the door, softly slipped into her lady's dressing-room, and fell to work in cleaning it.

Miss Flora came up, exclaiming on the ill-behaviour of most servants, telling Miss Betsy what a passion her mamma had been in. The other made little answer to what she said on that or any other score, having her thoughts very much taken up with the account just given her by Nanny: she recollected that Lady Mellasin had never dressed since that day, always making some excuse to avoid paying any grand visits, which she now doubted not but it was because she had not her necklace. It very much amazed her, as she well knew her ladyship was not wihout a good deal of ready cash, therefore was certain the sum must be large indeed for which her friend was arrested, that it reduced her to the necessity of applying to a pawnbroker; and who that friend could be, for whom she would thus demean herself, puzzled her extremely. It was not long, however, before she was let into the secret: but, in the mean time, other matters of more moment must be treated on.

CHAPTER XVII

Is of less importance than the former, yet must not be omitted

LADY Mellasin having vented her spleen on those who, by their stations, were obliged to bear it, and the object of it removed out of the house, became extremely cheerful the remaining part of the day. The fashion in which it might be supposed Miss Betsy would be accosted by the tarpaulin inamorato, and the reception she would give his passion, occasioned a good deal of merriment; and even Mr. Goodman, seeing his dear wife took part in it, would sometimes throw in his joke.

'Well, well,' cried Miss Betsy, to heighten the diversion, 'what will you say now, if I should take a fancy to the captain, so far as to prefer him to any of those who think it worth their while to solicit me on the score of love?'

'This is quite ungenerous in you,' cried Miss Flora; 'did you not promise to turn the captain over to me when you had done with him?' – 'That may not happen a great while,' replied the other; 'for, I assure you, I have seen him three or four times, when he has called here on business to Mr. Goodman; and think, to part with a lover of his formidable aspect, would be to deprive myself of the most conspicuous of my whole train of admirers. But suppose,' continued she, in the same gay strain, 'I resign to you Mr. Staple or Mr. Trueworth, would that not do as well?'

'Do not put me in the head of either of them, I beseech you,' said Miss Flora, 'for fear I should think too seriously on the matter, and it should not be in your power to oblige me.'

'All that must be left to chance,' cried Miss Betsy; 'but so far I dare promise you, as to do enough to make them heartily weary of their courtship to me, and at liberty to make their addresses elsewhere.'

After this, they fell into some conversation concerning the merits of the two last-mentioned gentlemen. They allowed Mr. Staple to have the finest face; and that Mr. Trueworth was the best shaped, and had the most graceful air in every thing he did. Mr. Staple had an infinity of gaiety both in his look and behaviour: Mr. Trueworth had no less of sweetness; and if his deportment seemed somewhat too serious for a man of his years, it was well atoned for by the excellence of his understanding. Miss Flora, however, said, upon the whole, that both of them were charming men; and Lady Mellasin added, that it was a great pity that either of them should have bestowed his heart where there was so little likelihood of ever receiving any recompence. 'Why so, my dear?' cried Mr. Goodman. 'If my pretty charge is at present in a humour to make as many fools as she can in this world, I hope she is not determined to lead apes in another. I warrant she will change her mind one time or other: I only wish she may not, as the old saying is, outstand her market.'

While they were thus discoursing, a servant brought a letter from Mr. Staple, directed to Miss Betsy Thoughtless, which was immediately delivered to her. On being told from whence it came, she gave it to Mr. Goodman, saying, 'I shall make no secret of the contents; therefore, dear guardian, read it for the benefit of the company.'

Mr. Goodman shook his head at the little sensibility she testified of his friend's devoirs; but said nothing, being willing to gratify the curiosity he doubted not but they were all in, Miss Betsy herself not excepted, as carless as she affected to be; which he did by reading, in an audible voice, these lines.

'To the most amiable and most accomplished of her sex.

Madam,
If the face be the index of the mind, (as I think one of our best poets takes upon him to assert) your soul must certainly be all made up of harmoney, and consequently take delight in what has so great a similitude of it's own heavenly nature. I flatter myself, therefore, you will not be offended that I presume to intreat you will grace with your presence a piece of musick, composed by the so justly celebrated

Signior Bononcini; and, I hope, will have justice done it in the
performance, they being the best hands in town that are employed.

I do myself the honour to inclose tickets for the ladies of Mr.
Goodman's family; and beg leave to wait on you this afternoon, in the
pleasing expectation, not only of being permitted to attend you to the
concert, but also of an opportunity of renewing those humble and
sincere professions I yesterday began to make of a passion, which only
charms such as yours could have the power of inspiring in any heart;
and can be felt by none with greater warmth, zeal, tenderness, and
respect, than by that of him who is, and ever must be, Madam, your
most passionate, and most faithful admirer,

T. STAPLE.

P.S. If there are any other ladies of your acquaintance, to whom you
think the entertainment may be agreeable, be pleased to make the
invitation. I shall bring tickets with me to accommodate whoever you
chuse to accompany you. Once more, I beseech you, Madam, to
believe me, as above, your, &c.'

Mr. Goodman had scarce finished reading this letter, when Lady
Mellasin and her daughter both cried out at the same time, 'O Miss
Betsy! how unlucky this happens! What will you do with the captain
now?'

'We will take him with us to the concert,' replied she: 'and, in my
opinion, nothing could have fallen out more fortunately. The captain
has appointed to visit me at five; Mr. Staple will doubtless be here
about that time, if not before, in order to usher us to the
entertainment; so that my tar cannot expect any answer from me to
his letter, and consequently I shall gain time.'

Though Mr. Goodman was far from approving this way of
proceeding, yet he could not forbear smiling, with the rest, at Miss
Betsy's contrivance; and told her, it was a pity she was not a man –
she would have made a rare minister of state.

'Well, since it is so,' said Lady Mellasin, 'I will have the honour of
complimenting the captain with the ticket Mr. Staple intended for
me.' Both Miss Flora and Miss Betsy pressed her ladyship to be of
their company; and Mr. Goodman likewise endeavoured to persuade
her to go: but she excused herself, saying, 'A concert was never
among those entertainments she took pleasure in.' On which they left
off speaking any farther on it: but Miss Betsy was not at a loss in her

own mind to guess the true reason of her ladyship's refusal, and looked on it as a confirmation of the truth of what Nanny had told her concerning the diamond-necklace.

There seemed, notwithstanding, one difficulty still remaining for Miss Betsy to get over; which was, the probability of Mr. Trueworth's making her a visit that afternoon; she did not chuse to leave him to go to the concert, nor yet to ask him to accompany them to it, because she thought it would be easy for a man of his penetration to discover that Mr. Staple was his rival; which she was by no means willing he should do before he had made a declaration to her of his own passion.

She was beginning to consider how she should manage in a point which she looked upon as pretty delicate, when a letter from that gentleman eased her of all the apprehensions she at present had on this score. The manner in which he expressed himself was as follows.

'To Miss Betsy Thoughtless.

Madam,

I remember, (as what can be forgot in which you have the least concern?) that the first time I had the honour of seeing you at Oxford, you seemed to take a great deal of pleasure in the pretty tricks of a squirrel, which a lady in the company had on her arm. One of those animals (which, they tell me, has been lately catched) happening to fall in my way, I take the liberty of presenting him to you; intreating you will permit him to give you such diversion as is in his power. Were the little denizens of the woods endued with any share of human reason, how happy would he think himself in the loss of his liberty, and how hug those chains which entitle him to so glorious a servitude!

I had waited on you in person, in the hope of obtaining pardon for approaching you with so trifling an offering; but am deprived of that satisfaction by the pressing commands of an old aunt, who insists on my passing this evening with her. But what need is there to apologize for the absence of a person so little known to you, and whose sentiments are yet less so! I rather ought to fear that the frequency of those visits I shall hereafter make, may be looked upon as taking too presuming an advantage of the permission you have been so good to give me. I will not, however, anticipate so great a misfortune, but endeavour to prevent it, by proving, by all the ways I am able, that I am, with the most profound submission, Madam, your very humble, obedient, and eternally devoted servant,

C. TRUEWORTH.'

Miss Betsy, after having read this letter, ordered the person who brought it should come into the parlour; on which he delivered to her the present mentioned in the letter, which she received with a great deal of sweetness, gave the fellow something to drink her health, and sent her service to his master, with thanks, and an assurance she should be glad to see him whenever it suited with his convenience.

All the ladies then began to examine the squirrel, which was, doubtless, the most beautiful creature of it's kind that could be purchased. The chain, which fastened it to it's habitation, was gold, the links very thick, and curiously wrought. Every one admired the elegance of the donor's taste.

Miss Betsy herself was charmed to an excess, both with the letter and the present; but as much as she was pleased with the respectful passion of Mr. Trueworth, she could not find in her heart to think of parting with the assiduities of Mr. Staple, nor even the blunt addresses of Captain Hysom, at least till she had exercised all the power her beauty gave her over them.

As the two last-mentioned gentlemen were the friends of Mr. Goodman, he went out somewhat before the hour in which either of them was expected to come, chusing not to seem to know what it was not in his power to amend, and determined, as he had promised Miss Betsy, not to interfere between her and any of those who pretended to court her.

These two lovers came to the door at the same time; and Mr. Staple saying to the footman that opened the door, that he was come to wait on Miss Betsy – 'I want to speak to that young gentlewoman, too,' cried the captain, 'if she be at leisure. Tell her my name is Hysom.'

Mr. Staple was immediately shewed up into the drawing-room, and the captain into the parlour, till Miss Betsy should be told his name. 'That spark,' said he to himself, 'is known here: I suppose he is one of those Mr. Goodman told me of, that has a mind to Miss Betsy; but, as she knew I was to be here, I think she might have left some orders concerning me; and not make me wait till that young gew-gaw had spoke his mind to her.'

The fellow not coming down immediately, he grew very angry, and began to call and knock with his cane against the floor; which, it may be easily imagined, gave some sport to those above. Miss Betsy, however, having told Mr. Staple the character of the man, and the diversion she intended to make of his pretensions, would not vex him too much; and, to atone for having made him attend so long, went to the top of the stairs herself, and desired him to walk up.

The reception she gave him was full of all the sweetness she could assume, and excused having made him wait, and laid the blame on the servant, who, she pretended, could not presently recollect his name. This put him into an exceeding good-humour. 'Nay, fair lady,' said he, 'as to that, I have staid much longer sometimes, before I could get to the speech of some people, who I have not half the respect for as I have for you. But you know,' continued he, giving her a kiss, the smack of which might be heard three rooms off, 'that I have business with you – business that requires dispatch; and that made me a little impatient.'

All the company had much ado to refrain laughing out-right; but Miss Betsy kept her countenance to a miracle. 'We will talk of business another time,' said she: 'we are going to hear a fine entertainment of musick. You must not refuse giving us your company; Lady Mellasin has got a ticket on purpose for you.' – 'I am very much obliged to her ladyship,' replied the captain; 'but I do not know whether Mr. Goodman may think well of it or not; for he would fain have put me off from visiting his charge here. I soon found, by his way of speaking, the wind did not fit fair for me from that quarter; so tacked about, shifted my sails, and stood for the port directly.'

'Manfully resolved, indeed!' said Mr. Staple; 'but I hope, captain, you have kept a good look-out, in order to avoid any ship of greater burden that might else chance to overset you.' – 'Oh, Sir! as to that,' replied the captain, 'you might have spared yourself the trouble of giving me this caution; there are only two small pinks in my way, and they had best stand clear, or I shall run foul on them.'

Though Mr. Staple had been apprized before hand of the captain's pretences, and that Miss Betsy intended to encourage them only by way of amusement to herself and friends, yet the rough manner in which his rival had uttered these words, brought the blood into his cheeks; which Lady Mellasin perceiving, and fearing that what was begun in jest might, in the end, become more serious than could be wished, turned the conversation; and, addressing herself to the captain on the score of what he had said concerning Mr. Goodman, made many apologies for her husband's behaviour in this point;

assured him, that he had not a more sincere friend in the world, nor one who would be more ready to serve him, in whatever was in his power.

The captain had a fund of good-nature in his heart; but was somewhat too much addicted to passion, and frequently apt to resent without a cause; but when once convinced he had been in the wrong, no one could be more ready to acknowledge and ask pardon for his mistake. He had been bred at sea: his conversation, for almost his whole life, had been chiefly among those of his own occupation; he was altogether unacquainted with the manners and behaviour of the polite world, and equally a stranger to what is called genteel raillery, as he was to courtly complaisance. It is not, therefore, to be wondered at, that he was often rude, without designing to be so, and took many things as affronts, which were not meant as such.

Lady Mellasin, who never wanted words, and knew how to express herself in the most persuasive terms whenever she pleased to make use of them, had the address to convince the captain that Mr. Goodman was no enemy to his suit, though he would not appear to encourage it.

While the captain was engaged with her ladyship in this discourse, Miss Betsy took the opportunity of telling Mr. Staple that she insisted upon it, that he should be very civil to a rival from whose pretensions he might be certain he had nothing to apprehend; and, moreover, that when she gave him her hand to lead her into the concert-room, he should give his to Miss Flora, without discovering the least marks of discontent: the lover looked on this last injunction as too severe a trial of his patience; but she would needs have it so, and he was under a necessity of obeying, or of suffering much greater mortification from her displeasure.

Soon after this, they all four went to the entertainment in Mr. Goodman's coach, which Lady Mellasin had ordered to be got ready. The captain was mightily pleased with the musick, and had judgment enough in it to know it was better than the band he had on board his ship. 'When they have done playing,' said he, 'I will ask them what they will have to go with me the next voyage.' But Mr. Staple told him it would be affront; that they were men who got more by their instruments than the best officer either by sea or land did by his commission. This mistake, as well as many others the captain fell into, made not only the company he was with, but those who sat near enough to hear him, a good deal of diversion.

Nothing of moment happening either here or at Mr. Goodman's, where they all supped together, it would be needless to repeat any particulars of the conversation; what has been said already of their different sentiments and behaviour, may be a sufficient sample of the whole.

CHAPTER XVIII

———————•———————

Treats on no fresh matters, but serves to heighten those already mentioned

MR. Goodman had staid abroad till very late that night the concert had been performed, so was not a witness of any thing that had passed after the company came home: but on Lady Mellasin's repeating to him every thing she remembered, was very well pleased to hear that she had reconciled the captain to him; though exremely sorry that the blunt ill-judged affection of that gentleman had exposed him to the ridicule, not only of Miss Betsy, but also of all her followers.

That young lady, in the mean time, was far from having any commiseration for the anxieties of those who loved her; on the contrary, she triumphed in the pains she gave, if it can be supposed that she, who was altogether ignorant of them in herself, could look upon them as sincere in others. But, I am apt to believe, ladies of this cast regard all the professions of love made to them (as, indeed, many of them are) only as words of course – the prerogative of youth and beauty in the one sex, and a duty incumbent on the other to pay: they value themselves on the number and quality of their lovers, as they do upon the number and richness of their cloaths; because it makes them of consideration in the world, and never take the trouble of reflecting how dear it may sometimes cost those to whom they are indebted for indulging this vanity.

That this, at least, was the motive which induced Miss Betsy to treat her lovers in the manner she did, is evident to a demonstration, from every other action of her life. She had a certain softness in her disposition, which rendered her incapable of knowing the distress of any one, without affording all the relief that was in her power to give; and had she sooner been convinced of the reality of the woes of love, the sooner she had left off the ambition of inflicting them, and, perhaps, have been brought to regard those who laboured under them, rather with too much than too little compassion. But of this the reader will be able to judge on proceeding farther in this history.

There were now three gentlemen, who all of them addressed this young lady on the most honourable terms; yet did her giddy mind make no distinction between the serious passion they had for her, and the idle gallantry she received from those who either had no design in making them, or such as tended to her undoing.

Impatient to hear in what manner Mr. Trueworth would declare himself, and imagining he would come the next day, as he had made so handsome an apology for not having waited on her the preceding one, she told Mr. Staple and Captain Hysom, in order to prevent their coming, that she was engaged to pass that whole afternoon and evening with some ladies of her acquaintance. Neither the captain nor Mr. Staple suspected the truth of what she said; but the former was in too much haste to know some issue of his fate to be quite contented with this delay.

Miss Betsy was not deceived in her expectations. Soon after dinner was over, she was told Mr. Trueworth had sent to know if she was at home, and begged leave to wait upon her. Lady Mellasin having a great deal of company that day in the dining-room, she went into an adjacent one to receive him. He was charmed at finding her alone; a happiness he could not flatter himself with on entering the house: he was assured, by the number of footman that he saw in the hall, that many visitors were there before him. This unexpected piece of good fortune (as he then thought it, especially as he found her playing with the squirrel he had sent to her the day before) so much elated him, that it brightened his whole aspect, and gave a double share of vivacity to his eyes. 'May I hope your pardon, Madam,' said he, 'for presuming to approach you with so trifling a present as that little creature?' – 'Oh, Mr. Trueworth!' answered she, 'I will not forgive you if you speak slight of my squirrel, though I am indebted to you for the pleasure he gives me. I love him excessively! You could not have made me a more obliging present.'

'How, Madam!' cried he; 'I should be miserable, indeed, if I had nothing in my power to offer more worthy your acceptance than that animal. What think you, Madam, of an adoring and passionately devoted heart?'

'A heart!' rejoined she; 'oh, dear! a heart may be a pretty thing, for aught I know to the contrary: but there is such an enclosure of flesh and bone about it, that it is utterly impossible for one to see into it; and, consequently, to know whether one likes it or not.'

'The heart, Madam, in the sense I mean,' said he, 'implies the soul; which being a spirit, and invisible, can only be known by it's effects. If the whole services of mine may render it an oblation, such as may obtain a gracious reception from the amiable Miss Thoughtless, I shall bless the hour in which I first beheld her charms, as the most fortunate one I ever had to boast of.' In ending these words he kissed her hand, with a look full of the greatest respect and tenderness.

She then told him, the services of the soul must needs be valuable, because they were sincere; but, as she knew not of what nature those services were he intended to render her, he must excuse her for not so readily accepting them. On which, it is not to be doubted, but that he assured her they should be only such as were dictated by the most pure affections, and accompanied by the strictest honour.

He was going on with such protestations as may be imagined a man, so much enamoured, would make to the object of his wishes; when he was interrupted by Miss Flora, who came hastily into the room, and told him that her mamma, hearing that he was in the house, expected he would not leave it without letting her have the pleasure of seeing him; that they were just going to tea, and that her ladyship intreated he would join company with those friends she had already with her.

Mr. Trueworth would have been glad to have found some plausible pretence for not complying with this invitation; but as he could not make any that would not be looked on as favouring of ill manners, and Miss Betsy insisted on his going, they all went together into the dining-room.

The lover had now no farther opportunity of prosecuting his suit in this visit; but he made another the next day, more early than before, and found nobody but Mr. Goodman with Miss Betsy, Lady Mellasin and Miss Flora being gone among the shops, either to buy something they wanted, or to tumble over goods, as they frequently did, merely for the sake of seeing new fashions. Mr. Trueworth having never been seen by Mr. Goodman, Miss Betsy presented him to him with these words – 'Sir, this is a gentleman from Oxford, an intimate friend of brother Frank's, and who did me the favour to bring me a letter from him.' There needed no more to make Mr. Goodman know, both who he was, and the business on which he was come. He received him with a great deal of good manners; but, knowing his absence would be most agreeable, after some few compliments, pretended he was called abroad by urgent business, and took his leave.

How much it rejoiced the sincerely devoted heart of Mr. Trueworth, to find himself once more alone with the idol of his wishes, may easily be conceived by those who have had any experience of the passion he so deeply felt: but his felicity was of short continuance, and he profited but little by the complaisance of Mr. Goodman.

He was but just beginning to pour forth some part of those tender sentiments, with which his soul overflowed, when he was prevented from proceeding, by a second interruption, much more disagreeable than the former had been.

Mr. Staple, and Captain Hysom, for whom Miss Betsy had not left the same orders she had done the day before, came both to visit her; the former had the advantage of being there somewhat sooner than the other, and accosted her with an air which made the enamoured heart of Mr. Trueworth immediately beat an alarm to jealousy. Mr. Staple, who had seen him there once before, when he brought her brother's letter to her, did not presently know him for his rival, nor imagined he had any other intent in his visits, than to pay his compliments to the sister of his friend.

They were all three engaged in a conversation which had nothing particular in it, when Miss Betsy was told Captain Hysom desired to speak with her; on which she bid the fellow desire him to walk in. 'He is in the back-parlour, Madam,' replied he: 'I told him you had company, so he desires you will come to him there; for he says he has great business with you, and must needs speak with you.' Both Miss Betsy and Mr. Staple laughed immoderately at this message; but Mr. Trueworth, who was not in the secret, looked a little grave, as not knowing what to think of it. 'You would scarce believe, Sir,' said Mr. Staple to him, 'that this embassy came from the court of Cupid; yet I assure you the captain is one of this lady's most passionate admirers.' – 'Yes, indeed,' added Miss Betsy; 'and threatens terrible things to every one who should dare to dispute the conquest of my heart with him. – But go,' continued she to the footman, 'tell him I have friends with me whom I cannot be so rude to leave, and that I insist on his giving us his company in this room.'

The captain, on this, was prevailed upon to come in, though not very well pleased at finding himself obliged to do so by the positive commands of his mistress. He paid his respects, however, in his blunt manner, to the gentlemen, as well as Miss Betsy; and having drawn his chair as near her as he could, 'I hoped, Madam,' said he, 'you would have found an opportunity of speaking to me before now; you must needs think I am a little uneasy till I know what I have to depend upon.' – 'Bless me, Sir!' cried she, 'you talk in an odd manner! – and then,' continued she, pointing to Mr. Trueworth, 'this gentleman here, who is a friend of my brother's, will think I have outrun my income, and that you come to dun me for money borrowed of you.' – 'No, no,' answered he, 'as to that, you owe me nothing but good-will, and that I think I deserve for the respect I have for you, if it were for nothing else: but, Madam, I should be glad to know some answer to the business I wrote to you upon?' – 'Lord, Sir!' replied she, 'I have not yet had time to think upon it, much less to resolve on any thing.' – 'That is strange,' resumed he; 'why, you have had three days; and sure that is long enough to think, and resolve too, on any thing.' – 'Not for me, indeed, captain,' answered she, laughing: 'but come, here are just four of us – what think you, gentlemen, of a game of quadrille, to kill time?'

Mr. Trueworth and Mr. Staple told her at once, that they approved the notion; and she was just going to call for cards and fishes, when the captain stopped her, saying, 'I never loved play in my life; and have no time to kill, as mayhap these gentlemen have, who, it is likely, having nothing else to do than to dress and visit: I have a great deal of business upon my hands; the ship is taking in her lading, and I do not know but we may sail in six or seven days, so must desire you will fix a day for us to be alone together, that I may know at once what it is you design to do.' – 'Fie, captain!' replied she, 'how can you think of such a thing? I assure you, Sir,' added she, with an affected disdain, 'I never make appointments with gentlemen.'

'That I believe,' said he: 'but you should consider that I live a great way off; it is a long walk from Mile End to St. James's, and I hate your jolting hackney-coaches: besides, I may come and come again, and never be able to get a word with you in private in an afternoon, and all the morning I am engaged either at the India House, or at

Change; therefore I should think it is better for both of us not to stand shilly-shally, but come to the point at once; for look ye, fair lady, if we happen to agree, there will be little enough time to settle every thing, as I am obliged to go soon.' – 'Too little, in my opinion, Sir,' answered she; 'therefore I think it best to defer talking any more of the matter till you come back.'

'Come back!' cried he; 'why, do you consider I shall be gone three years?' – 'Really, Sir,' said she, 'as I told you before, I have never considered any thing about it; nor can promise I shall be able to say any more to you at the end of twice the time you mention, than I can do at present, which I assure you is just nothing at all.'

Though both Mr. Trueworth and Mr. Staple had too much good manners to do any thing that might affront the captain, yet neither of them could restrain their laughter so well as to prevent some marks of the inclination they had for it, from being visible in their faces; and, willing to contribute something on their parts to the diversion they perceived she gave herself with a lover so every way unsuitable to her, one told her that it was a great pity she did not consult the captain's convenience; the other said, that it must needs be a vast fatigue for a gentleman, who was accustomed only to walk the quarter-deck, to take a stretch of four miles at once. 'And all to no purpose,' cried he that had spoken first. – 'Pray, Madam, give him his dispatch.'

As little acquainted as the captain was with raillery, he had understanding enough to make him see, that Miss Betsy's behaviour to him had rendered him the jest of all the company that visited her; and this he took so ill, that all the liking he before had to her was now turned into contempt. Finding they were going on in the ironical way they had begun – 'Look ye, gentlemen,' said he, with a pretty stern countenance, 'I would advise you to meddle only with such things as concern yourselves; you have nothing to do with me, or I with you. If your errand here be as I suspect it is, there sits one who I dare answer will find you employment enough, as long as you shall think it worth your while to dance attendance. – As for you, Madam,' continued he, turning to Miss Betsy, 'I think it would have become you as well to have given me a more civil answer; if you did not approve of my proposals, you might have told me so at first: but I shall trouble neither you nor myself any farther about the matter. I see how it is, well enough; and when next I steer for the coast of matrimony, shall take care to look out for a port not cumbered with rubbish: so, your servant!'

As he was going out of the house, he met Lady Mellasin and Miss Flora just entering, being returned from the ramble above-mentioned: they saw he was very angry, and would fain have persuaded him to turn back; telling him, that if any misunderstanding had happened between him and Miss Betsy, they would endeavour to make it up and reconcile them. To which he replied, that he thanked them for their love; but he had done with Miss Betsy for good and all; that she was no more than a young flirt, and did not know how to use a gentleman handsomely – said, he should be glad to take a bowl of punch with Mr. Goodman before he went on his voyage; but would not come any more to his house, to be scoffed at by Miss Betsy, and those that came after her.

Miss Flora told him, that it was unjust in him to deprive her mamma and herself of the pleasure of his good company for the fault of Miss Betsy; who, she said, she could not help owning, was of a very giddy temper. Lady Mellasin, to what her daughter had said, added many obliging things, in order to prevail on him either to return, or renew his visits hereafter: but the captain was obstinate; and, persisting in his resolution of coming there no more, took his leave; and Miss Flora lost all hope of receiving any benefit from his being rejected by Miss Betsy.

CHAPTER XIX

Will make the reader little the wiser

THE greatest part of the time that Mr. Trueworth and Mr. Staple staid with Miss Betsy, was taken up with talking of Captain Hysom; his passion, his behaviour, and the manner in which he received his dismission, afforded, indeed, an ample field for conversation: Lady Mellasin and Miss Flora, relating the answers he had given them on their pressing him to come back, Mr. Trueworth said, that it must be owned, that he had shewn a strength of resolution which few men in love could boast of.

'Love, Sir, according to my notions of that passion,' replied Mr. Staple, 'is not one to be felt by every heart; many deceive themselves in this point, and take for it what is in reality no more than a bare liking of a beautiful object: the captain seems to me to have a soul, as well as form, cast in too rough a mould to be capable of those refined and delicate ideas, which alone constitute and are worthy to be called love.'

'Yet,' said Lady Mellasin, 'I have heard Mr. Goodman give him an excellent character; and, above all, that he is one of the best-natured men breathing.' – 'That may be, indeed, Madam,' resumed Mr. Staple; 'and some allowances ought to be made for the manner in which he has been bred: though,' added he, 'I have known many commanders, not only of Indiamen, but of other trading-vessels, who have all their life-time used the sea, yet have known how to behave with politeness enough when on shore.'

Mr. Trueworth agreed with Mr. Staple, that though the amorous declarations of a person of the captain's age, and fashion of bringing up, to one of Miss Betsy's, exposed him to the deserved ridicule of as many as knew it, yet ought not his particular foible to be any reflection on his occupation, which merited to be held in the greatest veneration, as the strength and opulence of the nation was owing to it's commerce in foreign parts.

This was highly obliging to Mr. Staple, whose father had been a merchant; and Mr. Trueworth being the first who took his leave, perceiving the other staid supper, he said abundance of handsome things in his praise; and seemed to have conceived so high esteem of him, that Miss Betsy was diverted in her mind to think how he would change his way of speaking, when once the secret of his rivalship should come out, as she knew it could not fail to do in a short time.

But as easy as Mr. Staple was at present on this occasion, Mr. Trueworth was no less anxious and perplexed: he was convinced that the other visited Miss Betsy on no other score than that of love; and it appeared to him equally certain, by the freedom with which he saw him treated by the family, that he was likewise greatly encouraged, if not by Miss Betsy herself, at least by her guardian.

His thoughts were now wholly taken up with the means by which he might gain the advantage over a rival, whom he looked upon as a formidable one, not only for his personal accomplishments, but also for his having the good fortune to address her before himself. All he could do was to prevent, as much as possible, all opportunities of his entertaining Miss Betsy in private, till the arrival of Mr. Francis Thoughtless, from whose friendship, and the influence he had over his sister, he hoped much.

He waited on her the next day very early: Mr. Goodman happening to dine that day later than ordinary, on account of some friends he had with him, and the cloth not being drawn, Miss Betsy went and received him in another room. Having this favourable opportunity, he immediately began to prepare for putting into execution one of those strategems he had contrived for separating her from Mr. Staple. After some few tender speeches, he fell into a discourse concerning the weather; said, he was sorry to perceive the days so much shortened – that summer would soon be gone; and added, that as that beautiful season could last but a small time, the most should be made of it. 'I came,' said he, 'to intreat the favour of you and Miss Flora, to permit me to accompany you in an airing through Brompton, Kensington, Chelsea, and the other little villages on this side of London.'

Miss Betsy replied, that she would go with all her heart, and believed she could answer the same for Miss Flora, there being only two grave dons and their wives within, whom she would be glad to be disengaged from: 'But if not,' said she, 'I can send for a young lady in the neighbourhood, who will be glad to give us her company.'

She sent first, however, to Miss Flora, who immediately came in; and, the proposal being made, accepted it with pleasure; and added, that she would ask her mamma for orders for the coach to be got ready. 'It need not, Madam,' said Mr. Trueworth; 'my servant is here, and he shall get one from Blunt's.' But Miss Flora insisted on their going in Mr. Goodman's; saying, she was certain neither he nor her mamma would go out that day, as the company they had were come to stay; on which Mr. Trueworth complied.

When she had left the room – 'Ah, Madam!' said he to Miss Betsy, 'could I flatter myself with believing I owed this condescension to any other motive than your complaisance, to a person who has some share in your brother's friendship, I should be blessed indeed; but, ah! I see I have a rival – a rival dangerous to my hopes, not only on the account of his merits, but also as he had the honour of declaring his passion before me: the fortunate Mr. Staple,' added he, kissing her hand, 'may, perhaps have already made some impression on that heart I would sacrifice my all to gain; and I am come too late.'

'Rather too soon,' replied she, smiling; 'both of you equally too soon, admitting his sentiments for me to be as you imagine; for I assure you, Sir, my heart has hitherto been entirely my own, and is not very likely to incline to the reception of any guest of the nature you mean, for yet a long – long time. Whoever thinks to gain me, must not be in a hurry, like Captain Hysom.'

Mr. Trueworth was about to make some passionate reply, when Miss Flora returned, and told them the coach would be ready immediately, for she herself had spoke to the coachman, and bid him put the horses to with all the haste he could; on which the lover expressed his sense of the obligation he had to her for taking this trouble in the politest terms.

A person of much less discernment than this gentleman, might easily perceive, that the way to be agreeable to Miss Betsy, was not to be too serious; he therefore assumed all the vivacity he was master of, both before they went, and during the whole course of the little tour they made, in which it is not to be doubted but he regaled them with every thing the places they passed through could furnish.

The ladies were so well pleased, both with their entertainment and the company of the person who entertained them, that they seemed not in haste to go home; and he had the double satisfaction of enjoying the presence of his mistress, and of giving at least one day's disappointment to his rival: he was confirmed in the truth of this conjecture, when, on returning to Mr. Goodman's, which was not till some hours after close of day, the footman who opened the door told Miss Betsy that Mr. Staple had been to wait upon her.

After this it may be supposed he had a night of much more tranquillity than the preceding one had afforded him. The next morning, as early as he thought decency permitted, he made a visit to Miss Betsy, under the pretence of coming to enquire if her health had not suffered by being abroad in the night air, and how she had rested. She received him with a great deal of sprightliness; and replied, she found herself so well after it, as to be ready for such another jaunt whenever he had a fancy for it. 'I take you at your word, Madam,' cried he, transported to hear she anticipated what he came on purpose to intreat. 'I am ready this moment, if you please,' continued he; 'and we will either take a barge, and go up the river, or a coach to Hampstead, just to diversify the scene: you have only to say which you chuse.'

She then told him there was a necessity of deferring their ramble till the afternoon, because Miss Flora was abroad, and would not return till dinner-time. 'As to what route we shall take, and every thing belonging to it,' said she, 'I leave it entirely to you; I know nobody who has a more elegant taste, or a better judgment.' – 'I have taken care,' replied he, 'to give the world a high opinion of me in both, by making my addresses to the amiable Miss Betsy: but, Madam,' pursued he, 'since we are alone, will you give me leave to tell you how I have employed my hours this morning?' – 'Why – in dressing – breakfasting – and, perhaps, a little reading!' answered she. 'A small time, Madam, suffices for the two former articles with me,' resumed he; 'but I have, indeed, been reading: happening to dip into the works of a poet, who wrote near a century ago, I found some words so adapted to the situation of my heart, and so agreeable to the sense of the answer I was about to make yesterday to what you said, concerning the persistence of a lover, that I could not forbear putting some notes to them, which I beg you will give me your opinion of.'

In speaking these words, he took a piece of paper out of his pocket, and sung the following stanza.

I.

'The patriarch, to gain a wife
    Chaste, beautiful, and young,
Serv'd fourteen years, a painful life,
    And never thought it long.

II.

Oh! were you to reward such cares,
    And life so long would stay,
Not fourteen, but four hundred years,
    Would seem but as one day.'

Mr. Trueworth had a fine voice, and great skill in musick, having perfected himself in that science from the best masters when he was in Italy. Miss Betsy was so charmed both with the words and the notes, that she made him sing them several times over, and afterwards set them down in her musick-book, to the end that she might get them by heart, and join her voice in concert with her spinnet.

Mr. Trueworth would not make his morning visit too long, believing it might be her time to dress against dinner, as she was now in such a dishabille as ladies usually put on at their first rising: so, after having received a second promise from her of giving him her company that day abroad, took his leave, highly satisfied with the progress he imagined he had made in her good graces.

The wind happening to grow a little boisterous, though the weather otherwise was fair and clear, made Mr. Trueworth think a land journey would be more agreeable to the ladies, than to venture themselves upon the water: he therefore procured a handsome livery-coach; and, attended by his two servants, went to Mr. Goodman's. The ladies were already in expectation of him, and did not make him wait a moment.

Nothing extraordinary happening at this entertainment, nor at those others, which, for several succeeding days, without intermission, Mr. Trueworth prevailed on his mistress to accept, it would be superfluous to trouble the reader with the particulars of them.

Mr. Staple all this time was very uneasy: he had not seen Miss Betsy for a whole week; and, though he knew not as yet, that he was deprived of that satisfaction, by her being engrossed by a rival, yet he now began to be sensible she had less regard for him than he had flattered himself he had inspired her with; and this of itself was a sufficient mortification to a young gentleman, who was not only passionately in love, but also could not, without being guilty of great injustice to his own merits, but think himself not altogether unworthy of succeeding. This, however, was no more than a slight sample of the inquietudes which the blind god sometimes inflicts on hearts devoted to him; as will hereafter appear in the progress of this history.

CHAPTER XX

——————•——————

Contains an odd accident, which happened to Miss Betsy in the cloysters of Westminster Abbey

MR. TRUEWORTH, who was yet far from being acquainted with the temper of the object he adored, now thought he had no reason to despair of being one day in possession of all he aimed to obtain; it seemed certain, to him, at least, that he had nothing to apprehend from the pretensions of a rival, who at first he had looked upon as so formidable, and no other at present interposed between him and his designs.

Miss Betsy, in the mean while, wholly regardless of who hoped, or who despaired, had no aim in any thing she did, but merely to divert herself; and to that end laid hold of every opportunity that offered. Mr. Goodman, having casually mentioned, as they were at supper, that one Mr. Soulguard had just taken orders, and was to preach his first sermon at Westminster Abbey the next day, she presently had a curiosity of hearing how he would behave in the pulpit; his over-modest, and, as they termed it, sheepish behaviour in company, having, as often as he came there, afforded matter of ridicule to her and Miss Flora. These two young ladies therefore, talking on it after they were in bed, agreed to go to the cathedral, not doubting but they should have enough to laugh at, and repeat to all those of their acquaintance who had ever seen him.

What mere trifles, what airy nothings, serve to amuse a mind to not taken up with more essential matters! Miss Betsy was so full of the diversion she should have in hearing the down-looked bashful Mr. Soulguard harangue his congregation, that she could think and talk of nothing else, till the hour arrived when she should go to experience what she had so pleasant an idea of.

Miss Flora, who had till now seemed as eager as herself, cried all at once, that her head ached, and that she did not care for stirring out. Miss Betsy, who would fain have laughed her out of it, told her, she had only got the vapours; that the parson would cure her; and such like things: but the other was not to be prevailed upon by all Miss Betsy, or even Lady Mellasin herself, could say; and answered, with some sullenness, that positively she would not go. Miss Betsy was highly ruffled at this sudden turn of her temper, as it was now too late to send for any other young lady of her acquaintance to go with her; resolving, nevertheless, not to baulk her humour, she ordered a chair to be called, and went alone.

Neither the young parson's manner of preaching, nor the text he chose, being in any way material to this history, I shall therefore pass over the time of divine service; and only say, that after it was ended Miss Betsy passing towards the west gate, and stopping to look on the fine tomb, erected to the memory of Mr. Secretary Craggs, was accosted by Mr. Bloomacre, a young gentleman who sometimes visited Lady Mellasin, and lived at Westminster, in which place he had a large estate.

He had with him, when he came up to her, two gentlemen of his acquaintance, but who were entire strangers to Miss Betsy: 'What,' said he, 'the celebrated Miss Betsy Thoughtless! Miss Betsy Thoughtless! the idol of mankind! alone, unattended by any of her train of admirers, and contemplating these mementos of mortality!' – 'To compliment my understanding,' replied she, gaily, 'you should rather have told me I was contemplating the mementos of great actions.' – 'You are at the wrong end of the cathedral for that, Madam,' resumed he; 'and I don't remember to have heard anything extraordinary of the life of this great man, whose effigy makes so fine a figure here, except the favours he received from the ladies.'

'It were too much, then, to bestow them on him both alive and dead,' cried she; 'therefore we will pass on to some other.'

Mr. Bloomacre had a great deal of wit and vivacity; nor were his two companions deficient in either of these qualities: so that, between the three, Miss Betsy was very agreeably entertained. They went round from tomb to tomb; and the real characters, as well as epitaphs, some of which are flattering enough, afforded a variety of observations. In fine, the conversation was so pleasing to Miss Betsy, that she never thought of going home till it grew too dark to examine either the sculpture, or the inscriptions; so insensibly does time glide on, when accompanied with satisfaction.

But now ensued a mortification, which struck a damp on the sprightliness of this young lady: she ahd sent away the chair which brought her, not doubting but that there would be others about the church-doors. She knew not how difficult it was to procure such a vehicle in Westminster, especially on a Sunday. To add to her vexation, it rained very much, and she was not in a habit fit to travel on foot in any weather, much less in such as this.

They went down into the cloisters, in order to find some person whom they might send either for a coach or chair, for the gentlemen would have been glad of such conveniences for themselves, as well as Miss Betsy: they walked round and round several times, without hearing or seeing any body; but, at last, a fellow, who used to be employed in sweeping the church-doors, offered his service to procure them what they wanted, in case there was a possibility of doing it: they promised to gratify him well for his pains; and he ran with all the speed he could, to do as he had said.

The rain and wind increased to such a prodigious height, that scarce was ever a more tempestuous evening. Almost a whole hour was elapsed, and the man not come back; so that they had reason to fear neither coach nor chair was to be got. Miss Betsy began to grow extremcly impatient; the gentlemen endeavoured all they could to keep her in a good humour; 'We have a good stone roof over our heads, Madam,' said one of them, 'and that at present shelters us from the inclemency of the elements.' – 'Besides,' cried another, 'the storm cannot last always; and when it is a little abated, here are three of us, we will take you in our arms by turns, and carry you home.' All this would not make Miss Betsy laugh, and she was in the utmost agitation of mind to think what she should do; when, on a sudden, a door in that part of the cloister, which leads to Little Dean's Yard was opened, and a very young lady, not exceeding eleven years of age, but very richly habited, came running out, and taking Miss Betsy by the sleeve, 'Madam,' said she, 'I beg to speak with you.' Miss Betsy was surprized; but, stepping some paces from the gentleman, to hear what she had to say, the other drawing towards the door, cried, 'Please, Madam, to come in here!' On which she followed, and the gentlemen stood about some four or five yards distant. Miss Betsy had no sooner reached the threshold, which had a step down into the hall, and pulling her gently down, as if to communicate what she had to say with the more privacy, than a footman, who stood behind the door, immediately clapped it to, and put the chain across, as if he apprehended some violence might be offered to it. Miss Betsy was in so much consternation, that she was unable to speak one word; till the young lady, who stil had hold of her hand, said to her, 'You may thank Heaven, Madam, that our family happened to be in town, else I do not know what mischief might have befallen you.' – 'Bless me!' cried Miss Betsy, and was goiung on; but the other interrupted her, saying, hastily, as she led her forward, 'Walk this way; my brother will tell you all.' Miss Betsy then stopped short, 'What means all this?' said she: 'Where am I, pray, Miss? Who is your brother?' To which the other replied, that her brother was the Lord Viscount —, and that he at present was the owner of that house.

The surprize Miss Betsy had been put in by this young lady's first accosting her, was not at all dissipated by these words, but had now an equal portion of curiosity added to it: she longed to know the meaning of words, which at present seemed so mysterious to her, and with what kind of mischief she had been threatened, that she readily accompanied her young conductress into a magnificent parlour, at the upper end of which sat the nobleman she had been told of. 'I am extremely happy,' said he, as soon as he saw her enter, 'that Providence has put it in my power to rescue so fine a lady, from the villainy contrived against her.'

Miss Betsy replied, that she should always be thankful for any favours conferred upon her; but desired to know of what nature they were, for which she was indebted to his lordship; he then told her, that the persons she had been with had the most base designs upon her; that he had heard from a closet-window, where he was sitting, two of them lay a plot for carrying her off in a hackney-coach; and added, that being struck with horror at the foul intention, he had contrived, by the means of his sister, to get her out of their power; 'For,' said he, 'I know one of them to be so bloody a villain, that had I gone out myself, I must have fallen a sacrifice to their resentment.'

Miss Betsy was quite confounded; she knew not how to question the veracity of a nobleman, who could have no view or interest to deceive her; yet it was equally incongruous to her, that Mr. Bloomacre could harbour any designs upon her of that sort his lordship mentioned; she had several times been in company with that gentleman, and he had never behaved towards her in a manner which could give her room to suspect he had any dishonourable intentions towards her: but then, the treatment she had received from the gentleman-commoner at Oxford, reminded her, that men of an amorous complexion want only an opportunity to shew those inclinations, which indolence, or perhaps indelicacy, prevents them from attempting to gratify by assiduities and courtship.

After having taken some little time to consider what she should say, she replied that she was infinitely obliged to his lordship for the care he took of her, but might very well be amazed to hear those gentlemen had any ill designs upon her, two of whom were perfect strangers, and the other often visited at the house where she was boarded. As for the sending for a coach, the said it was by her own desire, if no chair could be procured: and added, that if his lordship had no other reason to apprehend any ill was meant to her, she could not, without injustice, forbear to clear up the mistake.

Lord — was a little confounded at these words; but, soon recovering himself, told her that she knew not the real character of the persons she had been with; that Bloomacre was one of the greatest libertines in the world; that, though she might agree to have a coach sent for, she could not be sure to what place it would carry her; and that he heard two of them, while the third was entertaining her, speak to each other in a manner which convinced him the most villainous contrivance was about to be practised on her.

A loud knocking at the door now interrupted their discourse; both his lordship and his sister seemed terribly alarmed: all the servants were called, and charge given not to open the door upon any account, to bar up the lower windows; and to give answers from those above, to whoever was there. The knocking continued with greater violence than it began, and Miss Betsy heard the gentlemen's voices talking to the servant; and, though she could not distinguish what they said, found there were very high words between them. My lord's sister ran into the hall to listen; then came back, crying, 'O what terrible oaths! – I am afraid they will break open the door!' – 'No,' replied Lord —; 'it is too strong for that: but I wish we had been so wise as to send for a constable.' One of the servants came down, and repeated what their young lady had said; adding, that the gentlemen swore they would not leave the place till they had spoke with the lady, who they said had been trepanned into that house. On this, 'Suppose, my lord,' said Miss Betsy, 'I go to the door and tell them that I will not go with them.' – 'No, Madam,' answered Lord —, 'I cannot consent my door should be opened to such ruffians; besides that they would certainly seize and carry you off by force, I know not what mischief they might do my poor men, for having at first refused them entrance.' She then said she would go up to the window, and answer them from thence; but he would not suffer her to be seen by them at all: and, to keep her from insisting on it, told her a great many stories of rapes, and other mischiefs, that had been perpetrated by Bloomacre, and those he kept company with.

All this did not give Miss Betsy those terrors, which, it is very plain his lordship and sister endeavoured to inspire her with; yet would she say no more of appearing to the gentlemen, as she found he was so averse to it.

At length the knocking ceased; and one of the footmen came down, and said that those who had given his lordship this disturbance had withdrawn from the door, and he believed they were gone quite out of the cloisters: but this intelligence did not satisfy Lord —; he either was, or pretended to be, in fear that they were still skulking in some corner, and would rush in if once they saw the door opened. There was still the same difficulty as ever, how Miss Betsy should get home; that is, how she should get safely out of the house; for, the rain being over, the servants said they did not doubt but they should be able to procure a chair or coach: after much debating on this matter, it was thus contrived.

Lord — had a window that looked into the yard of one of the prebendaries; a footman was to go out of the window to the back-door of that reverend divine, relate the whole story, and beg leave to go through his house: that request being granted, the footman went, and returned in less than half an hour, with the welcome news that a chair was ready, and waited in College Street. Miss Betsy had no way of passing, but by the same the footman had done, which she easily did, by being lifted by my lord into the window, and descending from it by the help of some steps placed on the other side by the servants of the prebendary.

It would be superfluous to trouble the reader with any speeches made by Lord —, and his sister, to Miss Betsy, or the replies she made to them; I shall only say, that passing through his house, and the College Garden, at the door of which the chair waited, she went into it, preceded by Lord —'s footman, muffled up in a cloak, and without a flambeau, to prevent being known, in case she should be met by Bloomacre, or either of his companions: and with this equipage she arrived safe at home, though not without a mind strangely perplexed at the meaning of this adventure.

CHAPTER XXI

———•———

Gives an explanation of the former, with other particulars, more agreeable to the reader in the repetition, than to the persons concerned in them

IT was near ten o'clock when Miss Betsy came home; and Mr. Goodman, who had been very uneasy at her staying out so late, especially as she was alone, was equally rejoiced at her return; but, as well as Lady Mellasin, was surprized on hearing by what accident she had been detained – they knew not how to judge of it – there was no circumstance in the whole affair which could make them think Mr. Bloomacre had any designs of the sort Lord — had suggested: yet did Mr. Goodman think himself obliged, as the young lady's guardian, to go to that gentleman, and have some talk with him concerning what had passed. Accordingly, he went the next morning to his house; but, not finding him at home, left word with his servant that he desired to speak with him as soon as possible: he came not, however, the whole day, nor sent any message to excuse his not doing so; and this neglect gave Mr. Goodman, and Miss Betsy herself, some room to suspect he was no less guilty than he had been represented, since had he been perfectly innocent, it seemed reasonable to them to think he would have come, even of his own accord, to have learned of Miss Betsy the motive of her leaving him in so abrupt and odd a manner – but how much they wronged him will presently appear, and they were afterwards convinced.

There was an implacable animosity between Lord — and Mr. Bloomacre, on account of the former's pretending a right to some lands which the other held, and could not be dispossessed of by law. As his lordship knew Mr. Bloomacre was not of a disposition to bear an affront tamely, he had no other way to vent his spleen against him, than by villifying and traducing him in all companies he came into; but this he took care to do in so artful a manner, as to be enabled either to evade, or render what he said impossible to be proved, in case he were called to an account for it.

The affair of Miss Betsy, innocent as it was, he thought gave him an excellent opportunity of gratifying his malice: he went early the next morning to the dean, complained of an insult offered to his house by Mr. Bloomacre, on the score of his sister having brought in a young lady, whom that gentleman had detained in the cloisters, and was going to carry off, by the assistance of some friends he had with him, in a hackney-coach.

The dean, who was also a bishop, was extremely incensed, as well he might, at so glaring a profanation of that sacred place; and the moment Lord — had taken his leave, sent for Mr. Bloomacre to come to him. That gentleman immediately obeying the summons, the bishop began to reprimand him in terms, which the occasion seemed to require from a person of his function and authority: Mr. Bloomacre could not forbear interrupting him, though with the greatest respect, saying nothing could be more false and base, than such an accusation; that whoever had given such an information was a villain, and merited to be used as such. The prelate, seeing him in this heat, would not mention the name of his accuser; but replied coolly, that it was possible he might be wronged; but to convince him that he was so, he must relate to him the whole truth of the story, and on what grounds a conjecture so much to the disadvantage of his reputation had been formed. On which Mr. Bloomacre repeated every thing that had passed; and added, that he was well acquainted with the family where the young lady was boarded, and that he was certain she would appear in person to justify him in this point, if his lordship thought it proper. 'But,' said the bishop, 'I hear you affronted the Lord —, by thundering at his door, and abusing his servants.' – 'No, my lord,' answered Mr. Bloomacre, 'Lord —, though far from being my friend, will not dare to alledge any such thing against me. We were, indeed, a little surprized to see the young lady, who was with us, snatched away in so odd a fashion by his sister, who we easily perceived had not the least acquaintance with her. We continued walking, however, in the cloister, till the man whom we had sent for a coach returned, and told us he had got one, and that it waited at the gate. We then, indeed, knocked at Lord —'s door; and being answered from the windows by the servants, in a very impertinent manner, I believe we might utter some words not very respectful either of his lordship or his sister, whose behaviour in this affair I am as yet entirely ignorant how to account for.'

The bishop paused a considerable time; but on Mr. Bloomacre's repeating what he had said before, concerning bringing the young lady herself to vouch the truth of what he had related to his lordship, replied, that there was no occasion for troubling either her or himself any farther; that he believed there had been some mistake in the business, and that he should think no more of it: on which Mr. Bloomacre took his leave.

Though the bishop had not mentioned the name of Lord — to Mr. Bloomacre, as the person who had brought this complaint against him, yet he was very certain, by all circumstances, that he could be indebted to no other for such a piece of low malice; and this, joined to some other provocations he had received from the ill-will of that nobleman, made him resolve to do himself justice.

He went directly from the deanry in search of the two gentlemen who had been with him in the Abbey when he happened to meet Miss Betsy; and, having found them both, they went to a tavern together, in order to consult on what was proper to be done, for the chastisement of Lord —'s folly and ill-nature.

Both of them agreed with Mr. Bloomacre, that he ought to demand that satisfaction which every gentleman has a right to expect from any one who has injured him, of what degree soever he be, excepting those of royal blood. Each of them was so eager to be his second in this affair, that they were obliged to draw lots for the determination of the choice: he who had the ill-luck, as he called it, to draw the shortest cut, would needs oblige them to let him be the bearer of the challenge, that he might at least have some share in inflicting the punishment, which the behaviour of that unworthy lord so justly merited.

The challenge was wrote – the place appointed for meeting was the field behind Montague House: but the gentleman who carried it, brought no answer back; his lordship telling him only that he would consider on the matter, and let Mr. Bloomacre know his intentions.

Mr. Bloomacre, as the principal, and the other as his second, were so enraged at this, that the latter resolved to go himself, and force a more categorical answer. He did so; and Lord — having had time to consult his brother, and, as it is said, some other friends, told him he accepted the challenge, and would be ready with his second at the time and place appointed in it.

Mr. Bloomacre did not go home that whole day, therefore knew nothing of the message that had been left for him by Mr. Goodman, till it was too late to comply with it; but this seeming remissness in him was not all that troubled the mind of that open and honest-hearted guardian of Miss Betsy. Mr. Trueworth and Mr. Staple had both been at his house the day before: the former, on hearing his mistress was abroad, left only his compliments, and went away, though very much pressed to come in by Miss Flora, who seeing him through the parlour-window, ran to the door herself, and intreated he would pass the evening there. Mr. Staple came the moment after, and met his rival coming down the steps that led up to the door; Mr. Trueworth saluted him, in passing, with the usual complaisance, which the other returned in a very cool manner, and knocked hastily at the door. 'I imagine,' said he to the footman who opened it, 'that Miss Betsy is not at home, by that gentleman's having so early taken leave: but I would speak with Mr. Goodman, if he be at leisure.'

He was then shewed into the back-parlour, which was the room where Mr. Goodman generally received those persons who came to him upon business. On hearing who it was that asked for him, he was a little surprized, and desired he would walk up stairs: but Mr. Staple not knowing but there might be company above, returned for answer, that he had no more than a word or two to say to him, and that must be in private; on which the other immediately came down to him.

This young lover having by accident been informed, not only that Mr. Trueworth made his addresses to Miss Betsy, but also that it was with him she had been engaged during all that time he had been deprived of seeing her, thought it proper to talk with Mr. Goodman concerning this new obstacle to his wishes. That worthy gentleman was extremely troubled to be questioned on an affair, on which he had given Miss Betsy his word not to interfere: but finding himself very much pressed by a person whose passion he had encouraged, and who was the son of one with whom he had lived in a long friendship, he frankly confessed to him that Mr. Trueworth was indeed recommended to Miss Betsy by her brother; told him he was sorry the thing had happened so, but had nothing farther to do with it; that the young lady was at her own disposal, as to the article of marriage; that he was ignorant how she would determine; and that it must be from herself alone he could learn what it was he might expect or hope.

Mr. Staple received little satisfaction from what Mr. Goodman had said; but resolved to take his advice, and, if possible, bring Miss Betsy to some eclaircissement of the fate he was to hope or fear. Accordingly, he came the next morning to visit her; a liberty he had never taken, nor would now, if he had not despaired of finding her in the afternoon.

She gave herself, however, no airs of resentment on that account: but when he began to testify his discontent concerning Mr. Trueworth, and the apprehensions he had of his having gained the preference in her heart, though the last who had solicited that happiness, she replied, in the most haughty tones, that she was surprized at the freedom he took with her; that she was, and ever would be, mistress of her actions and sentiments, and no man had a right to pry into either; and concluded with saying, that she was sorry the civilities she had treated him with, should make him imagine he had a privilege of finding fault with those she shewed to others.

It is not to be doubted but that he made use of all the arguments in his power to convince her, that a true and perfect passion was never unaccompanied with jealous fears. He acknowledged the merits of Mr. Trueworth: 'But,' added he, 'the more he is possessed of, the more dangerous he is to my hopes.' And then begged her to consider the torments he had suffered, while being so long deprived of her presence, and knowing, at the same time, a rival was blessed with it.

Miss Betsy was not at this time in a humour either to be persuaded by the reasons, or softened by the submissions, of her lover: and poor Mr. Staple, after having urged all that love, wit, despair, and grief, could dictate, was obliged to depart more dissatisfied than he came.

In going out he saw Mr. Goodman in the parlour, who gave him the 'Good morning!' as he passed. 'A sad one it has been to me,' answered he, with somewhat of horror in his countenance: 'but I will not endure the rack of many such.' With these words he flung out of the house, in order to go about what, perhaps, the reader is not at a loss to guess at.

CHAPTER XXII

———•———

*A duel begun, and another fought in the same
morning, on Miss Betsy's account, are here related,
with the manner in which the different antagonists
behaved to each other*

WELL may the God of Love be painted blind! Those devoted to his
influence are seldom capable of seeing things as they truly are; the
smallest favour elates them with imaginary hopes, and the least
coolness sinks then into despair: their joys, their griefs, their fears,
more frequently spring from ideal rather than effective causes. Mr.
Staple judged not that Miss Betsy refused to ease his jealous
apprehensions on the score of Mr. Trueworth, because it was her
natural temper to give pain to those that loved her, but because she
really had an affection for that gentleman. Looking on himself,
therefore, as now abandoned to all hope, rage and revenge took the
whole possession of his soul, and chaced away the softer emotions
thence.

Having heard Mr. Trueworth say he lodged in Pall Mall, he went
to the Cocoa Tree; and there informing himself of the particular
house where his rival might be found, sat down and wrote the
following billet.

'To Charles Trueworth, Esq.

Sir,
Both our wishes tend to the possession of one beautiful object; both
cannot be happy in the accomplishment: it is fit, therefore, the sword
should decide the difference between us, and put an end to those
pretensions on the one side or the other, which it is not probable
either of us will otherwise recede from. In confidence of your

complying with this proposal, I shall attend you in the Green Park, between the hours of seven and eight to-morrow morning. As the affair concerns only ourselves, I think it both needless and unjust to engage any of our friends in it; so shall come alone, and expect you will do the same to, Sir, your humble servant,

T. STAPLE.'

Mr. Trueworth was at home; and, on receiving this, immediately, and without the least hesitation, wrote and sent back, by the same messenger, the following answer.

'To T. Staple, Esq.

Sir,
Though I cannot but think the decision of our fate ought to be left entirely to the lady herself, (to whom, whatever be the fortune of the sword, it must at last be referred) yet, as I cannot, without being guilty of injustice to my own honour and pretensions, refuse you the satisfaction you require, shall not fail to meet you at the time and place mentioned in yours; till when, I am, Sir, your humble servant,

C. TRUEWORTH.'

By the stile of this letter, it may be easily perceived that Mr. Trueworth was not very well pleased with this combat, though the greatness of his courage and spirit would not permit him to harbour the least thought of avoiding it: yet, whatever his thoughts were on this occasion, he visited Miss Betsy the same day, and discovered no part of them in his countenance; his behaviour, on the contrary, was rather more sprightly than usual. He proposed to the two young ladies to go on some party of pleasure. Miss Betsy replied, with her accustomed freedom, that she should like it very well; but Miss Flora, who had been for three or four days past very sullen and ill-humoured, said one minute she would go, and the next that she would not; and gave herself such odd and capricious airs, that Miss Betsy told her she believed her head was turned: to which the other replied, tartly, that if the distemper was catching, it would be no wonder she should be infected, having it always so near her. Miss Betsy replied, that she knew no greater proof of madness than to punish one's self in the hope of mortifying another: 'But that shall never be my case,' continued she; 'as you will find.' Then turning to Mr. Trueworth, 'If you will accept of my company, without Miss Flora,' said she, laughing, 'we will take a walk into the Park.' It is not to be doubted but that the lover gladly embraced this opportunity of having his mistress to himself. 'It is like Miss Betsy Thoughtless,' cried Miss Flora; 'and only like herself, to go abroad with a man alone.' Miss Betsy regarded not this reproach; but, catching up her fan and gloves, gave Mr. Trueworth her hand, to lead her where she had proposed, leaving the other so full of spite, that the tears gushed from her eyes.

It is likely the reader will be pretty much surprized, that Miss Flora, who had always seemed more ready than even Miss Betsy herself, to accept of invitations of the sort Mr. Trueworth had made, should now, all at once, become so averse: but his curiosity for an explanation of this matter must be for a while postponed; others, for which he may be equally impatient, requiring to be first discussed.

Two duels having been agreed upon to be fought on the same morning, the respect due to the quality of L —, demands we should give that wherein he was concerned, the preference in the repetition.

The hour appointed being arrived, Lord — and his brother came into the field: Mr. Bloomacre and his friend appeared immediately after. 'You are the persons,' said Lord —, in an exulting tone, 'who made the invitation; but we are the first at table.' – 'It is not yet past the time,' replied Bloomacre, looking on his watch; 'but the later we come, the more eagerly we shall fall to.' In that instant all their swords were drawn; but they had scarce time to exchange one thrust, before a posse of constables, with their assistants, armed with staves and clubs, rushed in between them, beat down their weapons, and carried them all four to the house of the high-bailiff of Westminster.

That gentleman, by virtue of his office, made a strict examination into what had passed; and, having heard what both parties had to say, severely reprimanded the one for having given the provocation, and the other for the manner in which it was resented: he told them he had a right, in order to preserve the peace of Westminster, and the liberties of it, to demand, that they should find sureties for their future behaviour; but, in regard to their quality and character, he would insist on no more than their own word and honour that the thing should be mutually forgot, and that nothing of the same kind, which now had been happily prevented, should hereafter be attempted.

Lord — submitted to this injunction with a great deal of readiness; and Mr. Bloomacre, seeing no other remedy, did the same: after which the high bailiff obliged them to embrace, in token of the sincerity of their reconciliation.

Thus ended an affair which had threatened such terrible consequences. It made, however, a very great noise; and the discourse upon it was no way to the advantage of Lord —'s character, either for generosity or courage. Let us now see the sequel of the challenge sent by Mr. Staple to Mr. Trueworth.

These gentlemen met almost at the same time, in the place the challenger had appointed: few words served to usher in the execution of the fatal purpose; Mr. Staple only said, 'Come on, Sir! Love is the word, and Miss Betsy Thoughtless be the victor's prize.' With these words he drew his sword; Mr. Trueworth also drew his; and, standing on his defence, seeing the other was about to push, cried, 'Hold, Sir! your better fortune may triumph over my life, but never make me yield up my pretensions to that amiable lady: if I die, I die her martyr, and wish not to live but in the hope of serving her.' These words making Mr. Staple imagine, that his rival had indeed the greatest encouragement to hope every thing, added to the fury he was before possessed of, 'Die, then, her martyr!' said he; and running upon him with more force than skill, received a slight wound in his own breast, while aiming to the other's heart.

It would be needless to mention all the particulars of this combat; I shall only say, that the too great eagerness of Mr. Staple, gave the other an advantage over him, which must have been fatal to him from a less generous enemy: but the temperate Mr. Trueworth seemed to take an equal care to avoid hurting his rival, as to avoid being hurt by him; seeing, however, that he was about to make a furious push at him, he ran in between, closed with him, and Mr. Staple's foot happening to slip, he fell at full-length upon the earth, his sword at the same time dropped out of his hand, which Mr. Trueworth took up. 'The victory is yours,' cried he; 'take also my life, for I disdain to keep it.' – 'No,' replied Mr. Trueworth, 'I equally disdain to take an advantage, which mere chance has given me: rise, Sir, and let us finish the dispute between us, as becomes men of honour.' With these words he returned to him his sword. 'I should be unworthy to be ranked among that number,' said Mr. Staple, on receiving it, 'to employ this weapon against the breast, whose generosity restored it, were any thing but Miss Betsy at stake: but, what is life! what is even honour, without the hope of her! I therefore accept your noble offer; and death or conquest be my lot!' They then renewed the engagement with greater violence than before: after several passes,

Mr. Trueworth's dexterity could not hinder him from receiving a wound on his left-side; but he gave the other, at the same time, so deep a one in his right-arm, that it deprived him in an instant of the power of continuing the fight; on which Mr. Trueworth dropping the point of his sword, ran to him, 'I am sorry, Sir,' said he, 'for the accident that has happened; I see you are much hurt: permit me to assist you as well as I am able, and attend you where proper care may be taken of you.' – 'I do not deserve this goodness,' answered Mr. Staple; 'but it is the will of Heaven that you vanquish every way.'

Mr. Trueworth then seeing the blood run quite down upon his hand, stripped up the sleeve, and bound the wound from which it issued, as tight as he could with his handkerchief, after which they went together to an eminent surgeon near Piccadilly. On examination of his wounds, neither that in his arm, nor in his breast, appeared to be at all dangerous, the flesh being only pierced, and no artery or tendon touched. Mr. Trueworth seemed only assiduous in his cares for the hurts he had given his rival, without mentioning the least word of that which he had received himself, till an elderly gentleman, who happened to be with the surgeon when they came in, and had all the time been present, perceiving some blood upon the side of his coat, a little above the hip, cried out, 'Sir, you neglect yourself. I fear you have not escaped unhurt.' – 'A trifle,' said Mr. Trueworth, 'a mere scratch, I believe; it is time enough to think of that.' Nor would he suffer the surgeon, though he bled very fast, to come near him, till he had done with Mr. Staple. It was, indeed, but a slight wound which Mr. Truelove had received, though happening among a knot of veins, occasioned the effusion of a pretty deal of blood; for the stopping of which the surgeon applied an immediate remedy, and told him that it required little for a cure besides keeping it from the air.

Mr. Staple, who had been deeply affected with the concern this generous enemy had expressed for him, was equally rejoiced at hearing the wound he had given him would be attended with no bad consequences. Every thing that was needful being done for both, the old gentleman prevailed upon them to go with him to a tavern a few doors off, having first obtained the surgeon's leave; who told him a glass or two of wine could be of no prejudice to either.

This good-natured gentleman, who was called Mr. Chatfree, used to come frequently to Mr. Goodman's house, had some knowledge of Mr. Staple; and, though he was wholly unacquainted with Mr.

Trueworth, conceived so great an esteem for him, from his behaviour towards the person he had fought with, that he thought he could not do a more meritorious action, than to reconcile to each other two such worthy persons. What effect his endeavours, or rather their own nobleness of sentiments produced, shall presently be shewn.

CHAPTER XXIII

Among other things necessary to be told, gives an account of the success of a plot laid by Mr. Chatfree, for the discovery of Miss Betsy's real sentiments

THOUGH Mr. Goodman had as yet no intimations of the accidents of that morning, yet was he extremely uneasy; the looks, as well as words of Mr. Staple, in going of his house the day before, were continually in his mind, and he could not forbear apprehending some fatal consequence would, one time or another, attend the levity of Miss Betsy's behaviour and conduct, in regard to her admirers: he was also both surprized and vexed, that Mr. Bloomacre, from whom he expected an explanation of the Westminster Abbey adventure, had not come according to his request. This last motive of his disquiet was, however, soon removed: Mr. Bloomacre, who was no less impatient to clear himself of all blame concerning the transactions of that night, had no sooner finished his affair with Lord —, and was dismissed by the high-bailiff, than he came directly to Mr Goodman's, and recited to him, and all the ladies, the whole of what had passed.

Miss Betsy laughed prodigiously; but Mr. Goodman shook his head, on hearing the particulars related by Mr. Bloomacre; and, after that gentleman was gone, reproved, as he thought it his duty to do, the inconsiderateness of her conduct: he told her, that as she was alone, she ought to have left the Abbey as soon as divine service was ended; that, for a person of her sex, age, and appearance, to walk in a place where there were always a great concourse of young sparks, who came for no other purpose than to make remarks upon the ladies, could not but be looked on as very odd by all who saw her. 'There was no rain,' said he, 'till a long time after the service was ended, and you might then, in all probability, have got a chair; or if not, the walk over the Park could not have been a very great fatigue.'

Miss Betsy blushed extremely, not through a conscious shame of imagining what she had done deserved the least rebuke, but because her spirit, yet unbroke, could not bear controul: she replied, that as she meant no ill, those who censured her were most in fault. 'That is very true,' answered Mr. Goodman; 'but, my dear child, you cannot but know it is a fault which too many in the world are guilty of. I doubt not of your innocence, but would have you consider, that reputation is also of some value; that the honour of a young maid, like you, is a flower of so tender and delicate a nature, that the least breath of scandal withers and destroys it. In fine, that it is not enough to be good, without behaving in such a manner as to make others acknowledge us to be so.'

Miss Betsy had too much understanding not to be sensible what her guardian said on this occasion was perfectly just; and also that he had a right to offer his advice whenever her conduct rendered it necessary; but could not help being vexed, that any thing she did should be liable to censure, as she thought it merited none: she made no farther reply, however, to what Mr. Goodman said, though he continued his remonstrances, and probably would have gone on much longer, if not interrupted by the coming in of Mr. Chatfree. This gentleman having parted from the two wounded rivals, came directly to Mr. Goodman's, in order to see how Miss Betsy would receive the intelligence he had to bring her.

After paying his compliments to Mr. Goodman, and the other ladies, he came towards Miss Betsy; and looking on her with a more than ordinary earnestness in his countenance, 'Ah, Madam!' said he, 'I shall never hereafter see you without remembering what Cowley says of a lady who might, I suppose, be like you –

"So fatal, and withal so fair,
We're told destroying-angels are." '

Though Miss Betsy was not at that time in a humour to have any great relish for raillery, yet she could not forbear replying to what this old gentleman said, in the manner in which she imagined he spoke. 'You are at least past the age of being destroyed by any weapons I carry about me,' cried she: 'but, pray, what meaning have you in this terrible simile?' – 'My meaning is as terrible as the simile,' answered he; 'and though I believe you to be very much the favourite of Heaven, I know not how you will atone for the mischief you have been the occasion of this morning: but it may be,' continued he, 'you think it nothing that those murdering eyes of yours have set two gentlemen a fighting.'

Miss Betsy, supposing no other than that he had heard of the quarrel between Mr. Bloomacre and Lord —, replied merrily, 'Pray accuse my eyes of no such thing; they are very innocent, I assure you.' – 'Yes,' cried Mr. Goodman, and Lady Mellasin at the same time, 'we can clear Miss Betsy of this accusation.'

'What!' rejoined Mr. Chatfree, hastily, 'were not Mr. Staple and Mr. Trueworth rivals for her love?' – 'Mr. Staple and Mr. Trueworth!' said Miss Betsy, in a good deal of consternation; 'pray what of them?' – 'Oh, the most inveterate duel!' answered he; 'they fought above half an hour, and poor Mr. Staple is dead of his wounds.' – 'Dead!' cried Miss Betsy, with a great scream. Lady Mellasin and Miss Flora seemed very much alarmed; but Mr. Goodman was ready to sink from his chair, till Mr. Chatfree, unseen by Miss Betsy, winked upon him, in token that he was not in earnest in what he said.

The distraction in which this young lady now appeared, the concern she expressed for Mr. Staple, and her indignation against Mr. Trueworth, would have made any one think the former had much the preference in her esteem; till Mr. Chatfree, after having listened to her exclamations on this score, cried out on a sudden, 'Ah, Madam! what a mistake has the confusion I was involved in made me guilty of! Alas, I have deceived you, though without designing to do so! Mr. Staple lives, it is Mr. Trueworth who has fallen a sacrifice to his unsuccessful passion for you.' 'Trueworth dead!' cried Miss Betsy; 'O God! and does his murderer live to triumph in the fall of the best and most accomplished man on earth? Oh! may all the miseries that Heaven and earth can inflict, light on him! – Is he not secured, Mr. Chatfree? – Will he not be hanged?'

Mr. Chatfree could hold his countenance no longer; but bursting into a violent fit of laughter, 'Ah, Miss Betsy! Miss Betsy! I have caught you. Mr. Trueworth, I find, then, is the happy man.' – 'What do you mean, Mr. Chatfree?' cried Miss Betsy, very much amazed. 'I beg your pardon,' answered he, 'for the fright I have put you in; but be comforted, for Mr. Trueworth is not dead, I assure you; and, I doubt not, lives as much your slave as ever.' – 'I do not care what he is, if he is not dead,' said Miss Betsy; 'but, pray, for what end did you invent this fine story?' – 'Nay, Madam,' resumed he, 'it is not altogether my own inventing neither; for Mr. Trueworth and Mr. Staple have had a duel this morning, and both of them are wounded, though not so dangerously as I pretended, merely to try, by the concern you would express, which of them you were must inclined to favour; and I have done it i'faith – Mr. Trueworth is the man!'

Lady Mellasin, who had not spoke during all this conversation, now cried out, 'Aye, Mr. Chatfree, we shall soon have a wedding, I believe.' – 'Believe, Madam!' said he, 'why your ladyship may swear it! for my part, I will not give above a fortnight for the conclusion; and I will venture to wish the fair bride joy on the occasion, for he is a fine gentleman – a very fine gentleman, indeed! and I think she could not have made a better choice.' With these words he wiped his mouth, and advanced to Miss Betsy, in order to salute her; but, pushing him scornfully back, 'None of your slights, good Mr. Chatfree,' said she; 'if I thought you were in earnest, I would never see the face of Mr. Trueworth more.'

This did not hinder the pleasant old gentleman from continuing his raillery; he plainly told Miss Betsy that she was in love; that he saw the marks of it upon her, and that it was vain for her to deny it. Lady Mellasin laughed very heartily to see the fret Miss Betsy was in, at hearing Mr. Chatfree talk in this manner: but Miss Flora, to whom one would imagine this scene would have been diverting enough, never opened her lips to utter one syllable; but made such grimaces, as had they been taken notice of, would have shewn how little she was pleased with it.

Mr. Goodman had been so much struck with the first account given by Mr. Chatfree, that he was not to be rouzed by any thing that gentleman said afterwards; he reflected, that though the conse-quences of the encounter between the two rivals had been less fatal than he had been made to imagine, yet it might have happened, and indeed been naturally expected; he could not forbear, therefore, interrupting his friend's mirth, by remonstrating to Miss Betsy, in the most serious terms, the great error she was guilty of, by encouraging a plurality of lovers at the same time: he told her, that gentlemen of Mr. Trueworth's and Mr. Staple's character and fortune, ought not to be trifled with. 'Suppose,' said he, 'that one or both of them had indeed been killed, how could you have answered to yourself, or to the world, the having been the sad occasion?'

'Lord, Sir,' replied Miss Betsy, walking up and down the room in a good deal of agitation, 'what would you have me do? I do not want the men to love me; and if they will play the fool, and fight, and kill one another, it is none of my fault.'

In fine, between Mr. Chatfree's raillery, and Mr. Goodman's admonitions, this poor young lady was teazed beyond all patience; and, finding it impossible to put a stop to either, she flew out of the room, ready to cry with vexation.

She was no sooner gone, than Mr. Goodman took Mr. Chatfree into his closet; and, having learned from him all the particulars of the late duel, and consulted with him what was proper to be done to prevent any farther mischief of the like sort, they went together to Mr. Staple's lodging, in order to use their utmost endeavours to prevail on that gentleman to desist the prosecution of his addresses to Miss Betsy.

VOLUME THE SECOND

CHAPTER I

———•———

Will satisfy the reader's curiosity in some points, and increase it in others

THOUGH Mr. Goodman, under whose care and in whose house Miss Betsy had been for upwards of a year, knew much more of that young lady's humour and disposition than Mr. Chatfree, who saw her but seldom, could possibly do, and could not be brought to think, as he did, that the merits of Mr. Trueworth had made any effectual impression on her heart; yet he imagined, that to propogate such an opinion to Mr. Staple, would conduce very much to persuade him to break off his courtship, which was a thing very much desired by Mr. Goodman, as he was certain the continuance of it would be attended with almost insurmountable difficulties, and create many vexations and disputes, when Mr. Francis Thoughtless came to town.

The two old gentlemen went on together, discoursing on this affair, till they came to the lodgings of Mr. Staple; where they found him in an easy chair, leaning on a table, with papers and a standish before him. They perceived he had been writing, for the pen was not out of his hand when they entered the room: he threw it down, however, as soon as he saw them, and rose to receive them with a great deal of politeness, though accompanied with an air, which, in spite of his endeavours to conceal it, discovered he laboured under an extraordinary dejection of spirits.

'I am glad,' said Mr. Chatfree, pointing to the pen, 'to see you are able to make use of that weapon, as I feared your arm had been too much prejudiced by another.' – 'I have found some difficulty, indeed, in doing it,' replied the wounded gentleman; 'but something, which seemed to me a case of necessity, obliged me to exert my utmost efforts for that purpose.'

After the first civilities were over, and they were all seated, Mr. Goodman and Mr. Chatfree began to open the business upon which they came. Mr. Goodman represented to him, in the most pathetick terms, the deep concern he had been in, for having ever encouraged his addresses to Miss Betsy; and excused himself for having done so, by his ignorance, at the time, that Mr. Trueworth had been previously recommended by her brother. He then gave him some hints, that the civilities Miss Betsy had treated him with, he feared, were rather owing to that little vanity which is generally the companion of youth and beauty, than to that real regard which his passion and person merited from her; and said, he heartily wished to see him withdraw his affections from an object, where he could not now flatter him with the least hope of a suitable return.

'No, no!' cried Mr. Chatfree, interrupting him hastily, 'you may take my word, she is as much in love as a girl of her temper can be with Mr. Trueworth; and I do not doubt but you will all see the effects of it as soon as her brother comes to town.' Mr. Goodman, on this, took an opportunity of telling Mr. Staple, that the ascendant that young gentleman had over his sister, and the zeal he expressed for the interest of his friend, would certainly go a great way in determining the point; and added, that if it were true, as his friends suggested, that she really had an inclination for Mr. Trueworth, she would then avow it, and make a merit of it to her brother, as if done merely in regard to him.

Many other arguments were urged by these two gentlemen, in order to convince Mr. Staple of the little probability there was in succeeding with Miss Betsy: all which he listened to attentively, never interrupting what either of them said; till, perceiving they had ended all they had to offer on the subject, he made them this reply.

'Gentlemen,' said he, 'I am infinitely obliged to you both for this visit, and the friendly purpose of it; which, I perceive, was to give me that advice which you might reasonably think I wanted. I have heard, and I believe have not lost one word, at least, I am sure, no part of the meaning, of what you have delivered. I own there is a great justice in every thing you have alledged; and am pleased to think the arguments you bring, are such as, before your coming here, I had myself brought against the folly of my own unhappy passion for Miss Betsy. But, gentlemen, it is not that I am capable of being deterred from prosecuting it, by any thing I might have to apprehend, either by her own inclinations or her brother's persuasions; but for other reasons, which at present, perhaps, you may be ignorant of, yet are such as to conceal I should but half be just. Be pleased, Sir,' he continued, addressing himself to Mr. Goodman, and giving him a paper, 'to read that letter, and see what my resolutions are, and the motives I have for them.'

Mr. Goodman was beginning to look over the paper; but Mr. Staple requested he would read it aloud, as he desired that Mr. Chatfree should be partaker of the contents: on which he read, with an audible voice, these lines.

'To Charles Trueworth, Esq.

Sir,
When I proposed the decision of our fate by force of arms, I offered, at the same time, that the glory of serving Miss Betsy should be the victor's triumph. This your too great modesty declined: but, Sir, though you scorned to accept the advantage your superior skill acquired, your generosity, in spite of you, has gained. I love Miss Betsy; and would have maintained my claim against all who should have dared dispute her with me, while justice and while honour permitted me to do so: but though I am unfortunate, I never can be base. My life, worthless as it is, has twice been in your power; and I should be no less hateful to myself, than contemptible to the world, should I offer to interrupt the peace of him that gave it. May you be as successful in love as you have been in fight, and the amiable object be convinced of her own happiness in making yours! I desist for ever from the vain hopes I once was flattered with, and the first wish my soul now harbours is, to be worthy the title of your friend, as I am bound to avow myself, with the greatest sincerity, Sir, your most obliged and most humble servant,

T. STAPLE.'

'Nothing,' said Mr. Goodman, as soon as he had done reading, 'can equal your generosity in forming this resolution, but the wisdom in persisting in it; and if I find you do so, shall have more reason to congratulate you upon it, than I should think I had on the success of your wishes in marrying Miss Betsy.'

'I should laugh now,' cried Mr. Chatfree, 'if Mr. Trueworth, in a fit of generosity too, should also take it into his head to resign his pretensions, and chuse to wear the willow, instead of the myrtle-garland, because you do so.' – 'He has already proved his generosity,' replied Mr Staple, with a sigh, which he was unable to restrain, 'and has no need to give the severe testimony you mention, if he is so happy as you seem to think he is: but,' continued he, 'it is not my business to examine who yields, or who pursues, Miss Betsy. I am fixed in my determination to see her no more; and, as soon as I am recovered from the hurts I have received on her account, will go into the country, and seek a cure in absence for my unavailing passion.'

Neither Mr. Goodman nor Mr. Chatfree were so old as to have forgot how hard it is for a youthful heart to give up it's darling wishes, and sacrifice desire to discretion. They said abundance of handsome things, omitting nothing which they imagined might add to the fortitude of his present way of thinking. He, on the other hand, to take from them all remains of doubt concerning the sincerity of his intentions, sealed the letter he had wrote to Mr. Trueworth, and sent it to that gentleman, while they were in the room.

Mr. Goodman was extremely pleased in his mind, that an affair, which, for some time past, had given him a good deal of anxiety, was in so fair a way of being ended without farther mischief: he took no notice, however, on his return home, at least, not before Miss Betsy, of the visit he had been making, or that he knew any thing more of Mr. Staple, than what she had been told herself by Mr. Chatfree.

In the mean time, this young lady affected to appear more grave than ordinary: I say, affected to be so; for as she had been at first shocked by Mr. Chatfree's report, and afterwards teazed by his raillery, and then reprimanded on the score of her conduct by Mr. Goodman, she was not displeased in her heart at the dangerous proof which the two lovers had given her of their passion.

She lost, however, great part of the satisfaction this adventure might have afforded her, for want of a proper person to whom she might have talked freely on it. She had, indeed, many acquaintances, in some of whom she, doubtless, might have confided; but she did not chuse to be herself the reporter of this story to any one who had not heard of it from other hands; and Miss Flora, who knew the whole, and was her companion and bedfellow, was grown of late so sullen and peevish, as not to be capable of either giving or receiving any diversion in discourses of that nature.

It is certain, however, that there never was a more astonishing alteration in the temper of any one person in so short a time, than in that of Miss Flora: her once gay and sprightly behaviour, which, without being a beauty, rendered her extremely agreeable, was now become all dull and gloomy. Instead of being fond of a great deal of company, she now rather chose to avoid than covet the society of any one: she said but little; and, when she spoke, it was only to contradict whatever she heard alledged by others. A heavy melancholy, mixed with an ill-natured frown, perpetually loured upon her brow: in fine, if she had been a little older, she might have sat for the picture of Envy. Miss Betsy, by being most with her, felt most the effects of her bad humour; but as she thought she could easily account, the sweetness of her disposition made her rather pity than resent the change.

A young linen-draper, of whom Lady Mellasin sometimes bought things, had taken a great fancy to Miss Flora; and not doubting but she had a fortune in some measure answerable to the appearance she made, got a friend to intercede with Lady Mellasin, for leave to pay his respects to her daughter. This being granted, he made several visits to the house, and was very well received by Miss Flora herself, as well as by those who had the disposal of her; till, coming on the topick of fortune, Mr. Goodman plainly told him, that having many relations of his own to provide for, the most he could spare to Miss Flora was five hundred pounds. The draper's passion was very much damped on hearing his mistress's portion was like to be so small: he told Mr. Goodman, that though he was very much charmed with the person and behaviour of the young lady, and should be proud of the honour of an alliance with such a family, yet as he was a young man, and but lately set up for himself, he wanted money to throw into trade, and could not think of marrying without more than three times the sum offered. He added, that a young lady of her birth, and bringing up, would expect to live as she had been accustomed, which he could no way promise she should do, without a fortune sufficient to defray the expence.

Mr. Goodman thought the reasons he gave were very just; and as he was unwilling to stretch his hand any farther than he had said, and was too honest to promise more than he intended to perform, replied, with the same freedom that the other had spoke, that in truth he did not think Flora would make a fit wife for a tradesman; that the girl was young enough, not ugly; and it was his opinion that she should wait till a more suitable match should offer. In a word, Mr. Goodman's answer put a final stop to the courtship; and though Miss

Flora affected to disdain the mercenary views, as she termed them, of the draper, and never spoke of him but with the utmost contempt, yet her melancholy coming on soon after he had desisted his addresses, made Miss Betsy think she had reason to impute it to no other cause; and therefore, in mere compassion to this imaginary mortification, was so far from retorting any of those little taunts and malicious innuendoes, with which she was continually treated by the other, that she took all the pains she could to alleviate the vexation she saw her in, and soothe her into a better humour.

The reader will probably think as Miss Betsy did: but the falsity of this conjecture, and the cruel return the good-nature of that young lady met with, will in due time and place appear.

CHAPTER II

———•———

Contains some passages which, perhaps, may be looked upon as pretty extraordinary

ACCORDING to the common rule of honour among gentlemen, Mr. Trueworth had certainly behaved so, as not to have either that, or his good nature, called in question: but this was not enough to satisfy him; he could not be easy under the reflection, that the obligations he had conferred gave a painful gratitude to the receiver.

He was deeply affected with Mr. Staple's letter; he doubted not but that gentleman, in forcing himself to resign his pretensions to Miss Betsy, must suffer the extremest agonies; and heartily commiserating a case, which, had fortune so decreed, might have been his own, immediately wrote to him in the following terms.

'To T. Staple, Esq.

Sir,
I am ashamed to find the little I have done so much over-rated by a person, who, I am certain, is capable of the greatest things; but should be involved in more confusion still, should any consideration of me, or my happiness, prevail on you to become an enemy to your own. I am altogether unacquainted with what kind of sentiments either of us is regarded by the fair object of our mutual wishes. It is highly probable her young heart may, as yet, be quite insensible of those we have endeavoured to inspire it with: for my own part, as I have yet no reason to despair, so I have had also but little room for hope. You, Sir, have an equal chance, for any thing I know, or can boast of to the contrary; and, as you saw I refused to hazard my

pretensions on the point of the sword, neither justice nor honour requires you should forfeit yours, though an accident gave me the advantage of you in the field. It is by Miss Betsy herself our fate is to be judged. It is yet a moot-point whether either of us will succeed in the attempt of pleasing her. We may, perhaps, contend for an airy expectation; while another, more fortunate, shall bear away the prize from both: but if one of us is decreed to be the happy man, on which soever the lot shall fall, he ought not to incur the hatred of the other.

I gladly embrace the offer of your friendship; and whatever is the fortune of our love, should in that, as in all other events, endeavour to prove, that I am, with an equal sincerity, Sir, your very much obliged, and most humble servant,

C. TRUEWORTH.'

Mr. Staple read this letter many times over; but received not all the satisfaction which the author intended it should give him: although he acknowledged the generosity of his rival, yet he could not conceive there was a possibility for a man in love to be easy under the addresses of another, without knowing himself secure of not being prejudiced by them. He therefore concluded, that Mr. Chatfree was right in his conjecture; and that Miss Betsy only waited for her brother's coming to town, to declare in favour of Mr. Trueworth.

This gentleman had a great share of spirit, and some pride; and these making him disdain to pursue a fruitless aim, and suffering himself to be publickly overcome by Mr. Trueworth in love, as he had been in fight, very much contributed to enable him to keep that resolution he had formed in the presence of Mr. Goodman and Mr. Chatfree.

He answered to Mr. Trueworth's letter, however, with the utmost complaisance; but without letting him know any part of his intentions in relation to Miss Betsy, fearing lest any farther contest on this affair might draw from that gentleman fresh proofs of a generosity to which already he looked upon himself as too much obliged.

Miss Betsy, little suspecting what had passed between her two lovers since their meeting in the Green Park, received Mr. Trueworth, when he came to visit her the same day, as usual, with a great deal of good-humour. She took not any notice that she had heard of the duel, imagining that he would himself inform her of it; and he not thinking it would become him to do so, as having the advantage of his rival, it is probable there would have been no mention made of it, if Lady Mellasin hd not come into the room, and told him, that she would not have broke in upon his conversation with Miss Betsy, if it had been possible for her to have resisted the pleasure of congratulating him, not only on his safety, but also on his coming off victor in the field of battle.

The modesty of Mr. Trueworth would not suffer him to hear these last words without blushing; but, soon recovering himself, 'Fortune, Madam,' answered he, 'is not always the most favourable to the most deserving: her partial smiles will never make me vain or happy; unless,' continued he, looking tenderly on Miss Betsy, 'she would add to her indulgence here, and give me room to hope my services to this lady might one day be crowned with the same success as she this morning gave my sword.' – 'The one,' said Miss Betsy, smiling, 'has nothing to do with the other; and I do not know how to think a man, who really wishes nothing so much as to appear agreeable in the eyes of his mistress, would run the hazard of making the contemptible figure of a culprit at the bar of a court of judicature.'

They then fell into some discourse on duelling; and Mr. Trueworth could not help joining with the ladies, in condemning the folly of that custom, which, contrary to the known laws of the land, and oftentimes contrary to his own reason too, obliges the gentleman either to obey the call of the person who challenges him to the field, or, by refusing, submits himself not only to all the insults his adversary is pleased to treat him with, but also to be branded with the infamous character of a coward by all that know him.

Nothing material enough to be related happened in this visit, except that Miss Flora, who had been abroad when Mr. Trueworth came, and returned home a short time before he went away, talked much more in half an hour than she had done for some whole days past; but it was in so cold a manner, sometimes praising, sometimes blaming, his conduct in regard to the transactions of that morning, that he could not well determine in his mind, whether she was a friend or an enemy to the success of his passion. Miss Betsy herself was a little surprized; but nothing relating to that young lady dwelt much upon her mind, as she really thought she had no design in any thing she said or did. The behaviour of Mr. Staple ran much more in her head: she knew he was pretty much wounded, and therefore might suppose him unable to wait on her in person; but having expected he would send his compliments to her, either by letter or message, and finding he did neither the whole day, it seemed to her a thing too strange to be accounted for. She was, however, eased of the suspense she was in on that score, by receiving from him, as she was at breakfast the next morning, the following epistle.

'To Miss Betsy Thoughtless.'

Madam,

A brother's recommendations, superior merit, and your own inclination, have all united to plead my rival's cause, and gain the verdict against unhappy me! I ought more early to have seen the vanity of attempting to succeed where Mr. Trueworth was the candidate; yet, hurried by the violence of my passion, I rushed into an action, which, by adding to his glory, has shewn my demerits in a more conspicuous light than ever.

It would be needless to repeat what happened yesterday: I cannot doubt, Madam, but you are well acquainted with all the particulars of my folly, and the just punishment it met with. I have only to say, the generosity of my rival, and my conqueror, has restored me to my lost reason, and convinced me, that whatever preference he may be so happy as to have gained in your esteem, he is indebted for it to the excellence of your good sense, and not to that partial fancy, which frequently misguides the choice of persons of your sex and age.

I would have waited on you in person, to take my everlasting leave; but I am not certain how far I ought to depend on the strength of my resolution in your presence. Permit, therefore, my pen to do that which my tongue would falter in performing. Yes, Madam, I must forego, renounce for ever, those glorious expectations with which so lately I had flattered my fond heart; henceforth must think on you as the fallen father of mankind did on the tree of life; the merits of my too accomplished rival are the flaming swords which drive me from my once hoped for paradise; and, while I mourn my unhappy state, compel me to own it to be just. Farewel, O most amiable of your sex! farewel, for ever! I have troubled you too long, and have no excuse to make, but that it is the last you shall receive from me. May the blessed guardians of the fair and good be your constant directors, and shield you from all ills! Be assured, that till I cease to exist, I shall not cease to be, with the sincerest good wishes, Madam, your most faithful, though unfortunate, humble servant,

T. STAPLE.'

Miss Betsy was astonished to that degree, on reading so unexpected a declaration, that she could scarce believe she was awake for some moments, and thought it all a dream – she broke off, and made several pauses in the reading; crying out, 'Good God! It is impossible! What does the man mean! How came such stuff into his head? He is mad, sure!'

Mr. Goodman, who had some notion of what had put her into this ferment, and was willing to be more confirmed, asked her, in a pleasant way, what had occasioned it. 'Indeed, Sir,' replied Miss Betsy, endeavouring to compose herself, 'I have been so confounded, that I knew not where I was, or who was in the room.' – I ask your pardon; but this, I hope, will plead my excuse,' continued she, throwing the letter on the table; 'your friend has given over his suit to me, which I am very glad of; but the motives, which he pretends obliges him to it, are so odd and capricious, as not to be accounted for.'

'Given over his suit!' cried Lady Mellasin, hastily. 'Oh! pray let us hear on what pretence!' On which Mr. Goodman read the letter aloud, the very repetition of which renewed Miss Betsy's agitations. 'He has acted,' said Mr. Goodman, as soon as he had done reading, 'like a man of sense and resolution; and I see no cause why you should be disconcerted at the loss of a lover, whose pretensions you did not design to favour.' – 'He was very hasty, however,' cried Miss Betsy, scornfully, 'in concluding for me. What! did the man think I was to be won at once? Did he imagine his merits were so extraordinary, that there required no more to obtain, than barely to ask? But I give myself no concern on that score, I assure you, Sir: it is the insolence of his accusing me of being in love that vexes me. Who told him, I wonder, or how came such a thing into his head, that Mr. Trueworth had the preference in my esteem? By the manner in which he speaks of him in this letter, he has found more perfections in him than ever I did, and would make one think he were himself enamoured of his rival's merits.'

In answer to all this, he told her, with a serious air, that Mr. Staple was bound, by all those ties which engage a noble mind, to act in the manner he had done; that he had been twice indebted to Mr. Trueworth for his life; and that the whole behaviour of that gentleman towards him, both during the combat, and after it was over, demanded all the returns that gratitude could pay.

He afterwards ran into a detail of all the particulars of what had passed between the two rivals, many of which the ladies were ignorant of before. Lady Mellasin joined with her husband in extolling the greatness of soul which Mr. Trueworth had shewn on this occasion: but Miss Flora said little; and what she did, was rather in praise of Mr. Staple. 'Mr. Trueworth,' cried she, 'is a fine gentleman enough; but has done no more than what any man of honour would do; and, for my part, I think that Mr. Staple, in putting the self-denial he has now shewn in practice, discovers more of the hero and philosopher than the other has done.'

The conversation on this topick lasted some time, and probably would not have broke off so soon, if it had not been interrupted by two young ladies coming in to ask Miss Betsy and Miss Flora if they were not for the Park that morning. To which they having agreed, and promised to call on them in their way, went up into their chamber, in order to prepare themselves for the walk proposed.

CHAPTER III

──────●──────

Discovers to Miss Betsy a piece of treachery she little expected to hear of

MISS Flora, who had been deterred from saying all she had a mind to do, on the affair between Miss Betsy's two lovers, now took this opportunity of giving her tongue all the latitude it wanted. They were no sooner come into the chamber, than, 'Lord, my dear,' cried she, with a tone vastly different from that in which she had spoke to her of late, 'how vexed am I for you! It will certainly go all about the town, that you are in love with Trueworth; and there will be such cabals, and such whispering about it, that you will be plagued to death: I could tear him to pieces, methinks; for I am sure he is a vain fellow, and the hint must come first from himself.'

'I never saw any thing like vanity in him,' replied Miss Betsy; 'and I am rather inclined to believe Mr. Staple got the notion from the idle rattle of Mr. Chatfree.' – 'Mr.Chatfree,' said Miss Flora, 'thought of no such thing himself, till he had been at the tavern with Mr. Trueworth; but, if I was in your place, I would convince Mr. Staple, and the world, that I was not capable of the weakness imputed to me.'

'Why, what would you have me do?' cried Miss Betsy. 'I would have you write to Mr. Staple,' answered the other, 'and let him know the deception his rival has put upon him.' Miss Betsy, who had always an aversion to any thing of this kind, and thought it too great a condescension to write on any score to a man who had pretended love to her, shook her head at this proposal, and exclaimed against it with the utmost vehemence.

Miss Flora made use of all the arguments she could think on, to bring her off from what she called so ill-judged a pride: among other things, she told her, that, in compassion to the despair that gentleman had so feelingly expressed in his letter, she ought to give him the consolation of knowing, that if he had not gained so far on her affections as he wished, it was not because his rival had gained more; and added, that the steps she persuaded her to take, were such as common justice to her own character had a right to exact from her.

Miss Betsy heard, but was not to be prevailed upon by all she could say on this subject; but the other, who had a greater share of artifice than perhaps was ever known in one of her years, would not give over the design she had formed in her head; and, perceiving that the writing to a man was the greatest objection Miss Betsy had to letting Mr. Staple know she was not so much attached to his rival as he imagined, took another way of working her to her purpose, which she thought would be less irksome.

'Well, then, my dear Miss Betsy,' said she, in the most flattering accent, 'I will tell you the only method you can take, and I am glad I have been so lucky to hit upon it: you shall let me go and make Mr. Staple a visit, as of my own accord; I shall take care not to drop a syllable that may give him room to think you know of my coming; but yet, as he may suppose I am enough in your secrets to be mistress of this, or at least not altogether a stranger to it, he will, doubtless, say something to me concerning the matter; but if he should not, it will be easy for me, in the way of discourse, and as it were by chance, to express myself in such terms as will entirely clear you, and rid him of all the apprehensions he is under, of your being in love with Mr. Trueworth.'

Miss Betsy was not in her heart at all averse to Mr. Staple's having that eclaircissement Miss Flora had mentioned, and was much less shocked at this proposal than she had been at the former, offered to her consideration for that purpose; yet did not seem to come into it, till the other had lavished all the arguments that woman, witty and wilful to obtain her ends, could urge to prevail on her to do so; and at last consented not to the execution, without exacting from Miss Flora the most solemn vow of an inviolable secrecy.

This project being concluded on, and everything relating to it settled while they were dressing, they went together according to their promise, to the ladies who expected them, and then accompanied them into the Park: but as if this was to be a day of surprizes to Miss Betsy, she here met with something which gave her,

at least, an equal share with that she had received from the letter of
Mr. Staple.

They had not gone many yards in the Mall before they saw three
gentlemen coming towards them; one of whom, as they drew nearer
to each other, Miss Betsy and Miss Flora presently knew to be the
son of Alderman Saving, though he was grown fatter, more ruddy,
and in many respects much altered from what he was when he visited
at Mr. Goodman's.

As our young ladies had not heard of this gentleman's return to
England, it was natural for them, especially Miss Betsy, after what
had passed between them, to be in some little surprize at the sudden
sight of him; he was in some confusion too: but both parties had
presence enough of mind to recover themselves, so as to salute as
persons would do, who never had any thing more than an ordinary
acquaintance with each other.

After the civilities common to people who thus meet by accident,
Mr. Saving asked the ladies leave for himself and friends to join
company; which being readily granted, they all walked up the Mall
together; but the place being pretty full, were obliged to divide
themselves, and walk in couples, or as it happened. During this
promenade, Mr. Saving found an opportunity of saying to Miss
Betsy, unheard by any of the others, 'Madam, I have something to
acquaint you with, of great consequence to yourself: it is improper for
me either to come or write to you at Mr. Goodman's, therefore wish
you would appoint some place where I might speak with you.'

Miss Betsy was very much startled at his mentioning such a thing,
and replied, 'No, Mr. Saving, I do not make a practice of consenting
to assignations with men; nor have yet forgot that which I consented
to with you.' – 'I am very well able to clear myself of any fault on that
score,' said he: 'but, Madam, to ease you of those apprehensions,
which might, perhaps, make you think yourself obliged to keep me at
a distance, it is proper to acquaint you, that I am married, and that it
is only through a friendly regard for your honour and peace, that I
would warn you against the perfidy of a pretended friend.' Perceiving
she started at these words, and repeated them two or three times
over, 'Yes, Madam,' resumed he; 'and if you will permit me to speak
with you in a proper place, will bring with me an unquestionable
proof of the truth of what I say.'

One of the ladies happening to turn back to say something to Miss
Betsy, prevented him from adding farther; but what he had already

spoke, made a very deep impression on her mind. She could not conceive who the false friend should be that he had mentioned, unless it were Miss Flora; but though she had seen many instances of her insincerity, was not able to form any conjecture what she could have been guilty of to her, that Mr. Saving, who had been so long absent, could possibly be made acquainted with.

Thinking, however, that she ought not to deny herself the satisfaction of the eclaircissement he offered, especially as it was now to be given, not by a lover, but a friend, she sought and found a moment before they left the Mall, of saying to him without the notice of the company. 'Sir, I have considered on the hint you gave me; whatever concerns my honour, or my peace, must certainly merit my attention: I have an acquaintance in St. James's palace, whom I will visit as soon as dinner is over; if you walk a turn or two in the gallery leading to the Chapel Royal, you will see me pass that way between four and five o'clock.' To this Mr. Saving replied, that he would not fail to attend her there.

Miss Flora, who had been informed by Miss Betsy, after they had parted from Mr. Saving, that he was married, was full of the news when she came home: but Mr. Goodman, to whom the whole story of that affair had been related by the alderman, said, that the young gentleman had done very wisely, in complying with the commands of his father; and added, that the lady had a very agreeable person, a large fortune, and, above all, was extremely modest and discreet, so that there was no room to doubt his happiness. There was some farther discourse at table, concerning this new-wedded pair; but Miss Betsy took little part in it, as giving herself no pains for the interests of a person for whom she never had any thing but the most perfect indifference.

She was, notwithstanding, impatient enough for the account she expected to receive from him; and, without saying one word, either to Miss Flora, or any of the family, where she was going, went at the time prefixed to the place she had appointed to meet him.

Mr. Saving, to avoid being accused of want of punctuality in the affairs of friendship, as he had been in those of love, came somewhat before his time into the palace. As she ascended the great stairs, she saw him looking through one of the windows, waiting her approach; which greatly pleased her, as she would not have thought it proper to have walked there alone, nor would have been willing to have departed without the gratification of that curiosity his words had excited in her.

Excepting the time of divine service, and when the king, or any of the royal family go to chapel, few places are more retired than this gallery; none, besides the officers of the household passing on business into some of the apartments, scarce ever going into it; so that the choice Miss Betsy made, in her appointment with Mr. Saving, was extremely judicious.

As the business on which they met, was of a nature very different from love and gallantry, and time was precious to them both, they needed not many compliments to usher in what Mr. Saving had to say: he only, to excuse his behaviour to her, while he professed himself her lover, was beginning to relate the sudden manner in which he had been forced abroad; but she stopped him from going on, by telling him she had heard the whole story of that affair from Mr. Goodman, to whom the alderman had made no secret of it.

I have only, then,' said he, 'to acquaint you, Madam, that soon after my arrival in Holland, looking over some papers that my father had put into my portmanteau for my instruction in the business I was sent to negociate, I found among them a letter, which, doubtless, in the hurry he was in, he had shuffled with the others through mistake, which, pray, Madam,' continued he, giving her a paper, 'be pleased to peruse, and tell me whether honour and justice did not oblige me to take the first opportunity of cautioning you against the baseness and malice of a person you might otherwise, perhaps, confide in, on matters of more consequence to your peace than any thing on my account could be.'

Miss Betsy had no sooner taken the paper, and looked on the superscription, which was to Alderman Saving, than she cried out, with great amazement, 'Bless me! this is Miss Flora's hand.' – 'I think,' said Mr. Saving, 'that I might safely venture to affirm it upon oath, having often seen her writing; and have even some of it at this instant by me, in a song she copied for me, on my first acquaintance with her: but read, Madam,' pursued he, 'read the wicked scroll; and see the methods she took to prevail on a father to banish from his presence, and the kingdom, an only son, and to traduce that innocence and virtue, which she hated, because incapable of imitating.'

On this, Miss Betsy, trembling between a mixture of surprize and anger, hastily unfolded the letter, and found in it these lines, wrote in the same hand with the superscription.

Sir,

The real esteem I have for all persons of honesty and probity, obliges me to give you this seasonable warning of the greatest misfortune that can possibly befal a careful and a tender parent, as I know you are: but, not to keep you in suspense; your son, Sir, your only, your darling son! that son whom you have educated with so much tenderness, and who is so deservedly dear to you, is on the verge of ruin; his unhappy acquaintance with Mr. Goodman's family has subjected him to the artifices of a young girl, whose little affairs are in the hands of that gentleman. She is a great coquette, if I had said jilt too, I believe the injustice I should have done her character would not have been much; but as her share, either of fortune or reputation, is very small, I cannot condemn her for putting in practice all the strategems in her power of securing to herself a future settlement by marriage. I should, Sir, only be sorry that the lot should fall upon your son; as I know, and the world acknowledges, him to be a gentleman of much more promising expectations. It is, however, a thing I fear too near concluded; he loves her to distraction, will venture every thing for the gratification of his passion: she has a great deal of cunning, though little understanding in things more becoming of her sex; she is gay, vain, and passionately fond of gaming, and all the expensive diversions of the town. A shocking and most terrible composition for a wife! Yet such will she very speedily be made by the poor infatuated Mr. Saving, if you, Sir, in your paternal wisdom, do not find some way to put a stop to his intentions. The original of the picture I have been representing, is called Miss Betsy Thoughtless, a name well known among the gallant part of the town. I hope you will take the above intelligence in good part, as it is meant, with the greatest sincerity, and attachments to your interests, by, Sir, your most humble, but unknown servant,

A.Z.

P.S. Sir, your son is every day at Mr. Goodman's; and if you will take the trouble to set a watch over him, or send any person to enquire in the neighbourhood, it will be easy for you to satisfy yourself in the truth of what I have related.'

The consternation Miss Betsy was in on reading this cruel invective, was such as for some moments deprived her of the power of speaking. Mr. Saving could neither wonder at, nor blame, so just a resentment; yet, to mitigate it in part, he confessed to her a secret, which, till then, she had been wholly ignorant of.

'Though nothing, Madam,' said he, 'can excuse the crime she has been guilty of towards you, yet permit me to acquaint you, that the malice is chiefly levelled against me; and you are only wounded through my sides.'

'How can that be?' cried she. 'She does justice to your character, while she defames mine in the most barbarous manner.' – 'Mere artifice, Madam,' answered he, 'to work my father to her purpose, as I will presently convince you.'

He then told her, that before he ever had the honour of seeing her, he had treated Miss Flora with some gallantries; 'Which,' said he, 'her vanity made her take as the addresses of a serious passion, till those she found I afterwards made to you convinced her to the contrary. This Madam,' continued he, 'I am well assured of by her laying hold of every opportunity to reproach my inconstancy, as she has termed it. Finding how little I regarded all she said to me on that score, and still persisted in my devoirs to you, she doubtless had recourse to this most wicked strategem to cut me off from all hope, even though it had been in my power to have inclined you to favour my suit.'

Miss Betsy found this supposition so reasonable, and so conformable to the temper of Miss Flora, that she agreed with Mr. Saving in it. She did not now wonder at her wishing to be revenged on him; but could not brook with patience the method she took for being so: and said, that if Mr. Goodman did not do her justice on the author of so infamous a libel, she would immediately quit the house, and chuse another guardian.

'Hold, Madam,' said he; 'I must intreat you will give me leave to remind you of the consequences that may possibly attend your taking such a step. I own, with you, that treachery and calumny, such as hers, cannot be too severely exposed and punished: but, Madam, consider, that in order to do this, the accident which brought the letter into my possession, and the opportunity you have allowed me of presenting it to you, must be made known; the latter of which, you may be confident, she would not fail to make such representations of, as would not only hurt me, both with my father and my wife, but also furnish the malicious world, too apt to judge by appearances, with some pretence for casting a blemish on your own reputation.'

These remonstrances has some part of the effect they were

intended for on the mind of Miss Betsy; yet, having an aversion to dissimulation, and not knowing whether she could be able to conceal either her resentment, or the cause of it, she cried out hastily, without considering what she said, 'Why, then, did you let me know the injury done me, since it is improper for me to do any thing that might extort a reparation?'

'I could not, Madam,' replied he, 'behold you harbouring a snake in your bosom, without warning you of the sting. I am certain the easing you of my troublesome addresses has been no cause of mortification; and it was not that you should revenge what she has already done, but to put you upon your guard against any thing she may hereafter attempt to do, that I resolved to take the first opportunity of letting you see what she was capable of.'

Miss Betsy was by this time fully persuaded by his arguments; but could not forbear complaining of the difficulties it would be to her to look, or speak civilly, to sleep in the same bed, or behave in any respect as she had been accustomed, towards so unworthy a creature. She thanked him, however, for his good intentions to her; and, before they parted, promised to follow his advice, if it were only, as she said, from the consideration that to act in a different manner might be a prejudice to his domestick peace.

CHAPTER IV

Has very little in it, besides a collection of letters, some of which are much to the purpose, others less so

MISS Betsy, after having taken leave of Mr. Saving, went to the apartment of her friend; where she staid supper, not because she was at that time capable of being entertained either with the elegancies of the table, or the company, which happened to be pretty numerous, but merely to amuse and recover herself from the shock which the late discovery of Miss Flora's infidelity had given her.

On her coming home, she found the family not yet gone to bed, though it was then near one o'clock. Mr. Goodman was in high good-humour; and said to her, 'Miss Betsy, you have lost some hours of contentment by being abroad. Mr. Trueworth has been here, and did us the favour to pass the whole evening with us: but that is not all; three letters have been left for you. Two of them came by the post, and are, I know, by the superscriptions, from Mr. Francis Thoughtless and Lady Trusty; the other, I am informed, was left for you by a porter: but your curiosity must wait for these – I have still better news for you. Your eldest brother, Mr. Thomas Thoughtless, is coming home: I have received a letter from him, which tells me he has finished his tour, and we shall soon have him among us. See,' continued he, 'what he says.'

In speaking these words, he took the letter out of his pocket, and gave her to read. It contained these lines.

'To Mr. Goodman.

Worthy Sir,
I have been for upwards of a month detained on a party of pleasure,

at the chateau of Monsieur le Marquis de St. Amand; so was not so happy to receive yours of the seventh and twenty-second instant till yesterday, when I returned to Paris. I thank you for the long and particular account you give me of those affairs which are entrusted to your care. As to what you tell me concerning my brother Frank's having left the university, I am not sorry for it; nor can at all wonder, that a young fellow of his metal should be willing to exchange the hopes of a mitre for a truncheon. I have not heard from him since I left Florence; but believe it is owing to his want of knowing where to direct to me, my stages afterwards having been pretty uncertain: but finding by yours that he is now with Sir Ralph Trusty, shall accompany a letter I am obliged to send to that gentleman with one to him. I forgive my sister's not writing when you did, as you give me some hints she is likely soon to become a bride; a matter, I confess, sufficient to engross the whole thoughts of a young lady. Be pleased to assure her of my good wishes in this, and all other events. As you say she has two very advantageous offers, I flatter myself, through your good advice and inspection, she will take the best.

In my last, I mentioned somewhat of a design I had to pass a few months in the southern parts of this kingdom; but I have since changed my mind, and am determined on returning to my native country with all possible expedition. I believe you may expect me in three or four weeks at farthest. If, Sir, you could within that time hear of a house, agreeably situated, for my use, I should esteem it as a considerable addition to the favours our family, and myself in particular, have received from you since the death of our dear father. I should approve of St. James's Square, if rents are not too exorbitant; for, in that case, a house in any of the adjoining streets must content me. I would not willingly exceed an hundred, or an hundred and ten pounds, per annum; but would be as near the Park and Palace as possible.

I kiss Lady Mellasin's and her fair daughter's hands; and am, with very great respect, Sir, your most obliged, and most obedient servant,

T. THOUGHTLESS.'

Miss Betsy was very glad to find a brother, who had now been near five years abroad, was at last coming home, and much more so, that he intended to set up housekeeping in London; because, as doubting not he would be pleased to have her with him, she should have a fair pretence for quitting Mr. Goodman's house, and the society of Miss Flora, who had now rendered herself so irksome to her.

This did not hinder her, however, from reproaching Mr. Goodman for having mentioned to her brother any thing in relation to her lovers. 'You see, Sir,' said she, 'that the one of them has already abandoned me; and you will also see, in a short time, that the other will be little the better for his rival's resignation.'

To this Mr. Goodman pleasantly replied, that whatever she pretended at present, he believed better things from her good-sense, and the merits of Mr. Trueworth: to which Miss Betsy, unwilling to prolong the conversation, only told him he would find himself mistaken; and ran hastily up stairs, to examine the contents of those letters which, she had heard, lay on her toilette, ready for her perusal. The first she broke open was from Miss Forward; knowing it to be hers by the hand, and eager to see the event of a fate, which, by the history she had given her, had appeared so doubtful.

To Miss Betsy Thoughtless.

Dear Miss Betsy,
Since I saw you I have been driven to the last despair. The kind supply you left with me was quite exhausted; and I must infallibly have perished, through want of the common necessaries of life, and the cruel usage of my mercenary landlady, if my poor aunt in the country had not sent me a little present, which, for a small space of time, afforded relief; but accompanied with the melancholy account that my father was inexorable to her persuasions, would not hear of my return to L—e, and vowed never to see me more, or own me for his child. Soon was I again reduced to the lowest ebb of misery, had scarce sufficient to furnish the provisions of another day, and was even threatened to be turned out of doors by the inhuman hag; who, I very well remember, you said had her soul pictured in her countenance. But, my dear friend, in the midst of this distress, and when I thought no human help was near, my affairs took a most sudden and unexpected turn. Fortune threw in my way a kinsman of my mother's, whom I had never seen, or even heard of before: he compassionated my calamitous condition, removed me from that distant place, allows me a handsome maintenance, and has promised to continue it, till nature, and the endeavours of my good aunt, shall work my father to a more gentle temper.

I long to see you, and would have waited on you to return the money you were so kind to lend me; but knew not whether it were proper for me to do so, as I am wholly unacquainted with the family where you are. A visit from you would, therefore, now be doubly agreeable, as I am lodged in a house less unworthy to receive you, than that wretched one to which I before took the liberty to make you an invitation.

You may find me now at Mr. Screener's, the very next door to the Bedford Head, in Tavistock Street, in Covent Garden; where, I flatter myself, your good-nature will soon bring you to her, who is impatient for that happiness, and will always be, dear Miss Betsy, your very affectionate, and most humble servant,

A. FORWARD.

P.S. I had forgot to tell you that I am every Friday engaged at my above-mentioned good cousin's; and should never have forgiven myself, if, by this omission, you had lost your labour, and I the pleasure of your company.'

Miss Betsy, who little doubted the sincerity of this epistle, was very much touched with it, and resolved to comply with the invitation it contained in a short time. She now began to grow pretty sleepy; and would probably have deferred the persual of the other two letters till next morning, if Miss Flora had not come up to go to bed. To avoid, therefore, entering into any conversation with her, she took up the first that came to hand, and found the contents as follows.

'To Miss Betsy Thoughtless.

My dear sister,
As Mr. Goodman's endeavours for procuring me a commission, have not yet been attended with the desired success, I have been prevailed upon, by the solicitations of my friends, to give them my promise of passing some part of the hunting season in L—e; so shall not see you so soon as my last might make you expect. But I will not dissemble so far as to tell you, that to give you this information is the chief motive of my writing to you at present. No, my dear Betsy! it is one of much more consequence that now directs my pen. It is to give you such remonstrances, as, I fear, you stand but in too much need of; to beware how you disregard the smiles of fortune, and become the enemy of your own happiness. I received a letter yesterday from Mr. Trueworth; he complains sadly of my staying in the country, and seems to think my presence necessary for the advancement of his

courtship to you. I shall be always glad to be obliged by you on any score; but extremely sorry to find my interests with you, as a brother, should have more effect on you than your own reason, and the merits of one of the most deserving men on earth. I have no pretence to claim any authority over you by the ties of blood; but may certainly flatter myself with having some influence over you as a friend – enough, at least, I hope, to prevail on you to consider seriously on this matter; and am persuaded, that if you once bring yourself to do so, Mr. Trueworth will want no other advocate to plead his cause than your own understanding. I am willing to believe the assurance you gave me in your last, of your heart being free from any impressions yet endeavoured to be made upon it: did I think otherwise, I should be entirely silent on this occasion. I would be far, my dear sister, from opposing your inclinations; I would only wish to direct them where there is a prospect of the most felicity. Let me conjure you, therefore, to open your unprejudiced eyes, nor be wilfully blind to the good intended for you by your better stars. As you can never expect proposals of more advantage than those the love of Mr. Trueworth has inclined him to make you, I may be pretty confident, that you have not a friend in the world who would not highly condemn your want of giving due attention to it. Forgive the warmth with which I express myself, as it springs from the sincerest zeal for the establishment of your interest and happiness, than which nothing is more at the heart of him, who is, with the most tender regard, dear sister, your very affectionate friend, and brother,

F. THOUGHTLESS.'

While Miss Betsy was reading these letters, Miss Flora, who immediately followed her into the chamber, would fain have interrupted her by one impertinent question or another: but receiving no answer to any thing she said, gave over speaking, and went directly to bed; and Miss Betsy breaking open the third and last letter she had to peruse, found it contained as follows.

'To Miss Betsy Thoughtless.

My dear Miss Betsy,
I had wrote to you before, if I had not been prevented by an inflammation in my eyes, which, for some time past, has rendered my pen of no use to me; and I did not chuse to employ an amanuensis in what I have to say to you; but now take the first opportunity, being

somewhat better, of giving you that advice, which, it may be reasonably supposed, a person of your years and experience of the world may stand in need of; or, if not so, will be of some service in corroborating the good sentiments you are already inspired with.

It was with an extreme concern I heard what happened on your account at Oxford; and hope you have so well reflected on the danger you were in, the consequences that attended it, and how much worse might probably have ensued, as to be ever since more circumspect and careful with what company you trust yourself. I am far from reproaching you with the effects of an accident altogether unforeseen, and impossible to be even guessed at by you; but would beg you to keep always in your mind, that what has been, may, some time or other, be again; and that repeated inadvertencies may make Heaven weary of continuing it's protection. But, my dear Miss Betsy, it is not in my apprehensions of your own conduct, that the greatest part of my fear for you consists: the world, alas! and more particularly the place you live in, affords but too many wretches, of both sexes, who make it their business to entrap unwary innocence; and the most fair pretences are often the cover to the most foul designs! There are so many daily instances of the strictest caution not being always a sufficient security against the snares laid for our destruction, that I look on it as half a miracle, when a young woman, handsome, and exposed as you are, escapes unprejudiced, either in her virtue or reputation. Consider, my dear child, you who have no tender mother, whose precepts and example might keep you steady in the paths of prudence: no father, whose authority might awe the daring libertine from any injurious attack; and are but too much mistress of yourself. In fine, thus environed with temptations, I see no real defence for you but in a good husband. I have ever condemned rushing too early into marriage, and of risking, for the sake of one convenience, the want, perhaps, of a thousand others; but when an offer happens to be made, equally honourable and advantageous, and which affords an almost assured prospect of every thing necessary to compleat the happiness of that state, it cannot be too soon in life accepted. I hear, with pleasure, that an offer, such as I have been describing, is now presented to you; and it would give me an adequate concern to hear that you had rejected it. I need not tell you I mean Mr. Trueworth; for though there be many others who make their addresses to you on the same score, yet I am entirely ignorant of every thing relating to them; but I am well assured, not only by your brother's testimony, but by several gentlemen of this county, that in the fortune, person, and amiable qualities, of that gentleman, are comprized all that you either can or ought to wish in a husband. Trifle not, then, with a heart so deserving of you; scruple not to become a wife, when merit, such as his, invites, and so many reasons concur to urge you to consent. Believe me, there is more true felicity in the sincere and tender friendship of one man of honour, than in all the flattering pretensions of a thousand coxcombs. I have much more to say to you on this head; but shall defer, till you let me know with what kind of sentiments it is that you regard the gentleman I have been speaking of; which I beg you will do without disguise. Be satisfied that the secret of your real inclinations will be as safe in my keeping as your own; and that I am, wih the most perfect amity, my dear Miss Betsy, your constant friend, and humble servant,

M. TRUSTY.'

The time of night did not permit Miss Betsy to give these letters all the attention which the writers of them, doubtless, desired she should do; but she locked them carefully in her cabinet, resolving to consider the purport of them more seriously before she returned any answer.

CHAPTER V

•

Serves as a supplement to the former

THE next morning Miss Flora opened her lips almost as soon as she did her eyes, to talk to Miss Betsy on the design that had been agreed upon between them the day before, in relation to Mr. Staple. She told her she had employed her whole thoughts about it ever since, and that she had found out a way of introducing the discourse so as to give him no suspicion that she came from her; yet, at the same time, take away all his apprehensions of her being in love with Mr. Trueworth: and added, that she would go to his lodgings immediately after breakfast.

'Indeed,' replied Miss Betsy, sullenly, 'you shall do no such thing: I do not care what his apprehensions are, or any one else's. The men may all think and do as they will; I shall not fill my mind with any stuff about them.' – 'Hey-day!' cried Miss Flora, a good deal shocked at this sudden turn, 'what whim has got possession of you now?' – 'The whim you endeavoured to possess me with,' said Miss Betsy, scornfully, 'would have been a very ridiculous one, I am sure; but I have considered better on it, and despise such foolish fancies.' – 'Good-lack!' returned the other, 'you are grown wonderous wise, methinks; at least, imagine yourself so: but I shall go to Mr. Staple for all this. I cannot bear that he should think you are in love with Mr. Trueworth.' – 'I know no business,' said Miss Betsy, in a haughty tone, 'you have either with my love or hate: and I desire, for the future, you will forbear troubling your head in my affairs.'

Miss Flora then told her, that what she had offered was merely in regard to her reputation; and than ran over again all the arguments she had urged, in order to prevail on her to come into the measures she proposed: but whatever she said, either in the wheedling or remonstrating accent, was equally ineffectual; the other remained firm in her resolution, and behaved in a manner so different from what Miss Flora had ever seen her do before, that she knew not what to think of it. Having her own reasons, however, to bring her, if possible, to a less grave way of thinking, she omitted nothing in the power of artifice, that she imagined might be conducive to that end. All the time they were rising, all the time they were dressing, did she continue to labour on this score, without being able to obtain any other answers to what she said, than such as were peremptorily in the negative.

It is certain, that Miss Betsy was of so soft and tractable a disposition, that half the arguments Miss Flora had alledged, would, at another time, have won her to consent to things of much greater consequence than this appeared to be; but the discovery she had the day before made of her deceit, and the little good-will she had towards her, gave her sufficient reason to apprehend, that she had some farther designs than she pretended in this project, though of what nature it could be was not in her power to conceive. The thing in dispute seemed to her extremely trifling in itself; but the eagerness with which she was pressed to it by a person, of whose treachery she had so flagrant a proof, convinced her, that she ought not, on any account, to acquiesce.

Miss Flora, on the other hand, was disconcerted, beyond measure, at this unexpected change in Miss Betsy's humour; of which she was as little able to divine the cause, as the other was to guess the design she had formed: but, determining to accomplish her point, if possible, at any rate, she endeavoured all she could to dissemble her chagrin, and still affected a mighty regard for the honour of Miss Betsy, telling her she was resolved to serve her, whether she would or not; and that, how much soever she disapproved it, she should pursue her first intention, and undeceive Mr. Staple in the opinion he had of her being so silly as to fall in love with Mr. Trueworth.

Miss Betsy, on hearing this, and not doubting but she would do as she had said, turned towards her; and, looking full upon her, with a countenance composed enough, but which had yet in it somewhat between the ironical and severe, replied in these terms: 'Since you are so much bent,' said she, 'on making a visit to Mr. Staple, far be it from me, Miss Flora, to deprive that gentleman of the favour you intend him, provided you give me your promise, in the presence of Mr. Goodman, (and he will be your security for the performance of it) that you will mention neither my name, nor that of Mr. Trueworth; and, above all, that you will not pretend to have any knowledge of affairs you never have been trusted with.'

However inconsiderate or incautious Miss Betsy may appear to the reader, as to her conduct in general, it must be acknowleged, that at this time she shewed an uncommon presence of mind. This was, indeed, the only way to put a stop to, and quash at once, that scheme which her false friend had formed to do her a real prejudice under the pretence of serving her.

It is not in words to express the confusion Miss Flora was in, on hearing Miss Betsy speak in this manner. Bold as she was by nature, and habituated to repartee, she had not now the power of uttering one word. Innocence itself, when over-awed by authority, could not have stood more daunted and abashed; while the other, with a careless air, added, 'As soon as we go down stairs, I shall speak to Mr. Goodman about this matter.'

Whether Miss Betsy really intended to put this menace in execution, or not, is uncertain; for Miss Flora recovering her spirits, and her cunning, at the same time, affected to burst into a violent fit of laughter. 'Mr. Goodman!' said she; 'mighty pretty, indeed! You would trouble Mr. Goodman with the little impertinences we talk on between ourselves! But do so, if you think proper. I shall tell him the truth, that I made this proposal to you only to try you, and but acted the second part of what Mr. Chatfree had begun. You did not imagine, sure,' continued she, with a malicious sneer, 'that I loved you so well, that, for your sake, I would hazard my person and reputation, by going to see a young gay fellow at his own lodgings!'

'As for that,' cried Miss Betsy, with a look as contemptuous as she could possibly assume, 'I am equally well acquainted with the modesty and sincerity of Miss Flora, and know how to set a just value upon both.' In speaking these words, having now got on her cloaths, she flung out of the room without staying to hear what answer the other would have made.

After this, these two high spirits had little intercourse, never speaking to each other, but on such common affairs as were unavoidable between persons who lived in the same house, eat at the same table, and lay in the same bed. How Miss Flora employed her thoughts will very shortly be seen; but we must first examine what effects these late occurrences had on the mind of Miss Betsy.

Young as she was, she might be said to have seen a great deal of the world; and, as she had a fine understanding, and a very just notion of things, wanted only to reflect on the many follies and deceits which some of those who call themselves the beau monde are guilty of, to be enabled to despise them. The last letter she had received from Lady Trusty made a strong impression on her; and casting a retrospect on several past transactions she had been witness of, as well as those she had been concerned in herself, began to wonder at, and condemn the vanity of, being pleased with such shadowy things – such fleeting, unsubstantial delights, accompanied with noise and hurry in the possession, and attended with weariness and vexation of spirit. A multitude of admirers seemed now to her among this number: her soul confessed, that to encourage the addresses of a fop, was both dangerous and silly; and to flatter with vain hopes the sincere passion of a man of honour, was equally ungenerous and cruel.

These considerations were very favourable to Mr. Trueworth: she ran through every particular of that gentleman's character and behaviour, and could find nothing which could make her stand excused, even to herself, for continuing to treat him with the little seriousness she had hitherto done.

'What, then, shall I do with him?' said she to herself. 'Must I at once discard him – desire him to desist his visits, and tell him I am determined never to be his; or must I resolve to think of marrying him, and henceforward entertain him as the man who is really ordained to be one day my husband? I have, at present, rather an aversion, than an inclination to a wedded state; yet if my mind should alter on this point, where shall I find a partner so qualified to make me happy in it? But yet,' continued she, 'to become a matron at my years is what I cannot brook the thoughts of: if he loves me, he must wait; it will be sufficient to receive the addresses of no other; but, then, how shall I refuse those who shall make an offer of them, without giving the world room to believe I am pre-engaged?'

Thus did she argue with herself; the dilemma appeared hard to her: but what was the result of her reasoning, will best appear in the answer she sent to Lady Trusty's letter, which was in the following terms.

'To Lady Trusty.

Madam,

I received the honour of yours, and sincerely thank you for the good wishes and advice contained in it: be assured, Madam, I have a just sense of the value I ought to set upon them, and shall henceforth do the utmost in my power to deserve. I have, indeed, no parent to direct, and but few faithful friends to guide me through the perplexing labyrinth of life. I confess I have been too often misled by the prevalence of example, and my own idle caprice; it is, therefore, the highest charity to shew me to myself. I now see, and am ashamed of, the many inadvertencies I have been guilty of. The dangers which a young woman, like me, must necessarily be continually exposed to, appear to me, from what you say of them, in their proper colours, and convince me, that no person of understanding would condemn me, if, to avoid so many threatened ills, I flew to that asylum your ladyship has mentioned. I will own to you yet farther, Madam; that I am not insensible of the merits of Mr. Trueworth, nor of the advantages which would attend my acceptance of his proposals: but, I know not how it is, I cannot all at once bring myself into a liking of the marriage-state. Be assured of this, that I never yet have seen any man whom my heart has been more inclined to favour; and that, at present, I neither receive, nor desire the addresses of any other. There is no answering for events; but, in the way of thinking I now am, it seems not improbable, that I shall one day comply with what my friends take so much pains in persuading me to. In the mean time, I beseech you to believe I shall regulate my conduct so as to ease you of all those apprehensions you are so good to entertain on my account. I am, with a profound respect, Madam, your ladyship's most obliged and most devoted servant,

E. THOUGHTLESS.'

Miss Betsy also answered her brother's letter at the same time; but the purport of it being much the same with that she wrote to Lady Trusty, there is no occasion for inserting it.

CHAPTER VI

———————•———————

Seems to bring things pretty near a conclusion

MISS Betsy was now in as happy a disposition as any of her friends, or even Mr. Trueworth himself, could desire: she listened to the confirmations he was every day giving her of his passion, with the greatest affability, and much more seriousness and attention than she had been accustomed. The quarrel she had with Miss Flora making her willing to avoid her as much as possible, he was frequently alone with her whole hours together, and had all the opportunities he could wish of cultivating the esteem she made no scruple of confessing she had for him. As Mr. Staple was now gone out of town, pursuant to the resolution he had taken, and no other rival, at least none encouraged by Miss Betsy, had as yet seconded him, he had all the reason in the world to flatter himself, that the accomplishment of his wishes were not far distant.

Plays, operas, and masquerades, were now beginning to come into vogue; and he had the satisfaction to see his mistress refuse whatever tickets were offered her for those diversions, by any of the gentlemen who visited Lady Mellasin; and at the same time readily agreed to accompany him to those, or any other publick entertainments, whenever he requested that favour of her.

Miss Betsy's behaviour in this point, however, had more the air than the reality of kindness to Mr. Trueworth; for, in effect, it was not because she would not accept of tickets from any other person than himself, but because they were offered by gentlemen of Lady Mellasin's acquaintance; and, consequently, in respect to her, Miss Flora had the same invitation, with whom she was determined never more to be seen abroad.

This required some sort of contrivance, to be managed in such a fashion as to give no umbrage to Mr. Goodman or Lady Mellasin; for the former of which she had always a very great esteem, and did not chuse to afford the latter any cause of complaint against her, while she continued to live in the same house. The method she took, therefore, to avoid a thing so disagreeable to her, and at the same time to give no occasion of offence, was always to make choice of one diversion when she knew Miss Flora was pre-engaged to another.

To partake of these pleasures, which Mr. Trueworth, seeing into her temper, was almost every day presenting, she invited sometimes one lady, sometimes another, of those she conversed with; but the person who most frequently accompanied her, was Miss Mabel, a young lady, who lived in the next street, and whom she had been acquainted with ever since her coming to London, but had not been altogether so agreeable to her as she really deserved, and otherwise would have been, if Lady Mellasin and Miss Flora had not represented her as a prying, censorious, ill-natured creature; and, in fine, given her all the epithets which compose the character of a prude.

She was, indeed, both in principles and behaviour, the very reverse of Miss Flora; she was modest, without affectation; reserved, without austerity; chearful, without levity; compassionate and benevolent in her nature; and, to crown all, was perfectly sincere. Miss Betsy had never wanted penetration enough to see, and to admire the amiable qualities of this young lady, nor had been at all influenced by the character given of her by Lady Mellasin and Miss Flora, but being herself of too gay and volatile a temper, the more serious deportment of the other gave somewhat of a check to her's, and for that reason rendered her society less coveted by her. The letter of Lady Trusty, however, joined to the late accidents which had happened, having now given her a turn of mind vastly different from what it had been a very little time before, made her now prefer the conversation of Miss Mabel to most others of her acquaintance.

This young lady having been often in Mr. Trueworth's company, wtih Miss Betsy, saw enough into him to be assured the passion he professed for her was perfectly honourable and sincere; and as she had a real affection for her fair friend, and thought it a match greatly to her advantage, was perpetually remonstrating to her, that she could not treat with too much complaisance a lover so every way deserving of her.

It is certain, that what she said on this score had some weight with Miss Betsy: Mr. Goodman, also, was every day admonishing her in behalf of Mr. Trueworth, as he thought it his duty so to do, both as her guardian and her friend. In fine, never was a heart more beset, more forced, as it were, into tender sentiments than that of this young lady; first, by the merits and assiduities of the passionate invader, and, next, by the persuasion of all those who she had any reaosn to believe had her interest in view, and wished to see her happiness established.

Enemy as she was, by nature, to serious reflection, on any account, much more on that of marriage, everything now contributed to compel her to it; she could not avoid seeing and confessing within herself, that if ever she became a wife, the title could not be attended with more felicity than when conferred on her by a person of Mr. Trueworth's fortune, character, and disposition.

She was one day alone, and in a very considerative mood, when a letter was brought to her, which she was told came by the penny-post: as she was not accustomed to receive any by that carriage, it pretty much surprized her; but much more so when, having hastily opened it, she found the contents as follows.

'To Miss Betsy Thoughtless.

Madam,
It is with an inexpressible concern, that I relate to you a thing which I am but too sensible will give you some disquiet, nor could I have prevailed with myself on any terms to have done it, were it not to preserve you from falling into much greater affliction than the discovery I am about to make can possibly inflict: but, not to keep you in suspense, you are courted by a gentleman whose name is Trueworth; he is recommended by your brother, who, alas! knows him much less than he imagines. He has, indeed, a large estate; and does not want accomplishments to endear him to the fair-sex: I wish he had as much intrinsick honour and sincerity to deserve, as he has personal endowments to acquire, the favours so lavishly bestowed on him. I hope, however, you have not been so much deceived by the innocence of your own heart, and the fancied integrity of his, as to be so distractedly in love with him as he has the vanity to boast, and your companion and supposed friend, Miss Mabel, reports you are: if his designs upon you are such as they ought to be, he is at least ashamed

to confess they are so; and the lady I just mentioned, whispers it in all companies, that a marriage with you is of all things in the world the farthest from his thoughts. He plainly says, that he but trifles with you, till your brothers come to town, and will then find some pretence to break entirely with you – perhaps, on the score of fortune: but of that I am not positive; I only repeat some part of those unhandsome expressions his unworthy tongue has uttered.

But, Madam, as I have given you this intelligence, so I think it my duty to offer you some advice for your behaviour in so nice and critical a juncture. As he threatens to abandon you on the arrival of your brothers, I should think, that if you forbid him your presence till that time, it would not only be a sure touchstone of his affection, but also be a means of clearing your reputation from those blemishes it has received on his account. After what I have said, I believe it would be needless to add, that the less freely you converse with Miss Mabel, the less you will suffer, both in the judgment of the world and your own future peace of mind.

Slight not this counsel because given behind the curtain; but be assured it comes from one who is, with the sincerest attachment, Madam, your most humble, though concealed servant.'

If Miss Betsy had received this letter a very small time before she did, it might probably have wrought on her all the effect it was intended for; but she had scarce read it half through before the lucky discovery of Miss Flora's baseness, seasonably made to her by Mr. Saving, came fresh into her mind; and she was at no loss to guess at the malicious purpose, and the author of it, though wrote in a hand altogether a stranger to her.

She doubted not but it was a trick of Miss Flora's, to cause a separation between her and Mr. Trueworth; but the motives which had instigated her to do this, were not in her power to conceive.

'Revenge for her disappointed expectations,' said she to herself, 'might make her take the steps she did, on Mr. Saving's account: but what has Mr. Trueworth done to her? He never pretended to love her; he neither flattered nor deceived her vanity; it must be, therefore, only a wicked propensity, an envious, unsocial disposition, a love of mischief implanted in her nature, and uncorrected by reason or principle, that has induced her to be guilty of this poor, low, enervate spite: but I am resolved to mortify it.'

She was not long considering in what manner she should proceed to do as she had said; and I believe the reader will acknowledge she hit upon one as effectual for that end as could have been contrived.

She appeared extremely gay the whole time of dinner; and, as soon as it was over, 'I will present you with a dessert, Sir,' said she to Mr. Goodman; 'I will shew you what pains has been taken to break off my acquaintance with Mr. Trueworth, by some wretch, who either envies me the honour of his affections, or him the place they imagine he has in mine: but, I beseech you, read it,' continued she – 'and I will appeal to you, Lady Mellasin – and Miss Flora – if ever there was a more stupid plot.'

'Stupid enough, indeed!' cried the honest merchant, as soon as he had done reading; 'but it is yet more base. I am glad, however,' continued he, 'to find your good sense prevents you from being imposed upon by such artifices.' – 'This is so shallow a one,' answered she, 'that a very small share of understanding might serve to defend any one from being deceived by it. I pity the weakness, while I despise the baseness, of such mean incendiaries: Mr. Trueworth, however, will fare the better for this attempt against him; I will now make no scruple of prefering him to all mankind besides; and, perhaps, when my brothers arrive, shall consent to every thing he desires.'

Lady Mellasin could not help applauding the spirit and resolution she shewed on this occasion, and Mr. Goodman was quite charmed with it; and both of them joined in the severest exclamations against the folly and wickedness of the letter-writer: but Miss Flora said little; and, as soon as she could quit the table with decency, went up into her chamber, saying, she had a piece of work in her hand which she was in haste to finish.

If Miss Betsy had wanted any confirmation of the truth of her suspicions, the looks of Miss Flora, during this whole discourse, would have removed all doubt in her; and the opportunity of venting the spleen she had so justly conceived against her, without seeming to do so, gave her a most exquisite satisfaction.

CHAPTER VII

●

Is the better for being short

MISS Flora retired to her chamber, indeed, not to employ herself in the manner she pretended, but to give a loose to passions more inordinate and outrageous than it would naturally be believed could have taken possession of so young a heart.

But it is now high time to let the reader see into the secret springs which set her wicked wit in motion, and induced her to act in the manner she had done.

Through the whole course of the preceding pages, many hints have been given, that the inclinations of this yung lady were far from being unblameable; and it will not seem strange, that a person of the disposition she has all along testified, should envy and malign those charms she every day saw so much extolled, and preferred above her own; but we do not ordinarily find one, who, all gay and free like her, and who various times, and for various objects, had experienced those emotions which we call love, should all at once be inspired with a passion no less serious than it was violent, for a person who never made the least addresses to her on that account.

Yet so in effect it was: Mr. Trueworth had been but a very few times in her company, before she began to entertain desires for the lover of her fair friend. Whenever she had an opportunity of speaking to him alone, she made him many advances, which he either did not, or would not, interpret in the sense she meant them. This coldness, instead of abating, did but the more inflame her wishes; and, looking on the passion he had for Miss Betsy, as the only impediment to the gratification of her inclinations, she cursed his constancy, and the beauties which excited it. So true is that observation of Mr. Dryden –

'Love various minds does variously inspire;
He stirs in gentle natures gentle fire,
Like that of incense on the altar laid;
But raging flames tempestuous souls invade.
A fire which every windy passion blows;
With pride it mounts, and with revenge it glows.'

Miss Flora was not of a temper, either to bear the pangs of hopeless love in silent grief, or to give way too readily to despair. In spite of the indifference she found herself treated with by Mr. Trueworth, she was not without hope, that if she could by any means occasion a disunion between him and Miss Betsy, he would then be brought to cast his eyes on her, and return her flame with some degree of ardency.

It was for this end she had taken so much pains in endeavouring to persuade Miss Betsy either to write, or suffer her to go, to Mr. Staple, in order, as she pretended, to undeceive that gentleman in his opinion, that she was in love with Mr. Trueworth; but her intentions, in reality, were to make him believe that he himself was the favoured person, and had much the advantage over his rival in the affections of his mistress. This she doubted not, would make him quit his resolution of going into the country, and encourage him to renew his courtship with the same fervency as ever. The pride she knew Miss Betsy took in a multiplicity of lovers, and the equality with which she had carried herself between him and Mr. Trueworth, and which probably she would continue, seemed to afford her a fair prospect of giving Mr. Trueworth so much cause of discontent, as to make him break off with a woman who, after what had passed, made no distinction between him and the person he had twice vanquished in the field. She knew it would, at least, create a great deal of perplexity among them, and delay, if not totally prevent, the completion of what she so much dreaded.

But this scheme being rendered abortive, by the seasonable discovery Miss Betsy had made of her perfidiousness, she set her wits to work for some other new invention; and, believing that Miss Betsy's pride would immediately take fire on the least suspicion of any insult being offered, either to her beauty or reputation, procured an agent to write the above inserted letter, the effect of which has already been shewn.

This disappointment was the more grievous to her, as she had so little expected it: she broke the sticks of her fan, tore every thing came in her way, flew about the room like a princess in a tragedy; wanting the means of venting the rage she was possessed of in great things, she exercised it in small. A fine petticoat of Miss Betsy's happening to hang on the back of a chair, she threw a standish of ink upon it, as if by accident; and it was no breach of charity to believe, would have served the owner in a much worse manner, if her power had been equal to her will, and she could have done it without danger to herself.

To add to the fury and distraction of her mind, continuing still in her chamber, and happening to be pretty near the window, she saw Miss Betsy, Miss Mabel, and Mr. Trueworth, pass by in a landau, that gentleman having, it seems, invited these ladies on a party of pleasure: 'You shall not long enjoy this satisfaction,' cried she to herself, 'if it be in human wit to separate you!' But at this sight, the turbulent passions of her soul becoming more outrageous, 'O may the machine that conveys you be thrown from off it's wheels!' pursued she. 'May the wine you drink be poisoned! May the first morsel you attempt to swallow, mistake it's way, and choak you in the passage!'

Thus did she rave, not like one possessed with seven, but seven thousand fiends; and had perhaps remained in this wild way till her brain had been absolutely turned, if Lady Mellasin, having a great deal of company, had not positively commanded her to come down, after having sent several times in more mild terms to let her know what friends were there.

It was some days before the unhappy, and more wicked, Miss Flora could recollect her scattered senses enough for the contrivance of any farther mischief: but those evil spirits, to which she had yielded but too much the mastery of her heart, and all it's faculties, at length inspired her with, and enabled her in the execution of, a design of the most barbarous kind, and which for a time she saw had success even beyond her most sanguine expectations.

But while she was ruminating on projects, which had neither virtue nor generosity for their patrons, Miss Betsy passed her days in that chearfulness which is the constant companion of uncorrupted innocence, and a mind uninfluenced by any tempestuous passions; but as it is natural, even to the sweetest tempers, to take pleasure in the mortification of those who have endeavoured to injure us without cause given on our parts, she could not forbear being highly diverted to see the pains Miss Flora took to conceal the inward disturbance of her soul: the awkward excuses she made for the damage done her petticoat, gave her more satisfaction than she should have felt vexation for the spoiling the best thing she had in the world.

Miss Mabel, to whom Miss Betsy had imparted the whole of this affair, was not at all surprized at that part of the letter which related to herself, as she had often been informed, by several of her acquaintance, of the character given of her by that malicious girl; but neither of these young ladies could be able to imagine, as they suspected not her passion for Mr. Trueworth, from what source this pretended enmity to him was derived.

It would certainly have greatly contributed to the happiness of that gentleman, to have known in what manner his mistress had resented the injustice had been done him; but Miss Betsy forbore to let him into the secret, as being already sufficiently convinced of the sincerity of his affection, and would not put him to the trouble of giving her new proofs of it, by shewing him the ridiculous accusation anonymously formed against him.

CHAPTER VIII

Contains some incidents which will be found equally interesting and entertaining, or the author is very much mistaken

MR. Trueworth had all the reason imaginable, from the whole deportment of Miss Betsy towards him, to believe that there wanted little more for the conclusion of his marriage with her than the arrival of her two brothers; she had often told him, whenever he pressed her on that score, that she would give no definitive answer, till she had received the advice and approbation of the elder Mr. Thoughtless.

That gentleman was now expected in a few days, and Mr. Francis Thoughtless having intelligence of his being on his return, was also preparing to leave L—e, in order to meet him on his first arrival in London; but, during this short space of time, some events fell out, which put a great damp on the gaiety of those, who had with so much impatience wished for their approach.

Mr. Trueworth had an aunt, who, besides being the nearest relation he had living, and the only one in London, was extremely respected by him, on account of her great prudence, exemplary virtue, and the tender affection she had always testified for him. This good lady thought herself bound by duty, as she was led by love, to make a thorough enquiry into the character of the young person her nephew was about to marry; she was acquainted with many who had been in company with Miss Betsy, and were witnesses of her behaviour; she asked the opinion of those among them, whom she looked upon as the most candid, concerning the match now on the carpet, and was extremely troubled to find their answers were no way conformable to the idea Mr. Trueworth had endeavoured to inspire her with of his mistress's perfections: they all, indeed, agreed that she was handsome, well-shaped, genteel, had a good deal of wit, vivacity, and good-humour; but shook their heads when any of those requisites to make the married state agreeable were mentioned.

Poor Miss Betsy, as the reader has had but too much opportunities to observe, was far from setting forth to any advantage the real good qualities she was possessed of: on the contrary, the levity of her conduct rather disfigured the native innocence of her mind, and the purity of her intentions; so that, according to the poet –

'All saw her spots, but few her brightness took.'

The old lady not being able to hear any thing concerning her intended niece, but what was greatly to her dissatisfaction, was continually remonstrating to Mr. Trueworth, that the want of solidity in a wife was one of the worst misfortunes that could attend a marriage-state; that the external beauties of the person could not atone for the internal defects of the mind; that a too great gaiety *du cœur*, frequently led women into errors without their designing to be guilty of them; and conjured him to consider well before the irrevocable words, 'I take you for better and for worse,' were passed, how ill it would suit, either with his honour, or his peace of mind, if she whom he now wished to make his partner for life should, after she became so, behave in the same manner she did now.

Mr. Trueworth listened to what she said, wth all the attention she could desire; but was too passionately in love to be much influenced by it: not that he did not see there were some mistakes in the conduct of Miss Betsy, which he could wish reformed, yet he could not look upon them as so dangerous to her virtue and reputation, and therefore omitted no arguments, which he thought might justify his choice, and clear the accused fair one from all blame, in the eyes of a person whose approbation he was very desirous of obtaining.

The warmth with which he spoke, convinced his aunt, that to oppose his inclinations in this point was only warring with the winds; she desisted from speaking any more against the marriage, and contented herself with telling him, that since he was bent on making Miss Betsy his wife, she should be glad if, at least, he would remove her into the country, and prevent her returning to this town as long as possible.

This last council had a great deal of weight with Mr. Trueworth; he had often wished in his heart, when seeing her, as he often did, encompassed wth a crowd of such whom his good understanding made him despise, that if ever he became her husband, it might be in his power to prevail on her to break off acquaintance with the greatest part of those she at present conversed with; and now being admitted to entertain her with more freedom and seriousness than ever, he resolved to sound her sentiments on that score, and try to discover how far she could relish the retirements of a country life.

Accordingly, the next visit he made to her, he began to represent, in the most pathetick terms he was able, the true felicity that two people, who loved each other, might enjoy when remote from the noise and interruption of a throng of giddy visitors. 'The deity of soft desires,' said he, 'flies the confused glare of pomp and publick shews; it is in the shady-bowers, or on the banks of a sweet purling stream, he spreads his downy wings, and wafts ten thousand nameless pleasures on the fond, the innocent, and the happy pair.'

He was going on, but she interrupted him with a loud laugh; 'Hold, hold!' cried she, 'was there ever such a romantick description? I wonder how such silly ideas come into your head?' "Shady bowers! and purling streams!" Heavens, how insipid! Well,' continued she, 'you may be the Strephon of the woods, if you think fit; but I shall never envy the happiness of the Chloe that accompanies you in these fine recesses. What, to be cooped up like a tame dove, only to coo, and bill, and breed? O it would be a delicious life indeed!'

Mr. Trueworth now perceived, to his no small vexation, the late seriousness he had observed in Miss Betsy, and which had given him so much satisfaction, was no more than a short-lived interval, a sudden start of reason and recollection, soon dissipated, and that her temper, in reality, was still as light, as wild, and as inconsiderate as ever. The ridicule with which she treated what he said, did not, however, hinder him from proceeding in the praise of a country life; but happening to say, that innocence could no where else be so secure, she presently took up the word and with a disdainful air replied, that innocence in any one but an idiot, might be secure in any place; to which he retorted, that reason was at some times absent, even in those who had the greatest share of it at others.

Many smart repartees passed between them on this subject, in most of which Miss Betsy had the better; but Mr. Trueworth, not willing to give up the point, reminded her that Solomon, the most luxuriant, and withal the wisest of men, pronounced, that all the gaieties and magnificence of the earth were vanity and vexation of spirit. 'He did so,' replied she, with a scornful smile; 'but it was not till he had enjoyed them all, and was grown past the power of enjoying yet farther: when I am so, it is possible I may say the same.'

Mr. Trueworth, finding she was pretty much stung at some things he had said, and conscious that in his discourse he had in some measure forgot the respect due from a lover to his mistress, would not pursue the topick any farther; but, as artfully as he could, turned the conversation on things more agreable to Miss Betsy's way of thinking: he could not, however, after they had parted, forbear ruminating on the contempt she had shewn of a country life, and was not so easy as the submissiveness of his passion made him affect to be, on taking leave. This was, however, a matter of light moment to him, when compared with what soon after ensued.

I believe, that from the last letter of Miss Forward to Miss Betsy, the reader may suspect it was not by a kinsman she was maintained: but it is proper to be more particular on that affair, and shew how that unfortunate creature, finding herself utterly discarded by her father, and abandoned to the utmost distresses, accepted the offer made her by a rich Jew merchant, of five guineas a week to be his mistress.

But, as few woman who have once lost the sense of honour, ever recover it again, but, on the contrary, endeavour to lose all sense of shame also, devote themselves to vice, and act whatever interest or inclination prompts them to; Miss Forward could not content herself with the embraces nor allowances of her keeper, but received both the presents and caresses of as many as she had charms to attract.

Sir Bazil Loveit was a great favourite with her; and if, among such a plurality, one might be said to have the preference, it was he: this young baronet had been intimately acquainted with Mr. Trueworth abroad; they had travelled together through the greatest part of Italy, and had been separated only by Mr. Trueworth's being called home on account of some family affairs. Sir Bazil being but lately arrived, they had not seen each other since; till, meeting by accident in a coffee-house, they renewed their former friendship. After the usual compliments, Mr. Trueworth proposed passing the evening together; to which Sir Bazil replied, that he should be glad of the opportunity, but was engaged to sup with a lady: 'But,' said he, after a pause, 'it is where I can be free, and you shall go wih me.' To which the other having consented, Sir Bazil told him, as they were going towards the house, that there would be no occasion to use much ceremony; for it was only to a lady of pleasure he was conducting him: but added, that she was a fine girl, seemed to have been well brought up, had been but lately come upon the town, and behaved with more modesty than most of her profession.

Mr. Trueworth had never any great relish for the conversation of these sort of women; much less now, when his whole heart was taken up with an honest passion for a person who, in spite of the little errors of her conduct, he thought deserving of his affections: yet, as he had given his promise, he imagined that to go back on it would be too precise, and subject him to the raillery of his less scrupulous friend.

Miss Forward (for it was she to whom this visit was made) received them in a manner which justified the character Sir Bazil had given of her. There was, however, a certain air of libertinism, both in her looks and gestures, which would have convinced Mr. Trueworth, if he had not been told before, that she was one of those unhappy creatures, who make traffick of their beauty. The gentlemen had not been there above a quarter of an hour, before a maid-servant came into the room, and told Miss Forward, that a young lady, whose said her name was Thoughtless, was at the door in a chair, and desired to see her: 'O my dear Miss Betsy Thoughtless!' cried she, 'desire her to walk up immediately.' – 'This is lucky,' said Sir Bazil, 'I wanted a companion for my friend; now each man will have his bird.' – 'Hush,' cried Miss Forward, 'I can assure you she is virtuous; take care what you say.'

Mr. Trueworth was so much alarmed at hearing the name of Miss Betsy, that, being retired to a window in order to recover himself from the confusion, he heard not what Miss Forward had said to Sir Bazil: Miss Betsy presently entering the room, Miss Forward ran to embrace her, saying, 'My dear Miss Betsy, how glad I am to see you!' To which the other returned, 'My dear Miss Forward, how ashamed am I to have been so long absent! but one foolish thing or other has still prevented me coming.'

Sir Bazil then saluted her with a great deal of politeness, though with less respect than doubtless he would have done, had he seen her in any other place. Mr. Trueworth, who by this time had resolved in what manner he should act, now turned, and advanced towards the company; Miss Betsy, on seeing him, cried out in some surprize, 'Mr. Trueworth! Good God! who thought of finding you here?' – 'You did not, Madam, I dare answer,' replied he, with a very grave air, 'and I as little expected the honour of meeting you here.' – 'O you are acquainted, then,' said Sir Bazil, laughing; 'this is merry enough; I find we are all right!'

Mr. Trueworth made no direct answer to this; but endeavoured to assume a gaiety conformable to that of the company he was in: after some little time being passed in discoursing on ordinary affairs, Miss Forward took Miss Betsy into the next room to return the money she had been so kind to lend her at Mrs. Nightshade's; and told her, she had much to say to her, but could not be so rude to leave the gentlemen for any long time. While they were absent, which indeed was not above half a minute, 'This is a delicious girl,' said Sir Bazil to Mr. Trueworth, 'i'faith, Charles, you will have the best of the market tonight.' What reply Mr. Trueworth would have made is uncertain; the ladies returned that instant, and the conversation became extremely sprightly, though, on Sir Bazil's part, sometimes interspersed with expressions not altogether consistent with that decorum he would have observed towards women of reputation.

Miss Betsy, far from thinking any ill herself, took every thing as well meant, and replied to whatever was uttered by this gay young gentleman, with a freedom which, to those who knew her not perfectly, might justly render liable to censure. Mr. Trueworth would fain have taken some share, if possible, in this conversation, in order to conceal the perplexity of his thoughts, but all his endeavours were ineffectual; and though his words were sometimes gay, the tone with which he spoke them plainly shewed, that his heart was very far from corresponding with his expressions.

Sir Bazil having ordered a handsome supper, Miss Betsy staid till it was over, and then rose up, and took her leave; saying, she was obliged to go home and write some letters. As none of them had any equipage there, a hackney-coach was ordered to be called; and Mr. Trueworth offering to accompany her, Sir Bazil, on waiting on them down stairs, said to him some merry things on the occasion; which, though Miss Betsy did not comprehend, her lover understood the meaning of but too well for his peace of mind.

CHAPTER IX

———————•———————

Is yet more interesting than the former

ANY one may judge what a heart, possessed of so sincere and honourable a flame as that of Mr. Trueworth's, must feel, to see the beloved object so intimate with a common prostitute: it shall suffice, therefore, to say, that his anxieties were such as prevented him from being able to recover himself enough to speak to Miss Betsy on that subject as he would do. He forbore mentioning it at all, and said very little to her on any other, while they were in the coach: and, having seen her safe into Mr. Goodman's house, took his leave, and went home; where he passed a night of more vexation than he ever had before experienced.

Fain would he have found some excuse for Miss Betsy's conduct in this point; fain would he have believed her as innocent as she was lovely; but could not tell how to conceive there was a possibility for true virtue to take delight in the company of vice: but, were there even such a thing in nature, the shew of encouraging an infamous action he knew not how to brook in a woman he intended to make his wife.

He now acknowledged the justice of his aunt's remonstrances; and, by what the levity of Miss Betsy made him at present endure, forsaw what his honour and peace of mind must hereafter continually endure if he should once become a husband. Never were thoughts so divided, so fluctuating, as his! His good understanding, and jealousy of honour, convinced him there could be no lasting happiness with a person of Miss Betsy's temper; but then the passion he had for her, flattered him with the hopes, that as all the faults she was guilty of, sprung rather from want of consideration than design, she might be reasoned out of them, when once he had gained so far upon her affections, as to find he might take the liberty of painting them to her in their proper colours.

He often asked himself the question, whether he could be able to break with her or not; and finding, by the pangs which the very idea of an utter separation inflicted on him, that he could not, had no other measures to take than to submit with patience – to appear satisfied with every thing that pleased her – and to contrive all the methods he could, without her perceiving he did so, of stealing, by gentle degrees, into her mind, a disrelish of such things as were unbecoming in her.

He had but just rose from a bed which that night had afforded him but little repose; when he was told Sir Bazil Loveit, to whom he had given his directions the day before, was come to wait upon him. Mr. Trueworth was very glad ot if, being impatient to undeceive him in the opinion he found he had entertained of Miss Betsy. They had not been three minutes together before the other gave him an opportunity, by some facetious interrogatories concerning the transactions of the past night; and, among the rest, after looking round the room, asked how he had disposed of his pretty Betsy. To all which Mr. Trueworth replied, with a very serious air, 'Sir Bazil, though I must own there are many appearances to justify your mistake, yet I hope my word and honour will out-balance them. I do assure you, Sir, that lady, whom you think and speak so lightly of, is a woman of fortune, family, and reputation.' – 'I am sorry, then,' said Sir Bazil, very much surprized, 'I treated her in the manner I did. My Nancy, indeed,' continued he, meaning Miss Forward, 'told me she was virtuous, but I did not regard what she said on that score; I know it is a trick among them to set off one another, to draw in us men. But, pr'ythee, dear Charles, are you in earnest?' Mr. Trueworth, then, after having made a second asseveration that he was sincere in what he said, proceeded to give him some account of Miss Betsy's family, circumstances, and manner of life; adding, that nothing could be more surprizing to him, than to have met her in that place. 'But,' said he, 'she must certainly be unacquainted with the character of the woman she came to visit.'

'Such a thing might possibly happen,' replied Sir Bazil, 'and I think you would do well to give her a hint of it.' – 'Doubtless,' cried the other; 'I am doubly bound to do so; first, by my own honour; and, next, by the friendship I have for some of her kindred.' No farther discourse passed between them on this score; and the remaining time they were together being taken up on matters altogether foreign to the business of this history, there is no occasion for making any mention of it.

Sir Bazil staid so long, that when he had taken his leave, it was too late for Mr. Trueworth to make a morning visit to Miss Betsy, as he intended to have done, so was obliged to defer it till the afternoon; though, since his first acquaintance with her, he had never felt more impatience to see her.

As he had much in his head to say to her on the subject of the preceding day, he went as soon as he thought dinner was entirely over at Mr. Goodman's, in order to have an opportunity of talking with her before any other company came in. She was then in her chamber, dressing; but he waited not long before she came down, and appeared more lovely and dazzling in his eyes than ever. This happened to be the first day of her putting on a very rich and extremely well-fancied gown; and, either because it was more becoming than any of those he had seen her in before, or because of the pleasure ladies of her age and humour generally feel on such occasions, a more than usual brightness shone in her eyes, and was diffused through all her air; and, after having made her some compliments on the elegance of her taste in dress, 'I suppose, Madam,' said he, 'thus set forth, and equipped for conquest, you do not mean to stay at home this evening?' – 'No, indeed,' replied she; 'I am told there is a new tragedy to be acted to-night at Lincoln's Inn Fields, and I would not for the world miss the first night of a new play.'

On this, Mr. Trueworth asked if he might have leave to wait upon her there. 'With all my heart,' answered she. 'None of the gentlemen of my acquaintance know any thing of my going, so could not offer to gallant me; and there is only one lady goes with me.' – 'Miss Mabel, I guess?' cried Mr. Trueworth. 'No,' answered Miss Betsy; 'she is engaged to the other house tonight; so I sent to desire the favour of that lady you saw me with last night to give me her company.'

'You will have more, if you have hers, I doubt not,' said he: 'but sure, Madam, you cannot think of being seen with a woman of her fame, in a place so publick as the play-house!' Miss Betsy was astonished to hear him speak in this manner; and demanded of him, in somewhat of a haughty tone, what it was he meant. 'First, Madam,' resumed Mr. Trueworth, 'give me leave to ask you how long since, and by what accident, your intimacy with this woman commenced?' – 'Though your interrogatories,' replied she, 'are made in such a manner as might well excuse me from answering them, yet, for once, I may give you the satisfaction you desire. Miss Forward and I were together at the boarding-school; we mutually took a liking to each other, (I believe from a parity of humours and inclinations;) and, since her coming to London, have renewed that friendship we began in our more tender years.'

'Friendships begun in childhood, Madam,' answered he, with a very grave air, 'ought to be continued or broke off, according as the parties persevere in innocence, or degenerate into vice and infamy. This caution ought to be more peculiarly observed in persons of your sex, as reputation in you, once lost, is never to be retrieved. Remember, Madam, what your favourite author, Mr. Rowe, says on this occasion –

> "In vain with tears her loss she may deplore;
> In vain look back to what she was before;
> She sets, like stars that fall, to rise no more." '

Miss Betsy was so piqued at these remonstrances, that she had scarce patience to contain herself till he had given over speaking. 'Good lack!' cried she, 'how sententious you are grown! But, I hope, you have not the insolence to imagine I am guilty of any thing that might justly call my reputation in question?' – 'No, Madam,' replied he; 'far be it from me to suspect you of any thoughts but such as might become the purity of angels. But the more bright you are, the more we should lament to see the native lustre of your mind clouded and blemished by the faults of others. Permit me, Madam, to tell you, that to continue an intimacy with a woman of Miss Forward's character, must infallibly draw you into conveniences, which you want but to foresee to tremble at.'

'If you have the affection for me you pretend,' said she, haughtily, 'and could see the aversion I have to a censorious temper, it is yourself would have cause to tremble. I love Miss Forward, and neither know, nor will believe, any ill of her. Whenever I am convinced that she is unworthy my of friendship, it must be by her own actions, not by the report of others. Therefore, Mr. Trueworth, if you desire to continue on good terms with me, you must forbear to interfere with what company I keep, nor pretend to prescribe rules for my conduct, at least, till you have more right to do so.'

'I shall never, Madam, presume to prescribe,' replied he; 'but shall always think it my duty to advise you in a matter which so nearly concerns not only yourself, but all who have any relation to you, either by blood or affection.' Though these words, as well as all he had said on this occasion, were uttered in the most respectful accents, yet Miss Betsy, who was not able to imagine the least contradiction suited with the character of a lover, was offended beyond all measure. She frowned – she rose hastily from her chair – walked about the room in a disordered motion – told him, the nature of the acquaintance between them did not authorize the liberties he took – that she would not bear it – and desired that he would either leave her, or change the conversation to somewhat more agreeable.

Mr. Trueworth, who as yet had said little, in comparison with what he intended to say on this subject, was so much shocked at the impossibility he found of engaging her attention, that for some time he was incapable of speaking one word. During this pause, a servant presented a letter to Miss Betsy. 'O!' cried she, as soon as she looked on the superscription, 'it is from my dear Miss Forward. I hope nothing has happened to prevent her going with me to the play.' She made this exclamation merely to vex Mr. Trueworth; and, for that purpose also read the billet loud enough for him to hear what it contained, which was as follows.

'To Miss Betsy Thoughtless.

My dear Miss Betsy,
Since I received your message, I got a person to secure places for us in the box; so we need not go till six o'clock: but I am quite alone; and, if you are disengaged, should be glad you would come directly to her, who is ever, with the most perfect amity, my dear Miss Betsy, your very much obliged, and humble servant,

A. FORWARD.'

'Bid the messenger,' said Miss Betsy to the servant, 'tell the lady that I will wait upon her this moment; and then call me a chair. – I must comply with the summons I have just received,' said she, turning to Mr. Trueworth; 'so you must excuse my leaving you; for I will not strain your complaisance to accompany me where I am going: but shall be glad to see you when you are in a better humour.'

'I am ready, Madam, to attend you any where,' said Mr.

Trueworth, 'even to Miss Forward's; and will pass the whole evening with you, if you please, in her apartment: but, I beseech you, do not think of going to the play with a woman of her class; do not expose yourself in a place where so many eyes will be upon you. Reflect, for Heaven's sake, what your modesty will suffer, in seeing yourself gazed and pointed at by those to whom she sells her favours! and reflect yet farther, what they will judge of you!' – 'You grow scurrilous, Sir!' cried she, ready to burst with passion; 'I will hear no more.' Then, running to the door, asked if the chair was come; and, being told it was, 'Farewel, Sir,' said she, as she was going into it; 'when I want a spy to inspect, or a governor to direct my actions, the choice may perhaps fall on you.'

Mr. Trueworth, who, at this treatment, was not quite master of himself, retorted with some warmth, and loud enough to be heard by her, as the chairmen were carrying her to the steps of the house, 'The choice, Madam, perhaps, may not be yours to make.' With these words he went hastily away, half resolving in his mind never to see her more.

CHAPTER X

———•———

*Cannot fail of exciting compassion in some readers,
though it may move others to laughter*

THE few remonstrances Miss Betsy would vouchsafe to listen to from
Mr. Trueworth, had a much greater effect upon her mind, than her
pride, and the excessive homage she expected from her lovers, would
suffer to make shew of, or than he himself imagined. She had too
much discernment, heedless as she was, not to know he was above
any little malicious inuendoes; but, on the contrary, was extremely
cautious in regard to the character of whomsoever he spoke; she
feared, therefore, he had but too good grounds for the uneasiness he
expressed for her continuing a correspondence with Miss Forward;
she knew that she had been faulty, and could not be assured she was
not still so; and it was more owing to her impatience to be ascertained
of the truth, than to any real resentment she had conceived against
Mr. Trueworth, that she complied with the invitation of her now
suspected friend, and resolved to put the question home to her,
concerning her present manner of life, and the means by which she
was supported: she had found her removed from the lowerst degree
of penury and wretchedness, into a state equal to what she could have
been mistress of had she been re-established in the favour of her
father; and now, for the first time, began to think it strange she
should be so, from the mere bounty of a distant relation, to whom in
her utmost distress she had never applied, nor even once mentioned
in the recital of her melancholy history: 'I will talk to her,' said she to
herself; 'watch carefully, not only the replies she makes to what I say,
but also her very looks, unperceiving my suspicions; and, if I find the
least room to believe what Mr. Trueworth has insinuated, shall pity,

but will never see her more.'

In this prudent disposition did she enter the lodgings of Miss Forward; but had no opportunity for the execution of her purpose, some company, which she herself thought, by their behaviour, to be not of the best sort, happening to be just come before her, and departed not till it was time to go to the play. Miss Betsy was more than once about to tell Miss Forward that she had changed her mind, and would not go; but her complaisance, as having been the person who made the first proposal, as often stopped her mouth.

In fine, they went; but the house being very full, and the fellow who had been sent to keep places for them going somewhat too late, they were obliged to content themselves with sitting in the third row. This, at another time, would have been a matter of some mortification to Miss Betsy; but, in the humour she now was, to shew herself was the least of her cares. Never had she entered any place of publick entertainment with so little satisfaction; Mr. Trueworth's words ran very much in her mind; she had lost no part of them; and though she could not bring herself to approve of the freedom he had taken, yet, in her heart, she could not forbear confessing, that his admonitions testified the most zealous and tender care for her reputation; and, if given by any one except a lover, would have demanded more of her thanks than her resentment.

But, alas! those serious considerations were but of short duration: the brilliant audience; the musick; the moving scenes exhibited on the stage; and, above all, the gallantries with which herself and Miss Forward were treated by several gay young gentleman, who, between the acts, presented them with fruits and sweetmeats, soon dissipated all those reflections which it was so much her interest to have cherished, and she once more relapsed into her former self.

Towards the end of the play, there were two rakes of distinction that stuck very close to them, and when it was ended, took the liberty to invite them to sup at a tavern; Miss Betsy started at the motion, but was very well pleased to find Miss Forward shewed an equal dislike to it. 'You will give us leave, then,' cried one of the gentlemen, 'to guard you safe home, ladies?' – 'That I think, my dear,' said Miss Forward to Miss Betsy, 'may be granted, for the sake of being protected from the insults of those who may know less how to behave towards our sex.'

Miss Betsy making no opposition, they all four went into a

hackney-coach to Miss Forward's lodgings, it being agreed upon between them, that Miss Betsy should be set down there, and take a chair from thence to Mr. Goodman's. Nothing indecent, nor that could be any way shocking to the most strict modesty, being offered during their passage, on their alighting from the coach at Mr. Screener's door, Miss Forward thought, that to ask them to come in would incur no censure from her fair friend, as they had behaved with so much civility and complaisance: accordingly she did so; and they, who expected no less, took each man his lady by the hand, and immediately tripped up stairs.

Miss Betsy did not presently make any offer to go home, because she thought it would appear very odd in her to leave her companion with two strange gentlemen. She little guessed the designs they had in their heads, and doubted not but they would soon take leave; she did not, however, continue in this mistake for many minutes; for one of them drawing Miss Forward to a window, in order to speak to her with more privacy, the other, that he might have the better opportunity to do so, addressed himself to Miss Betsy, 'How killingly handsome you are!' said he, taking her by both her hands, and looking full in her face; 'what a pity you did not shine in the front tonight! By my soul you would have out-dazzled all the titled prudes about you!'

'Pish!' replied she, 'I went to see the play, not to be seen myself.' – 'Not to be seen! cried he; 'why then have you taken all this pains to empty the whole quiver of Cupid's arrows to new-point those charms you have received from nature? Why does the jessamine and the blooming violet play wanton in your hair? Why is the patch with so much art placed on the corner of this ruby lip, and here another to mark out the arched symmetry of the jetty brow? Why does the glittering solitaire hang pendant on the snowy breast, but to attract and allure us poor men into a pleasing ruin?'

Miss Betsy answered this raillery in it's kind; and, as she had a great deal of ready wit, would soon perhaps, had the same strain continued, have left the beau nothing to say for himself: but Miss Forward and the other gentleman having finished what they had to say, coming towards them, put an end to it. 'What do you think?' cried Miss Forward; 'this gentleman swears he won't go out of the house till I give him leave to send for a supper.' – 'You may do as you please,' said Miss Betsy; 'but I must be excused from staying to partake of it.' Whether she was really in earnest or not, is not very material; but her refusal was looked upon only as a feint, and they pressed her to tarry in such a manner, that she could not well avoid complying, even though she had been more averse, in effect, than for some time she pretended to be.

The conversation was extremely lively; and, though sprinkled with some double entendres, could not be said to have any thing indecent, or that could raise a blush in the faces of women who were accustomed to much company. Miss Betsy had her share in all the innocent part of what was said, and laughed at that which was less so. But, not to dwell on trifles, she forgot all the cautions given her by Mr. Trueworth, considering not that she was in company with two strange gentlemen, and of a woman whose character was suspected; and, though she had a watch by her side, regarded not how the hours passed on, till she heard the nighly monitor of time, cry, 'Past twelve o'clock, and a cloudy morning!'

After this she would not be prevailed upon to stay, and desired Miss Forward to send somebody for a chair. 'A chair, Madam!' cried that gentleman who, of the two, had been most particular in his addresses to her; 'you cannot, sure, imagine we should suffer you to go home alone at this late hour.' – 'I apprehend no great danger,' said she; 'though I confess it is a thing I have not been accustomed to.' He replied, that in his company she should not begin the experiment. On this a coach was ordered. Miss Betsy made some few scruples at committing herself to the conduct of a person so little known to her. 'All acquaintance must have a beginning,' said he; 'the most intimate friends were perfect strangers at first. You may depend on it I am a man of honour, and cannot be capable of an ungenerous action.'

Little more was said on the occasion; and being told a coach was at the door, they took leave of Miss Forward and the other gentleman, and went down stairs. On stepping into the coach, Miss Betsy directed the man where to drive; but the gentleman, unheard by her, ordered him to go to the bagnio in Orange Street. They were no sooner seated, and the windows drawn up to keep out the cold, than Miss Betsy was alarmed with a treatment which her want of consideration made her little expect. Since the gentleman-commoner, no man had ever attempted to take the liberties which her present companion now did: she struggled – she repelled with all her might, the insolent pressures of his lips and hands. 'Is this,' cried she, 'the honour I was to depend upon? Is it thus you prove yourself incapable of an ungenerous action?' – 'Accuse me not,' said he, 'till you have reason. I have been bit once, and have made a vow never to settle upon any woman while I live again; but you shall fare never the worse for that, I will make you a handsome present before we part; and, if you can be constant, will allow you six guineas a week.'

She was so confounded at the first mention of this impudent proposal; that she had not the power of interrupting him; but, recovering herself as well as she was able, 'Heavens!' cried she, 'what means all this? What do you take me for?' – 'Take you for!' answered he, laughing; 'pr'ythee, dear girl, no more of these airs: I take you for a pretty kind, obliging creature, and such I hope to find you, as soon as we come into a proper place. In the mean time,' continued he, stopping her mouth with kisses, 'none of this affected coyness.'

The fright she was in, aided by disdain and rage, now inspired her with an unusual strength: she broke from him, thrust down the window, and with one breath called him 'Monster! Villain!' with the next screamed out to the coachman to stop; and, finding he regarded not her cries, would have thrown herself out, if not forcibly witheld by the gentleman, who began now to be a little startled at her resolute behaviour. 'What is all this for?' said he: 'would you break your neck, or venture being crushed to pieces by the wheels?' – 'Any thing,' cried she, bursting into tears, 'I will venture; suffer any thing, rather than be subjected to insults, such as you have dared to treat me with.'

Though the person by whom Miss Betsy was thus dangerously attacked was a libertine, or, according to the more genteel and modish phrase, a man of pleasure, yet he wanted neither honour, nor good sense: he had looked on Miss Betsy as a woman of the town, by seeing her with one who was so, and her too great freedom in conversation gave him no cause to alter his opinion; but the manner in which she had endeavoured to rebuff his more near approaches, greatly staggered him. He knew not what to think, but remained in silent cogitation for some minutes; and, though he held her fast clasped round the waist, it was only to prevent her from attempting the violence she had threatened, not to offer any towards her. 'Is it possible,' said he, after this pause, 'that you are virtuous?' – 'I call Heaven to witness,' answered she, with a voice faltering through the excess of terror and indignation, 'that I never have entertained one thought that was not strictly so! that I detest and scorn those wretched creatures of the number of whom you imagine me to be one; and that I would sooner die the worst of deaths, than live with infamy! Yes, Sir, be assured,' continued she, gathering more courage, 'that whatever appearances may be this fatal night against me, I am of a family of some consideration in the world, and am blessed with a fortune, which sets me above the low temptations of designing men.'

As she had ended these words, they came to the bagnio; and, the coach immediately stopping, two or three waiters came running to open the door; on which Miss Betsy, more terrified than ever, shrieked in a most piteous manner; 'O God!' cried she, 'What's here? Where am I? What will become of me?' and, at that instant recollecting that no help was near; that she was in the power of a man whose aim was her eternal ruin; and that it was by her own indiscretion alone this mischief had fallen on her; with so overcome with the dread, the shame, the horror, as she then supposed, of her inevitable fate, that she was very near falling into a swoon.

The gentleman discovering, by the light of the lamps at the bagnio door, the condition she was in, was truly touched with it. 'Retire,' said he hastily to the fellows, 'we do not want you.' Then throwing himself on his knees before her, 'Let this posture, Madam,' continued he, 'obtain your pardon; and, at the same time, ease you of all apprehensions on my score.' – 'May I believe you?' said she, still weeping. 'You may,' replied he. Then rising, and placing himself on the seat opposite to her, 'I love my pleasures, and think it no crime to indulge the appetites of nature. I am charmed with the kind free woman, but I honour and revere the truly virtuous; and it is a maxim with me never to attempt the violation of innocence. These, Madam, are my principles in regard to your sex: but, to convince you farther – Here, fellow,' continued he to the coachman, who was walking backwards and forwards at some distance, 'get up upon your box, and drive where you were first directed.

Miss Betsy acknowledged the generosity of this behaviour; and, on his asking by what accident it had happened, that he found her in company with a woman of Miss Forward's character, she told him ingenuously the truth, that they knew each other when children in the country; but that she had not seen her more than three times since their coming to London, and was entirely ignorant of her conduct from that time.

He then took the liberty of reminding her, that a young lady more endangered her reputation by an acquaintance of one woman of ill fame, than by receiving the visits of twenty men, though professed libertines. To which she replied, that for the future she would be very careful what company she kept of both sexes.

This was the sum of the conversation that passed between them during their little stage to Mr. Goodman's; where being safely arrived, after having seen her within the doors, he saluted her with a great deal of respect, and took his leave.

CHAPTER XI

Shews what effects the transactions of the preceding night had on the minds of Miss Betsy and Mr. Trueworth

MR. Goodman and Lady Mellasin were gone to bed when Miss Betsy came home; but Miss Flora sat up for her, in complaisance, as she pretended, but in reality to see who it was came home with her. This malicious creature had been extremely fawning, for some days past, to Miss Betsy, but this night was more so than usual; doubtless, in the hope of being able to draw something out of her, which her cruel wit might turn to her disadvantage: but the other knew too well the disposition she had towards her, to communicate anything to her, which she would not wish should be made publick.

Never did any one pass a night with greater inquietudes than this young lady sustained; and she felt them the more terribly, as she had no friend to whom pride and shame would suffer her to impart the cause: she looked back with horror on the precipice she had fallen into, and considered it as a kind of miracle, that she had recovered from it unhurt, she could not reflect on what had passed; that by the levity of her conduct she had been thought a common prostitute, had been treated as such, and preserved from irrecoverable ruin by the mere mercy of a man who was a perfect stranger to her; without feeling anew that confusion which the most shocking moments of her distress inflicted. The most bitter of her enemies could not have passed censure more severe than she did on herself; and, in this fit of humiliation and repentance, would even have asked Mr. Trueworth pardon for the little regard she had paid to his advice.

The agitations of her mind would not suffer her to take one

moment of repose for the whole night; nor did the morning afford any more tranquillity: the disturbance of her heart flew up into her head, and occasioned so violent a pain there, that she was as unable as unwilling to get out of bed. She lay till some hours after the time in which they usually breakfasted, nor would take any refreshment, though the tea was brought to her bed-side. Amongst the crowd of tormenting ideas, the remembrance that she owed all the vexation she laboured under entirely to the acquaintance she had with Miss Forward, came strong into her thoughts; and she had not rose the whole day, if not moved to it by the impatience of venting her spleen on that unfortunate woman; which she did, in a letter to her, containing these lines.

'To Miss Forward.

I am sorry that the compassion, which your feigned contrition for one false step obliged me to take in your misfortunes, should make you imagine I would continue any conversation with you, after knowing you had abandoned yourself to a course of life, which I blush to think any of my sex can descend to brook the thoughts of, much more to be guilty of. If you had retained the least spark of generosity or good-will towards me, you would rather have avoided than coveted my company; as you must be sensible, that to be seen with you must render me in some measure a partaker of your infamy, though wholly innocent of your crimes. How base, how cruel, is such behaviour; especially to one, who had a real regard for you, even after you had confessed yourself unworthy of it! But I have been often told, and now I find the observation just, that women of your wretched principles, being lost to all hope of happiness themselves, take a malicious pleasure in endeavouring to destroy it in others.

But, for Heaven's sake, what could induce you to desire a continuation of a correspondence with me? What did you take me for? Did you imagine me so blind as not to see into the shameful means by which you are supported, or so weak as to forfeit all the reputation and respect I have in the world, merely to comply with your request? No! your conduct is too bare-faced to give me even the shadow of an excuse for ever seeing you again: do not, therefore, go about to varnish over actions, whose foulness will appear through all the colours you can daub them with. The friendship I once had for you has already pleaded all that yourself could urge in your defence; but the cause is too bad, and I must leave you to the miseries which attend remorse, and which a little time will infallibly bring on. Heavens! to be a common prostitute! to earn precarious bread, by being the slave of every man's licentious will. What is digging in the mines! What is begging! What is starving, when compared to this! But the idea is too shocking; modesty shudders at it. I shall drive both that and you as distant from my thoughts as possible; so, be assured, this is the last time you will ever hear from the much deceived, and ill-treated,

B. THOUGHTLESS.'

She was going to seal up the above letter, when a sudden thought coming into her head, she added, to what she had already wrote, this postscript.

'P.S. You may perhaps be instigated to answer this, either through resentment for the reproaches it contains, or through some remains of modesty, to attempt an apology for the occasion: but I would not wish you should give yourself that trouble; for, be assured, I shall read nothing that comes from you, and that whatever you send will be returned to you again unopened.'

She immediately sent this away by a porter; and, having satisfied the dictates of her indignation against Miss Forward, she had now done with her, and resolved to think of her no more; yet was the confusion of her mind far from being dissipated. 'What will Mr. Trueworth say,' cried she to herself, 'if ever the ridiculous adventure of last night should reach his ears, as nothing is more probable than that it may? What will my brother Frank say, on hearing such a story? What will Mr. Goodman and Lady Mellasin say? What a triumph for the envious Miss Flora! And what can I answer for myself, either to my friends or enemies?'

Little care as this young lady had seemed to have taken of her reputation, it was, notwithstanding, very dear to her. Honour was yet still more dear; and she could not reflect, that what she had done might call the one into question, and how near she had been to having the other irrecoverably lost, without feeling the most bitter agonies: she was not able to dress, or go down stairs that day; and gave orders to be denied to whoever should come to visit her.

In this perplexed situation of mind let us leave her for a while, and see with what sort of temper Mr. Trueworth behaved, after having seen her go to the very woman he had so much conjured her to avoid.

All the love he had for her would not keep him from resenting this last rebuff: he thought he had not deserved such usage; nor that his having professed himself her lover, gave her the privilege of treating him as her slave. The humour he was in making him unfit for company, he went directly to his lodgings; but had not been long there, before it came into his head that, possibly, the manner in which she had behaved was only a fit of contradiction; and that, after all, she might, when she was out of hearing, have given counter-orders to the chairmen, and was neither gone to Miss Forward's, nor would accompany her to the play. With such vain imaginations does love sometimes flatter it's votaries; and the sincere and ardent flame which filled the heart of Mr. Trueworth, made him greedily catch at every supposition in favour of the darling object.

Willing, however, to be more assured, he bethought himself of a strategem, which would either relieve all the doubts remaining in him of her obstinacy, or convince him they were but too just. He sent immediately to his barber for a black perriwig; and, muffled up in a cloak, so as to render it almost an impossibility for him to be known by any one, went to the theatre; and, with a heart divided betwixt hope and fear, placed himself in a part of the middle gallery, which had the full command of more than half the boxes. He saw a very brilliant circle; but not she, whom he so much dreaded to find, shine among them.

Having scrutinously examined all within the reach of his view, he quitted his present post, and removed to the other side of the house; where he soon discovered the persons he came in search of. He saw Miss Forward earnest in discourse with a gentleman that sat behind her; and Miss Betsy receiving fruit from another, with the same freedom and gaiety of deportment she could have done if presented by himself. He saw the nods, the winks, and the grimaces, which several in the pit made to each other, when looking towards these two ladies. Every moment brought with it some fresh matter for his mortification; yet would not his curiosity stop here. When the play was ended, he went hastily down stairs, and mingled with the crowd that stood about the door, in hopes of seeing Miss Betsy quit her company, take a chair, and go home. But how cruel a stab was it to a man who loved as he did, to find her go with a dissolute companion and two gentlemen, who, he had reason to believe, by the little he saw of their behaviour, were utter strangers to her, in a hackney-coach. He was once about to appear himself through his disguise, and tell Miss Betsy, that he thought he had more right to the honour of conducting her than those to whom she gave permission; but the greatness of his spirit assisted his prudence in restraining him from so rash an action.

After this sight, it is not in the power of words to represent what it was he felt. Reason was too weak to combat against the force of such various emotions as for a time had the entire possession of his soul; though he thought Miss Betsy unworthy of his love, yet still he loved her; and had she been witness of his present distracted state, she would have seen the power she had over him, no less manifest in the moments of his rage, than in those in which he had behaved with the greatest tenderness and respect.

His good-sense, however, at last convinced him, that as no solid happiness could be expected with a woman of Miss Betsy's temper, he ought to conquer his passion for her. This he resolved to attempt; yet thought, before he did so, it would become him to see her once more, to argue gently with her, and to try, at least, if there were not a possibility of making her see the errors she was guilty of.

With this intent he went the next day to visit her; but, being told she could see no company that day, was going from the door; when Miss Flora, who had watched for him at the parlour-window, came and desired him to walk in. His complaisance would not permit him to refuse her request; and, after the usual compliments, said he was sorry Miss Betsy was so ill. 'You need not be in much pain,' replied she, with a look which he thought had more than ordinary meaning in it; 'she is not greatly indisposed.' – 'Perhaps,' cried Mr. Trueworth, with some warmth, 'she is only so to me.' – 'I cannot say anything to that,' returned Miss Flora; 'but her orders were in general to all that came; and I believe, indeed, she is not perfectly well. She came home extremely late last night, and seemed in a good deal of disorder.' – 'Disorder, Madam!' interrupted Mr. Trueworth, impatiently. 'For Heaven's sake, on what occasion?' – 'I wish I could inform you,' answered she; 'but at present I am not favoured with her confidence, though there was a time when I was made partaker of her dearest secrets. I wish those she now intrusts them with may be no less faithful to her than I have been.' – 'I hope,' said he, 'she has none which, to be betrayed in, would give her pain.' With these words he rose up to go away. Miss Flora fain would have persuaded him to drink tea: but he excused himself, saying he was engaged; that he came only to enquire after the health of her fair friend, and could not have staid, if so happy as to have seen her.

Scarce could this passionate lover contain himself till he got out of the house. The manner in which Miss Flora had spoke of Miss Betsy, added fresh fuel to the jealousies he was before possessed of: but, how great soever his disturbance was, he found, on his return home, somewhat which made all he had known before seem light and trifling.

CHAPTER XII

───────── ● ─────────

*Contains some passages which, it is probable, will
afford more pain than pleasure; yet which are very
pertinent to the history, and necessary to be related*

THOUGH the words which Miss Flora had let fall to Mr. Trueworth,
concerning Miss Betsy, seemed as if spoken by mere chance, there
was couched under them a design of the most black and villainous
kind that ever entered the breast of woman, as will presently appear,
to the astonishment of every reader.

In order to do this, we must relate an incident in Miss Betsy's life
not hitherto mentioned, and which happened some little time before
her going to Oxford with her brother Frank.

On her first coming to town, a woman had been recommended to
her for starching, and making up her fine linen. This person she had
ever since employed, and took a great fancy to, as she found her
honest, industrious, and very obliging. The poor creature was
unhappily married; her husband was gone from her, and had listed
himself for a soldier. Being born in a distant country, she had no
relations to whom she could apply for assistance; was big with child,
and had no support but the labour of her hands. These calamitous
circumstances so much touched the commiserative nature of Miss
Betsy, that she frequently gave her double the sum she demanded for
her work, besides bestowing on her many things she left off wearing;
which, though trifles in themselves, were very helpful to a person in
such distress.

Miss Mabel, for whom she also worked at the same time, was no
less her patroness than Miss Betsy. In fine, they were both extremely
kind to her; insomuch as made her often cry out, in a transport of
gratitude, that these two good young ladies were worth to her all the

customers she had besides. They continued to prove themselves so indeed; for when her child was born, which happened to be a girl, they stood godmothers; and not only gave handsomely themselves, but raised a contribution among their acquaintance, for the support of the lying-in woman and her infant: the former, however, did not long enjoy the blessing of two such worthy friends; she died before the expiration of her month; and the latter, being wholly destitute, was about to be thrown upon the parish. Some well-disposed neighbour, who knew how kind Miss Mabel and Miss Betsy had been, came and acquainted them with the melancholy story: they consulted together; and each reflecting that she had undertaken the protection of this infant at the font, thought herself bound by duty to preserve if from those hardships with which children thus exposed are sometimes treated; they, therefore, as they were equally engaged, agreed to join equally in the maintenance of this innocent forlorn.

This was a rare charity indeed! and few there are, especially at their years, who so justly consider the obligations of a baptismal covenant. It was also the more to be admired, as neither of them had the incomes of their fortunes in their own hands, the one being under guardianship, and the other at the allowance of a father, who, though rich, was extremely avaricious.

As they were, therefore, obliged to be good œconomists in this point, and nurses in the country are to be had at a much cheaper rate than in the town, they got a person to seek out for one who would not be unreasonable in her demands, and at the same time do justice to her charge. Such a one, according to the character given of her by neighbours, being found, the child, decently cloathed, was sent down to her habitation, which was in a little village about seventeen miles from London. For the sake of concealing the part Miss Mabel had in this affair from the knowledge of her father, it was judged proper that Miss Betsy should seem to take the whole upon herself, which she did; and the nurse's husband came up every month and received the money from her hands, as also whatever other necessaries the child wanted.

Who would imagine that such a glorious act of benevolence should ever be made a handle to traduce and vilify the author! Yet what cannot malice, accompanied with cunning, do! It can give the fairest virtue the appearance of the foulest vice, and pervert the just estimation of the world into a mistaken scorn and contempt!

Miss Flora, after receiving the disappointment, as related in the sixth chapter of this volume, was far from desisting from the wicked design she had conceived of putting an end to the intercourse between Miss Betsy and Mr. Trueworth. Her fertile brain presented her with a thousand strategems, which she rejected, either as they were too weak to accomplish what she wished, or too liable to discovery, till at last she hit upon the most detestable project of representing what proceeded from the noblest propensity of Miss Betsy's nature, as the effect of a criminal compulsion: in fine, to make it appear so feasible, as to be believed that the child, who owed half it's maintenance to her charity, was entirely kept by herself, and the offspring of her own body.

Having well weighed and deliberated on this matter, it seemed to her such as Mr. Trueworth, on the most strict examination, could not discover the deception of: she therefore resolved to pursue it, and accordingly wrote the following letter.

'To Charles Trueworth, Esq.

Sir,
The friendship I had for some of your family, now deceased, and the respect due to your own character in particular, obliges me to acquaint you with truths more disagreeable than perhaps you ever yet have heard: but, before I proceed to the shocking narrative, let me conjure you to believe, that in me your better angel speaks, and warns you to avoid that dreadful gulph of everlasting misery into which you are just ready to be plunged.

I am informed, by those who are most versed in your affairs, and on whose veracity I may depend, that a treaty of marriage is on foot, and almost as good as concluded, between you and Miss Betsy Thoughtless. A young lady, I must confess, well descended; handsome, and endued with every accomplishment to attract the admiration of mankind; and if her soul had the least conformity with her exterior charms, you doubtless might have been one of the most happy and most envied men on earth: but, Sir, this seeming innocence is all a cheat; another has been beforehand with you in the joys you covet; your intended bride has been a mother without the pleasure of owning herself as such. The product of a shameful passion is still living; and though she uses the greatest caution in this affair, I have by accident discovered, is now nursed at Denham, a small village within two miles of Uxbridge, by a gardener's wife, who is called, by the country people, Goody Bushman. I give you this particular account, in order that you may make what enquiry you shall think proper into a fact, which, I am sorry to say, you will find but too real. I pity from my soul the unfortunate seduced young lady; she must be doubly miserable, if, by having lost her virtue, she loses a husband such as you: but if, after this, you should think it fit to prosecute your pretensions, I wish she may endeavour, by her future conduct, to atone for the errors of the past; but, alas! her present manner of behaviour affords no such promising expectations; and if you should set your honour and fortune, and all that is dear to you, against so precarious a stake as the hope of reclaiming a woman of her temper, it must certainly fill all your friends with astonishment and grief. But you are yourself the best judge of what it will become you to do; I only beg, that you will be assured this intelligence comes from one, who is, with the utmost sincerity, Sir, your well-wisher, and most humble, though unknown servant.'

She would not trust the success of the mischief she intended by this letter, till she had examined and re-examined every sentence; and, finding it altogether such as she thought would work the desired effect, got one who was always her ready agent in matters of this kind, to copy it over, in order to prevent any accident from discovering the real author; and then sent it, as directed, by the penny-post.

How far the event answered her expectations shall very shortly be related; but incidents of another nature requiring to be first mentioned, the gratification of that curiosity, which this may have excited, must for a while be deferred.

CHAPTER XIII

———————•———————

Is the recital of some accidents, as little possible to be foreseen by the reader as they were by the persons to whom they happened

IN youth, when the blood runs high, and the spirits are in full vivacity, affliction must come very heavy indeed, when it makes any deep or lasting impression on the mind. That vexation which Miss Betsy had brought upon herself, by going to the play with Miss Forward, was severe enough the whole night, and the ensuing day. A great while, it must be confessed, for a person of her volatile disposition; and when the more violent emotions had subsided, the terror she had lately sustained, had, at least, this good effect upon her; it made her resolve to take all possible precautions not to fall into the like danger again. As she had an infinite deal of generosity in her nature, when not obscured by that pride and vanity which the flatteries she had been but too much accustomed to, had inspired her with, she could not reflect how ill she had treated Mr. Trueworth, and the little regard she had paid to the tender concern he had shewn for her reputation, without thinking she ought to ask his pardon, and acknowledge she had been in the wrong. If Mr. Trueworth could have known the humour she was at present in, how readily would he have flown to her with all the wings of love and kind forgiveness! but as he had not the spirit of divination, and could only judge of her sentiments by her behaviour, it was not in his power to conceive how great a change had happened in his favour, through a just sensibility of her own error.

She, in the mean time, little imagined how he far he resented the treatment she had given him; especially as she heard he had been to wait upon her the day in which she saw no company; and, after having passed a night of much more tranquillity than the former had been, went down in the morning to breakfast with her usual chearfulness. She had not been many minutes in the parlour before she was agreeably surprized with the sight of her elder brother, Mr. Thomas Thoughtless, who, it seems, had arrived the night before. After the first welcomes were over, Mr. Goodman asked him, wherefore he did not come directly to his house; saying, he had always a spare bed to accommodate a friend; to which the other replied, that he had come from Paris with some company whom he could not quit, and that they had lain at the Hummums. Miss Betsy was extremely transported at his return, and said a thousand obliging things to him; all which he answered with more politeness than tenderness: and this young lady soon perceived, by this specimen of his behaviour to her, that she was not to expect the same affection from him, as she had received so many proofs of from her younger brother.

His long absence from England, and some attachments he had found abroad, had indeed very much taken off that warmth of kindness he would doubtless otherwise have felt for an only sister, and one who appeared so worthy of his love. As Mr. Goodman had acquainted him by letter, that he had hired a house for him, according to his request, the chief of their conversation turned on that subject; and, as soon as breakfast was over, they took a walk together to see it. On their return, he seemed very much pleased with the choice Mr. Goodman had made; and the little time he staid was entirely taken up with consulting Lady Mellasin, his sister, and Miss Flora, concerning the manner in which he should ornament it; for the honest guardian had taken care to provide all such furniture as he thought would be necessary for a single gentleman.

No intreaties were wanting to prevail on him to make that house his home, till his own was thoroughly aired, and in all respects fit for him to go into; but he excused himself, saying, he could not leave the friends he had travelled with, till they were provided for as well as himself; nor could all Mr. Goodman and the ladies urged, persuade him to dine with them that day.

It must be acknowledged, that this positive refusal of every thing that was desired of him, had not in it all that complaisance which might have been expected from a person just come from among a people more famous for their politeness than their sincerity.

But he had his own reasons, which the family of Mr. Goodman as yet were far from suspecting, which made him act in the manner he now did; and it was not, in reality, the want of French breeding, but the want of true old English resolution, that enforced this seeming negligence and abruptness.

After he was gone, Mr. Goodman went to Change; but was scarce entered into the walk, where he had appointed to meet some merchants, when he was accosted by two rough, ill-looking fellows, who demanded his sword, and told him they had a writ against him; that he was their prisoner, and must go with them.

Mr. Goodman, who had as little reason as any man living to suspect an insult of this nature, only smiled, and told them they were mistaken in the person. 'No, no,' said one of them, 'we are right enough, if you are Mr. Samuel Goodman!' – 'My name is Samuel Goodman,' replied he; 'but I do not know that it stands in any man's books for debt: but, pray,' continued he, 'at whose suit am I arrested?' – 'At the suit of Mr. Oliver Marplus,' said the other officer. 'I have no dealings with any such person,' cried Mr. Goodman: 'nor even ever heard the name of him you mention.' They then told him it was his business to prove that; they did but do their duty, and he must obey the writ. Mr. Goodman, on this, knowing they were not the persons with whom this matter should be contested, readily went where they conducted him, which was to a house belonging to him who appeared to be the principal of the two. As they were coming off Change, he bade his coachman drive his chariot home, and tell his lady, that he believed he should not dine with her that day; but he kept his footman with him, to send on what messages he should find convenient.

The officer, knowing his condition, and not doubting but he should have a handsome present for civility-money, used him with a great deal of respect when he had got him into his house; and, on his desiring to be informed of the lawyer's name employed in the action, he immediately told him, and also for what sum he was arrested, which was no less than two thousand five hundred and seventy-five pounds eight shillings. 'A pretty parcel of money, truly!' said Mr. Goodman; 'I wonder in what dream I contracted this debt.' He then called for pen, ink, and paper; and wrote a line to his lawyer in the Temple, desiring him to go to the other who they said was concerned against him, and find out the truth of this affair.

The honest old gentleman, having sent this letter by his servant, called for something to eat; and was extremely facetious and pleasant with the officers, not doubting but that what had happened was occasioned through some mistake or other, and should immediately be discharged when the thing was enquired into: but his present good-humour was changed into one altogether the reverse, when his own lawyer, accompanied by him who was engaged for his adversary, came to him, and told him there was no remedy but to give bail; that the suit commenced against him was on account of a bond given by Lady Mellasin to Mr. Oliver Marplus, some few days previous to her marriage. It is hard to say, whether surprize or rage was most predominant in the soul of this much-injured husband, at so shocking a piece of intelligence. He demanded to see the bond; which request being granted, he found it not, as he at first flattered himself, a forgery, but signed with his wife's own hand, and witnessed by Mrs. Prinks, her woman, and another person whom he knew not.

It is certain that no confusion ever exceeded that of Mr. Goodman's at this time: he sat like one transfixed with thunder; and was wholly incapable of uttering one syllable. He appeared to the company as lost in thought; but was, indeed, almost past the power of thinking, til his lawyer roused him with these words – 'Come, Sir,' said he, 'you see how the case stands; there is no time to be lost; you must either pay the money down, or get immediate security; for I suppose you would not chuse to lie here tonight.' This seasonable admonition brought him a little to himself: he now began to reflect on what it would best become him to do; and, after a pause of some moments, 'I believe,' said he, 'that I have now in my house more than the sum in bills that would discharge this bond; but I would willingly hear what this woman has to say before I pay the money, and will therefore give in bail.' Accordingly, he sent for two citizens of great worth and credit, to desire them to come to him; they instantly complied with this summons; and the whole affair being repeated to them, voluntarily offered to be his sureties.

Bail-bonds were easily procured; but it took up some time in filling them up, and discharging the fees, and other consequential expences, so that it was past one o'clock before all was over, and Mr. Goodman had liberty to return to his own habitation.

It was very seldom that Mr. Goodman staid late abroad; but whenever any thing happened that obliged him to do so, Lady Mellasin, through the great affection she pretended to have for him,

would never go to bed till his return. Mrs. Prinks for the most part
was her sole companion in such cases; but it so fell out, that this
night neither of the two young ladies had any inclination to sleep:
Miss Flora's head was full of the above-mentioned plot, and the
anxiety for it's success; the remembrance of the last adventure at
Miss Forward's was not yet quite dissipated in Miss Betsy; the
coldness with which she imagined herself treated by her elder
brother, with whom she had flattered herself of living, and being very
happy under his protection, gave her a good deal of uneasiness. To
add to all these matters of disquiet, she had also received that
afternoon a leter from Mr. Francis Thoughtless, acquainting her, that
he had the misfortune to be so much bruised by a fall he got from his
horse, that it was utterly impossible for him to travel, and she must
not expect him in town yet for some days.

The ladies were all together, sitting in the parlour, each chusing
rather to indulge her own private meditations, than to hold discourse
with the others, when Mr. Goodman came home. Lady Mellasin ran
to embrace him with a shew of the greatest tenderness; 'My dear Mr.
Goodman,' cried she, 'how much I have suffered from my fear lest
some ill accident should have befallen you!' – 'The worst that could
have happened has befallen me,' replied he, thrusting her from him;
'yet no more than what you might very reasonably expect would one
day or another happen.' – 'What do you mean, my dear?' said she,
more alarmed at his words and looks than she made shew of. 'You
may too easily inform yourself what it is I mean,' cried he, hastily, 'on
the retrospect of your behaviour; I now find, but too late, how much I
have been imposed upon. Did you not assure me,' continued he,
somewhat more mildly, 'that you were free from all incumbrances but
that girl, whom, since our marriage, I have tendered as my own?' And
then perceiving she answered nothing, but looked pale, and trembled,
he repeated to her the affront he had received; 'Which,' said he, 'in
all my dealings in the world, would never have happened, but on your
account.'

Though Lady Mellasin had as much artifice, and the power of
dissimulation, as any of her sex, yet she was at a loss thus taken
unprepared. She hesitated, she stammered, and fain would have
denied the having given any such bond; but, finding the proofs too
plain against her, she threw herself at his feet, wept, and conjured
him to forgive the only deception she had practised on him: 'It was a
debt,' said she, 'contracted by my former husband, which I knew not

of. I thought the effects he left behind him were more than sufficient to have discharged whatever obligations he lay under, and foolishly took out letters of administration. The demand of Marplus came not upon me till some time after; I then inconsiderately gave him my own bond, which he, however, promised not to put in force without previously acquainting me.'

This excuse was too weak, as well as all the affection Mr. Goodman had for her, to pacify the emotions of his just indignation. 'And pray,' cried he, in a voice divided between scorn and anger, 'of what advantage would it have been to me your being previously acquainted with it? Could you have paid the money without robbing or defrauding me? No, Madam!' continued he, 'I shall for the future give credit to nothing you can say; and as I cannot be assured that this is the only misfortune I have to dread on your account, shall consider what steps I ought to take for my defence.'

In speaking these words he rung the bell for a servant, and ordered that bed to which he had invited Mr. Thoughtless, should that instant be made ready for himself. All the tears and intreaties of Lady Mellasin were in vain to make him recede from his resolution of lying alone that night; and, as soon as he was told his orders were obeyed, he flung out of the room, saying, 'Madam, perhaps, we never more may meet between a pair of sheets!' Whether at that time he was determined to carry his resentment so far, or not, is uncertain; but what happened very shortly after left him no other part to take than that which he had threatened.

CHAPTER XIV

Gives a full explanation of some passages which hitherto have seemed very dark and mysterious

THIS was a night of great confusion in Mr. Goodman's family: Lady Mellasin either was, or pretended to be, in fits; Miss Flora was called up soon after she went to bed; but Mr. Goodman himself would not be prevailed upon to rise, though told the condition his wife was in, and that she begged with the utmost earnestness to see him.

This behaviour in a husband, lately so tender and affectionate, is a proof not only that the greatest love, once turned, degenerates into it's reverse, but also that the sweetest temper, when too much provoked by injuries, is not always the most easy to be reconciled. The perfect trust he had put in Lady Mellasin, the implicit faith he had given to all she said, and the dependance he had on the love she had professed for him, made the deception she was now convicted of appear in worse colours than otherwise it would have done.

The more he reflected on this ugly affair, the more he was convinced of the hypocrisy of his wife, in whom he had placed such confidence. 'We have been married near five years,' said he to himself; 'how comes it to pass, that the penalty of this bond was not in so long a time demanded? It must be that she has kept it off by large interest and for-bearance money; and who knows how far my credit may be endangered for the raising of it? It is likely, that while I thought every thing necessary for my family was purchased with ready-money, I may stand indebted to all the tradesmen this wicked woman has had any dealings with; nay, I cannot even assure myself that other obligations of the same kind with this I have already suffered for, may not some time or other call upon me for their discharge.'

With these disturbed meditations, instead of sleep, did he pass what was remaining of the night when he went to bed; yet he rose the next day full as early as he was accustomed to do after having enjoyed the best repose.

The first thing he did was to send for as many of those trades-people, as he either knew himself, or his servants could inform him, had at any time sent goods into his house. On their presenting themselves before him, he found, more to his vexation than surprize, (for he now expected the worst) that all of them, even to those who had supplied his kitchen, had bills of a long standing: he discharged all their several demands directly; and, having taken a receipt in full from each of them, desired they would henceforth suffer no goods to be left within his doors without the value being paid on the delivery.

Mr. Goodman had just dispatched the last of these people, when he was told a woman begged leave to speak with him: 'Another creditor, I suppose,' said he; and then ordered she should come in. As soon as she did so, 'Well, mistress,' cried he, seeing her a woman of a very plain appearance, 'what is it you require of me?' – 'Nothing, Sir,' replied she; 'but that you will permit me to acquaint you with a thing which it very much concerns you to be informed of?' – 'I should otherwise be an enemy to myself,' returned he; 'therefore, pray, speak what you have to say.'

'I am, Sir,' said she, 'the unfortunate wife of one of the most wicked men upon earth, and by my being so, have been compelled to be in some measure accessary to the injustice you have sustained: but, I hope, what I have to reveal will atone for my transgression.' Mr. Goodman then desired she would sit down, and without any farther prelude proceed to the business she came upon.

'The sum of what I have to relate,' rejoined she, 'is, that the bond on which you were yesterday arrested, and for the payment of which you have given security, is no more than an impudent fraud: but the particulars, that prove it such cannot but be very displeasing to you; however, I shall make no apology for relating them, as the perfect knowledge of the whole transaction may put you in a way to prevent all future injuries of the like nature.

'My husband, whose name is Oliver Marplus,' continued she, 'had the honour of waiting on a nobleman belonging to court, when Sir Solomon Mellasin had a post there: his lady, now unhappily yours, took a fancy to him, and entered into a criminal conversation with him, some time before her husband's death, and has ever since, unless very lately broke off, continued it. On my first discovering it, he begged me to be easy; and reminded me, that as he had nothing at present to depend upon, having lost his place, but her ladyship's bounty, I ought to wink at it, and be content that she should share his person, since I shared in the benefits arising from their intercourse. I knowing his temper too well not to know that any opposition I could make would be in vain, and seeing no other remedy, was obliged to feign a consent to what the love I then had for him rendered most terrible to me. Thus we went on, her ladyship still supplying him with money, for our support; till he being informed, that her marriage with you was near being consummated, he bethought himself of a strategem to prevent the change of her condition from depriving him of the continuance of her favour. It was this.

'Their private meetings were always in the Savoy, at a house of my husband's chusing for that purpose, the master of it being his intimate friend and companion. Myself, and two men, whom he made privy to the plot, and were to personate officers of justice, were to be concealed in the next room to the lovers, and as soon as we found they were in bed, burst open the door, rush in, and catch them in the very act of shame.

'All this was executed according as it was contrived; my husband jumped out of bed, pretended to struggle with the sham constables, and swore he would murder me: I acted my part, as they since told me, to the life; seemed a very fury; and said I did not care what became of me, if I was but revenged upon my rival. Lady Mellasin tore her hair, wept, and entreated me in the most abject terms to forgive, and not expose a woman of her rank to publick scorn and infamy. To which I replied, that it was not her quality should protect her! I loaded her with the most inveterate reproaches I could think of. Indeed, there required not much study for my doing so, for I heartily hated her. After some time passed in beseechings on her side, and railings on mine, one of the pretended constables took me aside, as if to persuade me to more moderation; while the other talked to her, and insinuated as if a sum of money might compromise the matter. My husband also told her, that though he detested me for what I had done, yet he wished her ladyship, for her own sake, would think of some way to pacify me; "For," said he, "a wife in these cases has great power."

'The terror she was in of appearing before a civil-magistrate, and of being liable to suffer that punishment the law inflicts upon an adultress, and consequently the loss of all her hopes of a marriage with you, Sir, made her readily agree to do any thing I should require. I seemed quite averse for a good while to listen to any terms of accommodation; but at length affected to be overcome by the persuasions of the men I brought with me, and her promise of allowing us a very handsome support as soon as she became your wife, and should have it in her power. This I made slight on; and told her, that I would not depend upon her promise for any thing. It was then proposed, that she should give a bond for a large sum of money to Mr. Marplus. "That you may do with safety," said he to her, "as I shall have it in my own hands; and, you may be assured, will never put it in force to your prejudice."

'In fine, Sir,' continued Mrs. Marplus, 'she agreed to this proposal; and, as it was then too late for the execution of what she had promised, on her making a solemn vow to fulfil it punctually the next day, I told her she was at liberty to go home that night, but that I would not withdraw the warrant I pretended to have taken out against her till all was over.

'She was, indeed, too much rejoiced at the expectation of getting off from the imaginary prosecution, to think of breaking her word: my wicked husband, however, had the success of his design more greatly at heart than to give her any long time for reflection. Accordingly, we went pretty early the next morning to her lodgings, accompanied by one of those who had assumed the character of constable, and who in reality had formerly served the parish where he still lives in that capacity, and a lawyer, previously directed to fill up the bond in the strongest and most binding terms that words could form. There was not the least demur or objection, on the part of her ladyship: she signed her name; and Mrs. Prinks, her woman, and the man we brought with us, set their hands as witnesses.

'You see, Sir,' pursued she, 'the drift of this contrivance; Lady Mellasin was the instrument, but it was you that was ordained to suffer: there was no fixed sum or sums stipulated for the support we were to receive from her; but Marplus was so continually draining her purse, that I have often been amazed by what arts she imposed on you to replenish it. Whenever she began to make any excuse for not complying with his demands, he presently threatened her with putting the bond in force against you; by which means he extorted from her almost whatever he required.

'One time in particular, he pretended to be under an arrest for three hundred pounds; and she not having so much money by her, was obliged to send Mrs. Prinks with her diamond necklace, to the pawnbroker's to make it up: yet, would you believe it, Sir, notwithstanding all he got from her ladyship, he kept me poor and mean, as you see; would not let me have a servant, but made me wash his linen, and do all his drudgery, while he strutted about the town like a fine fellow, with his toupee wig, and laced waistcoat; and, if I made the least complaint, would tell me, in derision, that, as I had no children, I had nothing else to do but to wait upon him. I bore all this, however, because I loved the villain; and, indeed, did not then know he was so great a one to me as I now find he is.

'He pretended to me that he was heartily weary of Lady Mellasin, hated her, and could no longer bear the pain of dissembling with her. "I will, therefore," said he, "demand a much larger sum of her than I know it is in her power to raise: her non-compliance will give me an excuse for compelling her husband to pay the penalty of the bond; and, when I have got the money, I will purchase an employment in some one or other of the publick offices, on which you and I may live comfortably together the remainder of our days."

'Accordingly, at his next meeting with Lady Mellasin, he told her he had a present occasion for a sum of money, and she must let him have five hundred pounds within four or five days at farthest. This, it seems, extremely alarmed her; she replied, that it was impossible for her to procure so much at once – complained that he had been too pressing upon her – and told him, that he ought not to expect she could always supply his extravagances in the manner she had lately done. High words arose between them on this account; she reproached him with the straits he had already put her to; said he must wait till money came into her hands. He swore the present exigence of his affairs required an immediate supply; that he saw no remedy but arresting you; and they parted in great anger.

'The next day he sent me to her with a letter: neither she nor Mrs. Prinks was at home, and I did not judge it proper to leave it with the servants, so carried it back again; he did not happen to ask me for it, and I never thought of returning it, which I am now very glad of, as it may serve to corroborate the truth of what I told you.'

In speaking this, she presented a paper to Mr. Goodman, which he took hastily out of her hands, and found it contained these words –

'To Lady Mellasin.

Madam,
Your excuses won't do with me. Money I must have; I know you may
raise it if you will, and I am amazed you should imagine I can believe
any thing you say to the contrary, when you have an old fellow who,
you yourself told me, knows no end to his wealth, and that you
married him only to make him my banker. Do not, therefore, offer to
trifle with me any longer; for if you do, by my soul I shall put the
bond in force! and then there will be an end of all love and friendship
between you and him, who has been for so many years, your constant
servant,

O. MARPLUS.'

'Oh! wretched woman!' cried Mr. Goodman, as soon as he had
done reading, 'to how low, how contemptible a fate, has vice reduced
her!' Mrs. Marplus, perceiving by his countenance the distraction of
his mind, would not prosecute her discourse, till he, recovering
himself a little, bid her go on, if any thing yet remained to be related
of this shocking narrative.
'I have told you, Sir,' resumed she, 'the preparations, the
consequence you are but too well acquainted with; I have only to
assure you, that I had not discovered my husband's baseness, but
with a view of your doing yourself justice: you have no occasion to
pay this bond; you can prove it a fraud by the joint evidence of myself
his wife, and another person no less deeply concerned in the
contrivance, and is ready to make his affidavit of every particular I
have recited; but then, whoatsoever is done, must be done with
expedition, or he will be past the reach either of you or me. I have
just now learned, that, instead of purchasing an employment, as he
pretended to me, he is privately preparing to go over to Holland,
Brussels, or some of those places, and settle there with a young
hussey, who they say is with child by him, and will leave me here to
starve. His lawyer, to whom he has assigned the bond, is to advance
fifteen hundred pounds upon it, on condition he has the residue of it
to himself, when you shall discharge the whole. Now it is in your
power, Sir, to save yourself the payment of so much money, and
relive a much-injured and distressed wife, by complaining to the
Court of Chancery of the imposition practised on you, and procure a
ne exeat regnum to prevent his escape.'

Here she gave over speaking; and Mr. Goodman, after a short pause, replied, that he could not at that instant resolve on any thing; but added, that he would take some advice, and then let her know how far she might be serviceable to him: on which she took her leave, after giving him directions where she might be found.

CHAPTER XV

———•———

Shews some part of the consequences produced by the foregoing occurrence

THOUGH Mr. Goodman very easily perceived the wife of Marplus had not made the discovery she had done through any principle of conscience, or true contrition for having been an accomplice in the base action she had revealed, but merely in revenge of a husband, who had used her ill, and was about to leave her, yet he thought it behoved him to draw all advantages he could from the knowledge of so astonishing, and so alarming a secret.

He therefore wasted no time, either in unavailing reflections on his own inconsiderateness, in marrying, at his years, a woman such as Lady Mellasin, nor in exclamations on her ingratitude and perfidiousness; but, convinced beyond a doubt of the wrongs he had sustained, bent his whole mind on doing himself justice, in as ample a manner as possible, on the aggressors.

The lawyer, to whom he had applied the day before, was not only a person who had transacted all the business he had in his way, but was also his acquaintance of a long standing, and very good friend; and it was no inconsiderable consolation, under so grievous a misfortune, that he was not at a loss whom he should consult on an affair that required the greatest integrity, as well as ability.

That gentleman, luckily for Mr. Goodman's impatience, came to enquire how he did after his last night's shock, just as he was preparing to wait on him, in order to acquaint him with the more stabbing one he had since received. This injured husband rejoiced, as much as the present unhappy circumstances of his mind would permit, at the sight of his friend; and related to him, in as brief a manner as he could, the sum of the whole story he had received from Mrs. Marplus.

'Good God!' said the laywer, as soon as Mr. Goodman had given over speaking, 'I am confounded: but, pray, Sir, how have you resolved to do? In what way will you proceed?' – 'That I must ask of you,' replied Mr. Goodman, hastily; 'you may be certain I shall not be passive in this matter. I only want to know what course I am to steer?' – 'Could you consent,' cried the lawyer, after a pause, 'to be divorced from Lady Mellasin?' – 'Consent!' said Mr. Goodman, with more warmth than before; 'the most terrible vexation I endure dwells in the consideration that she is still my wife! Were that name once erased, I think I should be easy.' – 'I hope then soon to see you so,' said the other; 'but the first thing we have to do is to get the affidavits of the two witnesses, and then arrest Marplus. I shall order it so with his lawyer, whom I have under my thumb, on account of some malpractices I have detected him in, that he shall not dare to procure bail for this unworthy client. In a word, Sir,' continued he, 'I do not doubt, the case being so plain, but to relieve you from paying the penalty of the bond; but, in the mean time, what will you do with Lady Mellasin? It is necessary she should be removed out of the house.' – 'The house is hell to me while she is in it!' said Mr. Goodman. They had some farther talk on this affair; and the manner in which Mr. Goodman was to conduct himself being settled, a footman was sent to bid Mrs. Prinks come down.

The confidant of all her lady's guilty secrets could not, now detected, behold the face of Mr. Goodman without the extremest terror and confusion: he perceived it, as she stood trembling scarce half within the door, not daring to approach. 'Come near,' said he; 'you are a servant, and below the effects of my resentment, which otherwise you might have cause to dread: I have a message to send by you to your lady; take care you deliver it in the words I give it.' On which she ventured to advance a few steps farther into the room, and he went on, with a more authoritative voice than she had ever heard him assume before, in this manner.

'Tell her,' said he, 'that for many reasons I find it wholly improper she should remain any longer under the same roof with me; desire her therefore to provide a lodging immediately for herself, and all belonging to her: you must all depart this very night, so it behoves her to be speedy in her preparations.' – 'To night, Sir!' cried Mrs.

Prinks. 'I have said it,' rejoined he, fiercely: 'be gone! it is not your business to reply, but to obey.' She spoke no more, but retired with much greater haste than she had entered.

Mr. Goodman and his lawyer were pursuing their discourse on the present melancholy occasion, when the butler came in to lay the cloth for dinner. As soon as he had finished, and set all the necessary utensils on the table, Mr. Goodman ordered him to go to Miss Betsy's chamber, and desire her to come down to dinner.

That young lady had passed the morning in a very disagreeable manner: the want of repose the night before had made her lie in bed till the day was very far advanced. When she got up, good-manners, good-breeding, and even common civility, obliged her to enquire after Lady Mellasin's health; and being told that she was still in bed, the same motives induced her to pay her compliments in person. On entering the chamber, a mournful scene presented itself to her eyes: Lady Mellasin sat up, supported by her pillows, with all the tokens of despair and grief in every feature of her face; Miss Flora had thrown herself on a carpet by the bed-side, her head leaning on the ruelle, and her eyes half drowned in tears; Mrs. Prinks stood at a little distance from them, pale and motionless as a statue. The approach of Miss Betsy made some alteration in their postures, and seemed to awaken them from that lethargy of silent woe: Lady Mellasin began to exclaim on the hardness of her fate, and the cruelty of Mr. Goodman; who, she said, seemed glad of a pretence to throw off that affection which she had flattered herself would have been as lasting as life; and bewailed herself in terms so tender and pathetick, that in spite of the little respect that Miss Betsy in reality had for her, and the just indignation she had for some time conceived against Miss Flora, her gentle, generous heart, was touched with the strongest emotions of pity and forgiveness.

As she was far from suspecting all the grounds Lady Mellasin had for this immoderate grief, and in her soul believing that Mr. Goodman would soon be brought to forgive both the affront and the damage his fortune had suffered on her account, she begged her ladyship would not indulge the dictates of despair, but reflect on the natural sweetness of Mr. Goodman's disposition; the great love he had for her; and, above all, his strict adherence to those principles of religion, which forbid a lasting resentment; and, in short, reminded her of every thing she could think of for her consolation.

None of them having yet breakfasted, she staid and drank coffee with them; nor would her compassionate temper have permitted her to quit them so soon as she did, if she had not been called away to a milliner, who was come with some things she had the day before ordered to be brought; and she had just dispatched this little affair, and got out of her dishabille, when she had received the above-mentioned message from Mr. Goodman.

On her coming into the parlour, where dinner was that moment serving up, 'I must request the favour of you, Miss Betsy,' said Mr. Goodman, 'to do the honours of my table today.' – 'I shall do the best I can, Sir,' replied Miss Betsy modestly; 'but am very sorry for the occasion which obliges me to take upon me an office I am so little accustomed to.' – 'You will be the better able to discharge it when it becomes your duty!' said Mr. Goodman, with a faint smile; 'but I believe this is the only time I shall put you to it. I have a kinswoman, who I expect will be so good as to take care of the affairs of my family henceforward.' – 'O Sir!' replied Miss Betsy, with a great deal of concern, 'I hope Lady Mellasin has not for ever forfeited her place!'

Mr. Goodman was about to make some reply, when they heard the voice of that lady whom Miss Betsy had just mentioned extremely loud upon the stairs. 'I will not be used in this manner,' cried she; 'if I must go, let him tell me so himself.' On this, Mr. Goodman grew extremely red: 'Go,' said he to the footman that waited at table, 'and tell Lady Mellasin that I will not be disturbed.' – 'Hold,' cried the lawyer; 'permit me, Sir, to moderate this matter.' In speaking these words, he rose hastily; and, without staying to hear what Mr. Goodman would say, ran to prevent Lady Mellasin from coming in. While he was gone, 'Yes, Miss Betsy,' said Mr. Goodman, 'you will lose your companion; Miss Flora, with her mother, leaves my house tonight.'

Miss Betsy, who had gone out of Lady Mellasin's chamber before Mrs. Prinks brought her this piece of intelligence from Mr. Goodman, was prodigiously surprized to hear him speak in this manner. 'It is a sudden turn, indeed,' pursued he; 'but the reasons which urge me to this separation will hereafter appear such as I neither could nor ought to have resisted.' Miss Betsy only replying, that he was certainly the best judge of what he did, no farther discourse happened on the subject, nor, indeed, on any other, for some moments.

At last, however, Mr. Goodman taking notice that she looked more than ordinarily serious, 'Perhaps,' said he, 'you may think my house

too melancholy for you when they are gone. The relation I intend to
bring home, though a perfect good woman, is pretty far advanced in
years; and, I believe, receives but few visits, especially from the
younger sort; but as the house I have hired for Mr. Thoughtless will
be ready in a day or two, I should imagine he would be glad to have
you with him till you marry: but this,' continued he, 'is at your own
option; I do but mention it, because I would have you entirely easy in
this point, and consider what it is will most contribute to make you
so.'

Miss Betsy had only time to thank him for his goodness before the
lawyer came down: that gentleman had found a more difficult talk
than he had expected, in bringing Lady Mellasin to submit to the
injunctions she had received from her husband; not that she had the
least spark of conjugal affection for him, as the reader may very well
suppose, or would have wished ever to see him more, if she could
have lived without him in the same manner she did with him; but the
thoughts of leaving her large and richly-appointed house – her fine
side-board of plate – her coach – her equipage, and all those other
ensigns of opulance and state she now enjoyed, were insupportable to
her, and, having in vain essayed what a feigned penitence and
tenderness could do, to work him to forgiveness, had how resolved to
try the effect of a more haughty and imperious deportment. 'I will
make him know I am his wife!' cried she; 'and whatever he is
possessed of, I am an equal sharer in: let him not therefore think
that, wherever he is master, I shall cease to be mistress.'

The lawyer then remonstrated to her, that though it were true, as
she said, that she had a right to partake of his fortune, yet it was still
in the power of a husband to oblige her to receive the benefit of that
right in what manner, and in what place, he should think proper: he
told her, Mr. Goodman was determined that she should quit his
house, and that all applications made by her to the contrary would be
fruitless, and exasperate him the more, and only serve to widen the
unhappy breach between them. 'If Mr. Goodman,' said he, 'has no
other complaint against your ladyship, than simply his paying the
penalty of the bond, and, it may be, some other trifling debts, I
cannot think he will, for any length of time, persevere in his present
inflexibility of temper.' These arguments, and some others he made
use of, enforced with all the rhetorick and art he was master of, at
last convinced her, that it was best for her to yield, with a seeming
willingness, to the fate it was not in her power to avoid; and she

promised him to send Prinks directly to hire an apartment for her, at a house near Golden Square, with the mistress of which she had some small acquaintance.

The whole time this gentleman had been with Lady Mellasin, the meat was kept on the table, but he would not stay to eat. 'We have not a minute to lose,' said he to Mr. Goodman; 'let us go, Sir, and dispatch what we have to do.' With these words, they both went hastily out of the doors, leaving Miss Betsy in a good deal of consternation at what they were about.

CHAPTER XVI

———————•———————

Is a kind of olio, a mixture of many things, all of them very much to the purpose, though less entertaining than some others

LADY Mellasin, who little expected that her husband was made so well acquainted, or even that he had the least thought of the worst part of her behaviour towards him, was ready enough to flatter herself, both from her experience of his uncommon tenderness for her, and from what his lawyer had insinuated, in order to prevail upon her to go away with the less noise, that when this gust of passion was blown over, he would be reconciled, and consent to her return.

These imaginations made her carry it with a high hand before the servants; and as they were packing up her things, while Mrs. Prinks was gone to prepare a lodging for her – 'Your master will be glad to fetch me home again,' cried she; 'poor man! he has been strangely wrong-headed of late. I suppose he will be ready to hang himself when he considers what he has done; for he may be sure I shall not very easily forgive the affront he has put upon me.'

How truly amiable is an unblemished character, and how contemptible is the reverse! Servants naturally love and respect virtue in those they live with, and seldom or ever either flatter or conceal the vices they do not greatly profit by. The airs Lady Mellasin gave herself on this occasion, were so far from making them believe her innocent, or their master blameable, that, as soon as they had gone out of her sight, they only turned her pride, and the fall it was going to sustain, into ridicule and grimace.

Miss Betsy, however, could not see them depart in this manner, without feeling a very deep concern: their misfortunes obliterated all the resentment she had at any time conceived against them; and she had never before been more angry, even with Miss Flora, for the treachery she had been guilty of to her, than she was now grieved at the sight of her humiliation.

She was sitting alone, and full of very serious reflections on this sudden change in the family, when her brother Thoughtless came in: she was glad of the opportunity of sounding his inclinations as to her living with him, and now resolved to do it effectually: she began with telling him the whole story of Lady Mellasin's and Miss Flora's removal; and then complained how dully she should pass the time with only Mr. Goodman, and an old gentlewoman who was to come to be his housekeeper. 'I thought you were about marrying,' said he; 'and expected, from what Mr. Goodman wrote to me, that my first compliment to you, on my arrival, would have been to have wished you joy. – You are not broke off with the gentleman, are you?'

The careless air with which he spoke these words, stung Miss Betsy to the quick; she took no notice, however, how much she was piqued at them, but replied, that the whole affair was mere suggestion; that it was true, indeed, she had for some time received the addresses of a gentleman recommended by her brother Frank; that he, and some other of her friends, were very much for the match, and she supposed had spoke of it as a thing concluded on, because they wished it to be so: but, for her own part, she never had as yet entertained one serious thought about the matter; and, at present, was far from having any disposition to become a wife; 'So that,' continued she, 'if I am doomed to stay in Mr. Goodman's house, till I am relieved that way, it is very probable I may be moped to death, and married to my grave.'

'Where is the necessity for that?' said he. 'Are there not places enough in town, where you may find good company to board or lodge with?' – 'Doubtless there are many such, Sir,' replied she, with some spirit; 'and if I am so unhappy as not to have any friend so kind to make me an invitation, shall be obliged to seek an asylum amongst strangers.'

Mr. Thoughtless looked a little confounded at these words: he had seen, from the beginning of her discourse, the aim to which it tended; and, as he had his own reasons for not complying with her desire, would not seem to understand her; but she now spoke too plain, and he was somewhat at a loss what answer to make, so as not

to give her any cause of accusing his want of affection, and at the
same time put her off from expecting he would agree to what she
would have him, in this point; when, fortunately for his relief, a letter,
just brought by the post, was presented to Miss Betsy. 'From L—e!'
said she, as soon as she took it into her hand. 'From brother Frank,
then, I suppose?' cried he. 'No,' answered she, 'from Lady Trusty;
you will excuse me, brother, while I look over the contents.' She
broke it open while she was speaking, and read to herself as follows.

'To Miss Betsy Thoughtless.

My dear Miss Betsy,
Sir Ralph received yesterday a letter from Mr. Thoughtless, dated
Calais, the third instant; so I doubt not but by this time I may
congratulate you on his safe arrival in London: but I am sorry to
acquaint you, that while you were embracing one brother, you were
in very great danger of losing another; but do not be too much
alarmed, I hope the worst is past. I believe he gave you an account
himself, that, by an unlucky fall from his horse, he was prevented
from going to London so soon as he had designed; but the mischief
done him by this accident was much greater than he imagined at the
time of his writing to you. What he took only for a common bruise,
proved to be a contusion; and, for want of proper care at first,
through the outrageousness of the pain, soon brought on a fever: for
two whole days we were in the utmost apprehensions for his life; but
now, thanks to the Author of all mercies, we are assured by the
physician that attends him, and who is esteemed the most skilfil this
county affords, that he is in a fair way of doing well. His delirium has
quite left him; and he has recovered the use of his reason so far as to
entreat I would send the warmest wishes of his heart to you, and to
desire you will make the same acceptable to his dear brother, if you
are yet so happy as to see him: he also enjoins you to pay his
compliments to Mr. Trueworth, in such words as are befitting the
friendship you know he has for him. I have much to say to you from
myself, on the score of that gentleman, and should be glad to add to
the advice I have already given you, but am deprived of that
satisfaction by the arrival of some company, who are come to pass a
week or fortnight with us; therefore must defer what I have to say till
another opportunity. Farewel! may Heaven keep you under it's
protection, and your guardian-angel never fail his charge! Be assured,

that though I do not write so long, nor so often to you, as I could wish, I am always, with the greatest sincerity, my dear Miss Betsy, your very affectionate friend, and humble servant,

                                                                    M. TRUSTY.

P.S. I wrote the above this morning, because one of our men was to have gone pretty early to town; but Sir Ralph having some letters of his own, which were not then ready, detained him; and I have now the pleasure to tell you, that the doctor, who is this moment come from your brother's chamber, assures me that he has found him wonderfully mended since his visit to him last night. Once more, my dear, adieu.'

Mr. Thoughtless, perceiving some tears in the eyes of Miss Betsy while she was reading, cried out, 'What is the matter, sister? I hope no ill news from the country!' – 'Be pleased to read that, Sir,' said she, giving him the letter, 'and see if I had not cause to be affected with some part of it.'

'Poor Frank!' said he, as soon as he had done reading, 'I am sorry for the accident that has happened to him; but more glad it is like to be attended with no worse consequences. Do not be melancholy, my dear sister; you find he is in a fair way of recovery, and I hope we shall soon have him with us. I long very much to see him,' continued he; 'and the more so, as I have spoke in his behalf to a general officer whom I contracted an intimacy with at Paris, and who has promised me all the service he can in procuring him a commission.'

They had some farther talk on family affairs; after which he told her he was troubled to leave her alone, but was obliged to return to some company he had made an elopement from when he came there. At parting, he saluted her with a great deal of affection – desired she would be chearful – and said, he dare believe she had too much merit ever to have any real cause to be otherwise.

This tenderness very much exhilerated her drooping spirits: she entertained fresh hopes of being in the house with a brother, who, she found, designed to live in the most elegant and polite manner, which was what she had at present the most at heart of any thing in the world. She now began to fancy he did not propose it to her, either because he did not think she would approve of it, or because he feared, that to testify any desire of removing her might offend Mr. Goodman, as she had boarded with him ever since she came to town; she, therefore, resolved to desire the favour of that gentleman to mention it to him, as of his own accord, and let her know what answer he should make. This idea gave her some pleasure for a while; but it was as soon dissipated: the thoughts of her brother Frank's misfortune, and the danger she could not be sure he was yet perfectly recovered from, came again into her mind; but this also vanished, on remembering the hopes Lady Trusty had given her: yet still she was discontented, though she knew not well at what. In fine, she was so little accustomed to reflect much on any thing, much less to be alone, that it became extremely irksome to her. 'What a wilderness is this house!' cried she to herself. 'What a frightful solitude! One would think all the world knew Lady Mellasin and Miss Flora were gone, that nobody comes near the door. How still! how quiet, is every thing!' Then would she start up from her chair, measure how many paces were in the room – look at one picture, then on another – then on her own resemblance in the great glass. But all this would not do; she wanted somebody to talk to – something new to amuse her with. 'I wonder,' said she, 'what is become of Trueworth! – I have not seen him these three days. Indeed, I used him a little ill at our last conversation: but what of that? If he loves me as well as he professes, he will not, sure, pretend to be affronted at any thing I do. My brother desires me to give his compliments; but if the man will not come to receive them, it is none of my fault. Yet, after all,' continued she, having paused a little, 'what privilege has our sex to insult and tyrannize over the men? It is certainly both ungenerous and ungrateful to use them the worse, for using us, perhaps, better than we deserve. Mr. Trueworth is a man of sense; and, if I were in his place, I would not take such treatment from any woman in the world. I could not much blame him if he never saw me more. Well – when next he comes, I will, however, behave to him with more respect.'

Thus did the dictates of a truly reasonable woman, and the idle humour of a vain coquette, prevail by turns over her fluctuating mind. Her adventure at Miss Forward's came fresh into her head: she was in some moments angry with Mr. Trueworth for offering his advice; in others, more angry with herself, for not having taken it. She remained in this perplexity till a servant, finding it grew late, and that his master did not sup at home, came in, and asked her if she would not please to have the cloth laid; to which she answered, with all her heart: on which, the table being immediately spread, she eat of something that was there, and soon after went to bed; where, it is probable, she lost in sleep both all the pleasure and the pain of her past meditations.

Mr. Goodman was all this while, as well as for several succeeding days also, busily employed on an affair no less disagreeable to him than it was new to him; but, by the diligence and adroitness of his lawyer, he got the affidavits, the warrant, and everything necessary for the intended prosecution of Marplus and Lady Mellasin, ready much sooner than many others would have done, or he himself had expected.

The fatigue and perplexity he was under, was, indeed, very great, as may be easily supposed; yet did it not render him neglectful of Miss Betsy. She had desired him to speak to her brother on her account, and he did so the first opportunity; not as if the thing had been mentioned by her, but as if he, in the present situation of his family, thought her removal expedient.

Mr. Thoughtless, from what his sister had said, expecting he should one time or other be spoke more plainly to upon that subject, had prepared himself with an answer. He told Mr. Goodman, that nothing could have been more satisfactory to him than to have his sister with him, if her being so were any ways proper. Said he, 'As I am a single man, I shall have a crowd of gay young fellows continually coming to my house; and I cannot answer that all of them would be able to behave with that strict decorum, which I should wish to see always observed towards a person so near to me. Her presence, perhaps, might be some check upon them, and theirs no less disagreeable to her. In fine, Mr. Goodman,' continued he, 'it is a thing wholly inconsistent with that freedom I propose to live in, and would not have her think on it.'

It was not that this gentleman wanted natural affection for his sister, that he refused what he was sensible she so much desired; but he was at present so circumstanced, that, to have complied, would, under a shew of kindness, have done her a real injury. He had brought with him a young and very beautiful mistress from Paris, of whom he was fond, and jealous to that extravagant degree, that he could scarce suffer her a moment from his sight: he had promised her the sole command of his house and servants, and that she should appear as his wife in all respects except the name. How could he, therefore, bring home a sister, who had a right to, and doubtless would have claimed, all those privileges another was already in possession of! And how would it have agreed with the character of a virtuous young lady, to have lived in the same house with a woman kept by her brother as his mistress!

But this was a secret Miss Betsy was as yet wholly unacquainted with; and when Mr. Goodman repeated to her what had passed between them on her score, and the excuse her brother had made for not complying with the proposal, she thought it so weak, and withal so unkind, that she could not forbear bursting into tears. The good-natured old gentleman could not see her thus afflicted without being extremely concerned, and saying many kind things to pacify her. 'Do not weep,' said he; 'I will make it my business, nay my study, to procure some place where you may be boarded to your satisfaction.' – 'I beg, Sir, that you will not mistake my meaning. I do assure you, Sir, I am not wanting in sensibility of your goodness to all our family, and to me in particular. I must, indeed, be strangely stupid not to think myself happy under the protection of a gentleman of so humane and benign a disposition. No, Sir, be persuaded there is no house in London, except that of an own brother, I would prefer to yours. I will, therefore, with your permission, continue here; nor entertain the least thought of removing, unless some accident, yet unforeseen, obliges me to it.'

Mr. Goodman then told her, that he should be glad she would always do what was most for her own ease. This was all the discourse they had upon this head; and when Miss Betsy began to consider seriously on the behaviour of Lady Mellasin and Miss Flora, she found there was little reason for her to regret the loss of their society; nor that she ought to think Mr. Goodman's house less agreeable for their being out of it. She received all such as she approved of, who had come to visit them, and by doing so, were acquainted with her; and as to those who still visited herself in particular, it was the same as ever. Mr. Goodman's kinswoman, now his housekeeper, was a well-bred, accomplished woman, and a chearful, agreeable companion. She seemed studious to oblige her: all the servants were ready to do every thing she desired; and it would have been difficult for her to have found any place where she could have been better accommo-dated, or have had more cause to be contented; and she would doubtless have thought herself more happy than she had ever been since her coming to Mr. Goodman's, if other things, of a different nature, had not given her some unquiet moments.

But, besides the unkindness of one brother, on whom she had built the most pleasing hopes, and the indisposition of another, for whom she had a very great affection, the late behaviour of Mr. Trueworth gave her much matter of mortification. She had not seen him for upwards of a week: she imputed this absence to the rebuff she had given him at his last visit; and, though she could not avoid confessing in her heart that she had treated him neither as a gentleman nor a friend, yet her vanity having suggested, that he was capable of resenting any thing she did, received a prodigious shock by the disappointment it now sustained.

CHAPTER XVII

———————•———————

Contains only such things as the reader might reasonably expect to have been informed of before

IT was the fate of Miss Betsy to attract a great number of admirers; but never to keep alive, for any length of time, the flame she had inspired them with. Whether this was owing to the inconstancy of the addressers, or the ill-conduct of the person addressed, cannot absolutely be determined; but it is highly probable that both these motives might sometimes concur to the losing her so many conquests. Mr. Trueworth had been the most assiduous, and also the most persevering, of all that had ever yet wore her chains. His love had compelled his judgment to pay an implicit obedience to her will; he had submitted to humour all the little extravagances of her temper, and affected to appear easy at what his reason could not but disapprove. He had flattered himself, that all that was blame-worthy in her would wear off by degrees, and that every error would be her last, till a long succession of repeated inadvertences made him first begin to fear, and then to be convinced, that however innocent she might be in fact, her manner of behaviour would ill suit with the character he wished should always be maintained by the woman he had made choice of for a wife.

His meeting her at Miss Forward's – her obstinately persisting in going to the play with that abandoned creature, after the remonstrances he had made her on that score – her returning home so late, and in disorder, conducted by a stranger – in fine, what he saw himself, and had been told, concerning the proceedings of that night, gave the finishing stroke to all his hopes, that she would ever, at least, while youth and beauty lasted, be brought to a just sensibility of the manner in which she ought to act.

If the letter, contrived and sent by the mischievous Miss Flora, had reached his hand but two days sooner, it would have had no other effect upon him than to make him spurn the invective scroll beneath his feet, and wish to serve the author in the same manner: but poor Miss Betsy had, by her own mismanagement, prepared his heart to receive any impressions to her prejudice; yet was the scandal it contained of so gross a kind, that he could not presently give into the belief of it: 'Good God!' he cried, 'it is impossible! If she has so little sense of honour or reputation, as the lightness of her behaviour makes some people too ready to imagine, her very pride is sufficient to secure her virtue: she would not, could not, condescend to the embraces of a man who thought so meanly of her as to attempt the gaining her on any other score than that of marriage! And yet,' pursued he, after a pause, 'who knows but that very pride, which seems to be her defence, may have contributed to her fall? She has vanity enough to imagine she may act with impunity what she would condemn in others. She might fancy, as the poet says –

"That faultless form could act no crime,
But Heav'n, on looking on it, must forgive."

'Why then,' continued he, 'should the foolish remains of the tenderness I once had for her, make me still hesitate to believe her guilty? No, no! the account before me has too much the face of truth; it is too circumstantial to be the work of mere invention. No one would forge a lie, and at the same time present the means of detecting it to be so. Here is the village specified, the nurse's name, and a particular direction how I may convince myself of the shameful truth. There is no room to doubt!'

To strengthen the opinion he now had of her guilt, the words Miss Flora had said to him, returned to his remembrance – that there was a time when Miss Betsy had trusted her with her dearest secrets. – 'Her dearest secrets!' cried he: 'what secrets can a virtuous young lady have, that shun the light, and require so much fidelity in the concealment of? No, no! it must be this Miss Flora meant by that emphatick expression. The other could not hide the consequence of her shameful passion from the family; Lady Mellasin and Miss Flora must know it, and perhaps many more; who, while they were witnesses of the respect I paid her, laughed at the folly of my fond credulity.'

Thus at some times did he believe her no less guilty than the letter said; but, at others, sentiments of a different nature prevailed, and pleaded in her favour; her adventure with the gentleman-commoner at Oxford came into his head: 'If the too great gaiety of her temper,' said he, 'led her into danger, she then had courage and virtue to extricate herself out of it.' He also recollected several expressions she had casually let fall, testifying her disdain and abhorrence of every thing that had the least appearance of indecency: but then relapsing into his former doubts, 'Yet who,' cried he again, 'can account for accident? she might, in one unguarded moment, grant what, in another, she would blush to think of.'

How terrible is the situation of a lover who endeavours all he can to reconcile his reason to his passion, yet to which side soever he bends his thoughts, finds in them things so diametrically opposite and incompatible, that either the one or the other must be totally renounced! Willing, therefore, to take the party which would best become his honour and reputation, Mr. Trueworth resolved to banish from his mind all the ideas of those amiable qualities he had admired in Miss Betsy, and remember only those which gave him occasion for disgust.

But this was a task not so easy to be accomplished as he imagined; for though the irregularity of Miss Betsy's conduct was of itself sufficient to deter him from a marriage with her, yet he found he stood in need of all helps to enable him to drive that once so pleasing object entirely from his mind.

To be therefore more fully confirmed how utterly unworthy she was of his regard, than could be made by this anonymous accusation, he went in person down to Denham; where, following the directions given him in the letter, the cottage where Goody Bushman lived was presently pointed out to him by the first person he enquired of. 'So far, at least,' said he to himself, 'the letter-writer has told truth.' He then sent his servants with his horses to wait his return at a publick-house in the village, and walked towards the place he came in search of.

He found the honest countrywoman holding a child in her arms on one side of the fire, two rosy boys were sitting opposite to her, with each a great piece of bread and butter in his hand. At sight of a strange gentleman she got off her seat; and, dropping a low curtsey, cried, 'Do you please to want my husband, Sir?' – 'No,' said Mr.

Trueworth; 'my business is with you, if you are Mrs. Bushman.' – 'Goody Bushman, an't please you, Sir,' replied she. And then, bidding the boys get farther from the chimney, reached him the handsomest joint-stool her cottage afforded, for him to sit down.

He told her that he had a kinswoman, who had some thoughts of putting a child to nurse in the country; that she had been recommended: 'But,' said he, 'can we have nothing to drink together? What sort of liquor does this part of the world afford?' – 'Alack, Sir,' replied she, 'you fine gentlemen, mayhap, may like nothing but wine; and there is none to be had any nearer than Uxbridge.' – 'Nor cyder!' cried he. 'I am afraid none good,' replied she; 'but there is pure good ale down the lane, if your honour could drink that.' – 'It is all one to me,' said Mr. Trueworth, 'if you like it yourself.' Then turning to him who seemed the eldest of the two boys, 'I suppose, my lad,' continued he, 'you can procure a tankard of this same ale.' – 'Yes, Sir,' cried his mother, hastily – 'Go to Philpot's, and bid them send a cann of their best ale; and, do you hear, desire my dame to draw it herself.' – Mr. Trueworth then gave the boy some money, and he went on his errand, prudently taking with him a large slice of bread that happened to lay upon the dresser.

'That is a fine child you have in your lap,' said Mr. Trueworth; 'is it your own?' – 'No,' answered she, 'this is a young Londoner.' – 'Some wealthy citizen's, I suppose,' rejoined he. 'No, by my truly, Sir!' said she; 'it has neither father nor mother, and belike must have gone to the parish, if a good sweet young lady had not taken pity of it, and given it to me to nurse; and, would you think it, Sir, is as kind to it, and pays as punctually for it, as if it were her own. My husband goes up to London every month to receive the money, and she never lets him come home without it, and gives him over and above sixpence or a shilling to drink upon the road: poor man, he loves a sup of good ale dearly, that's all his fault, though I cannot say he ever neglects his business; he is up early and down late, and does a power of work for a little money. Sir Roger Hill will employ nobody but him; and, good reason, because he makes him take whatever he pleases, and that is little enough, God knows; for he is a hard man: and if it were not for my nursing, we could not make both ends meet, as the saying is; but he is our landlord, and we dare not disoblige him.'

This innocent countrywoman would probably have run on with the whole detail of her family affairs, if Mr. Trueworth, desirous of turning the tide of her communicative disposition into a channel more satisfactory to his curiosity, had not interrupted her.

'This is a very extraordinary charity you have been telling me of,' said he, 'especially in a young lady: she must certainly be somewhat of kin to the child.' – 'None in the varsal world, Sir,' answered she, 'only her godmother.' The boy now bringing in the ale, Mr. Trueworth was obliged to taste it, and testify some sort of approbation, as the good woman had praised it so much; but he made her drink a hearty draught of it; after which, 'And pray,' resumed he, 'what is the name of the child?' – 'O, Sir!' replied she, 'the lady has given it her own name, Betsy; she is called Miss Betsy Thoughtless herself, though she is a woman grown, and might have had a child or two of her own; but you know, Sir, they are all called Miss till they are married.'

Mr. Trueworth, in the present disturbance of his thoughts, making no reply, she went on: 'She is a sweet young lady, I can tell you, Sir,' said she; 'I never saw her but once, and that was when I went to fetch the child; she used me with so much familiarity, not a bit proud, charged me to take care of her little Betsy, and told me, if she lived, I should keep her till she was big enough to go to school, and told me she would have her learn to write and read, and work, and then she would put her apprentice to a mantua-maker, or a milliner, or some such pretty trade; and then, who knows, Sir,' continued she, holding up the child at arms-length, and dancing it, 'but some great gentleman or other may fall in love with my little Betsy, and I may live to see her ride in her coach? I warrant she will make much of her old nurse.'

'There are many strange things happen in the world, indeed!' said Mr. Trueworth, with a sigh. After which, thinking there was no farther discovery to be made, he rose up to go away; but seeing the change of the money he had sent by the boy for the beer, lay upon the table, he gave it to him, saying, 'Here, my good boy, take this, and divide it with your brother, to buy apples.' Then turning to the nurse, took his leave of her with this compliment, 'Well, Mrs. Bushman, I believe you are a very honest careful woman, and shall not fail to remember you whenever it comes in my way. In the mean time,' added he, putting a crown piece into her hands, 'take this, and make merry with your husband.' The poor woman was so transported, that she knew not how to thank him sufficiently; she made twenty curtsies, crying, 'Heavens bless you, Sir; you are a right noble gentleman, I am sure. Marry, such guests come not every day!' And with such like expressions of gratitude, followed him till he was quite out of hearing.

What now could this enquiring lover think? Where was the least room for any conjecture in favour of Miss Betsy's innocence, to gain entrance into his breast? He had seen the child, had heard by whom, and in what manner it was delivered: the charge given with it, and the promises made for it's future protection; and whether the nurse was really so weak as to be imposed upon by this pretence of charity, or whether bribed to impose it upon others, the facts, as related in the letter, appeared to be so plain, from every circumstance, as to admit no possiblity of a doubt.

A marriage with Miss Betsy was, therefore, now quite out of the question with him: the manner of entirely breaking off with her, was the only thing that puzzled him. Loth was he to reproach her with the cause, and equally loth to be deemed so inconstant as to quit her without a justifiable one. He remained in this dilemma for the space of two days, at the expiration of which, after much debating with himself, he wrote, and sent to her, by a servant, the following epistle.

'To Miss Betsy Thoughtless.

Madam,

The very ill success I have met with, in the only business which brought me to this town, has determined me to quit it with all possible expedition, and not to think of a return, till I find myself in a disposition more capable of relishing it's pleasures. You have given me, Madam, too many instances how little agreeable my presence has ever been, not to convince me, that I stand in no need of an apology for not waiting on you in person, and that this distant way of taking my leave will be less unwelcome to you than a visit, which perhaps would only have interrupted your more gay amusements, and broke in, for some moments, on that round of pleasures, with which you are perpetually encompassed. May you long enjoy all the felicities the manner you chuse to live in can bestow, while I retire to solitude, and, lost in contemplation on some late astonishing occurrences, cry out with the poet –

"There is no wonder, or else all is wonder."

'If I speak in riddles, a very small retrospect on some remarkable passages in your own conduct, will serve for the solution; but that might probably be imposing on yourself too great a task. I shall therefore trouble you no farther than to assure you, that though I cease to see you, I shall never cease to be, with the most friendly wishes, Madam, your very humble servant,

C. TRUEWORTH.'

Mr. Trueworth having dispatched this letter, which he doubted not but would finish all his concerns with Miss Betsy, thought he had nothing more to do than to take leave of the friends he had in town, and retire to his seat in the country, and there endeavour to lose the remembrance of all that had been displeasing to him since he left it.

CHAPTER XVIII

Is of very small importance, yet contains such things as the reader may expect to hear

WHILE Mr. Trueworth was employing himself in exploring the truth of Miss Betsy's imaginary crime, and hunting after secrets to render her more unworthy of his love, that young lady's head was no less taken up with him, though in a widely different manner; she wanted not a just sense of the merits, both of his person and passion; and though a plurality of lovers, the power of flattering the timid with vain hopes, and awing the proudest into submission, seemed to her a greater triumph than to be the wife of the most deserving man on earth, yet when she consulted her heart, she found, and avowed within herself, she could part with the triumph with less reluctance in favour of Mr. Trueworth than of any other she yet had seen.

His absence, therefore, and the strange neglect he testified in not sending to acquaint her with the cause, gave her as much inquietude as a person of her humour could be capable of feeling; but whether it proceeded in reality from the first shootings of a growing inclination, or from that vanity which made her dread the loss of so accomplished a lover, cannot be easily determined: but to which soever of these causes it was owing, I think we may be pretty certain, that had he visited her in the situation her mind then was, he would have had no reason to complain of his reception.

She never went abroad without flattering herself with the expectation of hearing, on her return home, that he had been there, or at least that some letter or message from him had been left for her; and every disappointment involved her in fresh perplexity. In short, if

she had considered him with half that just regard, while he continued
to think her worthy of his affections, as she was beginning to do when
he was endeavouring to drive all favourable ideas of her from his
mind, they might both have been as happy as at present they were the
contrary.

She had been with Miss Mable, and two other ladies of her
acquaintance, to see that excellent comedy, called the Careless
Husband: she was very much affected with some scenes in it; she
imagined she saw herself in the character of Lady Betty Modish, and
Mr. Trueworth in that of Lord Morelove; and came home full of the
most serious reflections on the folly of indulging an idle vanity, at the
expence of a man of honour and sincerity. She was no sooner within
the doors, than the letter above-mentioned was put into her hands: as
they told her it had been left for her in the beginning of the evening,
by one of Mr. Trueworth's servants, and she knew, both by the
superscription, and device on the seal, that it came from that
gentleman, she ran hastily up stairs to her chamber, in order to
examine the contents; but what flutterings seized her heart – what an
universal agitation diffused itself through all her frame, on reading
even the first lines of this cruel epistle! 'Good Heaven!' cried she,
'going out of town, not to return!' And then, proceeding a little
farther; 'What,' added she, 'not see me before he goes! Sure the man
is either mad, or I am in a dream.'

Surprize, and some mixture of a tender remorse, were the first
emotions of her soul: but when she came to that part of the letter
which seemed to reflect upon her conduct, and the way in which she
chose to live, her native haughtiness re-assumed it's former power,
and turned her all into disdain and rage. 'No retrospect,' said she, 'on
my own behaviour, can ever justify the audacious reproaches he treats
me with. If I have been to blame, it is not his province to upbraid me
with it.'

As she was entirely ignorant of the base artifice that had been put
in practice against her, and was conscious of no fault Mr. Trueworth
had to accuse her of, but that of her going with Miss Forward to the
play, after the warning he had given her of the danger, it must be
confessed, she had a right to think the provocation too slight to draw
from him such resentful expressions, much less to induce him to
abandon her.

'Ungrateful man!' said she, bursting into tears of mingled grief and
spite, 'to treat me thus, when I was just beginning to entertain the

kindest thoughts of him! When I was ready to acknowledge the error I was guilty of, in not following his advice, and had resolved never to throw myself into such inconveniences again. 'Tis plain he never loved me, or he would not have taken so poor, so trifling, a pretence to break with me.'

Thus, for some moments, did she bewail, as it were, the ill-treatment she thought she had received from him. Then looking over the letter again, 'With what a magisterial air,' cried she, 'with what an affectation of superiority, does he conclude! "With the most friendly wishes, my humble servant!" Good lack! friendly! Let him carry his friendly wishes to those he may think will receive them as a favour!'

Upon revolving in her mind all the circumstances of her behaviour towards Mr. Trueworth, she could find nothing, except what passed at his last visit, that could give him any occasion of disgust, and even that she looked upon as a very insufficient plea for that high resentment he now expressed, much more for his resolving to throw off a passion he had a thousand and a thousand times vowed should be as lasting as his life.

The anonymous letter sent her by Miss Flora, some time since, now came fresh into her head; that passage in it which insinuated that Mr. Trueworth had no real design of marrying her, that he but trifled with her, and on the arrival of her brothers would find some pretence or other to break entirely with her, seemed now to tally exactly with his present manner of proceeding. 'The devil,' said she, 'may sometimes speak truth; Mr. Trueworth has but too well verified the words of that malicious girl; and what she herself then thought a falsehood is now confirmed by fact: yet, wherefore,' cried she, 'did he take all this pains, if he never loved me, never hoped any recompense for his dissimulation, what end could he propose by practicing it? What advantage, what pleasure, could it give him to affront the sister of his friend, and impose upon the credulity of a woman he had no design upon?' It would be endless to repeat the many contradictory surmizes which rose alternately in her distracted mind; so I shall only say, she sought, but the more she did so, the more she became incapable of fathoming, the bottom of this mysterious event.

The butler was laying the cloth in the parlour for supper when she came home; Mr. Goodman had waited for her some time, thinking she might be undressing, and now sent to desire she would come down: but she begged to be excused, said she could not eat, and then called for Nanny, who was the maid that usually attended her in her chamber, to come up and put her to bed.

This prating wench, who would always know the whole secrets of every body in the family, whether they thought fit to entrust her with them or not, used frequently to divert Miss Betsy with her idle stories: but it was not now in her power, that young lady had no attention for any thing but the object of her present meditations; which the other not happening to hit upon, was answered only with peevishness and ill-humour.

But as every little circumstance, if any was adapted to the passion we at that time are possessed of, touches upon the jarring string, and seems a missionary from fate, an accident, the most trifling that can be imagined, served to renew in Miss Betsy, the next morning, those anxieties which sleep had in some measure abated.

A ballad singer happening to be in the street, the first thing she heard, on her waking, was these words, sung in a sonorous voice, just under the window –

> 'Young Philander woo'd me long,
> I was peevish, and forbade him;
> I would not hear his charming song;
> But now I wish, I wish I had him!'

Though this was a song at that time much in vogue, and Miss Betsy had casually heard it an hundred times; yet, in the humour she now was, it beat an alarm upon her heart. It reminded her how inconsiderate she had been, and shewed the folly of not knowing how to place a just value on any thing, till it was lost, in such strong colours before her eyes, as one could scarce think it possible an incident in itself so merely bagatelle could have produced.

Again she fell into very deep reveries; and, divesting herself of all passion, pride, and the prejudice her vanity had but too much inspired her with, she found, that though Mr. Trueworth had carried his resentment farther than became a man who loved to that degree he pretended to have done; yet she could no way justify herself to her brother Frank, Lady Trusty or any of those friends who had espoused his cause, for having given him the provocation.

To heighten the splenetick humour she was in, Mr. Goodman, who, having been taken up with his own affairs, had not mentioned Mr. Trueworth to her for some days, happened this morning, as they sat at breakfast, to ask her how the courtship of that gentleman went on, and whether there was like to be a wedding or not. Perceiving she blushed, hung down her head, and made no answer, 'Nay, nay,' said he, 'I told you long ago I would not interfere in these matters; and have less reason now than ever to do so, as your eldest brother is in town, and who is doubtless capable of advising you for the best.' Miss Betsy was in a good deal of confusion; she knew not as yet whether it would be proper for her to acquaint Mr. Goodman with what had passed between Mr. Trueworth and herself, or to be silent on that head, till she should see what a little time might bring about. As she was thinking in what manner she should reply, Mr. Goodman's lawyer, luckily for her relief, came in, and put an end to a discourse which, in the present situation of her mind, she was very unfit to bear a part in.

But, as if this was to be a day of continued admonitions to Miss Betsy, she was no sooner dressed, and ready to quit her chamber, than she heard Miss Mabel's voice upon the stairs. As that young lady was not accustomed to make her any morning visits, she was a little surprized; she ran, however, to meet her, saying, 'This is a favour I did not expect, and therefore have the more cause to thank you.' – 'I do not know,' replied the other, as she entered the room, 'whether you will think I deserve thanks or no, when you hear the business that brought me; for I assure you I am come only to chide you.' – 'I think,' said Miss Betsy, with a sigh, 'that all the world takes the liberty of doing so with me! but, pray, my dear,' continued she, 'how am I so unhappy as to deserve it from you?'

'Why, you must know,' replied Miss Mabel, 'that I have taken upon me to be the champion of distressed love; you have broken a fine gentleman's heart, and I am come to tell you, that you must either make it whole again, as it was before he saw you, or repair the damage he has sustained by giving him your own.' – 'I plead Not Guilty,' said Miss Betsy, in a tone more sprightly than before: 'but, pray, who has gained so great an influence over you, as to send you on so doughty an errand?' – 'No, my dear, you are quite mistaken in the matter,' replied the other; 'I assure you I am not sent – I am only led by my own generosity, and the sight of poor Mr. Trueworth's despair.' – 'Trueworth!' cried Miss Betsy hastily; 'What do you mean?' – 'I mean,' replied the other, 'to engage you, if the little rhetorick I am mistress of can prevail on you to consider, that while we use a man of sense and honour ill, we do ourselves a real injury. The love our beauty has inspired, may, for a time, secure our power; but it will grow weaker by degrees, and every little coquette-air we give ourselves, lessen the value of our charms. I know there is at present some very great brulée between you and Mr. Trueworth: he is a match every way deserving of you; he has the approbation of all your friends; and, I have heard you acknowledge, you are not insensible of his merit. To what end, then, do you study to perplex and give unnecessary pains to a heart, which you, according to all appearances, will one day take a pride in rendering happy?'

'This is an extreme fine harangue, indeed!' replied Miss Betsy; 'but I would fain know for what reason it is directed to me. If Mr. Trueworth imagines I have used him ill, I think it no proof of his understanding, to make a proclamation of it; but, for Heaven's sake! how came you to be the confidante of his complaints?'

'Indeed, I have not that honour,' said Miss Mabel: 'finding myself a little ill this morning, I thought the air would do me good; so went into the Park, taking only a little girl with me, who lives next door, because I would not go quite alone. Being in the deshabille you see, I crossed the grass, and was passing towards the back of the Bird Cage Walk, where who should I see among the trees but Mr. Trueworth, if I may call the object that then presented itself to me by that name; for, indeed, Miss Betsy, the poor gentleman seems no more than the shadow of himself. He saw me at a distance, and I believe would have avoided me; but, perceiving my eyes were upon him, cleared his countenance as well as he was able, and accosted me with the usual salutations of the morning. "It is somewhat surprizing, Madam," said he, with an air of as much gallantry as he could assume, "to find a lady so justly entitled to the admiration of the world, as Miss Mabel is, shun the gay company of the Mall, and chuse an unfrequented walk, like this!" – "I might retort the same exclamation of surprize," replied I, "at so unexpectedly meeting with Mr. Trueworth here."

'After this, as you know, my dear,' continued she, 'I have lately, on your account, had the pleasure pretty often of Mr. Trueworth's company; I took the liberty to ask him where he had buried himself, that I had not seen him for so many days: to which he answered, not wthout a confusion, which I saw he attempted, though in vain, to conceal from me – "Yes, Madam, I have indeed been buried from all pleasure, have been swallowed up in affairs little less tormenting than those of the grave: but," added he, "they are now over, and I am preparing to return to my country seat, where I hope to re-enjoy that tranquillity which, since my leaving it, has been pretty much disturbed."

'Nothing could equal my astonishment at hearing him speak in this manner: "To your country-seat!" cried I; "not to continue there for any long time?" – "I know not as yet, Madam," replied he; and then, after a pause, "perhaps for ever!" added he. "Bless me," said I, "this is strange, indeed! Miss Betsy did not tell me a word of it; and I saw her but last night." – "She might not then know it, Madam," answered he: "but, if she had, I am not vain enough to imagine, she would think a trifle, such as my departure, worth the pains of mentioning."

'I then,' pursued Miss Mabel, 'endeavoured to railly him out of this humour. After having told him I had a better opinion of your understanding and generosity, than to be capable of believing you thought so lightly of his friendship and affection, I added, that this was only some little pique between you, some jealous whim: but he replied to all I said on this subject with a very grave air, pretended business, and took his leave somewhat abruptly for a man of that politeness I had till now always observed in him.'

'He carries it off with a high hand, indeed,' cried Miss Betsy: 'but it is no matter; I shall give myself no trouble whether he stays in town, or whether he goes into the country, or whether I ever see him more. What! does the man think to triumph over me?'

'I do not believe that is the case with Mr. Trueworth,' said the discreet Miss Mabel; 'but I know it is the way of many men to recriminate in this manner: and pray, when they do, who can we blame for it but ourselves, in giving them the occasion? For my part, I should think it an affront to myself to encourage the addresses of a person I did not look upon worthy of being treated with respect.'

She urged many arguments to convince Miss Betsy of the vanity and ill consequences of trifling with an honourable and sincere passion; which, though no more than what that young lady had already made use of to herself, and was fully persuaded in the truth of, she was not very well pleased to hear from the mouth of another.

Though these two ladies perfectly agreed in their sentiments of virtue and reputation, yet their dispositions and behaviour in the affairs of love were as widely different as any two persons possibly could be: and this it was, which, during the course of their acquaintance, gave frequent interruptions to that harmony between them, which the mutual esteem they had for each other's good qualities, would otherwise have rendered perpetual.

CHAPTER XIX

Is multum in parvo

THERE is an unaccountable pride in human nature, which often gets the better of our justice, and makes us espouse what we know within ourselves is wrong, rather than appear to be set right by any reason, except our own.

Miss Betsy had too much of this unhappy propensity in her composition: a very little reflection enabled her to see clearly enough the mistakes she sometimes fell into; but she could not bear they should be seen by others. Miss Mable was not only in effect the most valuable of all the ladies she conversed with, but was also the most esteemed and loved by her; yet was she less happy and delighted in her company, than in that of several others, for whom her good sense would not suffer her to have the least real regard. The truth is, that though she was very well convinced of her errors, in relation to those men who professed themselves her admirers, yet she loved those errors in herself, thought they were pretty, and became her; and therefore, as she could not as yet resolve to alter her mode of behaviour, was never quite easy in the presence of any one who acted with a prudence she would not be at the pains to imitate.

There were two young ladies, who had an apartment at the palace of St. James's, (their father having an office there) who exactly suited with her in the most volatile of her moments: they had wit, spirit, and were gay almost to wildness, without the least mixture of libertinism or indecency. How perfectly innocent they were, is not the business of this history to discuss; but they preserved as good a reputation as their neighbours, and were well respected in all publick places.

There it was Miss Betsy chiefly found an asylum from those perplexing thoughts which, in spite of her pride, and the indifference she had for mankind, would sometimes intrude upon her mind on Mr. Trueworth's account; here she was certain of meeting a great variety of company; here was all the news and scandal the town could furnish; here was musick, dancing, feasting, flattery: in fine, here was every thing that was an enemy to care and contemplation.

Among the number of those who filled the circle of those two court belles, there was a gentleman named Munden: he appeared extremely charmed with Miss Betsy at first sight; and after having informed himself of the particulars of her family and fortune, took an opportunity, as he was conducting her home one night, to entreat she would allow him to pay his respects to her where she lived. This was a favour Miss Betsy was never very scrupulous of granting; and consented the now more readily, as she thought the report of a new lover would gall Mr. Trueworth, who, she heard by some, who had very lately seen him, was not yet gone out of town.

Mr. Munden, to testify the impatience of his love, waited on her the very next day, as soon as he thought dinner would be over, at Mr. Goodman's: he had the satisfaction of finding her alone; but, fearing she might not long be so, suffered but a very few minutes to escape before he acquainted her with the errand on which he came: the terms in which he declared himself her admirer, were as pathetick as could be made use of for the purpose; but though this was no more than Miss Betsy had expected, and would have been strangely mortified if disappointed by his entertaining her on any other score, yet she affected, at first, to treat it with surprize, and then, on his renewing his protestations, to answer all he said with a sort of raillery, in order to put him to the more expence of oaths and asseverations.

It is certain, that whoever pretended to make his addresses to Miss Betsy, stood in need of being previously provided with a good stock of repartees, to silence the sarcasms of the witty fair, as well as fine speeches to engage her to more seriousness. Mr. Munden often found himself at his *ne plus ultra*, but was not the least disconcerted at it; he was a courtier; he was accustomed to attend at the levees of the great; and knew very well, that persons in power seldom failed to exercise it over those who had any dependance on them: and looking on the case of a lover with his mistress, as the same with one who is soliciting for a pension or employment, had armed himself with patience, to submit to every thing his tyrant should inflict, in the hope

that it would one day be his turn to impose those laws, according to
the poet's words –

> 'The humbled lover, when he lowest lies,
> But kneels to conquer, and but falls to rise.'

Miss Betsy was indeed a tyrant, but a very gentle one; she always
mingled some sweet with the sharpness of her expressions: if in one
breath she menaced despair, in the next she encouraged hope; and
her very repulses were sometimes so equivocal, as that they might be
taken for invitations. She played with her lovers, as she did with her
monkey; but expected more obedience from them: they must look gay
or grave, according as she did so; their humour, and even their very
motions, must be regulated by her influence, as the waters by the
moon. In fine, an exterior homage was the chief thing to be required;
for, as to the heart, her own being yet untouched, she gave herself
but little trouble how that of her lovers stood affected.

Mr. Munden, with less love perhaps than any man who had
addressed her, knew better how to suit himself to her humour: he
could act over all the delicacies of the most tender passion, without
being truly sensible of any of them; and though he wished, in reality,
nothing so much as attaining the affections of Miss Betsy, yet wishing
it without those timid inquietudes, those jealous doubts, those
perplexing anxieties, which suspense inflicts on a more stolid mind,
he was the more capable of behaving towards her in the way she
liked.

He was continually inviting her to some party of pleasure or other;
he gallanted her to all publick shews, he treated her with the most
exquisite dainties of the season, and presented her with many curious
toys. Being to go with these ladies, at whose appointment he first
commenced his acquaintance with her, and some other company, to a
masquerade, he waited on her some hours before the time; and
taking out of his pocket a ruby, cut in the shape of a heart, and
illustrated with small brilliants round about, 'I beg, Madam,' said he,
'you will do me the honour of wearing this to-night, either on your
sleeve or breast, or some other conspicuous place. There will be a
great deal of company, and some, perhaps, in the same habit as
yourself: this will direct my search, prevent my being deceived by
appearances, which otherwise I might be, and prophanely pay my
worship to some other, instead of the real goddess of my soul.'

This was the method he took to ingratiate himself into the favour of his mistress; and it had the effect, if not to make her love him, at least to make her charmed with this new conquest, much more than she had been with several of her former ones, though ever so much deserving her esteem.

In the midst of these gay scenes, however, Mr. Trueworth came frequently into her head. To find he was in town, made her flatter herself that he lingered here on her account; and that, in spite of all his resolution, he had not courage to leave the same air she breathed in: she fancied, that if she could meet him, or any accident throw him in her way, she should be able to rekindle all his former flames, and render him as much her slave as ever. With this view she never went abroad without casting her eyes about, in search of him; nay, she sometimes even condescended to pass by the house where he was lodged, in hopes of seeing him either going in or out, or from some one or other of the windows: but chance did not befriend her inclinations this way, nor put it in her power again to triumph over a heart, the sincerity of which she had but too ill treated, when devoted to her.

In the mean time, Mr. Goodman, in spite of the perplexities his own affairs involved him in, could not help feeling a great concern for those of Miss Betsy; he knew that Mr. Trueworth had desisted his visits to her; that she had got a new lover, who he could not find had consulted the permission of any one but herself to make his addresses to her; the late hours she kept, seldom coming home till some hours after the whole family, except the servant who sat up for her, were in bed, gave him also much matter of uneasiness; and he thought it his duty to talk seriously to her on all these points.

He began with asking her how it happened, that he had not seen Mr. Trueworth for so long a time: to which she replied, with the utmost indifference, that she took some things ill from that gentleman, and that, perhaps, he might have some subject of complaint against her; 'Therefore,' said she, 'as our humours did not very well agree, it was best to break off conversation.'

He then questioned her concerning Mr. Munden. 'I hope,' said he, 'you have taken care to inform yourself as to his character and circumstances.' – 'No, truly, Sir,' answered she, with the same careless air as before; 'as I never intend to be the better or the worse for either, I give myself no pain about what he is.' Mr. Goodman shook his head; and was going to reason with her on the ill consequences of such a behaviour, when some company coming in, broke off, for a time, all farther discourse between them.

CHAPTER XX

*Shews Miss Betsy left entirely to her own manage-
ment, and the cause of it, with some other particulars*

MR. Goodman, who had been a little vexed at being interrupted in
the remonstrances he thought so highly necessary should be made to
Miss Betsy, took an opportunity of renewing them the next morning,
in the strongest expressions he was master of.

Miss Betsy, with all her wit, had little to say for herself in answer
to the serious harangue made to her by Mr. Goodman on her present
fashion of behaviour; her heart avowed the justice of his reproofs, but
her humour, too tenacious of what pleased itself, and too impatient of
control, would not suffer her to obey the dictates either of his or her
own reason. She knew very well the tender regard he had for her, on
the account of her deceased father, and that all he spoke was
calculated for her good; but then it was a good she was not at present
ambitious of attaining, and thought it the privilege of youth to do
whatever it listed, provided the rules of virtue were unfringed; so that
all he could get from her was – that her amusements were innocent –
that she meant no harm in any thing she did – that it was dull for her
to sit at home alone; and, when in company, could not quit it abruptly
on any consideration of hours.

Mr. Goodman found, that to bring her to a more just sense of what
was really her advantage, would be a task impossible for him to
accomplish; he began heartily to wish she was under the care of some
person who had more leisure to argue with her on points so essential
to her happiness: he told her, that he indeed had feared his house
would be too melancholy a recess for her since the revolution that
had lately happened in his family, and therefore wished some more

proper place could be found for her. 'And for such a one,' said he, 'I shall make it my business to enquire; and there seems not only a necessity for my doing so, but that you should also choose another guardian; for as soon as the present unlucky business I am engaged in shall be over, it is my resolution to break up house-keeping, leave my business to my nephew, Ned Goodman, whom I expect by the first ship that arrives from the East Indies; and, having once seen him settled, retire, and spend the remainder of my days in the country.'

The melancholy accents with which Mr. Goodman spoke these words, touched Miss Betsy very much; she expressed, in terms the most affectionate, the deep concern it gave her that he had any cause to withdraw from a way of life to which he had so long been accustomed: but added, that if it must be so, she knew no person so proper, in whose hands the little fortune she was mistress of should be entrusted, as those of her brother Thoughtless, if he would vouchsafe to take that trouble upon him.

'There is no doubt to be made of that, I believe,' replied Mr. Goodman; 'and I shall speak to him about it the first time I see him.' They had some farther talk on Miss Betsy's affairs; and that young lady found he had very largely improved the portion bequeathed her by her father; for which, in the first emotions of her gratitude, she was beginning to pour forth such acknowledgements as he thought it too much to hear, and interrupted her, saying he had done no more than his duty obliged him to do, and could not have answered to himself the omission of any part of it.

It is so natural for people to love money, even before they know what to do with it, that it is not to be wondered at that Miss Betsy, now arrived at an age capable of relishing all the delicacies of life, should be transported at finding so considerable, and withal so unexpected, an augmentation of her fortune, which was no less than one third of what her father had left her.

The innate pleasure of her mind, on this occasion, diffused itself through all her form, and gave a double lustre to her eyes and air; so that she went with charms new pointed to a ball that night; for which the obsequious Mr. Munden had presented her with a ticket: but though she had all the respect in the world for Mr. Goodman, and indeed a kind of filial love for him, yet she had it not in her power to pay that regard to his admonitions she ought to have done. She came not home till between one and two o'clock in the morning; but was extremely surprized to find, that when she did so, the knocker was taken off the door; a thing which, in complaisance to her, had never before been done till she came in, how late soever she staid abroad: she was, nevertheless, much more surprized, as well as troubled, when, at the first rap her chairman gave, a footman, who waited in the hall for her return, immediately opened the door, and told her, with all the marks of sorrow in his countenance, that his master had been suddenly taken ill, and that his physician, as well as Mrs. Barns, the housekeeper, had given strict orders there should be no noise made in the house, the former having said his life depended on his being kept perfectly quiet.

It is not to be doubted, but that, on this information, she went with as little noise as possible up to her chamber; where Nanny, as she was putting her to bed, confirmed to her what the footman had said; and added, that she had heard the doctor tell Mrs. Barns, as he was going out, that he was very apprehensive his patient's disorder would not be easily remedied.

Distempers of the body, which arise from those of the mind, are, indeed, much more difficult to be cured than those which proceed from mere natural causes. Mr. Goodman's resentment for the ill usage he had sustained from a woman he had so tenderly loved, awhile kept up his spirits, and hindered him from feeling the cruel sting, which preyed upon his vitals, and insensibly slackened the strings of life: but the first hurry being over, and the lawyer having told him that every thing was drawn up, and his cause would be brought before the Commons in a few days, he sunk beneath the apprehensions; the thoughts of appearing before the doctors of the civil law, to several of whom he was known, to prove his own dishonour – the talk of the town – the whispers – the grimaces – the ridicule, which he was sensible this affair would occasion when exposed – the pity of some – and the contempt he must expect from others – all these things, though little regarded by him while at a distance, now they came more near at hand, and just ready to fall upon him, gave him such a shock, as all the courage he had assumed was not sufficient to enable him to resist.

He was seized at once with a violent fit of an apoplexy at a coffee-house, where a surgeon being immediately sent for, he was let blood, as is common in such cases. This operation soon recovered him, so far as speech and motion; but reason had not power to re-assume her seat in his distracted brain for many hours – he was brought home in a chair – the surgeon attended him – saw him put into bed, and sat by him a considerable time: but, finding him rather worse than better, told Mrs. Barns, he durst not proceed any farther, and that they must have recourse to a physician; which was accordingly done.

This gentleman, who was esteemed the most skilful of his profession, hearing Mr. Goodman frequently cry out, 'My heart! my heart!' laid his hand upon his bosom; and found, by the extraordinary pulsations there, that he had symptoms of an inward convulsion, wrote a prescription, and ordered he should be kept extremely quiet.

Towards morning, he grew more composed; and, by degrees, recovered the use of his understanding as perfectly as ever: but his limbs were so much weakened by that severe attack the fit had made upon him, that he could not sit up in his bed without support. The physician, however, had great hopes of him; said his imbecillity proceeded only from a fever of the nerves, which he doubted not but to abate, and that he would be well in a few days. How uncertain, how little to be depended upon, is art, in some cases! Mr. Goodman felt that within himself which gave the lye to all appearances; and, fully convinced that the hand of death had seized upon his heart, would not defer a moment putting all his affairs in such a posture as should leave no room for contention among the parties concerned, after his decease: he began with sending for Mr. Thoughtless; and consigned over to him the whole fortunes of Mr. Francis and Miss Betsy, the latter being obliged, as not being yet of age, to chuse him for her guardian in form. Having thus acquitted himself, in the most honourable manner, of the trust reposed in him for the children of his friend, he considered what was best to be done in relation to those of his own blood. By his death, the intended process against Lady Mellasin would be prevented, and consequently the third part of his effects would devolve on her, as being the widow of a citizen: he, therefore, having consulted with his lawer if such a thing were practicable, made a deed of gift to his nephew, Mr. Edward Goodman, of all his money in the Bank, stocks, and other publick funds. After this, he made his will; and the lawyer, perceiving he had left but few legacies, asked him how the residue of what he was possessed of should be disposed: to which he replied, 'Greatly as I have been wronged by Lady Mellasin, I would not have her starve; I have been calculating in my mind to what her dividend may amount, and believe it will be sufficient to enable her to live in that retired manner which best becomes her age and character.'

Mr. Goodman, thus having settled all his affairs in this world, began to make such preparations for another as are necessary for the best of men. In the mean time, as the least noise was disturbing to him, it was judged proper that Miss Betsy, who could not live without company, should remove. No boarding-place to her mind being yet found, and having done with all hopes of living with her brother, (as she was by this time informed of the true reasons he had for her not doing so) took lodgings in Jermyn Street; and finding the interest of her fortune, through the good management of her guardian, would allow it, hired a maid and foot-boy to wait upon her.

The adieu she received from Mr. Goodman was the most tender and affectionate that could be; she was very much moved with it, and sincerely lamented the loss she should sustain of so honest and worthy a friend: but her natural sprightliness would not suffer any melancholy reflections to dwell long upon her mind; and the hurry she was in of sending messages to all her acquaintance, with an account of the change of her situation, very much contributed to dissipate them. This important business was scarce over, and she well settled in her new habitation, when one of Mr. Goodman's footmen brought her a letter from her brother Frank, which had been just left for her by the post. It contained these lines.

'To Miss Betsy Thoughtless.

My dear sister,

I have been snatched from the brink of the grave, by the skill of one of the best physicians in the world, and the tender, and, I may say, maternal care of our most dear, and truly valuable friend, the excellent Lady Trusty. The first use I make of my recovered health, is to give an account of it to those whom, I flatter myself, will be obliged by the intelligence. I thank you for the many kind wishes you have sent me during the course of my illness, but hoped to have seen, before now, another name subscribed to your letters than that you received from your birth; and cannot help saying, I am a little surprized, that in the two last you favoured me with, you have been entirely silent on a subject you know I have always had very much at heart. I have also very lately received a letter from Mr. Trueworth, wherein he tells me, he is going to his country-seat – expresses the most kind concern for me, but mentions not the least syllable of you, or of his passion. I fear, my dear sister, there is some misunderstanding between you, which would very much trouble me, for your sake especially: but I shall defer what I have to say to you till I have the pleasure of seeing you. I am not yet judged fit to sit my horse for so long a journey; and the places in the stage-coach are all taken for to-morrow, but have secured one in Thursday's coach, and expect to be with you on Saturday. I accompany this to you with another one to my brother, and another to Mr. Goodman; so have no occasion to trouble you with my compliments to either. Farewel! I think I need not tell you that I am, with an unfeigned regard, my dear sister, your very affectionate brother, and humble servant,

F. THOUGHTLESS.

P.S. Sir Ralph and Lady Trusty are both from home at this time, or I am certain their good wishes, if no more, would have joined mine, that you may never cease to enjoy whatever it becomes you to desire! My dear Betsy, adieu!'

The joy which this letter would have afforded Miss Betsy had been compleat, if not somewhat abated by the apprehensions of what her brother would have to say to her when he should find she was indeed entirely broke off with Mr. Trueworth: but as the reader may probably desire to know in what manner he passed his time after that event, and the motives which induced him to stay in London, it is now highly proper to say something of both.

CHAPTER XXI

———•———

The author is under some apprehensions, will not be quite pleasing to the humour of every reader

IT is certain that Mr. Trueworth, at the time of his writing his last letter to Miss Betsy, was fully determined to go into the country; and was already beginning to make such preparations as he found necessary for his journey, when an accident of a very singular nature put a sudden stop to them, and to his intentions.

He was one day just dressed, and going out, in order to dine with some company, (for he now chose to be as little alone as possible) when one of his servants delivered a letter to him, which he said was brought by a porter, who waited below for an answer. As the superscription was in a woman's hand, and he was not accustomed to receive any billets from that sex, he broke it open with a kind of greedy curiosity, and found in it these lines.

'To Charles Trueworth, Esq.

Sir,

I am a woman of fortune, family, and an unblemished character; very young, and, most people allow, not disagreeable: you have done me the greatest injury in the world without knowing it; but I take you to be more a man of honour than not to be willing to make what reparation is in your power. If the good opinion I have of you does not deceive me, you will readily accept this challenge, and not fail to meet me about eleven o'clock in the morning, at General Tatten's bench, opposite Rosamond's Pond in St. James's Park; there to hear such interrogatories as I shall think fit to make you; and on your sincere answer to which depends the whole future peace, if not the life of her, who at present can only subscribe herself, in the greatest confusion, Sir, your unfortunate and impatient

INCOGNITA.'

Mr. Trueworth was a good deal surprized; but had no occasion to consult long with himself in what manner it would become a man of his years to behave in such an adventure, and therefore sat down and immediately wrote an answer in these terms.

'To the fair Incognita.

Madam,

Though a challenge from an unknown antagonist might be rejected without any danger of incurring the imputation of cowardice, and, besides, as the combat to which I am invited is to be that of words, in which your sex are generally allowed to excel, I have not any sort of chance of overcoming; yet, to shew that I dare encounter a fine woman at any weapon, and shall not repine at being foiled, will not fail to give you the triumph you desire; and to that end will wait on you exactly at the time and place mentioned in yours: till when, you may rest satisfied that I am, with the greatest impatience, the obliging Incognita's most devoted servant,

C. TRUEWORTH.'

Though Mr. Trueworth had not only heard of, but also experienced, when on his travels abroad, some adventures of a parallel nature with this; yet, as it never had entered his head that the English ladies took this method of introducing themselves to the acquaintance of those they were pleased to favour, the challenge of the Incognita – who she was – where she had seen him – what particular action of his had merited her good graces – and a thousand other conjectures, all tending to the same object, very much engrossed his mind. Indeed, he was glad to encourage any thoughts which served to drive those of Miss Betsy thence; whose idea, in spite of all his endeavours, and her supposed unworthiness, would sometimes intervene, and poison the sweets of his most jovial moments among his friends.

His curiosity (for it cannot be said was as yet instigated by a warmer passion) rendered him, however, very careful not to suffer the hour mentioned in the lady's letter to escape: but though he was at the place somewhat before the time, she was the first, and already waited his approach. As he turned by the corner of the pond, he began to reflect, that as she had given him no signal whereby she might be known, he might possibly mistake for his Incognita some other, whom chance might have directed to the bench; and was somewhat at a loss how to accost her in such a manner, as that the compliment might not make him be looked upon as rude or made, by a person who had no reason to expect it from him.

But the fair lady, who, it is likely, was also sensible she had been a little wanting in this part of the assignation, soon eased him of the suspense he was in, by rising from her seat, as he drew near, and soluting him with these words, 'How perfectly obliging,' said she, 'is this punctuality! It almost flatters me I shall have no reason to repent the step I have taken.' – 'A person who is injured,' replied Mr. Trueworth, 'has doubtless a right to complain; and if I have, though ever so unwarily, been guilty of any wrong, cannot be too hasty, nor too zealous, in the reparation: be pleased, therefore, Madam, to let me know the nature of my offence, and be assured that the wishes of my whole heart shall be to expiate it.'

In concluding these words, one of her gloves being off, he took hold of her hand, and kissed it with either a real or a seeming warmth. 'Take care what you say,' cried she, 'lest I exact more from you than is in your power to perform: but let us sit down,' pursued she, suffering him still to keep her hand in his, 'and begin to fulfil the promise you have made, by satisfying me in some points I have to ask, with the same sincerity as you would answer Heaven.' – 'Be assured I will,' said he, putting her hand a second time to his mouth; 'and this shall be the book on which I will swear to every article.'

'First, then,' demanded she, 'are you married, or contracted?' – 'Neither, by all that's dear!' said he. 'Have you no attachment,' resumed she, 'to any particular lady, that should hinder your engaging with another?' – 'Not any, upon my honour!' answered he.

I should before now have acquainted my reader, that the lady was not only masqued, but also close muffled in her hood; that Mr. Trueworth could discover no part even of the side of her face, which, growing weary of this examination, he took an opportunity to complain of. 'Why this unkind reserve, my charming incognita?' said he: 'I have heard of penitents who, while confessing crimes they were ashamed of, kept their faces hid; but I believe there never was a confessor who concealed himself – permit me to see to whom I am laying open my heart, and I shall do it with pleasure.' – 'That cannot be,' answered she, 'even for the very reason you have alledged: I have something to confess to you, would sink me into the earth with shame, did you behold the mouth that utters it. In a word, I love you! and after having told you so, can you expect I will reveal myself?' – 'Else how can I return the bounty as I ought,' cried he, 'or you be assured you have not lavished your favours on an insensible or ungrateful heart?'

'Time may do much,' said she; 'a longer and more free conversation with you may perhaps embolden me to make a full discovery of my face to you, as I have already done of my heart.' Mr. Trueworth then told her, that the place they were in would allow but very few freedoms; and added, that if he were really so happy as she flattered him he was, she must permit him to wait on her, where he might have an opportunity of testifying the sense he had of so unhoped, and as yet so unmerited, a blessing.

'Alas!' cried she, 'I am quite a novice in assignations of this sort – have so entire a dependance on your honour, that I dare meet you any where, provided you give me your solemn promise not to take any measures for knowing who I am, nor make any attempts to oblige me to unmask, till I have assumed courage enough to become visible of my own free will.'

Mr. Trueworth readily enough gave her the promise she exacted from him, not at all doubting but he should be easily able to find means to engage her consent for the satisfaction of his curiosity in these points. 'Well, then,' said she, 'it belongs to you to name a place proper for these secret interviews.'

On this, after a little pause, he answered, that since she judged it inconvenient for him to wait upon her at home, or any other place where she was known, he would be about the close of day at a certain coffee-house, which he named to her – 'Where,' continued he, 'I will attend your commands; and on your condescending to stop at the door in a hackney-coach, will immediately come down and conduct you to a house secure from all danger of a discovery.' She hesitated not a moment to comply with his proposal; yet, in the same breath she did so, affected to be under some fears, which before she had not made the least shew of – said, she hoped he would not abuse the confidence she reposed in him – that he would take no advantage of the weakness she had shewn – that though she loved him with the most tender passion, and could not have lived without revealing it to him, yet her inclinations were innocent, and pure as those of a vestal virgin – and a great deal more stuff of the like sort; which, though Mr. Trueworth could scarce refrain from smiling at, yet he answered; with all the seriousness imaginable – 'I should be unworthy, Madam, of the affection you honour me with, were I capable of acting towards you in a manner unbecoming of you, or of myself; and you may depend I shall endeavour to regulate my desires, so as to render them agreeable to yours.'

After some farther discourse of the like nature, she rose up and took her leave, insisting at parting, that he should not attempt to follow her, or take any method to find out which way she went; which injunction he punctually obeyed, not stirring from the bench till she was quite out of sight.

This adventure prodigiously amused him; never, in his whole life, had he met with any thing he knew so little how to judge of. She had nothing of the air of a woman of the town; and, besides, he knew it was not the interest of those who made a trade of their favours, to dispense them in the manner she seemed to intend; nor could he think her a person of the condition and character her letter intimated. He could not conceive, that any of those he was acquainted with, would run such lengths for the gratification of their passion, especially for a man who had not taken the least pains to inspire it. Sometimes he imagined it was a trick put upon him, in order to make trial how far his vanity would extend in boasting of it; it even came into his head, that Miss Betsy herself might get somebody to personate the amorous incognita, for no other purpose than to divert herself, and disappoint his high-raised expectation: but this last conjecture dwelt not long upon him; he had heard she now entertained another lover, which whom she was very much taken up, and, consequently, would not give herself so much trouble about one who had entirely quitted her. In fine, he knew not what to think: as he could not tell how to believe he had made such an impression upon any woman, without knowing it, as the incognita pretended; he was apt to imagine he should neither see nor hear any more of her. This uncertainty, however, employed his mind the whole day; and he was no less impatient for the proof, than he would have been, if actually in love with this invisible mistress.

The wished-for hour at last arrived; and he waited not long before he was eased of one part of his suspense, by being told a lady in a hackney-coach enquired for him: he was extremely pleased to find, at last, he had not been imposed upon by a trick of any of his frolicksome companions, and immediately flew to the coach-side; where, seeing it was indeed his incognita, he jumped directly in, with a transport which doubtless was very agreeable to her.

Though he had often heard some gentlemen speak of houses, where two persons of different sexes might at any time be received, and have the privilege of entertaining each other with all the freedom and privacy they could desire; yet, as he had never been accustomed to intrigues of this nature, and thought he should have no occasion to make use of such places, he had not given himself the trouble of asking where they might be found; therefore he had now no other recourse than either a tavern or a bagnio, the latter of which he looked upon, for more reasons than one, as the most commodious of the two; so ordered the coachman to drive to one in Silver Street: he excused himself, at the same time, to the lady, for not having been able to provide a better asylum for her reception; but she appeared perfectly content – told him she had put herself under his care – relied upon his honour and discretion, and left all to his direction.

Being come into the bagnio, they were shewn into a handsome large room, with a bed-chamber in it. Mr. Trueworth had his eye on every thing in an instant; and finding all was right, ordered a supper to be prepared, and then told the waiter he would dispense with his attendance till it was ready. As soon as he found himself alone with his incognita, 'Now, my angel,' said he, embracing her, 'I have an opportunity to thank you for the affection you have flattered me with the hopes of; but, at the same time, must complain of the little proofs you give me of it: the greatest stranger to your heart would be allowed the privilege of a salute; yet I am denied the privilege of touching those dear lips which have denounced my happiness.' – 'Do not reproach me,' answered she, 'with denying what is not yet in my power to grant: I cannot let you see my face; and you have promised not to force me.' – 'I have,' replied he, 'but that promise binds me not from indulging my impatient wishes with things you have not stipulated: your neck, your breasts, are free, and those I will be revenged upon.' With these words he took some liberties with her, which may better be conceived than described! – she but faintly resisted; and, perhaps, would have permitted him to take greater, thus masked; but the discovery of her face was what he chiefly wanted: 'You might, at least,' cried he, 'oblige me with a touch of those lovely lips I am forbid to gaze upon; 'here is a dark recess,' continued he, pointing to the inner-room, 'will save your blushes.'

He then raised her from the chair; and, drawing her gently towards the door, sung in a very harmonious voice, this stanza –

> 'Away with this idle, this scrupulous fear;
>   For a kiss in the dark,
>   Cry'd the amorous spark,
> 'There is nothing, no, nothing too dear!'

Having led her into the chamber, and seated her on the bed, which happened to be so disposed that no gleam of light came upon it from the candles in the next room, 'Now, my charmer,' said he, taking hold of her mask, 'you have no excuse for keeping on this invidious cloud.' – 'How impossible it is,' answered she, letting it fall into his hands, 'to refuse you any thing!'

What conversation after this passed between them, I shall leave to the reader's imagination; and only say, that the voice of the incognita being more distinguishable by the button of her mask being removed, Mr. Trueworth could not help thinking he had heard before accents very like those with which he was now entertained; though where, or from what mouth they had proceeded, he was not able to recollect.

This conjecture, however, rendering him more impatient than ever for the discovery, he omitted nothing in his power, either by words or actions, to dissuade her from re-assuming her vizard when they should quit that scene of darkness. 'How gladly would I comply,' cried she, 'but that I fear –' 'Fear what!' cried Mr. Trueworth, eagerly interrupting her. 'I fear to lose you,' replied she, fondly embracing him: 'My face is already but too well known to you; you have often seen it, but seen it without those emotions I endeavoured to inspire. How, then, can I now hope it will have the effect I wish!' – 'Unkindly judged,' said he: 'with what indifference soever I may have regarded you, the endearing softness, the enchanting transports, you have now blessed me with, would give new charms to every feature, and make me find perfections I never saw before. Come then, my goddess,' continued he, raising her, 'shine with full lustre on me, and fix me your adorer.' – 'Well,' cried she, 'you are not to be resisted, and I will venture.'

These words brought them to the chamber-door, and shewed the incognita to her amazed gallant to be no other than Miss Flora. 'Miss Flora Mellasin! Good Heavens!' cried he. 'You seem surprized and shocked,' said she: 'alas! my apprehensions were too just.' – 'Pardon me, Madam,' answered he, 'I am indeed surprized, but it is through an excess of joy! Could I have ever thought the favours I have received were bestowed by the amiable Miss Flora Mellasin!'

It is certain, that his astonishment at first was very great; but recovering himself from it in a short time, a thousand passages in Miss Flora's former behaviour towards him occurred to his remembrance, and made him wonder at himself for not having sooner found her out in the person of his incognita. They passed their time, till the night was pretty far advanced, in a manner very agreeable to each other; nor parted without reciprocal assurance of renewing this tender intercourse the next day, at the same place.

CHAPTER XXII

———•———

*Gives an account of a farther and more laudable
motive to induce Mr. Trueworth to put off his intended
journey into the country*

THOUGH it is impossible for a man of sense to have any real love for
a woman whom he cannot esteem, yet Mr. Trueworth found enough
in the agreeable person and sprightly humour of Miss Flora, to
dissipate those uneasy reflections which, in spite of him, had lurked
in his mind on Miss Betsy's account: the amour with this fond girl
afforded him a pleasing amusement for a time; and, without filling his
heart with a new passion, cleared it of those remains of his former
one, which he had taken so much pains to extirpate.

Whenever he thought of Miss Betsy, as it was impossible a young
lady he once loved with so much tenderness should not sometimes
come into his thoughts, it was only with a friendly concern for her
imagined fall. 'It is no wonder,' would he often say to himself, 'that so
young and lovely a creature, under the tuition of a woman of Lady
Mellasin's character, and the constant companion of one of Miss
Flora's disposition, endued with charms to excite the warmest wishes,
and unprovided with sufficient arms for her defence, should have
yielded to the temptations of an unwarrantable flame.' In fine, he
pitied her, but no more.

Thus entirely freed from all prepossession, and his heart almost in
the same situation as before he ever knew what it was to love, he was
easily persuaded by his friends to give over all thoughts of going into
the country, and stay to partake, in a moderate way, those pleasures
of the town, which the many uneasy moments he had sustained,
during his courtship with Miss Betsy, had kept him hitherto from
having any relish for.

But this state of indifference lasted not long; an object presented itself to him, inspiring him with a passion, which had so much of reason for it's guide, as made him think it rather his glory, than his misfortune, to be a second time enslaved.

Among all the friends and acquaintance he had in town, there was none he more valued and esteemed than Sir Bazil Loveit: they had been for some time inseparable companions; but accidents, either on the one side or the other, having hindered their meeting for several days, Mr. Trueworth went one morning to visit him at his house. He found him at home, but the hall so incumbered with trunks and boxes, that there was scarce a passage to the parlour-door. 'Welcome, my dear friend!' said Sir Bazil, who, having seen him from a window, ran down stairs to receive him: 'you find me in a strange disorder here; but I have got a couple of women out of the country; and that sex, I think, like a general officer, can never move without a waggon-load of trumpery at their tail.' – 'What, married!' cried Mr. Trueworth. 'No, 'faith,' said the other; 'but the arrival of two sisters last night from Staffordshire, gives me a sort of specimen of the hurry I am to expect when I become a husband.'

'The hurry,' said Mr. Trueworth, 'you seem to complain of, must needs be a very agreeable one; and I heartily congratulate you upon it. A single man, like you, makes but a very solitary figure in a great wild house: these ladies will fill the vacuum, and give a double life to your family.' – 'Nay,' resumed Sir Bazil, 'I shall not have them long with me; they hate London, and never come but once in two years, to buy cloaths and see fashions: besides, one of them is married, and the other fond of her sister, that I believe she would not quit her to be a duchess. Indeed, it is not much to be wondered at; our mother dying when she was very young, Harriot, for so she is called, was brought up under her sister, who is eight years older than herself, and they never have been asunder two days in their lives.'

Mr. Trueworth then expiated on the amiableness of such an harmony between persons of the same blood: to which Sir Bazil replied, that it was more than ordinarily fortunate for his sisters; 'For,' said he, 'the elder of them being married just before my mother's death, my father committed to her the care of the younger, as she was reckoned a woman of greater prudence than might be expected from her years. My brother Wellair, (for that is the name of the gentleman she married) though a very good husband in the main, is a great sportsman, takes rather too much delight in his hawks and hounds, and gives his wife but little of his company in the day; so that, if it were not for Harriot, she would pass her time uncomfortably enough. In short, the younger is improved by the lessons of the elder, and the elder diverted by the sprightliness and good-humour of the younger.'

Sir Bazil, who had an extreme regard for his sisters, could not forbear entertaining Mr. Trueworth on this subject all the time he was there; and, at parting, told him he would not ask him to stay dinner that day, because he supposed they would be very busy in unpacking their things, and setting themselves in order; but engaged him to come on the following.

Mr. Trueworth thought no farther on what had passed, than to remember his promise, which he accordingly fulfilled. Sir Bazil received him with open arms, and conducted him into the dining-room, where the two ladies were sitting. They were both very handsome: the elder was extremely graceful; and, at first glance, appeared to be the most striking beauty of the two; but, on a second, the younger had the advantage; she was not altogether so tall as her sister, nor had a skin of that dazzling whiteness; but her shape was exquisite – her complexion clear – her eyes sparkling – all her features perfectly regular, and accompanied with a sweetness which had in it somewhat irresistibly attractive.

After the first compliments were over, neither of them lost, by their manner of conversation, any part of that admiration which their eyes had gained. Mrs. Wellair talked pretty much; yet so agreeably, that nobody could be tired of hearing her. Miss Harriot spoke much less; but all she said discovered a delicacy of sentiment, and a judgment far above her years. Sir Bazil had a large estate; he lived up to the height of it; had a very elegant taste; and, in complaisance to his sisters, as well as to his friend, who had never dined with him before since he set up house keeping, had taken care that day to omit nothing in his bill of fare that could excite, or gratify, the most luxurious appetite; yet it was the wit, spirit, and good-humour, of the company, especially of Miss Harriot, which, to Mr. Trueworth, made the most agreeable part of the entertainment.

When the dessert was over, and the healths of absent friends toasted in Tokay and Frontiniac, they all adjourned into the drawing-room; where coffee and tea were soon brought in. Mrs. Wellair having been advised by her physicians to refrain from the use of any of those liquors, on account of some disorder she had complained of, took this opportunity of desiring leave to retire, in order to acquaint her husband, it being post-night, with her safe arrival in town.

Agreeable as her conversation was, Mr. Trueworth found no miss of her, as the lovely Harriot was left behind: on the contrary, he was rather rejoiced, in the hope she would now give her tongue a greater latitude than she had done in the presence of one whom, he easily perceived, she looked upon as her superior in understanding; as well as years; and, to provoke her to it, artfully introduced some discourse on the pleasures of the town; and said to Sir Bazil, it seemed to him a kind of miracle, that so young and beautiful a lady as Miss Harriot could content herself with the obscurity of a country life. 'Few of her age, indeed,' replied Sir Bazil, 'could chuse to live in the manner she does; but though I should, perhaps, not be of the same way of thinking, if I were a woman, and in her place, yet I cannot but say, my reason approves of her conduct in this point.'

'London,' said she, 'is a very magnificent, opulent city; and those who have their lot cast to live in it, may, doubtless, find sufficient to content them: but as for those amusements, which you gentlemen call the pleasures of the town, and which so many people take every winter such long journies merely to enjoy, I can see nothing in them which a reasonable person may not very well dispense with the want of.'

'What do you think of the Court, Madam?' cried Mr. Trueworth. 'As of a place I would always chuse to avoid,' replied she. 'I heartily pity the fatigue of those who are obliged to attend; and am tempted to laugh at the stupidity of those who undertake it without necessity. I am amazed to think how any one of common-sense can be at so great an expense for rich cloaths, to go to a place where she must suffer as great pain in shewing them. Bless me! to stand, for two or three hours together, mute as a fish – upright as an arrow; and, when the scene is over, walk backward like a crab, curtseying at every step, though their legs are so tired, they are scarce able to go through the ceremony!'

'A masquerade, then?' resumed Mr. Trueworth, willing to try her farther. 'What say you, Madam, to a masquerade? I hope you will allow no freedom of behaviour is wanting there?' – 'I should like a masquerade extremely,' answered she, 'if conducted in the same manner I have been told they are in Italy, and some other places, where only persons of condition are admitted, and none presume to say that under a vizard, which he either would or ought to be ashamed of when it is plucked off. But the venal ones you have here, are my utter detestation; they seem to me to license, under a shew of innocent diversion, not only folly, but all kind of prophaneness and indecency.'

'It must be owned, Madam,' said Mr. Trueworth, 'that your sentiments on both these subjects are extremely just: but you can have no such objection against a play or opera?' – 'No, Sir,' answered she; 'I look upon a good play as one of the most improving, as well as agreeable, entertainments a thinking mind can take; and as for an opera –' 'Aye, sister!' cried Sir Bazil, interrupting her, 'the opera! Take care what you say of the opera. My friend here is a passionate lover of musick; and, if you utter one syllable against his favourite science, you will certainly pass in his opinion for a stoick.' – 'I should deserve it,' said she; 'and be in reality as insensible as that sect of philosophers affect to be, if I were not capable of being touched by the charms of harmony.'

'Then, Madam,' said Mr. Trueworth, 'there are two of the pleasures of London, which are so happy to receive your approbation?' – 'Not only my approbation,' replied she, 'but my applause. I am, indeed, a very great admirer of both; yet can find ways to make myself easy without being present at either; and, at the distance of an hundred miles, enjoy in theory all the satisfaction the representation could afford.'

'This is somewhat extraordinary indeed, Madam,' cried Mr. Trueworth: 'be so good as to let us know by what method? – 'It is this, Sir,' answered she: 'as for the plays, I have a very good collection of the old ones by me, and have all the new ones sent down to me as they come out. When I was last in London, I was several times at the theatre; I observed how the actors and actresses varied their voices and gestures, according to the different characters they appeared in on the stage: and thus, whilst I am reading any play, am enabled to judge pretty near how it shews in representation. I have, indeed, somewhat more difficulty in bringing the opera home to me; yet I am so happy as to be able to procure a shadow of it, at least. We have two or three gentlemen in the neighbourhood who play to great perfection on the violin, and several ladies, who have very pretty voices, and some skill in musick. My sister touches the bass-viol finely; and I play a little on the harpsichord. We have all our parts in score before us, which we execute to the best of our power. It serves, however, to divert ourselves, and those friends who think it worth their while to come to hear us.'

Mr. Trueworth cried out, in a kind of rapture, as soon as she had done speaking, 'Who would not think himself happy to be one of the audience at such a performance!' He was going on; but Mrs. Wellair returned, on which he directed the compliments he was about to make Miss Harriot, equally to the other; which she returned with a great deal of politeness. The conversation afterwards turned on different subjects, and was very entertaining. Some other company coming in, Mr. Trueworth would have taken leave; but Sir Bazil would not permit him. He staid the whole evening; and, when he went home, carried such an idea of the lovely Harriot's perfection, that scarce any consideration would have been powerful enough to have made him quit the town while she continued in it.

CHAPTER XXIII

---•---

Returns to Miss Betsy's adventures, from which the two former were but a digression, though a very necessary one, as will hereafter appear

IF Miss Betsy had been made acquainted with the manner in which Mr. Trueworth passed his time, and the inducements he had to stay in London, doubtless her vanity would have been highly piqued: but she had not as yet this subject for mortification; on the contrary, she rather imagined he lingered here on her account; that it repented him of the letter he had sent her, though his spirit was too great to acknowledge it directly, and waited the arrival of her brother Frank, in hopes of engaging him to make his peace.

With these suggestions did she please herself whenever he came into her mind: but, indeed, she had but little room for meditation on his account; not only Mr. Munden plied her close with presents, treats, fine speeches, and all the tokens of impatient love, but she had also another conquest of a more late, and consequently, to a young lady of her humour, a more pleasing æra.

She had been one day at her mantua-maker's, to consult on some matters relating to her dress, and was a little surprized to see the woman come the next morning, before she was out of bed, to her lodgings. 'Hey day, Mrs. Modely!' cried she; 'what brings you here thus early?' – 'Indeed, Madam,' answered she, 'I could not well come out; I have eight or nine gowns n the house now, which should all have been finished and sent home today; the ladies will tear me to pieces about them: but I left all my business, and run away to acquaint you with a thing you little dream of. Ah, Miss Betsy! such a fine gentleman! such a vast estate! but it is no wonder,' continued she, 'you are so pretty, that you make all the men die for you.' –

'What is it you are talking of?' cried Miss Betsy; 'pr'ythee, dear Modely, explain.' – 'Lord!' replied the other, 'I am so transported that I know not how to contain myself! But I will tell you: you were yesterday at my house; Sir Frederick Fineer, who lodges in my first floor – the sweetest and most generous gentleman that ever lived, to be sure! (but that is nothing to the purpose) he saw you from his dining-room window when you came out of your chair; and, would you believe it! was so struck, that he immediately fell down in a swoon: you were but just gone when his valet de chambre (for he keeps three servants, two in livery, and one out) came down to me, and fetched me to his master. "Oh, Mrs. Modely!" said he to me, "what angel have you got below? – Tell me who she is? If she is not already married, I will give my whole estate to obtain her. I ask not what her fortune is; if I could once call that divine creature my wife, she should command all I am worth!"

'Indeed, Madam,' continued she, 'I was so much amazed, that I had not the power of speaking; and he, I suppose, interpreting my silence as a refusal of answering his demands, fell into such distractions, such ravings, as frighted me almost out of my wits; and, at last, to quiet him, I told him (I hope you will forgive me) your name, and where you lived, and that you were not married: on this he seemed pretty easy, and I left him; but, about two hours after, he sent for me again – desired I would go directly to you – make you a declaration of love in his name, and beg you would give him leave to visit you in person.'

'Bless me!' cried Miss Betsy; 'can the man neither speak nor write for himself?' – 'I told him, Madam,' resumed Mrs. Modely, 'that it would not be well taken from me; but he was quite mad, would listen to no reason, till I bethought myself of a strategem, which I fancy you will not disapprove: I made him believe that there was no need of my going to you; that you were to call upon me about a gown this afternoon; that I would persuade you to stay and drink tea, and he might come into the room, as if by chance, and entertain you with what discourse he thought proper. Now, I would fain have you come,' pursued she, 'for if you do but like his person, such an offer is not to be rejected.'

'I do not regard this offer,' said Miss Betsy; 'but I do not know but I may come just to divert myself a little.' – 'That is a dear good lady!' cried the other. 'About five, I believe, will be a proper time.' – 'Aye, thereabout,' replied Miss Betsy: 'but, dear Modely, don't let him know you have spoke a word to me concerning him.' – 'No, no,' said she; 'I shall not tell him I have seen you.'

During the whole time this woman staid, (which was, indeed, much longer than might have been expected from a person of that extraordinary business she pretended) nothing was talked of but Sir Frederick Fineer: she told Miss Betsy, that to her certain knowledge, he was of one of the best families in Cornwall; that he had a great estate in possession, and another in reversion; and, besides, was the next of kin to a coronet; that he kept company with nothing but lords and dukes, and that they were always courting his company.

Though Miss Betsy affected to treat all she said with indifference, yet she had given an attentive ear to it; and, after she was gone, began to rummage over all her ornaments; tried one, and then another, to see which would become her best, in order to secure a victory, which she imagined would afford so much triumph. 'Whether I marry him or not,' said she to herself, 'the addresses of a man of his rank will make me of some consideration in the world; and if ever I do become a wife, I should like to be a woman of quality: they may say what they will, but a title has prodigious charms in it; the name Fineer also becomes it. "Lady Fineer's servants there! Lady Fineer's coach to the door!" would sound vastly agreeable at the play or opera.'

She also pleased herself with the thought, that being courted by a person of Sir Frederick's quality and estate would immediately put to silence all the reproaches and remonstrances she might otherwise have expected to be persecuted with by her brother Frank, on Mr. Trueworth's account; and this imagination was of itself sufficient to give her an infinite satisfaction: in fine, she found so much in this new effect of her charms, to elevate and delight both her vanity and convenience, that she longed with as much impatience for a sight of her admirer as Mrs. Modely had told her he was under for a second interview with her.

Some part of the tedious moments were, however, taken up in a manner she was far from expecting; she was scarce risen from her toilette, when word was brought her that a young lady, who called herself Miss Flora Mellasin, was come to wait upon her. As she had never seen her since her being driven from Mr. Goodman's, the visit a little surprized her, and she would have been glad if common civility had dispensed with her receiving it; for though the pity she then had felt for her misfortunes had greatly effaced the memory of the injurious treatment she had met with from her, yet she never desired to continue any correspondence with her after they were once parted: besides, as she had no reason to look upon her coming as any proof of her friendship or good-will, but rather with a design of doing her some private prejudice, she resolved to behave entirely reserved towards her.

Her conjectures were not groundless: that complication of every worst passion that can fill the human heart, could not be perfectly satisfied, even amidst the most unbounded gratification of her amorous desires with the man that had excited them; the dread of losing him embittered all the transports of possession; she very well knew he had broke off with Miss Betsy, and doubted not but that event had happened through the artifice she had put in practice: yet, as there was a possibility that the adventure of Denham should be unravelled, and the innocency of Miss Betsy cleared up, she trembled lest such an eclaircissement should renew all his former tenderness for that once so much-loved rival, and herself be reduced to all the horrors of despair and shame. It was therefore to sound the inclinations of Miss Betsy, that alone brought her thither, in the wicked hope, that if there was the least probability of a reconciliation between them, she might find some opportunity of traversing all the steps that might be taken by either party for that purpose.

But Miss Betsy was too much upon her guard to give her any room to discover what her sentiments were in that point: she received her very coolly; and, even on her first entrance, told her that she was obliged to go out that evening; but the other taking no notice of the little pleasure Miss Betsy expressed on seeing her, told her she came out of friendship to visit her; that she had been told Mr. Trueworth and she were entirely parted; that if she had so great an affection for him as the world had been pleased to say, she must certainly stand in need of all the consolation that could be given her. 'But, I hope, my dear,' said she, 'you have too much good sense not to despise him now. Nothing is more common than that men should be false. Remember what the poet says –

"Ingratitude's the sin, which, first or last,
  Taints the whole sex, the catching court disease."

Miss Betsy was so provoked at being talked to in this manner, that she replied, that there was neither falsehood nor ingratitude in the case: if Mr. Trueworth had desisted his visits, it was only because he was convinced she desired not the continuance of them.

It is possible these words were more galling to the jealous heart of Miss Flora than any thing she could have said, though she spoke them with no other intent than to clear herself of the imputation of having been forsaken; a thing she looked upon as the worst blemish that could be cast upon her reputation. Miss Flora, finding no more was to be got out of her, took her leave for this time; resolving, however, in her own mind, to keep up an acquaintance with her, that seeming to her the most likely way both to satisfy her curiosity, and prevent any effort of what the extravagance of her passion made her apprehend.

Miss Betsy did not give herself much trouble in reflecting on what Miss Flora had said; but as soon as her watch reminded her of the appointed hour, she bid her footman fly and get a chair; on her coming to the house, Mrs. Modely herself opened the door at the first rap, and desired her to walk in. 'No, no,' said Miss Betsy, still sitting in the chair, 'I cannot stay; I only called to tell you that I will have the silver robings put upon the green night-gown, and will buy a new trimming for the pink.' – 'I shall be sure to obey your orders, Madam,' replied the other: 'but I must intreat you will do me the honour to come in and drink a dish of tea; the kettle boils, and I have just now had a present of a cannister of some of the finest Hyson in the world.' – 'I must leave you then as soon as I have tasted it,' said Miss Betsy, coming out of the chair; 'for I have twenty visits to make this evening.'

She had not been three minutes in the parlour, when the person for whom all this ceremony was affected, entered the room in somewhat of an abrupt manner. 'I come, Mrs. Modely, to complain,' said he – 'my servants tell me –' With these words he stopt short, and fixed his eyes full on Miss Betsy, with a kind of astonishment. – Mrs. Modely, pretending to be in a great fright, cried, 'For Heaven's sake, Sir Frederick! what is the matter? I hope nothing in my house has given your honour any cause of complaint?' – 'No, no! it is over now,' cried he; 'your house is become a temple, and this is the divinity that honours it with her presence – this Græcian Venus.' Miss Betsy was too much accustomed to company to be easily abashed; and answered briskly, 'If you mean the compliment to me, Sir, the Græcian Venuses are all painted fat, and I have no resemblance of that perfection.' – 'Only in your face, Madam,' returned he. 'Such sparkling eyes – such a complexion – such a mouth! In your shape you are Helen of Troy!' – 'That Helen of Troy,' said Miss Betsy, with an ironical smile, 'I think, was a Græcian princess, and must also be fat, or she would not have been reputed a beauty there.'

The baronet, finding by this he had been guilty of an absurdity when he intended a fine speech, thought to salve up the matter by saying, 'Sure, you are a Diana, then!' – 'Worse and worse!' cried Miss Betsy. 'I beseech you, Sir, compare me to no such boisterous goddess, that runs up and down, bare-footed and bare-legged, hunting wild boars in the forest!' – 'What shall I call you then?' resumed he. 'O, tell me by what name you will be worshipped?' – 'The lady's name, Sir Frederick,' cried Mrs. Modely, 'is Miss Betsy Thoughtless.' – 'Betsy!' said he; 'then Betsy let it be. Betsy shall henceforth become more famous than Cytherea was of old!'

He was going on with this fulsome stuff, in which he was often exposed by the ready wit of Miss Betsy, when a maid belonging to the house came in, and told her that a gentleman in a hackney-coach was at the door, and desired to speak with her. 'With me!' cried she, not able to guess who should have followed her there. 'Pray, call my footman, and bid him ask the person's name that enquires for me.' The maid did as she was ordered; and Miss Betsy's servant presently after brought her this intelligence – 'Mr. Munden, Madam,' said he, 'not finding you at home, has taken the liberty to call on you here, in order to conduct you where you are to pass the evening.' – 'He must be a happy man, indeed, that dare take such liberties,' cried Sir Frederick, somewhat fiercely. 'Many take more than they are allowed to do,' said Miss Betsy. 'Go,' continued she to the fellow, 'and tell him my mind is changed; that I cannot leave the company I am with, and will not go.' Mr. Munden having received this message, ordered the coachman to drive away, very much dissatisfied, as the reader may easily suppose.

Miss Betsy, the day before, had agreed to pass this evening with the ladies at St. James's, and some others, to play at commerce; a game then very much in vogue. Mr. Munden was to be one of the company; and calling at Miss Betsy's lodgings, in hopes of having some time with her before this meeting, the maid, who had not lived long enough with her mistress to know her humour, presently told him, she was only gone to her mantua-maker's, and gave him directions to the house; he also thinking it no indecorum to call on her at the house of a woman of that profession, had reason enough to be mortified at the repulse he met with for so doing.

As to Miss Betsy, though she was a little angry at the freedom Mr. Munden had taken, yet she was in reality much more pleased; and this for two reasons: first, because she saw it gave her new lover some jealous apprehensions; and, secondly, because it furnished her with a plausible pretence for complying with his entreaties to stay; which, she protested, she would not on any terms have been prevailed upon to do, but to prevent either him or Mrs. Modely from suspecting she would go where Mr. Munden had desired.

Mrs. Modely went out of the room several times, as if called away by some household affairs, that Sir Frederick might have an opportunity of declaring his passion to Miss Betsy; which he did in much the same rodomontade strain with which he had at first accosted her. A handsome supper was served in; after which, she being about to take her leave, he affected to be in a great fret, that a fine new chariot which, he said, he had bespoke, was not come home, that he might have seen her safe to her lodgings, with an equipage suitable to her merit, and the admiration he had of it: he would needs, however, attend her in another chair; which piece of gallantry, after a few faint refusals, she accepted.

VOLUME THE THIRD

CHAPTER I

———————•———————

Relates only to such things as the reader may
reasonably expect would happen

AS much taken up as Miss Betsy was with the pleasure of having
gained a new admirer, she could not forbear, after she came home,
making some reflection on the value of her conquest; she had found
nothing agreeable either in his person or conversation: the first
seemed to her stiff and aukward, and looked as if not made for his
cloaths; and the latter, weak, romantick, and bombast: in fine, he was
altogether such as she could not think of living with as a husband,
though the rank and figure she was told he held in the world, made
her willing to receive him as a lover. In short, though she could not
consent to sacrifice herself to his quality, she took a pride to sacrifice
his quality to her vanity.

No overtures of marriage having been made to her since Mr.
Munden began his courtship, and that gentleman growing, as she
fancied at least, a little too presuming, on finding himself the only
lover, she was not a little pleased at the opportunity of giving him a
rival whose quality might over-awe his hopes. In this idea, she was far
from repenting her behaviour towards him the night before: but how
little soever she regarded what mortification she gave the men, she
always took care to treat her own sex with a great deal of politeness;
and reflecting that she had been guilty of an omission, in not sending
her servant to excuse herself to the ladies who expected her, went
herself in the morning to make her own apology.

In the mean time, Mr. Munden, who it is certain was very much
out of humour, and impatient to let her know some part of the
sentiments her message had inspired him with, came to make her a

morning visit, having some business which he knew would detain him
from waiting on her in the afternoon. On finding she was abroad, he
desired the maid to favour him with her lady's standish; which she
accordingly bringing to him, he sat down, and, without taking much
consideration, wrote the following letter, and left for her on the table.

'To Miss Betsy Thoughtless.

Madam,
Amidst the enchanting encouragement with which you have been
pleased to admit my services, I would not, without calling your
honour and generosity in question, be altogether void of hope, that
you intended to afford them one day a recompence for ample
than a bare acceptance.

Judge, then, of my surprize at the repulse I met with at Mrs.
Modely's door. I could not think it any breach of the respect I owe
you, to call on you at the house of your mantua-maker; I could not
imagine it possible for you to have any engagements at such a place
capable of preventing you from keeping those that you had made with
persons for whom you profess an esteem: on the contrary, I rather
expected you would have permitted me to conduct you thence, with
the same readiness you have done from most of the other places
where you have been, since I first had the honour of being
acquainted with you.

I know very well, that it is the duty of every lover to submit, in all
things to the pleasure of the beautiful object whose chains he wears,
yet, Madam, as you have hitherto made mine easy, you must pardon
me, when I say, that this sudden transition from gentleness to cruelty,
appears to me to contain a mystery, which, though I dread, I am
distracted for the explanation of.

Some business of great moment prevents my waiting on you this
afternoon, but shall attend your commands to-morrow at the usual
hour; when, I still flatter myself, you will relieve the anxieties, and put
an end to the suspence, of him who is, with the greatest sincerity of
heart, Madam, your most humble, and most faithfully devoted
servant,

G. MUNDEN.'

Miss Betsy, at her return home, found also another billet directed
for her, which they told her had been brought by a servant belonging

to Sir Frederick Fineer: she gave that from Mr. Munden, however, the preference of reading first, not indeed through choice, but chance, that happening to be first put into her hands. As soon as she had looked it over, she laughed, and said to herself, 'The poor man is jealous already, though he knows not of whom, or why: what will become of him when he shall be convinced? I suppose he was sure of having me, and it is high time to mortify his vanity.'

She then proceeded to Sir Frederick's epistle; in which she found herself more deified than ever she had been by all her lovers put together.

'To the most wonderful of her sex, the incomparable Miss Betsy Thoughtless.

Divine charmer,
Though I designed myself the inexpressible pleasure of kissing your fair hands this evening, I could not exist till then without telling you how much I adore you: you are the empress of my heart, the goddess of my soul! the one loves you with the most loyal and obedient passion, the other regards you as the sole mover and director of all it's motions. I cannot live without you; it is you alone can make me blest, or miserable. O then pronounce my doom, and keep me not suspended between heaven and hell. Words cannot describe the ardency of my flame; it is actions only that can do it. I lay myself, and all that I am worth, an humble offering at your feet. Accept it, I beseech you; but accept it soon; for I consume away in the fire of my impatient wishes; and, in a very short time, there will be nothing left for you but the shadow of the man who is, with the most pure devotion, Madam, your beauty's slave, and everlasting adorer,

F. FINEER.'

'Good lack!' cried Miss Betsy, 'he is in a great haste, too; but I fancy he must wait a while, as many of better sense have done. What a romantick jargon is here! One would think he had been consulting all the ballads since fair Rosamond, and the Children in the Wood, for fine phrases to melt me into pity!'

She wondered, as indeed she had good reason, that a man of his birth, and who, it must be supposed, had an education suitable to it, should express himself in such odd terms; but then she was tempted to imagine, that it was only his over-care to please her that had made him stretch his wit beyond it's natural extent, and that if he had loved her less, he would have been able to have told her so in a much better stile. Possessed with this fancy, 'What a ridiculous thing this love is!' said she; 'What extravagancies does it sometimes make men guilty of! yet one never sees this madness in them after they become husbands. If I were to marry Sir Frederick, I do not doubt but he would soon recover his senses.'

How does a mind, unbroke with cares and disappointments, entirely free from passion, and perfectly at peace with itself, improve, and dwell on every thing that affords the least matter for it's entertainment? This young lady found as much diversion in anticipating the innocent pranks she intended to play with the authors of these two letters, as an infant does in first playing with a new baby, and afterwards plucking it to pieces; so true is the observation of the poet, that –

'All are but children of a larger growth.'

But this sprightliness of humour in Miss Betsy soon received a sad and sudden interruption: having sent, as she constantly did every day, to enquire after the health of Mr. Goodman, her servant returned with an account, that he had expired that morning. Though this was an event, which she, and all who knew him, had expected for some time, yet could she not be told of the death of a gentleman, under whose care and protection she so long had been, and who had behaved in all respects so like a parent towards her, without being very deeply affected with the news; she was then at dinner, but threw down her knife and fork, rose from the table, and retired to her chamber and wept bitterly: the more violent emotions of grief were soon assuaged, but her melancholy and dejection of spirits continued much longer; and, while they did so, she had the power of making the most just reflections on the vain pursuits, the fleeting pleasures, and all the noise and hurry of the giddy world. Love, and all the impertinences which bear that name, now appeared only worthy of her contempt; and, recollecting that Sir Frederick had mentioned visiting her that evening, she sent a servant immediately to Mrs. Modely's, desiring her to acquaint that gentleman, that she had just lost a very dear friend, and was in too much affliction to admit of any company.

This being the day on which Mr. Francis Thoughtless was expected to be in London, this affectionate sister perceiving, by his last letter to her, that his health was not perfectly established, was under a very great concern, lest he should be put to some inconvenience by Mr. Goodman's death, for a proper lodging on his first arrival; but she soon found her tender fears, on this occasion, altogether groundless.

Those objections which had hindered Mr. Thomas Thoughtless from taking her into his family, had not the same weight in relation to Mr. Francis, whose sex set him above meddling with those domestick concerns, the command of which he had given to another; and his reputation would suffer nothing by being under the same roof with the mistress of his brother's amorous inclinations.

He went to the inn where he knew the L—e stage puts up, welcomed Mr. Francis with open arms, as soon as he alighted from the coach, and gave him all the demonstrations of brotherly affection that the place they were in would admit of; then conducted him to his house, and insisted that he should not think of any other home, till he was better provided for, and settled in the world.

A servant belonging to the elder Mr. Thoughtless was immediately dispatched to Miss Betsy, with a letter from the younger; and it was from this man that she received the agreeable intelligence, that the two brothers were together. The terms in which Mr. Francis wrote to her were these –

'To Miss Betsy Thoughtless.

My dear sister,
Heaven be thanked, I am at last got safe to London; a place, which, I assure you, some months ago I almost despaired of ever seeing more. My brother has just given me an account of the death of honest Mr. Goodman; and, as I doubt not but you are very much concerned, as indeed we all have reason to be, for the loss of so sincere and valuable a friend, I am very impatient to see you, and give you what consolation is in my power; but the fatigue of my journey, after so long an illness, requires my taking some immediate repose; I shall, however, wait on you tomorrow morning; till when, believe me, as ever, with the greatest sincerity, dear sister, your affectionate brother, and humble servant,

F. THOUGHTLESS.

P.S. My brother purposes to come with me; but if any thing should happen to prevent his visit, you may depend on one from me. Once more, my dear sister, good night.'

In the present situation of Miss Betsy's mind, she could not have received a more sensible satisfaction, than what she felt on this young gentleman's arrival: but what ensued upon it will in due time and place appear.

CHAPTER II

———•———

Contains only some few particulars of little moment in themselves, but serve to usher in matters of more importance

MR. Goodman, who, both living and dying, had sincerely at heart the welfare of all with whom he had any concern, could not content himself to leave the world without giving to those who had been under his care such advice as he thought necessary for their future happiness.

Accordingly, the day preceding that which happened to be his last, he sent for Mr. Thoughtless; and on his being come, and seated by his bedside, he took his hand, and began to remonstrate to him in the most pathetick, though very gentle, terms, how unjustifiable to the eyes of Heaven, how disreputable to those of the world, it was to avow and indulge, in the publick manner he did, an unwarrantable flame.

'I never was severe,' said he, 'in censuring the frailties of youth and nature; but think the claim they have to pardon consists chiefly in an endeavour to conceal them; when gloried in, they lose the name of frailties, and become vices: besides, others by our example might be emboldened to offend; and, if so, what are we but accessary to their faults, and answerable for them, as well as for our own? You are at present,' continued he, 'the head of your family, have a large estate, are young, handsome, accomplished; in fine, have all the requisites to make a shining character in life, and to be a service and an honour to your country. How great a pity would it be, that such a stock of fortune's blessings, such present benefits, and such glorious expectations, should all be squandered in the purchase of one guilty pleasure!'

He then proceeded to a short discussion of the difference between a lawful and an unlawful communication between the sexes; he expatiated on the wife and laudable institution of marriage; the solid comforts arising from that state, in the choice of a worthy partner; the many advantages of an honourable alliance; the serene and lasting pleasures to be found in the society of a faithful, discreet, and endearing companion. 'A wife,' said he, with a sigh, which the memory of his own hard fate drew from him, 'may sometimes be bad, but a mistress we are sure is never good; her very character denies all confidence to be reposed in her; it is the interest of a wife to secure the honour of her husband, because she must suffer in his disgrace; a mistress, having no reputation of her own, regards not that of her keeper. It is the interest of a wife to be frugal of her husband's substance, because she must be a sharer in those misfortunes which the want of œconomy creates; but is the interest of a mistress to sell her favours as dear as she can, and to make the best provision she can for herself, because her subsistence is precarious, and depends wholly on the will of him who supports her. These, my dear friend,' continued he, 'are truths, which I hope you will not wait for experience to convince you of.'

It is probable Mr. Thoughtless did not relish this admonition; he seemed, however, to take it in good part, and returned for answer, that he should ever retain the most grateful sense of the kind concern he expressed for him; and added, that whatever inconveniences he might have been hurried into, by an inadvertent passion, he should always take care not to become the dupe of any woman.

Mr. Goodman then fell into some discourse concerning the younger Mr. Thoughtless; and the elder telling him, that, by his interest, he procured a comission for him on very easy terms, that worthy old gentleman appeared very much pleased, and said, he hoped they would always live together in that perfect amity which both good policy and nature demands between persons of the same blood.

'And now,' continued he, 'I have but one more thing to recommend to you, and that is in relation to your sister Miss Betsy: I doubt not of her innocence, but I fear her conduct; her youth, her beauty, the gaiety of her temper, and the little vanities of her sex, are every day exposing her to temptations fatal to reputation; I wish, therefore, she were well married; I know not how the courtship of Mr. Trueworth happened to be broke off; perhaps on some trifling

occasion either on the one or the other side: if so, it is likely Mr.
Francis, when he comes to town, may bring about a reconciliation.
According to my judgment of mankind, she cannot make a more
deserving choice. There is another gentleman, who now makes his
addresses to her, whose name is Munden; but I know nothing of his
character; he never applied to me, nor did she consult me on the
affair; it will, however, be a brother's part in you to enquire how far
he may be worthy of her.'

Perceiving Mr. Thoughtless listened to him with a good deal of
attention, he went on; 'I should also think it right,' said he, 'that while
she remains in a single state, she should be boarded in some social,
reputable family; I do not like this living by herself, her humour is too
volatile to endure solitude; she must have her amusements; and the
want of them at home naturally carries her in search of them abroad:
I could wish,' added, 'that you would tell her what I have said to you
on this subject; she is convinced I am her friend, I believe has some
regard for me, and, it may be, my dying admonitions will have greater
effect upon her than all she has heard from me before.'

Mr. Goodman, after this, beginning to grow extremely faint, and
altogether unable to hold any farther discourse, the brother of
Miss Betsy judged it convenient to retire; assuring the other, as he
took his leave, that no part of what he had said should be lost upon
him.

Though the promise he had made Mr. Goodman was chiefly
dictated by his complaisance, yet it was not wholly forgot after he had
left him. As to what that worthy gentleman had said, in relation to his
own manner of living, he thought he had talked well, but he had
talked like an old man, and that it was time enough for him to part
with his pleasures when he had no longer any inclination to pursue
them; but what had been alledged to him, concerning his sister's
conduct, made a much deeper impresssion on his mind: he
considered, that the honour of a family depended greatly on the
female part of it, and therefore resolved to omit nothing in his power
to prevent Miss Betsy from being caught by any snares that might be
laid to entrap her innocence.

He communicated to Mr. Francis Thoughtless, on his arrival, all
that Mr. Goodman had said to him on this score, and his own
sentiments upon it: that young gentleman was entirely of his brother's
opinion in this point; and they both agreed, that marriage was the
only sure refuge for a young woman of Miss Betsy's disposition and

humour. They had a long and pretty serious conversation on this head, the result of which was, that they should go together to her, and each exert all the influence he had over her, in order to draw from her some farther eclaircissement of her intentions than could yet be gathered from her behaviour.

Miss Betsy, who little suspected their designs, received them with all the tenderness that could be expected from a sister, especially her brother Frank; whose return, after so long an absence, gave her in reality an entire satisfaction: but she had scarce time to give him all the welcomes with which her heart overflowed, before the elder Mr. Thoughtless fell on the topick of Mr. Goodman, and the misfortune they sustained in the loss of so good a friend; after which, 'He has left you a legacy, sister,' said he. 'A legacy!' cried she, 'pray, of what kind?' – 'Such a one,' replied he, 'as perhaps you will not be very well pleased in receiving; nor would I chuse to deliver it, but for two reasons: first, that the injunctions of a dying friend are not to be dispensed with; and, secondly, that it is of a nature, I fear, you stand in too much need of.'

Miss Betsy, whose ready wit made her presently comprehend the meaning of these words, replied with some smartness, that whatever she stood in need of, she should certainly receive with pleasure, and that he might have spared himself the trouble of a prelude, for any thing that could be delivered by him, or bequeathed to her by Mr. Goodman.

He then told her, how that gentleman, the day before his death, had sent for him; 'For no other purpose,' said he, 'than to talk to me on your account, and to exhort me as your brother, and now your guardian, to have a watchful eye over all your actions; to remind you of some inadvertencies of the past, and to warn you against falling into the like for the future: sorry I am to find myself under a necessity of speaking to you in this manner; but harsh as it may seem at present, I doubt not, but you will hereafter own, is a proof of the greatest affection I could shew you.' He then repeated to her all that Mr. Goodman had said to him in relation to her; to which he also added many things of his own, which he thought might serve to strengthen and to enforce the arguments made use of by the other.

It is impossible to describe the various and disturbed emotions which discovered themselves in the countenance of Miss Betsy during the whole time her brother was speaking; she looked extremely grave at the manner in which he ushered what he had to deliver to her from Mr. Goodman; appeared confounded and perplexed at what she heard that gentleman had said concerning Mr. Trueworth; was quite peevish at the mention of Mr. Munden; but when told of the dangers to which she was exposed by living alone, and trusted with the management of herself, her eyes sparkled with disdain and rage at a remonstrance she looked upon as so unnecessary and so unjust.

If this message had been sent to her by any other than Mr. Goodman, whose memory, on account of the benefits she had received from him, was precious to her; or had it been repeated by any other mouth than that of her brother, she had certainly vented the indignation she was possessed, in the most bitter terms; but gratitude, respect, and love, denying her this remedy, she burst into tears. 'Good God!' cried she, 'what have I done to raise such cruel suggestions in the heart of any friend? Which of my actions can malice construe into a crime? I challenge my worst of enemies to prove me guilty of any thing that might justly cast a blemish on my reputation, much less to call my virtue into question.'

The two brothers seemed very much moved at the agonies that they saw her in, especially the elder; who, repenting he had gone so far, took her in his arms, and, tenderly embracing her, 'My dear sister,' said he, 'you wrong your friends, while you imagine yourself wronged by them; your reputation, I hope, is clear; your virtue not suspected: it is not to accuse you of any guilt, but to prevent your innocence from becoming a prey to the guilt of others, that Mr. Goodman sent you his dying admonition, or that I took upon me to deliver it.'

Mr. Francis Thoughtless seconded what the other had said; and both joining their endeavours to pacify the late tempest of her mind, she soon recovered that good-humour and chearfulness which was too natural to her to be long suspended by any accident whatever.

'I flattered myself,' said the younger of these gentlemen, 'that cautions of this kind would have been altogether unnecessary, and that before now you would have been disposed of to a man, under whose protection all that is dear to your sex had been secure; I need not tell you,' continued he, 'that I mean Mr. Trueworth.'

Miss Betsy looking a little confused, and not making any reply, the elder Mr. Thoughtless immediately took up the word, and said he had heard so high a character of that gentleman's merit, that he had wished for few things with more ardency than the honour of being allied to him; and that he never could find out what objection his sister had to accept of an offer so every way to her advantage.

To this Miss Betsy made answer, though not without some disorder and hesitation in her speech, that she had never made any objection either to his person or qualifications; but that she did not care to marry yet a while, and that he had not love enough to wait the event of her resolution in that point: that, besides, their humours did not suit, and there was little likelihood they would agree better after marriage; that there had been a little pique between them; that he gave himself airs of resenting something she had said, and thereupon had sent her a very impertinent letter; since which she had never seen him: 'So that,' added she, 'our breaking off acquaintance is wholly owing to himself.'

Mr. Francis, not doubting but this letter would explain what he so much desired to know the truth of, cried out to her hastily to let him see it. Miss Betsy already repenting that she had mentioned such a thing, as she was conscious there were some expressions in it which would greatly countenance the disagreeable remonstrances she had just now received; but she wanted artifice to pretend she had either lost or burnt it, and went that instant to her cabinet; where easily finding it, she gave it into her brother's hands, with these words – 'He reproaches me,' said she, 'with things I know nothing of, and in terms which, I think, do not very well become the passion he pretended to have for me.'

'That he once loved you,' said Mr. Francis, coolly, 'I am very certain. How his sentiments may be changed, and the reasons of their being so, this may, perhaps, give me room to guess.' He then read the letter aloud; and, while he was doing so, several times cast a look at Miss Betsy, which shewed he was highly dissatisfied with her, for having given any cause for the reflections contained in it.

'I see very well,' said he, returning her the letter, 'that he has done with you, and that it is your own fault. I shall, however, talk to him on the affair; and if there be a possibility of accommodating matters between you, shall endeavour it for your sake.'

Here Miss Betsy's spirit rouzed itself, in spite of the respect she had for her brothers. 'I beseech you, Sir,' said she to Mr. Francis, 'not to go about to force your sister upon any man. If Mr. Trueworth, of his own accord, renews the professions he has made, I shall, on your account, receive them as I did before any misunderstanding happened between us; but as to changing my condition, either in favour of him or any other man, I know not when, or whether ever, I shall be in the humour to do it. You may, however, if you please,' continued she, 'hear what he has to say for himself, and what mighty matters against me, that can excuse the abrupt manner of his quitting me.'

'I know not as yet,' replied Mr. Francis, with some vehemence, 'whether I shall interfere any farther in the thing; and am heartily sorry I have given myself any trouble about it, since you so little consider your own interest, or will follow the advice of those who are at the pains to consider for you.' – 'Come, come,' said the elder Mr. Thoughtless, 'you are both too fiery. I am confident my sister has too much good sense to suffer any little caprice to impede her real happiness; therefore, pr'ythee, Frank, let us drop this subject at present, and leave her to her own reflections.'

To which Miss Betsy answered, that there required but little reflection to instruct her what she ought to do; and that, though she could not consent to be kept always in leading-strings, the love and respect she had for her brothers would never permit her to do any thing without their approbation. There passed nothing more of consequence between them at this visit: but what had been said, served to engross pretty much the minds of each of them after they were separated.

CHAPTER III

●

Has somewhat more business in it than the former

THOUGH Miss Betsy was very conscious of the merits of Mr. Trueworth, and equally convinced of the friendship her brother Francis had for him, and had, thefore, doubted not but, when that young gentleman should arrive, he would reason strongly with her on the little regard she had paid to his recommendations, or the advantages of the alliance he had proposed; yet she did not expect the satisfaction of their first meeting would have been embittered by a resentment such as, it seemed to her, he had testified on the occasion.

She easily perceived the two brothers had consulted together, before they come to her, in what manner they should behave towards her; and this she looked upon as a sort of proof, that they intended to assume an authority over her, to which they had no claim. 'The love I have for them,' said she to herself, 'will always make me take a pleasure in obliging them, and doing every thing they desire of me; but they are entirely mistaken, if they imagine it in their power to awe me into compliance with their injunctions.

'And yet,' cried she again, 'what other aim than my happiness and interest can they propose to themselves, in desiring to have me under their direction? Poor Frank has given me proofs that I am very dear to him; and, I believe, my brother Thoughtless is not wanting in natural affection for me: why, then, should I reject the counsel of two friends, whose sincerity there is not a possibility of suspecting? They know their sex, and the dangers to which ours are exposed, by the artifices of base designing men. I have had some escapes, which I ought always to remember enough to keep me from falling into the like ugly accidents again. How near was I to everlasting ruin, by slighting the warning given me by Mr. Trueworth!'

This reflection bringing into her mind many passages of her behaviour towards that gentleman, she could not forbear justifying his conduct, and condemning her own. 'I have certainly used him ill,' pursued she, with a sigh; 'and if he should return, and forgive what is past, I think I ought, in gratitude, to reward his love!'

She was in this contemplating mood when her servant told her that Mrs. Modely had been to wait upon her; but, on hearing her brothers were with her, went away, saying she would come again; which she now was, and begged to speak with her.

Miss Betsy was at this moment just beginning to feel some sort of pleasure in the idea of Mr. Trueworth's renewing his addresses, and was a little peevish at the interruption: she ordered, however, that the woman should come up. 'Well, Mrs. Modely,' said she, as soon as she saw her enter, 'what stuff have you brought me now?'

'Ah, charming Miss Betsy,' replied she, 'you fine ladies and great fortunes think you may do any thing with the men. Poor Sir Frederick will break his heart, or run mad, that's to be sure, if you don't send him a favourable answer to this letter.' In speaking these words, she delivered a letter to Miss Betsy; which that young lady opened with a careless air, and it contained these high-flown lines.

'This humbly to be presented to the most beautiful of all beauties, the super-excellent Miss Betsy Thoughtless.

Adorable creature,
I am grieved to the very soul to hear you have any subject for affliction; but am very certain that, in being deprived of your divine presence, I endure a more mortal stab than any loss you have sustained can possibly inflict. I am consumed with the fire of my passion; I have taken neither repose nor food since first I saw you. I have lived only on the idea of your charms. Oh, nourish me with the substance! Hide me in your bosom from the foul fiend Despair, that is just ready to lay hold on me!

The passion I am possessed of for you is not like that of other men. I cannot wait the tedious forms of courtship: there is no medium between death and the enjoyment of you – the circle of your arms, or a cold leaden shroud – the one or the other must very shortly be my portion. But I depend upon the heaven of your mercy, and hope you will permit me to pour forth the abundance of my soul before you – to bask in the sunshine of your smiles; and to try, at least, if no spark of that amorous flame, which burns me up, has darted upon you, and kindled you into soft desires.

O, if any part of my impatient fires, by secret sympathy, should happily have reached your breast, never was there a pair so transcendently blest as we should be! The thought is rapture! Extasy too big for words – too mighty for description! And I must, therefore, for a few hours, defer any farther endeavours to convince you; till when I remain, absorbed in the delightful image, dear quintessence of joy, your most devoted, most obsequious, and most adoring vassal,

F. FINEER.'

In spite of the serious humour Miss Betsy was in, she could not read this without bursting into a violent fit of laughter; but soon composing herself, 'If I had not seen the author of this epistle,' said she to Mrs. Modely, 'I should have thought it had been sent me by some school-boy, and was the first essay of describing a passion he had heard talked of, and was ambitious of being supposed capable of feeling. But, sure,' continued she, 'the man must be either mad, or most impudently vain, to write to me as if he imagined I was in love with him, and would have him on his first putting the question to me.'

'Ah, my dear Madam!' said Mrs. Modely, 'do you consider that a young gentleman of ten thousand a year in possession, as much more in reversion, and the expectation of a coronet, is not apt to think he may have any body?' – 'If he does, he may find himself mistaken,' replied Miss Betsy haughtily; and then in the same breath softening her voice, 'But are you sure,' cried she, 'that he has so much?' – 'Sure, Madam!' said Mrs. Modely, 'Aye, as sure that I am alive! I have heard it from twenty people. They say he has a house in the country as big as a town, and above fifty servants in it; though he is but just come to London, and has not had time to settle his equipage as yet: but he has bespoke the finest coach, and the genteelest chariot, you ever saw; all in a new taste, and perfectly French; they are quite finished, all but the painting, and that only waits till he knows whether he may quarter your arms or not.'

'Bless me! cried Miss Betsy, 'does he think to gain me in the time of painting a coach?' – 'Nay, I don't know,' answered Mrs. Modely; 'but I think such an offer is not to be trifled with. He is violently in love with you, that is certain: he does not desire a penny of your fortune, and will settle upon you, notwithstanding, his whole estate, if you require it.'

Miss Betsy made no answer, but paused for a considerable time, and seemed, as it were, in a profound reverie. At last, coming out of it, 'He is for doing things in such a hurry,' said she; 'I have seen him no more than once, and scarce know what sort of a person he is: how, then, can I tell you whether I ever shall be able to bring myself to like him or not?'

'You may give him leave to wait on you, however,' cried the other. Here Miss Betsy was again silent for some moments; but Mrs. Modely repeating her request, and enforcing it with some arguments, 'Well, then, replied she, 'I shall not go to church this afternoon, and will see him if he comes. But, dear Modely,' continued she, 'don't let him assume on the permission I give him: tell him you had all the difficulty in the world to prevail on me to do it; for, in my mind, he already hopes too much, and fears too little, for a man so prodigiously in love.' Mrs. Modely on this assured her, she might trust to her management; and took her leave, very well pleased with the success of her negociation.

We often see the love of grandeur prevail over persons of the ripest years and knowledge. What guilty lengths have not some men run to attain it, even among those who have been esteemed the wisest and most honest of their time; when once a title, a bit of ribband cross their shoulder, or any other gew-gaw trophy of the favour of a court, has been hung out, how has their virtue veered and yielded to the temptation? It is not, therefore, to be wondered at, that a young heart, unexperienced in the fallacy of shew, should be dazzled with the tinsel glitter: the good sense of Miss Betsy made her see, that this last triumph of her charms was a vain, silly, and affected coxcomb; but then this coxcomb had a vast estate, and the enchanting ideas of the figure she should make, if in possession of it, in some measure out-balanced the contempt she had of the owner's person and understanding.

The glare of pomp and equipage, the pleasure of having it in her power of taking the upper-hand of those of her own rank, and of vying with those of a more exalted one, it is certain had very potent charms for her, but then there was a delicacy in her nature, that would not suffer the desire of attaining it to be altogether predominant: the thoughts of being sacrificed to a man for whom it was impossible for her to have either love or esteem; to be obliged to yield that, through duty, which inclinations shuddered at, struck a sudden damp to all the rising fires of pride and ambition in her soul, and convinced her, that greatness would be too dearly purchased at the expence of peace.

In fine, she considered on these things so long, that she grew weary of considering at all; so resolved to let the matter rest, give herself no farther pain, leave to chance the disposal of her fate, and treat all her lovers, as she hitherto had done, only as subjects of mere amusement.

She was now beginning to please herself with thoughts of how Mr. Munden, whom she expected that evening, would behave at the sight of his new rival, and how Sir Frederick Fineer would bear the preference of a man whom she was resolved to shew him had the same pretensions as himself: but though she happened to be disappointed in her expectation in this, she did not want other sufficient matter for her diversion.

Sir Frederick, to shew the impatience of his passion, came very soon after dinner: she received him with as grave an air as she could possibly put on; but it was not in her power, nor indeed would have been in any one else's, to continue it for any long time; his conversation was much of a piece with his letters, and his actions even more extravagant.

Never was such an Orlando Furioso in love: on his first approach, he had indeed the boldness to take one of her hands, and put it to his mouth; but, afterwards, whatever he said to her was on his knees. He threw himself prostrate on the carpet before her, grasped her feet, and tenderly kissed each shoe, with the same vehemence as he could have done her lips, and as much devotion as the pilgrims at Rome do the pantofle of his holiness! – 'Darts! – Flames! – Immortal joys! – Death! – Despair! – Heaven! – Hell! – Ever-during woe!' – and all the epithets in the whole vocabulary of Cupid's legend, begun and ended every sentence of his discourse. This way of entertaining her was so extraordinary, and so new to her, that she could not forbear sometimes returning it with a smile; which, in spite of her endeavours to perserve a serious deportment, diffused a gaiety through all her air.

Those who had told Sir Frederick, that the way to please this lady, was to soothe her vanity, either knew not, or had forgot to inform him, she had also an equal share of good sense; so that, mistaking the change he had observed in her looks for an indication of her being charmed with his manner of behaviour, he acted and re-acted over all his fopperies, and felt as much secret pride in repeating them, as a celebrated singer on the stage does in obeying the voice of an encore.

It is probable, however, that he would have continued in them long enough to have tired Miss Betsy so much as to have made her give him some demonstrative remark that the pleasantry he had seen her in, proceeded rather from derision than satisfaction, if, divine service being ended, some ladies, as they came from church, had not called to visit her. The sound of company coming up stairs, obliged him to break off in the middle of a rhapsody, which he, doubtless, thought very fine; and he took his leave somewhat hastily, telling her, the passion with which he was inflamed, was too fierce to be restrained within those bounds which she might expect before witnesses, and that he would wait on her the next day, when he hoped she would be at more liberty to receive his vows.

Eased of the constraint which decency, and the respect which she thought due to his quality, had laid her under while he was there, her natural sprightliness burst with double force. Mr. Munden, who came in soon after, felt the effects of it: he, indeed, enjoyed a benefit he little dreamt of. The absurd conversation of a rival he as yet knew nothing of, served to make all he said sound more agreeable than ever in the ears of his mistress: in this excess of good-humour, she not only made a handsome apology for the treatment he had received at Mrs. Modely's, (a thing she had never before vouchsafed to do to any of her lovers) but also gave him an invitation to squire her to a country dancing, in which she had engaged to make one the ensuing night.

CHAPTER IV

———•———

*If it were not for some particulars, might be as well
passed over as read*

MISS Betsy, one would think, had now sufficient matter to employ
her meditations on the score of those two lovers who at present laid
close siege to her, neither of whom she was willing to part with
entirely, and to retain either she found required some management:
Mr. Munden was beginning to grow impatient at the little progress
his long courtship had made on her affections; and Sir Frederick
Fineer, on the other hand, was for bringing things to a conclusion at
once; she was also every day receiving transient addresses from many
others; which, though not meant seriously by those who made them,
nor taken so by her, served occasionally to fill up any vacuum in her
mind; yet was it not in the power of love, gallantry, or any other
amusement, to drive the memory of Mr. Trueworth wholly out of her
head; which shews, that to a woman of sense, a man of real merit,
even though he is not loved, can never be totally indifferent.

But she was at this time more than ordinarily agitated on that
gentleman's account; she doubted not but her brother Frank either
had, or would shortly have, a long conference with him, on the
subject of his desisting his visits to her, and could not keep herself
from feeling some palpitations for the event; for though she was not
resolved to afford any recompence to his love, she earnestly wished
he should continue to desire it, and that she might still preserve
her former dominion over a heart which she had always looked
upon as the most valuable prize of all that her beauty had ever
gained.

Thus unreasonable, and indeed unjust, was she in the affairs of love: in all others she was humane, benevolent, and kind; but here covetous, even to a greediness, of receiving all, without any intention of making the least return. In fine, the time was not yet come when she should be capable of being touched with that herself which she took so much pains to inspire in others.

Though she could not love, she was pleased with being loved: no man, of what degree or circumstance soever, could offend her by declaring himself her admirer; and as much as she despised Sir Frederick Fineer for his romantick manner of expressing the passion he professed for her, yet to have missed him out of the number of her train of captives, would have been little less mortification to her than the loss of a favourite lover would have been to some other woman.

That inamorato of all inamoratoes, would not, however, suffer the flames which he flattered himself with having kindled in her, to grow cool; and, ambitious also of shewing his talents in verse as well as prose, sent to her that morning the following epistle –

'To the bright goddess of my soul, the adorable Miss Betsy Thoughtless.

Most divine source of joy!
To shew in what manner I pass the hours of absence from you, and at the same time represent the case of a lover racked with suspense, and tossed alternately between hopes and fears, I take the liberty to inscribe to you the inclosed poem, which, I most humbly beseech you to take as it is meant, the tribute of my duteous zeal, an humble offering presented at the shrine of your all-glorious beauty, from, lovely ruler of my heart, your eternally devoted, and no less faithful slave,

F. Fineer.

A true picture of my heart, in the different stages of it's worship; a poem, most humbly inscribed to the never-enough deified Miss Betsy Thoughtless.

When first from my unfinish'd sleep I start,
I feel a flutt'ring faintness round my heart;
A darksome mist, which rises from my mind,
And, like sweet sun-shine, leaves your name behind.
    When from your shadow to yourself I fly,
To drink in transport at my thirsty eye,
Each orb surveys you with a kindling sight,

And trembles to sustain the vast delight:
From head to foot, o'er all your heaven they stray,
Dazzled with lustre in your milky way:
At last you speak; and, as I start to hear,
My soul is all collected in my ear.
   But when resistless transport makes me bold,
And your soft hand inclos'd in mine I hold,
Then flooding raptures swim through ev'ry vein,
And each swollen art'ry throbs with pleasing pain.
   Fain would I snatch you to my longing arms,
And grasp in extasy your blazing charms:
O then, how vain the wish that I pursue!
I would lose all myself, and mix with you;
Involv'd – embodied, with your beauties join,
As fires meet fires, and mingle in their shine;
Absorb'd in bliss, I would dissolving lie,
Become all you, and soul and body die.
   Weigh well these symptoms, and then judge, in part,
The poignant anguish of the bleeding heart
Of him, who is, with unutterable love, resplendent charmer,
Your hoping, fearing, languishing adorer,

                                                    F. FINEER.

P.S. I propose to fly to the feet of my adorable about five o'clock this
afternoon; do not, I beseech you, clip the wings of my devotion, by
forbidding my approach.'

   How acceptable, to a vain mind is even the meanest testimony of
admiration! If Miss Betsy was not charmed with the elegance of this
offering, she was at least very well pleased with the pains he took in
composing it. In the humour she then was, she would perhaps have
rewarded the labour of his brain, with giving him an opportunity of
kissing her shoe a second time; but she expected her brother Frank
about the hour he mentioned, with some intelligence of Mr.
Trueworth, and had engaged to pass the evening abroad, as has been
already mentioned.
   She sent, however, a very complaisant message by the servant who
brought the letter; she ordered he should come up into her dining-
room, and then, with a great deal of sweetness, desired him to tell his
master, that she was under a necessity of spending the whole day with
some relations that were just come to town, therefore entreated he

would defer the honour he intended her till some other time.

Mr. Francis Thoughtless did, indeed, call upon her, as she imagined he would: he had been at the lodgings of Mr. Trueworth; but as that gentleman happened to be abroad at the time he went, and he was now obliged to go wth his brother on some business relating to the commission he was about to purchase, so he could not stay long enough with her to enter into any conversation of moment.

Miss Betsy had now full two hours upon her hands after her brother left her, to which she had appointed Mr. Munden to come to conduct her to the country-dancing; and as she had not seen Miss Mabel for a good while, and had heard that lady had made her several visits when she was not at home to receive them, she thought to take this opportunity of having nothing else to do, to return part of the debt which civility demanded from her to her friend. Accordingly, she set out in a hackncy-coach, but met with an accident by the way, which not only disappointed her intentions, but likewise struck a strange damp on the gaiety of hcr spirits.

As they were driving pretty fast through a narrow street, a gentleman's chariot ran full against them, with such rapidity, that both received a very great shock, insomuch that the wheels werc locked; and it was not without some difficulty, and the assistance of several peoplc, who seeing what had happened, ran out of their shops and houses, that the coachmen were able to keep their horses from going on; which, had they done, both the machines must inevitably have been torn to pieces: there were two gentlemen in the chariot, who immediately jumped out; Miss Betsy screaming, and frighted almost to death, was also helped out of the coach by a very civil tradcsman, before whose door the accident had happened; he led her into his shop, and made her sit down, while his wife ran to fetch a glass of water, and some hartshorn-drops.

Her extreme terror had hindered her from discovering who was in the chariot, or whether any one was there; but the gentlemen having crossed the way, and come into the same shop, she presently knew the one to be Sir Bazil Loveit, and the other Mr. Trueworth; her surprize at the sight of the latter was such as might have occasioned some raillery, if it had not been concealed under that which she had sustained before: Sir Bazil approached her with a very respectful bow, and made a handsomc apology for the fault his man had committed, in not giving way when a lady was in the coach; to which she modestly replied, that there could be no fault where there was no design of offending. Mr. Trueworth then drawing near, with a very cold and reserved air, told her he hoped she would receive no prejudice by the accident.

'I believe the danger is now over,' said she, struck to the very heart at finding herself accosted by him in a manner so widely different from that to which she had been accustomed: scarce had she the fortitude to bear the shock it gave her; but, summoning to her aid all that pride and disdain could supply her with, to prevent him from perceiving how much she was affected by his behaviour – 'I could not, however,' pursued she, with a tone of voice perfectly ironical, 'have expected to receive any consolation under this little disaster from Mr. Trueworth; I imagined, sir, that some weeks ago you had been reposing yourself in the delightful bowers, and sweet recesses, of your country-seat. How often have I heard you repeat with pleasure these lines of Mr. Addison's –

"Bear me, ye gods! t'Umbraia's gentle seats,
    Or hide me in sweet Bayia's soft retreats?"

'Yet still I find you in this noisy, bustling town.' She concluded these words with a forced smile; which Mr. Trueworth taking no notice of, replied with the same gravity as before, 'I purposed, indeed, Madam, to have returned to Oxfordshire; but events then unforeseen have detained me.'

While they were speaking, Sir Bazil recollecting the face of Miss Betsy, which till now he had not done, cried, 'I think, Madam, I have had the honour of seeing you before this?' – 'Yes, Sir Bazil,' replied she, knowing very well he meant at Miss Forward's, 'you saw me once in a place where neither you, nor anyone else, will ever see me again: but I did not then know the character of the person I visited.' To which Sir Bazil only replying, that he believed she did not, Mr. Trueworth immediately rejoined, that the most cautious might be *once* deceived.

The emphasis with which he uttered the word once, made Miss Betsy see that he bore still in his mind the second error she had been guilty of in visiting that woman; but she had no time to give any other answer than a look of scorn and indignation, Sir Bazil's footman telling him the chariot was now at liberty, and had received no damage: on which the gentlemen took their leave of her, Mr. Trueworth shewing no more concern in doing so, than Sir Bazil himself, or any one would have done, who never had more than a mere cursory acquaintance with her.

She would not be persuaded to go into the coach again, much less could she think of going on her intended visit; but desired a chair to be called, and went directly home, in order to give vent to those emotions which may easier be conceived than represented.

CHAPTER V

———•———

Seems to be calculated rather for the instruction than entertainment of the reader

HOW great soever was the shock Miss Betsy had sustained in this interview with Mr. Trueworth, he did not think himself much indebted to fortune for having thrown her in his way; he had once loved her to a very high degree; and though the belief of her unworthiness, the fond endearments of one woman, and the real merits of another, had all contributed to drive that passion from his breast, yet as a wound but lately closed is apt to bleed afresh on every little accident, so there required no less than the whole stock of the beautiful and discreet Miss Harriot's perfections, to defend his heart from feeling anew some part of it's former pain, on this sudden and unexpected attack.

Happy was it for him, that his judgment concurred with his present inclination, and that he had such unquestionable reasons for justifying the transition he had made of his affections from one object to another; else might he have relapsed into a flame which, if ever it had been attended with any true felicity, must have been purchased at the expence of an infinity of previous disquiets.

He was now become extremely conversant with the family of Sir Bazil, visited there almost every day, was well received by both the sisters, and had many opportunities of penetrating into the real sentiments and dispositions of Miss Harriot; which he found to be such as his most sanguine wishes could have formed for the woman to be blest with whom he would make choice of for a wife. When he compared the steady temper, the affability, the ease, unaffected chearfulness, mixed with a becoming reserve, which that young lady testified in all her words and actions, with the capricious turns, the pride, the giddy lightness, he had observed in the behaviour of Miss Betsy, his admiration of the one was increased by his disapprobation of the other.

How great a pity it is, therefore, that a young lady, like Miss Betsy, so formed by heaven and nature to have rendered any man compleatly happy in possessing her, inferior to her fair competitor neither in wit, beauty, nor any personal or acquired endowment, her inclinations no less pure, her sentiments as noble, her disposition equally generous and benign; should, through her own inadvertency, destroy all the merit of so many amiable qualities; and, for the sake of indulging the wanton vanity of attracting universal admiration, forfeit, in reality, those just pretensions to which otherwise she had been entitled to from the deserving and the discerning few!

Mr. Trueworth, as the reader may have observed, did not all at once withdraw his affections from the first object of them, nor transmit them to the second but on very justifiable motives. The levity of Miss Betsy, and other branches of ill conduct, had very much weaned her from his heart before the wicked artifices of Miss Flora had rendered her quite contemptible in his opinion, and had not wholly devoted himself to the beauties of Miss Harriot, till he was quite convinced the perfections of her mind were such as could not fail of securing the conquest which her eyes had gained.

He did not however presently declare himself; he saw the friendship between the two sisters would be somewhat of an obstacle to his hopes; he had heard that Miss Harriot had rejected several advantageous proposals of marriage, merely because she would not be separated from Mrs. Wellair; he also found, that Sir Bazil, though for what reason he could not guess, seemed not very desirous of having his sister disposed of: the only probable way, therefore, he thought, of obtaining his wishes, was to conceal them till he found the means of insinuating himself so far into the good graces both of the one and the other, as to prevent them from opposing whatever endeavours he should make to engage their sister to listen to his suit.

The stratagem had all the effect for which it was put in practice: the intimacy he had long contracted with Sir Bazil now grew into so perfect a friendship, that he scarce suffered a day to pass without an invitation to his house. Mrs. Wellair expressed the highest esteem and liking of his conversation; and Miss Harriot herself, not imagining of what consequence every word that fell from her was to him, said a thousand obliging things on his account; particularly, one day, after they had been singing a two-part song together, 'How often,' cried she to her sister, 'shall we wish for this gentleman, when we get into the country, to act the principal part in our little operas!'

All this he returned in no other manner than any man would have done who had no farther aim than to shew his wit and gallantry: so much of his happiness, indeed, depended upon the event, that it behoved him to be very cautious how he proceeded; and it is likely he would not have ventured to throw off the mask of indifference so soon as he did, if he had not been emboldened to it by an unexpected accident.

Among the number of those who visited the sisters of Sir Bazil, there was a young lady called Mrs. Blanchfield; she was born in the same town with them, but had been some time in London, on account of the death of an uncle, who had left her a large fortune: she had a great deal of vivacity and good-humour, which rendered both her person and conversation very agreeable; she passed in the eyes of most people for a beauty; but her charms were little taken notice of by Mr. Trueworth, though she behaved towards him in a manner which would have been flattering enough to a man of more vanity, or who had been less engrossed by the perfections of another.

By what odd means does fortune sometimes bring about those things she is determined to accomplish! Who could have thought this lady, with whom Mr. Trueworth had no manner of concern, and but a slight acquaintance, should even, unknowing it herself, become the happy instrument of having that done for him which he knew not very well how to contrive for himself? yet so it proved, in effect, as the reader will presently perceive.

Happening to call one morning on Sir Bazil while he was dressing 'O Trueworth!' said he, 'I am glad you have prevented me; for I was just going to your lodgings: I have something to acquaint you with, which I fancy you will think deserves your attention.' – 'I suppose,' replied Mr. Trueworth, 'you would not tell me any thing that was not really so: but, pray, what is is?'

'What! you have made a conquest here, it seems,' resumed Sir Bazil; 'and may say, with Caesar, "Veni, vidi, vici!" Did your guardian angel, or no kind tattling star, give you notice of your approaching happiness, that you might receive the blessing with moderation?' – Mr. Trueworth, not able to conceive what it was he meant, but imagining there was some mystery contained in this raillery, desired him to explain; 'For,' said he, 'the happiness you promise cannot come too soon.'

'You will think so,' replied Sir Bazil, 'when I tell you a fine lady, a celebrated toast, and a fortune of twenty thousand pounds in her own hands, is fallen in love with you.' – 'With me!' cried Mr. Trueworth; 'you are merry this morning, Sir Bazil?' – 'No, faith, I am serious,' resumed the other; 'the lady I speak of is Mrs. Blanchfield. I have heard her say abundance of handsome things of you myself; such as, that you were a very fine gentleman, that you had a great deal of wit, and sung well; but my sisters tell me, that when she is alone with them, she asks a thousand questions about you; and, in fine, talks of nothing else: so that, according to this account, a very little courtship would serve to make you master both of her person and fortune. What say you?'

'That I am neither vain enough to believe,' answered Mr. Trueworth, 'nor ambitious enough to desire, such a thing should be real.' – 'How!' cried Sir Bazil, in some surprize; 'why, she is reckoned one of the finest women in town; has wit, good-nature; is of a good family, and an unblemished reputation. Then, her fortune! Though I know your estate sets you above wanting a fortune with a wife, yet I must tell you a fortune is a very pretty thing: children may come; and a younger brood must be provided for.'

'You argue very reasonably indeed,' replied Mr. Trueworth: 'but, pray,' pursued he, 'as you are so sensible of this lady's perfections, how happened it that you never made your addresses to her yourself?' – 'I was not sure she would like me so well as she does you,' said he; 'besides, to let you into the secret, my heart was engaged before I ever saw her face, and my person had been so too by this time, but for an unlucky rub in my way.'

'What! Sir Bazil, honourably in love!' cried Mr. Trueworth. 'Aye, Charles! There is no resisting destiny,' answered he; 'I that have ranged through half the sex in search of pleasure; doated on the beauty of one, the wit of another, admired by turn their different charms, have at last found one in whom all I could wish in woman is comprized, and to whom I an unalterably fixed, beyond, even, I think, a possibility of change.'

'May I be trusted with the name of this admirable person', said Mr. Trueworth, 'and what impedes your happiness?' – 'You shall know all,' replied Sir Bazil: 'in the first place, she is called Miss

Mable.' – 'What! Miss Mable of Bury Street!' cried Mr. Trueworth
hastily. 'The same,' replied Sir Bazil: 'you know her, then?' – 'I have
seen her,' said Mr. Trueworth, 'in company with a lady I visited some
time ago; and believe she is, in reality, the original of that amiable
picture you have been drawing.'

'It rejoices me, however, that you approve my choice,' said Sir
Bazil: 'but her father is, without exception, the most sordid,
avaricious wretch, breathing; he takes more pleasure in counting over
his bags than in the happiness of an only child; he seems glad of an
alliance with me – encourages my pretensions to his daughter – is
ready to give her to me to-morrow, if I please: yet refuses to part with
a single shilling of her portion till he can no longer keep it; that is, he
will secure to me ten thousand pounds after his decease; and adds, by
way of cajole, that, perhaps, he will then throw in a better penny; but
is positively determined to make no diminution of his substance while
he lives. These,' continued he, 'are the only terms on which he will
give his consent; and this it is which has so long delayed my
marriage.'

Mr. Trueworth could not here forbear making some reflections on
the cruelty and injustice of those parents who, rather than divide any
part of their treasures with their children, suffer them to let slip the
only crisis that could make their happiness. After which, Sir Bazil
went on in his discourse.

'It is not,' said he, 'that I would not gladly accept my charming girl
on the conditions the old miser offers, or even without any farther
hopes of what he promises to do for her; but I am so unhappily
circumstanced as to be under a necessity of having ready-money with
a wife: old Sir Bazil, my father, gave my elder sister six thousand
pounds on her marriage with Mr. Wellair; and, I suppose, to shew his
affection to both his daughters was equal, bequeathed at his death
the same sum to Harriot, and this to be charged on the estate,
notwithstanding it was then under some other incumbrances. She can
make her demand, either on coming of age, or on the day of
marriage, which ever happens first: the one, indeed, is three years
distant, she being but eighteen; but who knows how soon the other
may happen? It is true, she seems at present quite averse to changing
her condition: but that is not to be depended upon; all young women
are apt to talk in that strain; but when once the favourite man comes
into view, away at once with resolution and virginity.'

Mr. Trueworth now ceased to wonder at the little satisfaction Sir

Bazil had shewn on any discourse, that casually happened concerning love or marriage, to Miss Harriot; and nothing could be more lucky for him than this discovery of the cause: he found by it that one obstacle, at least, to his hopes, might easily be removed; and that it was in his own power to convert entirely to his interest that which had seemed to threaten the greatest opposition to it.

A moment's consideration sufficed to make him know what he ought to do, and that a more favourable conjuncture could not possibly arrive for his declaring the passion he had so long concealed. 'Methinks, Sir Bazil,' said he, after a very short pause, 'there is not the least grounds for any apprehension of the inconvience you mention: whoever has in view the possession of Miss Harriot, must certainly be too much taken up with his approaching happiness to think of any thing besides.'

'Ah, friend!' cried Sir Bazil, 'you talk like one ignorant of the world.' – 'I talk like one who truly loves,' replied Mr. Trueworth, 'and is not ignorant of the merit of her he loves; and now,' continued he, perceiving Sir Bazil looked a little surprized, 'I will exchange secrets with you; and, for the one you have reposed in me, will entrust you with another which has never yet escaped my lips: I love your charming sister; the first moment I beheld her made me her adorer; her affability – her modest sweetness – her unaffected wit – her prudence – the thousand virtues of her mind – have since confirmed the impressions that her beauty made, and I am now all hers.'

As Sir Bazil had never discovered any thing in Mr. Trueworth's behaviour that could give him the least cause to suspect what now he was so fully informed of by his own confession, he was very much astonished. 'Is it possible!' cried he; 'are you in earnest? and do you really love Harriot?' 'Yes, from my soul I do!' replied Mr. Trueworth; 'and I wish no other blessing on this side Heaven than to obtain her. As to the six thousand pounds you speak of, I neither should demand, nor would accept it, till well assured the payment of it was quite agreeable to the situation of your affairs.'

'Would you then marry Harriot with nothing?' said Sir Bazil, 'or, what is tantamount to nothing, a small fortune, and that to be paid discretionary, rather than Mrs. Blanchfield, with twenty thousand pounds in ready specie?' – 'Not only rather than Mrs. Blanchfield,' replied Mr. Trueworth, 'but than any other woman in the world, with all those thousands multiplied into millions!'

'Amazing love and generosity!' cried Sir Bazil with some vehemence. 'Could she be capable of refusing, she were unworthy of you: but this you may be assured, that if all the influence I have over her can engage her to be yours, she shall be so.' Mr. Trueworth could testify the transport this promise gave him no otherwise than by a warm embrace; saying, at the same time, 'Dear Sir Bazil!' – 'Yes,' rejoined that gentleman, 'to give my sister such a husband as Mr. Trueworth, I would put myself to a much greater inconvenience than the prompt payment of her fortune, and shall not abuse your generous offer by –' 'I will not hear a word on that head,' cried Mr. Trueworth, hastily interrupting him; 'and if you would add to the favours you have already conferred upon me, do not ever think of it: pursue your inclinations with the deserving object of them, and be as happy with her as I hope to be, through your friendly assistance, with the adorable Miss Harriot!'

Here ensued a little contest between them; Sir Bazil was ashamed to accept that proof of friendship Mr. Trueworth made use of, joined to the consideration of his own ease, at last prevailed: after which Sir Bazil told him the ladies were gone to the shops, in order to make some purchases they wanted; but that he would take the first opportunity, on their return, to acquaint his sister with the sentiments he had for her; and appointed to meet him at the chocolate-house in the evening, to let him know the success.

CHAPTER VI

———————•———————

Shews the different operations of the same passion, in persons of different principles and dispositions

SIR Bazil had very much at heart the accomplishment of the promise he had made to Mr. Trueworth; and, indeed, no one thing could have seemed more strange than that of his being otherwise, when so many reasons concurred to engage his integrity: he had a real friendship for the person who desired his assistance; there were none among all his acquaintance for whom he had a greater regard, or who shared more of his good wishes; the natural affection he had for his sister made him rejoice in the opportunity of seeing her so happily disposed of; and the particular interest of his own passion might well render him not only sincere, but also zealous, in promoting an affair which would so fully answer all these ends.

The first breaking the matter to Miss Harriot he looked upon as the greatest difficulty; for he doubted not but when once a belief of Mr. Trueworth's inclinations was properly inculcated in her, his amiable person, and fine qualities, would enable him to make his way, as a lover, into a heart, which had already a high esteem for him as an acquaintance.

He resolved, however, not to delay making the discovery; and his sisters coming home soon after, he ran out of his dressing-room, and met them as they were going up stairs into their own chamber, with a whole cargo of silks, and other things they had been buying. 'Hold, hold!' cried he, not suffering them to pass; 'pray, come in here, and let me see what bargains you have been making?' – 'What understanding can you, that are a batchelor, have in these things?' said Mrs. Wellair, laughing. 'I have the more need then of being informed,' replied he, 'that I may be the better able to judge both of the fancy and frugality of my wife, whenever I am so happy to get one.'

'Well, well! I know all you men must be humoured,' said Mrs. Wellair, in the same gay strain. – 'Come, sister, let us unpack our bundles.' With these words they both went in, and the servant, who followed them with the things, having laid them down on a table, withdrew.

The ladies then began to open their parcels; and Sir Bazil gave his opinion first of one thing, and then of another, as they were shewn to him; till Miss Harriot, displaying a roll of very rich white damask, 'To which of you does this belong?' said Sir Bazil. 'To me,' answered she. 'Hah! I am glad on it, upon my soul!' rejoined he: 'this is an omen of marriage, my dear sister. I will lay my life upon it, that you become a bride in this gown!' – 'I must first find the man to make me so,' cried she briskly. 'He is not very far to seek, I dare answer,' said Sir Bazil. 'Why, then,' replied she, 'when he is found he must wait till my mind comes to me; and that, I believe, will not be in the wearing of this gown.'

'I am of a different way of thinking,' said he, somewhat more gravely than before: 'what would you say if I should tell you that one of the finest, most accomplished men in Europe, is fallen desperately in love with you, and has engaged me to be his intercessor?' – 'I should say nothing,' answered she, 'but that you have a mind to divert yourself, and put me out of humour with my new gown, by your converting it into a hieroglyphick.' In speaking these words she catched up her silk, and ran hastily up stairs, leaving Mrs. Wellair and her brother together.

'Poor Harriot!' said Sir Bazil, after she was gone; 'I have put her to the blush with the very name of matrimony – but I assure you, sister,' continued he to Mrs. Wellair, 'the thing I have mentioned is serious.' – 'Indeed!' cried that lady in some surprize. 'Yes, upon my honour,' resumed he; 'the gentleman I mean had not left me above a quarter of an hour before you came in, and I can tell you is one whom you know.' – 'If I know him,' replied she, after a pause, 'I fancy I need not be at any loss to guess his name, by the description you have given me of him; for I have seen no man, since my coming to town,, who so well deserves those encomiums as Mr. Trueworth.' – 'I am glad you think so,' said Sir Bazil; 'for I am certain your judgment will go a great way with Harriot: he is, in fact, the person I have been speaking of; and is so every way deserving of my sister's affection, that she must not only be the most insensible creature in the world, but also the greatest enemy to her own interest and happiness to refuse him.'

He then repeated to her all the conversation he had had that morning with Mr. Trueworth – the answers that gentleman had given him on the proposition he had made on Mrs. Blanchfield's account – his declaration of his passion for Miss Harriot – and every other particular, excepting that of the non-payment of her fortune; and that he concealed only because he would not be suspected to have been bribed by it to say more of his friend than he really merited.

Mrs. Wellair was equally charmed and astonished at this report; and, on Sir Bazil's telling her that Mr. Trueworth was under some apprehensions that the pleasure she took in having her sister with her would be an impediment to his desires, she very gravely replied, that she was very sorry Mr. Trueworth should imagine she was so wanting in understanding, or true affection to her sister, as, for the self-satisfaction of her company, to offer any thing in opposition to her interest or happiness.

After this they had a good deal of discourse together, concerning Mr. Trueworth's family and fortune, the particulars of both which Sir Bazil was very well acquainted with; and Mrs. Wellair, being thoroughly convinced, by what he said of the many advantages of the alliance proposed, assured him, in the strongest terms she was able, that she would do every thing in her power to promote it.

'I will entertain her on this subject while we are dressing,' said she: 'your pleasantry on this white damask will furnish me with an excellent pretence; I shall begin in the same strain you did, and then proceed to a serious narrative of all you have been telling me relating to Mr. Trueworth; to which I shall add my own sentiments of the amiableness of his person, parts, and accomplishments, and set before her eyes, in the light it deserves, the generosity of his passion, in refusing so great a fortune as Mrs. Blanchfield for her sake, and the respectfulness of it, in not daring to declare himself till he had engaged the only two who may be supposed to have any influence over her, in favour of his suit.'

'I know,' said Sir Bazil, 'that you women are the fittest to deal with one another; therefore, as I see you are hearty in the cause, shall wholly depend on your management: but, hark-ye, sister!' continued he, perceiving she was going out of the room, 'I have one more thing to add; I am to meet Trueworth at the chocolate-house this evening; he will be impatient for the success of the promise I have made him; now you know we shall have a great deal of company at dinner to-day, and I may not have an opportunity of speaking to you in private before the time of my going to him; for that reason we must have some watch-word between us, that may give an intimation in general how Harriot receives what you have said to her.'

'Oh, that is easy,' cried Mrs. Wellair; 'as thus: you shall take an occasion, either at table, or any time when you find it most proper, to ask me how I do; and by my answer to that question, you will be able to judge what success I have had.' – 'Very right,' replied Sir Bazil; 'and I will be sure to observe.' There passed no more between them; she went directly up stairs to do as she had said, and Sir Bazil to pay his mourning visit to Miss Mable, as he usually did every day.

The humours of these two worthy persons were extremely well adapted to make each other happy: Sir Bazil was gay, but he was perfectly sincere; Miss Mable had a great deal of softness in her nature, but it was entirely under the direction of her prudence; she returned the passion of her lover with equal tenderness, yet would not permit the gratification of it till every thing that threatened an interruption of their mutual ease should be removed. Sir Bazil made no secret of his affairs to her; she knew very well that he desired no more at present of her father than the six thousand pounds charged on his estate for Miss Harriot's fortune; and as the old gentleman testified the highest esteem for him, and satisfaction in the proposed match, she flattered herself that he would at last consent to so reasonable a request; but, till he did so, remained firm in her resolution of denying both her own and her lover's wishes.

The pleasure with which they always saw each other was now, however, greatly enhanced by his acquainting her with the almost assured hope he had, that the difficulty which had so long kept them asunder would be soon got over; and he should have the inexpressible satisfaction of complying with the conditions her father had proposed, without the least danger of incurring any inconvenience to himself.

The clock striking two, he was obliged to leave her, and go home to receive the company he expected. He behaved among his friends with his accustomed vivacity; but casting his eyes frequently towards Miss Harriot, he imgained he saw a certain gloom upon her countenance, which made him fearful for the effects of Mrs. Wellair's solicitations; till, recollecting the agreement between him and that lady, he cried out hastily to her, 'How do you do, sister?' To which she answered, with a smile, 'As well as can be expected, brother;' and then, to prevent Miss Harriot, or any one else, from wondering what she meant by so odd a reply, added, 'after the ugly jolt I have had this morning over London stones in a hackney-coach.'

Sir Bazil easily understood, that by the words 'As well as can be expected,' his sister meant as much as could be hoped for from the first attack on a maid so young and innocent as Miss Harriot; and doubted not but that so favourable a beginning would have as fortunate a conclusion.

Those guests who had dined with him staid supper also; but that did not hinder him from fulfilling his engagement with Mr. Trueworth. He begged they would excuse a short excursion which, he said, he was obliged to make on extraordinary business; and accordingly went at the time appointed for the meeting that gentleman.

Mr. Trueworth received the intelligence he brought with him with transports befitting the sincerity of his passion. He thought he had little to apprehend, since Mrs. Wellair vouchsafed to become his advocate. 'It is certainly,' said Sir Bazil, 'as greatly in her power to forward the completion of your wishes, as it was to have obstructed them. But, my dear friend,' continued he, 'there is no time to be lost: the business that brought my sisters to town will soon be over; and Mrs. Wellair will then be on the wing to get home to her husband and family. You must dine with me to-morrow; I shall be able by that time to learn the particulars of Harriot's behaviour, on her first hearing an account of the affection with which you honour her; and by that you may the better judge how to proceed.' This was the substance of all the discourse they had together at that time. Sir Bazil went home, and Mr. Trueworth adjourned to a coffee-house, where he met with something not very pleasing to him. It was a letter from Miss Flora, containing these lines.

'To Charles Trueworth, Esq.

My dear Trueworth,
For such you still are, and ever must be, to my fond doating heart; though I have too much cause to fear you cease to wish it – else why this cruel absence? I have not seen you these three days! – an age to one that loves like me. I am racked to death with the apprehensions

of the motives of so unexpected a neglect! If my person or passion were unworthy your regard, why did you accept them with such enchanting softness? And if ever I had any place in your affection, what have I done to forfeit it? But, sure, you cannot think of abandoning me! – of leaving me to all the horrors of despair and shame! – No! it is impossible! Ingratitude consists not with that strict honour you pretend to; and that, I still flatter myself, you are in reality possessed of. You may have had some business: but how poor a thing is business when compared with love! And I may reply, with our English Sappho, in one of her amorous epistles –

> "Business you feign; but did you love like me,
> I should your most important business be."

But whither does my hurrying spirits transport me! If I am still so happy to retain any share of your heart, I have said too much; if I am not, all I can say will be ineffectual to move you. I shall, therefore, only tell you that I can live no longer without seeing you, and will call on you at the coffee-house this evening about eight; till when I am, though in the utmost distraction, my dear, dear Trueworth, your passionately tender, and devoted servant,

F. MELLASIN.

P.S. Having heard you say letters were left for you at this place, and that you stepped in once or twice every day, I thought it more proper to direct for you here than at your own lodgings. Once more adieu. – Do not fail to meet me at the hour.'

Scarce could the ghost of a forsaken mistress, drawing his curtains at the dead of night, have shocked Mr. Trueworth more than this epistle. He had, indeed, done no more than any man of his age and constitution would have done, if tempted in the manner he had been; yet he reproached himself severely for it. He knew how little this unhappy creature had her passions in subjection; and, though all the liking he ever had for her was now swallowed up in his honourable affections for Miss Harriot, yet he was too humane and too generous not to pity the extravagance of a flame he was no longer capable of returning. He wanted her to know there was a necessity for their parting; but knew not how to do it without driving her to extremes! He hated all kind of dissimulation; and, as neither his honour nor his inclinations would permit him to continue an amorous correspondence with her, he was very much at a loss how to put an end to it, without letting her into the real cause; which, as yet, he thought highly improper to do.

It cost him some time in debating within himself how he should behave in an affair which was, indeed, in the present situation of his heart, pretty perplexing: he considered Miss Flora as a woman of condition – as one who tenderly loved him – and as one who, on both these accounts, it would not become him to affront. He reflected also, that a woman, who had broke through all the rules of virtue, modesty, and even common decency, for the gratification of her wild desires, might, when denied that gratificiation, be capable of taking such steps as might not only expose her own character, but with it so much of his as might ruin him with Miss Harriot. He found it, therefore, highly necessary to disguise his sentiments, and act towards her in such a manner as should wean her affections from him by degrees, without his seeming to intend or wish for such an event.

He had but just come to this determination, when he was told from the bar that a lady in a hackney-coach desired to speak with him. He went directly to her; but, instead of ordering the man to drive to any particular house, bid him drive as slowly as he could round St. James's Square.

This very much startling her, she asked him what he meant. 'Are all the houses of entertainment in the town,' said she, 'shut up, that we must talk to each other in the street?' – 'It is impossible for me, Madam,' answered he, 'to have the pleasure of your company this evening. I am engaged with some gentleman at the house where you found me, and have given my promise to return in ten minutes.' These words, and the reserved tone in which he spoke them, stabbed her to the heart. 'Ungenerous man!' cried she, 'is it thus you repay the most tender and ardent passion that ever was!' – 'You ladies,' said he, 'when once you give way to the soft impulse, are apt to devote yourselves too much to it; but men have a thousand other amusements, which all claim a share in the variegated scenes of life. I am sorry, therefore, to find you disquieted in the manner your letter intimates. Love should be nursed by laughing, ease, and joy: sour discontent, reproaches, and complaints, deform it's native beauty, and render that a curse, which otherwise would be the greatest of our blessings. I beg you, therefore,' continued he, with somewhat more softness in his voice, 'for your own sake, to moderate this vehemence. Be assured I will see you as often as possible; and shall always think of you with the regard I ought to do.'

Perceiving she was in very great agonies, he threw his arms about her waist, and gave her a very affectionate salute; which, though no more than a brother might have offered to a sister, a little mitigated the force of her grief. 'I see I am undone!' cried she. 'I have lost your heart, and am the most wretched creature upon earth!' – 'Do not say so,' replied he. 'I never can be ungrateful for the favours you have bestowed upon me; but discretion ought to be observed in an amour, such as ours. I have really some affairs upon my hands, which for a time will very much engross me. Make yourself easy, then; resume that gaiety which renders you so agreeable to the world; and, depend upon it, that to make me happy, you must be so yourself.' – 'When, then, shall I see you?' cried she, still weeping, and hanging on his breast. 'As soon as convenience permits I will send to you,' said he; 'but there is a necessity for my leaving you at present.'

He then called to the coachman to drive back to the house where he had taken him up. It is not to be doubted but she made use of all the rhetorick of desperate dying love, and every other art she was mistress of, to engage him to prefix some time for their meeting; but he would not suffer himself to be prevailed upon so far: and he left her with no other consolation than a second embrace, little warmer than the former had been, and a repetition of the promise he had made of writing to her in a short time.

CHAPTER VII

——•——

May be called an appendix to the former, as it contains only some passages subsequent to the preceding occurrences

WHAT pain soever the good-nature and generosity of Mr. Trueworth had made him suffer, at the sight of the unfortunate Miss Flora's distress, it was dissipated by recalling to his mind the pleasing idea Sir Bazil had inspired in him, of succeeding in his wishes with the amiable Miss Harriot.

What sleep he had that night, doubtless, presented him with nothing but the delightful images of approaching joys; and, possibly, might give him some intimation of what was in those moments doing for him by those who were waking for his interest.

Mrs. Wellair, who was extremely cautious how she undertook any thing, without being fully convinced it was right, and no less industrious in accomplishing whatever she had once undertook, had employed all the time she had with her sister, before dinner, in representing to her, in the most pathetick terms, the passion Mr. Trueworth had for her, the extraordinary merits he was possessed of, and the many advantages of an alliance with him: but Miss Harriot was modest to that excess, that to be told, though from the mouth of a sister, she had inspired any inclinations of the sort she mentioned, gave her the utmost confusion. She had not considered the difference of sexes, and could not hear that any thing in her had reminded others of it, without blushing. The effects of her beauty gave her rather a painful than a pleasing sensation; and she was ready to die with shame at what the most part of women are studious to acquire, and look on as their greatest glory.

She offered nothing, however, in opposition to what Mrs. Wellair had said concerning the person or amiable qualities of Mr. Trueworth; neither, indeed, had she a will to do it. She had been always highly pleased with his conversation, and had treated him with the same innocent freedom she did her brother; and she was now afraid, that it was her behaving to him in this manner that had encouraged him to think of making his addresses to her as a lover. She looked back with regret on every little mark of favour she had shewn him, lest he should have construed them into a meaning which was far distant from her thoughts; and these reflections it was that occasioned that unusual pensiveness which Sir Bazil had observed in her at dinner, and which had given him some apprehensions proceeded from a cause less favourable to his friend.

Mrs. Wellair was not at all discouraged by the manner in which her sister had listened to this overture: she knew that several proposals of the same nature had been made to her in the country; all which she had rejected with disdain – a certain air of abhorrence widely different to what she testified on account of Mr. Trueworth; and this prudent lady rightly judged, that he had little else to combat with than the over-bashfulness of his mistress.

At night, on going to bed, she renewed the discourse; and pursued the theme she had begun with such success, that she brought Miss Harriot to confess she believed there was no man more deserving to be loved than Mr. Trueworth. 'But, my dear sister,' said she, 'I have no inclination to marry, nor to leave you: I am quite happy as I am, and desire to be no more so.' To which the other replied, that was childish talking; that she would, doubtless, marry some time or other; that she might, perhaps, never have so good an offer, and could not possibly have a better; therefore advised her not to slip the present opportunity; but, whenever Mr. Trueworth should make a declaration of his passion to herself, to receive it in such a manner as should not give him any room to imagine she was utterly averse to his pretensions.

Miss Harriot suffered her to ruge her on this point for a considerable time; but at last replied, in a low and hesitating voice, that she would be guided by her friends, who, she was perfectly convinced, had her interest at heart, and knew much better than herself what conduct she ought to observe. To which Mrs. Wellair replied, that she doubted not but the end would abundantly justify the advice that had been given her.

The first thing this lady did in the morning, was to go to her brother's chamber, and acquaint him with all that had passed between herself and Miss Harriot; after which they agreed together, that Mr. Trueworth should have an opportunity that very day of making his addresses to her.

Though Sir Bazil thought it needless to add any thing to what was already done, yet he could not forbear taking an occasion, when they were at breakfast, to mention Mr. Trueworth's name, and the many good qualities he was possessed of. Mrs. Wellair joined in the praises her brother gave him; but Miss Harriot spoke not a word: on which, 'Are you not of our opinion, sister?' cried he to her. 'Yes, brother,' answered she; 'Mr. Trueworth is certainly a very fine gentleman.' – 'How cold is such an expression,' resumed Sir Bazil, 'and even that extorted!' – 'You would not, sure, Sir,' said she, a little gaily, 'have me in raptures about him, and speak as if I were in love with him?'

'Indeed, but I would!' cried Sir Bazil; 'and, what is more, would also have you be so: he deserves it from you; and, as you must some time or other be sensible of the tender passion, you cannot do it at more suitable years.' – 'I see no necessity,' replied she, 'for my being so at any years.'

'It is a sign, then,' said he, 'that you have not consulted nature. Have you never read what Lord Lansdown has wrote upon this subject? If you have not, I will repeat it to you –

> "In vain from Fate we strive to fly;
> For, first or last, as all must die,
> So, 'tis decreed by those above,
> That, first or last, we all must love."

'Poets are not always prophets,' answered she, laughing. 'It depends upon Mr. Trueworth himself,' said Sir Bazil, 'to prevent you from giving the lie to the prediction. If he fails, I shall believe no other man in the world will ever have the power to engage you to fulfil it; he dines here to-day. Sister Wellair and I are obliged to go abroad in the afternoon; so must desire you to make tea, and entertain him, as well as you can, till we come back.'

'I see you are both in the plot against me,' cried she; 'but I shall endeavour to behave so as not to affront your guest; yet, at the same time, be far from making good your oracle.'

A gentleman coming in to Sir Bazil, broke off their discourse, and relieved Miss Harriot from any farther persecution at this time. It was not that she disliked either the person or conversation of Mr. Trueworth, or that she was tired with the praises given him by her brother and sister; on the contrary, she found a thousand things which they had not mentioned, to admire in him: in fine, he was, in reality, less indifferent to her than she herself imagined; but there was a certain shyness in her disposition, which mingled some share of pain with the pleasure of hearing him spoke of as her lover.

She was sensible this propensity, which nature had implanted, was a weakness in her; but, though she used her utmost efforts for overcoming it, she found herself unequal to the task. In vain she considered, that the addresses of a man of such perfect honour and politeness as Mr. Trueworth, could not but be accompanied with the most profound respect: in vain she called the mind the example of other ladies, whom she had seen behave in the company of those who professed themselves their lovers, with the greatest ease and sprightliness; the very sight of Mr. Trueworth, as she saw him from her chamber-window, talking with her brother in the garden, threw her heart into palpitations, which all the reason she was mistress of could not enable her to quiet; but, when obliged to go down and sit with him at table, her confusion increased, by being more near the object which occasioned it. She endeavoured to treat him with the same freedom she had been accustomed; but it was not in her power: in fine, never woman suffered more in constraining herself to be silent and demure, than she did in constraining herself to be talkative and gay.

What, then, became of her, when Sir Bazil and Mrs. Wellair, after making a formal excuse for a short absence, went out, and left her exposed to the solicitations of a passion which her timid modesty had made her so much dread.

The moment Mr. Trueworth saw himself alone with her, he approached her with the most tender and respectful air. 'How often, Madam, have I languished for an opportunity, such as this, of telling you how much my soul adores you! My dear friend, Sir Bazil, has assured me he has prepared you to forgive the boldness of my flame, and that, for his sake, you will vouchsafe to listen to my vows; but it is from myself alone you can be convinced of the ardency of the love you have inspired.'

'My brother, Sir,' answered she, blushing, 'has, indeed, informed me that I have obligations to you of a nature which I was as far from expecting as I am far from deserving.' Here Mr. Trueworth began to run into some praises on the charms which had subdued his heart; which, though no more than dictated by his real sentiments, seemed to her too extravagant, and beyond what her modesty would suffer her to endure. 'Hold, Sir!' cried she, interrupting him; 'if you would have me believe your professions are sincere, forbear, I beseech you, to talk to me in this manner. It is an ill-judged policy, methinks, in you men, to idolize the women too much you wish would think well of you. If our sex are, in reality, so vain as you generally represent us, on whom but yourselves can the fault be laid? And if we prove so weak as to imagine ourselves such as either the flattery or the partial affection of the lover paints us, we shall be apt to take every thing as our due, and think little gratitude is owing for the offering he makes us of his heart.'

Mr. Trueworth was perfectly ravished at hearing her speak thus; but durst not express himself with too much warmth on the occasion. 'It must be confessed, Madam,' replied he, 'that the beauties of the person, when not accompanied by those of the mind, afford but a short-lived triumph to the fair possessor; they dazzle at first sight, and take the senses, as it were, by surprize; but the impression soon wears off, and the captivated heart gains it's former liberty: nay, perhaps, wonders at itself for having been enslaved; whereas those darts which fly from the perfections of the mind, penetrate into the soul, and fix a lasting empire there. But when both these charms shall happen to be united, as in the lovely Harriot,' continued he, taking one of her hands and kissing it; 'when in the most enchanting form that nature ever made, is found a soul enriched with every virtue, every grace – how indissoluble is the chain! how glorious the bondage!'

'Love is a theme I have never made my study,' answered she; 'but, according to my notions of the matter, those gentlemen who pretend to be affected by it, give themselves more trouble than they need. As that passion is generally allowed rather to be the child of fancy, than of real merit in the object beloved, I should think it would be sufficient for any man, in his addresses to a lady, to tell her that she happens to hit his taste – that she is what he likes; without dressing her up in qualities which, perhaps, have no existence but in his own imagination'.

'Where love is founded on beauty alone, as I have already said,' resumed Mr. Trueworth, 'the instructions you give, Madam, are certainly very just; for, indeed, no farther could be warranted by sincerity: but where reason directs the lover's choice, and points out those excellences which alone can make him happy in the possession of his wishes, ideas more sublime will naturally arise, and we can never too much admire, or praise, what is immediately from the divine source of perfection! It is not, O charming Harriot!' pursued he, looking on her with the utmost tenderness; 'it is not these radiant eyes, that lovely mouth, nor that sweet majesty that shines through all your air, but it is the heaven within that I adore: to that I pay my present worship, and on that build all my hopes of future bliss!'

Miss Harriot was about to make some reply; but his looks, the vehemence with which he uttered these last words, and the passionate gesture which accompanied them, made her relapse into her former bashfulness, from which she had a little recovered herself, and again deprived her of the power of speech.

'You give up the point, then, my angel!' cried he, perceiving she was silent; 'and I am glad you do; for had you continued to prohibit my expatiating on these matters, which made me your adorer, I must have maintained the argument even against your lovely self, to whom I shall for ever yield in all things else.'

After this he fell, insensibly as it were, into some discourse concerning the divine ordinance of marriage; and then proceeded to give her the most amiable picture that words could form of that state, when two persons of virtue, honour, and good sense, were by love and law united, and found themselves equally bound by duty and inclination to promote each other's happiness.

There are some ladies who listen very contentedly to the most warm and amorous addresses that can be made to them, yet will not suffer the least word of marriage till after a long and tedious preparation is made for a sound which they pretend to think so dreadful. These, no doubt, will say, that Mr. Trueworth went too far for a lover on the first declaration of his passion; but he was emboldened to act in the manner he did by the brother of his mistress, and had the satisfaction to perceive she was not offended at it: she had a great share of solid understanding, was an enemy to all sorts of affectation; and as she knew the end proposed by his courtship was marriage, saw no reason why he should be fearful of mentioning it to her; and though her modesty would not permit her to take much part in a conversation of this nature, yet she was too artless, and indeed, too sincere, to counterfeit a displeasure which she did not feel.

CHAPTER VIII

Is more full of business than entertainment

WHILE Mr. Trueworth was thus prosecuting a suit, which every time he saw the lovely Harriot redoubled his impatience to accomplish, Mr. Francis Thoughtless had been twice at his lodgings without finding him at home: but on that gentleman's leaving his name the second time, and saying he would come again the next morning, the other thought himself under an indispensible necessity of staying to receive his visit.

The meeting of these two was extremely civil and polite, but far from that cordial familiarity which used to pass between them, especially on the side of Mr. Francis. After Mr. Trueworth had congratulated him on the recovery of his health, and coming to town, they fell into some discourse on ordinary affairs, without the least mentioning of Miss Betsy, by either party, for a considerable time; till her brother, growing a little impatient that the other should say nothing to him on an affair in which he had made him his confidant, and which he had taken so much pains to forward, said to him, with an air, partly gay, and partly serious, 'I was surprized on my arrival to be told, that a passion so violent as that you pretended for my sister, should all on a sudden vanish, and that a thing which I once thought so near being concluded, was entirely broken off.'

'Things of that nature,' replied Mr. Trueworth, coldly, 'are never concluded till accomplished: accidents sometimes intervene to separate persons who have seemed most likely to be united for ever; which, indeed, never was the case between me and that lady.'

'Yet, Sir,' rejoined the other, a little irritated at his manner of speaking, 'I think, that when a gentleman has made his addresses to a young lady of family and character for any length of time, and in the publick manner you did, some cause ought to be assigned for his deserting her.'

'I am under no obligation,' said Mr. Trueworth, very gloomily, 'to give an account of my behaviour to any one whatever; but, in consideration of our friendship, and the love I once had for your sister, I shall make no scruple to tell you, that a woman of her humour would suit but ill with a man of mine: as to any farther eclaircissement of this affair, it is from herself alone you must receive it.' – 'She shewed me a letter from you, Sir,' cried Mr. Francis, hastily. 'That might then suffice to inform you,' answered Mr. Trueworth, 'that in what I have done, I but obeyed the dictates of my honour.' – 'Honour!' cried the other, fiercely, and laying his hand on his sword, 'What is it you mean, Sir? Did honour oppose your marriage with my sister?'

'No menaces!' said Mr. Trueworth, with a gravity which was pretty near disdain: 'you know me incapable of fear; I have fought for your sister, but will never fight against her. I injure not her reputation; on the contrary, I would defend it, if unjustly attacked, even at the hazard of my life: but as to love or marriage, these are things now out of the question; we both, perhaps, have other views, and the less is said of what is past is the better.'

Mr. Francis naturally took fire on the least suspicion of an indignity offered to him; but when once convinced of his mistake, was no less ready to repent and acknowledge it; he had seen many instances of the honour, generosity, and sincerity of Mr. Trueworth: he had also been witness of some of the levity and inconsiderateness of his sister; and the reflection of a moment served to make him see this change had happened merely through her own ill conduct.

His rage abated even while the other was speaking; but a deep concern remained behind; and, throwing himself down in a chair, 'Into what vexations,' cried he, 'may not a whole family be plunged, through the indiscretion of one woman?'

'Judge not too rashly,' said Mr. Trueworth; 'Miss Betsy may one day see a man so happy as to inspire her with sentiments far different from those she hitherto has entertained; and she also may be more happy herself, with a man who loves her with less delicacy than I did.'

The brother of Miss Betsy seemed not to take any notice of these words; but, rising in some confusion, 'Well, Sir,' said he, 'I shall trouble you no more upon this subject; and am sorry I have done it now.' Mr. Trueworth then told him, that though the intended alliance between them was broke off, he saw no occasion that their friendship should be so too; that he should be glad of an opportunity to return the favours he had received from him, in relation to his sister, though his endeavours on that score had not met with the desired success; and that he hoped they should not live as strangers while they continued in the same town: to all this Mr. Franics made but very short replies, either taking what he said as words of course, or because the disorder of his own mind would not permit him to prolong the conversation.

It is likely Mr. Trueworth was not much troubled at the hasty leave this young gentleman took; for though he always had a very sincere regard for him, yet the point on which he now had come, was tender, and could not be touched upon without giving him some pain: he had no time, however, to make many reflections on the conversation that had passed between them. A letter was brought him by a porter who, waiting for an answer, he immediately opened it, and found the contents as follows.

'To Charles Trueworth, Esq.

Sir,
Extraordinary merits seldom fail of having as extraordinary effects: you have made a conquest of a heart without knowing it, which not the utmost endeavours of any other could ever subdue. I am commissioned to acquaint you, that a lady of some consideration in the world, and a large fortune in her own hands, thinks you alone deserve to be the master both of that and of herself: but as she is apprehensive of your being already engaged, begs you will be so generous as to confess the truth; that, if so, she may put a timely stop to the progress of her growing passion; if not, you will, doubtless, hear more from her by the hand of, Sir, your unknown servant.

P.S. Please to send this back, with your answer wrote on the other side of the paper, which you may put up under a cover sealed up, but without any direction. Sincerity and secrecy are earnestly requested.'

Mr. Trueworth could not avoid looking on this adventure as a very odd one: yet, whether the proposal was real or feigned, the matter was wholly indifferent to him; and he hesitated not a moment in what part he should take in it; but sat down immediately, and wrote, as desired, the following answer.

'To the unknown.

Sir, or Madam,
Though I know the honour with which you flatter me is more the
effect of fortune than desert, it would certainly make me vain and
happy, were I not denied the power of accepting. The heart required
of me by the lady is already disposed of – irrecoverably disposed of;
and I can only repay her goodness by sincerely wishing a return of
hers, and with it all those felicities she would so lavishly bestow on
her most obliged, and most humble servant,

C. TRUEWORTH.

P.S. The lady may depend, that my secrecy shall be equal to the
sincerity I have shewn in this.'

He had no sooner dispatched the messenger who brought this, than
a second came, and presented him with another, and had orders also
to wait for an answer: he presently knew it came from Miss Flora,
and expected the contents to be such as he found them on perusing.

'To Charles Trueworth, Esq.

Most cruel and ungenerous man!
Loth I am to give you epithets like these: my heart shudders, and my
trembling hand is scarce able to guide my pen in those reproaches
which my reason tells me you deserve: how unkind, how stabbing to
the soul, was your behaviour at our last meeting! yet, even then, you
promised me to write; I depended on that promise, and hope had not
quite forsook me; every knocking at the door I expected was a
messenger from you; in vain I expected, in vain I looked, in vain I
listened for the welcome mandate; and every disappointment threw
me into fresh agonies. I have sent twice to the coffee-house, been
there once in person; but could hear nothing of you. O, what secret
recess now hides you from me? What can have caused so terrible a
reverse in my so lately happy fate? I fear to guess; for madness is in
the thought! O do not drive me to extremes!! Many women, with not
half my love, or my despair, have ran headlong into actions which, in
my cooler moments, I dread to think on. Be assured, I cannot live,
will not live, without you! Torture me not any longer with suspense!
Pronounce my doom at once! But let it be from your own mouth that
I receive it; that you, at least, may be witness of the death you inflict,

and be compelled to pity, if you cannot love, the most unfortunate, and most faithful, of her sex,

F. MELLASIN.

P.S. I have charged the man who brings you this, to find you wherever you are, and not to leave you without an answer.'

Mr. Trueworth was in the utmost perplexity of mind on reading this distracted epistle. Of all the hours of his past life he could not recollect any one which gave him so much cause of repentance as that wherein he had commenced an amour with a woman of so violent a temper: he had never loved her; and all the liking he ever had for her being now utterly erased by a more laudable impression, the guilty pleasures he had enjoyed with her were now irksome to his remembrance; and the more she endeavoured to revive the tender folly in him, the more she grew distasteful to him.

It so little becomes a woman, whose characteristick should be modesty, to use any endeavours to force desire, that those who do it are sure to convert love into indifference, and indifference into loathing and contempt: even she who, with the greatest seeming delicacy, labours to rekindle a flame once extinguished, will find the truth of what Morat says in the play –

> 'To love once pass'd we cannot backward move;
> Call yesterday again, and we may love.'

Mr. Trueworth, however, had so much pity for that unfortunate creature, that he would have given, perhaps, good part of his estate that she no longer loved him: but how to turn the tide of so extravagant a passion, he could not yet resolve; and it being near the time in which he knew they would expect him at Sir Bazil's, where he now dined every day, and the messenger who brought him the letter also growing impatient to be dispatched, he wrote in haste these few lines.

'To Miss Flora Mellasin.

Madam,
Business of the greatest consequence now calls upon me, and I have no time to write as I would do; but depend upon it I will send to you to-morrow morning, and either appoint a meeting, or let you know my real sentiments in a letter; till when, I beg you will make yourself more easy, if you desire to oblige him who is, with the most unfeigned good wishes, Madam, your most humble, and most

obedient servant,

C. TRUEWORTH.

P.S. I shall take it as a favour, Madam, that you will henceforward forbear to make any enquiry concerning me at the coffee-house, or elsewhere.'

Having given this to Miss Flora's porter, he hasted away to Sir Bazil's; there to compose his mind, after the embarrassments it had sustained that morning.

CHAPTER IX

●

Contains very little to the purpose

MR. Francis Thoughtless had no sooner left the lodgings of Mr. Trueworth, than he went directly to those of his sister Betsy; where, in the humour he then was, the reader will easily suppose, he could not be very good company. After telling her he had seen Mr. Trueworth, and had had some conversation with him on her account, 'I am now convinced,' said he, 'of what before I doubted not, that by your own ill management, and want of a just sense of what is for your interest and happiness, you have lost an opportunity of establishing both, which can never be retrieved: nor is this all; your manner of behaviour not only ruins yourself, but involves all belonging to you in endless quarrels and perplexities.'

These were reproaches which Miss Betsy had too much spirit to have borne from any one but a brother; and even to him she was far from yielding that she had in any measure deserved them. 'I defy Trueworth himslf,' cried she, with all the resentment of a disappointed lover in her heart, 'to accuse me of one action that the strictest virtue could condemn!'

'Ah, sister!' replied he, 'do not let your vanity deceive you on this score: I see very plainly that Mr. Trueworth regards you with too much indifference to retain resentment for any treatment you have given him; that he once loved you, I am well assured; that he no longer does so, is owing to yourself: but I shall mention him no more; the passion he had for you is extinguished, I believe, beyond all possibility of reviving, nor would I wish you to attempt it. I would only have you remember what Mr. Goodman uttered concerning you with almost his dying breath: for my own part, I have not been a witness of your conduct, since the unhappy brulée I fell into on your account at Oxford, which I then hoped would be a sufficient warning for your future behaviour.'

If Miss Betsy had been less innocent, it is probable she would have replied in a more satisfactory manner to her brother's reproaches; but the real disdain she always had for whatever had the least tendency to dishonour, made her zealous in defending herself only in things of which she was not accused, and silent in regard of those in which she was judged blame-worthy.

'What avails your being virtuous!' said Mr. Francis; 'I hope, and believe, you are so: but your reputation is of more consequence to your family; the loss of the one might be concealed, but a blemish on the other brings certain infamy and disgrace on yourself and all belonging to you.'

On this she assumed the courage to tell him his way of reasoning was neither just nor delicate. 'Would you,' said she, 'be guilty of a base action, rather than have it suspected that you were so?' – 'No,' answered he; 'but virtue is a different thing in our sex to what it is in yours: the forfeiture of what is called virtue in a woman is more a folly than a baseness; but the virtue of a man is his courage, his constancy, his probity; which if he loses, he becomes contemptible to himself, as well as to the world.'

'And certainly,' rejoined Miss Betsy, with some warmth, 'the loss of innocence must render a woman contemptible to herself, though she should happen to hide her transgression from the world.' – 'That may be,' said Mr. Francis; 'but then her kindred suffer not through her fault: the remorse, and the vexation for what she has done, is all her own. Indeed, sister,' continued he, 'a woman brings less dishonour upon a family by twenty private sins, than by one publick indiscretion.'

'Well,' answered she, 'I hope I shall always take care to avoid both the one and the other, for my own sake. As to indulging myself with the innocent pleasures of the town, I have the example of some ladies of the first quality, and best reputation, to justify me in it.'

Mr. Thoughtless was about to make some reply, which, perhaps, would have been pretty keen, but was prevented by the coming in of her maid, who delivering a letter to her, and saying, 'From Sir Frederick Fineer, Madam!' she hastily broke it open; and having read it, bid the maid let Sir Frederick's servant know she would be at home.

'There, brother,' said she, giving him the letter, 'read that, and be convinced I have not lost every good offer in losing Mr. Trueworth.' – 'I wish you have not,' answered he sullenly. He took the paper, however, and read the contents of it, which were these.

'To the divine arbitress of my fate, the omnipotently lovely Miss Betsy Thoughtless.

O Goddess! more cruel than the avenging Nemisis, what have I done, that, like Ixion, I must still be tortured on the wheel of everlasting hopes and fears? I hoped yesterday to have approached the shrine of your resplendent charms; but you had quitted the sacred dome which you inhabit, and vouchsafed to bless some happier mansion with your presence – perhaps a rival: oh, forbid it Heaven! forbid it, all ye stars that, under the Supreme, rule all beneath the moon! The thought is terrible, and shocks the inmost cavities of my adoring jealous soul. I kneel while I am writing, and implore you to grant me permission to sip a cup of nectar and ambrosia at your tea-table this afternoon; and if you can, without injustice to superior merit, debar all other intruders thence, that I may have liberty to pour forth my ejaculations at your feet. I am, with the most ardent devotion, brightest refulgency of beauty, your most adoring, and everlasting slave,

F. FINEER.'

As little as Mr. Francis at this time was disposed to mirth, he could not, in spite of his ill-humour, refrain laughing on reading some expressions in this heroically-learned epistle: 'I need not ask,' said he, throwing the letter contemptuously on the table, 'who, or what, this new adorer of yours is; it is easy to see he is either mad or a fool, or thinks to make you so.'

'I have as bad an opinion of his intellects as you have,' replied she; 'but I assure you he is a baronet, and the presumptive heir of a much greater title; and has an estate large enough to keep me a coach and twelve, if the custom of the country permitted.'

Mr. Francis paused for a few moments; and, after looking over the letter again, 'I wish,' said he, 'instead of a fool of fashion, he is not a knave in the disguise of a coxcomb: his stupidity seems to me to be too egregious to be natural; all his expressions have more the appearance of a studied affectation, than of a real folly. Take care, sister; I have heard there are many impostors in this town, who are continually on the watch for young ladies who have lost their parents, and live in the unguarded manner you do.'

Miss Betsy seemed to treat her brother's suspicions on this head with a good deal of contempt: she told him, that the person at whose house she became acquainted with Sir Frederick, knew his circumstances perfectly well; that he had a prodigious estate, was of a very ancient and honourable family, and conversed with several people of the first quality in England: 'However,' added she, 'you may call here this afternoon, and see him yourself, if you please; for, according to my judgment, he has not wit enough to be an impostor.'

Mr. Francis replied, that he would be glad to see so extraordinary a person if he were not obliged to go upon some business relating to the commission he was soliciting, which he feared would detain him beyond the hour: 'But, with your leave,' said he, 'I will take this letter with me, and hear what my brother thinks of it.'

To this Miss Betsy readily agreed; and he went away in somewhat of a better humour than he had entered, or that he had put her into by the severe reprimands he had given her.

She had a very tender regard for her brothers, but did not think it their province to prescribe rules for her behaviour; she looked upon herself as a better judge in what manner it would become her to act, than they could possibly be, as having lived more years in London than either of them had done months; and, if she was willing to be advised, would not submit to be directed by them.

Thus did her pride a while support her spirits: but when she reflected on the affair of Mr. Trueworth, and the reasons she had given him for speaking and thinking of her in that cool manner she found he now did, she began to be somewhat less tenacious; and acknowledged within herself, that her brother Frank, exclusive of his friendship for that gentleman, had sufficient cause to blame her conduct in that point; and the heat of passion which had been raised by some expressions he had uttered being over, she ceased to take unkindly what she was now sensible had only been occasioned by his zeal for her welfare.

She now saw in their true light all the mistakes she had been guilty of; all her dangers, all her escapes; and blushed to remember, how she had been plunged into the one, merely by her own inadvertency; and been blessed with the other, ony by the interposition of some accident, altogether unforeseen, and even unhoped for, by her.

She had also a more just and lively idea of the merits of Mr.

Trueworth than ever she had been capable of entertaining while he professed himself her lover: the amiableness of his person – his fine understanding – his generosity – his bravery – his wit – and the delicacy and elegance of his conversation – seemed to her impossible to be equalled; she considered, too, that his estate was much beyond what her fortune could expect, and that even his family was superior to hers; and could not help being very sensibly affected that she had so rashly thrown away her pretensions to the heart of so valuable a man.

'It is true,' said she, 'that if I had an inclination to marry, I have other offers: Mr. Munden, by his way of living, must have a good estate, perhaps not inferior to that of Mr. Trueworth; the man has good sense, and wants neither personal nor acquired endowments; and I have tried both his love and his constancy; besides, he lives always in town, has a taste for the pleasures of it – a woman could not be very unhappy in being his wife. Then there is Sir Frederick Fineer – he is a fool, indeed; but he is a man of quality: and I know several ladies, who are the envy of their own sex, and the toast of the other, and yet have fools for their husbands.'

In this manner did she continue reasoning within herself, till her head began to ache, and she was luckily relieved from it by the last-mentioned subject of her meditations.

He approached her with his accustomed formalities; first saluting the hem of her garment, then her hand, and lastly her lips, which she receiving with an air more than ordinarily serious, and also making very short replies to the fine speeches he had prepared to entertain her with – 'What invidious cloud,' said he, 'obscures the lightning of your eyes, and hides half the divinity from my ravished sight?' – 'People cannot always be in the same humour, Sir Frederick,' answered she. 'Yours should be always gay,' rejoined he, 'if once you were mine, you should do nothing but love, and laugh, and dress, and eat, and drink, and be adored. Speak, then, my angel,' continued he; 'when shall be the happy day? Say, it shall be to-morrow?'

Here it was not in her power to retain any part of her former gravity. 'Bless me!' cried she, 'to-morrow!' – What, marry to-morrow? Sure, Sir Frederick, you cannot think of such a thing! Why, I have not so much as dreamt of it!' – 'No matter,' answered he; 'you will have golden dreams enough in my embraces; defer, then, the mutual bliss no longer – let it be to-morrow.' – 'You are certainly mad, Sir Frederick!' said she; 'but if I were enough so too, as really to consent to such a hasty nuptial, where, pray, are the preparations for it?'

'Oh, Madam, as to that,' resumed he, 'people of quality always marry in a deshabille; a new coach – chariot – servants – liveries – and rich cloaths for ourselves – may all be got ready before we make our publick appearance at court, or at church.' – 'But there are other things to be considered,' said Miss Betsy, laughing outright. 'None of any importance,' replied he: 'I will jointure you in my whole estate; the writings shall be drawn to-night, and presented to you with the wedding-ring.'

'This would be wonderful dispatch indeed!' said she; 'but, Sir, I have two brothers whom I must first consult on the affair.' Sir Frederick seemed extremely struck at these words; but recovering himself as soon as he was able, 'I thought, Madam,' cried he, 'you were entirely at your own disposal.' – 'I am so, Sir,' answered she; 'but I love my brothers, and will do nothing without their approbation.' – 'Ah, cruel fair!' cried he, 'little do you know the delicacy of my passion; I must owe you wholly to yourself: your brothers, no doubt, will favour my desires, but it is your own free-will alone can make me blessed. Tell me not, then, of brothers,' continued he, 'but generously say you will be mine.'

Miss Betsy was about to make some reply, when word was brought that a servant of the elder Mr. Thoughtless desired to speak with her: on which she arose hastily, and went to the top of the stair-case, to hear what message he had to deliver to her; and was pleasingly surprized when he told her that his master desired the favour of her company to supper immediately at his house. As she never had an invitation there before, she was at a loss to guess what could have caused so sudden an alteration: she asked the fellow what company was there; he told her, only Mr. Francis and another gentleman, whose name he knew not, but believed they wanted her on some affairs concerning the late Mr. Goodman, because, as he was waiting, he heard them often mention that gentleman and Lady Mellasin.

Though she could not conceive on what purpose she was to be consulted on any thing relating to Mr. Goodman, yet she was extremely glad that any occasion had happened to induce her brother to send for her to his house; and ordered the man to acquaint his master that she would not fail to wait upon him with as much expedition as a chair could bring her.

On her return to Sir Frederick, she told him she had received a summons from her elder brother, which she was under an indispensable necessity of complying with; so desired he would defer, till another opportunity, any farther discourse on the subject they had been talking of. Having said this, she called hastily for her fan and gloves, and at the same time gave orders for a chair. Sir Frederick seemed very much confounded; but, finding that any attempt to detain her would be impracticable, took his leave, saying, 'You are going to your brother's, Madam?' To which she answering, she was so, 'I beg then, Madam,' rejoined he, 'that you will not mention any thing concerning me, or the passion I have for you, till I have the honour of seeing you again. Be assured,' continued he, 'I have mighty reasons for this request; and such as, I flatter myself, you will allow to be just.' He said no more; but, perceiving she was ready, led her down stairs; and having put her into a chair, went into that which waited for himself, little satisfied with the success of his visit.

Though the motives on which Miss Betsy's company was desired in so much hurry, by a brother who had never before once invited her, may seem strange, yet as that incident was but the consequence of other matters which yet remain untold, regularity requires they should first be discussed.

CHAPTER X

———•———

Contains an account of some transactions which, though they may not be very pleasing in the repetition, nor are of any great consequence to Miss Betsy, would render this history extremely deficient if omitted

As Lady Mellasin has made so considerable a figure in the former parts of this history, the reader may, perhaps, now begin to think she has been too long neglected; it is, therefore, proper to proceed directly to some account how that guilty and unfortunate woman behaved, after being driven in the manner already related from the house of her much-injured husband. Mr. Goodman was advised by his lawyers to be extremely private in the prosecution he was going to commence against her, and by no means to let her know the secret of her criminal conversation with Marplus had been discovered to him: this seemed a caution necessary to be observed, in order to prevent her from taking any measures, either to invalidate the evidence of the witnesses, or prevail upon them to abscond when the proof of what they had sworn against her should be expected. The whole detection of her guilt was designed to come at once upon her like a thunderclap, and thereby all the little efforts of artifice and chicanery to which she, doubtless, would otherwise have had recourse, be rendered of no use, nor give the least impediment to justice.

Accordingly, this zealous assertor of his client's cause went to visit her, as of his own good-will; flattered her with the hope that her husband would soon be prevailed upon to take her home again, and lent her several small sums of money to supply her necessities; saying, at the same time, that when matters were made up between them, and all was over, he very well knew that Mr. Goodman would return it to him with thanks.

This strategem had the effect it was intended for; it not only kept her from attempting any thing of the nature above-mentioned, but also from running Mr. Goodman into debt; which certainly she might have done, on some pretence or other, in spite of all the care and means that could have been taken to destroy her credit.

It must be acknowledged, indeed, that acting in this manner was a prodigious piece of dissimulation; but, at the same time, it must be acknowledged also, that it was abundantly justified by the cause, and practised for the most laudable end, to serve an honest, worthy, gentleman, his friend and client, against a woman who had wronged him in the tenderest point, and who was capable of making use of the vilest methods to elude the punishment her crimes deserved; and, as a great author tells us –

> 'It is a kind of stupid honesty,
> Among known knaves, to play upon the square.'

Lady Mellasin, however, was lulled into so perfect a security by her dependance on the good-nature of her husband, and the tender affection he had always shewn to her, as well as by the high character she had always heard of the lawyer's veracity, that she was more easy than could have been expected in a woman of her situation, even though it had been as she was made to believe.

She received, and returned, with her usual politeness and gaiety, the visits that were made her by all those who thought proper to continue an acquaintance with her: she pretended that it was only a little family contest that had separated her from Mr. Goodman for a short time; and always mentioned him with so much kindness and respect, as made every one believe there was nothing between them but what would be easily made up.

This was, indeed, the most prudent method she could take; not only to preserve her own reputation to the world, but also to give Mr. Goodman a high idea of her conduct, if what she said should happen to be repeated to him.

She was every day in expectation that, through her own good management, and the intercession of the lawyer, whom she now took to be her staunch friend, all would be over, and she should be recalled home; when a citation to appear before the doctors of the civil law was delivered to her by an officer belonging to that court.

It is more easy to conceive than describe her distraction at so unlooked-for a turn; she now found that her intrigue with Marplus was discovered, and that all she had to dread was like to fall upon her by that event; her perplexity was also greatly increased by her not being able to find out by whom, or by what means, she had been betrayed: she sent immediately in search of Marplus, whom, since his arresting Mr. Goodman, she had never once seen nor heard any thing of; but all the information she could get of him was, that he had been thrown into prison by Mr. Goodman, and, after confinement of a few days, had been released, and was gone nobody knew where, but, as it was supposed, out of England; that his wife had likewise removed from her lodgings, but whether with an intention to follow him or not, no certain intelligence could be given.

As this unhappy woman, therefore, neither knew on what foundation the accusation against her was built, nor what evidences could be produced to prove it, she might very well be bewildered in her thoughts, and not know what course to take; yet, amidst all these matters of astonishment, oppressed with grief, and struck with horror at the near prospect of approaching infamy, she had courage, and presence enough of mind, to enable her to do every thing that was necessary for her defence in so bad a cause.

Mr. Goodman's indisposition putting a stop to the process, she had time to consult with those whom she found most qualified for the purpose. Her chief agent was a pettifogger, or understrapper in the law, one who knew all those quirks and evasions, which are called the knavish part of it; and as the extreme indigence of his circumstances made him ready to undertake any thing, though ever so desperate, provided it afforded a prospect of advantage, so he had impudence and cunning enough to go through with it, even to the hazard of his ears.

This man kept up her spirits, by assuring her, he would find ways and means so to puzzle the cause, that nothing should be clearly proved against her: but there was no opportunity for him to exercise his abilities in this way, for Mr. Goodman's death soon after furnished him with another. Lady Mellasin was no sooner informed, by spies she kept continually about Mr. Goodman's house, that his life was despaired of, than they set about making his will, the first article of which, after the prelude usual in such writings, was this.

'Imprimis, I give and bequeathe to my dear and well-beloved wife, Margaret, Lady Mellasin Goodman, the full sum of thirty thousand pounds of lawful money of Great Britain, over and above what otherwise she might lay claim to as my widow, in consideration of the great wrong I have done her, throough the insinuations of malicious and evil-minded persons; which I now heartily repent me of, and hope that God and she will forgive me for it.'

Then followed some other legacies to several of his kindred, and those of his friends, whom he had been known to have been the most intimate with; but the sums to each were very trifling, and did not amount, in the whole, to above seven or eight hundred pounds. As everyone who had the least acquaintance with Mr. Goodman, was very well convinced that he had always intended his nephew for his heir, the pretended will went on in this manner.

'Item, I give and bequeathe to my dear nephew, Edward Goodman, the son of Nathanial Goodman, and of Catherine his wife, late of Bengal in the East Indies, the whole residue of my effects, whatsoever and wheresoever they shall be found at my demise; provided that he, the said Edward Goodman, shall take to be his lawful wife, Flora Mellasin, only daughter and remaining issue of Sir Thomas Mellasin, and of the above-mentioned Margaret his wife: but in case that either party shall refuse to enter into such marriage, then that he, the said Edward Goodman, shall be obliged to pay to the said Flora Mellasin the full sum of five thousand pounds of lawful money of Great Britain, in consideration of the misfortuncs she has suffered by the injury I have done her mother.'

This impudent piccc of forgery was signed Samuel Goodman, in a character so like that gentleman's, that, when compared with other papers of his own hand-writing, the difference could not be distinguished by those who were best acquainted with it: two persons also, of the lawyer's procuring, set their names as witnesses.

Notwithstanding the flagrancy of this attempt, Lady Mellasin flattered herself with the hopes of it's success; and, on Mr. Goodman's death, threw in a caveat against the real will, and set up this pretended one.

On the other hand, though one would imagine there needed but little skill for the detection of so gross an imposition, yet Mr. Goodman's lawyer thought proper to get all the help he could to corroborate the truth. This piece of forgery was dated about ten days before Mr. Goodman died; he knew that the elder Mr. Thoughtless came every day to visit him during the whole time of his sickness; and that Miss Betsy, at the time this will was supposed to be made, actually lived in the house, and that neither of these two could be totally ignorant of such a transaction, in case any such had been.

It was therefore at the lawyer's request, that Miss Betsy was sent for to her brother's house; she answered, wtih a great deal of readiness, to all the questions he put to her, according to the best of her knowledge; particularly as to that concerning the making the will: she said, that she had never heard the least mention of any lawyer but himself coming to Mr. Goodman's during the whole time of his sickness; and that she verily believed no will but that drawn up by him, and which all the family knew of, could possibly be made by Mr. Goodman's orders, or in his house; and as to the article in the pretended will, relating to Miss Flora, nothing could be a more palpable forgery, because Mr. Goodman had offered five hundred pounds with her in marriage to a linen-draper, not above six weeks before his parting with Lady Mellasin; 'Which,' added she, 'is a very plain proof that he never intended her for his nephew.'

All the time Miss Betsy staid, the whole discourse was on this affair; and she had no opportunity, as the lawyer was present, to acquaint her brothers with any thing concerning Sir Frederick Fineer, as otherwise it was her full intention to have done, after the surprizing injunction he had laid upon her of secrecy, in regard of his passion, and every thing relating to him.

CHAPTER XI

———•———

Is very well deserving the attention of all those who are about to marry

WHILE Miss Flora was buoyed up with the expectation that her mother would soon be reconciled with Mr. Goodman, she abated not of her former gaiety, and thought of nothing but indulging her amorous inclinations with the man she liked: but when once those expectations ceased, her spirits began to fail; she now found it necessary, for her interest as well as pleasure, to preserve, if possible, the affection of her lover; she knew not what dreadful consequences the prosecution Mr. Goodman was about to exhibit against her mother, might be attended with, and trembled to think she must share with her the double load of infamy and penury; and rightly judged, that a man of Mr. Trueworth's fortune, honour, and good-nature, would not suffer a woman, with whom he continued a tender communication, to be oppressed with any ills his purse could relieve her from. The apprehensions, therefore, that she might one day be reduced to stand in need of his support, assisted the real passion she had for him, and made her feel, on the first appearance of his growing coldness towards her, all those horrors, those distractions, which her letters to him had so lively represented.

On his ceasing to make any fixed appointment with her, and from seeing her every day, to seeing her once in three or four days, gave her, with reason, the most terrible alarms; but when, after an absence of near a week, she had followed him to the coffee-house, the cool and indifferent reception she there met with, gave, indeed, a mortal stab to all her hopes; and she longer hesitated to pronounce her own doom, and cry out, she was undone.

The excuse he made of business was too weak – too trite – too common-place – to gain any credit with her, or alleviate her sorrows; she knew the world too well to imagine a gay young gentleman, like him, would forego whatever he thought a pleasure for any business he could possibly have: she doubted not but there was a woman in the case; and the thoughts that, while she was in vain expecting him, he was soliciting those favours from a rival she had so lavishly bestowed and languished to repeat, fired her jealous brain, even to a degree of frenzy.

Awhile she raved with all the wild despair of ill-requited burning love: but other emotions soon rose in her distracted bosom, not to controul, but add fresh fuel to the flame already kindled there. 'My circumstances!' cried she, 'my wretched circumstances! – What will become of me? Involved in my mother's shame, he will, perhaps, make that a pretence for abandoning me to those misfortunes I thought I might have depended on him to relieve.'

However, as the little billet, in answer to her last letter to him, contained a promise that he would write to her the next day, she endeavoured, as much as she was able, to compose herself till that time, though she was far from hoping the explanation she expected to receive in it would afford any consolation to her tormented mind.

Mr. Trueworth also, in the mean time, was not without his own anxieties: a man of honour frequently finds more difficulty in getting rid of a woman he is weary of, and loves him, than obtaining a woman he loves and is in pursuit of; but this gentleman had a more than ordinary perplexity to struggle through. Few women would go the lengths Miss Flora had done for the accomplishment of her desires; and he easily saw, by the whole tenor of her behaviour, she would go as great, and even more, to continue the enjoyment of them.

Glad would he have been to have brought her by degrees to an indifference for him; to have prevailed on her to submit her passion to the government of her reason, and to be convinced that an amour, such as theirs had been, ought to be looked upon only as a transient pleasure; to be continued while mutual inclination and convenience permitted, and, when broke off, remembered but as a dream.

But this he found was not to be done with a woman of Miss Flora's temper; he therefore thought it best not to keep her any longer in suspense, but let her know at once the revolution in her fate, as to that point which regarded him, and the true motive which had occasioned it; which he accordingly did in these terms.

'To Miss Flora Mellasin.

Madam,

It is with very great difficulty I employ my pen to tell you it is wholly inconvenient for us ever to meet again in the manner we have lately done; but I flatter myself you have too much good-sense, and too much honour, not to forgive what all laws, both human and divine, oblige me to. I am entering into a state which utterly forbids the continuance of those gallantries which before pleaded their excuse: in fine, I am going to be married; and it would be the highest injustice in me to expect that fidelity which alone can make me happy in a wife, if my own conduct did not set her an example.

Though I must cease to languish for a repetition of those favours you blessed me with, yet be assured I shall always remember them with gratitude, and the best good wishes for the prosperity of the fair bestower.

I send you back all the testimonies I have received of your tenderness that are in my power to return: it belongs to yourself to make use of your utmost endeavours for the recovery of the heart which dictated them. This I earnestly intreat of you; and in the hope that you will soon accomplish a work so absolutely necessary for your peace and reputation, I remain, as far as honour will permit, Madam, your most obliged, and most humble servant,

C. TRUEWORTH.'

Mr. Trueworth flattered himself that so plain a declaration of his sentiments and intentions would put a total end to all future correspondence between them; and, having looked it over, after he had finished, and found it such as he thought proper for the purpose, put it under a cover, with all the letters he had received from Miss Flora, not excepting the first invitation she had made him, under the title of the 'Incognita,' and sent away the packet by a porter; for he had never intrusted the servants with the conveyance of any epistle from him to that lady.

Miss Flora, from the moment her eyes were open in the morning, (if it can be supposed she had any sleep that night) had been watching, with the most racking impatience, for the arrival of Mr. Trueworth's messenger. She wished, but dreaded more, the eclaircissement which she expected would be contained in the mandate he had promised to send; yet was distracted for the certainty, how cruel soever it might prove.

At length it came, and with it a confirmation of even worse than the most terrible of her apprehensions had suggested. The sight of her own letters, on her opening it, almost threw her into a swoon; but, when her streaming eyes had greedily devoured the contents of the billet that accompanied them, excess of desperation struck her for some moments stupid, and rendered her mind inactive as her frame.

But, when awakened from this lethargy of silent grief, she felt all the horrors of a fate she had so much dreaded. Frustrated at once in every hope that love or interest had presented to her, words cannot paint the wildness of her fancy; she tore her hair and garments, and scarce spared that face she had taken so much pains to ornament, for wanting charms to secure the conquest it had gained.

But with the more violence these tourbillions of the mind rage for a while, the sooner they subside, and all is hushed again; as I remember to have somewhere read –

'After a tempest, when the winds are laid,
The calm sea wonders at the wreck it made.'

So this unhappy and abandoned creature, too much deserving of the fate she met with, having exhausted her whole stock of tears, and wasted all the breath that life could spare in fruitless exclamations, the passions which had raised these commotions in her soul became more weak, and the beguiler Hope once more returned, to lull her wearied spirits into a short-lived ease.

She now saw the folly of venting her rage upon herself – that to give way to grief and despair would avail her nothing, but only serve to render her more miserable – that, instead of sitting tamely down, and meanly lamenting her misfortune in the loss of a lover, on whom she had built so much, she ought rather to exert all the courage, resolution, and artifice, she was mistress of, in contriving some way of preventing it, if possible.

'He is not yet married!' said she – 'the irrevocable words are not yet past! I have already broke off his courtship to one woman – why may I not be as successful in doing so with another? He cannot love the present engrosser of his heart more than he did Miss Betsy Thoughtless! It is worth, at least, the pains of an attempt!'

The first step she had to take towards the execution of her design, was to find out the name, condition, and dwelling, of her happy rival;

and this, she thought, there would be no great difficulty in doing, as she doubted not but Mr. Trueworth visited her every day, and it would be easy for her to employ a person to watch where he went, and afterwards to make the proper enquiries.

But, in the mean time, it required some consideration how to behave to that gentleman, so as to preserve in him some sort of esteem for her, without which, she rightly judged, it would be impossible for her ever to recover his love, in case she should be so fortunate as to separate him from the present object of his flame.

She knew very well, that all testimonies of despair in a woman no longer loved, only create uneasiness in the man who occasioned it, and but serve to make him more heartily wish to get rid of her; she, therefore, found it best, as it certainly was, to pretend to fall in with Mr. Trueworth's way of thinking – seem to be convinced by his reasons, and ready to submit to whatever suited with his interest or convenience. It was some time before she could bring herself into a fit temper for this sort of dissimulation; but she at last arrived at it, and gave a proof how great a proficient she was in it by the following lines.

'To Charles Trueworth, Esq.

Dear Sir,
I am apt to believe you as little expected as desired an answer to the eclaircissement of yesterday; nor would I have given you the trouble of this, but to assure you it shall be the last of any kind you ever shall receive from me. Yes, I have now done with reproaches and complaints. I have nothing to alledge against you – nothing to accuse you of. Could the fond folly of my tender passion have given me leisure for a moment's reflection, I had forseen that the misfortune which is now fallen upon me was inevitable. I am now convinced that I ought not to have hoped that the unbounded happiness I so lately enjoyed, could be of any long duration – that a man of your fortune and figure in the world must one day marry – names and families must be supported; and yours is too considerable for you to suffer it to be extinct. I must not, I will not, therefore, repine at a thing which, in my cooler moments, I cannot but look upon as essential to your honour and convenience. Had you quitted me on any other score, I cannot asnwer but I might have been hurried into extravagancies displeasing to you, and unbecoming of myself: but here I must resign; and am determined to do so with the same patience, in shew at least,

as if I had never loved. I will not tell you the agonies I have sustained in the cruel conflict between my reason and my passion, in making this resolution: it is sufficient for you to know that the former has the victory. More might too much affect your generous nature; besides, when woes are remediless, they are best borne in silence.

Farewel! – Oh, farewel for ever! May you find every thing in the happy she you make your choice of to give you lasting bliss! and, to compleat all, may she love you with the same ardency, tenderness, and disinterestedness, as her who must now only subscribe herself, at an eternal distance, dear, dear Sir, your most faithful friend, and humble servant,

F. MELLASIN.'

This letter, which, it must be confessed, was wrote artfully enough, had all the effect it was intended for on the mind of Mr. Trueworth. It not only afforded him an infinity of contentment, as he hoped she would soon be enabled to banish all those disturbed emotions which naturally attend the breaking off an acquaintance such as theirs had been, but it also established in him a very high idea of her good understanding, disinterested affection, honour, and sincerity: but how long he continued in this favourable opinion as to the three last-mentioned qualifications, will hereafter be shewn.

In the mean time, something happened which, as he was a man just even to the extremest nicety, gave him, according to his way of thinking, a great deal of reason to reproach himself.

CHAPTER XII

———•———

Miss Betsy's innocence, as to the Denham affair, fully cleared up to Mr. Trueworth by a very extraordinary accident

MR. Trueworth had made so great a progress in his courtship, that the sincerity of Miss Harriot got the better of her bashfulness, even so far as to confess to him, it was with pleasure she yielded to the persuasions of her friends in favour of his love, and that he had infinitely the preference of all mankind in her esteem; in fine, her behaviour was such as left nothing wanting, but the ceremony, to assure him of his happiness.

Sir Bazil also having concluded every thing with the father of his mistress, brought that young lady acquainted with his sisters; who, highly approving their brother's choice, soon treated her, and were treated by her, with the same affection and familiarity as if already united.

There were few hours, excepting those allotted by nature and custom for repose, which this amiable company did not pass together. The old gentleman, who was extremely good-humoured when nothing relating to the parting with his money came on the carpet, would frequently make one among them; and being one day more than ordinarily chearful, told Mr. Trueworth that, as he found the two weddings were to be solemnized in one day, and he should give his daughter's hand to Sir Bazil, desired he might also have the honour of bestowing Miss Harriot's upon him: to which Mr. Trueworth replied, that he should joyfully receive her from any hands, but more particularly from his; and that he took the offer he made as a very great favour. On this, the other grew very gay, and said abundance of merry things, to the no small expence of blushes both in his daughter and Miss Harriot.

It is impossible for any lover, while waiting for the consummation of his wishes, to enjoy a more uninterrupted felicity than did Sir Bazil and Mr. Trueworth – continually blest with the society of their mistresses, and receiving from them all the marks that a virtuous affection could bestow: yet both of them found it requisite to contrive every day some new party of pleasure or other, in order to beguile the necessary, though to them tedious, time it took up in drawing of writings, and other preparations for the much longer-for nuptials; which Mrs. Wellair did not fail to do all on her part to hasten, being impatient to return to her family, whence she had been absent longer than she had intended.

Sir Bazil and Mr. Trueworth having been talking a little walk in the Park one morning, the former finding himself so near the habitation of Miss Mabel, could not forbear calling on her, though she was to dine that day at his house, and Mr. Trueworth accompanied him. That lady was then at her toilette, but made no scruple of admitting them into her dressing-room, where they had scarce seated themselves, when her woman, who was waiting, was called out by a footman to speak to some people, who, he said, were very importunate to see Miss Mabel, and would take no answer from him.

'Rude guests, indeed,' cried Miss Mabel, 'that will not take an answer from a servant! – Who are they?' – 'I never saw them before, Madam,' replied the footman: 'but the one is a woman of a very mean appearance, and the other, I believe, is a soldier. I told them your ladyship had company, and could not be seen; but the man said he only begged one word with you; that he has just come from abroad, and wanted to know where he might see his child, and a deal of such stuff. The woman is almost as impertinent as the man; and I cannot get them from the door.'

'I will lay my life upon it, Madam,' said the waiting maid, 'that this is the father of the child that you and Miss Betsy Thoughtless have been so good to keep ever since the mother's death.' – 'I verily believe thou hast hit upon the right!' cried Miss Mabel. 'Pr'ythee go down; and, if it be as thou imaginest, bid them come up – I will see them.'

The maid went as she was ordered, and immediately returned with two persons, such as the footman had described. The woman was the first that advanced, and, after dropping two or three curtseys to each of the company, addressed herself to Miss Mabel in these words – 'I do not know, Madam,' said she, 'whether your ladyship may remember me; but I nursed poor Mrs. Jinks, your ladyship's sempstress and clear-starcher, all the time of her lying-in, when your ladyship and Madam Betsy Thoughtless were so good as to stand godmothers, and afterwards took the child, that it might not go to the parish.'

'I remember you very well,' said Miss Mabel: 'but, pray, what is your business with me now?' – 'Why, Madam,' said she, 'your ladyship must know, that Mrs. Jinks's husband has seen his folly at last – has left the army, and is resolved to take up and settle in the world: so, Madam, if your ladyship pleases, he would willingly have his child.'

'O doubtless, he may have his child!' rejoined Miss Mabel. – 'But, hark'e, friend,' continued she, turning to the man, 'are you able to keep your child?' – 'Yes, Madam,' answered he, coming forward, 'thank God, and good friends. I had an uncle down in Northampton-shire, who died a while ago, and left me a pretty farm there; and so, as my neighbour here was telling you, I would not have my child a burden to any body.' – 'If we had thought it a burden,' said Miss Mabel, 'we should not have taken it upon us; however, I am glad you are in circumstances to maintain it yourself. Your wife was a very honest, industrious woman, and suffered a great deal through your neglect; but I hope you will make it up in the care of the child she has left behind.'

'Aye, Madam,' replied he, wiping his eyes,' 'I have nothing else to remember her! I did not use her so well as she deserved, that's certain: but I have sowed all my wild oats, as the saying is; and I wish she were alive to have the benefit of it.'

'That cannot be,' interrupted the woman; 'so don't trouble good Madam with your sorrowful stories. If her ladyship will be so good only to give us directions where to find the child; for we have been to Madam Betsy's, and her ladyship was not at home; so we made bold to come here.' – 'Yes, Madam,' cried he, 'for my colonel comes to town in a day or two, and I shall get my discharge, and have no more to do with the service; so would willingly have my child to take down with me to the farm.'

Miss Mabel made no other answer to this, than saying it was very well; and immediately gave them the direction they requested to Goody Bushman's, at Denham. 'I cannot tell you exactly where the house is,' said she: 'but you will easily find her; the husband is a gardener, and she has been a nurse for many years.'

The fellow seemed exremely pleased, thanked her as well as he could in his homely fashion, and desired she would be so kind as to give his duty to the other lady, and thank her also, for her part of the favours both his wife and child had received; nor had he forgot his manners so far as not to accompany the testimonies of his gratitude with a great many low scrapes, till he got quite out of the room.

After this, Sir Bazil began to grow a little pleasant with Miss Mabel concerning the motherly part she had been playing. 'You do me more honour than I deserve,' said she, laughing; 'for it was but half a child I had to take care of; so, consequently, I could but be half a mother. I am glad, however,' continued she, more seriously, 'that my little god-daughter has found a father.'

While they were talking in this manner, the old gentleman happening to come in, and hearing Sir Bazil was above with his daughter, sent to desire to speak with him in his closet.

Miss Mabel being now alone with Mr. Trueworth, thought she saw something in his countenance which very much surprized her. 'You are pensive, Sir!' said she. 'I hope the mention we have been making of Miss Betsy has given you no alarm.' – 'A very great one,' answered he; 'but not on the account you may, perhaps, imagine. I have wronged that lady in the most cruel manner; and, though the injury I have done her went no farther than my own heart, yet I never can forgive myself for harbouring sentiments which, I now find, were so groundless and unjust.'

As it was not possible for Miss Mabel to comprehend the meaning of these words, she intreated him, somewhat hastily, to explain the mystery they seemed to contain: on which he made no scruple of repeating to her the substance of the letter he had received; his going down to Denham, in order to convince himself more fully; and the many circumstances which, according to all appearances, corro-borated the truth of that infamous scandal.

Never was astonishment equal to that Miss Mabel was in on hearing the narrative of so monstrous a piece of villainy. 'Good God!' cried she, 'I know Miss Betsy has many enemies, who set all her actions in the worst light, and construe every thing she says and does into meanings she is ignorant of herself: but this is so impudent, so unparalleled a slander, as I could not have thought the malice of either men or devils could have invented!'

'Indeed, Madam,' said Mr. Trueworth, 'should fortune ever discover to me the author of this execrable falsehood, I know no revenge I could take that would be sufficient, both for traducing the innocence of that lady, and the imposition practised upon myself.' Miss Mabel agreed with him, that no punishment could be too bad for the inventors of such cruel aspersions; and, having a little vented her indignation on all who were capable of the like practices, 'I suppose, then,' said she, 'that it was owing to this wicked story that you desisted your visits to Miss Betsy?'

'Not altogether, Madam,' answered he: 'I had long before seen it was not in my power to inspire that lady with any sentiments of the kind that would make me happy in the married state. I loved her; but my reason combated with my passion, and got the better.'

'I understand you, Sir,' replied she; 'and though I hope, nay, believe in my soul, that poor Miss Betsy is innocent as a vestal, yet I cannot but own, that the too great gaiety of her temper, and the pride of attracting as many admirers as to have eyes to behold her, hurries her into errors, which, if persevered in, cannot but be fatal both to the peace and reputation of a husband. Where you are now fixed, you doubtless have a much better prospect of being truly happy. It is, however, a great pity, methinks,' continued this amiable lady, 'that so many rare and excellent qualities as Miss Betsy is possessed of, should all be swallowed up and lost in the nonsensical vanity of being too generally admired.'

They had time for no more; Sir Bazil returned: he had only been sent for to examine the soul copy of the marriage-articles, which the old gentleman had just brought from his lawyer's, on purpose to shew them to him some time that day; and they now took their leave, that the lady might have time to dress; Sir Bazil looking on his watch, said, it was then a quarter past two, and they should dine at three, so begged she would not waste too much time in consulting her glass; 'For,' added he, 'you know you have always charms for me.' – 'And I am not ashamed, then,' replied she, with a smile, 'even before Mr. Trueworth, to confess, that I desire to have none for any other.'

He kissed her hand on this obliging speech, and ran hastily down stairs, followed by Mr. Trueworth; whose temper had not quite recovered its accustomed vivacity.

CHAPTER XIII

Seems to promise a very great change for the better, both in the humour and conduct of Miss Betsy, in regard to those who professed themselves her lovers

AS little as Miss Betsy had accustomed herself to compare and judge of things, she wanted not the power, whenever it pleased her to have the will to do so: the words of Sir Frederick Fineer, on taking leave of her at his last visit, sunk pretty deeply into her mind; nor could she remember them without a mixture of surprize, resentment, and confusion. No man, excepting Mr. Saving, whose reasons for it she could not but allow were justifiable, had hitherto ever presumed to make his addresses to her in a clandestine manner; and Sir Frederick Fineer seemed to her, of all men, to have the least excuse for doing so; and she would not have hesitated one moment to come into her brother Frank's opinion, that he was no other than an impostor, if the dependance she had on the good faith of Mrs. Modely had not prevented her from entertaining such a belief.

Besides, all the pleasure her gay young heart as yet had ever been capable of taking in the conquests she had made, consisted in their being known; and this proceeding in Sir Frederick was too mortifying to that darling propensity, to be easily forgiven, even though he should make it appear, that the motives on which he requested this secrecy were such as could not be dispensed with.

'What can the man mean?' said she: 'I suppose, by his desiring his courtship to me should be a secret, he intends a marriage with me should be so too – that I should live with him only as the slave of his loose pleasures; and, though a lawful wife, pass me in the eyes of the world for a kept mistress. Was ever such insolence! such an unparalleled insult; both on my person and understanding! Heaven be my witness, that it is only his quality could induce me; nay, I know not as yet whether even that could be sufficient to induce me to become his wife, and can he be so ridiculously vain as to imagine I would accept him on any cheaper terms than that cclat his rank and fortune would bestow upon me?'

She spent all that part of the night which she could spare from sleep, in meditating on this affair; and at last came to a resolution of seeing him no more, whatever he might pretend in justification of his late request.

She also had it in her head to return unopened any letter he should send: but curiosity prevailed above her resentment in this point; and when his servant came in the morning, and presented her with his master's compliments, and a billet at the same time, she had not the power of denying herself the satisfaction of seeing what excuse he would make: the contents of it were as follows.

'To the delight of my eyes, the life of my desires, the only hope and joy of my adoring soul, the divine Miss Betsy Thoughtless.

Since last I left your radiant presence, my mind has been all dark and gloomy – my anxieties are unutterable – intolerable – I know not what cruel constructions you may have put upon the petition I made you, of not mentioning me to your brothers – but, sure, you cannot think I apprehend a refusal from that quarter: no, my birth and fortune set me above all doubts of that nature; and I am very certain that both they, and all your kindred, would rather force you, if in their power, to accept the hand I offer; but it is not to them, but to yourself alone, I can submit to yield. Heaven, it is true, is in possessing you; but then I would owe that heaven only to your love; you may think, perhaps, that this is too great a delicacy; but know, fair angel, that there is another motive – a motive which, though derived from the same source, binds me in a different way. Fain would I court you; fain marry you; with all the pomp and splendour your superior beauty merits; but neither my virtue, my honour, nor my religion, will permit it: the mystery is this.

Upon examining into the cause why we see so many jarring pairs united in the sacred yoke of matrimony, I found it wholly owing to the want of that true affection which, to make perfect happiness, ought to precede the nuptial ceremony; that sordid interest, the persuasion of friends, or some such selfish view, either on the one side or the other, had given the hand without the heart, and inclination had no share in beckoning to the altar.

Being convinced of this truth by innumerable examples, and resolved to avoid the fate of others, I made a vow, and bound myself by the most solemn imprecations, never to marry any woman, how dear soever she might be to me, that would not assure me of her love, by flying privately with me to the altar, without consulting friends, or asking any advice but of her own soft desires.

This, my adorable charmer, being the case, I am certain you have too high a sense of the duty owing to all that's holy, to exact from me a thing which you cannot but be certain, must entail eternal perdition on my perjured soul.

Let us haste, then, to tie the blissful knot, and surprize our friends with a marriage they little dreamt of. As Phœbus each night hurries himself into the lap of Thetis, to render his appearance the more welcome the next day, so shall the next morning after our marriage behold us shine forth at once no less gorgeous than the bright ruler of the day, dazzling the eyes of the admiring world.

I am fired with the imagination, and am wrapped in extasies unutterable; but will fly this evening to your divine feet, where I hope to persuade you to delay our mutual happiness no longer than to-morrow, and exchange my present appellation of lover into that of husband; assuring yourself, I shall then be, as now, with the most consummate devotion to your all-conquering charms, sweet goddess of my hopes, your passionate adorer, and everlasting slave,

F. FINEER.

P.S. I beseech you will give necessary orders for preventing any impertinent intruder from breaking in upon our converse, for, exclusive of my vow, I should detest, as the poet says –

> "With noise and shew, and in a crowd to woo;
> For true felicity dwells in two."

Once more, my dear divinity, adieu.'

Miss Betsy read this letter over several times, and made herself mistress of the sense, as she thought, of every part of it; she had always found, in every thing he said or did, a great deal of the affected and conceited coxcomb; but in this she imagined she discovered more of the designing knave: the vow he mentioned was an excuse too shallow to pass on a discernment such as hers; but her vanity still suggesting that he was really in love with her, and that if he intended any villainy towards her, it was enforced by the violence of his passion, it came into her head, that there was a possibility of his being already married, or contracted to some lady whom he durst not break with, but being bent on gaining her at all events, he had formed this pretence of a vow, in order to gain her to a clandestine marriage, thinking, that after it was over, and there was no remedy, she would be content to live with him in a private manner, since it would then be impracticable for her to do so in a publick one.

This, indeed, she could not be certain of; but she was so, that it did not become a woman of any family and character to receive the addresses of a man, how superior soever he might be in point of fortune, who either was ashamed, or had any other reasons to hinder him from avowing his passion to her relations.

She had no sooner fixed herself in this determination, than she went to her cabinet, with an intent to pack up all the letters she had received from him, and inclose them in one to Mrs. Modely; but recollecting, she had given one of them to her brother Frank, which he had not yet returned, she thought she would defer, till another opportunity, this testimony of the disregard she had for himself and all that came from him.

To prevent, however, his troubling her with any more visits, messages, or epistles, she sat down to her escrutore, and immediately wrote her presentiments to his agent, in the following terms.

'To Mrs. Modely.

Dear Modely,
As it is not my custom to write to men, except on business, of which I never reckoned love, nor the professions of it, any part, I desire you will tell Sir Frederick Fineer, that the only way for him to keep his oath inviolated, is to cease entirely all farther prosecutions of his addresses to me; for as my birth and fortune, as well as my humour, set me above encouraging a secret correspondence with any man, on what pretence soever it may be requested, he may expect, nay, assure himself, that on the next visit he attempts to make me, or letter or message he causes to be left for me, I shall directly acquaint my brothers with the whole story of his courtship; the novelty of which may possibly afford us some diversion.

I thank you for the good I believe you intended me, in your recommendation of a lover, whose title and estate you might think had some charms in them, and the oddities of whose temper you were perhaps unacquainted with.

I desire, however, you will henceforth make no mention of him; but, whenever I send for you, confine your conversation to such matters as befit your vocation; for, as to others, I find you are but little skilled in what will please her who is, notwithstanding this raillery, my dear Modely, your friend and servant,

B. THOUGHTLESS.

P.S. To shew how much I am in earnest, I should have sent the baronet all the epistles he has been at the pains of writing to me, but I am just going out, and I have not leisure to look them up; I will not fail, however, to let him have them in a day or two; they may serve any other woman as well as me, and save him abundance of trouble in his next courtship. You see I have some good-nature, though nothing of that love I suppose he imagined his merits had inspired me with. Adieu.'

Miss Betsy was highly diverted, after sending this dispatch, to think how silly poor Modely would look on finding herself obliged to deliver such a message to her grand lodger, and how dismally mortified he would be on the receiving it.

CHAPTER XIV

───────●───────

Shews that Miss Betsy, whenever she pleased to exert herself, had it in her power to be discreet, even on occasions the most tempting to her honour and inclinations

SOON after Miss Betsy had sent away what she thought would be a final answer to Sir Frederick, her brother Frank came in; she immediately shewed him the letter she had received that morning, and related to him in what manner she had behaved concerning it, with which he was extremely pleased, and said more tender things to her than any she had heard from him since he came to town.

'This is a way of acting, my dear sister,' said he, 'which, if you persevere in, will infallibly gain you the esteem of all who know you; for while you encourage the addresses of every idle fop, believe me, you will render yourself cheap, and lose all your merit with the sensible part of mankind.'

If she was not quite of his opinion in this point, she offered no arguments in opposition to the remarks he made; and assured him, as she had done once before, that she would never give any man the least grounds to hope she approved his pretensions, till she had first received the sanction of both his and her brother Thoughtless's approbation.

He then told her that they had received intelligence, that the India ship, which they heard was to bring Mr. Edward Goodman, was safely arrived in the Downs; so that, in all likelihood, that gentleman would be in London in two or three days at farthest; 'Which I am very glad of,' said he; 'for, though I believe the lawyer a very honest, diligent man, as any can be of his profession, the presence of the heir will give a life to the cause, and may bring things to a more speedy issue.'

He also told her that a gentleman of her brother's acquaintance had the day before received a letter from Sir Ralph Trusty, intimating that he should be obliged, by the death of Mr. Goodman, there being affairs of consequence between them, to come to town much sooner than he had intended, and that he should bring his lady with him: 'And then, my dear sister,' said he, 'you will be happy, for a time at least, in the conversation and advice of one who, I am certain, in her good wishes for you, deserves to be looked upon by you as a second mother.'

He was going on in some farther commendations of that worthy lady, when Miss Betsy's man came to the dining-room door, and told her that Mr. Munden was below in the parlour, and would wait on her if she was at leisure. Mr. Francis perceiving she was hesitating what answer to make, cried hastily, 'Pray, sister, admit him. This is lucky! now I shall see now much he excels Mr. Trueworth in person and parts.' – 'I never told you,' answered she, 'that he did so in either; but perhaps he may in his good opinion and esteem for me: however, I think you promised never to mention Trueworth again to me; I wish you would keep your word. – 'Well, I have done,' said he; 'do not keep the gentleman waiting.' On which she bade the footman desire Mr. Munden to walk up.

That gentleman was a good deal disconcerted in his mind concerning the little progress his courtship had made with Miss Betsy – he had followed her for a considerable time – been at a great expence in treating and making presents to her – he had studied her humour, and done every thing in his power to please her; yet thought himself as far from the completion of his wishes as when he began his addresses to her: he had not for several days had an opportunity of speaking one word to her in private; she was either abroad when he came, or so engaged in company that his presence served only to fill a vacant seat in her dining-room – he therefore determined to know what fate he was to expect from her.

As he had not been told any body was now with her, and had never seen Mr. Francis before, he was a little startled on his coming into the room, to find a young, gay gentleman, seated very near her, and lolling his arm, in a careless posture, over the back of the chair in which she was sitting: on his entrance, they both rose to receive him with a great deal of politeness, which he returned in the same manner; but added to the first compliments, that he hoped he had been guilty of no intrusion.

'Not at all, Sir,' replied the brother of Miss Betsy; 'I was only talking to my sister on some family affairs, which we may resume at any time, when no more agreeable subjects of entertainment fall in our way.' – 'Yes, Mr. Munden,' said Miss Betsy, 'this is that brother whose return to town you so often heard me wish for – and this, brother,' continued she, turning to Mr. Francis, 'is a gentleman who sometimes does me the honour of calling upon me; and whose visits to me I believe you will not disapprove.'

She had no sooner ended these words than the two gentleman mutually advanced, embraced, and said they should be proud of each other's acquaintance; after which they entered into a conversation sprightly enough for the time it lasted, which was not long; for Mr. Francis, looking on his watch, said he was extremely mortified to leave such good company, but business of a very urgent nature called him to a different place at that hour.

As much as Mr. Munden was pleased to find himself so obligingly introduced by his mistress to the acquaintance of her brother, he was equally glad to be rid of him at this juncture, when he came prepared to press her so home to an eclaircissement as should deprive her of all possibility of keeping himself any longer in suspense.

It was in vain for her now to have recourse to any of those evasions by which she had hitherto put him off; and she found herself under a necessity, either of entirely discarding him, or giving him some kind of assurance that the continuance of his pretensions would not be in vain.

Never had she been so plunged before – never had any of her lovers insisted in such plain terms her declaring herself; and she was compelled, as it were, to tell him, since he was so impatient for the definition of his fate, it was from her brothers he must receive it, for she was resolved, nay, had solemnly promised, to enter into no engagement without their knowledge and approbation. 'But suppose,' said he, 'I should be so happy as to obtain their consent, may I then assure myself you will be mine?' – 'Would you wish me to hate you?' cried she, somewhat peevishly. 'Hate me!' answered he; 'no, Madam, it is your love I would purchase, almost at the expence of life.'

'Persecute me then no more,' said she, 'to give you promise, or assurances, which would only make me see you with confusion; and think of you with regret; it is sufficient I esteem you, and listen to the professions of your love: let that content you, and leave to myself the grant of more.' – 'Yet, Madam –' resumed he; and was going on, but was interrupted by the maid, who came hastily into the room, and said, 'Madam, here is Miss Mabel!'

She had no sooner spoke these words, than the lady she mentioned followed her into the room. Miss Betsy was never more glad to see her than now, when her presence afforded her so seasonable a relief: 'My dear Miss Mabel,' said she, 'this is kind indeed, when I already owe you two visits!' – 'I believe you owe me more,' answered she with a smile: 'but I did not come to reproach you; nor can this, indeed, be justly called a visit, since it is only a mere matter of business brings me hither at this time.'

Mr. Munden, on this, thought proper to take his leave; but, in doing so, said to Miss Betsy, with a very grave air, 'I hope, Madam, you will have the goodness to consider seriously on what we have been talking of: I will do myself the honour to wait upon your brothers to-morrow, and afterwards on yourself.' With these words he withdrew, without staying for an answer.

'I know not,' said Miss Mabel, after he was gone, 'whether what I have to say to you will be of sufficient moment to excuse me for depriving you of your company, since I only called to tell you, that we are eased of your little pensioner at Denham, by the father's unexpectedly coming to claim his own.'

Miss Betsy replied, that she guessed as much, for she had heard those people had been at her lodgings when she was not at home, and had said somewhat of their business to her servant. 'I am also to pay you,' resumed the other, 'my quota of the last month's nursing.' In speaking these words she took out of her pocket the little sum she stood indebted for, and laid it on the table.

Though Miss Betsy had the most perfect regard and good wishes for Miss Mabel, and Miss Mabel the same for Miss Betsy, yet neither of them was in the secrets of the other: they visited but seldom; and, when they did, talked only on indifferent affairs. In fine, though they both loved the amiable qualities each found in the other, yet the wide contrariety between their dispositions occasioned a coolness in their behaviour which their hearts were far from feeling.

Miss Mabel stayed but a very few minutes after having dispatched the business she came upon; nor was Miss Betsy at all troubled at her departure, being at present, what she very rarely was, in a humour rather to be alone than in any company whatever.

She no sooner was at liberty than she began to reflect on the transactions of that morning: she had done two things which seemed pretty extraordinary to her; she had entirely dismissed one lover, a piece of resolution she did not a little value herself upon; but then she was vexed at the too great encouragement, as she thought it, which she had given to another.

'What shall I do with this Munden?' said she to herself. 'If my brothers should take it into their heads to approve of his pretensions, I shall be as much teazed on his account as I was on that of Mr. Trueworth: I have no aversion, indeed, to the man, but I am equally as far from having any love for him; there is nothing in his person, or behaviour, that might make a woman ashamed of being his wife; yet I can see nothing so extraordinary in him as to induce me to become so.

'Why, then,' continued she, 'did I not tell him at once I would not have him; and that, if he was weary of paying his respects to me, he might carry them where they would be more kindly received? It was a very silly thing in me to send him to my brothers: they are in such haste to get me out of the way of what they call temptation, that I believe they would marry me to any man that was of a good family, and had an estate. If I must needs have a husband to please them, I had better have taken Trueworth; I am sure there is no comparison between the men; but it is too late to think of that now; for it is very plain, both by his behaviour to me when last I saw him, and by what he said to my brother Frank, that he has given over all intentions on that score.'

She was in the midst of these cogitations, when a servant belonging to the ladies whom she visited at St. James's, came, and presented her with a letter, containing these lines.

'To Miss Betsy Thoughtless.

Dear creature,
My sister and self had an invitation to a party of pleasure, where there will be the best company, the best musick, and the best entertainment in the world; but my father having unluckily forced her to pass some days with an old aunt, who lies dangerously sick at Hampstead, I know nobody can so well supply her vacant place as your agreeable self; therefore, if you are not already too deeply engaged this evening, would beg the favour of you to share with me in the proposed diversion: we shall have two young gentlemen of rank for our conductors and protectors; but I flatter myself you will make

no scruple to go any where with her who is, with the most perfect amity, dear Miss Betsy, your most humble, and most obedient servant,

A. AIRISH.

P.S. Let me know whether I can be so happy as to have you with me; and if so, I will call on you about five, and drink tea, for we shall not go to the assembly 'till eight.'

This proposal put Miss Betsy out of all her serious reflections; and she returned for answer to the lady, that she would not fail to be at home, and ready to attend her at the appointed hour.

Accordingly, as soon as ever dinner was over, she went to dress, and thought of nothing but how to make as brilliant a figure as any she should meet with at the assembly. Miss Airish came somewhat before the hour she had mentioned in her letter, accompanied by two rakes of quality, whom Miss Betsy had seen two or three times before with her and her sister, and by one of whom she had once been treated with some familiarities, which had made her ever since very cautious of giving him any opportunity to attempt the like.

As much, therefore, as she had pleased herself with the idea of this evening's pleasures, she no sooner saw who were to be their conductors, than she resolved not to put herself in their powers; yet knew not how, without affronting Miss Airish, to avoid complying with the promises she had made of accompanying her.

They all came singing and romping into the room; but the perplexity of Miss Betsy's mind made her receive them with a very serious air. The men accosted her with a freedom conformable enough to their own characters, but not very agreeable to one of her's; and she rebuffed, with a good deal of contempt, him with whom she had most reason to be offended.

'Lord! How grave you look!' said Miss Airish, observing her countenance: 'pr'ythee, my dear creature, put on a more chearful aspect; this is to be a night of all spirit, all mirth, all gaiety!' – 'I am sorry I cannot be a partaker of it,' said Miss Betsy, who, by this time, had contrived an excuse. 'Lord! What do you mean? not partake of it!' cried Miss Airish hastily; 'sure you would not offer to disappoint us?' – 'Not willingly,' replied Miss Betsy; 'but I was just going to send to let you know I have received a message from my elder brother, to come to his house, in order to meet some persons there on very extraordinary business: but, I hope,' added she, 'that my not going will be no hindrance to the diversion you propose.'

'It would have been none, Madam,' said one of the gallants, 'if this assembly were like others; but we are only a select company of gay young fellows, who resolve to try how far nature may be exhilarated by regaling every sense at once: to prevent all quarrels, every man is to bring a lady with him, who is to be his partner in singing, dancing, playing, or whatever they two shall agree upon. We two,' continued he, 'pitched upon the two Miss Airishes; but one of them being gone another way, we thought of you; otherwise we could have found ladies who would have obliged us.'

'Very likely,' replied Miss Betsy; 'and I suppose it may not be too late to seek them.' – 'But I had rather have you than all the world,' cried he whom Miss Betsy was most apprehensive of: 'you know I have always shewn a particular tendre for you; therefore, pr'ythee,' continued he, catching her in his arms, and eagerly kissing her, 'my dear girl, send some excuse to your brother, and let us have you with us.'

'Unhand me, my lord!' cried she, struggling to get loose; 'what you ask is impossible, for I neither can nor will go!' The resolution with which she spoke these words, and the anger which at the same time sparkled in her eyes, made them see it would be but lost labour to endeavour to persuade her; they looked one at another, and were confounded what to do; till Miss Airish, vexed to the very heart at Miss Betsy's behaviour, hit upon an expedient to solve the matter: 'Well,' said she, 'since Miss Betsy cannot go, I will introduce your lordship to a young lady, who, I am sure, will not refuse us; besides, I know she is at home, for I saw her looking out of her chamber-window as we came by: but we must go directly, that she may have time to dress.'

On this they both cried, with all their hearts; and one of them, taking her hand, skipped down stairs with her in the same wild way they came up: the other followed, only turning his head towards Miss Betsy, crying with a malicious sneer –

'How unregarded now that piece of beauty stands!'

Miss Betsy, though sufficiently piqued, was very glad to get rid of them; and the more so, that by their happening to call on her, instead of her meeting them at Miss Airish's apartment, she had the better opportunity of excusing herself from going where they desired.

CHAPTER XV

———————•———————

The terrible consequence which may possibly attend our placing too great a dependance on persons whose principles we are not well assured of, are here exemplified in a notable act of villainy and hypocrisy

MISS Betsy no sooner found herself alone, than she began to reflect very seriously on the preceding passage: she knew very little of these two young noblemen, yet thought she saw enough in their behaviour to make any woman, who had the least regard for her honour or reputation, fearful to trust herself with them in any place where both might be so much endangered; she was, therefore, very much amazed that Miss Airish should run so great a risque; and, to find that she did so, joined to some other things which she had of late observed in the conduct of both the sisters, contributed to diminish the love and esteem she once had for them.

She found, however, too many objects of satisfaction in the visits she made to those ladies to be willing to break acquaintance with them; and, as she doubted not but that she had highly disobliged the one, by not complying with her invitation, and that this would infallibly occasion a rupture with the other also, if not in time reconciled, she went the next morning to their apartment, in order to make her peace.

On her enquiring for that lady, the footman told her she was but just come home, and, he believed, was going to bed; but he would tell the chamber-maid she was there. 'No, no!' cried Miss Betsy; 'only give my compliments to your lady, and tell her I will wait on her this afternoon.' She was going away with these words, but Miss Airish, lying on the same floor, heard her voice, and called to her to come in.

Miss Betsy did as she was desired, and found her in a much better

humour than she expected. 'O, my dear!' said she, 'what a night have
you lost by not being with us! Such a promiscuous enjoyment of
every thing that can afford delight or satisfaction! – Well, after all,
there is nothing like playing the rake a little sometimes – it gives such
a fill-up to the spirits.'

'Provided it be innocent, I am of your mind,' replied Miss Betsy; 'I
suppose every thing was managed with decency among you.' – 'O
quite so!' cried the other; 'all harmless libertinism: it is true, there
were private rooms; but, you know, one might chuse whether one
would go into them or not.' – 'I am not sure of that,' said Miss Betsy:
'I am glad, however, you were so well pleased with your
entertainment; and equally so, that you were not hindered from
enjoying it by my not being able to share with you in it.'

'I am obliged to you, my dear,' replied Miss Airish; 'I was a little
vexed with you at first, indeed, but knew you could not help it: the
lady we called upon went very readily with us; so, as it happened,
there was no disappointment in the case.'

'It was only to be convinced of that,' said Miss Betsy, 'that I came
hither thus early; but I will now take my leave – repose I am sure is
necessary for you, after so many waking hours.' The other did not
oppose her departure, being, in effect, desirous of taking that rest
which her exhausted spirits wanted.

Never had Miss Betsy felt within herself a greater or more sincere
satisfaction than she now did, for having so prudently avoided falling
into inconveniences, the least of which, as she very rightly judged,
would have been paying too dear a price for all the pleasures she
could have received.

Sweet indeed are the reflections which flow from a consciousness
of having done what virtue, and the duty owing to the character we
bear in life, exact from us! but poor Miss Betsy was not to enjoy, for
any long time, so happy a tranquillity; she was rouzed out of this
serenity of mind by an adventure of a different kind from all she had
ever yet experienced, and which, if she were not properly guarded
against, it ought to be imputed rather to the unsuspecting goodness
of her heart, than to her vanity, or that inadvertency which had
occasioned her former mistakes.

She was sitting near the window, leaning her arms upon the slab,
very deep in contemplation, when, hearing a coach stop at the door,
she looked out, imagining it might be somebody to her, and saw Mrs.
Modely come out: she wondered what business that woman should

now come upon, after the letter she had sent her; and resolved to chide her for any impertinent message she should deliver.

Mrs. Modely, whose profession was known to the people of the house, always ran up without any other ceremony than asking if Miss Betsy was at home and alone: being now told she was so, she flew into the room, with a distraction in her countenance which very much surprized Miss Betsy; but before she had time to ask the meaning, the other, throwing herself down in a chair, increased her astonishment by these words.

'O, Madam!' cried she, 'I am come to tell you of the saddest accident – poor Sir Frederick Fineer! – O that he had never seen you! – O that I had never meddled between you! – I am undone, that is to be sure – ruined for ever! – I shall never get another lodger – nay, I believe I shall never recover the fright I am in!'

Here she burst into a violent fit of tears; and her sobs interrupting the passage of her words, gave Miss Betsy opportunity to enquire into the mystery of her behaviour. 'For Heaven's sake, what is the matter?' said that young lady; 'pr'ythee, cease these exclamations, and speak to be understood!'

'Ah, dear Miss Betsy!' resumed the other, 'I scarce know what I say or do; poor Sir Frederick has run himself quite through the body!' – 'What! killed himself!' cried Miss Betsy hastily. 'He is not dead yet,' replied Mrs. Modely; 'but there he lies, the most dismal object that ever eyes beheld! the agonies of death in his face – the sword sticking in his breast; for the surgeon says, that the moment that is drawn out, his life comes with it.'

Perceiving Miss Betsy said nothing, and looked a little troubled, she went on in this manner. 'But this is not the worst I have to tell you, Madam,' continued she; 'his death is nothing, but it is his soul – his soul, Miss Betsy! hearing them say he could not live above three hours at most, I sent for a parson; and there the good man sits and talks, and argues with him; but, would you think it, he will not pray, nor be prayed for, nor confess his sins – nor say he is sorry for what he has done – nor do any thing that is right till he has seen you.'

'Me!' said Miss Betsy; 'what would he see me for?' – 'Nay, I know not; but it is his whim, and he is obstinate: therefore, my dear Madam, in christian charity, and in compassion to his soul, hear what he has to say.'

'What good can I do him by going, Mrs. Modely?' said Miss Betsy. 'None, as to his share in the world,' answered she: 'but, dear Madam, consider the other, think what a sad thing it is for a man to die without the rites of the church; I'll warrant he has sins enough upon him, as most young gentlemen have; and, sure, you would not be the cause of his being miserable to all eternity!'

'Indeed, Mrs. Modely, I do not care to go,' said Miss Betsy. 'The sight is very terrible, indeed,' cried the other; 'but you need not stay two minutes; if you but just step in and speak to him, I fancy it will be enough: but, Lord! he may be dead while we are talking; and if he should leave the world in this manner, I should not be able to live in my house; and I have a lease of eleven years to come – I should think I saw his ghost in every room – so, dear, dear Miss Betsy! for my sake, if not for his, go with me – I came in a hackney-coach for haste, and it is still at the door.'

'Well, Modely, you shall prevail,' answered Miss Betsy: 'but you shall stay in the room all the time I am there.' – 'That you may be sure I will,' returned the other: 'but come, pray Heaven we are not too late!'

They said little more to each other till they came to the house of Mrs. Modely; where the first sound that reached the ears of Miss Betsy were groans, which seemed to issue from the mouth of a person in the pangs of death.

Mrs. Modely led her into Sir Frederick's chamber, which was judiciously darkened, so as to leave light enough to discern objects, yet not so much as to render them too perspicuous. Miss Betsy saw him lying on the bed, as Mrs. Modely described, with a sword sticking upright in his breast, a clergyman, and another person, who appeared to be the surgeon, were sitting near him. 'Miss Betsy is so good,' said Mrs. Modely, 'to come to visit you, Sir Frederick.' – 'I am glad of it,' replied he, in a low voice. – 'Pray, Madam, approach.'

'I am sorry, Sir Frederick, to find you have been guilty of so rash an action,' said Miss Betsy, drawing towards the bed. 'I could not live without you,' rejoined he; 'nor would die without leaving you as happy as it is in my power to make you: I have settled two thousand pounds a year upon you during your natural life; but, as I would consult your honour in every thing I do, and people might imagine I made you this settlement in consideraton of some favours which I had too true a regard for you ever to desire, you must enjoy it as my widow, and with it the title of Lady Fincer.'

Miss Betsy was so much amazed at this proposal that she had not the power to speak; but Mrs. Modely cried out, 'Was ever any thing so generous!' – 'Truly noble, indeed!' added the surgeon; 'and worthy of himself and the love he has for this lady.' – 'Bless me!' said Miss Betsy, 'would you have me marry a dying man? – You ought, Sir Frederick, to have other thoughts, as you are going out of the world.'

'Aye, Sir Frederick,' cried the parson, 'think of your immortal part.' – 'I can think of nothing,' answered he, groaning bitterly, 'of my own happiness till I have fixed that of Miss Betsy.' – 'Lord, Madam!' cried Mrs. Modely, softly, 'you would not be so mad to refuse: what! two thousand pounds a year, and a ladyship, with liberty to marry who you will!'

'This is the most generous offer I ever heard of,' said the parson: 'But I wish the lady would resolve soon; for it is high time Sir Frederick should prepare for another world.' – 'He cannot live above an hour,' rejoined the surgeon: 'even if the sword is not withdrawn; therefore, good Madam, think what you have to do.'

While they were speaking, Sir Frederick redoubled his groans, and they went on pressing her to accept the terms he offered. 'Do not plunge a man into a sad eternity, merely for his love to you,' said the parson. 'All the world would condemn you, should you refuse,' cried the surgeon. 'A virgin-widow with two thousand pounds a year!' added Mrs. Modely.

In this manner did they urge her; and the parson getting on the one side of her, and the surgeon on the other, plied her so close with arguments, both on the advantages accruing to herself, and the compassion owing from her to a gentleman who had committed this act of desperation on himself, merely through his love for her, that she neither could nor knew how to make any answer; when Sir Frederick, giving two or three great groans, which seemed more deep than before, and the surgeon, pretending to take Miss Betsy's silence for consent, cried out, 'Madam, he is just going – we must be speedy!' And then turning to the parson, 'Doctor,' said he, 'proceed to the ceremony; pass over the prelude, and begin at the most essential part, else my patient won't live to the conclusion.'

The parson knew very well what he had to do, having his book ready, began at – 'Sir Frederick Fineer, Baronet, wilt thou have this woman to be thy wedded wife?' and so on. To which Sir Frederick answered in the same dismal accents he had hitherto spoken, 'I will!' Then the parson, turning to Miss Betsy, said, 'Betsy Thoughtless, wilt thou have this man to be thy wedded husband?' and so forth. Miss Betsy, in the confusion of her mind, not well knowing what she said or did, replied in the affirmative; on which he was hurrying over the rest of the ceremony; but she, recollecting herself, cried out, 'Hold, doctor! I cannot be married in this manner.' But he seemed not to regard her words, but read on; and the surgeon taking hold of her hand, and joining it with Sir Frederick's, held it, in spite of her resistance, till the ring was forced upon her finger.

This action so incensed her, that the instant she got her hand at liberty, she plucked off the ring, and threw it on the ground. 'What do you mean?' said she. 'Do you think to compel me to a marriage? – Modely, you have not used me well!' With these words she was turning to go out of the room, but perceived, not till then, that Mrs. Modely had slipped out, and that the door was locked; she then began to call, 'Mrs. Modely, Mrs. Modely!' To which no answer was made.

'Come, come, Madam,' said the surgeon, 'this passion will avail you nothing; you are effectually married, whatever you may imagine to the contrary.' – 'Yes, yes,' rejoined the parson, 'the ceremony is good and firm: I will stand to what I have done before any bishop in England.' – 'There wants only consummation,' cried the surgeon; 'and that we must leave the bridegroom to compleat before he dies.' With these words they both went out, making the door fast after them.

Miss Betsy made use of her utmost efforts to pass at the same time they did, but they pushed her back with so much violence as almost threw her down; and Sir Frederick at the same time jumping off the bed, and throwing away the sword, which she imagined sheathed in his body, catched her suddenly in his arms.

It is hard to say whether rage for the imposition she now found had been practised on her, or the terror for the danger she was in, was the passion now most predominant in the soul of Miss Betsy; but both together served to inspire her with unusual strength and courage.

'Your resistance is vain,' cried he; 'you are my wife, and as such I shall enjoy you: no matter whether with your will or not.' She made no answer to these words; but, collecting all her force, sprung from him, and catching hold of one of the posts at the bed's foot, clung so fast round it, that all his endeavours to remove her thence were ineffectual for some moments, though the rough means he made use of for that purpose were very near breaking both her arms.

Breathless at last, however, with the continual shrieks she had sent out for help, and the violence she had sustained by the efforts of that abandoned wretch, who had as little regard to the tenderness of her sex, as to any other principle of humanity, she fell almost fainting on the floor; and was on the point of becoming a victim to the most wicked strategem that ever was invented, when on a sudden the door of the chamber was burst open, and a man, with his sword drawn, at that instant rushed in upon them.

'Monster! cried he that entered, 'what act of villainy are you about to perpetrate?' Miss Betsy rising from the ground, at the same time, said to him, 'Oh, whoever you are, that Heaven has sent to my deliverance, save me, I conjure you, from that horrid wretch!' – 'Fear nothing, Madam,' answered he. He had time for no more; the intended ravisher had snatched up his sword, and was advancing towards him with these words, 'That woman is my wife,' said he; 'how dare any one interfere between us?' – 'O, it is false! it is false! believe him not! cried Miss Betsy. Her protector made no reply; but, flying at his antagonist, immediately closed with him, and wrenched the sword out of his hand, which, throwing on the ground, he set his foot upon, and snapped it in pieces.

The obscurity of the room, joined to the excessive agitations Miss Betsy was in, had till now hindered her from discovering, either by the voice or person, who it was to whom she owed her safety: on his drawing back one of the window-curtains to give more light into the place, that he might see with whom he had been engaged, she presently saw, to her great amazement and confusion, that her deliverer was no other than Mr. Trueworth.

But how great soever was her astonishment, that of Mr. Trueworth was not less, when, looking on the face of the pretended Sir Frederick Fineer, he presently knew him to be a fellow who had served in quality of valet de chambre to a gentleman he was acquainted with in France, who had robbed his master, and only through his lenity and compassion had avoided the punishment his crimes deserved.

'Rascal!' cried Mr. Trueworth, 'have you escaped breaking on the wheel at Paris, to attempt deeds more deserving death in England!' The wretch, who hitherto had behaved with a very lofty air, now finding he was discovered, fell at Mr. Trueworth's feet, and begged he would have mercy on him – alledged, that what he had done was occasioned by mere necessity – said, he was told the lady had a great fortune, and might be easily gained, and such like stuff; which putting Mr. Trueworth beyond all patience, he gave him three or four blows with the flat of his sword, before he sheathed it, saying, at the same time, 'Execrable dog! If thou wert not unworthy of death from any hand but that of the common hangman, thou shouldst not live a moment to boast the least acquaintance with this lady.' Then turning to Miss Betsy, who was half dying with the various emotions she was possessed of, 'Madam,' said he, 'I will not ask by what means you came into this villain's company; only permit me to conduct you hence, and see you safely home.'

Miss Betsy was seized with so violent a fit of trembling through all her frame, that she had neither voice to thank him for the extraordinary assistance she had received from him, nor strength enough to bear her down stairs, if he had not with the greatest politeness, and most tender care, supported her at every step she took.

They found no creature below; the house seemed as if forsaken by all it's inhabitants; but the parlour-door being open, Mr. Trueworth placed his fair charge in an easy chair, while he ran to find somebody to get a coach.

After much knocking and calling, Mrs. Modely came out of a back room, into that where Miss Betsy was. As soon as that young lady saw her, 'Oh, Mrs. Modely!' cried she, 'I could not have believed you would have betrayed me in this cruel manner!' – 'Bless me, Madam!' replied she, in a confusion which she in vain endeavoured to conceal, 'I know not what you mean. I betray you! When you were talking with Sir Frederick I was sent for out; when I came back, indeed, I saw the parson and surgeon pass through the entry in a hurry, and at the same time hearing a great noise, was going up as soon as I had pulled off my things: but I hope,' continued she, in a whining tone, 'nothing has happened to my dear Miss Betsy.' – 'Whatever has happened,' said Mr. Trueworth, fiercely, 'will be enquired into: in the mean time, all we require of you is to send somebody for a coach.'

Mrs. Modely then ringing a bell, a maid-servant appeared, and what Mr. Trueworth had requested was immediately performed; but, though Miss Betsy now saw herself safe from the mischief which had so lately threatened her, she had still emotions very terrible to sustain, and would have, doubtless, thrown her into a swoon, if not vented in a violent flood of tears.

Being arrived at the house where Miss Betsy lodged, just as Mr. Trueworth was helping her out of the coach, they were met by the two Mr. Thoughtlesses coming out of the door: they started back at a sight which, it must be confessed, had something very alarming in it – they beheld their sister all pale and trembling – her eyes half drowned in tears – her garments torn – her hair hanging loosely wild about her neck and face – every token of despair about her – and in this condition conducted by a gentleman, a stranger indeed to the one, but known by the other to have been once passionately in love with her; might well occasion odd sort of apprehensions in both the brothers, especially in the younger.

The sudden sight of her brothers made a fresh attack on the already weakened spirits of Miss Betsy; and she would have sunk on the threshold of the door, as Mr. Trueworth quitted her hand, in order to present it to Mr. Francis, if the elder Mr. Thoughtless, seeing her totter, had not that instant catched her in his arms.

'Confusion!' cried Mr. Francis, 'what does all this mean? Trueworth, is it thus you bring my sister home?' – 'I am heartily sorry for the occasion,' said Mr. Trueworth, 'since –' He was going on; but Mr. Francis, fired with a mistaken rage, prevented him, crying out, ' 'Sdeath, Sir! how came you with my sister?' – Mr. Trueworth, a little provoked to find the service he had done so ill requited, replied, in a disdainful tone, 'She will inform you! after that, if you have any farther demands upon me, you know where I am to be found; I have no leisure now to answer your interrogatories.'

With these words he stepped hastily into the coach, and ordered to be drove to the Two Red Lamps in Golden Square.

Miss Betsy's senses were entirely lost for some moments, so that she knew nothing of what passed. Mr. Francis hearing what directions Mr. Trueworth had given the coachman, was for following him, and forcing him to an explanation; but the elder Mr. Thoughtless prevailed on him to stay till they should hear what their sister would say on this affair.

She was carried into her apartment, rather dead than alive; but being laid on a settee, and proper means applied, she soon returned to a condition capable of satisfying their curiosity.

CHAPTER XVI

———————•———————

Will not tire the reader

MISS Betsy having her heart and head full of the obligation she had to Mr. Trueworth, and on the first discovery of her senses, thinking he was still near her, cried out, 'Oh, Mr. Trueworth! how shall I thank the goodness you have shewn me! – I have no words to do it; it is from my brothers you must receive those demonstrations of gratitude, which are not in my power to give.'

The brothers loked sometimes on her, and sometimes on each other, with a good deal of surprize all the time she was speaking; till, perceiving she had done, 'To whom are you talking, sister?' said Mr. Francis; 'here is nobody but my brother and myself.'

'Bless me!' cried she, looking round the room, 'how wild my head is! – I knew not where I was – I thought myself still in the house of that wicked woman who betrayed me, and saw my generous deliverer chastising the monster that attempted my destruction.'

'Who was that monster?' demanded the elder Mr. Thoughtless, hastily. 'A villain without a name,' said she; 'for that of Sir Frederick Fincer was but assumed, to hide a common cheat – a robber!' – 'And who, say you,' rejoined Mr. Francis, 'was your deliverer?' – 'Who, but that best of men!' answered she, 'Mr. Trueworth! – O, brothers! if you have any regard for me, or for the honour of our family, you can never too much revere or love the honour and the virtue of that worthy man.'

'You see, Frank, how greatly you have been to blame,' said the elder Mr. Thoughtless; 'and how much more you might have been, if I had not dissuaded you from following that gentleman; who, I now

perceive, was the saviour, not the invader, of our sister's innocence.'
– 'I blush,' said Mr. Francis, 'at the remembrance of my rashness – I
ought, indeed, to have known Trueworth better.'

There passed no more between them on this subject; but on
finding Miss Betsy grew more composed, and able to continue a
conversation, they obliged her to repeat the particulars of what had
happened to her; which she accordingly did with the greatest veracity
imaginable, omitting nothing of moment in the shocking narrative.

The calling to mind a circumstance so detestable to her natural
delicacy, threw her, however, into such agonies, which made them
think it their province, rather to console her under the affliction she
had sustained, than to chide her for the inadvertency which had
brought it on her.

They stayed supper with her, which, to save her the trouble of
ordering, Mr. Thoughtless went to an adjacent tavern, and gave
directions for it himself – made her drink several glasses of wine, and
both of them did every thing in their power, to chear and restore her
spirits to their former tone: after which they retired, and left her to
enjoy what repose the present anxieties of her mind would permit her
to take.

Though the condition Miss Betsy was in, made these gentlemen
treat her with the above-mentioned tenderness, yet both of them
were highly incensed against her, for so unadvisedly encouraging the
pretensions of a man, whose character she knew nothing of but from
the mouth of a little mantua-maker – her consenting to sup with him
at the house of that woman, and afterwards running with her into his
very bed-chamber, were actions, which to them seemed to have no
excuse.

Mr. Francis, as of the two having the most tender affection for her,
had the most deep concern in whatever related to her. 'If she were
either a fool,' said he, stamping with extreme vexation, 'or of a vicious
inclination, her conduct would leave no room for wonder! But for a
girl, who wants neither wit nor virtue, to expose herself in this
manner, has something in it inconsistent! – unnatural! – monstrous!

'I doubt not,' cried he again, 'if the truth could be known, but it
was some such ridiculous adventure as this that lost her the affection
of Mr. Trueworth, though her pride and his honour joined to conceal
it.'

The elder Mr. Thoughtless was entirely of his brother's opinion in
all these points; and both of them were more confirmed than ever,

that marriage was the only sure guard for the reputation of a young woman of their sister's temper. Mr. Munden had been there the day before; and, as he told Miss Betsy he would do, declared himself to them; so it was resolved between them, that if, on proper enquiry, his circumstances should be found such as he said they were, to clap up the wedding with all imaginable expedition.

But no business, how important or perplexing soever it be, can render gratitude and good manners forgotten or neglected by persons of understanding and politeness. These gentlemen thought a visit to Mr. Trueworth neither could or ought to be dispensed with, in order to make him those acknowledgements the service he had done their sister demanded from them.

Accordingly, the next morning, Mr. Thoughtless, accompanied by his brother, went in his own coach, which he made be got ready, as well in respect to himself as to the person he was going to visit.

They found Mr. Trueworth at home; who, doubtless, was not without some expectation of their coming. On their sending up their names, he received them at the top of the stair-case with so graceful an affability and sweetness in his air, as convinced the elder Mr. Thoughtless, that the high character his brother Frank had given of that gentleman, was far from exceeding the bounds of truth.

It is certain, indeed, that Mr. Trueworth, since the eclaircissement of the Denham affair, had felt the severest remorse within himself, for having given credit to that wicked aspersion cast upon Miss Betsy; and the reflection, that fortune had now put it in his power to atone for the wrong he had been guilty of to that lady, by the late service he had done her, gave a secret satisfaction to his mind, that diffused itself through all his air, and gave a double sprightlines to those eyes which, by the report of all who ever saw him, stood in need of no addition to their lustre.

The elder Mr. Thoughtless, having made his compliments on the occasion which had brought him thither, the younger advanced, though with a look somewhat more downcast than ordinary – 'I know not, Sir,' said he, 'whether any testimonies of the gratitude I owe you will be acceptable, after the folly into which a mistaken rage transported me last night.' – 'Dear Frank!' cried Mr. Trueworth, smiling, and giving him his hand, in token of a perfect reconciliation, 'none of these formal speeches – we know each other; you are by nature warm, and the little philosophy I am master of, makes me think whatever is born with us pleads it's own excuse! besides, to see me with your sister in the condition she then was, entirely justifies your mistake.' – 'Dear Trueworth!' replied the other, embracing him, 'you are born every way to overcome!'

Mr. Thoughtless returning to some expressions of his sense of the obligation he had conferred upon their whole family – 'Sir, I have done no more,' said Mr. Trueworth, 'than what every man of honour would think himself bound to do for any woman in the like distress, much more for a lady so deserving as Miss Betsy Thoughtless. I happened, almost miraculously, to be in the same house with her when she stood in need of assistance; and I shall always place the day in which my good stars conducted me to the rescue of her innocence, among the most fortunate ones of my whole life.'

In the course of their conversation, the brothers satisfied Mr. Trueworth's curiosity, by acquainting him with the means by which their sister had been seduced into the danger he had so happily delivered her from; and Mr. Trueworth, in his turn, informed them of the accident that had so seasonably brought him to her relief: which latter, as the reader is yet ignorant of, it is proper should be related.

'Having sent,' said he, 'for my steward to come to town, on account of some leases I am to sign, the poor man had the misfortune to break his leg as he was stepping out of the stagecoach, and was carried directly to Mrs. Modely's; where, it seems, he has formerly lodged. This casualty obliged me to go to him. As a maid-servant was shewing me to his room, (which is up two pair of stairs) I heard the rustling of silks behind me; and casting my eyes over the banister, I saw Miss Betsy, and a woman with her, who I since found was Mrs. Modely, pass hastily into a room on the first floor.

'A curiosity,' continued he, 'which I cannot very well account for, induced me to ask the nurse who attends my steward, what lodgers there were below. To which she replied, that they said he was a baronet, but that she believed nothing of it; for the two fellows who passed for his servants were always with him, and, she believed, ate at the same table, for they never dined in the kitchen. "Besides," said she, "I have never seen two or three shabby, ill-looked men, that have more the appearance of pick-pockets, than companions for a gentleman, come after him; and, indeed, I believe he is no better than a rogue himself."

'Though I was extremely sorry,' pursued Mr. Trueworth, 'to find Miss Betsy should be the guest of such a person, yet I could not forbear laughing at the description this woman gave of him; which, however, proved to be a very just one. I had not been there above half an hour before I heard the shrieks of a woman, and fancied it the voice of Miss Betsy, though I had never heard it made use of in that manner. I went, however, to the top of the stair-case; where, hearing the cries redoubled, I drew my sword, and ran down. The door of the chamber was locked; but, setting my foot against it, I easily bursted it open, and, believe, entered but just in time to save the lady from violation.

'On seeing the face,' added he, 'of this pretended baronet, I immediately knew him to be a fellow who waited on a gentleman I was intimate with at Paris. What his real name is I either never heard or have forgot; for his master never called him by any other than that of Quaint, on account of the romantick and affected manner in which he always spoke. The rascal has a little smattering of Latin; and, I believe, has dipped into a good many of the ancient authors. He seemed, indeed, to have more of the fop than the knave in him; but he soon discovered himself to be no less the one than the other; for he ran away from his master, and robbed him of things to a considerable value. He was pursued and taken; but the gentleman permitted him to make his escape, without delivering him into the hands of justice.'

After this mutual recapitulation, the two brothers began to consider what was to be done for the chastisement of the villain, as the prosecuting him by law would expose their sister's folly, and prove the most mortal stab that could be given to her reputation. The one was for cutting off his ears; the other for pinning him against the very wall of the chamber where he had offered the insult. To which Mr. Trueworth replied, 'I must confess his crime deserves much more than your keenest resentments can inflict; but these are punishments which are only the prerogative of law; to which, as you rightly judge, it would be improper to have recourse. I am afraid, therefore, you must content yourselves with barely caning him; that is,' continued he, 'if he is yet in the way for it; but I shrewdly suspect he has before now made off, as well as his confederates, the parson and the surgeon: however, I think it would be right to go to the house of this Modely, and see what is to be done.'

To this they both readily agreed; and they all went together: but, as they were going – 'O what eternal plagues,' said Mr. Francis, 'has the vanity of this girl brought upon all her friends!' – 'You will still be making too hasty reflections,' cried Mr. Trueworth; 'I hope to see Miss Betsy one day as much out-shine the greatest part of her sex in prudence, as she has always done in beauty.'

By this time they were at Mrs. Modely's door; but the maid, whom she had tutored for the purpose, told them that Sir Frederick Fineer was gone – that he would not pay her mistress for the lodgings, because she had suffered him to be interrupted in them – and that she was sick in bed with the fright of what had happened, and could not be spoke to.

On this Mr. Trueworth ran up to his steward's chamber, not doubting but he should there be certainly informed whether the mock baronet was gone or not; the two Mr. Thoughtlesses waited in the parlour til his return, which was immediately, with intelligence, that the wretch had left the house soon after himself had conducted Miss Betsy thence.

They had now no longer any business here; but the elder Mr. Thoughtless could not take leave of Mr. Trueworth without intreating the favour of seeing him at his house: to which he replied, that he believed he should not stay long in town, and while he did so, had business that very much engrossed his time, but at his return should rejoice in an opportunity of cultivating a friendship with him. With this, and some other compliments, they separated; the two brothers went home, and Mr. Trueworth went where his inclinations led him.

CHAPTER XVII

———•———

Love in death; an example rather to be wondered at than imitated

ON Mr. Trueworth's going to Sir Bazil's, he found the two ladies with all the appearance of the most poignant grief in their faces: Mrs. Wellair's eyes were full of tears; but those of her lovely sister seemed to flow from an exhaustless spring.

This was a strange phænomenon to Mr. Trueworth; it struck a sudden damp on the gaiety of his spirits; and he had but just recovered his surprize enough to ask the meaning, when Mrs. Wellair prevented him, by saying, 'O, Mr. Trueworth, we have a melancholy account to give you – poor Mrs. Blanchfield is no more!'

'Dead!' cried he. 'Dead!' repeated Miss Harriot; 'but the manner of it will affect you most.' – 'A much less motive,' replied he, 'if capable of giving pain to you, must certainly affect me: but I beseech you, Madam,' continued he, 'keep me not in suspense.'

'You may remember,' said Miss Harriot, sighing, 'that some time ago we told you that Mrs. Blanchfield had taken leave of us, and was gone down to Windsor. It seems she had not been long there before she was seized with a disorder, which the physicians term a fever on the spirits; whatever it was, she lingered in it for about three weeks, and died yesterday: some days before she sent for a lawyer, and disposed of her effects by will; she also wrote a letter to me, which last she put into the hands of a maid, who has lived with her almost from her infancy, binding her by the most solemn vow to deliver to me as soon as possible after she was dead, and not till then, on any motive whatsoever.

'The good creature,' pursued Miss Harriot, 'hurried up to town this morning, to perform her lady's last injunctions: this is the letter I received from her,' continued she, taking it out of her pocket, and presenting it to him; 'read it, and join with us in lamenting the fatal effects of a passion people take so much pains to inspire.'

The impatience Mr. Trueworth was in for the full explanation of a mystery, which, perhaps, he had some guess into the truth of, hindered him from making any answer to what Miss Harriot had said upon the occasion; he hastily opened the letter, and found in it these lines.

'To Miss Harriot Loveit.

Dear, happy friend!
As my faithful Lucy, at the same time she delivers this into your hands, brings you also the intelligence of my death, the secret it discovers cannot raise in you any jealous apprehensions: I have been your rival, my dear Harriot; but when I found you were mine, wished you not to lose what I would have given the world, had I been the mistress of it, to have gained. The first moment I saw the too agreeable Mr. Trueworth, something within told me, he was my fate – that according as I appeared in his eyes, I must either be happy, or no more: it has proved the latter; death has seized upon my heart, but cannot drive my passion thence. Whether I shall carry it beyond the grave I shall know before this reaches you; but at present I think it is so incorporated with my immortal part, as not to be separated by the dissolution of my frame.

I will not pretend to have had so much command over myself, as to refrain taking any step for the forwarding my desires: before I was convinced of his attachment to you, I caused a letter to be wrote to him, making him an offer of the heart and fortune of a person, unnamed indeed, but mentioned as one not altogether unworthy of his acceptance. This he answered as requested, and ingenuously confessed, that the whole affections of his soul were already devoted to another. I had then no more to do with hope, nor had any thing to attempt but the concealing my despair: this made me quit London, and all that was valuable to me in it. I flattered myself, alas! that time and absence would restore my reason; but, as I said before, my doom was fixed – irrevocably fixed! and I soon found, by a thousand symptoms of an inward decay, that to be sensible of that angelick man's perfections, and to live without him, are things incompatible in nature: even now, while I am writing, I feel the icy harbingers of death creep through my veins, benumbing as they pass. Soon, very soon, shall I be reduced to a cold lump of senseless clay; indeed, I have now no wish for life, nor business to transact below. I have settled my worldly affairs, and disposed of the effects that Heaven has blessed me with, to those I think most worthy of them. My last will is in the hands of Mr. Markland the lawyer; I hope he is an honest man; but lest he should prove otherwise, let Mr. Trueworth know I have made him master of half that fortune, which once I should have rejoiced to lay wholly at his feet: all my jewels I intreat you to accept; they can add nothing to your beauty, but may serve to ornament your wedding-garments; Lucy has them in her possession, and will deliver them to you.

And now, my dear Miss Harriot, I have one favour to beg of you; and that is, that you exert all the influence your merits claim over the heart of Mr. Trueworth, to engage him to accompany you in seeing me laid in the earth. I know your gentle, generous nature, too well, to doubt you will deny me this request; and the very idea that you will ask, and he will grant, gives, methinks, a new vigour to my enfeebled spirits. O if some departed souls are permitted, as some say they are, to look down on what passes beneath the moon, how will mine triumph – how exult to see my poor remains thus honoured! thus attended! I can no more but this – may you make happy the best of men, and may he make you the happiest of women! Farewel – enternally farewel – be assured, that I as lived, so I die, with the greatest sincerity, dear Miss Harriot, yours, &c.

J. BLANCHFIELD.

P.S. Be so good to give my last adieus to Mrs. Wellair; she will find I have not forgot her, nor my little godson, in my bequests.'

How would the vain unthinking sop have exulted on such a proof of his imagined merit! how would the sordid avaricious man, in the pleasure of finding so unexpected an accession to his wealth, have forgot all compassion for the hand that gave it! Mr. Trueworth, on the contrary, blushed at having so much more ascribed to him than he would allow himself to think he deserved, and would gladly have been deprived of the best part of his fortune, rather than have received an addition to it by such fatal means.

The accident, however, was so astonishing to him, that he scarce believed it real; nor could what he read in the letter under her own hand, nor all Mrs. Wellair and Miss Harriot alledged, persuade him to think, at least to acknowledge, that the lady's death was owing to a hopeless flame for him.

While they were speaking, Sir Bazil came in; he had been at home when his sister received the letter, and had heard what Lucy said of her mistress's indisposition, and was therefore no stranger to any part of the affair.

'Well, Trueworth,' said he to that gentleman, 'I have often endeavoured to emulate, and have even envied, the great talents you are master of; but am now reconciled to nature for not bestowing them on me, lest they might prove of the same ill consequences to some women, as yours have been to Mrs. Blanchfield.'

'Dear Sir Bazil,' replied Mr. Trueworth, 'do not attempt to force me into an imagination which would render me at once both vain and wretched. Chance might direct the partial inclination of this lady to have kinder thoughts of me, than I could either merit or return; but I should be loth to believe that they have produced the sad event we now lament.'

'I am of opinion, indeed,' said Sir Bazil, 'that there are many who deceive themselves, as well as the world, in this point. People are apt to mistake that for love, which is only the effect of pride, for a disappointment: but it would be unjust to suppose this was the case with Mrs. Blanchfield; the generous legacy she has bequeathed to you, and the tenderness with which she treats my sister, leaves no room to suspect her soul was tainted with any of those turbulent emotions, which disgrace the name of love, and yet are looked upon as the consequence of that passion; she knew no jealousy, harboured no revenge; the affection she had for you was simple and sincere; and, meeting no return, preyed only upon herself and by degrees consumed the springs of life.'

'I am glad, however,' said the elder sister of Sir Bazil, 'to find that Mr. Trueworth has nothing to reproach himself with on this unhappy score: some men, on receiving a letter of the nature he did, would, through mere curiosity of knowing on whose account it came, have sent an answer of encouragement; it must be owned, therefore, that the command he had over himself in this generosity to his unknown admirer, demanded all the recompense in her power to make.'

Mr. Trueworth, whose modesty had been sufficiently wounded in this conversation, hastily replied, 'Madam, what you by an excess of goodness are pleased to call generosity, was, in effect, no more than a piece of common honesty: the man capable of deceiving a woman who regards him, is no less a villain than he who defrauds his neighbour of the cash intrusted into his hands: the unfortunate Mrs. Blanchfield did me the honour to depend on my sincerity and secrecy: I did but my duty in observing both; and she, in so highly over-rating that act of duty, shewed indeed the magnanimity of her own mind, but adds no merit to mine.'

'I could almost wish it did not,' said Miss Harriot, sighing. 'Madam!' cried Mr. Trueworth, looking earnestly on her, as not able to comprehend what she meant by these words. 'Indeed,' resumed she, 'I could almost wish, that you were a little less deserving than you are, since the esteem you enforce is of so dangerous a kind.' She uttered this with so inexpressible a tenderness in her voice and eyes, that he could not restrain himself from kissing her hand in the most passionate manner, though in the presence of her brother and sister; crying, at the same time, 'I desire no more of the world's esteem, than just so much as may defend my lovely Harriot from all blame for receiving my addresses.'

They afterwards fell into some discourse concerning what was really deserving admiration, and what was so only in appearance; in which many mistakes in judging were detected, and the extreme weakness of giving implicitly into the opinions of others, exposed by examples suitable to the occasion.

But these are inquisitions which it is possible would not be very agreeable to the present age; and it would be madness to risk the displeasure of the multitude for the sake of gratifying a few: so the reader must excuse the repetition of what was said by this agreeable company on that subject.

CHAPTER XVIII

———•———

Displays Miss Betsy in her penitentials, and the manner in which she behaved after having met with so much matter for the humiliation of her vanity; as also some farther particulars, equally worthy the attention of the curious

WHILE Miss Betsy had her brothers with her, and was treated by them with a tenderness beyond what she could have expected, just after the unlucky adventure she had fallen into, she felt not that remorse and vexation which it might be said her present situation demanded.

But when they were gone, and she was left entirely to those reflections, which their presence and good-humour had only retarded, how did they come with double force upon her! To think she had received the addresses, and entertained with a mistaken respect the lowest and most abject dreg of mankind – that she had exposed herself to the insults of that ruffian – that it had not been in her power to defend herself from his taking liberties with her the most shocking to her delicacy – and that she was on the very point of becoming the victim of his base designs upon her; made her feel over again, in idea, all the horrors of her real danger.

By turns, indeed, she blessed Heaven for her escape; but then the means to which she was indebted for that escape, was a fresh stab to her pride. 'I am preserved, 'tis true,' said she, 'from ruin and everlasting infamy: but then by whom am I preserved? by the very man who once adored, then slighted, and must now despise, me. If nothing but a miracle could save me, O why, good Heaven! was not that miracle performed by any instrument but him! What triumph to him! what lasting shame to me, has this unfortunate accident produced!

'Alas!' continued she, weeping, 'I wanted not this proof of his honour – his courage – his generosity – nor was there any need of my being reduced in the manner he found me, to make him think me undeserving of his affection.'

Never was a heart torn with a greater variety of anguish than that of this unfortunate young lady: as she was yet ignorant of what steps her brothers intended to take in this affair, and feared they might be such as would render what had happened to her publick to the world, she fell into reflections that almost turned her brain; she represented to herself all the sarcasms, all the comments, that she imagined, and probably would have been made on her behaviour – her danger, and her delivery – all these thoughts were insupportable to her – she resolved to hide herself for ever from the town, and pass her future life in obscurity: so direful to her were the apprehensions of becoming the object of derision, that, rather than endure it, she would suffer any thing.

In the present despondency of her humour, she would certainly have fled the town, and gone directly down to L—e, if she had not known that Sir Ralph and Lady Trusty were expected here in a very short time; and she was so young when she left that country, that she could not think of any family to whom it was proper for her to go, without some previous preparations.

All her pride – her gaiety – her vanity of attracting admiration – in fine, all that had composed her former character, seemed now to be lost and swallowed up in the sense of that bitter shame and contempt in which she imagined herself involved; and she wished for nothing but to be unseen, unregarded, and utterly forgotten, by all that had ever known her, being almost ready to cry out, with Dido –

'Nor art, nor nature's hand, can ease my grief,
Nothing but death, the wretch's last relief;
Then farewel, youth, and all the joys that dwell
With youth and life – and life itself, farewel!'

The despair of that unhappy queen, so elegantly described by the poet, could not far transcend what poor Miss Betsy sustained during this whole cruel night: nor did the day afford her any more tranquillity – on the contrary, she hated the light – the sight even of her own servants was irksome to her – she ordered, that whoever came to visit her, except her brothers, should be denied admittance –

complained of a violent pain in her head – would not be prevailed upon to take the least refreshment; but kept herself upon the bed, indulging all the horrors of despair and grief.

In the afternoon Mr. Francis Thoughtless came – seemed a little surprized to find his brother was not there; and told Miss Betsy, that, having been called different ways, they had appointed to meet at her lodgings, in order to have some serious discourse with her concerning her future settlement: to which she replied, that her late fright hung so heavy on her spirits, that she was in little condition at present to resolve on any thing.

She spoke this with so dejected an air, that Mr. Francis, who truly loved her, in spite of all the resentment he had for the errors of her conduct, could not forbear saying a great many tender things to her; but nothing afforded her so much consolation as the account he gave her, that no prosecution would be commenced against the sham Sir Frederick Fineer. 'The villain', said he, 'is run away from his lodgings, but, questionless, might easily be found out, and brought to justice; but the misfortune is, that in cases of this nature, the offended must suffer as well as the offender: to punish him, must expose you. You see, therefore, to what your inadvertency has reduced you – injured to the most shocking degree, yet denied the satisfaction of revenge.'

Miss Betsy only answering with her tears – 'I speak not this to upbraid you,' resumed he; 'and would be far from adding to the affliction you are in; on the contrary, I would have you be chearful, and rejoice more in the escape you have had, than bewail the danger you have passed through: but then, my dear sister, I would wish you also to put yourself into a condition which may defend you from attempts of this vile nature.'

He was going on with something farther, when the elder Mr. Thoughtless came in. 'I have been detained,' said that gentleman, 'longer than I expected; my friend is going to have his picture drawn; and, knowing I have been in Italy, would needs have my judgment upon the painter's skill.' 'I suppose, then,' said Mr. Francis, 'your eyes have been feasted with the resemblance of a great number of beauties, either real or fictitious.' – 'No, faith,' replied the other; 'I believe none of the latter: the man seems to be too much an artist in his profession to stand in any need of having recourse to that stale strategem of inviting customers by exhibiting shadows, which have no substances but in his own brain; and, I must do him the justice to say, that I never saw life imitated to more perfection.'

'Then you saw some faces there you were acquainted with,' said the younger Mr. Thoughtless. 'Two or three,' answered the elder; 'but one, which more particularly struck me, as I had seen the original but twice – but once, indeed, to take any notice of: it was of your friend, the gentleman we waited on this morning.'

'What, Trueworth!' demanded Mr. Francis. 'The same,' resumed the other: 'never was there a more perfect likeness – he is drawn in miniature; I believe, by the size of the piece, intended to be worn at a lady's watch; but I looked on it through my magnifier, and thought I saw his very self before me.'

He said much more in praise of the excellence of this artist; as, indeed, he was very full of it, having a desire his favourite mistress's picture should be drawn, and was transported to have found a person who, he thought, could do it so much justice.

Though Miss Betsy sat all this time in a pensive posture, and seemed not to take any notice of this discourse, yet no part of it was lost upon her. 'You extol this painter so much, brother,' said she, 'that if I thought my picture worth drawing, I would sit to him myself. Pray,' continued she, 'where does he live, and what is his name?' Mr. Thoughtless having satisfied her curiosity in these points, no more was said on the occasion; and the brothers immediately entered into a conversation upon the business which had brought them thither.

The elder of them remonstrated to her, in the strongest terms he was able, the perpetual dangers to which, through the baseness of this world, and her own inadvertency, she was liable every day to be exposed. 'This last ugly incident,' said he, 'I hope may be hushed up; Mr. Trueworth, I dare say, is too generous to make any mention of it; and those concerned in it will be secret for their own sakes: but you may not always meet the same prosperous chance. It behoves us, therefore, who must share in your disgarce, as well as have a concern in your happiness, to insist on your putting yourself into a different mode of life: Mr. Munden makes very fair proposals; he has given me leave to examine the rent-roll of his estate, which accordingly I have ordered a lawyer to do. He will settle an hundred and fifty pounds per annum on you for pin-money, and jointure you in four hundred; and I think your fortune does not entitle you to a better offer.'

'Brother, I have had better,' replied Miss Betsy, with a sigh. 'But you rejected it!' cried Mr. Francis, with some warmth; 'and you are not to expect a second Trueworth to fall to your share.' – 'Let us talk no more of what is past,' said the elder Mr. Thoughtless; 'but endeavour to persuade our sister to accept of that which at present is most for her advantage.'

Both these gentlemen, in their different turns, made use of every argument that could be brought on the occasion, to prevail on Miss Betsy to give them some assurance, that as now there was no better prospect for her, she would trifle no longer with the pretensions of Mr. Munden, but resolve to marry him, in case the condition of his affairs was proved, upon enquiry, to be such as he had represented to them.

She made, for a great while, very little reply to all this; her head was now, indeed, very full of something else; she sat in a kind of reverie, and had a perfect absence of mind during this latter part of their discourse: she heard, but heard without attention, and without considering the weight of any thing they urged; yet, at last, merely to get rid of their importunities and presence, that she might be alone to indulge her own meditations, she said as they said, and promised to do whatever they required of her.

Mr. Thoughtless having now, as he imagined, brought her to the bent he wished, took his leave: but Mr. Francis staid some time longer; nor had, perhaps, gone so soon, if Miss Betsy had not discovered a certain restlessnes, which made him think she would be glad to be alone.

This was the first time she had ever desired his absence; but now, indeed, most heartily did so: she had got a caprice in her brain, which raised ideas there she was in pain till she had modelled, and brought to the perfection she wanted. What her brother had cursorily mentioned concerning the picture of Mr. Trueworth, had made a much deeper impression on her mind than all the serious discourse he had afterwards entertained her with; she longed to have in her possession so exact a resemblance of a man who had once loved her, and for whom she had always the most high esteem, though her pride would never suffer her to shew it to any one who professed himself her lover. 'This picture,' said she, 'by looking on it, will remind me of the obligation I have to him; I might forget it else; and I would not be ungrateful: though it is not in my nature to love, I may, nay, I ought, after what he has done for me, to have a friendship for him.'

She then began to consider whether there was a possibility of becoming the mistress of what she so much desired – she had never given her mind to plotting – she had never been at the pains of any contrivances but how to ornament her dress, or place the patches of her face with the most graceful art; and was extremely at a loss what strategem to form for the getting this picture into her hands: at first, she thought of going to the painter, and bribing him to take a copy of it for her own use. 'But then,' said she, 'a copy taken from a copy goes still farther from the original; besides, he may betray me, or he may not have time to do it; and I would leave nothing to chance. No! I must have the very picture that my brother saw, that I may be sure is like, for I know he is a judge.

'Suppose,' cried she again, 'I go under the pretence of sitting for my picture, and look over all his pieces – I fancy I may find an opportunity of slipping Trueworth's into my pocket – I could send the value of it the next day, so the man would be no sufferer by it.'

This project seemed feasible to her for a time; but she afterwards rejected it, on account she could not be sure of committing the theft so artfully as not to be detected in the fact: several other little strategems succeeded this in her inventive brain; all which, on second thoughts, she found either impossible to be executed, or could promise no certainty in their effects.

Sleep was no less a stranger to her eyes this night than it had been the preceding one; yet of how different a nature were the agitations that kept her waking: in the first, the shock of the insult she had sustained, and the shame of her receiving her protection from him by whom, of all men living, she was at least willing to be obliged, took up all her thoughts – in the second, she was equally engrossed by the impatience of having something to preserve him eternally in her mind.

After long revolving within herself, she at last hit upon the means of accomplishing her desires – the risque she ran, indeed, was somewhat bold; but as it succeeded without suspicion, she had only to guard against accidents that might occasion a future discovery of what she had done.

Early the next morning she sent to Blunt's – hired a handsome chaise and pair, with a coachman and two servants, in a livery different from that she gave her own man; then dressed herself in a riding-habit and hunting-cap, which had been made for her on her going down to Oxford, and she had never been seen in by Mr. Trueworth; so that she thought she might be pretty confident, that when he should come to examine who had taken away his picture, the description could never enable him to guess at the right person.

With this equipage she went to the house where the painter lived: on enquiring for him by name, he came immediately to know her commands. – 'You have the picture here of Mr. Trueworth,' said she; 'pray, is it ready?' – 'Yes, Madam,' answered he, 'I am just going to carry it home.' – 'I am glad, then, Sir,' resumed Miss Betsy, 'that I am come time enough to save you that trouble: Mr. Trueworth went to Hampstead last night; and being to follow him this morning, he desired I would bring it with me, and pay you the money.' – 'O, Madam, as to the money,' said he, 'I shall see Mr. Trueworth again!' and then called to the man to bring down his picture. – 'Indeed I shall not take it without paying you,' said she; 'but, in the hurry, I forgot to ask him the sum – pray, how much is it?' – 'My constant price, Madam,' replied he, 'is ten guineas, and the gentleman never offered to beat me down.'

By this time the man had brought the picture down in a little box, which the painter opening, as he presented it to her, cried, 'Is it not a prodigious likeness, Madam?' – 'Yes, really, Sir,' said she, 'in my opinion there is no fault to be found.' – She then put the picture into her pocket, counted ten guineas to him out of her purse, and told him, with a smile, that she believed he would very shortly have more business from the same quarter – then bid the coachman drive on.

The coachman having previous orders what to do, was no sooner out of sight of the painter's house, then he turned down the first street, and carried Miss Betsy home: she discharged her retinue, undressed herself with all the speed she could; and whoever had now seen her, would never have suspected she had been abroad.

This young lady was not of a temper to grieve long for any thing: how deep soever she was affected, the impression wore off on the first new turn that offered itself. All her remorse, all her vexation, for the base design laid against her at Mrs. Modely's, were dissipated the moment she took it into her head to get possession of this picture; and the success of her enterprize elated her beyond expression.

It cannot be supposed that it was altogether owing to the regard she had for Mr. Trueworth, though in effect much more than she herself was yet sensible of, that she took all this pains; it looks as if there was also some little mixture of female malice in the case. Her brother had said that the picture seemed to be intended to be worn at a lady's watch – she doubted not but it was so; and the thoughts of disappointing her rival's expectations contributed greatly to the satisfaction she felt at what she had done.

CHAPTER XIX

———•———

*Presents the reader with some occurrences which, from
the foregoing preparations, might be expected, and also
with others that may seem more surprizing*

MISS Betsy was not deceived in her conjecture in relation to the
picture being designed as an offering to some lady: Mr. Trueworth
had not, indeed, sat for it to please himself, but to oblige Miss
Harriot, who had given some hints that such a present would not be
unwelcome to her.

It is a common thing with painters to keep the pieces in their own
hands as long as they can, after they are finished, especially if they
are of persons endued by nature with any perfections which may do
honour to their art: this gentleman was like others of his profession;
he found it to his credit to shew frequently Mr. Trueworth's picture
to as many as came to look over his paintings, and had detained it for
several days beyond the time in which he had promised to send it, on
pretence that there were still some little touches wanting on the
drapery.

Mr. Trueworth growing a little impatient at the delay, as Miss
Harriot had asked two or three times, in a gay manner, when she
should see his resemblance, went himself in order to fetch it away:
the painter was surprized at the sight of him, and much more so
when he demanded the picture. He told him, however, the whole
truth without hesitation, that he delivered it to a lady not above an
hour before he came, who paid him the money for it, and said that
she had called for it on his request.

Nothing had ever happened that seemed more strange to him; he
made a particular enquiry concerning the face, age, complexion,
shape, stature, and even dress of the lady, who had put this trick

upon him: and it was well for Miss Betsy, that she had taken all the precautions she did, or she had infallibly been discovered; a thing which, perhaps, would have given her a more lasting confusion, than even her late unlucky adventure with the mock baronet.

She was, however, among all the ladies of his acquaintance, almost the only one who never came into his head on this occasion: sometimes he thought of one, sometimes he thought of another; but on recollecting all the particulars of their behaviour towards him, could find no reason to ascribe what had been done to any of them. Miss Flora was the only person he could imagine capable of such a thing; he found it highly probable, that her love and invention had furnished her with the means of committing this innocent fraud; and though he was heartily vexed that he must be at the trouble of sitting for another picture, yet he could not be angry with the woman who had occasioned it: on the contrary, he thought there was something so tender, and so delicate withal, in this proof of her passion, that it very much enhanced the pity and good-will he before had for her.

But while his generous heart was entertaining these too favourable and kind sentiments of her, she was employing her whole wicked wit to make him appear the basest of mankind, and also to render him the most unhappy.

She had found out every thing she wanted to know concerning Mr. Trueworth's courtship to Miss Harriot; and flattered herself, that a lady bred in the country, and unacquainted with the artifices frequently practised in town, to blacken the fairest characters, would easily be frightened into a belief of any thing she attempted to inspire her with.

In the vile hope, therefore, of accomplishing so detestable a project, she contrived a letter in the following terms.

'To Miss Harriot Loveit.

Madam,

Where innocence is about to suffer merely through it's incapacity of suspecting that ill in another it cannot be guilty of itself, common honesty forbids a stander-by to be silent. You are on the brink of a precipice which, if you fall into, it is not in the power of human art to save you. Death only can remove you from misery, remorse, distraction, and woes without a name! Trueworth, that sly deceiver of your sex, and most abandoned of his own, can only bring you a polluted heart and prostituted vows! He made the most honourable professions of love to a young lady of family and character – gained her affections – I hope no more: but, whatever was between them, he basely quitted her, to mourn her ill-placed love and ruined fame. Yet this, Madam, is but his least of crimes: he has since practised his betraying arts on another, superior to the former in every female virtue and accomplishments – second to none in beauty, and of a reputation spotless as the sun, till an unhappy passion for that worst of men obscured it's brightness, at least in the eyes of the censorious. He is, however, bound to her by the most solemn engagements that words can form, under his own hand-writing; which, if she does not in due time produce against him, it will be owing only to her too great modesty. These two, Madam, are the most conspicuous victims of his perfidy. Pray Heaven you may not close the sad triumvirate, and that I may never see such beauty and such goodness stand among the foremost in the rank of those many wretches he has made!

In short, Madam, he has deceived your friends, and betrayed you into a mistaken opinion of his honour and sincerity. If he marries you, you cannot but be miserable, he being the right of another: if he does not marry you, your reputation suffers. Happy is it for you, if the loss of reputation is all you will have to regret! He already boasts of having received favours from you; which, whoever looks in your face, will find it very difficult to think you capable of granting: but yet, who knows what strange effects too great a share of tenderness in the composition may not have produced!

Fly, then, Madam, from this destructive town, and the worst monster in it, Trueworth! Retire in time to those peaceful shades from whence you came; and save what yet remains of you worthy your attention to preserve!

Whatever reports to your prejudice the vanity of your injurious deceiver may have made him give out among his loose companions, I still hope your virtue has hitherto protected you, and that this warning will not come too late to keep you from ever verifying them.

Be assured, Madam, that in giving this account, I am instigated by no other motive than merely my love of virtue, and detestation of all who would endeavour to corrupt it; and that I am, with perfect sincerity, Madam, your well-wisher, and humble servant,

UNKNOWN.'

Miss Flora, on considering what she had wrote, began to think she had expressed herself in somewhat too warm a manner; but she let it pass on this account: 'By the virulence', said she, 'with which I have spoken of Trueworth, his adored Miss Harriot will certainly imagine it comes from one of those unhappy creatures I have represented in it; and, if so, it will gain the more credit with her. If she supposes that rage and despair have dictated some groundless accusations against her love, she, nevertheless, will believe others to be fact, and that at least he has been false to one.'

She, therefore, went to the person who was always her secretary in affairs of this nature; and, having got it copied, was going to the post-house, in order to send it away; for she never trusted any person but herself with these dispatches.

She was within three or four yards of the post-house, when she saw Mr. Trueworth at some distance, on the other side of the street. Her heart fluttered at this unexpected sight of him – she had no power to refrain from speaking to him – she staid not to put her letter in, but flew directly across the way, and met him just as he was turning the corner of another street.

'Oh, Mr. Trueworth!' cried she, as they drew near each other, 'I have prayed that I might live once more to see you; and Heaven has granted my petition!'

'I hope, Madam,' said he, 'that Heaven will always be equally propitious to your desires in things of greater moment.' – 'There can scarce be any of greater moment,' answered she; 'for, at present, I have a request to make you of the utmost importance to me, though no more than I am certain you would readily grant to any one you had the least acquaintance with. But,' continued she, 'this is no proper place for us to discourse in. Upon the terms we now are, it can be no breach of faith to the mistress of your vows to step with me, for three minutes, where we may not be exposed to the view of every passenger.'

Mr. Trueworth had not been very well pleased with the rencounter, and would gladly have dispensed with complying with her invitaton; but thought, after what she had said, he could not refuse, without being guilty of a rudeness unbecoming of himself as well as cruel to her: yet he did comply in such a manner as might make her see his inclination had little part in his consent. He told her he was in very great haste, but would snatch as much time as she mentioned from the business he was upon. Nothing more was said; and they went together into the nearest tavern; where, being seated, and wine brought in, 'Now, Madam,' said he, with a cold civility, 'please to favour me with your commands.'

'Alas!' replied she, 'it belongs not to me to command, and my request you have already granted.' – 'What, without knowing it!' cried he. 'Yes,' resumed she; 'I thought an intimacy, such as ours had been, ought not to have been broke off, without a kind farewell. I blame you not for marrying; yet, sure, I deserve not to be quite forsaken – utterly thrown off: you might at least have flattered me with the hope that, in spite of your matrimonial engagement, you would still retain some sparks of affection for your poor Flora.' – 'Be assured,' said he, 'I shall always think on you with tenderness.' – 'And can you then resolve never to see me more?' rejoined she passionately. 'I hoped,' replied he, 'that you had acquiesced in the reasons I gave you for that resolution.' – 'I hoped so, too,' said she; 'and made use of my utmost efforts for that purpose: but it is in vain; I found I could not live without you; and only wished an opportunity to take one last embrace before I leave the world and you for ever.' In speaking these words, she threw herself upon his neck, and burst into a flood of tears.

How impossible was it for a heart such as Mr. Trueworth's to be unmoved at a spectacle like this! Her love, her grief, and her despair, shot through his very soul. Scarce could he refrain mingling his tears with hers. 'My dear Flora,' cried he, 'compose yourself – by Heaven I cannot bear to see you thus!' He kissed her cheek while he was speaking, seated her in a chair, and held her hand in his with the extremest tenderness.

This wicked creature was not so overcome with the emotions of her love and grief, as not to see the pity she had raised in him; and, flattering herself that there was in it some mixture of a passion she more wished to inspire, fell a second time upon his bosom, crying, 'Oh, Trueworth! Trueworth! here let me die; for death hath nothing in it so terrible as the being separated from you!'

Mr. Trueworth was a man of strict honour, great resolution, and passionately devoted to the most deserving of her sex: yet he was still a man – was of an amorous complexion; and thus tempted, who can answer, but in this unguarded moment he might have been guilty of a wrong to his dear Harriot, for which he would afterwards have hated himself, if an accident of more service to him than his own virtue, in so critical a juncture, had not prevented him.

He returned the embrace she gave, and joined his lips to hers with a warmth which she had not for a long time experienced from him: a sudden rush of transport came at once upon her with such force, that it overwhelmed her spirits, and she fell into a kind of fainting between his arms. He was frightened at the change he observed in her; and hastily cutting the lacings of her stays, to give her air, the letter above-mentioned dropped from her breast upon the ground. He took it up, and was going to throw it upon the table; but in that action seeing the name of Miss Harriot on the superscription, was struck with an astonishment not easy to be conceived. He no longer thought of the condition Miss Flora was in; but, tearing open the letter, he began to examine the contents.

Miss Flora in that instant recovering her senses, and the remembrance of what had been concealed in her bosom, flew to him, endeavouring to snatch the paper from his hands; but he had already seen too much not to be determined to see the rest. 'Stand off!' cried he, in a voice half choked with fury; 'I am not yet fully acquainted with the whole of the favours you have bestowed upon me in this paper!' Confounded as she was, cunning did not quite forsake her. 'I am ignorant of what it contains,' said she; 'I found it in the street! – It is not mine! – I wrote it not!'

With such like vain pretences would she have pleaded innocence; yet all the time endeavoured, with her whole strength, to force the proof of her guilt from him; insomuch that, though he was very tall, he was obliged with one hand to keep her off, and with the other to hold the paper at arms length, while he was reading it; and could not forbear frequently interrupting himself, to cast a look of contempt and rage on the malicious authoress. 'Vile hypocrite!' cried he: and then again, as he got farther into the base invective, 'Thou fiend in female form!'

She now finding all was over, and seized with a sudden fit of frenzy, or something like it, ran to his sword, which he had pulled off and laid in the window, and was about to plunge it in her breast. He easily wrested it from her; and, putting it by his side, 'O thou serpent! – thou viper!' cried he. 'If thou wert a man, thou shouldest not need to be thy own executioner!' The tide of her passion then turning another way, she threw herself at his feet, clung round his legs, and, in a voice rather screaming than speaking, uttered these words – 'O pardon me! – pity me! Whatever I have done, my love of you occasioned it!' – 'Curse on such poisonous love!' rejoined he. 'Hell, and it's worst effects, are in the name, when mentioned by a mouth

like thine!' Then finding it a little difficult to disentangle himself
from the hold she had taken of him, 'Thou shame and scandal to that
sex to which alone thou owest thy safety!' cried he furiously, 'quit me
this instant, lest I forget thou art a woman! – lest I spurn thee from
me, and use thee as the worst of reptiles!'

On hearing these dreadful words, all her strength forsook her; the
sinews of her hand relaxed, and lost their grasp. She fell a second
time into a fainting-fit; but of a nature as different from what the
former had been as were the emotions that occasioned it. Mr.
Trueworth was now too much and too justly irritated to be capable of
relenting: he left her in this condition, and only bid the people at the
bar, as he went out of the house, send somebody up to her assistance.

The humour he was at present in rendering him altogether unfit
for company, he went directly to his lodgings; where examining the
letter with more attention than he could do before, he presently
imagined he was not altogether unacquainted with the hand-writing.
He very well knew it was not that of Miss Flora, yet positive that he
had somewhere seen it before: that which he had received concerning
Miss Betsy and the child at Denham came fresh into his head; he
found them, indeed, the same on comparing; and, as the reader may
suppose, this discovery added not a little to the resentment he was
before inflamed with against the base inventress of these double
falsehoods.

CHAPTER XX

———•———

Contains divers things

MISS Betsy was all this time enjoying the little fraud she had been guilty of: the idea how Mr. Trueworth would be surprized at finding his picture had been taken away, and the various conjectures that would naturally rise in his mind upon so odd an accident, gave her more real pleasure than others feel on the accomplishment of the most material event.

She was, indeed, of a humour the most perfectly happy for herself that could be: chearful, gay – not apt to create imaginary ills, as too many do, and become wretched for misfortunes which have no existence but in their own fretful dispositions. On any real cause, either for grief or anger, that happened to her, nobody, it is certain, felt them with a more poignant sensibility; but then she was affected with them but for a short time. The turbulent passion could obtain no residence in her mind; and, on the first approaches of their opposite emotions, entirely vanished, as if they had never been. The arrows of affliction, of what kind soever they were, but slightly glanced upon her heart, nor pierced it, much less were able to make any lasting impression there.

She now visited as usual – saw as much company as ever; and hearing no mention made, wherever she went, of her adventure with the mock baronet, concluded the whole thing was, and would remain, an eternal secret, and therefore easily forgot it; or, if it came into her head, remembered it only on account of her deliverer.

She was now on exceeding good terms with her brothers, who were full of spirits themselves. The elder Mr. Thoughtless, who loved play but too well, had lately had some lucky casts; and Mr. Francis had accomplished his affairs – his commission was signed, and every thing contributed to render the whole family perfectly easy in themselves, and obliging to each other.

In the midst of this contentment of mind, Mr. Edward Goodman came to town from Deal. The two Mr. Thoughtlesses, on account of the many obligations they had to his uncle, and the good character they had heard of himself, received him with abundance of respect and affection.

This young Indian had a great deal of the honest simplicity of his uncle, both in his countenance and behaviour, and wanted not politeness and good manners sufficient to render his conversation very agreeable.

He was sent from Bengal at about four years of age, and received the first rudiments of his education at one of the best schools in England; where he continued till he had attained to his nineteenth, and then returned to his native country, and was now about twenty-four.

Mr. Thoughtless had now got so much the better of his mistress as to prevail on her to content herself with keeping in her own apartment whenever he had any company by whom it was improper for her to be seen.

He made a handsome entertainment for Mr. Goodman soon after his arrival; to which the lawyer who had the care of his affairs, with his wife, a well-bred, discreet woman, were also invited. Miss Betsy, at the request of her brother, presided at the head of the table.

Dinner was ordered to be ready about three, and the invitation accordingly made; but the lawyer not coming, his wife, perceiving they waited for him, was a little perplexed; but she was soon eased of it, by his coming in less than a quarter of an hour after the time he was expected.

This gentleman was the very person who made Mrs. Blanchfield's will; and, to apologize for his stay, he related to them the cause that had detained him; which was, that a demur being made to the payment of some part of the money bequeathed by that lady to Mr. Trueworth, he had been obliged to go with him, in order to rectify the mistake which had occasioned it. In giving this account, he imagined not that any person present had the least concern in it, or even was acquainted with either of the parties he mentioned.

Miss Betsy said nothing, but had her own reflections on what he had been saying: she, however, had the satisfaction of hearing her two brothers ask those questions she longed to put to him herself. By the answers he made, she doubted not but the deceased had been courted by Mr. Trueworth – had loved him, and was to have been married to him, by her having made him so considerably a legacy.

The rest of their conversation that whole day was chiefly on matters concerning the late Mr. Goodman, the baseness of Lady Mellasin, and the measures that were taken to detect the fraud she had been guilty of; all which was very dry and insipid to Miss Betsy at this time, as, indeed, it would have been had it turned on any other subject. She was not, therefore, very sorry when the company broke up, that she might be at home, and at full liberty to indulge meditations which promised her more satisfaction than any thing she could hear abroad.

She had set it down in her mind, from what the lawyer had said, as a sure fact, that Mr. Trueworth, since his desisting his courtship to her, had loved another; and also, that her rival in his affection was now no more. 'He need not,' said she to herself, 'be at the trouble of sitting a second time for his picture in compliment to her; nor can what I have done be a subject of disquiet to either of them.'

She then would take his picture out of the cabinet, where she had concealed it, and examine it attentively. 'Good God!' cried she, 'how uncertain is the heart of man! How little dependence ought we to place on all the professions of love they make us! Just so he looked, with all this tenderness in his eyes, when his false tongue protested he never could think of marrying any woman but myself.' But these uneasy, and, indeed, unjust reflections, lasted not above a minute. 'Mrs. Blanchfield,' said she, 'had a large fortune; it was that, perhaps, he was in love with, and finding no hope of gaining me, he might be tempted, by his ambition, to make his addresses to her; but whatever were his thoughts on her account, she is now dead; and who knows what may happen? That he once loved me is certain; if he should return to his first vows, the obligation I have received from him would not permit me to treat him with the same indifference I have done. I am not in love with any man,' continued she; 'but if ever I marry, he certainly, exclusive of what he has done for me, deserves, in every respect, to have the preference; and I should, with less regret, submit to the yoke of wedlock with him than any other I have seen.'

Thus she went on, forming ideal prospects all that night, and part of the ensuing day; when the elder Mr. Thoughtless came in, and gave her the most unwelcome interruption she could receive.

He told her that he had just received an account, to his entire satisfaction, in every thing relating to Mr. Munden; and that no reasonable objection could be made, either as to the family, the estate, or the character of that gentleman. 'Therefore,' said he, 'as you have thought fit to encourage his pretensions, and he has continued them a sufficient length of time to defend you from the censure of a too quick consent, you cannot, I think, in honour, but reward his passion without delay.'

Miss Betsy was, at present, in a disposition very unfit to comply with her brother's advice; but, after all that had been urged by him, and by Mr. Francis, she could not assume courage wholly to refuse.

She hesitated – she began a sentence without ending it – and when she did, her answers were not all of a piece with that ready wit which she had always testified on other occasions.

Mr. Thoughtless, perceiving she was rather studious to evade giving any determinate answer, than willing to give such a one as he desired she should, began to expostulate with her on the capriciousness of her humour and behaviour; he conjured her to reflect on her late adventure with the impostor, Sir Frederick Fineer; and how ill it became her to countenance the addresses of a wretch like him, and, at the same time, trifle with a man of fortune and reputation.

She suffered him to go on in this manner for a considerable time, without giving him the least interruption; but by degrees recovering her spirits, 'I shall take care, Sir,' said she, 'never to fall into the like adventure again; neither do I intend to trifle with Mr. Munden: but marriage is a thing of too serious a nature to hurry into, without first having made trial of the constancy of the man who would be a husband, and also of being well assured of one's own heart.'

Mr. Thoughtless then told her, with some warmth, that he found she was relapsing into a humour and way of thinking which could not in the end but bring ruin on herself and disgrace to all her family; and added, that for his part he should meddle no more in her affairs. The tender soul of Miss Betsy was deeply affected at these words: she loved her brothers, and could not bear their displeasure; the thought of having any disagreement with them was dreadful to her; yet the putting a constraint on her inclinations to oblige them was no less so. In this dilemma, whether she complied, or whether she refused, she found herself equally unhappy.

One moment she was opening her mouth to yield a ready assent to all that was requested of her on the score of Mr. Munden; the next to confess, that she neither liked nor loved that gentleman, and knew not whether she should ever be able to resolve on a marriage with him; but her sincerity forbade the one, and her fears of offending gave a check to the other; and both together kept her entirely silent.

'You ought, methinks, however,' resumed Mr. Thoughtless, 'to have spared Mr. Munden the trouble of laying open his circumstances, and me that of examining into them.' – 'I should undoubtedly have done so, Sir,' answered she, 'if I had been entirely averse to the proposals of Mr. Munden; therefore, both you and he are too hasty in judging. You know, brother, that Sir Ralph and my dear Lady Trusty will be in town in a very few days; and I am willing to have the approbation of as many of my friends as possible, in a thing of so much consequence to my future peace.'

Mr. Thoughtless was now somewhat better satisfied than he had been; and after recommending to her a constancy of mind and resolution, took his leave of her.

This conversation having a little dissipated those gay imaginations she was before possessed of, she began to consider seriously what she meant by all this, and what it availed her to give both her lover and brothers so much matter of complaint against her: she reflected that she had now gone so far with that gentleman, that neither honour towards him, nor regard to her own reputation, would well suffer her to go back. 'Since it is so, then,' said she to herself, 'to what end do I take all this trouble to invent excuses for delaying what must one day necessarily be?

'Yet, wherefore must it be?' continued she; 'I have made no promise; and if a better offer should happen, I see no reason that obliges me to reject it: for example, if Mr. Trueworth or such a one as Mr. Trueworth, (if his equal is to be found in nature) neither my brothers, nor the world, I fancy, would condemn me for quitting Mr. Munden.

'Why, then,' cried she, 'need I make all this haste to put myself out of the way of fortune? I am young enough; have lost no part of what has attracted me so many admirers; and, while my heart and hand are free, have, at least, a chance of being more happy than Mr. Munden can make me.'

In a word, being fully persuaded in her mind that the lady, who had supplanted her in Mr. Trueworth's affections, was dead, she imagined there was a probability he might renew his addresses to herself; she wished, at least, to make the experiment; and, to that end, resolved to give no promise to Mr. Munden: yet would she not allow herself to think she loved the other, but only that she would give him the preference, as he was a match of more advantage.

Nothing is more certain, nor, I believe, more obvious to the reader, than that this young lady, almost from the time of Mr. Trueworth's quitting her, had entertained a growing inclination for him, which the late service he had rendered had very much increased: but this her pride would not suffer her to own, even to herself, as the comick poet truly says –

> 'For whatso'er the sages charge on pride,
> The angels fall, and twenty faults beside;
> On earth, 'tis sure, 'mong us of mortal calling,
> Pride saves man oft, and woman too, from falling.'

CHAPTER XXI

———— • ————

Presents the reader with some prognosticks, on events in futuro

THE reader will easily suppose that, in the present disposition of Miss Betsy's heart, Mr. Munden met with but an indifferent reception from her; she avoided his company as much as possible; and, when obliged to receive a visit from him, could not bring herself to treat him with any thing more than a cold civility. He complained of her cruelty – told her he had expected better things from her after her brothers had approved his flame: he pressed her, in the most pathetick terms he was master of, to let him know when the happy day would arrive, which should put an end to the long series of his hopes and fears.

It is certain, that if this gentleman had loved with that warmth and sincerity which some men have done, he must have been very unhappy during his courtship to Miss Betsy; but he was altogether insensible of the delicacies of the passion he professed – he felt not the pains he affected to languish under – he could support the frowns, or even the slights, of his mistress, without any other anxiety than what his pride inflicted.

It was, therefore, rather owing to this last propensity in his nature, than any emotions of a real tenderness for Miss Betsy, which had made him persevere in his addresses to her. All his aquaintance knew he had courted her a long time; some of them had been witness of her treatment of him: and he was unwilling it should be said of him, that he had made an offer of his heart in vain.

He had, at first, indeed, a liking for her person; he had considered her beauty, wit, and the many accomplishments she was possessed of, were such as would render his choice applauded by the world. The hopes of gaining her in a short time, by the encouragement she had given his addresses, had made him pursue her with vigour; but the delays – the scruples – the capriciousness of her humour – the pretences she of late had made to avoid giving him a definitive answer – had, at length, palled all the inclination he once had for her; and even desire was deadened in him, on so many disappointments.

It is, therefore, a very ill-judged thing in the ladies, to keep too long in play the man they ever design to marry: and, with all due deference to that great wit and poet, Sir John Suckling, there are very few examples which verify his maxim, that –

> ' 'Tis expectation makes the blessing dear.'

According to my opinion, which is founded on observation, another author, who wrote much about the same time with Sir John, has given us a more true idea of what a tedious courtship may produce, especially on the side of the man. In a matrimonial dialogue, he makes the husband excuse the coldness complained of by his wife, in these terms –

> 'Unequal lengths, alas! our passions run;
> My love was quite worn out, ere yours begun.'

This being the case with Mr. Munden, it rendered Miss Betsy little less indifferent to him, in reality, than he had ever been to her: to which another motive, perhaps, might also be added, viz. that of his indulging himself with amusements with other fair-ones, of a more kind complexion; for continency (as will hereafter appear) was not among the number of that gentleman's virtues.

But enough of Mr. Munden for the present. It is now highly proper to give the reader some account what Mr. Trueworth was doing while Miss Betsy was entertaining sentiments for him, which he had long since ceased the ambition of inspiring her with.

Difficult was it for him to get over the mingled astonishment and vexation which the detection of the wickedness of Miss Flora had involved him in. The remembrance of those guilty moments, in which he had indulged a tender intercourse with a woman of her abandoned principles, filled him with the most bitter remorse, and rendered him almost hateful to himself.

To recollect that he had been the instrument of her base designs on Miss Betsy, and how cruelly he had wronged that lady by a too rash belief, was, of itself, sufficient to inflame his rage; but when he reflected on this last act of baseness, which, if not providentially discovered, might have made his dear Harriot entertain suspicions of him fatal to her peace, if not totally destructive of their mutual happiness, the shock of such a misfortune, though happily frustrated, was more than he could bear with any tolerable degree of patience.

Rage, disdain, and revenge, for the vile contriver of so black an attempt, were the first emotions that took possession of his mind; but the violence of those passions evaporating by degrees, he began to think more coolly, and to reason with himself, from which that depravity of morals and manners, women are sometimes guilty of, proceeded.

'Chastity,' said he, 'is but one branch of virtue, but a material one, and serves as a guard to all the others; and if that is once overcome, endangers the giving entrance to a thousand vices. A woman entirely free from those inordinate desires, which are, indeed, but the disgrace of love, can scarce be capable of envy, malice, or revenge, to any excess.

'That sex,' cried he again, 'are endued by nature with many perfections which ours cannot boast of; it is their own faults when they sink beneath us in value; but the best things, when once corrupted, become the worst. How dear, therefore, ought a woman to prize her innocence! As Shakespeare says –

> '– They are all white – a sheet
> Of spotless paper, when they first are born;
> But they are to be scrawl'd upon, and blotted
> By every goose-quill.'

He was in the midst of these contemplations, when a letter from Miss Flora was brought to him: she still flattered herself with being able to work on his good nature by submissions, and a seeming contrition for what she had done; and had accordingly wrote in the most moving terms she was mistress of; but he knowing, by the hand-writing on the superscription, from whom it came, would not even open it; and his indignation rekindling afresh, he took a piece of paper, in which he wrote only this line –

'I read no letters from incendiaries.'

This served as a cover to the letter, which he sent directly by the messenger that brought it.

If the mind of Mr. Trueworth had been less taken up than it was at present, this ugly accident would doubtless have dwelt much longer upon it; but affairs of a more important, and more pleasing nature, demanded his whole attention.

The day prefixed for the celebration of his marriage with Miss Harriot, and also of that of Sir Bazil and Miss Mabel, had been delayed on account of Mrs. Blanchfield's death. None of these generous persons could think of indulging the joys they so much languished for till all due rites were paid to the memory of that amiable lady.

Mr. Trueworth and Miss Harriot went into deep mourning; Sir Bazil and Mrs. Wellair also put on black; Miss Mabel did the same, in compliment to them, for she had not the least acquaintance with the deceased.

Nor was this all; Mr. Trueworth, to testify his gratitude and respect, ordered a very curious monument of white marble to be erected over her remains, the model of which he drew himself, after one he had seen in Italy, and was much admired by all judges of architecture and sculpture.

If, by a secret and unfathomable intuition, the souls of the departed are permitted any knowledge of what is done below, that of Mrs. Blanchfield's must feel an extreme satisfaction, in such proofs of the esteem of him she had so tenderly and so fatally loved, as well as those of her fair friend and rival.

That generous young lady would fain have prolonged their mourning for a whole month, and consequently have put off her marriage till that time; but this, if Mr. Trueworth would have been prevailed upon to have submitted to, Sir Bazil and Mrs. Wellair would not agree to: he thought he had already sacrified enough of the time of his promised happiness, and Mrs. Wellair was impatient to get home, though equally loath to leave her sister till she had disposed of herself.

They were arguing on this topick one evening – Mr. Trueworth opposed Miss Harriot as much as he durst do without danger of offending her; but Sir Bazil plainly told her, that if she continued obstinate, Miss Mabel and he would finish their affairs without her. Mrs. Wellair urged the necessity there was for her return; and Mr. Trueworth, encouraged by what these two had said, added, that he was certain Mrs. Blanchfield did not mean, by what she had done, to obstruct his happiness a moment: to which Miss Harriot, with a most obliging smile, replied, 'Well, obediencce will very shortly be my duty, and I will give you a sample of it before-hand. Here is my hand,' continued she, giving it to him; 'make it your own as soon as you please.'

It is not to be doubted but Mr. Trueworth kissed the hand she gave him with the utmost warmth and tenderness; but before he could make any reply to so kind a declaration, Sir Bazil cried out, 'Well said, Harriot! love has already wrought wonders in your heart; you will grant to a lover what you refuse to us.' – 'Not to a lover, Sir,' answered she, 'but to a person who is about to be my husband. I think it is as ill-judged a reserve in a woman to disown her affection for the man she has consented to marry, as it would be imprudence to confess it before she has consented.'

After some farther conversation on this head, (in the course of which Mr. Trueworth had the opportunity of being more confirmed than ever, that the disposition of his mistress was, in every respect, such as he wished to find it) all that was yet wanting for the completions of the nuptials was settled.

The second day after this was fixed for the celebration of the ceremony; after which it was determined that the two bridegrooms, with their brides, the father of Miss Mabel, Mrs. Wellair, and two other friends, should all set out together for Sir Bazil's seat in Staffordshire; and that Mrs. Wellair should write to her husband to meet them there, that the whole family might be together on so joyful an occasion.

CHAPTER XXII

———•———

*Will prove, by a remarkable instance of a high-raised
hope suddenly disappointed, the extreme weakness of
building our expectations upon mere conjecture*

THOUGH it is not to be imagined that the preparations for marriages,
such as those of Sir Bazil Loveit and Mr. Trueworth, could be an
entire secret to the town, especially as neither of the parties had any
motive to induce them to desire it should be so, yet Miss Betsy never
heard the least syllable of any such thing being in agitation. Those of
her acquaintance, whom she at presently chiefly conversed with, were
either ignorant of it themselves, or had never happened to mention it
in her presence; so that, knowing nothing of Mr. Trueworth's affairs
of late, more than what the lawyer had casually related at her
brother's, it is not to be wondered at, that she imagined him wholly
disengaged since the death of that lady who had so kindly
remembered him in her will.

Neither ought it (her vanity considered) to appear strange, that she
was apt to flatter herself with a return of his affection to herself, when
the memory of the late object of it should be utterly erased.

When there is the least possibility that what we ardently wish may
come to pass, the minutest circumstance, in favour of our hopes,
serves to assure us that it certainly will do so.

Miss Betsy was going to make a visit at Whitehall; but, in crossing
the Park, happened to meet the two Miss Airishes, who asked her to
take a turn with them: to which she replied, that she would gladly
accompany them, but had sent word to a lady that she was coming to
pass the whole evening with her. 'Nay,' said the elder Miss Airish,
'we have an engagement too at our own apartment, and can stay only
to walk once up the Mall, and down again.' Miss Betsy replied, that

would be no great loss of time; and so went with them. They had not proceeded many yards in their promenade, before Miss Betsy saw Mr. Trueworth, with Sir Bazil, coming directly towards them. The gentlemen bowed to her as they approached more near. A sudden thought that moment darting into Miss Betsy's head, she dropped her fan, as if by accident, as they were passing each other, just at Mr. Trueworth's feet: he stopped hastily to take it up, and presented it hastily to her. 'I am sorry, Sir,' said she, 'to give you this trouble.' – 'Whatever services, Madam, are in my power,' replied he, 'will be always a pleasure to myself.' – No more was said – the gentlemen and the ladies pursued their different routs. This little adventure, however, had a prodigious effect on Miss Betsy: she thought she saw something so gay and sparkling in the eyes of Mr. Trueworth, as denoted his mourning-habit belied his heart, and that he was not much affected with the death of her for whom decency and gratitude had obliged him to put it on. After the gentlemen were out of hearing, the two Miss Airishes began to give their judgments upon them – the one cried, they both were very pretty fellows; but the other accused them of want of politeness. – 'As they saw we had no man with us,' said she, 'they might, methinks, have offered their service to gallant us, especially as one of them seems to be acquainted with Miss Betsy.' But that young lady little regarded what was said on the occasion, being too much taken up with her own cogitations: she repeated internally the words of Mr. Trueworth; and as she was persuaded he was now at liberty to offer her all manner of services, she interpreted, that by whatever services were in his power, he meant to renew his services to her as a lover. This imagination elated her to a very high degree, but hindered her from holding any conversation with the two ladies she was with, as it was improper for her to say any thing on the subject which so much engrossed her thoughts. They all walked together up to Buckingham House, then turned back, and the two Miss Airishes took leave of her at St. James's – they went into the Palace, and she was proceeding towards Spring Garden, when she at a distance perceived Sir Bazil Loveit, Mr. Trueworth, Miss Mabel, and two ladies, whose faces she was entirely unacquainted with.

The reader will not be at a loss to guess, that these two were no other than Mrs. Wellair and Miss Harriot – they had been that afternoon to take leave of some friends, and had appointed to meet the gentlemen in the Mall: in their way thither they had called upon

Miss Mabel, and brought her with them. This little troop being all in the same sable livery, seemed so much of a family, as threw Miss Betsy into some sort of surprize: she knew not that Miss Mabel had the least acquaintance with Sir Bazil, nor even any more with Mr. Trueworth than having seen him a few times in her company. As they drew nearer, she made a motion to Miss Mabel, as if she was desirous of speaking to her; upon which that lady advanced towards her, with these words: 'I am sorry, Madam,' said she, 'as you are alone, that it is improper for me to ask you to join us.' – 'I am very glad, Madam, you do not,' replied Miss Betsy, very much piqued, 'because I should be obliged to refuse you.' She no sooner uttered these words than she passed hastily on, and Miss Mabel returned to her company, who waited for her at some paces distance.

It must be acknowledged, that Miss Betsy had cause to be alarmed at a speech of this nature, from a lady of Miss Mabel's politeness and good humour; she thought there must be some powerful reasons, which had obliged her to make it; and what those reasons could be, seemed at present an impenetrable secret. She was too much disconcerted to be able to pass the whole evening, as she had promised the lady she went to, she would do; she therefore pretended a sudden indispostion, took her leave, and went home, in order to be at full liberty to ruminate on what had passed in the Park.

She had not been many minutes in her own apartment, before she was interrupted in her meditations by the coming of her two brothers. Several bustos, pictures, pieces of old china, and other curiosities, belonging to a nobleman, lately deceased, being to be exposed to sale, the elder Mr. Thoughtless had an inclination to become a purchaser of such of them as he should find agreeable to his fancy, but was willing to have his sister's judgment in the matter; and it was to engage her to go with him the next morning about twelve o'clock, when the goods were to be exhibited to publick view, that had occasioned him and Mr. Francis to make her this visit. It is not to be doubted, but that she was willing to oblige him in that point; she assured him she would be ready against he came to call on her.

When she was alone, she began to run over in her mind, all the particulars of what had passed that evening in the Park, and found something very extraordinary on the whole. It had seemed extremely odd to her, that Mr. Trueworth and Sir Bazil did not join her and the two Miss Airishes; but then she thought she could easily account for their not doing so, and that Mr. Trueworth did not chuse to enter into any conversation with her, because Sir Bazil had happened to see her at Miss Forward's, and might possibly have entertained no favourable idea of her on that score; she, therefore, with a great deal of readiness, excused Mr. Trueworth for this omission, especially as she was possessed of the fancy, that the compliment with which he returned her fan, and the look he assumed during that action, seemed to tell her he wished for an opportunity of adding something more tender. But when she came to consider on the second meeting, she was indeed very much at a loss to fathom the meaning of what she had seen; she knew a thousand accidents might have occasioned an acquaintance between Miss Mabel and Sir Bazil; and also, that the little she had with Mr. Trueworth might have been casually improved; but could not find the least shadow of reason why that lady should tell her it was improper for to ask her to join company with them. Though she had of late seen that lady less frequently than usual; yet, whenever they did meet, it was with the greatest civility and appearance of friendship: she had, in reality, a sincere regard for her, and imagined the other looked upon her with the same; and therefore could not but believe the shyness she put on in the Park, when speaking to her, must have some very powerful motive to occasion it. Suspense was, of all things, what Miss Betsy could least bear: she resolved to be convinced, though at the expence of that pride she would not have forfeited on any other account. – 'In spite of the ill-manners she has treated me with,' said she, 'I will go once more to her – satisfy my curiosity as to the manner of her behaviour, and then never see her more.'

To be more sure of finding her at home, she thought it best to make the visit she intended in the morning; accordingly, she sent to her brother, that being obliged to go to a lady, who had desired to see her, she could not wait for his coming to call on her, but would not fail to meet him at the place of sale, about the hour he had mentioned. This promise she thought it would be easy for her to perform, as she designed to stay no longer with Miss Mabel than would be sufficient to get some light into a thing which at present gave her so much perplexity.

She went about eleven o'clock; but was strangely surprized, on her coming to the house, to find all the windows shut up; and after the chairman had knocked several times, the door was opened by Nanny, the little prating wench, who had lived at Mr. Goodman's. – 'Nanny,' cried Miss Betsy, 'bless me! do you live here?' – 'Yes, Madam,' answered she, 'I have lived here ever since my master Goodman died.' – 'I am glad of it,' returned Miss Betsy: 'but, pray, is your lady at home?' – 'O, dear Madam,' said the girl, 'my lady! – why, Madam, don't you know what's done to-day?' – 'Not I,' replied she – 'pr'ythee what dost mean? What done?' – 'Lord, Madam,' said Nanny, 'I wonder you should not know it! – my lady is married today.' – 'Married!' cried Miss Betsy hastily; 'to whom?' – 'To one Sir Bazil Loveit, Madam,' replied the other; 'and Mr. Trueworth is married too, to one Miss Harriot, Sir Bazil's sister: my old master gave both the brides away. I believe the ceremony is over by this time; but as soon as it is, they all bowl away for Sir Bazil's seat in Staffordshire: they say there will be open house kept there, and the Lord knows what doings. All the servants are gone – none but poor me left to look after the house.' – 'Mr. Trueworth married!' cried Miss Betsy, in the greatest confusion; 'I thought his mistress had been dead.' – 'No, no, Madam,' said Nanny; 'you mean Mrs. Blanchfield – I know all that story – I was told it by one who comes often here: Mr. Trueworth, I assure you, never courted her; she was only in love with him, and on hearing his engagement with Miss Harriot, took it to heart, poor soul, and died in a few days, and has left him half her fortune, and a world of fine things to Miss Harriot.'

She was going on with this tittle-tattle; but Miss Betsy was scarce in a condition to distinguish what she said; she leaned her head back against the chair, and was almost fainting away. The maid perceiving the change in her countenance, cried out, 'Lord, Madam, you are not well! – shall I get you any thing? But, now I think on it, there is a bottle of drops my lady left behind her in the dressing-room; I'll run and fetch them.' She as going to do as she said; but Miss Betsy, recovering of herself, called to her to stay, saying she had no occasion for any thing. 'Lord, Madam,' said she, 'I did not think the marriage of Mr. Trueworth would have been such a trouble to you, or I would not have told you any thing of it. I am sure you might have had him if you would; I remember well enough how he fought for you with Mr. Staple, and how he followed you up and down wherever you went. For that matter, Miss Harriot has but your leavings.' – 'I give myself no trouble who has him,' replied Miss Betsy, disdainfully: 'it is not him I am thinking of; I was only a little surprized that Miss Mabel should make such a secret of her affairs to me.' – 'You know, Madam,' said Nanny, 'that my lady is a very close woman: but I wonder, indeed, she should tell you nothing of it; for I have heard her speak the kindest things of you.' – 'Well, it is no matter,' replied Miss Betsy. 'Farewel, Nanny.' Then bid the chairmen go on. The confusion she was in hindered her from directing the chairmen where to go; so they were carrying her home again, till she saw herself at the end of the street where she lived; but then, recollecting all at once where she had appointed to meet her brothers, she ordered them to go to Golden Square.

It seemed as if fate interested itself in a peculiar manner for the mortification of this young lady; every thing contributed to give her the most poignant shock her soul could possibly sustain. It was not enough that she had heard the cruel tidings of what she looked upon as the greatest of misfortunes, her eyes must also be witness of the stabbing confirmation. The place of sale was within two houses of Sir Bazil's; but, as she had never heard where that gentleman lived, could have no apprehensions of the spectacle she was to be presented with. On her chair turning into the square, she saw that side of it, to which she had directed the men to carry her, crouded with coaches, horses, and a great concourse of people; some waiting for the bridal bounty, but more as idle spectators. At first, she imagined it was on the account of the sale; but the same instant almost shewed her her mistake.

Several footmen, with wedding-favours in their hats, two of whom she knew by their faces, as well as by their liveries, belonged to Mr. Trueworth, were just mounting their horses. The crowd was so thick about the door, that it was with some difficulty the chair passed on; and she had an opportunity of seeing much more than she desired. There were three coaches and six: in the first went Sir Bazil and the new-made Lady Loveit, the father of Miss Mabel, and a young lady whom Miss Betsy had sometimes seen in her company; in the second were seated Mr. Trueworth, his bride, Mrs. Wellair, and a grave old gentleman; the third was filled by four maid-servants, and the two valet de chambres of the two bridegrooms, with a great deal of luggage before and behind. The ladies and gentlemen were all in extreme rich riding-habits; and the footmen, eleven in number, being all in new liveries, and spruce fellows, the whole cavalcade altogether made a very genteel appearance.

Miss Betsy, in spite of the commotions in her breast, could not forbear standing a little in the hall, after she had got out of her chair; till the whole had passed. 'Well!' said she to herself, with a deep sigh, 'all is over, and I must think no more of Trueworth! But wherefore am I thus alarmed? He has long since been lost to me – nor did I love him!'

She assumed all the courage her pride could supply her with, and had tolerably composed herself before she went up into the sale-room; yet not so much but a paleness, mixed with a certain confusion, appeared in her countenance. Mr. Munden, who happened to be there, as well as her brothers, took notice of it, and asked if she was not well: to which she replied, with an uncommon presence of mind, that she was in perfect health, but had been frightened as she came along by a great black ox, who, by the carelessness of the driver, had like to have run his horns quite into the chair. Mr. Munden, who never wanted politeness, and knew how to put on the most tender air whenever he pleased, expressed an infinity of concern for the accident she mentioned: and this behaviour in him she either relished very well, or seemed to do so.

What credit her brothers gave to the story of the ox is uncertain: they, as well as all the company in the room, had been drawn to the windows by the noise of the cavalcade which had set out from Sir Bazil's. Every one was talking of it when Miss Betsy entered; and, it is very probable, the two Mr. Thoughtlesses might imagine it had an effect upon her, in spite of the indifference she had always pretended: they were, however, too prudent to take any notice, especially as Mr. Munden was present.

Whatever were the troubles of this young lady, her spirits enabled her to conceal them; and she gave her opinion of the goods to be disposed of with as much exactitude as if her mind had been taken up with no other thing.

Mr. Thoughtless made a purchase of the twelve Cæsars in bronze, and two fruit-pieces of Varelst's: and Mr. Munden, on Miss Betsy's expressing her liking of two very large curious jars, bought them, and presented them to her.

Nothing material passed here: but, the sale being over for that day, every one returned to their respective habitations, or whatever business or inclination called them.

VOLUME THE FOURTH

CHAPTER I

———•———

*Contains, among other particulars, an example of
forgiving goodness and generosity, worthy the imitation
of as many as shall read it*

THE constraint Miss Betsy had put on herself while in the presence
of the company she had been with, had been extremely painful to
her; but, when she got home, she gave a loose to tears, that common
relief of sorrows: yet, amidst all those testimonies of a violent
affection for Mr. Trueworth, she would not allow herself to imagine
that she was possessed of any for him; nor that the vexation she was
in proceeded from any other motive than that of finding a heart, that
had once been devoted to her, capable of submitting to the charms of
any other woman.

All she could bring herself to acknowledge was only that she had
been very much to blame in treating the proposals of Mr. Trueworth
in the light manner she had done: she now wondered at herself for
having been so blind to the merits of Mr. Trueworth's family, estate,
person, and accomplishments; and accused herself, with the utmost
severity, for having rejected what, she could not but confess, would
have been highly for her interest, honour, and happiness, to have
accepted.

Thus deeply was she buried in a too late repentance, when a letter
was brought to her, the superscription of which was wrote in a hand
altogether unknown to her. On opening it, she found the contents as
follows.

'Marshalsea Prison.

To Miss Betsy Thoughtless.

Madam,

After the just though severe resolution your last informed me you had taken of never seeing nor receiving any thing from me more, I tremble to approach you. Fearing you would not vouchsafe to open this, knowing from whence it came, I got a person to direct it for you; and cannot assure myself you will, even now, examine the contents so far as to see the motive which emboldens me to give you this trouble.

I have long since rendered myself unworthy your friendship – it is solely your compassion and charity that I now implore. The date of this petition, in part, will shew you the calamity I labour under. I have languished in this wretched prison for upwards of a month, for debts my luxury contracted, and which I vainly expected would be discharged by those who called themselves my admirers: but, alas! all the return they make for favours they so ardently requested, is contempt. I have been obliged to make away with every thing their gallantry bestowed, for my support.

All the partners of my guilty pleasures – all those who shared with me in my riots, are deaf to my complaints, and refuse a pitying ear to the distress they have in a great measure contributed to bring upon me. My creditors, more merciful than my friends or lovers, have consented to withdraw their actions; and I shall have my discharge on paying the fees of this loathsome prison. Three guineas will be sufficient to restore my liberty; which, if I am so fortune once more to obtain, I will think no labour, though ever so hard or abject, too much, if it can enable me to drag on my remains of life in true penitence.

Dear Madam, if, by favouring me with the sum I mention, you are so good as to open my prison-gate, Heaven will, I doubt not, reward the generous bounty: and, if the Almighty will vouchsafe to hear the prayers of an abandoned creature like me, I shall never cease to invoke his choicest blessings may be showered down on the head of my charming deliverer.

I shall send to-morrow morning a poor honest woman, whom I can confide in, for your answer. I beseech you to be assured that, if once freed from this detested place, no temptations, of what kind soever, shall ever prevail upon me to return to my yet more detested former course of life; and am determined to fly to some remote corner of the kingdom, as distant from London as from L——e; and there endeavour to earn a wretched pittance, by means how low soever I care not.

Your grant of the request I make you at this time, will save both the soul and body of her who is, with the most unfeigned contrition, Madam, your most humble, and most unfortunate servant,

A. FORWARD.'

Utterly impossible was it for this unhappy creature to have sent her petition at a more unlucky time. Miss Betsy, full of the idea of the misfortune she had sustained in the loss of Mr. Trueworth, could not be reminded of Miss Forward, without being also reminded that the first occasion of his disgust was owing to her acquaintance with that woman.

'Infamous creature!' cried Miss Betsy, as soon as she had done reading; 'she deserves no compassion from the world, much less from me. No, no! there are but too many objects of charity to be found; and I shall not lavish the little bounty I am able to bestow, on a wretch like her!'

These were the first reflections of Miss Betsy on receiving so unexpected a petition; but they soon subsided, and gave way to others of a more gentle nature. 'Yet,' said she, 'if the poor wretch is sensible of her faults, and truly resolved to do as she pretends, it would be the utmost cruelty to deny her the means of fulfilling the promise she makes of amendment.

'How unhappy is our sex!' continued she, 'either in a too much or too little sensibility of the tender passion! She was, alas! too easily influenced by the flatteries of the base part of mankind; and I too little grateful to the merits of the best.'

In fine, the natural goodness of her disposition got the ascendant over all considerations that opposed the grant of Miss Forward's request. 'My acquaintance with her has been fatal to me,' said she; 'but that was less owing to her fault than my own folly.'

Accordingly, she sent by the woman who came next morning, as mentioned in the letter, four guineas, inclosed in a piece of paper, and wrote to her in these terms.

'To Miss Forward.

Madam,
Though I cannot but look upon your misfortunes as justly fallen on you, yet heartily commiserate them. If your penitence is sincere, I doubt not but you will, some way or other, be enabled to pursue a more laudable course of life than that which has brought you into this

distress. I add one guinea to the sum you requested; and wish it were in my power to do more, being your real well-wisher, and humble servant,

E. THOUGHTLESS.'

Though no one could have more refined notions of virtue, nor a greater abhorrence for vice, than this young lady, yet never did she hate the persons of the guilty; nor would judge with that severity of their faults which some others, much less innocent, are apt to do.

It pleased her to think that, by this donation, she should gladden the heart of an afflicted person, who had been of her acquaintance, how unworthy soever of late she had rendered herself; and this little interruption of her meditations contributed a good deal to compose her mind, after the sudden shock it had sustained on the score of Mr. Trueworth's marriage.

But she had very shortly another and more agreeable relief. Sir Ralph and Lady Trusty came to town; which she no sooner was informed of, and where a house had been taken for their reception, than she went early the next morning to pay her respects, and testify the real satisfaction she conceived at their arrival.

Nothing of business would probably have been said to her on this first visit, if her two brothers had not come in immediately after. The first compliments on such an occasion being over – 'Sir Ralph,' said the elder Mr. Thoughtless, 'we have wished for your coming to town on many accounts; but none so much as that of my sister, who is going to be married, and has only waited to intreat you will do her the favour of disposing of her hand.'

The good baronet replied, that there was nothing he should do with greater pleasure, provided it were to a person worthy of her. 'That, Sir,' said the elder Mr. Thoughtless, 'we have taken care to be convinced of; and I doubt not but you will think as we do, when you shall be informed of the particulars.' Miss Betsy blushed, but uttered not a word, either to oppose or to agree to what had been said.

Lady Trusty perceiving her in some confusion, led her into another room, in order to talk seriously to her on many things she had in her head.

CHAPTER II

———•———

Is very full of business

THE two brothers of Miss Betsy having some reason to apprehend she would still find some pretence, if possible, to evade fulfilling the promise she had made them in regard to Mr. Munden; and also that he, finding himself trifled with, might become weary of prosecuting so unavailing a suit, and break off as Mr. Trueworth had done, resolved to omit nothing in their power for bringing to a conclusion an affair which seemed to them so absolutely necessary for securing the honour of their family in that of their sister.

They suspected that their putting off the marriage till the arrival of Sir Ralph and Lady Trusty, was only to gain time, and invent some excuse to get that lady on her side: they, therefore, judged it highly proper to acquaint her previously with the motives which made them so impatient to see their sister disposed of, and by that means prevent her ladyship from being prepossessed by any ideas the other might prepare for that purpose.

Accordingly, Mr. Francis Thoughtless having been informed by letter of the day in which they intended to be in town, he went on horseback, and met them at the inn where they dined, about twenty miles from London.

That good lady was so much troubled at the recital he made her of Miss Betsy's late adventures, that she could not forbear letting fall some tears; and, though she laid the blame of her ill-conduct chiefly on her having lived so long under the tuition and example of a woman such as Lady Mellasin, yet she could not but allow there was a certain vanity in her composition, as dangerous to virtue as to reputation, and that marriage was the only defence for both.

Sir Ralph, who was an extreme facetious, good-natured man, was a little pleasant on what his lady had said on this occasion. 'You forget, my dear,' cried he, 'how many ladies of late have broke the conjugal hoop, and think themselves justified in doing so, by having been prevailed upon to enter into it without inclination. Remember the words of the humorous poet Hudibras –

> "Wedlock without love, some say,
> Is but a lock without a key;
> And 'tis a kind of rape to marry
> One, who neglects, cares not for ye;
> For what does make it ravishment,
> But being 'gainst the mind's consent?"

'Does Miss Betsy,' continued he, to Mr. Francis, 'love the gentleman you would have her marry?' To which the other replied, that the temper of his sister was too capricious for any one to be able to judge of the real situation of her heart, or even for herself to be fully assured of it.

He then proceeded to inform him how long Mr. Munden had courted her, and of the great encouragement she had always given to his addresses; her submitting the decision of the affair to the elder Mr. Thoughtless's inspection into the circumstances of his estate, which being found agreeable to the report made of it, she now only waited, or pretended to wait, for the approbation of Sir Ralph, as being, by her father's will, constituted her guardian.

'Well, then,' said Sir Ralph, 'since it is so, and you are all desirous it should be a match, I shall not fail to give my verdict accordingly.'

As impatient as the two brothers were to see her married, and out of the way of those temptations she at present lay under, they could not be more so than Lady Trusty now was: she doubted not that the virtue and good-sense of that young lady would render her a very good wife, when once she was made one; and therefore heartily wished to see her settled in the world, even though it were to less advantage than her beauty, and the many good qualities she was possessed of, might entitle her to expect.

It was in order to do every thing in her power to bring about what she thought so good a work, that she had drawn Miss Betsy from the company, and retired with her into the closet, in the manner already related.

Miss Betsy, who knew nothing of all this, or even that her brother had gone to meet them on the road, was extremely surprized to find, by the discourse with which Lady Trusty entertained her, that no part of what had happened to her, ever since the death of Mr. Goodman, was a secret to her ladyship.

She presently saw, however, it must be by her brother Frank that this intelligence had been given; and was not at all at a loss to guess the motive of his having done it. 'I find, Madam,' said she, 'that all the errors and inadvertencies I have been guilty of are betrayed to you; and am far from being sorry they are so, since the gentle reproofs you take the trouble to give me, are so many fresh marks of the friendship with which you vouchsafe to honour me, and which I shall always esteem as my greatest happiness. I flatter myself, however,' continued she, 'that the remembrance of what has lately befallen me, and the imminent dangers I have escaped, will enable me to regulate my conduct in such a manner as to give your ladyship no farther pain on my account.'

Lady Trusty, on this, embraced her with the utmost tenderness; and told her, that there were few things she either wished or hoped for with greater ardency than to see her happily settled, and freed from all temptations of what kind soever.

This worthy lady then fell on the subject of Mr. Munden; and recapitulated all the arguments which had been already urged, to persuade her to come to a determination. In fine, she left nothing unsaid that was suitable to the occasion.

Miss Betsy listened to her with the most submissive attention; and, after a short pause, replied in these terms – 'Madam,' said she, 'I am convinced, by my own reason as well as by what your ladyship has been pleased to say, that I have, indeed, gone too far with Mr. Munden to be able to go back with honour; and, since I find he has the approbation of all my friends, shall no longer attempt to trifle with his pretensions.'

'You will marry him, then?' cried Lady Trusty. 'Yes, Madam,' answered Miss Betsy; and added, though not without some hesitation, 'Since my marriage is a thing so much desired by those to whose will I shall always be ready to submit, Mr. Munden has certainly a right to expect I should decide in his favour.'

She said no more, but hung down her head, and Lady Trusty was going to make some reply – perhaps to ask how far her heart acquiesced in the consent her tongue had given – but was prevented by Sir Ralph, who, pushing open the door of the room where they were, told her she engrossed his fair charge too long – that it was now time for himself and her brothers to have some share in their conversation.

'Some polite wives, Sir Ralph,' said Lady Trusty, laughing, 'would not have excused so abrupt a breaking in upon their privacy; and I assure you, if you had interrupted us a moment sooner, you might have spoiled all, for Miss Betsy has but just given me her promise to marry Mr. Munden.'

'I should have been heartily sorry indeed,' said he, 'if my over zeal had rendered me a Marplot on this occasion: but come,' continued he, 'since the young lady has at last resolved, let us carry the joyful news to her brothers.'

In speaking these words he gave one of his hands to Lady Trusty, and the other to Miss Betsy, and led them into the dining-room, where the Mr. Thoughtlesses were: 'Well, gentlemen,' said he, 'your sister has at last consented to give you a brother; pray, thank her for the addition she is going to make to your family.'

'I hope,' said the elder Mr. Thoughtless, 'she will find her own happiness in doing so.' The yonger added something to the same purpose. After this the conversation turned chiefly on the solid satisfaction of a married life, in which Miss Betsy took but little part, only saying to her two brothers, 'Well, since both of you have so high an opinion of matrimony, and will needs have me, who am by some years younger than either of you, lead the way, I hope I shall soon see you follow the example.'

'Our elder brother,' said Mr. Francis, 'may, doubtless, marry whenever he pleases; and, as for my part, when it can be proved that I have an offer made me equally advantageous to what you have rejected, and I should refuse it, I could not be angry with the world for condemning my want of judgment.'

'No more of that,' cried Sir Ralph; 'you see she hears reason at last.' Lady Trusty would fain have persuaded the gentlemen to stay dinner there; but they excused themselves, as expecting company at home, and said, if possible they would return toward evening: she would not, however, permit Miss Betsy to take leave; and her continuing there that whole day happened to bring things somewhat sooner a conclusion, than perhaps they otherwise would have been.

Mr. Munden, as soft and compalisant as he carried it to Miss Betsy, was very much disgusted in his mind at her late behaviour; he found she loved him not, and was far from having any violent inclination for her himself; but the motives which had made him persevere in his courtship, after being convinced of the indifference she had for him, made him also impatient to bring the affair to as speedy a result as possible. Sir Ralph was the last person to whom she had referred the matter; he had heard by accident of that gentleman's arrival, and went to her lodgings, in order to see in what manner she would now receive him; but not finding her at home, called at the house of Mr. Thoughtless, who had always been very propitious to his suit.

On the two brothers returning from Sir Ralph's, they met him just coming out of the house; the elder desired him to walk in – told him, with a great deal of freedom, that Sir Ralph was come to town; that the business having been communicated to him, he approved of the match, and his sister had consented. Mr Munden received this information with all the seeming transport of a man passionately in love; he made them a thousand retributions for the part they had taken in his interest; and they expressed no less satisfaction in the accomplishment of his desires. After some few compliments on both sides, the elder Mr. Thoughtless informed him, that Miss Betsy was to stay the whole day with Sir Ralph and Lady Trusty; that himself and brother had promised to return thither in the evening, and that he should be glad if he would accompany them, in order that when they were all together, every thing might be settled for the completion of the nuptials.

It is not to be doubted but that the lover readily embraced this proposition; and an hour for his waiting on them being prefixed, he took his leave, the company that was to dine with Mr. Thoughtless that instant coming in.

CHAPTER III

———•———

Will not let the reader fall asleep

I BELIEVE the reader will easily perceive, that it was owing to the apprehensions of Miss Betsy's fluctuating disposition, that her brothers testified so great an impatience for bringing the affair of her marriage to a conclusion; and also, that it was to confirm her in her resolution, and reconcile her to the promise she had made, that Lady Trusty had kept her with her that whole day.

The arguments urged by that worthy lady, the obliging and chearful manner in which they were delivered, joined to the facetious and entertaining remarks which Sir Ralph had occasionally made, had indeed a great effect, for the present, on the too wavering and uncertain mind they were intended to fix.

Though she was far from expecting Mr. Munden could come that evening with her brothers, or even from imagining he could as yet be informed of what had passed in his favour, yet she was not displeased when she saw him enter; and if she looked a little confounded, it was rather to be attributed to modesty than anger.

That gentleman having made his first compliments to Sir Ralph and Lady Trusty, on his being presented to them, flew directly to Miss Betsy, and expressed his sense of the happiness her brothers had made him hope, in terms the most passionate that words would form. She received what he said to her, on this occasion, with a sweetness which must have infinitely charmed a heart truly sensible of the tender passion, that even Mr. Munden, though less delicate than he pretended, could not but be greatly affected with it.

In fine, the behaviour of both towards each other, gave great contentment to all the friends of Miss Betsy; and her elder brother, for form's sake, recapitulating the proposal of Mr. Munden, concerning her settlement and jointure, Sir Ralph gave that approbation in publick which he before had done in private: the intended bridegroom and Mr. Thoughtless agreed to go the next morning to Mr. Markland the lawyer, and give him the necessary instructions for drawing up the marriage articles.

They broke not up company till the night was pretty far advanced; and Mr. Thoughtless not having his own coach there, a hackney set them all down at their respective habitations.

Thus far all went extremely well: the parties chiefly concerned seemed perfectly satisfied with each other, and with themselves, for the agreement they had mutually entered into; and there appeared not the least likelihood of any future difficulty that would arise to interrupt, or delay the consummation of the so much desired nuptials.

Miss Betsy had not as yet had time to meditate on what she had given her promise to perform: the joy she found her compliance had given all her friends – the endearing things they said to her upon the occasion, and the transport Mr. Munden had expressed, on seeing himself so near the end of all his wishes – had kept up her spirits; and she imagined, while in their presence, that her inclination had dictated the consent her lips had uttered.

But when she was alone, shut up in her own apartments – when she no longer received the kind caresses of her smiling friends, nor the flattering raptures of her future husband – all the lively ideas which their conversation and manner of behaviour towards her had inspired, vanished at once, and gave place to fancies, which must justly bear the name of splenetic.

'I must now look upon myself,' said she, 'as already married: I have promised – it is too late to think of retracting. A few days hence, I suppose, will oblige me to the performance of my promise; and I may say, with Monimia in the play –

> "I have bound up for myself a weight of cares;
> And how the burden will be borne, none knows."

'I wonder,' continued she, 'what can make the generality of women so fond of marrying? It looks to me like an infatuation; just as if it were not a greater pleasure to be courted, complimented, admired, and addressed, by a number, than be confined to one, who, from a slave, becomes a master; and, perhaps, uses his authority in a manner disagreeable enough.

'And yet it is expected from us. One has no sooner left off one's bib and apron, than people cry – "Miss will soon be married!" – and this man, and that man, is presently picked out for a husband. Mighty ridiculous! they want to deprive us of all the pleasures of life, just when one begins to have a relish for them.'

In this humour she went to bed; nor did sleep present her with images more pleasing: sometimes she imagined herself standing on the brink of muddy, troubled waters; at others, that she was wandering through desarts, overgrown with thorns and briars, or seeking to find a passage through some ruined building, whose tottering roof seemed ready to fall upon her head, and crush her to pieces.

These gloomy representations, amidst her broken slumbers, when vanished, left behind them an uncommon heaviness upon her waking mind: she rose, but it was only to throw herself into a chair, where she sat for a considerable time, like one quite stupid and dead to all sensations of every kind.

At last, remembering that they were all to dine at her brother's that day by appointment, she rouzed herself as well as she was able, and started from the posture she had been in; 'I see I am at the end of all my happiness,' said she, 'and that my whole future life is condemned to be a scene of disquiet; but there is no resisting destiny – they will have it so; I have promised, and must submit.'

On opening a little cabinet, in which she always kept those things she most valued, in order to take out some ornaments to put on that day, the picture of Mr. Trueworth stared her in the face. 'Ah!' said she, taking it up, and looking attentively upon it, 'if my brother Frank and Lady Trusty had been in town when the original of this made his addresses to me, I should then, as now, have been compelled to have given my hand. It is likely, too, I should have yielded with the same reluctance. Blinded by my vanity – led by mistaken pride – I had not considered the value I ought to have set upon his love. He had not then done any thing for me more than any other man, who pretended courtship to me, would have done. I know not how it is, I did not then think him half so agreeable as I now find he is. What a sweetness is there in these eyes!' cried she, still looking on the picture. 'What an air of dignity in every feature! – wit – virtue – bravery – generosity – and every amiable quality that can adorn mankind, methinks are here comprized.

'But to what purpose do I now see all these perfections in him?' went she on. 'He is the right of another; he has given himself to one, who knows better than my unhappy self to do justice to such exalted merit: he thinks no more of me; and I must henceforth think no more of him!'

She ended these words with a deep sigh, and some tears; then laid the picture up, and endeavoured to compose herself as well as she could.

She was but just dressed when Mr. Munden came to wait on her, and conduct her to her brother's, where they were to dine: he told her he had been with the elder Mr. Thoughtless at the lawyer's, about the writings; 'So that now, my angel!' said he, 'I flatter myself that my days of languishment are near a period.'

He took the freedom of accompanying these words with a pretty warm embrace. – 'Forbear, Mr. Munden,' cried she, with the most forbidding coldness; 'you have yet no right to liberties of this nature.'

'Cruel and unkind Miss Betsy!' resumed he; 'must nothing, then, be allowed to love, and all be left to law?' He then went on with some discourses of the passion he had for her, and the joy he felt in the thoughts of his approaching happiness: to all which she made very short replies; till at last it came into her head to interrupt him in the midst of a very tender exclamation, by saying, 'Mr. Munden, I forgot to mention one thing to you; but it is not yet too late – I suppose you design to keep a coach?'

This a little startled him; and, looking upon her with a very grave air – 'Madam,' said he, 'you are sensible my estate will not permit me to oblige you in this point.' – 'And can you imagine I will ever marry to trudge on foot?' cried she.

'I should be both sorry and ashamed,' replied he, 'to see you do that; but there are other conveniences, which will, I hope, content you, till fortune puts it in my power to do otherwise.'

He then reminded her of the expectations she had frequently heard him make mention of, concerning his hopes of soon obtaining both an honourable and lucrative employment; and assured her, that as soon as he had procured a grant of it, he would set up an equipage accordingly.

But this did not at all satisfy her; she insisted on having a coach directly, and gave him some hints, as if she would not marry without one; which very much nettling him, he desired she would remember

her promise, which was absolutely given, without the least mention of
a coach being made.

'I would not have you,' said she, 'insist too much on that promise,
lest I should be provoked to give you the same answer Leonora, in
the play, gives to her importunate lover –

> "That boasted promise ties me not to time;
> And bonds without a date, they say, are void."

Mr. Munden could not now contain his temper – he told her he
could not have expected such treatment after his long services, and
her favourable acceptance of them – that he thought he merited, at
least, a shew of kindness from her; and, in fine, that she did not act
towards him as became a woman of honour.

This was a reproach which the spirit of Miss Betsy was too high to
bear; she, blushing with indignation, and casting the most disdainful
look upon him, was about to make some answer, which, perhaps, in
the humour he then was, would have occasioned him to retort in such
a manner as might have broken off all the measures which had been
so long concerting, if a sudden interruption had not prevented it.

Mr. Francis Thoughtless, not knowing anything of Mr. Munden's
being there, and happening to pass that way, called on his sister, to
know if she was ready to go to his brother's, it being near dinner-
time; he immediately perceived, by both their countenances, that
some brulée had happened between them; and, on his asking, in a
gay manner, the cause of it, Mr. Munden made no scruple to relate
the sum of what had passed. The brother of Miss Betsy, though in
his heart very much vexed with her, affected to treat what Mr.
Munden had said, as a bagatelle; and, calling to his sister's footman
to get a hackney-coach to the door, made them both go with him to
his brother's; saying, they would there adjust every thing.

CHAPTER IV

———————•———————

Contains, among other particulars, certain bridal admonitions

THOUGH Mr. Francis Thoughtless did not judge it convenient to reproach his sister in the presence of Mr. Munden, on the complaints of that gentleman, yet she had no sooner vented the little spleen she had been that instant possessed of, than she began to excuse herself of having been too poignant to a person whom she had promised to make her husband.

To atone, therefore, for the severity of her late behaviour – 'This is a good, handsome, clean hack,' said she with a smile; 'one would think my fellow had pitched on such a one on purpose, to keep me from regretting my not having one of my own.'

'I only wish, Madam,' replied Mr. Munden, 'that you might be reconciled to such things as are in my power to accommodate you with, till I am so happy to present you with every thing you can desire.' – 'Let us talk no more of that,' cried she; 'be assured that, whatever I may have said, I am far from thinking the happiness of life consists in grandeur.'

Mr. Munden, on these words, kissed her hand; and she permitted him to hold it between his till they came out of the coach.

This, indeed, had been the very last effort of all the maiden pride and vanity of Miss Betsy; and Mr. Munden henceforward had no reason to complain of her behaviour towards him.

Sir Ralph Trusty, in regard to his age and character, had the honour of nominating the day for the celebration of their nuptials; and Miss Betsy made no excuses, or order to protract the time, but agreed with as much readiness as her future bridegroom could have wished.

The good Lady Trusty, as well as the two Mr. Thoughtlesses, however, being not yet able to assure themselves that nothing was to be feared from the uncertainty of her temper, did every thing in their power to keep her in good-humour with her fate; and to their endeavours it may, perhaps, be ascribed, much more than to the force of her own resolution that she ceased to be guilty of any thing that might give the least cause of discontent to Mr. Munden, or betray that which, in spite of all she could do, preyed upon herself.

To these assiduities of her friends, another motive might also be added for the keeping up her spirits, which was, that of her mind being continually employed: Mr. Munden had taken a very handsome house – the upholsterer received all the orders for the furnishing it from her – there were, besides, many other things necessary for the rendering it compleat, that were not in his province to supply; the going, therefore, to shops and warehouses for that purpose, took a very great part of her time. What could be spared from these, and some other preparations for her wedding, either Lady Trusty, or her brothers, had the address to engage: one or other of them were always with her, till the night was far advanced, and sleep became more welcome than any meditations she could indulge.

The appointed day at length arrived – she was conducted to the altar by Sir Ralph Trusty; where, being met by Mr. Munden, the ceremony of marriage was performed, none being present at it but Lady Trusty and her two brothers; for as she could not have celebrated it with that pomp and eclat agreeable to a woman of her humour, she had earnestly desired it might be done with all the privacy imaginable.

The indissoluble knot now tied, they proceeded to Pontac's; where an elegant entertainment being prepared for them by Mr. Munden's orders, they dined; and afterwards went all together to a lodging Mr. Munden had hired, for a small time, in a little village five or six miles from London.

This he had done to oblige his bride, who had told him she desired to be lost to the world till the first discourse of their marriage should be over, to avoid the visits and congratulations of their friends on that occasion.

It would be needless to tell the reader that there was a general scene of joy amidst this little company: Mr. Munden expressed, and indeed, felt, an infinity of transport, on having triumphed over so many difficulties, which had for a long time continually risen to impede his wishes. The two Mr. Thoughtlesses were extremely overjoyed, on thinking a period was put to all their cares in relation to their sister: Lady Trusty also, and Sir Ralph, looking on this marriage, as things were circumstanced, highly convenient for Miss Betsy, were very much pleased; so that it must necessarily follow, that an event, which cost so much pains to bring about, must occasion a general content in the minds of all those who had so strenuously laboured for it.

Amidst this scene of joy, Miss Betsy herself was the only person whose countenance discovered the least pensiveness; nor was hers any more than what might be attributed to the modesty of a virgin bride.

Lady Trusty, however, who had observed her all day with an attentive eye, thought it proper to give her some admonitions concerning her future behaviour, before she took her leave.

To this end, she drew her into another room, apart from the company; and having told her she had something of moment to say to her, began to entertain her in the following manner.

'My dear child,' said she, 'you are now, I fear, more through your compliance with the desires of your friends than through your own inclination, entered into a state, the happiness of which greatly depends on the part you act in the first scenes of it: there are some women who think they can never testify too much fondness for their husbands, and that the name of wife is a sufficient sanction for giving a loose to the utmost excesses of an extravagant and romantick passion; but this is a weakness which I am pretty certain you will stand in no need of my advice to guard against. I am rather apprehensive of your running into a contrary extreme, equally dangerous to your future peace, as to that of your husband. A constant and unmoved insensibility will in time chill the most warm affection, and, perhaps, raise suspicions in him of the cause, which would be terrible indeed: beware, therefore, I conjure you, how you affect to despise, or treat with any marks of contempt, or even of too much coldness, a tenderness which he has a right to expect you should return in kind, as far, at least, as modesty and discretion will permit you to bestow.

'As to your conduct in family affairs,' continued this good lady, 'I would have you always confine yourself to such things as properly

appertain to your own province, never interfering with such as belong
to your husband: be careful to give to him all the rights of his place,
and, at the same time, maintain your own, though without seeming to
be too tenacious of them. If any dispute happen to arise between you
concerning superiority, though in matters of the slightest moment,
rather recede a little from your due than contend too far; but let him
see you yield more to oblige him than because you think yourself
bound to do so.

'Mr. Munden, I flatter myself, has every qualification to make you
happy, and to shew that your friends, in advising you to marry him,
have not misled your choice: but as perfection is not to be found on
this side the grave, and the very best of us are not exempt from the
frailties of human nature, whatever errors he may happen to fall into,
as it does not become you to reprimand him, I wish you would never
take notice you have observed them. A man of the strictest honour
and good sense may sometimes slip – be guilty of some slight
forgetfulness – but then he will recover of himself, and be ashamed
of his mistake; whereas reproaches only serve to harden the indignant
mind, and make it rather chuse to persevere in the vices it detests,
than to return to the virtues it admires, if warned by the
remonstrances of another.

'But, above all things,' added she, 'I would wish you to consider
that those too great gaieties of life you have hitherto indulged, which,
however, innocent, could not escape censure while in a single state,
will now have a much worse aspect in a married one.

'Mistake me not, my dear,' pursued she, after a pause, finding, by
Miss Betsy's countenance, that what she had said on this score had
stung her to the quick; 'I would not have you deprive yourself of
those pleasures of life which are becoming your sex, your age, and
character; there is no necessity that, because you are a wife, you
should become a mope: I ony recommend a proper medium in these
things.'

Her ladyship was going on, when Miss Betsy's servants, whom she
had ordered to bring such part of her baggage as she thought would
be needful while she staid in that place, came with it into the
chamber; on which this kind adviser told her fair friend that she
would refer what she had farther to say on these subjects till another
opportunity.

Miss Betsy replied, that she would treasure up in her heart all the
admonitions she should at any time be pleased to give her; and that

she hoped her future conduct would demonstrate that no part of what her ladyship had said was lost upon her.

With these words they returned into the dining-room; and the close of day soon after coming on, Sir Ralph and his lady, with the two Mr. Thoughtlesses, took leave of the bride and bridegroom, and came back to town.

CHAPTER V

———————•———————

Seems to demand, for more reasons than one, a greater share of attention than ordinary, in the perusal of it

THE fair wife of Mr. Munden (Miss Betsy now no more) had promised nothing at the altar that she was not resolved religiously to perform: she began seriously to consider on the duties of her place; she was ignorant of no part of them; and soon became fully convinced that on a strict observation of them depended her honour – her reputation – her peace of mind – and, in fine, all that was dear to a woman of virtue and understanding.

To give the more weight to these reflections, she also called to her mind the long perseverance of Mr. Munden – his constant assiduities to please her – his patient submitting to all the little caprices of her humour; and establishing in herself an assured belief of the ardour and sincerity of his affection to her, her gratitude, her good-nature, and good-sense, much more than compensated for the want of inclination; and without any of those languishments, those violent emotions, which bear the name of love, rendered her capable of giving more real and more valuable proofs of that passion than are sometimes to be found among those who profess themselves, and are looked upon by the world, as the most fond wives.

In spite of her endeavours, the thoughts of Mr. Trueworth would, however, sometimes come into her mind; but she repelled them with all her might: and as the merits of that gentleman would, in reality, admit of no comparison with any thing that Mr. Munden had to boast of, she laboured to overbalance the perfections of the one, by that tender and passionate affection with which she flattered herself she now was, and always would be, regarded by the other.

Thus happily disposed to make the bonds she had entered into easy to herself, and perfectly agreeable to the person with whom she was engaged, he had, indeed, a treasure in her beyond what he could ever have imagined, or her friends, from her former behaviour, had any reason to have expected; and, had he been truly sensible of the value of the jewel he possessed, he would have certainly been compleatly blessed: but happiness is not in the power of every one to enjoy, though Heaven and fortune deny nothing to their wishes. But of this hereafter.

At present, all was joy and transport on the side of the bridegroom – all complaisance and sweetness on that of the bride. Their whole deportment to each other was such as gave the most promising expectations of a lasting harmony between them, and gladdened the hearts of as many as saw it, and interested themselves in the felicity of either of them.

They continued but a few days in the retirement which had been made choice of for the consummation of their nuptials, Mr. Munden was naturally gay, loved company, and all the modish diversions of the times; and his wife, who, as the whole course of this history has shewn, had been always fond of them to an excess, and whose humour, in this point, was very little altered by the change of her condition, readily embraced the first proposal he made of returning to town, believing she should now have courage enough to appear in publick, without testifying any of that shamefacedness on account of her marriage, which she knew would subject her to the ridicule of those of her acquaintance who had a greater share of assurance.

For a time, this new-married pair seemed to have no other thing in view than pleasure. Mr. Munden had a numerous acquaintance his wife not a few. Giving and receiving entertainments, as yet, engrossed their whole attention – each smiling hour brought with it some fresh matter for satisfaction; and all was chearful, gay, and jocund.

But this was a golden dream, which could not be expected to be of any long continuance. The gaudy scene vanished at once, and soon a darkening gloom overspread the late enchanting prospects. Mr. Munden's fortune could not support these constant expences. He was obliged to retrench somewhere; and, not being of a humour to deny himself any of those amusements he was accustomed to abroad, he became excessively parsimonious at home, insomuch that the scanty allowance she received from him for housekeeping, would scarcely furnish out a table fit for a gentleman of an estate far inferior to that he was in possession of, to sit down to himself; much less to ask any friend who should casually come in to visit him, to partake of.

Nothing can be more galling to a woman of any spirit, than to see herself at the head of a family without sufficient means to support her character as such in a handsome manner. The fair subject of this history had too much generosity, and, indeed, too much pride, in her composition, to endure that there should be any want in so necessary an article of life; and, as often as she found occasion, would have recourse for a supply to her own little purse.

But this was a way of going on which could not last long. She complained of it to Mr. Munden; but, though the remonstrances she made him were couched in the most gentle terms that could be, he could not forbear testifying a good deal of displeasure on hearing them. He told her that he feared she was a bad œconomist; and that, as she was a wife, she ought to understand that it was one of the main duties of her place to be frugal of her husband's money, and be content with such things as were suitable to his circumstances.

The surly look with which these words were accompanied, as well as the words themselves, made her easily perceive, that all the mighty passion he had pretended to have had for her, while in the days of courtship, was too weak to enable him to bear the least contradiction from her now he became a husband.

She restrained, however, that resentment which so unexpected a discovery of his temper had inspired her with, from breaking into any violent expressions; and only mildly answered, that she should always be far from desiring any which would be of real prejudice to his circumstances; but added, that she was too well acquainted with his fortune, not to be well assured it would admit of keeping a table much more agreeable to the rank he held in life, and the figure he made in other things.

'I am the best judge of that,' replied he, a little disdainfully; 'and also, that it is owing to your own want of management that my table is so ill supplied. I would wish you, therefore, to contrive better for the future; as you may depend upon it that, unless my affairs take a better turn, I shall not be persuaded to make any addition to my domestick expences.'

'I could wish then, Sir,' cried she, with a little more warmth, 'that henceforth you would be your own purveyor; for I confess myself utterly unable to maintain a family like ours on the niggard stipend you have allotted for that purpose.'

'No, really, Madam,' answered he, very churlishly, 'I did not marry in order to make myself acquainted with how the markets go, and become learned in the prices of beef and mutton. I always looked on that as the province of a wife; it is enough for me to discharge all reasonable demands on that score: and, since you provoke me to it, I must tell you, Madam,' continued he, 'that what my table wants of being compleat, is robbed from it by the idle superfluities you women are so fond of, and with which, I think, I ought to have no manner of concern.'

As she was not able to comprehend the meaning of these words, she was extremely astonished at them; and, in a pretty hasty manner, demanded a detail of those superfluities he accused her of: on which, throwing himself back in his chair, and looking on her with the most careless and indifferent air he could assume, he replied in these terms.

'I know not,' said he, 'what fool it was that first introduced the article of pin-money into marriage-writings. Nothing, certainly, is more idle; since a woman ought to have nothing apart from her husband; but, as it is grown into a custom, and I have condescended to comply with it, you should, I think, of your own accord, and without giving me the trouble of reminding you of it, convert some part of it, at least, to such uses as might ease me of a burden I have, indeed, no kind of reason to be loaded with. As, for example,' continued he, 'coffee, tea, chocolate, with all the appendages belonging to them, have no business to be enrolled in the list of house-keeping expences, and consequently not to be taken out of what I allow you for that purpose.'

Here he gave over speaking; but the consternation his wife was in preventing her from making any immediate answer, he resumed his discourse. 'Since we are upon this topick, my dear,' said he, 'it will be the best to tell you at once what I expect from you – it is but one thing more – which is this. You have a man entirely to yourself; I am willing he should eat with the family; but as to his livery and wages, I think it highly reasonable you should be at the charge of.'

The innate rage which, during the whole time he had been talking, swelled her breast to almost bursting, would now no longer be confined. 'Good Heavens!' cried she, 'to what have I reduced myself! – Is this to be a wife! – Is this the state of wedlock! – Call it rather an Egyptian bondage! – The cruel task-masters of the Israelites could exact no more. Ungrateful man! pursued she, bursting into tears, 'is this the love, the tenderness, you vowed?'

Overwhelmed with passion, she was capable of uttering no more; but continued walking about the room in a disordered motion, and all the tokens of the most outrageous grief and anger. He sat silent for some time; but, at last, looking somewhat more kindly on her than he had done – 'Pr'ythee, my dear,' said he, 'don't let me see you give way to emotions so unbecoming of yourself, and so unjust to me. You shall have no occasion to complain of my want of love and tenderness – you know what my expectations are; and when once I have gained my point, you may be sure, for my own sake, I shall do every thing suitable to it. I would only have you behave with a little prudence for the present.'

In concluding these words, he rose and took hold of her hand; but approached her with an air so cold and indifferent, as was far from atoning, with a woman of her penetration, for the unkindness of his late proposal. 'No, Mr. Munden!' cried she, haughtily turning from him, 'do not imagine I am so weak as to expect, after what you have said, any thing but ill-usage.'

'I have said nothing that I have cause to repent of,' answered he; 'and hope that, when this heat is over, you will do me the justice to think so too. I leave you to consider it, and bring yourself into a better humour against my return.' He added no more; but took his hat and sword, and went out of the room.

She attempted not to call him back; but retired to her chamber, in order to give a loose to passions more turbulent than she had ever known before.

CHAPTER VI

———•———

Contains a second matrimonial contest, of worse consequence than the former

WHOEVER considers Miss Betsy Thoughtless in her maiden character, will not find it difficult to conceive what she now endured in that of Mrs. Munden. All that lightened her poor heart, all that made her patiently submit to the fate her brothers had, in a manner, forced upon her, was a belief of her being passionately loved by the man she made her husband: but thus cruelly undeceived by the treatment she had just met with from him, one may truly say, that if it did not make her utterly hate and despise him, it at least destroyed at once, in her, all the respect and good-will she had, from the first moment of her marriage, been endeavouring to feel for him.

It is hard to say whether her surprize at an eclaircissement she had so little expected, her indignation at Mr. Munden's mean attempt to encroach upon her right, or the shock of reflecting, that it was by death alone she could be relieved from the vexations with which she was threatened by a man of his humour, were most predominant in her soul; but certain it is, that all together racked her with most terrible convulsions.

She was in the midst of these agitations, when Lady Trusty came to visit her. In the distraction of these thoughts she had forgot to give orders to be denied to all company, which otherwise she would doubtless have done, even without excepting that dear and justly valued friend.

She endeavoured, as much as possible, to compose herself, and prevent all tokens of discontent from appearing in her countenance, but had not the power of doing it effectually enough to deceive the penetration of that lady; she immediately perceived that something extraordinary had happened to her; and, as soon as she was seated, began to enquire into the cause of the change she had observed in her.

Mrs. Munden, on considering what was most prudent in a wife, from the first moment of her becoming so, had absolutely resolved always to adhere, as strictly as possible, to this maxim of the poet –

> 'Secrets of marriage should be sacred held,
> Their sweets and bitters by the wife conceal'd.'

But finding herself pretty strongly pressed by a lady to whom she had the greatest and most just reason to believe she ought to have nothing in reserve, she hesitated not long to relate to her the whole story of the brulée she had with her husband.

Lady Trusty was extremely alarmed at the account given her; and because she would be sure not to mistake any part of it, made Mrs. Munden repeat several times over every particular of this unhappy dispute; then, after a pause of some minutes, began to give her advice to her fair friend in the following terms.

'It grieves me to the soul,' said that excellent lady, 'to find there is already any matter of complaint between you – you have been but two months married; and it is, methinks, by much too early for him to throw off the lover, and exert the husband: but since it is so, I would not have you, for your own sake, too much exert the wife; I fear he is of a rugged nature – it behoves you, therefore, rather to endeavour to soften it, by all the means in your power, than to pretend to combat with unequal force; you know the engagements you are under, and how little relief all the resistance you can make will be able to afford you.'

'Bless me, Madam!' cried Mrs. Munden, spiritously, 'would your ladyship have me give up, to the expence of house-keeping, that slender pittance allowed for cloaths and pocket-money in my marriage articles?'

'No, my dear,' cried Lady Trusty; 'far be it from me to give you any such counsel: on the contrary, I am apprehensive that, if you should suffer yourself to be either menaced, or cajoled, out of even the smallest part of your rights, it is possible that a man of Mr. Munden's disposition might hereafter be tempted to encroach upon the whole, and leave you nothing you could call your own.

'It is very difficult, if not wholly impossible,' continued she, 'to judge with any certainty, how to proceed with a person whose temper one does not know; I am altogether a stranger to that of Mr. Munden, nor can you as yet pretend to be perfectly acquainted with it: all I can say, therefore, is, that I would have you maintain your own privileges, without appearing to tenacious of them.'

'I have then no other part to take,' said Mrs. Munden, 'than just to lay out, in the best manner I can, what money he is pleased to allow, without making any addition, what accidents soever may happen to demand it.'

'I mean so,' replied Lady Trusty; 'and whenever there is any deficiency, as some there must necessarily be, in what might be expected from your way of living, I would not have you seem to take the least notice of it: behave, as if entirely unconcerned, contented, and easy; leave it to him to complain; and when he does so, you will have an opportunity, by shewing the bills of what you have laid out, of proving, that it is not owing to your want of good management, but to the scarcity of the means put into your hands, that his table is so ill supplied; but still let every thing you urge on this occasion be accompanied with all the softness it is in your power to assume.'

To this Mrs. Munden, with a deep sigh, made answer, that though she was an ill dissembler, and besides had little room, from her husband's late carriage towards her, to flatter herself with any good effect of her submission, yet she would endeavour to follow her ladyship's counsel, in making the experiment, however irksome it might be to her to do so.

They had a very long conversation together on this head; during the whole course of which Lady Trusty laboured all she could to persuade the other to look on her situation in a much less disagreeable light then, in reality, it deserved.

But how little is it in the power of argument to reason away pain! one is much more deeply affected with what one feels than what one hears: the heart of Mrs. Munden was beset with thorns, which all the words in the world would have been ineffectual to remove; disappointed in every thing that could have rendered this marriage supportable to her – her good-nature abused – her spirit humbled and depressed – no considerations were of force to moderate her passions, but that melancholy one that, as her misfortunes were without a remedy, the best, and indeed the only relief that fate permitted, was in patiently submitting.

She acted, nevertheless, in every respect, for several days, conformable to the method Lady Trusty had prescribed, and restrained her temper so as neither by word or action to give Mr. Munden any just cause of offence: he also kept himself within bounds, though it was easy for her to perceive, by his sullen deportment, every time he was at table, how ill he was satisfied with the provisions set before him.

A cold civility on the one side, and an enforced complaisance on the other, hindered the mutual discontent that reigned in both their hearts from being perceptible to any who came to visit them, and also from breaking into any indecencies between themselves; till one day a gentleman of fine consideration in the world happening, unexpectedly, to come to dine with them, Mr. Munden was extremely shocked at being no better prepared for his entertainment.

'What!'my dear,' said he to his wife, 'have you nothing else to give us?' To which she replied, with a great presence of mind, 'I am quite ashamed and sorry for the accident; but you know, my dear, we both intended to dine abroad to-day, so I gave a bill of fare accordingly; and this gentleman came too late to make any addition to what I had ordered.'

It may be easily supposed the guest assured them that there needed no apologies, that every thing was mighty well, and such like words of course: so no more was said upon this subject.

But the pride of Mr. Munden filled him with so much inward rage and spite, that he was scarce able to contain himself till his friend had taken leave; and he no sooner was at liberty to say what he thought proper, without incurring the censure of being unmannerly or unkind, than he began to reproach her in the most unjust and cruel terms, for having, as he said, exposed him to the contempt and ridicule of a person who had hitherto held him in the highest esteem.

She made no other reply than that she was no less confounded than himself at what had happened – that it was not in her power to prevent it – that she could wish to be always prepared for the reception of any friend – and that she was certain, when he reflected on the cause, he would be far from laying any blame on her.

In speaking these words, she ran to her cabinet; and, as Lady Trusty had directed, produced an account to what uses every single shilling she had received from him had been converted since the last dispute they had with each other on this score.

In presenting these papers to him, 'Read these bills,' said she, 'and be convinced how little I deserve such treatment from you: you will find that there are no items inserted of coffee, tea, or chocolate; articles,' continued she, with an air a little disdainfully, 'which you seemed to grumble at, though yourself and friends had the same share in, as well as me and mine.'

'Rot your accounts!' cried he, tearing the papers she had given him into a thousand pieces; 'have you the folly to imagine I will be troubled with such stuff? It is sufficient I know upon the whole what ought to be done; and must plainly tell you, once for all, that you should rather think of retrenching your expences, than flatter yourself with expecting an increase of my allowance to you.'

'My expences! my expences,' reiterated she with vehemence, 'what does the man mean?' – 'My meaning,' answered he, sullenly, 'would need no explanation, if you had either any love for me, or prudence enough to direct you to do what would entitle you to mine: but since you are so ignorant, I must tell you, that I think my family too much encumbered; you have two maids – I do not desire you to lessen the number, but they are certainly enough to wait upon you in the morning; I have a man, for whom I never have any employment after that time, and he may wait at table, and attend you the whole afternoon; I see therefore no occasion you have to keep a fellow merely to loiter about the house, eat, drink, and run before your chair when you make your visits. I insist, therefore, that you either discharge him, or consent to give him his livery and wages, and also to allow for his board out of your own annual revenue of pin-money.'

What usage was this for a young lady, scarce yet three months married; endued with every qualification to create love and esteem, accustomed to receive nothing but testimonies of admiration from as many as beheld her, and addressed with the extremest homage and tenderness by the very man who now seemed to take pride in the power he had obtained of thwarting her humour, and dejecting that spirit and vivacity he had so lately pretended to adore.

How utterly impossible was it for her now to observe the rules laid down to her by Lady Trusty! Could she, after this, submit to put in practice any softening arts she had been advised, to win her lordly tyrant into temper? Could she, I say, have done this, without being guilty of a meanness, which all wives must have condemned her for?

But though the answers she gave to the proposal made her by this ungenerous husband, were such as convinced him she would never be prevailed upon to recede from any part of what was her due by contract, and though she testified her resentment, on his attempting such a thing, in terms haughty enough, yet did she confine herself wtihin the limits of decency, not uttering a single word unbecoming of her character, either as the woman of good understanding, or the wife.

Mr. Munden's notions of marriage had always been extremely unfavourable to the ladies – he considered a wife no more than an upper-servant, bound to study and obey, in all things, the will of him to whom she had given her hand: and how obsequious and submissive soever he appeared when a lover, had fixed his resolution to render himself absolute master when he became a husband.

On finding himself thus disappointed in his aim, he was almost ready to burst with an inward malice; which not daring to wreak, as perhaps at that time he could have wished, he vented it in an action mean and spiteful indeed, but not to be wondered at in a man possessed of so small a share of affection, justice, or good-nature.

The reader may remember, that Mr. Trueworth, in the beginning of his courtship to Miss Betsy, had made her a present of a squirrel; she had still retained this first token of love, and always cherished it with an uncommon care: the little creature was sitting on the ridge of it's cell, cracking nuts, which his indulgent mistress had bestowed upon him: the fondness she had always shewn of him put a sudden thought into Mr. Munden's head; he started from his chair, saying to his wife, with a revengeful sneer, 'Here is one domestick, at least, that may be spared!' With these words he flew to the poor harmless animal, seized it by the neck, and throwing it with his whole force against the carved work of the marble chimney, it's tender frame was dashed to pieces.

All this was done in such an instant, that Mrs. Munden had not time to make any attempt for preventing it; but the sight of so disastrous a fate befalling her little favourite, and the brutality of him who inflicted it, raised emotions in her, which she neither endeavoured, nor, at that instant, could have the power to quell.

'Monster!' cried she, 'unworthy the name man; you needed not have been guilty of this low piece of cruelty, to make me see to what a wretch I am sacrificed.' – 'Nor was there any occasion for exclamations such as these,' replied he, scornfully, 'to make me know that I am married to a termagant!'

Many altercations of the like nature passed between them; to which Mrs. Munden was the first that put a period: finding herself unable to restrain her tears, and unwilling he should be witness of that weakness in her, she flew out of the room, saying at the same time, that she would never eat, or sleep with him again.

CHAPTER VII

●

Gives an exact account of what happened in the family of Mr. Munden, after the lamentable and deplorable death of his lady's favourite squirrel; with several other particulars, much less significant, yet very necessary to be told

IF Mr. Munden had set his whole invention to work, in order to find the means of rendering himself hateful in the eyes of his wife, he could not have done it more effectually than by his savage treatment of her beloved squirrel: many circumstances, indeed, concurred to set this action of his in the most odious light that could possibly be given it.

In the first place, the massacre of so unhurtful a creature, who never did any thing to provoke it's fate, had something in it strangely splenetic and barbarous.

In the next, the bloody and inhuman deed being perprated by this injurious husband, merely in opposition to his wife, and because he knew it would give her some sort of affliction, was sufficient to convince her, that he took pleasure in giving pain to her, and also made her not doubt but he would stop at nothing for that purpose, provided it were safe, and came within the letter of the law.

It grieved her to be deprived of a little animal she so long had kept, with whose pretty tricks she had so often been diverted; and it must be confessed, that to be deprived of so innocent a satisfaction, by the very man she had looked upon as bound by all manner of ties to do every thing to please her, was enough to give the most galling reflections to a woman of her delicacy and spirit.

But there was still another, and, by many degrees, a more aggravating motive for her indignation: if she had purchased this squirrel with her own money, or if it had been presented to her by any other hands than those of Mr. Trueworth, not only the loss would have been less shocking to her, but also the person, by whom she sustained that loss, would, perhaps, have found less difficulty in obtaining her forgiveness.

She kept her promise, however, and ordered a bed to be made ready for her in another room. Mr. Munden came not home that night till very late; and being told what his wife had done, took not the least notice of it; but happening to meet her the next morning, as she was coming down stairs, 'So, Madam,' said he, 'I suppose you fancy this obstinate disobedience to your husband is mighty becoming in you!'

'When a husband,' answered she, 'is ignorant of the regard he ought to have for his wife, or forgets to put it in practice, he can expect neither affection nor obedience, unless the woman he has married happens to be an idiot.'

They passed each other with these words; and she went directly to Lady Trusty, being impatient to acquaint her with the behaviour of her husband towards her since she last had seen her.

This worthy lady was astonished beyond measure at the recital; it seemed so strange to her, that a gentleman of Mr. Munden's birth, fortune, and education, should ever entertain the sordid design of obliging his wife to convert to the family uses what had been settled on her for her own private expences, that she could not have given credit to it from any other mouth than that of the weeping sufferer: his killing of the squirrel also, though a trifle in itself, she could not help thinking denoted a most cruel, revengeful, and mean mind.

But how much soever she condemned him in her heart, she forebore expressing the whole of her sentiments on this occasion to his wife, being willing, as they were joined to each other by the most sacred and indissoluble bonds, rather to heal, if possible, the breach between them, than to add any thing which might serve to widen it.

She told her that, though she could not but confess that Mr. Munden had behaved towards her, through this whole affair, in a manner very different from what he ought to have done, or what might have been expected from him, yet she was sorry to find that she had carried things to that extremity; particularly she blamed her for having quitted his bed: 'Because,' said she, 'it may furnish him with some matter of complaint against you; and, likewise, make others suspect you have not that affection for him which is the duty of a wife.'

Mrs. Munden making no answer to this, and looking a little perplexed – 'I do not mean, by what I have said,' resumed Lady Trusty, 'to persuade you to take any steps towards a reconciliation; that is, I would not have you confess you have been in the wrong, or tell him you are sorry for what you have done: that would be taking a blame upon yourself you do not deserve; and he would imagine he had a right to expect the same on every trifling occasion. It may be, he might be imperious and ill-natured enough to create quarrels merely for the sake of humbling your spirit and resentment into submission.

'But as to live in the manner you are likely to do together,' continued she, 'cannot but be very displeasing in the eye of Heaven, and must also expose both of you to the censure and contempt of the world, when once it comes to be known and talked of, some means must be speedily found to bring about an accommodation between you.'

'O, Madam!' cried the other, hastily interrupting her, 'how impossible is it for me ever to look with any thing but disdain and resentment on a man who, after so many protestations of eternal love, eternal adoration, has dared to treat me in this manner! No!' added she, with greater vehemence than before, 'I despise the low, the grovelling mind; light and darkness are not more opposites than we are, and can as easily agree.'

'You must not think, nor talk in this fashion,' said the good lady; 'all you can accuse him of will not amount to a separation; besides, consider how odd a figure a woman makes who lives apart from her husband; there is an absolute necessity for a reconciliation; and, as it is probable that neither of you will pursue any measures for that purpose, it is highly proper your friends should take upon them to interpose in the affair.'

It was a considerable time before Mrs. Munden could be persuaded, by all the arguments Lady Trusty made use of, that either her duty, her interest, or her reputation, required she should forgive the insults she had received from this ungrateful and unworthy husband.

The good lady would not, however, give over till she had prevailed on her not only to listen to her reasons, but also to be at last perfectly convinced by them: this point being gained, the manner in which the matter should be conducted was the next thing that employed her thoughts.

It seemed best to her that the two Mr. Thoughtlesses should not be made acquainted with any part of what had passed, if the business she so much wished to see accomplished could be effected without their knowledge: her reason for it was this; they were both men of pretty warm dispositions, especially the younger; and as they had been so assiduous in promoting this match, so early a breach, and the provocations given for it by Mr. Munden, might occasion them to shew their resentment for his behaviour in a fashion which would make what was already very bad, much worse.

'Sir Ralph is a man in years,' said she; 'has been your guardian; and I am apt to believe that, on both these accounts, his words will have some weight with Mr. Munden: the friendship which he knows is between us, will also give me the privilege of adding something in my turn; and, I hope, by our joint mediation, this quarrel may be made up, so far, at least, as that you may live civilly together.'

Mrs. Munden made no other reply to what her ladyship had said, than to thank her for the interest she took in her affairs, and the trouble she was about to give Sir Ralph on her account.

The truth is, this young lady would in her heart have been much better satisfied that there had been a possiblity of being separated for ever from a person who, she was now convinced, had neither love nor esteem for her, rather than to have consented to cohabit with him as a wife, even though he should be prevailed upon to request it in the most seemingly submissive terms.

While they were in this conversation, a message came from Mr. Edward Goodman, containing an invitation to Sir Ralph and Lady Trusty, to an entertainment that gentleman had ordered to be prepared the next day for several of his friends, on a particular occasion; which, because the reader as yet is wholly ignorant of, it is highly proper he should be made acquainted with.

CHAPTER VIII

─────────●─────────

Presents the reader with some passages which could not conveniently be told before, and, without all doubt, have been for a long time impatiently expected

THE spirits of Lady Mellasin had for several months been kept up by the wicked agents she had employed in the management of the worst cause that ever was taken in hand: those subtle and most infamous wretches, in order to draw fresh supplies of money from that unhappy woman, had still found means to elude and baffle all the endeavours of Mr. Goodman's honest lawyer to bring the manner to a fair trial.

But, at last, all their diabolical inventions, their evasions, their subterfuges, failing, and the day appointed which they knew must infallibly bring the whole dark mystery of iniquity to light, when all their perjuries must be explored, and themselves exposed to the just punishment of such flagitious crimes, not one of them had courage to stand the dreadful test, nor face that awful tribunal they had so greatly abused.

Yet so cruel were they, even to the very woman, all the remains of whose shattered fortune they had shared among them, as not to give her the least warning of her fate; nor, till the morning which she was made to hope would decide every thing in her favour, did she know she was undone, deserted, and left alone to bear the brunt of all the offended laws inflict on forgery.

What words can represent the horror, the confusion, of her guilty mind, when neither the person who drew up the pretended will, nor neither of those two who had set their names as witnesses, appearing, she sent in search of them, and found they were all removed from their habitations, and fled no one could inform her where.

Scarce had she the time to make her escape out of the court, before word was given to an officer to take her into custody: not daring to go home, nor knowing to whom she could have recourse for shelter in this exigence, she ran, like one distracted, through the streets, till she came to one of the gates of St. James's Park; where, meeting with a porter, she sent him to her lodgings, to order her daughter Flora and Mrs. Prinks to come that instant to her.

Mrs. Prinks immediately obeyed the summons, but Miss Flora had the audacity to desire to be excused, being then dressing to go on a business which, indeed, she then imagined was of much more consequence to herself than any thing relating to her mother could possibly be.

After this dissolute and unfortunate creature was left by Mr. Trueworth, in the manner described in the third volume of this history, she gave a loose to agonies which only those who have felt the same can be capable of conceiving.

Her shrieks, and the request Mr. Trueworth had made on his going out, brought up the woman of the house herself, to administer what relief was in her power to a lady who seemed to stand in so much need of it.

Having prevailed on her to come down stairs, she seated her in a little room behind the bar; and as she saw the violence of her passions threw her into frequent faintings, neglected nothing which she thought might be of service to recover her spirits and compose her mind.

As she was thus charitably employed, a young gentleman who used the house, and was very free with all belonging to it, happened to come it. Miss Flora, besides being handsome, had something extremely agreeable and engaging in her air; and had her heart been possessed of half that innocence her countenance gave the promise of, her character would have been as amiable as it was now the contrary.

There are some eyes which shine through their tears, and are lovely in the midst of anguish; those of Miss Flora had this advantage, and she appeared, in spite of her disorder, so perfectly charming to the stranger, that he could not quit the place without joining his endeavours to those of the good-natured hostess, for her consolation, and had the satisfaction to find them much more effectual for that purpose.

The afflicted fair-one, finding herself somewhat better, thanked the good woman, in the politest terms, for the pains she had been at; but the gentleman would not be denied seeing her safe home in a coach; saying, the air, on a sudden, might have too violent an effect on her so lately recovered spirits; and that it was not fit she should be alone, in case of accidents.

Miss Flora was easily prevailed upon to accept his obliging offer; he attended her home – stayed about half an hour with her – and entreated she would give him permission to come the next day and enquire after her health.

She knew the world too well, and the disposition of mankind in general, not to see that there was something more than mere compassion in the civilities he had shewn to her: she examined his person – his behaviour – and found nothing in either that was not perfectly agreeable; and though she had really loved Mr. Trueworth to the greatest excess that woman could do, yet, as she knew he was irrecoverably lost, she looked upon a new attachment as the only sure means of putting the past out of her head.

A very few visits served to make an eclaircissement of the thoughts they had mutually entertained of each other; and as he had found by the woman of the tavern, that the distress of this young lady had been occasioned by a love-quarrel with a gentleman who had brought her into that house, he began with expressing the utmost abhorrence of that injustice and ingratitude which some were capable of: 'But,' said he, 'if some of us have neither love nor honour for those that love us, we all certainly love our own happiness; and he must be stupid and insensible, indeed,' added he, embracing her with the warmest transport, 'who could not find it eternally within these arms!'

'You all talk so,' answered she, with the most engaging smile she could put on: 'but as my youth – innocence – and, perhaps, a little mixture of female vanity – have once misled me, it behoves me to be extremely cautious how the tender impulse gets a second time possession of my heart.'

In short, she put him not to a too great expence of vows and protestations before she either was, or pretended to be, convinced of the sincerity of his passion, and also rewarded it in as ample a manner as his soul could wish.

It is certain, that for a time this new gallant behaved with the extremest fondness towards her – did every thing the most ardent lover could do to please her – he treated her – carried her to all publick places of entertainment – and, what in her present circumstances was most necesary to her, was continually making her very rich and valuable presents.

But it could not be expected that an amour, entered into in this manner, and which had no solid esteem on either side for it's foundation, would be of any long continuance; the gentleman had a great deal of good-nature, but was gay and inconstant as the most variable of his sex – he found a new charm in every face that presented itself to him; and, as he wanted no requisites to please the fair, he too seldom failed in his attempts upon them.

Miss Flora was not ignorant that he had many amusements of this kind, even while he kept up the most tender correspondence with her; but perceiving that reproaches and complaints were equally in vain with a man of his humour, she had the cunning to forbear persecuting him with either; and by appearing always easy, degagée, and unconcerned, preserved her acquaintance with him, and received proofs of his liberality long after she had lost those of his inclination.

On being told that he was going on a party of pleasure into the south of France, she exercised all her wit and artifice to engage him to permit her to be one of the company; but he treated this request as a mere bagatelle – said the thing was utterly impracticable – that none of the gentlemen took any ladies with them – so he would not have her think of it.

It was in order to take her leave of him before his departure, that she was going to his lodgings when Lady Mellasin had sent for her into the Park.

The cool reception he had given her, sent her home in a very ill-humour, which was greatly heighted by a letter which she found Mrs. Prinks had left for her on the table.

That woman having joined her lady in the Park, and consulted together what was to be done, they took a hackney-coach, and drove to an obscure part of the town, where they hired lodgings in a feigned name; after which Mrs. Prinks hurried home, packed up what cloaths and othere necessaries she thought would be immediately wanted; and, after having wrote a short account to Miss Flora of the misfortune that had happened, and given her directions where to come, returned, with all haste, to her disconsolate lady.

CHAPTER IX

———•———

Contains the catastrophe of Lady Mellasin's and her daughter Flora's adventures while on this side the globe

WHILE this unhappy little family were in their concealment, each of them set their whole wits to work to find some means by which Lady Mellasin might be extricated from that terrible dilemma she had brought herself into.

But as this was a thing in it's very nature, as affairs had been managed, morally impossible to be accomplished, all their endeavours to that purpose only served to shew them the extreme vanity of the attempt, and consequently to render them more miserable.

Despair, at length, and the near prospect of approaching want, so humbled the once haughty spirit of Lady Mellasin, that she resolved on writing to Mr. Edward Goodman – to make use of all her rhetorick to soothe him into forgiveness for the troubles she had occasioned him – and, in fine, to petition relief from the very man whom she had made use of the most villainous arts to prejudice.

The contents of her letter to that much-injured gentleman were as follows.

'To Edward Goodman, Esq.

Sir,
Appearances are so much against me that I scarce dare say I am innocent, though I know myself so, as to any intention of doing you injustice: I cannot, however, forbear giving you a short sketch of the imposition which has been practiced upon me, and in my name attempted to be put on you.

The will, which has occasioned this long contest between us, was brought me by a person who told me he had drawn it up exactly acccording to my late husband's instructions, the very evening before he died; the subscribing witnesses gave me the same assurance; and also added, that Mr. Goodman was so well convinced of my integrity, and the wrong he had done me by suspecting it, that had he lived only to the next morning, he had resolved to send for me home, and be reconciled to me in the face of the world: so that, if the thing was a piece of forgery, these men are only guilty – I am entirely free from any share in it.

But as these proceedings, which I have unhappily been prevailed upon to countenance, have given you a great deal of trouble and expence, I sincerely ask your pardon for it: this is all the atonement I can make to Heaven for offences more immediately my own.

I am very sensible, notwithstanding, that, by what I have done, I have not only forfeited my claim to such part of the effects of Mr. Goodman as appertain to the widow of an eminent and wealthy citizen, but, likewise, all my pretensions to the friendship and favour of the person he has made his heir: yet, Sir, however guilty I may seem to you, or how great my faults in reality may have been, I cannot help being of opinion that, when you remember I was once the wife of an uncle, whose memory you have so much cause to value, you will think the name and character I have borne, ought to defend me from publick infamy, parish-alms, and beggary.

Reduced as I am, it would ill become me to make any stipulations, or lay a tax on the goodness I am necessitated to implore. No, Sir; as I can now demand nothing, so, also, I can hope for nothing but from your compassion and generosity; and to these two amiable qualities alone shall ascribe whatever provision you shall think fit to make for me out of that abundance I was once in full possession of.

I shall add no more, than to intreat you will consider, with some portion of attention and good-nature, on what I have lately been, and what I at present am, the most unfortunate, and most forlorn of womankind,

M. MELLASIN GOODMAN.

P.S. My daughter Flora, the innocent partner of my griefs and sufferings, will have the honour to deliver this to you, and, I hope, return with a favourable answer.'

Lady Mellasin chose to send Miss Flora with this letter, as

believing her agreeable person, and manner of behaviour, would have a greater effect on that youthful heart of the person it was addressed to, than could have been expected from the formal and affected gravity of Mrs. Prinks.

It is not unlikely, too, but that she might flatter herself with the hopes of greater advantages by her daughter's going in person to Mr. Goodman's, than those which her letter had petitioned for. She had often heard and read of men whose resentment had been softened and melted into tenderness on the appearance of a lovely object: as the poet somewhere or other expresses it –

> 'Beauty, like ice, our footing does betray;
> Who can tread sure on the smooth, slipp'ry way?'

Miss Flora herself was also very far from being displeased at going on this errand; and as it was not proper for her to dress in the manner she would have done on making a visit to any other person, it cost her some time, before her setting out, to equip herself in such a deshabille as she thought would be most genteel and become her best.

She had the good fortune to find Mr. Goodman at home, and was immediately introduced to him. He was a little surprized at a visit made him by a young lady whom he had never seen before; but not enough to prevent him from receiving her with the utmost complaisance. He saluted her, seated her in a chair, and then asked her what commands she had to favour him with: on which, taking out the letter, and giving it to him, 'This, Sir,' said she, with a deep sigh, 'will inform you of the request that brings me here.'

Mr. Goodman read it hastily over; but, while he was doing so, could not forbear shaking his head several times; yet spoke nothing till after a pause of some minutes. 'Madam,' said he, 'as this is a business which I could not expect to have heard of, I must confess myself altogether unprepared how to proceed in it. If Lady Mellasin,' added he, 'will give herself the trouble to send in three or four days, she may depend on an answer from me.'

The coldness of these words, and the distant air he assumed while speaking them, so widely different from that with which he had accosted this lady on her first entrance, made her presently see she had nothing to hope from this embassy on her own account, and made her also tremble for that of her mother.

As he urged her not to stay, nor even gave the least hint that he was desirous of her doing so, she rose, and, with a most dejected air, took her leave; telling him, in going out, that she should not fail of acquainting Lady Mellasin with his commands; who, she doubted not, would be punctual in obeying them.

Mr. Goodman was, indeed, too well acquainted with the character of Miss Flora to be capable of receiving any impression from the charms nature had bestowed upon her, even though they had been a thousand times more brilliant than in effect they were, and she had not been the daughter of a woman who had rendered herself so justly hateful to him.

Lady Mellasin was shocked to the very soul at being told the reception her daughter had met with; and could not help looking upon it as a very bad omen of her future success. She doubted but by his saying that he must have time for deliberation, he meant that he would do nothing in this point, without having first consulted his friends; and she had no reason to expect that any of those he conversed with would give counsel in her favour.

To be reduced from a state of opulence and respect to one of poverty, contempt, and wretchedness, is terrible indeed! but much more so when accompanied with a consciousness of having deserved, by our vices and ill conduct, all the misfortunes we complain of.

Lady Mellasin having no pleasing reflection of having done her duty in any one point of life, it would not have been strange if, thus destitute of comfort from within, all succour from without, she had yielded herself to the last despair.

She, nevertheless, amidst all the distraction of her thoughts, still continued to testify a resolution seldom to be found among women of her abandoned principles; never departing from this maxim, that, in the worst of events, nothing was to be neglected. On the third day she sent Mrs. Prinks to wait upon Mr. Goodman for his answer; having experienced the little effect her daughter's presence had produced.

It is a thing well worth the observation of all degrees of people, that the truly generous never keep long in suspense the persons they think proper objects of their bounty. A favour that costs too much pains in obtaining, loses great part of it's value – it palls upon the mind of the receiver, and looks more like being extorted than bestowed.

Mr. Cowley, though a man whose great merit, one would think, should have set him above the necessity of making any request of a pecuniary nature, was certainly obliged, sometimes, to solicitations that were very uneasy to him, and drew from him this emphatick exclamation –

'If there's a man, ye gods, I ought to hate,
Attendance and dependance be his fate!'

It soon occurred to Mr. Goodman in what manner it would best become him to act towards this unhappy woman; and also what conditions ought to be stipulated on her part. He had been told, both by the lawyer and the two Mr. Thoughtlesses, that it was his late uncle's intention that she should not be left without a decent provision; and being willing to conform, as much as possible, to all the desires of a person whom he had always esteemed as a parent, he passed by the injury which, since his death, she had attempted to do to himself; and, within the time he had mentioned to Miss Flora, wrote an answer to the request in the following terms.

'To Lady Mellasin Goodman.

Madam,
Though you cannot but be sensible that your late base attempt to invalidate my dear uncle's will, excludes you from receiving any benefit from it; yet, as I am determined, as far as in my power, to make the example of that excellent man the rule of all my actions, I shall not carry my resentment, for the injustice you have done me, beyond what he expressed for those much greater injuries he sustained by your infidelity and ingratitude. It was not his intention you should starve; nor is it my desire you should do so.

I am willing, Madam, to allow you a pension of one hundred pounds per annum, to be quarterly paid into whose hands soever you shall think fit to appoint for that purpose; but it must be on condition that you retire forthwith, and pass the whole remainder of your days in some remote part of the kingdom. The farther you remove from a town where your ill conduct has rendered you so obnoxious, the better.

This, Madam, is what I insist upon; and is, indeed, no more than what your own safety demands from you. A very strict search is making after your accomplices; and if they, or any of them, shall happen to be found, it will be in vain for you to flatter yourself with escaping that punishment which the offended laws inflict on crimes of this nature: nor would it be in my power to shield you from that fate which even the meanest and most abject of those concerned with you must suffer.

As I should be extremely sorry to see this, I beg you, for your own sake, to be speedy in your resolution, which, as soon as you inform me, I shall act accordingly. I am, yours, &c.

E. GOODMAN.'

This he ordered to be delivered to any one who should say they came from Lady Mellasin; and Mrs. Prinks accordingly received it.

Lady Mellasin, in the miserable circumstances to which she had reduced herself, was transported to find she should not be entirely without support. As for her being obliged to quit London, she was not in the least shocked at it, as there was no possibility for her even to appear publickly in it; and she was rather desirous, than averse, to be out of a place which could no longer afford her those pleasures and amusements she had once so much indulged herself in the enjoyment of.

But when she considered on her banishment, and ran over in her mind what part of England she should make choice of for her asylum, the whole kingdom appeared a desart to her, when driven from the gaieties of the court and capital: she therefore resolved to go farther, and enter into a new scene of life, which might be more likely to obliterate the memory of the former. She had heard much talk of Jamaica – that it was a rich and opulent place – that the inhabitants thought of little else but how to divert themselves in the best manner the country afforded, and that they were not too strict in their notions either as to honour or religion – that reputation was a thing littler regarded among them: so that, in case the occasion that had brought her thither should happen to be discovered, she would not find herself in the less estimation.

She, therefore, hesitated not to write a second letter to Mr. Goodman, acquainting him with her desire to go to that plantation; and hinting to him that, if it would be giving him too great a trouble to remit the quarterly payments he mentioned, she should take it as a particular favour if he would be pleased to bestow on her such a sum as he should think proper, in lieu of the annuity he had offered.

Mr. Goodman was extremely pleased with this proposal; and several letters having passed between them concerning the conditions, he agreed to give her two hundred pounds in specie, to provide herself with sufficient necessaries for the voyage, and eight hundred more to be deposited in the hands of the captain of the ship, to be paid on her arrival; with which she appeared very well satisfied, and gave him the most solemn assurances never to trouble him again.

But Miss Flora was all distraction at this event: the thoughts of leaving dear London were equally irksome to her with those of death itself. Fain would she have staid behind; but what could she do? Without reputation – without friends – without money – there was no remedy but to share her mother's fortune. Mrs. Prinks also, who, by living so long with Lady Mellasin, known to be in all her secrets, and agent in her iniquitous proceedings, could have no character to recommend her to any other service, continued with the only person she, indeed, was fit to live with; and they all embarked together on board a ship that was then ready to sail.

All Mr. Goodman's friends congratulated him on the service he had done his country, in ridding it of three persons who, by perverting the talents Heaven had bestowed upon them, to the most vile purpose, were capable of doing the greatest mischiefs to the more innocent and unwary. It was on this occasion that he made the invitation before-mentioned.

CHAPTER X

———•———

Returns to the affairs of Mrs. Munden

THERE were present at the entertainment made by Mr. Goodman, several other of his friends, besides Sir Ralph and Lady Trusty, the two Mr. Thoughtlesses, and Mrs. Munden. The husband of that lady had also received an invitation to be one of the guests; but he pretended a previous engagement would not permit him to accept the favour intended him.

He made his excuse, however, in terms so polite, and seemingly sincere, that none of the company, excepting those who were in the secret of the disagreement between him and his wife, had any apprehensions that his absence was occasioned by any other motive that what his message had expressed.

Sir Ralph Trusty and his lady, who were the only persons who had the least suspicion of the truth of this affair, could not help being a good deal concerned at it; but they forbore taking any notice, till the latter, perceiving Mrs. Munden had retired to a window at the farther end of the room, in order to give herself a little air, stept hastily towards her, and, in a low voice, accosted her in these terms.

'I see plainly, my dear,' said she, 'through the excuse your husband has made for not complying with Mr. Goodman's invitation; and am heartily sorry to find this fresh proof of the disunion between you. It is high time something should be attempted to put things on a better footing. I will desire Sir Ralph to send for Mr. Munden to-morrow, and we will try what can be done.'

'Your ladyship is extremely good,' replied the other; 'and I shall be always ready to submit to whatever you shall think proper for me: but

I am determined to be entirely passive in this affair, and shall continue to live with Mr. Munden in the same manner I do at present, till a very great alteration in his behaviour shall oblige me to think I ought, in gratitude, to make some change in mine.'

Lady Trusty would not prolong the conversation, for fear of being observed; and they both rejoined the company. After this, there passed nothing of sufficient moment to acquaint the reader with; so that I shall only say, that, after a day, and great part of the ensuing night, spent in feasting, merriment and all that could exhilarate the spirits and excite good-humour, every one retired to their respective dwellings, highly satisfied with the manner in which they had been entertained by the younger merchant.

Lady Trusty was far from being forgetful of the promise she had made to her fair friend; and, after a serious consultation with Sir Ralph in what manner it was most proper to proceed, prevailed upon that gentleman, who was little less zealous than herself in doing good offices, to write the following billet to Mr. Munden.

'To George Munden, Esq.

Sir,
A business which, I am perfectly well assured, is of the utmost consequence both to your present and future happiness, obliges me to intreat the favour of seeing you this morning at my house; it not being so proper (for reasons I shall hereafter inform you of) for me to wait on you at yours.

As I have no other interest in what I have to impart, than merely the pleasure I shall take in doing you a service, and discharging what I think the duty of every honest man, I flatter myself you will not fail of complying immediately with my request; and, at the same time, believe me to be, what I am, with the greatest sincerity, Sir, your well-wisher, and most humble and most obedient servant,

RALPH TRUSTY.'

This letter being sent pretty early in the morning, Mr. Munden was but just out of bed when he received it – a breakfast much less pleasing to him than his chocolate. He doubted not but his wife had made Lady Trusty acquainted with the whole secret of his family-affairs; and therefore easily guessed on what score he was sent for in this pressing manner by Sir Ralph; and, as it was highly disagreeable to him to enter into any discussions on that head, it was some time before he could resolve within himself what answer he should send.

But whatever deficiencies there might be in this gentleman, none, excepting those of his own family, to whom he did not think it worth his while to be complaisant, could ever accuse him of want of politeness – a character so dear to him, that, perhaps he would not have forfeited it, even for the attainment of any other of the more shining and valuable virtues of his sex.

Perplexing, therefore, as he knew this interview must necessarily be to him, he could not think of behaving in an uncourtly manner to a gentleman of Sir Ralph Trusty's rank and fortune; and having ordered that the servant who brought the letter should come up, desired him, in the most affable terms, to acquaint his master that nothing should deprive him of the honour of attending him the moment he was dressed.

Sir Ralph Trusty, in his younger years, had lived very much in London, had kept the best company in it; and though he was perfectly sincere in his nature, and had a thorough contempt for all those idle superfluous ceremonies, which some people look upon as the height of good-breeding, and value themselves so much upon, yet he knew how to put them in practice when ever he found they would facilitate any point he had to gain; and as Mr. Munden was altogether the courtier in his behaviour, he thought it best to address him in his own way, and receive him rather in a manner as if he was about to praise him for some laudable action he had done, than make any remonstrances to him on a conduct which he wanted to convince him required some amendment.

After having said a great many obliging things to him, in order to bring him into a humour proper for his purpose, the politick old baronet began in these terms to open the business on which he had desired to speak with him.

'I have not words to make you sensible,' continued he, 'how much your absence was regretted yesterday by all the company at Mr. Goodman's, especially by the two Mr. Thoughtlesses, who, indeed, on all occasions, express the highest esteem and regard for you, both as a friend and brother; but I was more particularly affected, when, on coming home, my wife acquainted me with what she imagined the real cause that deprived us of you.

'She told me,' added he, 'that having the other day surprized Mrs. Munden in tears and great confusion, she would not leave her until she wrested from her a secret, which I am equally ashamed and sorry to repeat; but which you can be at no loss to guess at.'

Though Mr. Munden had foreseen on what account he was sent for, and had prepared himself for it, yet he could to forbear testifying some confusion; but, recovering himself from it as soon as he could, 'Yes, Sir Ralph, I easily perceive,' answered he, 'that my wife has been making some complaints against me to your lady, which, doubtless, have laid me under her displeasure, as I know the accuser has the advantage of the accused, in the opinion of those to whom they appeal.'

'Not at all,' cried Sir Ralph hastily; 'I dare answer that my wife is no less concerned for your sake, than for that of Mrs. Munden, at the unfortunate disagreement that has happened between you.'

As he was speaking these words, Lady Trusty, either by design or accident, passed by the door of the room where they were sitting. 'Come in, my dear,' said Sir Ralph to her, 'and justify yourself from being swayed against right reason, by any partial affection to your fair friend.'

'If you mean in the case of Mrs. Munden, as I suppose you do,' replied she, 'I can acquit myself with very great ease from any imputation on that score; and am ready, even before her husband, to give it as my judgment, that, in all disputes between persons who are married to each other, especially when carried to any height, neither of them are wholly faultless; for, though one may be the first aggressor, the other seldom, if ever, behaves so as not to incur some part of the blame.'

'Your ladyship is all goodness,' said Mr. Munden, very respectfully; 'and, in what you have said, discover not only a penetration, but also a love of justice, which can never be too much admired and applauded. What your ladyship has observed between me and Mrs. Munden, is exactly the thing; it is certain, that both of us have been to blame; I have, perhaps, acted in a manner somewhat too abruptly towards her, and she in one too resentful, and too imperious, towards me; and though I am willing to allow my dear Betsy all the merit of those good qualities she is possessed of, yet I cannot help giving her some part of the character Mr. Congreve ascribes to Zara in his Mourning Bride, and saying –

> "That she has passion, which outstrips the winds,
> And roots her reason up."

Lady Trusty, who, for the sake of Mrs. Munden's reputation, was so eager to patch up a reconciliation at any rate between her and her husband, would not seem to defend her behaviour as a wife, while she gently accused him of having too far exerted the authority of a husband.

In a word, both Sir Ralph and his lady managed in so artful a manner, still blending cajolings with remonstrances, that, when they came to enter into a discussion on this affair, Mr. Munden, whatever he thought in his heart, could not forbear seeming to yield to the justice of their reasonings.

He consented, though not without some scruples, and a much greater share of inward reluctance than his complaisance would permit him to make shew of, to add one guinea per week to his allowance for the expences of his table. As to the rest, he readily enough agreed to meet his wife half way towards a reconciliation; assured them, that he was far from requiring any other submission on her part, than what he would set her the example of in himself, and that he wished nothing more than to exchange forgiveness with her.

On this, Lady Trusty dispatched a servant directly to Mrs. Munden, to let her know she must needs speak with her immediately, which summons was no sooner delivered than complied with.

This prudent lady having cast about in her mind all that was proper to be done, in order to accomplish the good work she laboured for, and had so much at heart, would not leave it in the power of chance to disappoint what she had so happily begun; and having prevailed over the ill-nature and sourness of the husband, thought it equally necessary to prevent the resentment, or inadvertency, of the wife from frustrating her endeavours.

On being told that Mrs. Munden was come, she ran down stairs to receive her, led her into a parlour, and informed her, as briefly as she could, all that part which she thought would be most satisfactory to her, of the conversation which had passed between them and Mr. Munden on her score.

Finding what she said was received by the other more coolly than she wished, she took that privilege which her rank, her age, and the friendship she haf always shewn to her, might justly claim, to remonstrate to her, that it did not become her situation and character to stand too much upon punctilios at this time; when all that either was, or ought to be, dear to womankind, depended on a speedy accommodation with her husband: 'The unhappy brulée,' said she, 'has lasted too long – your servants must certainly know it – you cannot be assured of their secrecy – the whole affair, perhaps, with large additions to it, will soon become the talk of the town – every one will be descanting upon it; and how much soever Mr. Munden may be in fault, you cannot hope to escape your share in the censure.'

Poor Mrs. Munden, who looked upon this lady as a second mother, would not attempt to offer any thing in opposition to the arguments she used; and, besides, could not forbear avowing, within herself, the justice of them. 'Well, Madam,' answered she, with a deep sigh, 'I shall endeavour to follow your ladyship's advice; and, since I am a wife, will do my best to make the yoke I have submitted to, sit as lightly upon me as possible.'

Lady Trusty perceiving her spirits were very much depressed, omitted nothing, that the shortness of time would allow, to persuade her to believe, that her condition was not so unhappy, in reality, as she at present imagined it to be; and having brought her to somewhat of a more chearful temper, conducted her into the room where Sir Ralph and Mr. Munden were still discoursing on the matter in question.

'Welcome, my fair charge,' cried the former, taking her by the hand, and drawing her towards Mr. Munden; 'I have once already had the honour of giving you to this gentleman – permit me to do so a second time; I hope with the same satisfaction, on both sides, as at first.'

'On mine, by Heaven, it is!' replied Mr. Munden, flying hastily to embrace her, as she moved slowly forward; 'if my dearest Betsy will promise to forget what is past, the pains I have suffered, during this interruption of my happiness, will be a sufficient security for her, that I shall be very careful for the future to avoid doing any thing that may again subject me to the like misfortune.'

These words, and the tender air which he assumed in speaking them, were so much beyond what Mrs. Munden could have expected from him, after his late treatment of her, that all her pride, her anger, and even her indifference, subsided at that instant, and gave place to sentiments of the most gentle nature.

'You must believe,' answered she, with an infinity of sweetness in her voice and eyes, 'that I have also had my share of anguish: but whatever inquietudes you have sustained on my account must be forgotten on your part, as it shall be mine to make atonement for them by every thing in my power, which can flatter me with the hopes of doing so.'

Insensible and morose as Mr. Munden was, he could not avoid, on this obliging behaviour in his fair wife, being touched in reality with some soft emotions, which he so well knew how to magnify the appearance of, that not only herself, but the bye-standers, imagined he was the most transported man alive.

Impossible it is to express how much Sir Ralph, and his good lady, rejoiced to see this happy event: they entertained them very elegantly at dinner, in the afternoon they went all together to take the air in Kensington Gardens; and a great deal of company coming in the evening to visit Lady Trusty, every thing contributed to keep up the spirit and good-humour of the newly re-united pair.

CHAPTER XI

Contains some few particulars which followed the reconciliation

THOUGH this reconciliation wsa not altogether sincere on the side of Mr. Munden, yet being made in the presence of Sir Ralph and Lady Trusty, it kept him from giving any flagrant remonstrations, at present, that it was not so; and he continued to live with his amiable wife in the most seeming good harmony for some time.

She, on her part, performed with the utmost exactitude all she had promised to him; and though she could not be said to feel for him all that warmth of affection which renders the discharge of our duty so great a pleasure to ourselves, yet her good-nature and good-sense well supplied that deficiency, and left him no room to accuse her of the least failure in what might be expected from the best of wives.

During this interval of tranquillity, she lost the society of two persons, the tenderness of whose friendship for her she had experienced in a thousand instances: Mr. Francis Thoughtless, who had stayed so long in town, merely through the indulgence of his commanding officer, was now obliged to repair to his regiment, then quartered at Leeds in Yorkshire; and Sir Ralph Trusty, having finished his affairs in town, his lady returned with him to their country-seat.

Thus was she almost at once deprived of the only two persons to whom she could impart her mind without reserve, or on whose advice she could depend in any exigence whatever; for, as to her elder brother, he was too eager in the pursuit of his pleasures, and too much absorbed in them, to be truly solicitous for any thing that did not immediately relate to them; she saw him but seldom, and, when she did so, there was a certain distance in his behaviour towards her which would not permit her to talk to him with that freedom she could have wished to do.

She had not, however, any fresh motive to regret their depature on this account; Mr. Munden continued to behave to her in much the same manner as he had done since the breach had been made up between them: he was, indeed, very much abroad; but as she was far from being passionately fond of him, and only desired he would treat her with civility when with her, the little she enjoyed of his company was no manner of affliction to her.

She still retained some part of that gaiety, and love of a variety of conversation, which had always been a predominant propensity in her nature; and though in all her excursions, and the liberties she took, she carefully avoided every thing that might taint her virtue, or even cast a blemish on her reputation, yet were they such, as a husband who had loved with more ardency, would not, perhaps, have been very easy under: on his part, also, the late hours he came home at – the messages and letters which were daily brought to him by porters, might have given much disquiet to a wife, not defended from jealousy by so great a share of indifference: but in this they were perfectly agreed – neither offered to interfere with the amusements of the other, nor even pretended to enquire into the nature of them.

Though this was a mode of living together, which was far from being capable of producing that happiness for which the state of marriage was ordained, yet was it perfectly easy to persons who had so little real affection for each other; and, however blameable in the eyes of the truly discreet, escaped the censure of the generality of mankind, by it's being so frequently practised.

But I shall not expatiate on their present manner of behaviour to each other, since it was not of any long continuance, but proceed to the recital of a little adventure, which, though it may seem trifling to the reader in the repetition, will hereafter be found of some consequence.

It was a mighty custom with Lady Mellasin and Miss Flora, when they had nothing of more consequence to entertain them, to go among the shops, and amuse themselves with enquiring after new fashions, and looking over that variety of merchandize which is daily brought to this great mart of vanity and luxury.

Mrs. Munden, while in a virgin state, and a boarder at Mr.

Goodman's, used frequently to accompany those ladies when bent on such sort of rambles; and she still was fond enough of satisfying her curiosity this way, at such times as she found nothing else to do, or was not in a humour to give or receive visits.

Happening one day to pass by the well-furnished shop of an eminent mercer, and seeing several silks lie spread upon the counter, she was tempted to step in, and examine them more nearly. A great number of others were also taken from the shelves, and laid before her; but she not seeming to approve any of them, the mercer told her he had some curious pieces out of the loom that morning of a quite new pattern, which he had sent his man with to a lady of quality, and expected he would be back in a few minutes, so intreated she would be pleased either to stay a little, or give him directions where she might be waited upon.

Mrs. Munden complied with the former of these requests; and the rather, because, while they were talking, she heard from a parlour, behind the shop, a harpsichord very finely touched, accompanied with a female voice which sung, in the most harmonious accents, part of this air, composed by the celebrated Signior Bononcini –

> 'M'insegna l'amor l'inganno,
> Mi togl'al cor, l'assanno,
>   Mi da l'ardir amor,
>   Mi da l'ardir amor.'

The attention Mrs. Munden gave to the musick, preventing her from speaking, the mercer said he was sorry she was obliged to wait so long: 'I rather ought to thank you, Sir, for detaining me, since I have an entertainment more elegant than I could have expected elsewhere.'

'The lady sings and plays well indeed, Madam,' said he: 'she is a customer of mine, and sometimes does my wife the favour of passing an hour with her.'

The lady still continued playing; and Mrs. Munden expressing a more than ordinary pleasure in hearing her, the complaisant mercer asked her to walk into the parlour; to which she replied, she would gladly accept his offer, provided it would be no intrusion: he assured her it would not be accounted so in the least; and with these words conducted her into the room.

A few words served to introduce her to his wife, who being a very genteel, pretty sort of woman, received her with great civility: but the fair musician was no sooner told the effects her accents had produced on Mrs. Munden, than, though she was a foreigner, and spoke very broken English, she returned the compliment made her by that lady on the occasion, in a manner so perfectly free, and withal so noble, as discovered her to have been bred among, and accustomed to converse with, persons in the highest stations in life.

Vain as Mrs. Munden was of her perfections, she was always ready to acknowledge and admire those she found in others of her sex. There was something in this lady, that attracted her in a peculiar manner; she took as much delight in hearing her talk, as she had done in hearing her sing; she longed to be of the number of her acquaintance, and made her several overtures that way; which the other either did not, or would not, seem to understand.

The mercer's man returning with the silks his master had mentioned, Mrs. Munden thought, after the obliging entertainment she had received, she could do no less than become a purchaser of something: accordingly she bought a piece of silk for a night-gown; though at the time she had not the least occasion for it, nor, on her coming into the shop, had any intention to increase her wardrobe.

Having now no longer a pretence to stay, she gave the mercer directions where to send home the silk, and then took her leave: but could not do it without telling the lady, that she should think herself extremely happy in having the opportunity of a much longer conversation with her.

On her speaking in this manner, the other appeared in very great confusion; but having, after a pretty long pause, a little recovered herself, 'It is an honour, Madam,' said she, 'I would be extremely ambitious of; and had certainly taken the liberty to request it of you, if there were not a cruel peculiarity in my fate, which deprives me of all hopes of that, and many other blessings, I could wish to enjoy.'

Mrs. Munden was so much surprized at these words, that she could only reply, she was sorry a lady, who appeared so deserving, should be denied any thing she thought worthy of desiring.

It might well, indeed, seem a little strange that a lady so young, beautiful, and accomplished, should have any motive to induce her to speak in the terms she had done. Mrs. Munden had a good deal of curiosity in her composition; she thought there was something extraordinarily mysterious in the circumstances of this stranger; and was very desirous of penetrating into the secret.

About an hour after she came home, the mercer's man brought the silk: she enquired of him the name, condition, and place of abode, of the young lady she had seen at his master's; but received not the least information from him as to any of the questions she had put to him. He told her, that thought she often bought things at their shop, yet his master always carried them home himself, and he was entirely ignorant of every thing relating to her.

This a little vexed her, because she doubted not but that, if she once found out her name, quality, and where she lived, her invention would supply her with the means of making a more particular discovery. She resolved, therefore, on going again to the shop, under the pretence of buying something, and asking the mercer himself, who she could not imagine would have any interest in concealing what she desired to know.

Some company coming in, prevented her from going that afternoon; but she went the next morning after breakfast. The mercer not happening to be at home, she was more than once tempted by her impatience to ask for his wife, and as often restrained by the reflection that such a thing might be looked upon as a piece of impertinence in a person so much a stranger: she therefore left the house without speaking to any body but the man she had seen the day before.

Her curiosity, however, would not, perhaps, have suffered her to stop here, if something of more moment had not fallen out to engage her attention, and put the other out of her head for the present.

The nobleman on whom Mr. Munden depended for the gift so often mentioned in this history, had been a long time out of town, and was but lately returned. He had heard in the country that Mr. Munden was married, and that his wife was very beautiful and accomplished.

On Mr. Munden's going to pay his compliments to him on his arrival, 'I congratulate you,' said he; 'I am told you are married, and have got one of the prettiest and most amiable women in London for a wife.'

'As to beauty, my lord,' replied he, 'there is no certain standard for it; and I am entirely of the poet's mind, that –

" 'Tis in no face, but in the lover's eye.'

'But whatever she is,' continued he, 'I am afraid she would be too vain if she knew the honour your lordship does her, in making this favourable mention of her.'

'Not at all,' rejoined the peer; 'but I shall not take her character from common fame – you must give me leave to be a judge of the perfections I have heard so much talk of: besides,' pursued he, 'I have a mind to see what sort of a house you keep; I think I will come some day, and take a dinner with you.'

It is not to be doubted but that Mr. Munden omitted nothing that might assure his lordship, that it was an honour which he was extremely ambitious of, and should be equally proud of receiving, though he durst not have presumed to have asked it.

The very next day being appointed for this grand visit, he went home to his wife, transported with the gracious behaviour of his patron towards him. He threw a large parcel of guineas into her lap; and charged her to spare nothing that might entertain their noble guest in a manner befitting his high rank, and the favours he expected one day to receive from him.

Mr. Munden could not have given any commands that would be more pleasing to his fair wife: feasting and grand company were her delight. She set about making the necessary preparations with the greatest alacrity imaginable; and it must be acknowledged that, considering the shortness of the time, she had sufficient to have employed the most able and experienced housewife.

CHAPTER XII

———————————•———————————

Is only the prelude to greater matters

IT MIGHT be justly reckoned a piece of impertinence to take up the reader's time with a repetition of the bill of fare of the entertainment made on the above occasion; it will be sufficient to say that every thing was extremely elegant; that it was composed of the best chosen dishes, which were all served up in the greatest order; and that there was as great a variety of them as consisted with the table of a private gentleman, without incurring the censure of profuseness.

Such as it was, however, the noble lord seemed highly delighted with it; he praised every thing that came before him, almost to a degree of flattery; and took all opportunities of being yet more lavish in his encomiums on the beauty, wit, and elegance of the fair provider.

Mr. Munden was transported within himself at the satisfaction his patron expressed; and his wife also felt a secret joy on hearing the fine things said of her, which sparkled in her eyes, and gave an additional lustre to all her charms.

This nobleman, though past what is called the prime of life, was far from having arrived at those years which bring on decay; he was, besides, of a sanguine, vigorous complexion – had a very graceful person – a fine address – a great affluence of wit – and something so soft and engaging in his manner of behaviour to the ladies, as rendered him still a prodigious favourite with them.

He was too good a judge of what is amiable in womankind, not to discover immediately the many perfections Mrs. Munden was mistress of: he felt the whole force of her charms; and as he loved beauty more for his own sake than for that of the possessor, and never liked without desiring to enjoy, his eyes told her, at every glance, that he languished for an opportunity of declaring in a different manner the sentiments he had for her.

Mrs. Munden perfectly understood the language in which she found herself addressed: but, had she been less learned in it, an explanation soon presented itself.

Her husband, stepping to the head of the stair-case to give some orders to a servant, the peer took hold of one of her hands, and kissing it with the utmost raptures, 'Divine creature,' cried he, 'how unjust is fortune! that a face and person so formed for universal admiration, is not placed in a higher and more conspicious sphere of life!'

She had not time to make any reply – Mr. Munden returned that moment – nor had the noble lord the least opportunity, while he staid, of speaking one word to her that was improper for a husband to be witness of.

He prolonged the time of his departure to a greater length than could have been expected from a person whose high office in the state permitted him much fewer hours of leisure than those in middling stations of life are happy enough to enjoy: when he went away, he assured both the husband and the wife that he quitted them with the utmost reluctance, and that he had never passed a day more agreeably in his whole life.

Mr. Munden was now in such high good-humour, that he no sooner found himself alone with his fair wife, than he took her in his arms, and kissed her very heartily – a favour not common with him since the first week of their marriage. He told her, moreover, she had behaved like an angel – that nothing could be more elegant than the dinner she had prepared – and that he could not have expected such a variety of covers, and so fine a dessert, for the money he gave her for that purpose.

'I think myself very happy,' answered she, 'that you approve so well of my management: but I fancy,' continued she with a smile, 'you will have some better opinion of my œconomy when I tell you that it cost less than you imagine.'

'Is it possible!' cried he, in a pleasing surprize: 'I rather thought you had been kind enough to have added somewhat out of your own pocket, to render the entertainment so perfectly compleat.'

'No, I assure you,' resumed she; 'there remains no less than these

three guineas of the sum you allowed me for this day's expence.'
With these words, she laid the the pieces she had mentioned on the
table, which he was so ungenerous as to take immediately up and put
it into his own pocket.

'Nay, Mr. Munden,' said she, while he was putting up the money,
'this is not dealing altogether so fairly by me as I have done by you: I
expected that the trouble I have been at, deserved, at least, to be
rewarded with what I have saved by my frugality.'

'Take care, my dear,' said he, laughing, 'how you lessen the merit
of what you have done; I am willing to take it as an obligation to me;
and, sure, you value an obligation to me at a much higher rate than
three pieces.'

Though all this passed on both sides in a jocose way, yet, as it
served to shew the niggardliness of Mr. Munden's temper, cannot be
supposed to have increased either the love or respect his wife had for
him.

She made, however, no other answer to what he had last said, than
to tell him she found he was fashionable enough to suffer virtue to be
it's own reward; and then turned the conversation, and continued in
the same chearful humour as before any mention had been made of
the three guineas. Mr. Munden did not go abroad the whole evening:
but whether he chose to sup at home for the pleasure of enjoying his
wife's company, or for the sake of partaking of the remainder of those
dainties which had been so highly praised at dinner, is a point which,
perhaps, might admit of some dispute.

It is certain, indeed, the yet unsubdued vanity of this young lady
made her feel so much innate satisfaction in the admiration their
noble visitor had expressed of her person and accomplishments, as
gave a double sprightliness to her conversation that whole evening;
and might, perhaps, render her more than ordinarily lovely in the
eyes of her husband.

It is very far from being an improbability that some people may be
apt to imagine she built a little too much on the veracity of the praises
bestowed upon her by that nobleman: but those who think this way,
will be convinced of their error when they shall presently find how far
her conjectures were justified in this point.

She was sitting the next morning in a careless posture at one of the
windows that looked into the street, ruminating sometimes on one
thing, and sometimes on another, when she could not help
obvserving a fellow on the other side of the way, who kept walking

backwards and forwards, before the house, which, though he frequently passed thirty or forty paces, yet he took care never to lose sight of.

This seemed a little odd to her, as she sat there a considerable time, and the man still continued on his post: she doubted not but that he wanted to speak with some one or other of her family, but had not the least notion his business was with herself.

Being told breakfast waited for her, she went into her dressing-room, where she usually took it, and thought no farther of the man till Mr. Munden was dressed and gone out; but in less than a minute after he was so, she received intelligence from her footman, that there was a person had a letter for her, and said he would deliver it into no hands but her own.

On this she ran immediately down stairs; and found, to her great surprize, that he was no other than the fellow that she had seen loitering so long about the house. 'I am ordered, Madam,' said he, 'to give you this;' and at the same time presented her with a letter. 'From whom does it come?' demanded she. 'I am ignorant,' answered he, 'both of the person who sent it, and the business it contains: my orders were only to deliver it into your own hands;' and with these words went away with all the speed he could.

It must be confessed, a married woman ought not to have received a letter brought her in this manner, and without knowing whence it came: but curiosity prevailed above discretion; and she, hastily opening it, found it contained these lines.

'To Mrs. Munden.

Loveliest of your sex,
As not to adore you would be the greatest proof of insensibility, so not to wish, and even attempt every thing consistent with the character of a man of honour, for the obtaining some reward for that adoration, would be the most stupid piece of self-denial, becoming only of a stoick, or one more dead to all the joys of life. The force of your charms has made the conquest of a heart which only waits a favourable opportunity of throwing itself at your feet, not altogether without hope, in spite of the circumstances you are in, of being, in some measure, acceptable to you; at least it shall be so, if the most ardent and perfect passion that ever was, joined with the power of rendering you all manner of services, can give it merit in your eyes.

A very short time, I flatter myself, will explain to you what at present may seem a mystery: benignant Love will furnish the most faithful of his votaries with the means of declaring himself at full; and the flame with which he is inspired, instruct him also to give you such testimonies of his everlasting attachment, as the good understanding you are mistress of you will not permit you to reject; till when, I only beseech you to think, with some share of tenderness, on your concealed adorer.'

Utterly impossible is it to describe the situation of Mrs. Munden's mind, after having several times read over this epistle, and well examined the purport of it: she doubted not, one moment, but that it was dictated by the noble lord she had seen the day before, and whose behaviour to her had, in some degree, corresponded with the sentiments contained in it. If her vanity was delighted with the conquest she had made, her pride was shocked at that assurance which the daring lover seemed to flatter himself with of gaining her; and her virtue much more alarmed at the attempts which his rank and fortune might embolden him to make for that end.

At first she was resolved to shew the letter to her husband the moment he came home, and acquaint him with her sentiments on the matter, that he might take proper precautions to prevent her from being exposed to any future attacks from this dangerous nobleman.

But, on more mature deliberation, her mind changed: Mr. Munden was, at present, in tolerable good humour with her – she was willing, if possible, to preserve it in him; and, as she could not but think an information of this kind would give him a great deal of uneasiness, so she had also reason to apprehend the effects of it might, in some measure, innocent as she was, fall upon herself.

He had never yet discovered the least emotions of jealousy; and she knew not what suspicions her having received such a letter from one person might raise in him in relation to others. 'He may, possibly,' said she to herself, 'look upon every man that visits me as an invader of his right; and, consequently, I shall be debarred from all conversation with the sex.

'Besides,' continued she, 'I am not certain that this letter was sent me by the noble lord, or that he has in reality entertained any designs to the prejudice of my virtue; there is, indeed, a strong probability of it, even by his behaviour towards me yesterday: yet it may not be so; appearances often deceive us; and I might take that for the effect of love which proceeded only from complaisance; but, whatever his intentions are, it would certainly be the extremest folly and madness in me to inflame Mr. Munden against a person on whom his interest so much depends.

'It is no matter, therefore,' went she still on, 'whether it be the noble lord in question, or any other person who presumes to think so meanly of me as to address me in this audacius manner; it is, doubtless, in my power to keep out of the way of receiving any farther insults from him; and I am sufficiently capable myself of being guardian of my own honour, without disturbing a husband's peace about it.'

Thus ended the debate she had with herself on this occasion: she committed her letter to the flames; and resolved, that if ever the author was hardy enough to discover himself, to treat him with all the contempt due to him from affronted virtue.

CHAPTER XIII

Contains what every reader of an ordinary capacity may, by this time, easily guess at

SOME of my readers will, doubtless, think Mrs. Munden entirely justified in making a secret of the above-mentioned letter to her husband, as she did so in regard to his peace; but others, again, who maintain that there ought to be no reserve between persons so closely united, will condemn her for it: I shall forbear to give my vote upon the matter; and only say, that if she had not acted with less prudence soon after, she might saved herself a very great shock, and her husband much vexation.

It was no more than three days after the great man had dined there, that Mr. Munden received a billet from him, which contained as follows.

'To George Munden, Esq.

Dear Munden,
I have so few days that I can call my own, that I am willing to make those few as happy as I can; and on that motive desire yours and your amiable wife's company to dinner with me to-morrow: I leave you to make both my request and compliments acceptable to her; and am, with all sincerity, dear Munden, yours, &c. &c.

* * * * *

P.S. I shall have a female relation with me, who will rejoice in an opportunity of becoming acquainted with Mrs. Munden.'

Mr. Munden desired the servant who brought this, to give his own and wife's most humble duty to his lord, and assure his lordship they would not fail to attend his commands.

Some friends being with him when this invitation was brought, hindered him from saying any thing of it at that time to his wife; but they were no sooner gone, than, with an air and voice elated even to an excess, he told her of the high favour conferred upon them by his right honourable patron.

Mrs. Munden was now more than ever convinced of the base designs Lord **** had upon her, and that the letter she had received was sent by him: she therefore immediately determined within herself to let him see, by her not complying with this invitation, that she was neither ignorant what his intentions were, nor would do any thing that might give him the least encouragement to prosecute them.

But as she still judged it was wholly improper to acquaint Mr. Munden with any thing of the affair, she could form no other contrivance to avoid accompanying him in this visit, than by pretending herself seized with a sudden indisposition; which she resolved to do some few hours before the arrival of that wherein they should set out.

If she had persisted in this mind, it would have been highly laudable indeed: but, alas! the next morning inspired her with very different sentiments; vanity, that sly subverter of our best resolutions, suggested to her that there was no necessity for her behaving in the manner she had designed.

'What should I fear?' said she to herself; 'what danger threatens either my virtue or my reputation? A wife may certainly go any where with her husband: besides, a lady will be there, a relation of his lordship's; he can communicate nothing to me in their presence that I should blush to hear; and it would be rather ridiculous prudery, than discretion in me, to deny myself the satisfaction of such good company.'

It must be acknowledged, (for it but too plainly appears from every circumstances of this lady's conduct, both before and after marriage) that the unhappy propensity in her nature for attracting universal admiration, rendered her little regardful either of the guilt or the disquiets to which her beauty was accessary: if she was admired and loved, she cared not to what end; in short, it made her, perfectly uncorrupted and pure as her own inclinations were, rather triumph in, than regret, the power she had of inspiring the most inordinate and vicious ones in others.

Thus, more delighted than alarmed, she equipped herself with all the arts and labboured industry of female pride, for securing the conquest she had gained: safe as she imagined herself from all the encroachments of presumptuous love, she pleased herself with the thoughts of being looked upon by the adoring peer as Adam did upon the forbidden fruit – longing, wishing, but not daring to approach.

She had but just finished her embellishments, and was looking in the great glass to see if all was right, when Mr. Munden sent up stairs to know if she was ready, and to tell her his noble patron had sent his own chariot to fetch them: on hearing this she immediately tripped down stairs, singing, as she went, this part of an old song –

> 'With an air and a face,
> And a shape and a grace,
> Let me charm like beauty's goddess.'

Oh, how will the prudent, reserved part of the sex lament, that a young lady, endued with so many perfections, so many amiable qualities, should thus persevere in a vanity of which she had already experienced such vexatious consequences!

Lord **** received them in a fashion which fully gratified the ambition of Mr. Munden, and the yet less warrantable expectations of his wife; the lady mentioned in the letter was already with him; who, on his lordship's presenting Mrs. Munden to her, saluted her with abundance of sweetness and good-breeding: she was a person of about thirty years of age; had been extremely handsome, and still retained the remains of charms which must have been very powerful in their bloom; nor was her conversation less agreeable than her person; she said little, indeed, but what she said was extremely to the purpose, and very entertaining; there was, notwithstanding, a certain air of melancholy about her, which she in vain attempted to conceal, though it was easy to perceive she made use of her utmost efforts for that purpose.

His lordship was extremely gay and spiritous, as, indeed, were all the company, during the whole time at dinner: but it was no sooner over, than he said to Mr. Munden, 'Dear Munden, I have a business to communicate to you which these ladies must forgive me if I make a secret of to them.' With these words he took Mr. Munden into another room, and spoke to him in the following manner.

'A person,' said he, 'has been guilty of an action in regard to me, which it is neither consistent with my honour or my humour to put up with: I will shew you,' continued he, giving him an unsealed letter, 'what I have wrote to him upon the occasion; and that will instruct you how I intend to proceed, and, at the same time, convince you of the confidence I respose in your friendship.'

Mr. Munden took the letter out of his lordship's hands, and found the contents as follows.

'To William W——, Esq.

Sir,
Though the affront you have offered me deserves the severest treatment, yet, in consideration of our former intimacy, I shall wave my peerage, and require no other satisfaction from you than what any private gentleman has a right to demand of another, in a case of the like nature.

I shall be in the Green Park to-morrow about eight in the morning, where I believe you have honour enough to meet me: bring with you any one person you think fit; the gentleman who puts this into your hands will accompany me.

Not that I mean our friends should be engaged in the quarrel; but think it proper that there should be some witnesses that no foul play is attempted on either side. I am, expecting your ready compliance, Sir, yours, &c.

* * * * *.'

'You see, Munden,' said he, perceiving he had done reading, 'the assurance I build on the sincerity of your attachment to me.' – 'Your lordship does me an infinity of honour,' replied the other with a low bow, 'and I have nothing to regret, but that my sword must lie idle while your lordship's is employed.'

'As for that,' resumed the peer, 'I always thought it the utmost folly and injustice to set two people on cutting one another's throats, merely in compliment to their friends: but, my dear Munden,' pursued he, looking on his watch, 'I would have you go immediately; I believe you will find him at the Cocoa Tree; he is generally there about this hour – but if not, they will direct you where to find him.'

He sealed the letter while he was speaking; which being again delivered to Mr. Munden, they both returned into the room where the ladies were. Mr. Munden stayed no longer than while his footman called a hackney-coach to the door; as he was going out, the nobleman said to him, 'I doubt not but you will be back as soon as possible; in the mean time we three will amuse ourselves with a game at ombre.'

Mrs. Munden was a good deal surprized at her husband's departure; but had much more reason to be so, as well as alarmed, in a moment or two after.

Cards were but just laid upon the table, when a servant came hastily, and told the lady a messenger had brought word that her mother was suddenly seized with an apoplectic fit; that it was not yet known whether the old lady would recover, and that she must come home that instant.

On this she started up, seemed in a most terrible fright, and took her leave with a precipitation natural enough to the occasion, in a daughter possessed of any share of duty or affection.

This part of the history must be very unintelligible indeed, if the reader has not by this time seen, that all this was but a feint contrivance by the amorous nobleman, in order to get an opportunity of employing the whole battery of his rhetorick against the virtue he was impatient to triumph over.

This pretended kinswoman was, in fact, no more than a cast-off mistress of his lordship's; but, having her dependance entirely upon him, was obliged to submit in every thing to his will, and become an assistant to those pleasures with others which she could no longer afford him in her own person.

She was brought to his house that day for two reasons; first, as he knew not what fears, and what apprehensions, the beauty of Mrs. Munden might raise in her husband, and render him suspicious of the true motive of his being sent away, had no other company been there; and, secondly, to prevent that fair-intended victim of his unwarrantable flame from being too suddenly alarmed at finding herself alone with him.

Mrs. Munden, however, had no time to examine into the meaning of what she saw; and all she could recollect in that instant was, that she was in the house, and wholly in the power, of a person who had designs upon her, to which neither her honour, nor her inclinations, would permit her to acquiesce, and trembled for the event: but concealing the disorders of her mind as much as possible, 'Well, my lord,' said she, taking up the cards, and beginning to shuffle them, 'since we are deprived of a third person by this melancholy accident, what thinks your lordship of a game at picquet?'

'I think,' answered he, looking upon her with eyes which redoubled all her terrors, 'that to waste the precious time in cards, and throw away the golden opportunity of telling you how much my soul adores you, would be a stupidity which neither love nor fortune could forgive me for.'

In speaking these words he snatched one of her hands; and, in spite of her endeavours to withdraw it, pressed it to his mouth with an eagerness which would have convinced her, if she had not been so before, of the vehemence of those desires with which he was inflamed.

'Fie, my lord!' cried she, with an air as haughty and reserved as it was in the power of any woman to assume, 'this is not language with which the wife of him you are pleased to call your friend, could expect to be entertained.'

'Unreasonably urged!' cried he: 'ought my friendship for the husband to render me insensible to the beauties of the wife? or would your generous consenting to reward my passion, dissolve the union between us? No; on the contrary, it would rather be cemented; I should then love him not only for his own, but for your sake also, and should think myself bound to stretch my power to it's extremest limits to do him service: be assured, my angel, that in blessing me, you fix the happiness of your husband, and establish his future fortune in the world.'

These words, joined to Mr. Munden's being gone away, she knew not on what errand, made her shudder with the apprehensions that he might have been tempted, by the hopes of interest, to become yielding to the dishonourable intentions of his patron: but, willing to be more confirmed, 'I hope, my lord,' answered she, 'that you cannot think Mr. Munden has so mean a soul to accept of an establishment on such condition.'

'I could name some husbands, and those of the first rank, too,' said he, 'who, to oblige a friend, and for particular reasons, have consented to the complaisance of their wives in this point; but I desire no such sacrifice from Mr. Munden; there is no necessity for it; I have now sent him on a pretence too plausible for him to suspect the real motive of my wanting to get rid of him: I had a lady here also for no other end than to prevent him from feeling any disquiet on leaving us alone together – I shall always take the same precautions – all our interviews shall be as private as your own wishes, and my happiness be an eternal secret to the whole world as well as to your husband.

'Come, then, my charmer,' added he, attempting to take her in his arms, 'we have no time to lose – away, then, with all idle scruples – yield to my embraces – assist my raptures – and be assured that my whole soul, my fortune, and all my power can give, shall be at your disposal!'

It was the discomposure of Mrs. Munden's mind which alone hindered her from interrupting him during the former part of his speech; but the close of it, joined with the action which accompanied it, obliged her to collect all her scattered spirits; and flying to the other end of the room, in order to avoid his grasp, 'Forbear, my lord!' said she: 'know, I despise your offers; and set my virtue at a much higher rate than all the advantages you, or the whole world, would give in exchange.'

Lord **** finding he had to do with a mistress of uncommon spirit, thought best to alter the manner of his addresses to her; and approaching her with an air much more humble and submissive than he had hitherto done, 'How I adore,' cried he, 'this noble disinterestedness in you! you will grant nothing but to love alone – be it so: your beauty is, indeed, above all other price. Let your husband reap all the advantages, and let it be yours to have the pleasure, like Heaven, to save from despair the man who cannot live without you.'

Perceiving, or at least imagining he perceived, some abatement in the fierceness of her eyes, on the change of his deportment, he persisted in it – he even threw himself on his knees before her; took hold of her hands, bathed them alternately with tears, then dried them with his kisses: in a word, he omitted nothing that the most passionate love, resolute to accomplish it's gratification, could suggest to soften her into compliance.

At another time, how would the vanity of this lady have been elated to see a person of such high consideration in the world thus prostrate at her feet! but at this, the reflection how much she was in his power, and the uncertainty how far he might exert that power, put to silence all the dictates of her pride, and rendered her, in reality, much more in awe of him, than he affected to be of her: she turned her eyes continually towards the door, in hopes of seeing Mr. Munden enter; and never had she wished for his presence with the impatience she now did.

The noble lord equally dreaded his return; and finding the replies she made to his pressures somewhat more moderate than they had been on the first opening his suit, flattered himself that a very little compulsion would compleat the work: he therefore resolved to dally no longer; and having ushered in his design with a prelude of some warm kisses and embraces, was about to draw her into another room.

She struggled with all her might; but her efforts that way being in vain, she shrieked, and called aloud for help. This a little shocked him; he let her go: 'What do you mean, Madam?' said he. 'Would you expose yourself and me to the ridicule of my servants?' – 'I will expose myself to any thing,' answered she, 'rather than to the ruin and everlasting infamy your lordship is preparing for me!'

'Call not by so harsh a name,' cried he, 'the effects of the most tender passion that ever was: by heavens, I love you more than life! nay, life without you is not worth the keeping.' Speaking these words, he was about to lay hold of her again; and her cries having brought no body to her assistance, she must infallibly have been lost, if her better angel had not in that instant directed her eyes to a bell which hung in the pannel of the wainscot just behind the door of the room into which he was forcing her; she snatched the handle, and rung it with such vehemence that it resounded through the house.

This action made him release her with a kind of indignant fling; and a servant immediately coming up, 'I believe,' said she to him, 'my servant is below; pray order him to call me a chair this moment.' The peer, not often accustomed to such rebuffs, was so much confounded at the strength of her resolution, that he had not power to utter one word; and she, fearing another assault, ran to the door, which the footman hastily shut after him; and having opened it, 'Your lordship,' said she, 'has used me in a manner neither worthy of yourself nor me; I leave you to blush at the remembrance.'

She waited not to hear what reply he would have made, but flew down stairs into the hall; where a chair being presently brought, she threw herself into it, extremely disconcerted in her dress as well as mind.

CHAPTER XIV

———————•———————

Contains a brief recital of several very remarkable, and equally affecting, occurrences, of which the last-mentioned extraordinary adventure was productive, and which may justly enough be looked upon as yet more extraordinary than even the adventure itself

MR. MUNDEN, who was no less pleased and vain on the confidence his noble patron seemed to repose in him, than he was ambitious of the favours he hoped to receive from him, had been extremely diligent in the execution of that commission he had been entrusted with; but found much more difficulty in it than he could have imagined.

He was told at the bar of the Cocoa Tree, that the gentleman he inquired for had not been there since morning; that Sir John F— had taken him home with him to dinner, and that in all probability they were still together.

Mr. Munden, on this, ordered the coachman to drive to Mark Lane, with all the speed he could; but had, on his coming there, the mortification to hear that Mr. W— had left Sir John about a quarter of an hour before, and was gone to the other end of the town: on which he drove back to the Cocoa Tree, thinking he might now meet him there; but was again disappointed.

They informed him, however, that Mr. W— had just called in, but staid no longer than to tell them he would be there again in half an hour. Mr. Munden was impatient at this delay, but could not think of returning to Lord **** without having done the business he was sent upon: he therefore sat down, and waited till the other came, which was somewhat sooner than the time he had been made to hope.

These gentlemen, though far from being intimately acquainted, were not altogether strangers, having frequently met at the levee of Lord ****. They now saluted each other with the utmost politeness; after which, Mr. Munden drawing him to the most retired part of the room, 'I have had a chace after you, Sir,' said he, 'for a good part of this afternoon, and which would have been impertinent in me, if not excuseable by my being under an indispensable obligation of seeing you.'

'Then, Sir,' replied the other, 'whatever the business be, I shall think myself happy in being found.' – 'This, Sir, will inform you,' said Mr. Munden, giving himm the letter. 'From Lord ****!' cried Mr. W—, as soon as he saw the superscription. 'It is so,' answered Mr. Munden; 'and I am heartily sorry for the occasion.'

Mr. W— made no reply to what Mr. Munden said, till he had examined the contents of the letter; and then, after putting it into his pocket with a careless air, 'I see into the meaning of this,' said he: 'an ugly accident, which I have but lately discovered, has, I believe, misrepresented me to his lordship. Could I be capable of what he at present thinks I am, I should be utterly unworthy of the condescension he vouchsafes me by this invitation: but, Sir, all this is founded on a mistake, which may casily be rectified; I will not give his lordship the trouble of going to the Green Park; I will wait on him at his own house at the hour he mentions; and if what I have to say to him does not fully convince him of my innocence, will follow either to that, or any other place he pleases; though no consideration in the world, except his own commands, should compel me to draw my sword against a breast I so much love and reverence.'

Mr. Munden replied, that he should be extremely glad to find an affair, which at present seemed to threaten such fatal consequences, was amicably made up; and, after having assured him that he would deliver what he had said to his lordship in the most exact manner, was about to take his leave; but could not do it so soon as he desired, the other still detaining him by beginning some subject or other of conversation, which, how frivolous soever, Mr. Munden could not break off too suddenly, without incurring the censure of abruptness and ill-manners.

Lord **** in the mean time was in the utmost agitation; not for the return of Mr. Munden, for he very well knew the message he would bring, but that he had taken a great deal of pains to no purpose: the beauty of Mrs. Munden had inspirerd him with the most eager desire of enjoying her; the gaiety of her temper, joined to the temptations in his power to offer, had given him an almost assured hope of gaining her – and now, to find himself thus repulsed – repulsed with such disdain – left a surprize upon him which very much increased the shock of his disappointment.

Besides, as he doubted not but she would inform her husband of all that had passed between them, it gave the most mortal stab to that haughtiness too incident to opulence and grandeur, to reflect he had given a man, so much beneath him, an opportunity of triumphing over him in his mind.

He had not recovered his confusion, and was walking backwards and forwards in his drawing-room, with a disordered motion, when Mr. Munden returned; to whom he never spoke, nor looked upon. The satisfaction this gentleman had felt on finding the business of his embassy was like to terminate so happily, was very much damped at seeing himself received in this manner.

'I did not expect to find your lordship alone,' said Mr. Munden. – 'I believe not,' replied he: 'but an unlucky accident at home deprived me of my cousin's company; and your wife, it seems, did not think herself safe with me.'

These last words, and the contemptuous tone in which they were expressed, put him into the extremest consternation: 'I hope, my lord,' cried he, 'that Mrs. Munden cannot have so far forgot herself as to have acted in any manner unbecoming of the respect due to your lordship.' – 'Fine women will have their caprices,' resumed the peer: 'but no matter; let no more be said of it.'

Mr. Munden then proceeded to repeat what Mr. W— had said to him; but his lordship took no notice, and seemed entirely unconcerned all the time he was speaking; till the other adding, that, if his lordship thought proper, he would attend him in the morning, in order to be at hand in case the event should require his presence, the peer replied peevishly, 'No, no; you need not come – I believe there will be no occasion; if there be, I can send for you.'

After this, Mr. Munden, easily perceiving his company was rather troublesome than agreeable, made a low obeisance, and withdrew, almost distracted in his mind at this sudden turn of temper in his patron, and no less impatient to hear what his wife had to say on that account.

It was not in one of the best of humours, as the reader may easily imagine, that he now came home; nor did he find Mrs. Munden in one very proper to alleviate his vexation. She was extremely pensive;

and when he asked her, in somewhat of an imperious voice, the reason of having left Lord **** in so abrupt a manner – 'When you,' said she, 'forsook the guardianship of my honour, it was time for me to take the defence of it upon myself; which I could do no other way than by flight.'

'What is it you mean?' cried he. 'I am certain my lord has too much friendship for me to offer any rudeness to you.' – 'Be not too certain,' answered she, 'of the friendship of that base great man.' She then began to repeat the discourse with which his lordship had entertained her, after being left alone with him; but had gone through a very small part of it before her husband interrupted her, saying, with a kind of malicious sneer, that he was positive there was nothing at all in what she apprehended – that it was impossible for the noble lord to be in earnest when he talked to her in such terms – that she had been deceived by her own vanity, to mistake for a serious design upon her virtue what was only meant for mere gallantry; and then added, with more passion, that he feared her idle resentment had lost him all his interest with the best of friends.

'Good Heavens!' cried she, 'defend me, and all virtuous women, from such gallantries! But know, Sir,' continued she, with a great deal of vehemence, 'that, but for that idle resentment, as you are pleased to call it, my ruin and your dishonour would have been compleated by this best of friends.'

'How!' said Mr. Munden, eagerly; 'he did not, sure, proceed to action?' Perceiving he was now in a disposition to listen with more attention to what she said, than hitherto he had done, she hesitated not to acquaint him with every particular of his lordship's behaviour to her, and the means by which she had defended herself.

During this recital, Mr. Munden bit his lips, and appeared in very great emotions. He spoke not a word, hoever, till his fair wife, pitying the anxieties she saw him under, desired him to think no more of this accident, since it was so happily got over. 'It may be so in your opinion,' answered he fiercely; 'but not in mine. I foresee the consequences; though you, perhaps, think not of them. It is true, my lord's behaviour is not to be justified; nor can yours in regard to me be so: you ought to have considered the dependence I had on him, and not have carried things with so high an hand. You might have doubtless evaded this attempt by more gentle and less affrontive methods: but that cursed pride of yours must be gratified, though at the expence of all my expectations.' With these words he flung out of the room; and this was all the return she met with from her ungrateful husband, for having resisted, with such courage and resolution, temptations which some women would have thought themselves absolved for yielding to the force of.

Ill-natured and perverse as Mr. Munden was, it must be confessed that his present situation, nevertheless, merited some compassion: he had a great share of ambition – loved both pleasure and grandeur to an excess; and, though far from being of a generous disposition, the pride and vanity of his humour made him do many things, through ostentation, which his estate would not well support. He kept company with persons of rank and fortune much superior to his own; and, as he bore an equal part in their expences whenever he was with them, he stood in need of some addition to his revenue: well, therefore, might he be chagrined at an accident that cast so dark a cloud over that prospect of interest and perferment he had flattered himself with from Lord ****.

But though this was the main point, it was not the sole subject of his discontent. The motives for his being sent by Lord **** to Mr. W——, the pretended quarrel between them, and the trifling excuses made by the latter to detain him from making too quick a return, were all too obvious for him not to be assured that gentleman was privy to, and agreed to be an assistant in, the design his lordship had upon his wife.

Mr. W——, though the representative of a borough in C——, was, indeed, no more than a creature of Lord ****; to whose interest alone he was indebted for his seat in parliament: but it was not because Mr. Munden knew him to be obliged to do everything enjoined by his lordship, that restrained the resentment he conceived against him from breaking out, but because he considered that a quarrel between them on this score might occasion the affair to become publick, and expose both himself and wife to the ridicule of as many as should hear it.

Wrath, when enervate, especially if inflamed by any just provocation, is certainly very dreadful to be borne; and what this injured husband sustained in the first emotions of it, must have excited the pity of every reader of this history, if he had not afterwards meanly vented it where he had not the least occasion for disgust, but rather of the highest tenderness and admiration.

In the midst of these perplexities, however, let us leave him for a while, and return to her whose beauty had been the innocent cause of all this trouble to him, and danger to herself.

Wonderful, indeed, were the effects this last adventure produced in her. Many times before she had been on the very verge of ruin, and as often indebted merely to fortune for her preservation from the mischiefs into which her inadvertency had almost plunged her: but none of those dangers, those escapes, had ever been capable of making any lasting impression on her mind, or fixing her resolution to avoid running again into the same mistakes.

The cruel reproaches and reflections cast on her by Mr. Munden, filled her not now with the least resentment; for though she deserved them not upon the score he made them, yet she was conscious that she did so for going to the house of Lord ****, after having the strongest reasons to believe he had dishonourable intentions upon her.

She blushed to remember, that she had given herself leave to be pleased at the thoughts of appearing amiable in the eyes of that great man. 'Good God!' cried she, 'what infatuation possessed me! Am I not married? Is not all I am the property of Mr. Munden? Is it not highly criminal in any one to offer to invade his right? And can I be so wicked to take delight in the guilt to which I am in a manner accessary?

'The vanities of my virgin state,' continued she, 'might plead some excuse; but nothing now can be urged in my defence for persevering in them. The pride of subduing hearts is mine no more: no man can now pretend to love me but with the basest and most shameful views. The man who dares to tell me he adores me, contradicts himself by that very declaration; and while he would persuade me he has the highest opinion of me, discovers he has in reality the meanest.'

In fine, she now saw herself, and the errors of her past conduct, in their true light. 'How strange a creature have I been!' cried she; 'how inconsiderate with myself! I knew the character of a coquet both silly and insignificant; yet did every thing in my power to acquire it. I aimed to inspire awe and reverence in the men; yet, by my imprudence, emboldened them to the most unbecoming freedoms with me. I have sense enough to discern real merit in those who professed themselves my lovers; yet affected to treat most ill those in whom I found the greatest shrae of it. Nature has made me no fool; yet not one action of my life has given any proof of common reason.

'Even in the greatest and most serious affair of life – that of marriage,' added she with a deep sigh, 'have I not been governed wholly by caprice? I rejected Mr. Trueworth only because I thought I did not love him enough; yet gave my hand to Mr. Munden, whom, at that time, I did not love at all; and who has since, alas! taken little care to cultivate that affection I have laboured to feel for him.'

In summing up this charge against herself, she found that all her faults and her misfortunes had been owing either to an excess of vanity, a mistaken pride, or a false delicacy. The two former appeared now too contemptible in her eyes for her not to determine utterly to extirpate; but the latter she found less reason to correct, since it happened only in regard to Mr. Trueworth, and could never happen again, as both their marriages had put a total end to all tender communication between them.

This change in Mrs. Munden's humour, great and sudden as it was, did not, however, prove a transient one – every day, every hour, confirmed her in it; and if at any time her natural vivacity made her seem a little pleased on hearing her wit, her beauty, or any other perfection or accomplishment, too lavishly extolled, she presently checked herself for it; and assumed a look of reserve, which, though less haughty than she had sometimes put on upon different occasions, had not the less effect, and seldom failed to awe the flatterer into silence – a proof of which the reader will be immediately presented with.

CHAPTER XV

———•———

Contains such things as will be pleasing to those whose candid dispositions interest them in favour of the heroine of this history

NOTHING so much encourages an unwarrantable passion for a married woman, as to know she has a husband regardless of her charms. A young gay gentleman, a companion of Mr. Munden's, privy to most of his secrets, and partner with him in many a debauch, had seen Mrs. Munden at Miss Airish's, where she still continued to visit. He had entertained a kind of roving flame for her, which his friendship for her husband could not prevent him from wishing to gratify; but, though they often met, he never could get an opportunity of declaring himself: all he could do was sometimes to whisper in her ear that she was divinely handsome – that he adored her – and that he died for her – and such like stuff; which she was too often accustomed to hear to take much notice of.

The indifferent opinion which most men of pleasure, or, in other words, genteel rakes of the town, have of women in general, joined to the too great gaiety he had observed in Mrs. Munden's behaviour, made him imagine there required little more for the gaining her than the making his addresses to her. The means of speaking to her in private seemed to him the sole difficulty he had to get over: and, in order to do so, he wrote to her in the following terms.

'To Mrs. Munden.

Madam,
A fine woman would reap little advantage from the charms she is mistress of, if confined to the languid embraces of a single possesser.

Marriage takes off the poignancy of desire: a man has no relish for beauties that are always the same, and always in his power; those endearments generally make his happiness become disgustful to him by being his duty; and he naturally flies to seek joys yet untasted, in the arms of others. This, fair angel, is the case with us all – you have too much good-sense not to know it, or to expect your husband should vary from his sex in this particular.

Let those unhappy women, therefore, to whom nature has been niggard of her bounties, pine in an abandoned bed. You are formed to give and to receive the most unbounded joys of love – to bless and to be blest with the utmost profusion of extasies unspeakable.

To tell you how infinitely I adore you, and how much I have languished for an opportunity of declaring my passion, would require a volume instead of a letter: besides, my pen would but faintly express the sentiments of my soul – they will have more energy when whispered in your ear. I know such a thing is impossible at your own house, or at any of those where you visit. Favour me, then, I beseech you, with taking a little walk in the Privy Garden near the water-side, to-morrow about eleven; from which place, if my person and passion be not altogether disagreeable to you, we may adjourn to some other, where I may give you more substantial demonstrations how much I am, with the utmost sincerity, dear Madam, your eternally devoted, and most faithful admirer.

P.S. I do not sign my name for fear of accidents; but flatter myself my eyes have already said enough to inform you who I am.'

If this letter had come but a very small time before it did, it is possible that, though Mrs. Munden would even then have been highly offended at the presumption, yet her vanity and curiosity might have excited her to give the meeting required in it by the author; though it had only been, as she would then have imagined, merely to see who he was, and laugh at his stupidity for addressing her in that manner.

Not but she had some distant guess at the person; but whether it was him, or any other, who had taken this liberty, she now gave herself not the least concern: she was only desirous to put an entire stop to those audacious hopes she found he had entertained, and to keep herself from receiving any future solicitations, from the same quarter at least.

To send back his letter without any other token of her resentment and disdain at the contents, she thought would not be sufficient; and her ready wit, after a little pause, presented her with a method more efficacious. It was this.

She folded up the epistle in the same fashion it was when she received it, and inclosed it in another piece of paper; in which she wrote these lines.

'Sir,

As I cannot think any man would be weak enough to dictate an epistle of this nature to the wife of Mr. Munden, I must suppose you made some mistake in the direction, and sent that to me which was intended for some other woman, whose character it might better agree with.

I must intreat you, however, to be more careful for the future; for if any such impertinence should a second time arise, I shall think myself obliged to make a confidante of my husband, whose good-sense and penetration will, doubtless, enable him to discover the author, and his spirit and courage instruct him in what manner to resent the affront offered to his ever-faithful, and most affectionate wife,

B. MUNDEN.'

This had all the effect she wished it should have – the beau was ashamed of the fruitless attack he had made – wrote to her no more – avoided her sight as much as possible – and, whenever chance brought him into her company, behaved towards her with all the distance and respect imaginable.

This lady, now fully convinced how dangerous it was to be too much admired for her external charms, ceased even to wish they should be taken notice of; and set herself seriously about improving those perfections of the mind which she was sensible could alone entitle her to the esteem of the virtuous and the wise.

Mr. Munden, who had never been disquieted at the former part of his wife's behaviour, was equally insensible of this alteration in her: his cares, indeed, were too much taken up for re-establishing himself with his right honourable patron, to give any attention to what passed at home.

After much debating with himself, he thought it best to proceed so as not to let the noble lord imagine he was acquainted with any part of the attempt made upon his wife; but, though he attended his levee as usual, and seemed rather more obsequious than ever, he had the mortification to find himself very coolly received. He stood undistinguished in the circle which constantly waited the motions of that great man – was scarcely spoken to by him, and then with a kind of indrawn reserve, which made him justly enough apprehensive that he had little now to hope for from him.

The truth is, he saw through the policy of this dependant – he could not doubt but Mrs. Munden had told him of the violence he had offered to her – he was conscious of the baseness of it; but he was not angry with himself for it, though with the person he would have injured; and could not forgive him for the knowledge of his crime, though the other was willing to forgive the crime itself.

The treatment he received at Lord ****'s made him extremely churlish to his wife; he looked upon her as the primary cause of his misfortune, cursed his marriage with her, and even hated her for the beauties and good qualities which should have endeared her to him. Nothing she could say or do had the power of pleasing him; so that she stood in need of all her courage and fortitude to enable her to support, with any tolerable degree of patience, the usage she received.

To heighten her misfortune, the late levity of her temper had hindered her from cultivating an acquaintance with any one person, on whose secrecy, sincerity, and sedateness, she could enough depend for the disburdening her mind of those vexations with which it was sometimes overwhelmed.

But this was a matter of disquiet to her which she had not long to complain of. Heaven sent her a consolation of which she had not the least distant expectation, and restored her to a friend, by whom she had thought herself utterly forsaken, and whom she had not herself scarce thought of for a long time.

Lady Loveit was now but just returned from the country, where she had continued ever since her marriage to Sir Bazil. A famous French milliner being lately arrived from Paris with abundance of curiosities, her ladyship went to see if there was any thing she should think worth the purchasing. Mrs. Munden was led by the same curiosity; and it was at this woman's house that these ladies happened to meet after so long an absence from each other.

Mrs. Munden was a little confused at first sight of her, as bringing to her mind some passages which it was never in her power to think on with the indifference she wished to do. They embraced, however, with a great deal of affection – made each other the usual

compliments on the mutual change of their condition; for Lady
Loveit, by some accident, had heard of Mrs. Munden's marriage.

Though both these ladies were much more taken up with each
other than with examining the trifles they came to see, yet neither of
them would quit the shop without becoming customers. Lady Loveit
perceiving that Mrs. Munden had neither coach nor chair at the
door, after having asked what part of town she lived in, and finding it
was not too much out of her way, desired she would give her leave to
set her down in her chariot.

Mrs. Munden readily accepted the offer; and, being come to the
door of her house, would have persuaded Lady Loveit to alight and
come in: but she excused herself; and, at the same time, gave her a
pressing invitation to her house as soon as an opportunity permitted.
'I know, Madam,' said she, smiling, 'that it is my duty to pay the first
visit to your ladyship – yet, as you are here –' 'I should not stand on
that punctilio with you,' interrupted Lady Loveit, with the same
good-humour; 'but I expect company at home; and I know not but
that they already wait for me.' The other then told her she would do
herself the favour to attend her ladyship in a day or two: and this was
all that passed at this first interview.

Mrs. Munden was extremely rejoiced at the opportunity of
renewing her acquaintance with this lady; in which she had not the
least room to doubt but that she should find what she so much
wanted, a faithful adviser and an agreeable companion. They had
always loved each other – there was a great parity of sentiment and
principle between them; and as nothing but their different ways of
thinking, in point of conduct towards the men, had hindered them
from becoming inseparable friends, that bar being removed by Mrs.
Munden's change of temper, and her being now what Lady Loveit
always was, no other remained to keep them from communicating
their thoughts with the utmost freedom to each other.

The visit promised by Mrs. Munden was not delayed beyond the
time she mentioned. Lady Loveit received her without the least
reserve; and they soon entered into conversation with the same
sprightliness as before the change of their conditions.

Mrs. Munden had resolved within her self not to make the least
mention of Mr. Trueworth's name; but feeling, notwithstanding, a
good deal of impatience to hear something of him, artfully entered
into a discourse which she knew must draw the other in to say
something concerning him.

'I need not ask,' said she, 'how you liked the country; it is pretty plain, from your continuing there such a length of time, that you found more pleasures at Sir Bazil's seat than any you had left behind.' – 'The house is well situated, indeed,' replied Lady Loveit; 'yet I have passed the least part of my time there since I left London; nor have we staid away so long entirely through choice, but have in a manner been detained by a succession of accidents altogether unforeseen.

'It took up six weeks,' continued she, 'to receive the visits which were every day crowded upon us from all parts of the country. This hurry being over, we could do no less than accompany Mr. Wellair and his lady, who had been with us all this while, to their house, where we staid about a fortnight; after which, Sir Bazil having promised my brother and sister Trueworth to pass some time with them in Oxfordshire, we crossed the country to that gentleman's fine seat; where, you may suppose, his arrival was welcomed in much the same manner Sir Bazil's had been in Staffordshire. Besides all his relations, intimate friends, tenants, and dependants, I believe there was scarce a gentleman or lady, twenty miles round, who did not come to congratulate him on his marriage and return.

'For the reception of those guests,' went she still on, 'the generous Mr. Trueworth omitted nothing that might testify his joy on the occasion of their coming. Feasting employed their days, and balls their nights. But, alas! in the midst of these variegated scenes of pleasure, death, sudden death! snatched away the source of all our joys, and turned the face of gladness into the most poignant grief.'

'Death! did your ladyship say?' cried Mrs. Munden, with an extraordinary emotion. 'Is, then, Mr. Trueworth dead?' – 'No, Madam,' replied the other, wiping away some tears which the memory of this fatal accident drew from her eyes; 'Mr. Trueworth lives; and, I hope, will long do so, to be an honour to his country, and a comfort to all those who are so happy as to know him; for certainly there never was a man more endued with qualities for universal good: but it was his wife, his amiable wife, that died!'

'His wife!' cried Mrs. Munden, interrupting her a second time: 'is he already a widower?' – 'Too soon, indeed, he became so!' answered Lady Loveit. 'Scarce three months were elapsed from that day which made her a bride to that which made her a lifeless corpse: we were all together, with some other company, one evening in the turret, which, by the help of some large telescopes Mr. Trueworth had placed there, commands the prospect of three counties at once, when my poor sister was seized suddenly ill. As she was supposed to be pregnant, her complaint at first was taken no other notice of then to occasion some pleasantries which new-married women must expect to bear: but she soon grew visibly worse – was obliged to be carried down stairs, and put directly into bed. The next morning she discovered some symptoms of a fever; but it proved no more than the forerunner of the small pox, of which distemper she died before her danger was apprehended, even by the physician.'

'How I pity both the living and the dead!' said Mrs. Munden. 'Mr. Trueworth, certainly, could not support so great a loss with any degree of moderation?' – 'The shock at first,' replied Lady Loveit, 'was as much as all his philosophy and strength of reason could enable him to combat with. Sir Bazil, though deeply affected for the loss of so amiable a sister, was obliged to conceal his own sorrows, the better to allieviate those he saw him in; and this kept us for two whole months at his house after the ceremony of the funeral was over. We had then prevailed on him to return with us to London; every thing was prepared for our departure, when an unlucky accident happened to myself, which detained us for yet a considerable time longer.

'We were diverting ourselves one day with angling,' continued she; 'when, in endeavouring to cast my rod at too great a distance, I stooped so far over the bank, that I plunged all at once, head foremost, into the water. The pond, it seems, was pretty deep; and I was in some danger. Sir Bazil and Mr. Trueworth, seeing me fall, jumped in at the same instant; and, by their assitance, I was brought safe to shore. I was immediately carried into the house, stripped of my wet garments, and put into a warm bed: but the fright had so great an effect upon me, that it caused an abortion, which, as I was then in the fifth month of my pregnancy, had like to have proved fatal to me. I was close prisoner in my chamber for several weeks; and, on my being just able to leave it, was advised to have recourse first to the Bristol and then to the Bath waters, for the better establishment of my health. Accordingly, we went to both those places – staid as long at each as I found needful for the purpose that brought me thither; and on my perfect recovery, Sir Bazil having some business at his estate, returned to Staffordshire – made a short excursion to Mrs. Wellair's, and then we bowled up to London.

'This,' added she, 'is the whole history of my eleven month's absence. I should also have told you that we had not Mr. Trueworth's company in our last ramble. One of the members for his county having vacated his seat by accepting an employment, Mr. Trueworth was prevailed upon, by a great number of gentlemen and freeholders, to oppose his being rechosen by setting up for a candidate himself. The election was to come on in a few days after our departure; and we have since heard that he succeeded in his attempt.'

Lady Loveit having finished her long narrative, and received the compliments of Mrs. Munden for the trouble she had given her, was beginning to ask some questions concerning her own affairs; but some ladies coming in, broke off, for the present, all conversation on this head; and Mrs. Munden soon after took leave, though not without receiving an assurance from the other of having her visit returned in a short time.

CHAPTER XVI

———●———

Presents the reader, among many other particulars, with a full, though as concise an account as can be given, of the real quality and condition of the lady that Mrs. Munden had seen, and been so much charmed with, at the mercer's

MRS. Munden carried enough home with her from Lady Loveit's to employ her mind, for that whole night at least. What she had been told in relation to the death of Mrs. Trueworth, raised a strange contrariety of ideas in her, which it was impossible for her either to reconcile, or oblige either the one or the other totally to subside.

She thought it great pity that so virtuous, so beautiful, and so accomplished, a young lady, as she had been told Mrs. Trueworth was, should thus early be snatched away from all the joys of love and life; but could not lament so melancholy an accident in a manner she was sensible it deserved: envy had ever been a stranger to her breast; yet, since her own marriage, and that of Mr. Trueworth with his lady, she had sometimes been tempted to accuse Heaven of partiality, in making so wide a difference in their fate; and, though the blame of her misfortunes lay wholly on herself, had been apt to imagine that she had only been impelled, by an unavoidable impulse, to act as she had done, and was fated, by an invincible necessity, to be the enemy of her own happiness.

Thus did this fair predestinarian reason within herself whenever the ill-usage of Mr. Munden made her reflect on the generosity of Mr. Trueworth. She repined not at the felicities she supposed were enjoyed by Mrs. Trueworth, but regretted that her own lot had been cast so vastly different.

But though all these little heart-burnings now ceased by the death of that so late happy lady, and even common humanity demanded the tribute of compassion for her destiny, of which none had a greater share, on other occasions, than Mrs. Munden, yet could she not on this pay it without some interruptions from a contrary emotion: in these moments, if it may be said she grieved at all, it was more because she knew that Mr. Trueworth was grieved, than for the cause that made him so.

Her good-sense, her justice, and her good-nature, however, gave an immediate check to such sentiments whenever she found them rising in her; but her utmost efforts could not wholly subdue them: there was a secret something in her heart which she would never allow herself to think she was possessed of, that, in spite of all she could do, diffused an involuntary satisfaction at the knowledge that Mr. Trueworth was a widower.

If Lady Loveit could have foreseen the commotions her discourse raised in the breast of her fair friend, she would certainly never have entertained her with it; but she so little expected her having any tenderness for Mr. Trueworth, that she observed not the changes in her countenance when she mentioned that gentleman, as she afterwards frequently did, on many occasions, in the course of the visits to each other: nor could Mrs. Munden, being ignorant herself of the real cause of the agitation she was in, make her ladyship a confidante in this, as she did in all her other affairs, the little happiness she enjoyed in marriage not excepted.

Lady Loveit had, indeed, a pretty right idea of her misfortune in this point, before she heard it from herself: Sir Bazil, though not at all conversant with Mr. Munden, was well acquainted with his character and manner of behaviour; and the account he gave of both to her on being told to whom he was married, left her no room to doubt how disagreeable a situation the wife of such a husband must be in. She heartily commiserated her hard fate; yet, as Lady Trusty had done, said every thing to persaude her to bear it with a becoming patience.

Perceiving she had lost some part of her vivacity, and would frequently fall into very melancholy musings, Sir Bazil himself, now fully convinced of her merit and good qualities, added his endeavours to those of his amiable consort, for the exhilarating her spirits: they would needs have her make one in every party of pleasure, either formed by themselves, or wherein they had a share; and obliged her to come as often to their house as she could do without giving offence to her domestick tyrant.

An excess of gaiety, when curbed, is apt to degenerate into it's contrary extreme: it must, therefore, be confessed, that few things could have been more lucky for Mrs. Munden than this event; she had lost all relish for the conversation of the Miss Airishes, and those other giddy creatures which had composed the greatest part of her acquaintance; and too much solitude might have brought on a gloominess of temper equally uneasy to herself and to those about her; but the society of these worthy friends, the diversions they prepared for her, and the company to which they introduced her, kept up her native liveliness of mind, and at the same time convinced her that pleasure was no enemy to virtue or to reputation, when partook with persons of honour and discretion.

She had been with them one evening, when the satisfaction she took in their conversation, the pressures they made to detain her, joined to the knowledge that there was no danger of Mr. Munden's being uneasy at her absence, (he seldom coming home till towards daybreak) engaged her to stay till the night was pretty far advanced; yet, late as it was, she was presented with an adventure of as odd a kind as ever she had been surprized with.

She was undressing, in order to go to bed, when she heard a very loud knocking at the street-door; after which her footman came up, and told her that a woman was below, who said she must speak with her immediately. 'I shall speak to nobody at this time of the night,' said Mrs. Munden; 'therefore go down and tell her so.' The fellow went; but returned in a moment or two, and told her that the person would take no denial, nor would go out of the house without seeing her. 'Some very impudent creature, sure!' said Mrs. Munden – 'but do you go,' added she in the same breath, to the maid that waited on her, 'and ask her name and business: if she will tell neither, let her be turned out of the house.'

She was in a good deal of perplexity to think who should enquire for her at that late hour; when the servant she had sent to examine into the matter, came back, and, before she had well entered the chamber, cried out, 'Lord, Madam! I never was so astonished in my life! I wonder Tom could speak in such a rude manner; the woman, as he called her, is a very fine lady, I am sure, though she has no hoop nor stays on – nothing but a fine rich brocade wrapping-gown upon her: she looks as if she was just going to bed, or rather coming out of bed, for her head-cloaths are in great disorder, and her hair all about her ears.'

'Well, but her name and business,' demanded Mrs. Munden hastily. 'Nay, Madam,' replied the maid, 'she will tell neither but to yourself; so, pray, dear Madam, either come down stairs, or let her be brought up: I am sure she does not look as if she would do you any hurt.'

Mrs. Munden paused a little on what she had heard; and believing there must be something very extraordinary indeed, both in the person and the visit, resolved to be convinced of the truth; therefore, having given a strict charge that both the footmen should be ready at her call in case there should be any occasion for them, went into the dining-room, and ordered that the person who enquired for her should be introduced.

Her whole appearance answered exactly to the description that had been given of her by the maid; but it was her face which most alarmed Mrs. Munden, as being positive she had seen it before, though when or where she could not at that instant recollect.

But the stranger soon eased her of the suspense she was in; when, throwing herself at her feet, and bursting into a flood of tears, 'You once offered me your friendship, Madam,' said she: 'a consciousness of my own unworthiness made me refuse that honour; but I now come to implore your compassion and charitable protection. I have no hope of safety, or of shelter, but in your goodness and generosity.'

The accents of her voice now discovered her to be no other than the lady Mrs. Munden had seen at the mercer's: she was strangely confounded, but not so much as to hinder her from raising the distressed fair-one with the greatest civility, and seating her in a chair, 'Though I cannot comprehend, Madam,' answered she, 'by what accident you are reduced to address me in these terms, yet you may rely upon my readiness to assist the unfortunate, especially a person, whom I cannot but look upon as far from deserving to be so.'

'Oh! would to God,' cried the other, very emphatically, 'that my history could preserve that kind opinion in you! but, alas! though I find myself obliged to relate it to you, in order to obtain the protection I intreat, I tremble lest, by doing so, I should forfeit those pretensions to your mercy, which otherwise my sex, and my distress, might justly claim.'

These words were sufficient to have aroused the curiosity of a woman who had less of that propensity in her nature than Mrs. Munden; she told her that, by being made the confidante of her affairs, she should think herself obliged to excuse whatever she found not worthy of her approbation.

'Prepare yourself, then, Madam,' said her still weeping guest; 'summon all your goodness to forgive the frailties of youth and inadvertency, and to pity the sad consequences which sometimes attend the pride of flattered beauty and vain desire of ambition.'

This expression sunk more deeply in the mind of Mrs. Munden than the person who uttered it imagined: she made no reply, however; and the other began the narrative she had promised in these or the like terms.

The history of Mademoiselle de Roquelair.

'I need not tell you, Madam,' said she, 'that I am not a native of this kingdom; my bad pronunciation of the language speaks it for me: I am, indeed, by birth a Parisian, and daughter of the Sieur de Roquelair, a man of some estimation in the world.

'The great hopes conceived of me in my infancy, encouraged him to be almost profuse in the expences of my education; no accomplishment befitting of my sex and rank was denied me: in fine, it was easy to see he had an affection for me above all his other children; and that the partial opinion he had of my person and understanding, made him build the highest expectations on my future fortune.

'But, alas! what he intended for my happiness proved my undoing; I had but just attained my fifteenth year of age, when the little beauty I was mistress of was taken notice of by the Duke de M—, as I was walking one evening in the Thuilleries, with a young companion of my own sex: he passed us twice without speaking, but at the third turn accosted us with a gallantry natural to persons of his high rank; the praises he bestowed on me were such as might excuse some vanity in a heart so young and inexperienced as mine then was.

'On our leaving the walk,s a gentleman of his retinue followed; and, as I afterwards was informed, enquired who I was, and many other particulars concerning me: the next morning, being at mass in the church of St. Sulpice, I saw the duke again; and, on my coming out, had a letter put into my hands, which, as soon as I got to a convenient place, I opened, and found it, as I before imagined, from the duke.

'After magnifying the power of my wit, my beauty, my fine shape, and a thousand charms with which his amorous fancy painted me, and protesting, with the most solemn imprecations words could form, his everlasting adoration of me, he intreated I would meet him at the same place where he had first seen me, and appointed an hour in which he knew least company would be there.

'I was imprudent enough to comply with this request: my illustrious lover was there before me – he saluted me with the utmost transport in his voice and eyes – led me to a retired part of the walk – made me the most splendid offers – and endeavoured to persuade me, that being his mistress was a station more respectable than being the wife of a private gentleman, or even of a little marquis.

I was unprepared to confute the arguments he urged; and, to confess the truth, felt but too much satisfaction in hearing him speak: my tongue obeyed the dictates of my heart, and told him that I would be his, though I cannot say that I was tempted by any extraordinary liking of his person, but merely by my ambition of pleasing a prince of the blood-royal.

'It was agreed between us, that a proper place should be provided for my reception, and I should quit my father's house entirely; and this was to be accomplished at the end of three days: but, before the expiration of that time, a person who had seen me in the Thuilleries carried home intelligence with what company I had been, and my father, who preferred virtue above grandeur, took all imaginable precautions to prevent my continuing so dangerous an intercourse.

But what cannot the power of gold effect? Though I was locked up in my chamber, no letters or messages permitted to be delivered to me, an agent of the duke's, by a large bribe, corrupted one of the servants, by whose assistance I got out of the house when all the rest of the family were asleep; and a chariot, waiting for me at the end of the street, carried me to a magnificent hotel; where I found my noble lover, and every thing I could wish, ready to receive me.

'Here I lived, for near two whole years, in a pomp which excited the envy, and set me above the scandal, of the censorious: but, at length, malice overtook me; the baseness of those about me accused me to my prince of having wronged his bed; he too easily gave credit to their aspersions; and not only withdrew his affection and his favours from me, but cruelly discarded me without the least provision for my future support.

'My father, who would never see me in my exalted state, equally shunned me in my fallen one; but, at last, through the intercession of some friends, he was prevailed upon to forgive what was past, provided I would leave Paris for ever, and spend the remainder of my days in a monastery: to this, in the distracted condition I then was, I yielded; and a convent at Roan was made choice of for my retreat; the abbess was wrote to concerning me; and every thing was prepared for my departure; when chance brought me acquainted with Mr. Thoughtless.

'You start, Madam,' continued she, perceiving Mrs. Munden looked very much confused; 'but know, at once, that I am that very unfortunate woman your brother brought with him from Paris, who has ever since lived with him, and whom you must have heard of.'

The amazement Mrs. Munden was in, on finding her the mistress of her brothers, was such as would not permit her to make any other reply than to desire she would go on with what she had farther to relate: on which Mademoiselle de Roquelair resumed her discourse in this manner.

'This gentleman,' said she, 'was very well acquainted with my story; but it did not hinder him from entertaining a passion for me – he declared it to me; the aversion I had to a recluse life, the allurements of the world, and his more persuasive rhetorick, soon won me to yield to his desires; I made a second elopement – we embarked together, and came to England; where I have had the command of his family, and lived with him in all things like a wife, except the name. But fortune, always my enemy, conjured up a spirit of jealousy in him, for my torment at first, and, at last, for my utter ruin. His fears of losing me, as he pretended, secluded me from all society; denied me all the publick diversions of the town; and though I lived amidst the very seat of pleasures, kept me as much a stranger to them as if I had been a thousand leagues removed: but, oh! this night, this night, Madam, has compleated all his too suspicious temper long since threatened! The poor mercer, at whose house you saw me, came this night to bring a piece of silk I had bespoke of him: Mr. Thoughtless came home immediately after; and being told who was above with me, flew up stairs, burst open the door, which by some accident was locked, rushed in with his drawn sword, swearing he would sacrifice us both: the man, to avoid his fury, jumped out of the window into the yard; Mr. Thoughtless ran down the back stairs, in order, I suppose, to make him in that place the victim of his rage: whether he has effected it, I know not; for, trembling at my own danger, I took that opportunity of running directly out of the house; though where to go I knew not – I had no friend – no acquaintance to whom I could apply; I found myself all alone in the street, and exposed to insults, even worse than those from which I fled. My good genius, (for so I hope it was) in that dreadful instant, reminded me of you; I had heard a high character of your goodness; and was assured of it, even by the little I had seen of you, when you were pleased to think me worthy of your notice.

'This, Madam,' added she, 'has brought me to you; and I once more beseech shelter and protection under your roof for this night at least, till I can recollect in what manner I can dispose of my wretched self.'

Though Mrs. Munden was apprehensive this lady had favoured herself too much in the recital she had made, yet she could not think of refusing what she asked: she ordered a bed to be instantly prepared for her; and having conducted her to the chamber where she was to lie, told her she would defer, till the next morning, any farther discourse on the subject they had been talking of, as it was very late, and she expected Mr. Munden home; so wishing her a good repose, returned to her own apartment, to reflect at more leisure on this strange adventure.

CHAPTER XVII

———•———

Is less entertaining than some of the former

THE husband of Mrs. Munden being engaged abroad till his usual hour, she had just time to get into bed before he came home; which she was very glad of, as it prevented him from asking any question concerning her sitting up so much beyond her custom; and she was not willing to say any thing to him of her new guest, till she had talked farther with her, and also examined into the truth of the affair which brought her thither.

The more she reflected on the account that lady had given of herself, the less reason she found to give credit to some passages in it: she could not think that a prince, such as the Duke of M—, would, on a mere suggestion, cast a woman out to misery and beggary, whom he had so passionately loved; and yet less could she believe that her brother, a man not fiery by nature, could have acted in the manner she had represented, without a much greater provocation than what she pretended.

Besides, the mercer bringing home goods so late at night to a customer, and being locked up with her, seemed so inconsistent with innocence, that she could not help being of opinion, that the cause must be bad indeed which had no better plea for it's defence.

It also afforded her a good deal of matter for vexation, that by expressing, in such warm terms, the great liking she took of this lady when they accidentally met at the mercer's, she had encouraged her to make choice of her house for an asylum in her distress, and by this means rendered herself interested in the concerns of a stranger, who, at the best, it did not well become her to take part with.

But her most alarming apprehensions were in relation to her brother: she knew not but, if irritated to the high degree Mademoiselle de Roquelair had described, he might in reality have been guilty of some rash action, which might endanger his reputation, and even his life.

Her mind being thus employed, it is easy to believe sleep had little power over her eyes: late as she went to bed, she rose pretty early in the morning; and, impatient to know something farther of the transactions of the preceding night, she dispatched a servant to her brother's house under pretence of enquiring after his health, not doubting but, by the answer he would bring, she should be able to form some conjecture whether any thing of the nature Mademoiselle de Roquelair seemed to apprehend, had really happened or not.

The man returning with the intelligence that Mr. Thoughtless was very well, and not yet stirring, gave her great consolation: she then went up to the chamber of Mademoiselle; and, after giving her the usual salutation of the morning, sat down by her bed-side, and began talking in this manner.

'Madam,' said she, 'I have been considering on your story; and as I sincerely pity the misfortunes to which you have reduced yourself, should be glad to know by what method you propose to extricate yourself from them, and what farther assistance you require from me, or is in my power to grant, wtihout acting unbecoming of my character.'

'I should be utterly unworthy,' answered the other, weeping, 'of the compassion you have shewn, and even of the life you have preserved, should I entreat any thing of you that might either injure your reputation, or prejudice the good understanding between you and your brother. As to my misfortunes, they are, alas! past remedy; I neither hope, nor shall endeavour, for a reconciliation with Mr. Thoughtless; I have long since been ashamed and weary of the errors of my conduct, though I wanted strength of resolution to reform them: but be assured, Madam, I have now no other wish than to pass my future life in that only retreat for wretches like myself – a monastery.'

Her streaming eyes, her moving accent, and, above all, the seeming contrition she expressed for her faults, raised such a flow of tenderness in the soul of Mrs. Munden, that she resolved from that instant to do every thing in her power to save her.

'As the religion of your country,' said she, 'and in which you were bred, affords a great number of those safe and sure asylums for persons who have made ill use of their liberty, you cannot, indeed, do better than to fly to some one of them for refuge from temptations, which you have too much experienced the force of; and if you persevere in this good disposition, I will endeavour to procure the means of rendering you able to accomplish so laudable a desire.'

'Ah, Madam,' cried Mademoiselle de Roquelair, 'it is all I ask of Heaven, or you; the accidents of my life have convinced me there can be no real happiness without virtue, and that the most certain defence of virtue is religion: if I could now flatter myself with the means of being received within those sacred walls, from which the fatal love of Mr. Thoughtless drew me, I should think my guardian angel had not quite forsook me.'

On this, the good-natured believing Mrs. Munden said many kind things to her – made her take some refreshment as she lay in bed, in which she advised her to continue some time, and endeavour to compose herself to sleep, she seeming to stand in need of it very much. In going out of the chamber, she told her she should return in a few hours; but if she wanted any thing in the mean time, on her ringing a bell by her bedside, a maid-servant would immediately attend upon her.

She was, indeed, bent to try all possible methods for the accomplishment of what she promised. 'How guilty soever this unhappy woman is,' said she within herself, 'my brother, in common justice, ought at least to leave in her in the same condition in which he found her: she was then going to a nunnery; and it is now his duty to send her to one; for it cannot be expected her father will make a second offer of that sort.'

With these reflections, together with others on the manner in which it would be most proper to address Mr. Thoughtless on this score, was her mind taken up, till the hour she imagined he might be stirring: the disturbances which must necessarily have happened in his family the night before, made her suppose he might lie longer than usual; but she chose rather to wait a while for his rising, than hazard losing the opportunity of speaking to him by his being gone abroad.

That gentleman had, in fact, passed the most disagreeable night he had ever known: he had loved Mademoiselle de Roquelair with such an extravagance of fondness, that he had sometimes been even prompted by it to marry her; but the too great warmth of her constitution, and the known inconstancy of her temper, as often deterred him from it, and also made him restrain her from any of those liberties he would otherwise have allowed her: he had thought himself no less secure of her person than she always pretended he was of her heart; and now to find all his tenderness for her abused, all his precautions frustrated, might well raise in him passions of the most desperate kind.

The inclinations of this woman were, in reality, too vicious to be bound by any obligations, or withheld from their gratifications, by any of the methods taken for that purpose: she loved variety – she longed for change, without consulting whether the object was suitable or not – the mercer had a person and address agreeable enough; he was of an amorous complexion, and readily improved the advances she made him: he frequently came to her under the pretence of bringing patterns of silks, or other things in his way of trade; and all this, as she imagined, without raising any suspicion in the family. No interruption happening in their repeated interviews, she sometimes kept him with her till near the hour in which Mr. Thoughtless usually came home, which was seldom till one or two o'clock.

But on this unlucky night it so fell out that a very ill run of play, and the loss of all the money he had about him, brought him home much sooner than was his custom: a servant being at the door, prevented his knocking; so that the lovers had not the least notice how near he was to them. He went directly into his dressing-room, which was backwards on the ground-floor, and sat musing for some time, casting up the sums he had lost, cursing fortune within himself, and protesting never to touch a card or throw a dice again; when, on a sudden, he was alarmed with the sound of a man's voice laughing very heartily; he stamped with his foot; and a servant immediately coming up, 'Is there any company above?' demanded he, hastily. 'None, Sir, but the mercer that comes to Madam with silks,' replied the man. 'A mercer at this time of night!' cried Mr. Thoughtless. 'How long has he been here?' – 'I cannot tell exactly, Sir,' said he; 'but, I believe, three or four hours.' – 'A long visit; and on business too!' resumed Mr. Thoughtless; and, after a little pause, 'Go,' continued he, 'bid Mademoiselle de Roquelair come down to me.'

If this unfaithful woman had been but mistress of artifice enough to have made any one of the family her friend, she would certainly have been told that Mr. Thoughtless was come home, and her gallant might easily have slipt out of the house without his knowledge; but, on the contrary, her imperious behaviour towards them, set them all in general against her: this fellow in particular, whom she had used worse than the rest, rejoiced that his master was likely to find out what he wished him to know, but never durst acquaint him with.

On his going up stairs, he found they were shut in the bed-chamber; and, running to his master with this account, 'Locked in the chamber!' said Mr. Thoughtless, starting up. 'Yes, Sir,' answered the servant; 'and nobody would answer, though I knocked two or three times;' which, by the way, if he did at all, it was too softly for them to hear.

'Confusion!' cried Mr. Thoughtless, now worked up to the highest pitch of jealous rage; 'I'll try if they will open to me!' With these words he drew his sword, and flew up stairs, burst open the door, and rushed into the room with all the fury of an incensed lion. The astonished guilty pair had neither thought nor means to escape; the lover, on the first burst of the door, jumped out of the window into the yard – Mademoiselle ran screaming to one corner of the room. 'Abandoned woman!' cried Thoughtless, 'your punishment shall be the second course!' then, followed by his man with lights, ran in pursuit of the person who had injured him.

This unhappy woman, not daring to stand the tempest of his rage when he should return, took the opportunity of his having quitted the chamber to make her escape; though, at the time she did so, as she had truly told Mrs. Munden, she neither knew where nor to whom she should apply for refuge.

The mercer, in the mean time, was found by Mr. Thoughtless, but in a condition more exciting pity than revenge: the poor man had broke both his legs with his fall, and was otherwise very much hurt; but on seeing by whom, and in what manner he was approached, the terror of immediate death made him exert all the strength that was left in him to cry out for pardon; which word he repeated over and over again in the most lamentable tone that could be. Mr. Thoughtless, on this, turned hastily away, bidding his servants raise and carry him into the hall, where a chair being presently brought, he was put into it, and sent home to make the best excuse he could to his wife for the mischief that had happened to him.

Every room was afterwards searched for Mademoiselle de Roquelair; but she not being found, and a maid-servant remembering that, in the midst of the confusion, the street-door had been left open, the flight of that lady was not to be doubted.

Though these disturbances had taken up the greatest part of the night, Mr. Thoughtless was able to enjoy little repose after going to bed; and rose rather sooner than usual – he was up and dressed when his sister came; but was a good deal surprized to be told of her being there, as she had never visited him before without a formal invitation.

'Good morrow, my dear sister,' said he, as soon as she was introduced; 'this is a favour quite unexpected: pray, what brings you abroad thus early?' – 'You men,' answered she, 'who keep such late hours, may well think it early; but for us women, who live more regularly, it is no wonder to see us breathe the morning air: but I assure you I rose somewhat sooner than ordinary to-day on your account.' – 'On mine! As how, pray?' demanded he. 'I am come,' answered she, 'to solicit in behalf of a person who has fallen under your displeasure – Mademoiselle de Roquelair.'

'Mademoiselle de Roquelair!' cried he, hastily interrupting her: 'what knowledge can you have of that infamous creature?' She then ingenuously related to him how they had met by accident at the mercer's – the offer she had then made of her friendship; and how, as she supposed, emboldened by that mistaken encouragement, she had flown to her house for shelter the preceding night: 'You see how dangerous it is,' said he, ''to make friendship at first sight; but surely the wretch cannot flatter herself with the least distant hope of a reconciliation?'

'Far be it from me, Sir,' replied Mrs. Munden very gravely, 'to become the negociator of such a treaty, or even to attempt a vindication of her behaviour: no, it is your own honour, for which alone I am concerned; and that, I think, requires you should send her to a monastery; since, as she says, you deprived her of the opportunity of entering into one.'

'All mere pretence!' cried he: ' 'tis true, there was some talk of such a thing; but she has inclinations of a different sort.' To which Mrs. Munden replied, that inclinations, though ever so corrupt, might be reformed by reason, adversity, and experience – that she hoped her penitence was sincere – and what before her was her aversion, was now become her choice. She then urged the request she came upon, in terms so moving and pathetick, that Mr. Thoughtless, irritated as he was, could not withstand the energy of her words: he told her he would consider on what she had said, and give his answer the next day; but, in the mean time, desired she would advise her unworthy guest to send for her baggage immediately; saying, he would have nothing in his house that should remind him of her.

Mrs. Munden, pretty well satisfied with having obtained thus much, took her leave; and returned to Mademoiselle de Roquelair, with an account of what she had done.

CHAPTER XVIII

———————•———————

Contains a most shocking instance of infidelity and ingratitude

MADEMOISELLE de Roquelair, on finding how far the good-nature of Mrs. Munden had made her interest herself in her behalf, expressed the transports of her gratitude in terms which gave some pain to the modesty of that lady to receive: 'What I have done,' said she, 'is to promote the cause of virtue; and I hope my endeavours that way will not be lost on your account.' – 'You are all goodness,' replied the other; 'but I blush to think that, being already indebted for so many favours, I must still become your petitioner for more: though I have lived fifteen months in this town, I am a perfect stranger to the greatest part of it, quite unacquainted with it's customs, and know not where, and in what manner, to address myself for lodgings. In the midst of my distractions, I found shelter under your hospitable roof; may I presume to flatter myself with the continuance of that charitable protection, till I receive an answer from Mr. Thoughtless?'

Mrs. Munden paused a little at this request; but, thinking it would be cruel in this distress to have recourse to strangers, and to whom she could communicate nothing of her mind, made this reply – 'Though it would be highly inconvenient, Madam,' said she, 'for you to remain in my house for any length of time; yet as, in all probability, your affairs will be determined in a few days, I would not have you think of leaving me till you are prepared to leave the kingdom. Please, therefore,' continued she, 'to make an inventory of what things you have at my brother's, and I will give orders for their being brought directly hither.'

Mademoiselle de Roquelair was beginning to give some fresh testimonies of the sense she had of this last obligation; but Mrs. Munden would not suffer her to proceed; and, pointing to a standish that stood on the table, desired her to write the memorandums she had mentioned. 'Obedience, Madam, is better than sacrifice,' said the other; and immediately did as she was directed: after which Mrs. Munden went down to give the orders she had promised.

She sent this inventory by her own man, and instructed him to procure persons for bringing thither every thing belonging to Mademoiselle de Roquelair: but as this could not be done, and that lady dressed, before the hour of dinner, which was just at hand, she judged it improper she should appear at table till she could do so with greater decency; she therefore bid one of the maids prepare something apart, and serve it up to her in her own chamber.

She then began to consider what she should say to Mr. Munden in relation to this affair: she knew not but he might already be apprized of what had passed; or if even he were not so, she thought it would be impossible to keep her in the house without his privity; so resolved to be quite open in the affair.

She was right in her conjecture: Mademoiselle de Roquelair had happened to ring the bell for something she wanted; Mr. Munden hearing it, and knowing his wife was abroad, asked who was above; and this question occasioned the man, who was then dressing him, to give an account, as far as was in his power to do, of the last night's accident.

This a little surprized him, yet not enough to keep him from the Park, where he constantly walked every day an hour or two before dinner; but on his return, he immediately interrogated his wife concerning her new guest; on which she told him, without the least reserve, every circumstance of this transaction; he listened attentively to what she said, but testified neither any dislike or approbation of her conduct in this respect: he said no more to her after she had done speaking; but behaved with the same sullen silence he had always done since her adventure with Lord ****; and as soon as dinner was over, went out to pass the remainder of the day, and best part of the night, according to custom.

Mrs. Munden's good-nature would not suffer her to go abroad the whole afternoon; she passed all the hours, till bed-time, with Mademoiselle Roquelair, and did every thing in her power both to comfort her in the affliction she was under, and to fortify her in the good resolution she seemed to have taken: the next morning she received, as she expected, the following billet from her brother.

'To Mrs. Munden.

Dear Sister,
In compliance with your desires, and to be certain of getting eternally rid of the sight of a woman who has so much abused the kindness I had for her, I consent to grant her request of being enabled to go into a monastery: a friend of mine has great dealings with a merchant at Bologne; I will see him this afternoon, and pay into his hands the sum which I am told is sufficient for that purpose. If you give yourself the trouble to call on me to-morrow morning, I will give you his order for her receiving it on her arrival. I cannot think of entering your house while she is in it; but am always, dear sister, your affectionate brother,

T. THOUGHTLESS.'

Mrs. Munden having imparted the contents of this letter to Mademoiselle de Roquelair, she seemed as much contented as a person in her circumstances could be: she dined below that day; and Mr. Munden treated her with the same politeness and complaisance he always used towards persons over whom he had no power.

The next morning did not fail of carrying his fair wife to her brother's about the hour in which she imagined he would expect her; but on the moment of her entrance, she had the mortification of being accosted by him in these terms: 'My dear sister,' said he, 'I was just going to send to you, to prevent your giving yourself this needless trouble. The gentleman I went to is out of town, and will not return these two days: so nothing can be done in this woman's affair till he comes back.' She told him she was extremely sorry; 'Because,' said she, 'delays are sometimes dangerous: but I hope, my dear brother, no second considerations will make you frustrate the good intentions of this unhappy penitent.' – 'No, no!' cried he; 'I wish she may persevere in them as steadfastly as I shall to the promise I have made.' Satisifed with this assurance, she made her leave, little suspecting, while she was labouring wtih all her might in this good office, that cruel and ungenerous return which was about to be made for her compassion.

Mr. Munden had seen Mademoiselle de Roquelair no more than

once; but that once was sufficient to make him become enamoured – her beauty fired him – the known wantonness of her inclinations encouraged him – he scarce doubted of success; but in case of a failure, and if she should even acquaint his wife with his attempt, her character furnished him with the pretence of having made it only to try how far her conversion was sincere.

He therefore hesitated not a moment if he should endeavour the accomplishment of his desires; and, for the doing so, no time was to be lost, as she was so suddenly to depart. Mrs. Munden was no sooner gone out, than he went softly up stairs to the chamber of this too lovely and less more virtuous stranger: she was sitting in a pensive posture, leaning her head upon her hand, when he came in; but rose to receive him with that respect which she thought due from her to the husband of her protectress.

After the salutations of the morning were over, 'Is it possible,' cried he, taking one of her hands, and looking earnestly on her face, 'that such youth, such beauty, charms in such profusion, should be condemned to a cloyster? No! it cannot be! All the powers of love and pleasure forbid you to make so unnatural a choice!' Transported and amazed at hearing him speak in this manner, she could not forbear telling him, with her eyes, that her thoughts corresponded with his words; but willing her tongue should preserve the decency of the character she had assumed, at least till he should make a farther declaration of his sentiments; 'If I were, indeed,' answered she, 'all that can be described of beautiful, I could not, sure, be an offering too amiable for Heaven!'

'Heaven never gave you these perfections,' resumed he, 'to be concealed in a dark lonesome cell! Those melting lips of yours were never formed to kiss the feet of a cold lifeless image, or pour forth oraisons to unhearing saints, but to make blest some warm, some happy he, who knows and has the power of returning the raptures they bestow!' These last words were attended with such vehement and repeated pressures of the lips he praised, as left her no room to doubt the aim of his desires; as did the manner of her receiving them also convince him of his success.

'But are you in earnest, resolved to be a nun?' replied he. 'Since fate will have it so,' replied she with a deep sigh, and a look so languishing and so sweet as pierced his very soul. 'Make me your fate, then,' cried he impatiently: 'be mine, and not all the saints in the kalendar shall snatch you from me.' – 'You are then – you must be,

my fate!' said she, returning his embrace with equal eagerness: 'you
have the power of fate; and are no less resistless. Henceforth I'll seek
no other heaven but your love – your breast my altar – and your arms
my cell!'

It will be easily supposed that, after this, she refused no liberties he
thought fit to take. Nothing but the last favour was wanting to
compleat his wishes; and to that he would not venture to proceed, for
fear of an interruption: but they agreed to meet at the Portuguese
ambassador's chapel at six o'clock that same evening. Mutual kisses
and embraces having sealed the covenant, he went down to dress,
and left her to compose her countenance against Mrs. Munden's
return.

This very wicked woman, who had never any real thoughts of
going into a monastery, and only intended to appropriate the money
she expected from Mr. Thoughtless to such uses as might induce
some man of fortune to make choice of her for a mistress, now gave
herself little pain whether he granted her request or not, imagining
she had found in Mr. Munden all she wished for, or could hope, in a
gallant.

She affected, however, to Mrs. Munden, to be under some
concern for this delay of her intended journey; but said she would
employ the time she staid in such acts of devotion as should best
prepare her to become a member of that sacred society which she
soon hoped to be among. 'I have not been,' added she, 'for a long
time, at confession; but I will go this afternoon, and ease my
conscience of it's load of guilt.'

Thus impiously did she profane the name of religion, by making it
the veil to cover the most shameful depravities of nature. On the
arrival of the appointed hour, with looks of sanctity, and a heart full
of impurity, she hasted to the place of rendezvous. The punctual Mr.
Munden waited for her at the chapel-door, and conducted her where
they had all the freedom they could wish of indulging their vicious
inclinations.

They broke off this amorous intercourse much sooner than either
of them desired; Mademoiselle de Roquelair not being able to find a
plausible excuse to make to Mrs. Munden for staying beyond the
time which her pretended devotions might be reasonably supposed to
take up: but, to atone for this misfortune, a strategem was contrived
between them, not only for their meeting next day, but also for their
continuing together a much longer time. It was thus.

She told Mrs. Munden that the reverend father to whom she had confessed, informed her that a young lady, of a very worthy family in England, having passed her year of probation at a monastery in Bologne, and returned hither only to take an eternal leave of her friends, and of the world, was now just ready to go back, in order to be initiated. 'To this family,' added she, 'the good father has offered to introduce me to-morrow; and if the young lady approves of my being the companion of her voyage, as he assures me she certainly will, how happy shall I think myself!'

The truth of all this not being suspected by Mrs. Munden, she congratulated her upon it. It is easy to deceive the innocent; but, it must be owned, this wicked woman had subtlety enough to have imposed on a person more skilled in the artifices of the world than was the amiable lady on whom she practised it.

But, not to detain the reader's attention on so ungrateful a subject, I shall only say, that one assignation was still productive of another; and the credulity of the injured wife served only as a matter of mirth to the transgressing husband and his guilty partner.

But now the time was come when the subterfuges must necessarily be at an end, or become too gross not to be seen through. Mr. Thoughtless had seen his friend – had paid the money into his hands, and received a bill from him on the merchant at Bologne. When he delivered it to Mrs. Munden – 'Sister,' said he, 'this paper will entitle your guest to the receipt of three hundred louis-d'ors on her arrival at Bologne: but I expect you will oblige her to depart immediately; for it is neither consistent with your reputation to keep her in your house, nor with my peace of mind that she should continue in the kingdom.' To which she replied, with a smile, 'That there was nothing more certain than that his commands, in this point, would be punctually obeyed.'

This lady was rejoiced at having accomplished what she thought so good a work; but, having perceived in Mademoiselle de Roquelair some abatement of her first eagerness for a religious life, she thought proper, on giving her the bill, to repeat to her the words her brother had said on that account: to which the other coolly answered, 'Your brother, Madam, need be under no apprehensions of my offending him in this point, or of giving you any farther trouble.'

This, though no more than what the lovers expected, was yet a dreadful shock to them both: great part of the time they were together that evening was taken up in talking of it. Mademoiselle de

Roquelair protested that death was less cruel than being torn from
her dear Munden thus early – thus in the infancy of their happiness;
and gave some hints that she wished he would hire private lodgings
for her: but she knew little of the temper of the man she had to deal
with. He loved her as a mistress, but hated the expence of keeping
her as a mistress: he therefore evaded all discourse on that head; and
told her he fancied that, by pretences such as already had been made,
she might still continue in the house. 'Means, at least,' said he,
'might be found out to protract our mutual misfortune, and give us
more time to consider what we have to do.'

She agreed, however, to make the experiment; and poor Mrs.
Munden was imposed upon, by some new invention, from one day to
another, for upwards of a week: but, at last, beginning to fear there
was something more at the bottom fo these delays than was
pretended, and her brother having sent twice in that time to know if
his desires had been complied with, she resolved at once to put a
period to inconveniences which she thought she could so easily get
rid of.

Mademoiselle de Roquelair having staid abroad extremely late
one night, she took the opportunity of her having done so, of
speaking more plainly to her than her good-nature and complaisance
had hitherto permitted her to do: she went up to her chamber next
morning; and, with an air which had something of severity in it, 'You
keep odd hours, Madam,' said she, 'for a person who affects to be so
great a penitent; but I suppose you are now prepared to ease me of all
concern on your account.' – 'I shall trouble you no longer,' cried the
other, 'till the young lady I told you of is ready to depart.' – 'You will
do well,' resumed Mrs. Munden, 'to remain with her till she is so;
for, Madam, I must insist on your removal hence this day.' – 'You
will not turn me out of doors?' cried Mademoiselle de Roquelair. 'I
hope you will not oblige me to an act so contrary to my nature,'
replied Mrs. Munden. 'Say, rather, contrary to your power,' returned
that audacious woman; and, coming up to her with the most
unparalleled assurance, 'This house, which you forbid me,' pursued
she, 'I think Mr. Munden is the master of; and I shall, therefore,
continue in it till my convenience calls me from it, or he shall tell me
I am no longer welcome!'

Impossible is it to describe, and difficult even to conceive, Mrs.
Munden's astonishment at these words; to hear a woman thus doubly
loaded with guilt and obligations – a woman, who but a few days past

had been prostrate at her feet, imploring pity and protection, now all at once ungratefully contemning the benefits she had received, and insolently defying the authority to which she had flown for shelter; all this must certainly give a shock almost beyond the strength of human reason to sustain. 'Mr. Munden!' cried the injured fair-one, with a voice hardly intelligible, 'Mr. Munden!' She could utter no more; but flew down stairs with such rapidity that her feet scarce touched the steps.

Mr. Munden was not quite ready to go out – she found him in his dressing-room; and, throwing herself into a chair, half suffocated with passion, related to him, as well as she was able, the manner in which she had been treated; to which he replied, with a good deal of peevishness, 'Pr'ythee, do not trouble me with these idle stories; Mademoiselle de Roquelair is your guest – I have no concern in your little quarrels.' – 'I hope,' said she, 'you will do me that justice which every wife has a right to expect, and convince the French hypocrite that I am too much the mistress of this house for any one to remain in it without my permission.' – 'So you would make me the dupe of your resentment!' replied he scornfully; 'but positively I shall not do a rude thing to oblige you or any body else.' In speaking these words, having now adjusted his dress, he flung out of the room without giving her time to add any thing farther on a subject he was wholly unprepared to answer.

What a perplexing whirl of wild imaginations must such a behaviour from a husband excite in a wife, conscious of having done nothing to provoke it! Happy was it for her that love had the least share in her resentment – all her indifference could not enable her to support, with any degree of patience, so palpable a contempt – she returned directly to her own chamber; where, shutting herself up, she gave a loose to agitations too violent for words to represent.

CHAPTER XIX

———————•———————

*Relates such things as the reader will, doubtless, think
of very great importance, yet will hereafter be found of
much greater then he can at present imagine*

AFTER this much-injured wife had vented some part of the
overflowing passions of her soul in tears and exclamations, she began
to consider, with more calmness, in which manner she ought to
behave, in so amazing a circumstance. She had not the least
propensity in her nature to jealousy; yet she could not think that any
thing less than a criminal correspondence between her husband and
this Frenchwoman, could induce the one, or embolden the other, to
act as they had done towards her.

'Neither divine nor human laws,' said she, 'nor any of those
obligations by which I have hitherto looked upon myself as bound,
can now compel me any longer to endure the cold neglects, the
insults, the tyranny, of this most ungrateful, most perfidious man! I
have discharged the duties of my station; I have fully proved I know
how to be a good wife, if he had known how to be even a tolerable
husband: wherefore, then, should I hesitate to take the opportunity,
which this last act of baseness gives me, of easing myself of that heavy
yoke I have laboured under for so many cruel months?'

She would not, however, do anything precipitately; it was not
sufficient, she thought, that she should be justified to herself, she was
willing also to be justified in the opinion of her friends: her brother
was the first person to be consulted; she resolved, therefore, to go
immediately to him; but as it was necessary to put something in order
before her departure, in case she should return no more, she called
the maid, who always waited on her in her chamber, to assist her on
this occasion.

She locked up her jewels, and what other trinkets she had of value, in an amber-cabinet, and made her wearing-apparel be also disposed of in proper utensils, leaving out only some linen, and other necessaries, for the present use, which she also caused to be packed up. The poor maid, who loved her mistress dearly, and easily guessed the meaning of these preparations, could not refrain weeping all the time she was thus employed. 'Ah, Madam!' cried she, 'what a sad thing it is that married gentlemen will be so foolish! – Hang all the French, I say!' – 'What do'st mean, Jenny?' said Mrs. Munden. 'Ah, Madam!' replied she, 'I should have told you before, but that I was afraid of making you uneasy: but, since I find you know how things are, I shall make no secret of it. You may remember, Madam, that you gave me leave last Monday to go to see my sister – she lives in St. Martin's Lane – it would have been nearer for me, indeed, to have gone through the Mews; but, I know not how it happened, I went by Charing Cross; and, just as I was going to cross the way, who should I see pop out of a hackney-coach but my master and this Frenchwoman – they hurried together, arm in arm, into a bagnio – and you know, Madam, some of those places have but an ugly name: for my part, I was so confounded that I scarce knew whether I stood upon my head or my heels; but I did not say a word of what I had seen when I came home, till just now John came down and told us all how that wicked woman had affronted you.'

Mrs. Munden then recalled that Mr. Munden's man was in the room when she related the behaviour of Mademoiselle de Roquelair; which she now was not sorry for, nor of the fresh proof given her by this maid of the perfidy of her husband.

'Well, Jenny,' said she, 'I am not yet determined how I shall proceed; I am going to my brother's, and shall take Tom with me: if I do not come back to-night, he shall bring you instructions what things to send me; but, in the mean time, say nothing to your master of what we have been talking.'

Mrs. Munden could not forbear shedding tears, as she was going into her chair, at the thoughts of this exile, voluntary as it was, from a house she had so much right to call her own; but the poor maid roared out so loud at seeing her depart, that it brought all the servants out of the kitchen to know what was the matter; which, being told by Jenny, occasioned so general a grief among them for the loss of so good a mistress, that had Mademoiselle de Roquelair remained in the house, and the same servants also been continued, it is possible she would have had little either of respect or obedience from them.

But fortune spared this mortification, in order to inflict a much greater one on her ingratitude and treachery. Mr. Munden had not quitted the presence of his wife many minutes before he began to reflect seriously on this accident; he found it might prove a very vexatious one, if the consequences it seemed to threaten were not in time prevented: he highly blamed Mademoiselle de Roquelair for her behaviour to Mrs. Munden; not so much because it might give that lady room to suspect in what manner he had wronged her, as because it plainly shewed that the other intended to pin herself on him, and oblige him to support her – a thing which did not at all suit with his humour; he had gratified his passion almost to a surfeit – a very little longer time would have made him as heartily wish to get rid of her, as he had ever done to gain her; and although it could not be said he was as yet altogether cloyed with the pleasures she so lavishly bestowed, yet a little examination into the extent of his inclinations, convinced him that he could bear the loss of her for ever without pain.

While the blood runs high, and the fire is rampant for possession, prudence is of little force; but when the one begins to flag, the other resumes it's empire over the mind, and never rests till it finds means to retrieve what it has lost: he could now consider that the money remitted to Bologne by Mr. Thoughtless could be received by nobody but Mademoiselle de Roquelair herself, and that it was probable that gentleman, if told the usage that had been given to his sister, might be provoked to recal his order, and prevent the payment of it at all. This seemed, however, a plausible pretence for persuading her to go away directly, and also for making a merit to his wife of what he did.

Having fully determined within himself how to proceed in this affair, he shortened his morning's walk, and came home some hours before the usual time: he was at first a little fretted on being told Mrs. Munden was gone to her brother's, not doubting but the errand on which she went was to complain of the treatment she had received; but Jenny carefully concealing what her mistress had said to her concerning her intentions of coming back no more, he passed it lightly over, imagining her accusations and reproaches would cease, the object of them being once removed.

He found no difficulty in prevailing on Mademoiselle de Roquelair to go to Bologne. Three hundred louis-d'ors was too tempting a sum to be forfeited merely for the want of a little jaunt, especially as she considered that she might accomplish her business there and return to London within the compass of a very few days; and he told her that he would hire lodgings for her against her coming back.

'Well, then, my angel,' said he, 'no time is to be lost: as this is not post day, if you set out immediately for Dover, you may be at Bologne, and have received the money before any letter can reach that place to prevent it; for it is very likely that the spite my wife has towards you, may work upon the resentment of her brother to attempt such a thing.' Everything being concluded upon for this expedition, he went himself to procure a post-chaise, appointing her to meet him at a place he mentioned to her in an hour at farthest.

As he had promised to send all her baggage to the lodgings which he should provide for her return, she had nothing to do but to pack up some few necessaries to take with her. This little work being soon over, a hackney-coach carried her to the house that had been agreed upon; where she saw a post-chaise already at the door, and the diligent Mr. Munden waiting for her coming: as she proposed to reach Canterbury that same night, and it was then past two o'clock, the lovers were obliged to take a very hasty leave.

This double, deceitful man, having a farther view in what he did than she had any notion of, told her, at parting, that it would be proper for her to stay at Bologne till she received a letter from him with an account in what street and part of the town the lodgings he should provide for her were situated, to the end she might come directly into them on her arrival: he spoke this with an air so full of tenderness and care for her repose, that she had not the least suspicion of his drift; and replied, that she would not fail to do as he advised, but desired he would be as speedy as possible in writing to her; 'For,' cried she, embracing him, 'I shall think every day a year till I return to the arms of my dear Munden!'

Having thus, in reality, discarded, his mistress, though without her knowing he had done so, he went home, in order to boast to his wife of the complaisance he had shewn to her in this affair; but, finding she was not yet come back, he called for her maid, and bid her tell her, the moment she should return, that he had complied with her request, and made the Frenchwoman go out of the house.

After having said this, he went out again, and came not home till late at night; when he was confounded beyond measure on finding a letter from Mrs. Munden, which had been left for him by her own footman in the beginning of the evening; and contained these lines.

'To Mr. Munden.

Sir,

As you cannot but be sensible that the mutual engagements between us have been strictly adhered to on my part, and almost in every particular falsified on yours, you ought not to be surprized that I have at last resolved to put a final end to a way of life so unpleasing in the eyes of Heaven, and so disagreeable to ourselves: it never was in my power to make you truly happy, nor in your will to make me even tolerably easy; I therefore fly for ever from your ill-usage, and once more put myself under the protection of my friends, to whom I also shall commit the care of settling with you the terms of our separation; which being once agreed upon, you will not be troubled either with the complaints, or the reproaches, of your much-injured wife,

B. MUNDEN.

P.S. I have removed nothing out of your house but what was my own before marriage.'

Upon enquiring further into the matter, he was informed that Mrs. Munden had, indeed, removed a large India-chest, a bureau, cabinet dressing-table; and, in fine, every thing that belonged immediately to herself; and also that his family was now reduced to two, her own man and maid having followed her.

All this convincing him how much she was in earnest, involved him in the most perplexing cogitations; not that he regretted the parting with her through any remains of affection, or that his hardened heart was touched with a just sensibility of her merit, or with any repentance of his ill treatment of her; but that he knew such an affair must necessarily be attended with some noise and confusion, and in many respects give him a good deal of embarrassment: it was therefore these last two reasons which alone determined him to make use of all his artifice to bring about a second reconciliation.

That beautiful lady, in the mean time, had thoughts much more composed; her brother had received her in the most affectionate manner – had approved her conduct in regard to her unfaithful husband – had assured her of the continuance of his friendship and protection; and, before she could request it of him, invited her, and such of her servants as she chose should attend her, to remain in his house as long as she should think fit. He desired her to take upon her the sole command and management of his house and family, and assigned the best apartment for her particular use: in fine, he omitted nothing that might convince her of a sincere welcome.

On discoursing together concerning her obtaining a separate maintenance, it was the opinion of both of them, that Mr. Markland the lawyer should be advised with, as he was a man who could not but be well experienced in such affairs; and accordingly a servant was dispatched to that gentleman, to desire he would come to them the next day.

But though she had reason to be highly satisfied with the reception given her by her brother, yet she could not be quite easy till she should hear what judgment her dear Lady Loveit would pass on the step she had taken. She went the next morning to pay a visit at that lady's toilette; she related to her sincerely every particular of the provocation she had received, the manner in which she had resented it, and the resolution she had taken of living in an eternal state of separation from so bad a man: to which Lady Loveit replied, that though she was extremely sorry for the occasion, yet she thought if she had acted otherwise, it would have been an injustice not only to herself, but to all wives in general, by setting them an example of submitting to things required of them neither by law nor nature.

This encouragement, from a lady of her known scrupulous disposition, made Mrs. Munden not doubt but she would be equally absolved by Lady Trusty and her brother Frank; to both whom she wrote an account of all she had done.

On her return from Lady Loveit's, she found a letter from Mr. Munden, in answer to that she had sent to him the day before: the contents whereof were as follow.

'To Mrs. Munden.

Madam,
The unaccountableness of your behaviour astonishes me! For heaven's sake, how can you answer to yourself the having quitted your husband's house for so trifling a pretence? It is true, I did not at first give much regard to your complaint against Mademoiselle de Roquelair; but, on considering it, I obliged her to depart immediately. I do assure you she set out yesterday for Dover, and I believe by this time is as far as Calais on her way to Bologne; so that there now remains no excuse for your absenting yourself: and if you should continue to do so, it will be a very plain proof that you are extremely

wanting in that duty and affection which the laws both of God and man expect from you. But I flatter myself that is not the case; and therefore expect you will return with all possible expedition to him who will be always ready to prove himself your most affectionate husband,

G. MUNDEN.

P.S. I know not what you mean by terms of separation: a wife who elopes from her husband forfeits all claim to every thing that is his, and can expect nothing from him till she returns to her obedience; but were it otherwise, and the law entirely on your side in this point, you might be certain that I look upon the happiness of possessing you in too just a light to be easily brought into any agreement that would deprive me of you.'

Though Mr. Munden wanted not cunning in most things, yet in writing this epistle he seemed not to consider the spirit or the penetration of his wife, who, he might have known, had too great a share of both to be either intimidated by the majesterial air of some of the expressions, or soothed by the fawning, unsincere compliments, of the others.

This vain attempt therefore only served to remind her of the many proofs she had received both of his ill-nature and deceit towards her; and, instead of weakening the resolution she had taken of not living with him again, rather rendered it more strong and permanent.

CHAPTER XX

———•———

More of the same

MR. MARKLAND did not, like too many of his profession, ever flatter his clients with an assurance of success in any cause of which he himself was doubtful: he plainly told Mrs. Munden, that he feared not all the ill-usage she had sustained would be sufficient to compel her husband to allow her a separate maintenance. 'Honour and generosity may, indeed,' added he, 'oblige him to do that which, I am very apprehensive, the law will not enforce him to.'

'Alas!' cried Mrs. Munden, bursting into tears, 'if I can have no relief but from his honour and generosity, I must be miserable!' – 'Not so, my dear sister,' said Mr. Thoughtless, 'while you have a brother who has it in his power to support you against all the injuries of fortune, and the injustice of a husband so unworthy of you.'

She thanked him in terms which so affectionate an offer demanded from her, but could not help appearing very much dejected at what Mr. Markland had said to her: on which, 'Madam,' said he, 'though the letter of the law may not be altogether so favourable for you in this point as you certainly deserve, yet, notwithstanding that, and how refractory soever Mr. Munden may be in his principles or dispositions, I hope there may be means found to bring him to do you justice. I will wait on him – will talk to him in a proper manner; and do flatter myself with being able to give you a good account of what I have done.'

It is not to be doubted but both the brother and the sister earnestly intreated he would exert all his abilities in an affair which they easily saw would be difficult enough to manage; but the answers of this honest, good-natured gentleman, soon convinced them that there was no need of any persuasions to induce him to do every thing in his power for the service of ill-treated innocence.

Mrs. Munden having told him that about eleven o'clock was the most certain time for her husband to be spoke with, he went the next morning at that hour: on sending up his name, Mr. Munden guessed the errand on which he came; but that did not hinder him from ordering he should be introduced, nor, when he was so, from receiving him with that politeness he always used to strangers.

Mr. Markland began with telling him he was extremely sorry for the occasion on which he waited on him that morning; 'I little imagined,' said he, 'that when I drew up the articles for an union between you, Sir, and Mrs. Munden, I should ever have been employed in transacting a deed of separation: but, since it has unhappily proved so, I hope, at least, it may be done as amicably as the nature of the thing will admit.'

Mr. Munden at first affected to treat this proposal in a manner somewhat ludicrous; but perceiving it was not well taken by the other, 'You will pardon me, Sir,' cried he; 'I protest I am under the greatest consternation in the world, that my wife should have the assurance to trouble a gentleman of your character on so foolish an affair: upon my honour, Sir, there is nothing in it but mere whim – caprice!'

'If I did not think it sufficiently serious,' replied Mr. Markland, 'and were not also well convinced you will hereafter find it so, I should not have given either myself or you the trouble of this visit: but, Sir,' continued he, 'you may depend that the lady's complaints will have their weight.'

'All womanish spite, upon my soul, Sir!' resumed Mr. Munden; 'I defy her to accuse me of any one action that can justify her quitting my house, much less to prove any real injury received from me; without which, you know, Sir, there can be no pretence for separation.'

'You cannot as yet, Sir, be sensible what is in her power to prove,' said the lawyer: 'but God forbid this unhappy dissention should ever come to that! for, admitting she should be wanting in such proofs as the strictness of the law requires in these cases, the very attempt must necessarily involve you in an infinity of disquiet. Consider, Sir,' pursued he, 'when the affairs of a family are laid open, and every dispute between the husband and the wife exposed before a court of judicature, or even in a petition to a Lord Chancellor, the whole becomes a publick talk, and furnishes a matter of ridicule for the unthinking scoffers of the age.'

'I can easily prevent all this,' cried Mr. Munden hastily, 'by procuring a warrant from the Lord Chief Justice to force her immediately home.' – 'You may certainly do so,' cried Mr. Markland, with a half smile; 'but, Sir, are you sure of keeping her at home when you have got her there? Is it not in her power to leave you again the same day, nay, even the same hour, in which you compelled her to return? so that your whole time may be spent in an unavailing chase, somewhat of a piece with the fable of the Sisyphæan stone, which, as often as the driver forced to the height he aimed at, rolled back to it's beloved descent. In short, Sir, as Mrs. Munden is determined to live apart, you have no way to preserve her but by confinement; and I appeal to your own judgment how that would look in the eyes of the world, and what occasion for complaint it would afford to all her friends, who would, doubtless, have a strict watch on your behaviour.'

These words threw Mr. Munden into a deep reverie, which the other would not interrupt, being willing to see how far this last remonstrance had worked upon him; till, coming out of it, and vexed that he had shewn any discomposure; 'Well, Sir,' said he, 'if she resolves to persist in this obstinacy, let her enjoy her humour; I shall give myself no pain about it; but she must not expect I shall allow one penny towards her maintenance.'

It was on this head that Mr. Markland found he had occasion to employ all the rhetorick he was master of: he urged the unreason-ableness, the injustice, the cruelty, of denying the means of subsistence to a lady whose whole fortune he enjoyed; said such a thing was altogether unprecedented among persons of condition; and, to prove what he alledged, produced many instances of wives who, on parting from their husbands, were allowed a provision proportionable to the sums they had brought in marriage.

All these arguments were enforced in terms so strong and so pathetick, that Mr. Munden could make no other answer than, that he did not desire to part – that it was her own fault – and that if she would not return to her duty, she ought to be starved into a more just sense of it – and that he was very sure the law would not compel him to do any thing for her: on which Mr. Markland again reminded him of the vexation, the fatigue, the disgrace, with which a suit commenced by either party must be attended, in whose favour soever the decision should be made.

He talked so long on the subject, that Mr. Munden, either to get rid of him, or becuase he was really uncertain what to do, at last told him that he would consider on what he had been saying, and let him know his resolution in a week's time. Mr. Markland then replied, that he would trouble him no farther for the present; and after having prefixed a day for waiting on him again, took his leave.

The mind of Mr. Munden was, indeed, in the utmost confusion amidst that variety of vexatious incidents which he had now to struggle with – the little probability he found there was of re-establishing himself in the favour of his patron – the loss of all his hopes that way – the sudden departure of a wife whom, though he had no affection for, he looked upon as a necessary appendix to his house – the noise her having taken such a step would make in the town – the apprehensions of being obliged to grant her a separate maintenance; all these things put together, it is certain, were sufficient to overwhelm a man of less impatient temper.

He cursed his amour with the Frenchwoman, as having been the cause of this last misfortune falling on him; and, to prevent all farther trouble on her account, ordered that the baggage she had left behind should be immediately put on board a vessel, and sent after her to Bologne: he also wrote to her at the same time, acquainting her with the disturbance which had happened; and that it was highly necessary for his future peace that he should see her no more, nor even hold any correspondence with her.

Mrs. Munden, in the mean time, was far from being perfectly easy; though Mr. Markland gave her hopes that her husband would very speedily be brought to settle things between them in a reasonable way; and her brother was every day giving her fresh assurances of his friendship and protection, whether that event proved favourable or not: yet all this was not enough to quell some scruples which now rose in her mind; the violence of that passion which had made her resolve to leave Mr. Munden being a little evaporated, the vows she had made him at the altar were continually in her thoughts; she could not quite assure herself that a breach of that solemn covenant was to be justified by any provocations; nor whether the worst usage on the part of the husband could authorize resentment in that of a wife.

She was one day disburdening her disquiets on this score to her dear Lady Loveit, in terms which made that lady see, more than ever she had done before, the height of her virtue, and the delicacy of her sentiments, when Sir Bazil came hastily into the room with a paper in his hand; and after paying his compliments to Mrs. Munden, 'My dear,' said he to his lady, 'I have very agreeable news to tell you; I have just received a letter from my brother Trueworth, which informs me that he is upon the road, and we shall have him with us this evening.' – 'I am extremely glad,' replied she; 'and, likewise, that he is so good to let us know it, that I may make some little preparations for his welcome.'

Mrs. Munden could not be told that Mr. Trueworth was so near, and might presently be in the same room with her, without the utmost confusion; which she fearing would be observed, laid hold of the pretence Lady Loveit's last words furnished her with, of taking her leave; and, rising hastily up, 'I will wait on your ladyship,' said she, 'at a more convenient time; for I perceive you are now going to be busy.' – 'Not at all,' replied the other; 'three words will serve for all the instructions I have to give; therefore, pr'ythee, dear creature, sit down.' In speaking these words, she took hold of one of her hands, and Sir Bazil of the other, in order to replace her on the settee she had just quitted; but she resisting their efforts, and desiring to be excused staying any longer, 'I protest,' cried Lady Loveit, 'this sudden resolution of leaving us would make one think you did it to avoid Mr. Trueworth! and, if that be the case, I must tell you, that you are very ungrateful, as he always expresses the greatest regard for you.' – 'Aye, aye!' said Sir Bazil, laughing; 'old love cannot be forgot: I have heard him utter many tender things of the charming Miss Betsy Thoughtless, even since his marriage with my sister.'

'I ought not, then,' replied she, 'to increase the number of obligations I have to him by that compassion which I know he would bestow on my present distress: but I assure you, Sir Bazil, I would not quit you and my dear Lady Loveit thus abruptly, if some letters I have to write, and other affairs which require immediate dispatch, did not oblige me to it.'

On this they would not offer to detain her; and she went home to give a loose to those agitations which the mention of Mr. Trueworth always involved her in.

CHAPTER XXI

●

Affords variety of amusement

MRS. MUNDEN was so ignorant of her own heart, in relation to what it felt on Mr. Trueworth's account, that she imagined she had only fled his presence because she could not bear a man who had courted her so long should see her thus unhappy by the choice she had made of another.

'I am well assured,' cried she, 'that he has too much generosity to triumph in my misfortune, and too much complaisance to remind me of the cause: yet would his eyes tacitly reproach my want of judgment; and mine, too, might perhaps, in spite of me, confess, as the poet says, that –

> "I, like the child, whose folly prov'd it's loss,
> Refus'd the gold, and did accept the dross."

This naturally leading her into some reflections on the merits of Mr. Trueworth, she could not help wondering by what infatuation she had been governed when rejecting him, or, what was tantamount to rejecting him, treating him in such a manner as might make him despair of being accepted. – 'What, though my heart was insensible of love,' said she, 'my reason, nay, my very pride, might have influenced me to embrace a proposal which would have rendered me the envy of my own sex, and excited the esteem and veneration of the other.' Thinking still more deeply, 'O God!' cried she with vehemence, 'to what a height of happiness might I have been raised! and into what an abyss of wretchedness am I now plunged! – Irretrievably undone – married without loving or being beloved – lost in my bloom of years to every joy that can make life a blessing!'

Nothing so much sharpens the edge of affliction as a consciousness of having brought it upon ourselves, to remember that all we could wish for, all that could make us truly happy, was once in our power to be possessed of; and wantonly shunning the good that Heaven and fortune offered, we headlong run into the ills we mourn, rendering them doubly grievous.

This being the case with our heroine, how ought all the fair and young to guard against a vanity so fatal to a lady, who, but for that one foible, had been the happiest, as she was in all other respects the most deserving, of her sex! But to return.

A just sensibility of the errors of her past conduct, joined with some other emotions, which the reader may easily guess at, though she as yet knew not the meaning of herself, gave her but little repose that night; and, pretty early the next morning, she received no inconsiderable addition to her perplexities.

The time in which Mr. Munden had promised to give his answer to the lawyer was now near expired; yet he was as irresolute as ever: loath he was to have the affair between him and his wife made publick, and equally loath to comply with her demands. Before he did either, it therefore came into his head to try what effect menaces would produce; and accordingly wrote to her in these terms.

'To Mrs. Munden.

Madam,

Though your late behaviour has proved the little affection you have for me, I still retain too much for you to be able to part with you. No! be assured, I never will forego the right that marriage gives me over you – will never yield to live a widower while I am a husband; and, if you return not within four and twenty hours, shall take such measures as the law directs, to force you back to my embraces. By this time to-morrow you may expect to have such company at your levee as you will not be well pleased with, and from whose authority not all your friends can screen you: but, as I am unwilling to expose you, I once more court you to spare yourself this disgrace, and me the pain of inflicting it. I give you this day to consider on what you have to do. The future peace of us both depends on your result; for your own reason ought to inform you, that being brought to me by compulsion will deserve other sort of treatment than such as you might hope to find on returning of your own accord to your much-affronted husband,

G. MUNDEN.'

This letter very much alarmed both the sister and the brother: the former trembled at the thoughts of seeing herself in the hands of the officers of justice; and the latter could not but be uneasy that a disturbance of this kind should happen in his house. They were just going to send for Mr. Markland, to consult him on what was to be done, when that gentleman, whom chance had brought that way, luckily came in. He found Mr. Thoughtless in great discomposure, and Mrs. Munden almost drowned in tears. On being informed of the occasion, 'I see no reason,' said he gravely, 'for all this: I cannot think that Mr. Munden will put in execution what he threatens; at last, not till after I have spoke to him again. I rather think he writes in this manner only to terrify you, Madam, into a submission to his will. However,' continued he, after a pretty long pause, 'to be secure from all danger of an affront this way, I think it would be highly proper you should retire to some place where he may not know to find you, till I have once more tried how far he may be prevailed upon to do you justice.'

This advice being highly approved of, 'My wife's sister,' resumed he, 'has a very pleasant and commodious house on the bank of the river on the Surrey side – she takes lodgers sometimes; but at present is without: so that, if you resolve to be concealed, you cannot find a more convenient retreat; especially as, it's being so near London, nothing of moment can happen here but what you may be apprized of in little more than an hour.'

Mrs. Munden testifying as much satisfaction at this proposal as a person in her circumstances could be capable of feeling, Mr. Markland told her that he was ready to conduct her immediately to the place he mentioned; and her brother adding that he would accompany them, and see his sister safe to her new abode, they all set out together on their little voyage; Mrs. Munden having first given directions to her servants where they should follow her with such things as she thought would be wanted during her stay there.

On their arrival, they found Mr. Markland had spoken very modestly of the place he recommended: the house was pleasant almost beyond description, and rendered much more so by the obliging behaviour of it's owner.

They all dined together that day; and, on parting, it was agreed that Mrs. Munden should send her man every morning to town, in order to bring her intelligence of whatever accidents had happened in relation to her affairs on the preceding day.

As much as this lady had been rejoiced at the kind reception she had met with from her brother under her misfortunes, she was now equally pleased at being removed for a time from him, not only because she thought herself secure from any insults that might be offered by her husband, but also because this private recess seemed a certain defence against the sight of Mr. Trueworth – a thing she knew not well how to have avoided in town, without breaking off her acquaintance with Lady Loveit.

After the gentlemen were gone, the sister-in-law of Mr.Markland led her fair guest into the garden, which before she had only a cursory view of. She shewed her, among many other things, several curious exotick plants, which, she told her, she had procured from the nurseries of some persons of condition to whom she had the honour to be known: but Mrs. Munden being no great connoisseur that way, did not take much notice of what she said concerning them; till, coming to the lower end, she perceived a little wicker-gate. 'To where does this lead?' cried she. 'I will shew you presently, Madam,' replied the other; and, pulling it open, they both entered into a grass-walk, hemmed in on each side with trees, which seemed as old as the creation. They had not gone many paces, before an arbour, erected between two of these venerable monuments of antiquity, and overspread with jessamines and honeysuckles, attracted Mrs. Munden's eyes. 'Oh, how delightful is this!' said she. 'It would have been much more so, Madam, if it had been placed on the other side of the walk,' said the gentlewoman; 'and, if I live till next spring, will have the position of it altered. You will presently see my reasons for it,' continued she, 'if you please to turn your eyes a little to the right.' Mrs. Munden doing as she was desired, had the prospect of a very beautiful garden, decorated with plots of flowers, statues, and trees cut in a most elegant manner. 'Does all this belong to you?' demanded she, somewhat surprized. 'No, Madam,' answered the other; 'but they are part of the same estate, and, at present, rented by a gentleman of condition, who lives at the next door. The walk we are in is also common to us both, each having a gate to enter it at pleasure; though, indeed, they little frequent it, having much finer of their own.' With such like chat they beguiled the time, till the evening dew reminded them it was best to quit the open air.

Mrs. Munden passed this night in more tranquillity than she had done many preceding ones: she awoke, however, much sooner than was her custom; and, finding herself less disposed to return to the embraces of sleep than to partake that felicity she heard a thousand chearful birds tuning their little throats in praise of, she rose, and went down into the garden: the contemplative humour she was in, led her to the arbour she had been so much charmed with the night before; she threw herself upon the mossy seat, where scenting the fragrancy of the sweets around her, made more delicious by the freshness of the morning's gale, 'How delightful, how heavenly!' said she to herself, 'is this solitude! how truly preferable to all the noisy, giddy pleasures, of the tumultuous town! yet how have I despised and ridiculed the soft sincerity of a country life!' Then recollecting some discourse she formerly had with Mr. Trueworth on that subject, 'I wonder,' cried she, 'what Mr. Trueworth would say if he knew the change that a little time has wrought in me! he would certainly find me now more deserving of his friendship than ever he could think me of his love: but he is ignorant, insensible, of my real sentiments; and if Sir Bazil and Lady Loveit should tell him with what abruptness I fled their house at the news of his approach, I must appear in his eyes the most vain, stupid, thankless, creature I once was. But, such is my unhappy situation, that I dare not even wish he should discover what passes in my heart: the just sensibility of his amiable qualities, and of the services he has done me, which would once have been meritorious in me to have avowed, would now be highly criminal.'

With these reflections she took out Mr. Trueworth's picture, which she always carried about her; and, looking on it with the greatest tenderness, 'Though I no more must see himself,' said she, 'I may, at least, be allowed to pay the tribute of my gratitude to this dumb representative of the man to whom I have been so much obliged.' At this instant, a thousand proofs of love given her by the original of the copy in her hand, occurring all at once to her remembrance, tears filled her eyes, and her breast swelled with involuntary sighs.

In this painfully pleasing amusement did she continue for some time; and had, doubtless, done so much longer, if a sudden rustling among the leaves behind her, had not made her turn her head to see what had occasioned it: but where are the words that can express the surprize, the wild confusion, she was in, when the first glance of her eyes presented her with the sight of the real object, whose image she had been thus tenderly contemplating! She shrieked – the picture dropped from her hand – the use of her faculties forsook her – she sunk from the seat where she was sitting, and had certainly fainted quite away but for the immediate assistance of the person who had caused the extraordinary emotions.

Her fancy, indeed, strong as it was, had formed no visionary appearance – it was the very identical Mr. Trueworth whom chance had brought to make the discovery of a secret which, of all things in the world, he had the least suspicion of.

He was intimately acquainted with the person to whom the house adjoining to that where Mrs. Munden lodged belonged; and, hearing where he was, on his return from Oxfordshire, had come the evening before, intending to pass a day or two with him in this agreeable recess.

As he was never a friend to much sleeping, he rose that morning, and went down into the garden before the greatest part of the family had quitted their beds: he saw Mrs. Munden while at too great a distance to know who she was; yet did her air and motion, as she walked, strike him with something which made him willing to see what sort of face belonged to so genteel a form. Drawing more near, his curiosity was gratified with a sight he little expected: he was just about to accost her with the salutation of the morning, when she went into the arbour, and seated herself in the manner already described. The extreme pensiveness of her mind had hindered her from perceiving that any one was near; but the little covert under which she was placed being open on both sides, he had a full view of every thing she did. Though she was in the most negligent night-dress that could be, she seemed as lovely to him as ever; all his first flames rekindled in his heart, while gazing on her with this uninterrupted freedom: he longed to speak to her, but durst not, lest, by doing so, he should be deprived of the pleasure he now enjoyed; till, observing she had something in her hand which she seemed to look upon with great attention, and sometimes betrayed agitations he had never seen in her before, he was impatient to discover, if possible, the motive; he therefore advanced as gently as he could towards the back of the arbour; which having no wood-work, and the leafy canopy only supported by ozier boughs placed at a good distance from each other, he had a full opportunity of beholding all that the reader has been told. But what was his amazement to find it was his own picture! – that very picture, which had been taken from the painter's, was the object of her meditations! He heard her sighs – he saw her lovely hand frequently put up to wipe away the tears that fell from her eyes while looking on it; he also saw her, more than once, (though, doubtless, in those moments, not knowing what she did) press the lifeless image to her bosom with the utmost tenderness: scarce could he give credit to the testimony of his senses, near as he was to her; he even strained his sight to be more sure; and, forgetting all the precautions he had taken, thrust himself as far as he was able between the branches of which the arbour was composed.

On perceiving the effect this last action had produced, the gate, though not above twenty paces off, seemed to slow a passage to fly to her relief; and, setting his foot upon a pedestal of a statue, quick as thought, or the flash of elemental fire, sprang over the myrtle-hedge that parted the garden from the walk. 'Ah, Madam!' cried he, catching her in his arms to hinder her from falling, 'what has the unhappy Trueworth done to render his presence so alarming! How have I deserved to appear thus dreadful in your eyes!'

That admirable presence of mind which Mrs. Munden had shewn on many occasions, did not on this entirely leave her: the time he was speaking those few words sufficed to enable her to recollect her scattered spirits; and, withdrawing herself from the hold he had taken of her, and removing a little farther on the bench, as if to give him room to sit, 'Sir,' said she, with a voice pretty well composed, 'the obligations I have to you demand other sort of sentiments than those you seem to accuse me of; but I thought myself alone, and was not guarded against the surprize of meeting you in this place.' – 'I ought, indeed,' replied he, 'to have been more cautious in my approach, especially as I found you deep in contemplation; which, perhaps, I have been my own enemy by interrupting.'

Till he spoke in this manner, she was not quite assured how far he had been witness of her behaviour; but what he now said confirming her of what she had but feared before, threw her into a second confusion little inferior to the former. He saw it – but saw it without that pity he would have felt had it proceeded from any other motive; and, eager to bring her to a more full eclaircissement, 'If you really think, Madam,' said he, 'that you have any obligations to me, you may requite them all by answering sincerely to one question. Tell me, I beseech you,' continued he, taking up the picture, which she had neither thought nor opportunity to remove from the place where it had fallen; 'resolve me how this little picture came into your possession?' What was now the condition of Mrs. Munden! She could neither find any pretence to evade the truth, nor fit words to confess it; till Mr. Trueworth repeating his request, and vowing he would never leave her till she granted it, 'What need have I to answer?' said she, blushing. 'You know it what manner it was taken from the painter's; and the sight of it in my hand is sufficient to inform you of the whole.'

'Charming declaration! – transporting, ravishing, to thought!' cried he, kissing her hand. 'O had I known it sooner, engaged as I then was to one who well deserved my love; could I have guessed Miss Betsy Thoughtless was the contriver of that tender fraud; I know not what revolution might have happened in my heart! the empire you had there was never totally extirpated; and kindness might have regained what cruelty had lost!' – 'Do not deceive yourself, Sir,' said she, interrupting him with all the courage she could assume; 'nor mistake that for love which was only the effect of mere gratitude.' These words were accompanied with a look which once would have struck him with the most submissive awe; but he was now too well acquainted with the sentiments she had for him to be deterred by any other outward shew of coldness. 'Call it by what name you please,' cried he, 'so you permit me the continuance of it, and vouchsafe me the same favours you bestow on my insensible resemblance.' In speaking this, he threw his arms about her waist, not regarding the efforts she made to hinder him, and clasped her to his breast with a vehemence which in all his days of courtship to her he never durst attempt. 'Forbear, Sir,' said she; 'you know I am not at liberty to be entertained with discourses, or with actions, of this nature. Loose me this moment! or be assured, all the kind thoughts I had of you, and on which you have too much presumed, will be converted into the extremest hatred and detestation!' The voice in which she uttered this menace convincing him how much she was in earnest, he let go his hold, removed some paces from her, and beheld her for some moments with a silent admiration. 'I have obeyed you, Madam!' cried he, with a deep sigh; 'you are all angel – be all angel still! Far be it from me to tempt you from the glorious height you stand in: yet how unhappy has this interview made me! I love you without daring even to wish for a return! nay, so fully has your virtue conquered, that I must love you more for the repulse you have given my too audacious hopes. You may at least pity the fate to which I am condemned.'

'It would be in vain for me,' replied she, in a voice somewhat broken by the inward conflict she sustained, 'to endeavour to conceal what my inadvertencies have so fully betrayed to you; and you may assure yourself, that I shall think on you with all the tenderness that honour, and the duties of my station, will admit. But remember, Sir, I am a wife; and, being such, ought never to see you more: in regard, therefore, to my reputation and peace of mind, I must intreat you will henceforth avoid my presence with the same care I will do yours.'

'Severe as this injunction is,' replied he, 'my soul avows the justice of it; and I submit.' – 'Farewel, then!' said she, rising from her feet. 'Oh, farewel!' cried he, and kissed her hand with emotions not to be expressed. 'Farewel for ever!' rejoined she, turning hastily away to prevent his seeing the tears with which her eyes were overcharged, and in that cruel instant overflowed her cheeks. She advanced with all the speed she could towards the wicker-gate; but, when there, could not forbear giving one look behind; and, perceiving he had left the walk, and was proceeding through the garden, with folded arms, and a dejected pace, 'Poor Trueworth!' cried she, and pursued him with her eyes till he was quite out of sight.

Some readers may, perhaps, blame Mr. Trueworth, as having presumed too far on the discovery of the lady's passion; and others, of a contrary way of thinking, laugh at him for being so easily repulsed: but all, in general, must applaud the conduct of Mrs. Munden. Till this dangerous instance, she had never had an opportunity of shewing the command she had over herself; and, as Mr. Eastcourt justly says –

> 'Ne'er let the fair-one boast of virtue prov'd,
> Till she has well refus'd the man she truly lov'd.'

CHAPTER XXII

───────●───────

Is less pleasing than the former

AFTER this solemn parting between Mr. Trueworth and Mrs. Munden, that lady's mind was in too much disorder to think what was become of the little picture that had occasioned it; till, an hour or two after, the maid of the house came running into the chamber with it in her hand. 'Does this pretty picture belong to you, Madam?' said she. Mrs. Munden started; but, soon recovering herself, answered that it did – said that it was the picture of her youngest brother – and that she believed she might pull it out of her pocket with her handkerchief, or some how or other drop it in the walk. 'Aye, to be sure, it was so,' said the maid; 'for it was there I found it: as I was going to the pump for some water, I saw something that glittered just by the little arbour, on which I ran and took it up; but my mistress told me she believed it was yours; for she knew your ladyship was in the walk this morning.' – 'I am glad thou hast found it,' replied Mrs. Munden; 'for it would have vexed me to the heart to have lost it.' – 'Aye, to be sure, Madam!' cried she; 'for it is a sweet picture – your brother is a handsome gentleman – I warrant there are a thousand ladies in love with him.' Mrs. Munden could not forbear smiling at the simplicity of the wench; but, willing to be rid of her, rewarded her honesty with a crown-piece, and dismissed her.

She was rejoiced, indeed, to have this picture once more in her possession; not only because some other might have found and kept it, but also because she thought she might indulge herself in looking on it without any breach of that duty to which she was resolved so strictly to adhere. To be secure, however, from a second rencounter with the original in that place, she kept close in the house, and stirred not out of it all the time he was there: but her apprehensions on this score were needless; Mr. Trueworth religiously observed the promise he had made her; and, lest he should be under any temptation to break it while so near her, took leave of his friend that same day, and returned to London; but carried with him sentiments very different from those he had brought down, as will hereafter appear.

As to Mrs. Munden, she found that she had no less occasion for exerting the heroine when alone, than when encircled in the arms of Mr. Trueworth: the accident which had betrayed the secret of her heart to him had also discovered it to herself. She was now convinced that it was something more than esteem – than friendship – than gratitude – his merits had inspired her with; she was conscious that, while she most resisted the glowing pressure of his lips, she had felt a guilty pleasure in the touch which had been near depriving her of doing so; and that, though she had resolved never to see him more, it would be very difficult to refrain wishing to be for ever with him.

This she thought so highly criminal in herself, that she ought not to indulge the remembrance of so dear, so dangerous, an invader of her duty; yet when she considered that, merely for her sake, and not through the weak resistance she had made, his own honour had nobly triumphed over wild desire in a heart so young and amorous as his, it increased that love and admiration which she in vain endeavoured to subdue: and she could not help crying out, with Calista in the play –

> 'Oh, had I sooner known thy wond'rous virtue,
> Thy love, thy truth, thou excellent young man!
> We might have both been happy.'

But, to banish as much as possible all those ideas which her nicety of honour made her tremble at, it was her fixed determination to retire into L—e as soon as she had ended her affairs with her husband, and pass the remainder of her days, where she should never hear the too dear name of Trueworth.

She did not, therefore, neglect sending her servant to town; but he returned that day, and several succeeding ones, without the least intelligence; no letter nor message from Mr. Munden having been left for her at her brother's: on which she began to imagine that he never had, in reality, intended to put his threats in execution.

Mr. Markland, in the mean time, had been twice to wait upon him; but the servants told him that their master was extremely indisposed, and could not be seen: this he looked upon as a feint to put off giving him an answer as he had promised; and both Mr. Thoughtless and his sister were of the same opinion when they heard it. Mr. Markland went again and again, however; but was still denied access: near a whole week passing over in this manner, Mrs. Munden grew very uneasy, fearing she should be able to obtain as little justice as favour from her husband.

But, guilty as he had been in other respects, he was entirely innocent in this: the force of the agitation he had of late sustained, joined to repeated debauches, had over-heated his blood, and thrown him into a very violent fever, insomuch that in a few days his life was despaired of; the whispers of all about him – the looks of the physician that attended him – and, above all, what he felt within himself, convincing him of the danger he was in – all his vices, all his excesses, now appeared to him such as they truly were, and filled him with a remorse which he had been but too much addicted to ridicule in others: in fine, the horrors of approaching dissolution, rendered him one of those many examples which daily verify these words of Mr. Dryden –

> 'Sure there are none but fear a future state!
> And when the most obdurate swear they do not,
> Their trembling hearts belie their boasting tongues!'

Among the number of those faults which presented him with the most direful images, that of the ill-treatment he had given a wife, who so little deserved it, lay not the least heavy upon his conscience: he sent his servants to Mr. Thoughtless, at whose house he imagined she still was, to intreat he would prevail on her to see him before he died; but that gentleman giving a very slight answer, as believing it all artifice, he engaged the apothecary who administered to him, and was known by Mr. Thoughtless, to go on the same errand; on which the brother of Mrs. Munden said she was not with him at present, but he would send to let her know what had happened. Accordingly, he dispatched one of his men immediately to her with the following billet.

'To Mrs. Munden.

Dear sister,
Mr. Cardiack, the apothecary, assures me that your husband is in fact ill, and in extreme danger; he is very pressing to see you: I will not

pretend to advise you what to do on this occasion – you are the best judge; I shall only say that, if you think fit to comply with his request, you must be speedy; for, it seems, it is the opinion of the gentlemen of the faculty, that he is very near his end. I am, dear sister, yours affectionately,

T. THOUGHTLESS.'

Not all the indifference she had for the person of Mr. Munden – not all the resentment his moroseness and ill-nature had excited in her – could hinder her from feeling an extreme shock on hearing his life was in danger: she sought for no excuses, either to evade or delay what he desired of her; she went directly to him, equally inclined to do so by her compassion, as she thought herself obliged to it by her duty.

As she entered the chamber, she met the apothecary coming out: in asking him some questions, though she spoke very low, Mr. Munden thought he distinguished her voice; and cried out, as loud as he was able, 'Is my wife here?' On which, approaching the bed, and gently opening one of the curtains, 'Yes, Mr. Munden,' replied she; 'I am come to offer all the assistance in my power; and am sorry to find you are in any need of it.' – 'This is very kind,' said he, and stretched out one of his hands towards her, which she took between hers with a great deal of tenderness: 'I have been much to blame,' resumed he; 'I have greatly wronged you; but forgive me – if I live, I will endeavour to deserve it.'

'I hope,' said she, 'Heaven will restore your health, and that we may live together in a manner becoming persons united as we are.' – 'Then you will not leave me?' cried he. 'Never,' answered she, 'till your behaviour shall convince me you do not desire my stay.'

Here he began to make solemn protestations of future amendment; but his voice failing him, through extreme weakness, a deep sigh, and tender pressure of his cheek to hers, as she leaned her head upon the pillow, gave her to understand what more he would have said: on this she assured him she was ready to believe every thing he would have her – intreated him to compose himself, and endeavour to get a little rest. 'In the mean time,' said she, 'I will order things so that I may lie in the same room with you, and quit your presence neither night nor day.'

Here he pressed his face close to hers again, in token of the satisfaction he felt in hearing what she said; and the nurse who attended him that instant presenting him with some things the physician had ordered should be given him about that hour, joined her entreaties with those of Mrs. Munden, that he would try to sleep; to which he made a sign that he would do so: and, the curtains being drawn, they both retired to the farther end of the room.

As he lay pretty quiet for a considerable time, Mrs. Munden recollected that there was a thing which friendship and good manners exacted from her: she had wrote, the very day before, to Lady Loveit, acquainting her with the motive which had obliged her to quit her brother's house, and desiring she would favour her with a visit, as soon as convenience would permit, at the place of her retirement. As she doubted not but the good-nature of this lady would prevail on her to comply with her request, she could not dispense with sending her an immediate account of the sudden revolution in her affairs, and the accident which had occasioned this second removal.

She had no sooner dispatched a little billet for this purpose, than the groans of Mr. Munden, testifying that he was awake, drew both her and the nurse again to the bed-side: they found him in very great agonies, and without the power of speech; the doctor and apothecary were sent for in a great hurry; but, before either of them came, the unhappy gentleman had breathed his last.

Mrs. Munden had not affected any thing more in this interview than what she really felt; her virtue and her compassion had all the effect on her that love has in most others of her sex; she had been deeply touched at finding her husband in so deplorable a situation; the tenderness he had now expressed for her, and his contrition for his past faults, made a great impression on her mind; and the shock of seeing him depart was truly dreadful to her: the grief she appeared in was undissembled – the tears she shed unforced; she withdrew into another room; where, shutting herself up for some hours, life, death, and futurity, were the subject of her meditations.

CHAPTER XXIII

———•———

Contains a very brief account of every material occurrence that happened in regard of our fair widow, during the space of a whole year, with some other particulars of less moment

MR. THOUGHTLESS was not at home when the news of Mr. Munden's death arrived; but, as soon as he was informed of it, he went to his sister; and, on finding her much more deeply affected at this accident than he could have imagined, pressed her, in the most tender terms, to quit that scene of mortality, and return to his house: the persuasions of a brother, who of late had behaved with so much kindnes towards her, prevailed on her to accept of the invitation; and, having given some necessary orders in regard to the family, was carried away that same night in a chair, with the curtains close drawn.

She saw no company, however, till after the funeral; and, when that was over, Lady Loveit was the first admitted. As Mrs. Munden was still under a great dejection of spirits, which was visible in her countenance, 'If I did not know you to be the sincerest creature in the world,' said Lady Loveit, 'I should take you to be the greatest dissembler in it; for it would be very difficult for any one less acquainted with you, to believe you could be really afflicted at the death of a person whose life rendered you so unhappy.'

'Mistake me not, Lady Loveit,' answered she; 'I do not pretend to lament the death of Mr. Munden, as it deprives me of his society, or as that of a person with whom I could ever have enjoyed any great share of felicity, even though his life had made good the professions of his last moments: but I lament him as one who was my husband, whom duty forbids me to hate while living, and whom decency requires me to mourn for when dead.'

'So, then,' cried Lady Loveit, 'I find you take as much pains to grieve for a bad husband, as those who have the misfortune to lose a good one do to alleviate their sorrows: but, my dear,' continued she, with a more serious air, 'I see no occasion for all this. I am well assured that your virtue, and the sweetness of your temper, enabled you to discharge all the duties of a wife to Mr. Munden while alive; and with that I think you ought to be content: he is now dead – the covenant between you is dissolved – Heaven has released you – and, I hope, forgiven him; decency obliges you to wear black – forbids you to appear abroad for a whole month – and at any publick place of diversion for a much longer time; but it does not restrain you from being easy in yourself, and chearful with your friends.'

'Your ladyship speaks right,' said Mrs. Munden: 'but yet there is a shock in death which one cannot presently get over.' – 'I grant there is,' replied Lady Loveit; 'and if we thought too deeply on it, we should feel all the agonies of that dreadful hour before our time, and become a burden to ourselves and to the world.'

It is certain, indeed, that the surprize and ptiy for Mr. Munden's sudden and unexpected fate had at the first overwhelmed her soul; yet, when those emotions were a little evaporated, she rather indulged affliction, because she thought it her duty to do so, than endeavoured any way to combat with it.

It was not, therefore, very difficult to reason her out of a melancholy which she had in a manner forced upon herself, and was far from being natural to her; and when once convinced that she ought to be easy under this stroke of Providence, became entirely so.

The painful task she had imposed upon her mind being over, more agreeable ones succeeded: the remembrance of Mr. Trueworth – his recovered love – the knowledge he had of hers – and the consideration that now both of them were in a condition to avow their mutual tenderness without a crime, could not but transfuse a sensation more pleasing than she had ever before been capable of experiencing.

In the mean time, that gentleman passed through a variety of emotions on her account; nor will it seem strange he should do so to any one who casts the least retrospect on his former behaviour; he had loved her from the first moment he beheld her; and had continued to love her for a long series of time with such an excess of passion, that not all his reason on her ill-treatment of him, and her supposed unworthiness, was scarce sufficient to enable him wholly to

desist: a new amour was requisite to divide his wishes – the fondness
and artful blandishments of Miss Flora served to wean his heart from
the once darling object – but there demanded no less than the
amiable person, and more amiable temper, of Miss Harriot, to drive
thence an idea so accustomed to preside. All this, however, as it
appeared, did not wholly extinguish the first flame; the innocence of
the charming Miss Betsy fully cleared up – all the errors of her
conduct reformed – rekindled in him an esteem; the sight of her,
after so many months absence, made the seemingly dead embers of
desire begin to glow, and, on the discovery of her sentiments in his
favour, burst forth into a blaze: he was not master of himself in the
first rush of so joyous a surprize – he forget she was married – he
approached her in the manner the reader has already been told; and
for which he afterwards severely condemned himself, as thinking he
ought to be content with knowing she loved him, without putting her
modesty to the blush by letting her perceive the discovery he had
made.

As Lady Loveit, without suspecting the effect which her discourse
produced, had been often talking of the ill-treatment she received
from Mr. Munden, and the necessity she had been under of quitting
his house, the sincere veneration she now had for her made him
sympathize in all the disquiets he was sensible she sustained; but
when he heard this cruel husband was no more, and, at the same
time, was informed in what manner she behaved, both in his last
moments, and after his decease, nothing, not even his love, could
equal his admiration of her virtue and her prudence.

What would he not now have given to have seen her! but he knew
such a thing was utterly impracticable; and to attempt it might lose
him all the tenderness she had for him: his impatience, however,
would not suffer him to seem altogether passive and unconcerned at
an event of so much moment to the happiness of them both; and he
resolved to write, but to find terms to express himself so as not to
offend either her delicacy, by seeming too presuming, or her
tenderness, by a pretended indifference, cost him some pains; but, at
length, he dictated the following little billet.

'To Mrs. Munden.

Madam,
I send you no compliments of condolance; but beg you to be assured,

that my heart is too deeply interested in every thing that regards you, to be capable of feeling the least satisfaction while yours remains under any inquietude: all I wish at present is, that you would believe this truth; which, if you do, I know you have too much justice, and too much generosity, to lavish all your commiseration on the insensible dead, but will reserve some part for the living, who stand most in need of it. I dare add no more as yet, than that I am, with an esteem perfect and inviolable, Madam, your most obedient, most devoted, and most faithful servant,

C. TRUEWORTH.

These few lines, perhaps, served more to raise the spirits of Mrs. Munden than all she could receive from any other quarter; she nevertheless persevered in maintaining the decorum of her condition; and as she had resolved to retire into L——e in case of a separation from her husband, she thought it most proper to fix her residence in that place in her state of widowhood, at least for the first year of it.

Accordingly, she wrote to Lady Trusty to acquaint her with her intentions, and received an answer such as she expected, full of praises for her conduct in this point, and the most pressing invitations to come down with all the speed she could.

What little business she had in London was soon dispatched, and all was ready for her quitting it within a month after the death of Mr. Munden: places for herself and her maid were taken in the stagecoach – all her things were packed up, and sent to the inn; she thought nothing now remained but to take leave of Lady Loveit, whom she expected that same evening, being the last she was to stay in town; but, near as her departure was, fortune in the mean time had contrived an accident, which put all her fortitude, and presence of mind, to as great a trial as she had ever yet sustained.

Lady Loveit, having got a cold, had complained of some little disorder the day before; and though nothing could be more slight than her indisposition, yet, as she was pretty far advanced in her pregnancy, the care of her physician, and the tenderness of Sir Bazil, would not permit her by any means to expose herself to the open air.

Mrs. Munden being informed by a messenger from her of what had happened, found herself under an absolute necessity of waiting on her, as it would have been ridiculous and preposterous, as well as unkind, to have quitted the town for so long a time without taking leave of a friend such as Lady Loveit.

She could not think of going there without reflecting at the same time how strong a probability there was of meeting Mr. Trueworth; she knew, indeed, that he did not live at Sir Bazil's, having heard he had lately taken a house for himself; but she knew also, that his close connection with that family made him seldom let slip a day without seeing them; she therefore prepared herself as well as she was able for such an interview, in case it should so happen.

That gentleman had dined there; and on finding Lady Loveit was forbid going abroad, and Sir Bazil unwilling to leave her alone, had consented to stay with them the whole day: they were at ombre when Mrs. Munden came, but on her entrance threw aside the cards; Lady Loveit received her according to the familiarity between them, and Sir Bazil with little less freedom; but Mr. Trueworth saluted her with a more distant air. 'I had not the honour, Madam,' said he, 'to make you any compliments on either of the great changes you have undergone; but you have always had my best wishes for your prosperity.'

Mrs. Munden, who had pretty well armed herself for this encounter, replied with a voice and countenance tolerably well composed, 'Great changes indeed, Sir, have happened to us both in a short space of time.' – 'There have so, Madam,' resumed he; 'but may the next you meet with bring with it lasting happiness!' She easily comprehended the meaning of these words, but made no answer, being at loss what to say, which might neither too much embolden, nor wholly discourage, the motive which dictated them.

After this, the conversation turned on various subjects, but chiefly on that of Mrs. Munden's going out of town: Mr. Trueworth said little; Lady Loveit, though she expressed an infinite deal of sorrow for the loss of so amiable a companion, could not forbear applauding her resolution in this point; but Sir Bazil would fain have been a little pleasant on the occasion, if the grave looks of Mrs. Munden had not put his raillery to silence. Perceiving the day was near shut in, she rose to take her leave; it was in vain that they used all imaginable arguments to persuade her to stay supper; she told them, that as the coach went out so early, it was necessary for her to take some repose before she entered upon the fatigue of her journey; Lady Loveit on this allowed the justice of her plea, and said no more.

The parting of these ladies was very moving; they embraced again and again, promised to write frequently to each other, and mingled tears as they exchanged farewels. Sir Bazil, who had really a very high esteem for her, was greatly affected, in spite of the gaiety of his temper, on bidding her adieu; and happy was it for Mrs. Munden that the concern they were both in hindered them from perceiving that confusion, that distraction of mind, which neither she nor Mr. Trueworth were able to restrain totally the marks of as he approached to make her those compliments, which might have been expected on such an occasion, even from a person the most indifferent; his tongue, indeed, uttered no more than words of course, but his lips trembled while saluting her; nor could she in that instant withhold a sigh, which seemed to rend her very heart: their mutual agitations were, in fine, too great not to be visible to each other, and left neither of them any room to doubt of the extreme force of the passion from which they sprang.

The motive which had made her refuse staying supper at Sir Bazil's, was to prevent Mr. Trueworth from having any pretence to wait upon her home, not being able to answer how far she could support her character, if exposed to the tender things he might possibly address her with on such an opportunity; and she now found, by what she had felt on parting with him, how necessary the precaution was that she had taken.

After a night less engrossed by sleep than meditation, she set out for L—e, where she arrived without any ill accident to retard her journey; and was received by Sir Ralph and Lady Trusty with all those demonstrations of joy, which she had reason to expect from the experienced friendship of those worthy persons.

As this was the place of her nativity, and her father had always lived there in very great estimation, the house of Lady Trusty at first was thronged with persons of almost all conditions, who came to pay their compliments to her fair guest; and as no circumstance, no habit, could take from her those charms which nature had bestowed upon her, her beauty and amiable qualities soon became the theme of conversation through the whole country.

She was not insensible of the admiration she attracted,; but was now far from being elated with it: all the satisfaction she took out of her dear Lady Trusty's company was in reading some instructive or entertaining book, and in the letters of those whom she knew to be her sincere friends; but she had not been much above two months in the country before she received one from a quarter whence she had not expected it. It was from Mr. Trueworth, and contained as follows.

'To Mrs. Munden.

Madam,
I have the inexpressible pleasure to hear that you are well by those whom you favour with your correspondence; but, as they may not think any mention of me might be agreeable to you, I take the liberty myself to acquaint you that I live; and flatter myself that information is sufficient to make you know that I live only to be, with the most firm attachment, Madam, your eternally devoted servant,

C. TRUEWORTH.

These few lines assuring her of his love, and at the same time of his respect, by his not presuming once to mention the passion of which he was possessed, charmed her to a very high degree, and prepared her heart for another, which, in a few weeks after, he found a pretence for sending to her. It contained these lines.

'To Mrs. Munden.

I am now more unhappy than ever; Lady Loveit is gone out of town, and I have no opportunity of hearing the only sounds that can bless my longing ears: in pity, therefore, to my impatience, vouchsafe to let me know you are in health – say that you are well – it is all I ask. One line will cost you little pains, and be no breach of that decorum to which you so strictly adhere; yet will be a sovereign specifick to restore the tranquillity of him who is, with an unspeakable regard, Madam, your unalterable, and devoted servant,

C. TRUEWORTH.'

Mrs. Munden found this epistle so reasonable, and withal couched in such respectful terms, that she ought not to refuse compliance with it; and, accordingly, wrote to him in this manner.

'To Charles Trueworth, Esq.

Sir,
The generous concern you express for my welfare demands a no less grateful return. As to my health, it is no way impaired since I left London; nor can my mind labour under any discomposure, while my friends continue to think kindly of me. I am, with all due respect, Sir, yours, &c.

B. MUNDEN.'

Upon this obliging answer he ventured to write again, intreating her to allow a correspondence with him by letters while she remained in L—e; urging, that this was a favour she could not reasonably deny to any friend who desired it with the same sincerity she must be convinced he did.

Mrs. Munden paused a little; but finding that neither her virtue nor her reputation could any way suffer by granting this request, her heart would not permit her to deny both him and herself so innocent a satisfaction; and by the next post gave him the permission he petitioned for, in these words.

'To Charles Trueworth, Esq.

Sir,

I should be unjust to myself, as well as ungrateful to the friendship with which you honour me, should I reject any proofs of it that are consistent with my character to receive and to return: write, therefore, as often as you think proper; and be assured I shall give your letters all the welcome you can wish, provided they contain nothing unsuitable to the present condition of her who is, as much as you ought to expect, Sir, yours, &c.

B. MUNDEN.'

After this, an uninterrupted intercourse of letters continued between them for the whole remainder of the year. Mr. Trueworth was for the most part extremely cautious in what manner he expressed himself; but whenever, as it would sometimes so happen, the warmth of his passion made him transgress the bounds which had been prescribed him, she would not seem to understand, because she had no mind to be offended.

Thus equally maintaining that reserve which she thought the situation she was in demanded, and at the same time indulging the tenderness of her heart for a man who so well deserved it, she enjoyed that sweet contentment which true love alone has the power of bestowing.

CHAPTER XXIV

———•———

Is the last; and, if the author's word may be taken for it, the best

INNOCENT and pure as the inclinations of Mrs. Munden were, it is highly probable, however, that she was not sorry to see the time arrive which was to put an end to that cruel constraint her charming lover had been so longer under; and, while it gave him leave to declare the whole fervency of the passion he was possessed of, allowed her also to confess her own without a blush.

Mr. Trueworth, who had kept an exact account of the time, contrived it so that a letter from him should reach her hands the very next day after that in which she was to throw off her mourning weeds. It was in these terms he now wrote.

'To Mrs. Munden.

Madam,

The year of my probation is expired – I have now fully performed the painful penance you enjoined; and you must expect me shortly at your feet, to claim that recompence which my submission has in some measure merited. You cannot now, without an injustice contrary to your nature, forbid me to approach you with my vows of everlasting love; nor any longer restrain my impatient lips from uttering the languishments of my adoring heart: nor can I now content myself with telling you, at the distance of so many miles, how very dear you are to me. No! you must also read the tender declarations in my eyes, and hear it in my sighs. The laws of tyrant custom have been fulfilled in their most rigorous forms; and those of gentler love, may, sure, demand an equal share in our obedience. Fain would my flattering hopes persuade me that I shall not find you a too stubborn rebel to that power, to whose authority all nature yields a willing homage, and that my happiness is a thing of some consequence to you. If I am too presuming, at least forgive me; but let your pen assure me you do so by the return of the post; till when I am, with a mixture of transport and anxiety, Madam, your passionately devoted, and most faithful adorer,

C. TRUEWORTH.'

Though this was no more than Mrs. Munden had expected, it diffused through her whole frame a glow of satisfaction unknown to those who do not love as she did: she thought, indeed, as well as he, that there was no need of continuing that cruel constraint she so long had imposed upon herself; and hesitated not if she should acknowledge what he before had not the least cause to doubt. The terms in which she expressed herself were these.

'To Charles Trueworth, Esq.

Sir,

I know there is a great share of impatience in the composition of your sex, and wonder not at yours – much less have I any pretence to excuse you of presumption, as you are too well acquainted with the just sensibility I have of your merits not to expect all the marks of it that an honourable passion can require. An attempt to conceal my heart from you will be vain – you saw the inmost recesses of it at a time when you should most have been a stranger there: but what was then my shame to have discovered, is now my glory to avow; and I scruple not to confess, that whatever makes your happiness will confirm mine. But I must stop here, or, when I see you, shall have nothing left to add in return for the pains so long a journey will cost you. Let no anxieties, however, render the way more tedious; but reflect that every step will bring you still nearer to a reception equal to your wishes, from her who is, with an unfeigned sincerity, yours &c.

B. MUNDEN.'

This was the first love-letter she had ever wrote; and it must be owned that the passion she was inspired with had already made her a pretty good proficient that way: but though the prudish part of the sex may perhaps accuse her of having confessed too much, yet those of a more reasonable way of thinking will be far from pronouncing sentence against her – the person of Mr. Trueworth – his admirable endowments – the services he had done her, might well warrant the tenderness she had for him – his birth, his estate, his good character, and her own experience of his many virtues, sufficiently authorized her acceptance of his offers; and it would have been only a piece of idle affectation in her to have gone about to have concealed her regard for a person whom so many reasons induced her to marry, especially as chance had so long before betrayed to him her inclinations in his favour.

Thus fully justified within herself, and assured of being so hereafter to all her friends, and to the world in general, she indulged the most pleasing ideas of her approaching happiness, without the least mixture of any of those inquietudes, which pride, folly, ill-fortune, or ill-humour, too frequently excite, to poison all the sweets of love and imbitter the most tender passion.

As she had not made Lady Trusty the confidante of any part of what had passed between her and Mr. Trueworth; deterred at first through shame, and afterwards by the uncertainty of his persisting in his addresses, that lady would have been greatly surprized at the extraordinary vivacity which now on a sudden sparkled in her eyes, if there had not been other motives besides the real one by which she might account for it.

Mrs. Munden had received intelligence that Lady Loveit was safely delivered of a son and heir; and, what was yet more interesting to her, that Mr. Thoughtless was married to a young lady of a large fortune, and honourable family: letters also came from Mr. Francis Thoughtless, acquainting them that he had obtained leave from his colonel to leave the regiment for two whole months; and that, after the celebration of his brother's nuptials, he would pass the remainder of his furlow with them in L—e.

These, indeed, were the things which at another time would have highly delighted the mind of Mrs. Munden; but at this her thoughts were so absorbed in Mr. Trueworth, whom she now every hour expected, that friendship, and even that natural affection which had hitherto been so distinguishable a part of her character, could not boast of but a second place.

Lady Trusty observing her one day in a more than ordinarily chearful humour, took that opportunity of discoursing with her on a matter which had been in her head for some time. 'Mr. Munden has been dead a year,' said she; 'you have paid all that regard to his memory which could have been expected from you, even for a better husband; and cannot now be blamed for listening to any offers that may be made to your advantage.' – 'Offers, Madam!' cried Mrs. Munden; 'on what score does your ladyship mean?' – 'What others can you suppose,' relied she gravely, 'than those of marriage? There are two gentleman who have solicited both Sir Ralph and myself to use our best interest with you in their behalf; neither of them are unworthy your consideration; the one is Mr. Woodland, whom you have frequently seen here; his estate at present, indeed, is no more than eight hundred pounds a year, but he has great expectations from a rich uncle: the other is our vicar, who, besides two large benefices, has lately had a windfall of near a thousand pounds a year by the death of his elder brother; and it is the opinion of most people, that he will be made a bishop on the first vacancy.'

'So much the worse, Madam,' said the spiritous Mrs. Munden; 'for if he takes the due care he ought to do of his diocese, he will have little time to think of his wife: as to Mr. Woodland, indeed, I have but one objection to make, but that is a main one; I do not like him, and am well assured I never can. I therefore beg your ladyship,' continued she, with an air both serious and disdainful, 'to advise them to desist all thoughts of me on the account you mention, and to let them know I did not come to L—e to get a husband, but to avoid all impertinent proposals of that kind.'

'It is not in L—e,' replied Lady Trusty, a little piqued at these last words, 'but in London you are to expect proposals deserving this contempt: here are no false glosses to deceive or impose on the understanding – here are no pretenders to birth, or to estate; every one is known for what he really is; and none will presume to make his addresses to a woman without a consciousness of being qualified to receive the approbation of her friends.'

'I will not dispute with your ladyship on this point,' replied Mrs. Munden: 'I grant there is less artifice in the country than the town, and should scarce make choice of a man that has been bred, and chuses to reside always, in the latter; but Madam, it is not the place of nativity, nor the birth, nor the estate – but the person, and the temper of the man, can make me truly happy: I shall always pay a just regard to the advice of my friends, and particularly to your ladyship; but as I have been once a sacrifice to their persuasions, I hope you will have the goodness to forgive me when I say, that if ever I become a wife again, love, an infinity of love, shall be the chief inducement.'

'On whose side?' cried Lady Trusty hastily. 'On both, I hope, Madam!' replied Mrs. Munden with a smile.

'Take care, my dear,' rejoined the other; 'for if you should find yourself deceived in that of the man, your own would only serve to render you the more unhappy.'

The fair widow was about to make some answer, which perhaps would have let Lady Trusty into the whole secret of her heart, if the conversation had not been broke off by a very loud ringing of the bell at the great gate of the courtyard before the house; on which, as it was natural for them, they both ran to the window to see what company were coming.

The first object that presented itself to them was a very neat running footman, who, on the gate being opened, came tripping up towards the house, and was immediately followed by a coach, with one gentleman in it, drawn by six prancing horses, and attended by two servants in rich liveries, and well mounted. Lady Trusty was somewhat surprized, as she never had seen either the person in the coach, or the equipage, before; but infinitely more so when Mrs. Munden, starting from the window in the greatest confusion imaginable, cried, 'Madam, with your leave – I will speak to him in the parlour!' – 'Speak to whom?' said Lady Trusty. The other had not power to answer and was running out of the room, when a servant of Sir Ralph's came up to tell her a gentleman, who called himself Trueworth, was come to wait on her. 'I know – I know!' cried she, 'conduct him into the parlour.'

Prepared as she was by the expectation of his arrival, all her presence of mind was not sufficient to enable her to stand the sudden rush of joy which on sight of him bursted in upon her heart: nor was he less overcome – he sprang into her arms, which of themselves opened to receive him; and, while he kissed away the tears that trickled from her eyes, his own bedewed her cheeks. 'Oh, have I lived to see you thus!' cried he, 'thus ravishingly kind!' – 'And have I lived,' rejoined she, 'to receive these proofs of affection from the best and most ill-used of men! Oh, Trueworth! Trueworth!' added she, 'I have not merited this from you.' – 'You merit all things!' said he; 'let us talk no more of what is past, but tell me that you now are mine; I came to make you so by the irrevocable ties of love and law, and we must now part no more! Speak, my angel – my first, my last, charmer!' continued he, perceiving she was silent, blushed, and hung down her head; 'let those dear lips confirm my happiness, and say the time is come that you will be all mine.' The trembling fair now, having gathered a little more assurance, raised her eyes from the earth, and looking tenderly on him, 'You know you have my heart,' cried she; 'and cannot doubt my hand.'

After this a considerable time was passed in all those mutual endearments which honour and modesty would permit, without Mrs. Munden once remembering the obligations she was under of relieving Lady Trusty from the consternation she had left her in.

That lady had, indeed, heard her servant say who was below; but as Mrs. Munden had never mentioned the name of Mr. Trueworth the whole time she had been with her, and had not any suspicion of the correspondence between them, much less could have the least notion of her affection for a gentleman whom she had once refused, in spite of the many advantages an alliance with him offered, nothing could be more astonishing to her than this visit, and the disorder with which Mrs. Munden went down to receive it.

She was still ruminating on an event which appeared so extraordinary to her, when the now happy lovers entered the room, and discovered, by their countenances, some part of what she wished to know: 'I beg leave, Madam,' said Mrs. Munden, 'to introduce to your ladyship a gentleman whose name and character you are not unacquainted with, Mr. Trueworth.'

'I am, indeed, no stranger to both,' replied Lady Trusty, advancing to receive him, 'nor to the respect they claim:' he returned this compliment with a politeness which was natural to him; and, after they were seated, her ladyship beginning to express the satisfaction she felt in seeing a gentleman of whose amiable qualities she had so high an idea, 'Your ladyship does me too much honour,' said he; 'but I fear you will repent this goodness, when you shall find I am come with an intent to rob you of a companion who, I know, is very dear to you.'

'If you should succeed in the robbery you mention,' answered she, smiling, 'you will make me ample atonement for it by the pleasure you will give me in knowing what I have lost is in such good hands.'

Mr. Trueworth had no time to make any reply to these obliging words; Sir Ralph, who had dined abroad, came in that instant, not a little surprized to find so gay an equipage, and altogether unknown to him, before his door; but on his lady's acquainting him with the name of their new guest, welcomed him with a complaisance not at all inferior to what she had shewn. There requires little ceremony between persons of good-breeding to enter into a freedom of conversation; and the good old baronet was beginning to entertain Mr. Trueworth with some discourses, which at another time would have been very agreeable to him; but that obedient lover having undertaken, in order to save the blushes of his fair mistress, to make them fully sensible of the motive which had brought him into L—e, delayed the performance no longer than was necessary to do it without abruptness.

Mrs. Munden, who, in desiring he should break the matter, had not meant he should do it suddenly, or in her presence, looked like the sun just starting from a cloud all the time he was speaking, and was ready to die wtih shame; when Sir Ralph said, that since all things were concluded between them, and there was no need for farther courtship, he could not see any reason why their marriage should not be immediately compleated: but Lady Trusty, in compassion to her fair friend's confusion, opposed this motion. The next day after the succeeding one was, however, appointed without any shew of reluctance on the side of Mrs. Munden, and the inexpressible satisfaction of Mr. Trueworth.

He had lain the night before at an inn about eight miles short of Sir Ralph's seat; and, as he had no acquaintance either with him or his lady, had intended to make that his home during his stay in the country: but Sir Ralph and Lady Trusty would not consent to his departure; and all he could obtain from them was, permission to send back his coach, with one servant to take care of the horses.

No proposals having yet been made concerning a settlement for Mrs. Munden, by way of dowry, Mr. Trueworth took Sir Ralph aside the next morning, and desired he would send for a lawyer, which he immediately did – a gentleman of that profession happening to live very near; and, on his coming, received such instructions from Mr. Trueworth for drawing up the writings, as convinced Sir Ralph both of the greatness of his generosity, and the sincerity of his love, to the lady he was about to make his wife.

Expedition having been recommended to the lawyer, he returned soon after dinner with an instrument drawn up in so judicious a manner, that it required not the least alteration. While Sir Ralph and Mr. Trueworth were locked up with him in order to examine it, Mrs. Munden received no inconsiderable addition to the present satisfaction of her mind by the arrival of her brother Frank. After the first welcome being given – 'You are come, captain,' said Lady Trusty, 'just time enough to be a witnes of your sister's marriage, which is to be celebrated to-morrow.' – 'Marriage!' cried he; 'and without acquainting either of her brothers with her intentions! But I hope,' continued he, 'it is not to disadvantage, as your ladyship seems not displeased at it?' – 'I assure you, captain,' resumed Lady Trusty, 'I knew nothing of the affair till yesterday, nor had ever seen before the gentleman your sister has made choice of: but love and destiny,' added she, 'are not to be resisted.' These words, and the serious air she assumed in speaking them, giving him cause to fear his sister was going to throw herself away, he shook his head, and seemed in a good deal of uneasiness; but had not an opportunity to testify what he felt any otherwise than by his looks; Sir Ralph and Mr. Trueworth in that instant entering the room. The extreme surprize he was in at the sight of the latter, was such as prevented him from paying his respects to either in the manner he would have done if more master of himself; but Mr. Trueworth, guessing the emotions of his mind, locked him in his arms, saying, 'Dear Frank! I shall at last be so happy as to call you brother.' – 'Heavens! is it possible?' cried he. 'Am I awake, or is this illusion!' Then running to Mrs. Munden, 'Sister,' said he, 'is what I hear a real fact? Are you, indeed, to be married to Mr. Trueworth?' – 'You hear I am,' answered she, smiling, 'and hear it from a mouth not accustomed to deceit.' He then flew to Mr. Trueworth, crying, 'My dear, dear Trueworth! I little hoped this honour!' Then, turning to Lady Trusty, 'Oh, Madam!' said he, 'how agreeably have you deceived me!' – 'I knew it would be so,' replied she; 'but I told you nothing but the truth.'

The extravagance of the young captain's joy being a little over, Mr. Trueworth presented Mrs. Munden with the parchment he had received from the lawyer. 'What is this?' demanded she. 'Take it, take it!' cried Sir Ralph; 'it is no less than a settlement of eight hundred pounds a year on you in case of accidents.' – 'I accept it, Sir,' said Mrs. Munden to Mr. Trueworth, 'as a fresh proof of your affection: but Heaven forbid I should ever live to receive any other advantage from it.' He kissed her hand with the most tender transports on these obliging words; after which they all seated themselves: and never was there a joy more perfect and sincere than what each of these worthy company gave demonstrations of in their respective characters. The next morning compleated the wishes of the enamoured pair, and the satisfaction of their friends.

An account of this event was dispatched the next post to all who had any welfare in the interest of the new-wedded lovers. Mr. Thoughtless, though very much engrossed by his own happiness, could not but rejoice in the good fortune of his sister. Sir Bazil, who, since his thorough knowledge of Mrs. Munden, had a high esteem of her, was extremely glad; but his lady was warm even to an excess in her congratulations: in fine, there were few of her acquaintance who did not in some measure take part in her felicity.

Thus were the virtues of our heroine (those follies that had defaced them being fully corrected) at length rewarded with a happiness retarded only till she had rendered herself wholly worthy of receiving it.